# The Feeling of Being Valued

## Erica H. Campbell

Sylifi

Copyright © 2026 by Erica H. Campbell

All rights reserved.

No part of this book may be reproduced in any form or by any electronic or mechanical means, including information storage and retrieval systems, without written permission from the author, except for the use of brief quotations in a book review.

# Contents

| | |
|---|---:|
| Chapter 1 | 1 |
| Chapter 2 | 19 |
| Chapter 3 | 38 |
| Chapter 4 | 55 |
| Chapter 5 | 73 |
| Chapter 6 | 91 |
| Chapter 7 | 110 |
| Chapter 8 | 127 |
| Chapter 9 | 146 |
| Chapter 10 | 163 |
| Chapter 11 | 181 |
| Chapter 12 | 197 |
| Chapter 12.5 | 215 |
| Chapter 13 | 224 |
| Chapter 14 | 241 |
| Chapter 15 | 261 |
| Chapter 16 | 280 |
| Chapter 17 | 300 |
| Chapter 18 | 321 |
| Chapter 19 | 341 |
| Chapter 20 | 361 |
| Chapter 21 | 381 |
| Chapter 22 | 401 |
| Chapter 23 | 419 |
| Chapter 24 | 438 |
| Chapter 25 | 456 |
| Chapter 26 | 474 |
| Chapter 27 | 492 |
| Chapter 28 | 512 |
| Chapter 29 | 533 |
| Chapter 30 | 554 |
| Epilogue | 572 |
| About the Author | 579 |

## Chapter One

I stared at the inside of my locker outside my college gym's changing room, pretending to try and find something, desperately hoping Marissa would walk on by me after she got done terrorizing her latest victim. She had always been a bit of a bitch, but since a couple years ago, what with her dad leaving her mom for a girl just a year older than herself, she'd gotten much worse. I almost understood, I could hear the whispers when it first happened, the pity, the small snickers directed at her. By becoming the biggest threat in the school, she'd shut everyone up pretty fast. I wished I was that bold, that confident. I was only here on scholarship, I would never have been able to afford this place otherwise. I went to public school most of my childhood, and only got into this school because I had won a dumb essay contest in middle school and got into a fancy high school with a partnership with the university.

It was a nice school, it was clean and there were no fights, per-say, and it was essentially an 8 year track from high school through college if you could pay, but I had to work so, *so* hard to keep up the scholarship. Overall, I didn't belong here, and people like Marissa knew that. I was only here because of a contest years ago, and even though I had gone to the same high school as these girls, they never saw me as one of them. While Marissa got whispers and hidden laughter, I got called "rat" and "charity" to my face constantly. It wasn't a welcoming environment, but if I ever wanted to move out of my parent's tiny apartment and do something with my life, it was what I had to do.

I heard the sound of something snapping, and I peeked through the slits in the locker door. Marissa was leaning into the other girl's face, a broken pen in her hand.

"If I *ever* catch you trying to talk shit about me again, I will snap your fucking finger like I snapped this pen, do you understand?"

The girl nodded quickly, her eyes wide. I shuddered. Marissa would *do* it, too. She had already been caught putting glue in a girl's hair, pushing one down a flight of stairs, and another time she was found to have been making a classmate eat erasers to "clean her name off the bitches' tongue". And that was just since starting college, in high school she'd ruined lives... She was almost untouchable. The only thing she got in trouble for was the glue, and the school just called it "a prank taken too far". The stairs was explained away as her tripping by mistake, knocking into the other girl, and the erasers were "non toxic" and the girl "ate them herself" so there was no crime done, according to Marissa's family lawyer.

In my mind, I'd thought Marissa would level out after she got into college, away from all the high school drama, the petty stuff. After all, they always said "high school is nothing like the real world", but to Marissa, it didn't matter. With her money and influence over the school from her family, she could treat college as just another 4 years of high school, and once she graduated and joined her mother's tech company, I had little doubt that she'd just keep being herself there, too.

She pushed the other girl against the lockers, making them clang, and turned to walk away. I looked at her, our eyes meeting for a second. Her round face drawn in with her half lidded sneer, a look she almost always had, a look that said "you're not worth my time" without as many words. Her brown hair framed that cruel expression with a wave of layered curls, accenting her green eyes and making her look like a princess or dutchess who had just seen something disdainful. My throat closed, and I felt myself shrink back.

"What's wrong, Rat? You want me to give you attention too?" She said, her voice low and dangerous.

I smiled, trying to fake a kindness I didn't feel and I forced a laugh. "Oh, no, I was just getting my gym clothes, I'll be going now!"

I grabbed the clothes on top of the pile and walked away, my heart pounding. The other girl glared at me, angrily. I had abandoned her, and I knew it, but I couldn't have done anything anyway, and it's not like I could make any new friends at this point anyway...

I changed quickly and sent a text to my only friend in school, a girl named Henrietta who was here from Germany. Her family owned a company that sold blood around the world, and the other girls had taken to making fun of her accent, and calling her "Frau Bludsauger" as a reference to her family's business. The mutual bullying and ostracization we experienced drew us together, making me one of *her* only friends as well.

*'Hey gril, srry im late, had a lady m sitch, omw in'*

The reply was instantaneous

*'Oh gods, are you ok?'*

I shot back a confirmation I was, and headed into the gym proper. It was a good gym, it had rows of equipment, mostly focused on cardio, but there was some basic weight equipment as well, for toning and staying trim. Henri and I, though, we stuck to the cardio. I jogged over to her sitting on a weight bench and gave her a quick hug.

"Hey girl, ready to pump it up?" I asked, cheerfully, trying to ignore the shakiness I'd felt from dealing with Marissa just a moment before.

"Ha, ja, of course. But are you really ok, Amber?" She asked, her german accent still slipping in despite years of trying to hide it.

I nodded and climbed onto a treadmill.

"It's ok, it wasn't me she was targeting, it was another girl, the one whose dad owns the bank on West Main? I don't know her name. I was just caught in the crossfire."

"Ok, sweet thing, if you say so, let us get pumped up then!"

She stepped onto the machine next to me and we started off, matching each other's pace. We had an unspoken contest going, to see who could out pace and outlast the other each time. If I raised the speed on my treadmill, she'd bump up hers, if she raised her incline, I'd do mine too. Last woman standing won, and the loser had to buy the winner a smoothie. We never had actually said it out loud, but it was still our thing, and we never started without the other.

I flicked on the TV in front of us as we ran, and watched the news as I jogged, focusing on the reports of local crime, the stocks, the upcoming election, and apparently, the spread of the compression energy particles to our town. They had gotten into the water supply in a small Russian town years ago from a lab catastrophe, and had been spreading ever since. They only affected about 1-3% of the population, but if you had the genetic mutation that allowed them to 'latch on' to your body mass as an energy source, it'd eat you away until you were out of usable genetic material. For some people that meant they'd lose an arm or a head, or have lopsided, twisted bodies. For others, they'd just get smaller. In some cases, it'd cause a catalyst trigger that could compress you and your surroundings all at once as the particles 'ate' all the mass around the victim, burning through their body quickly. It was dangerous, and people died a lot because of it.

If they were in our town's water supply already... That could be... fun. I fantasized about Marissa getting infected, and losing chunks of her body, or better yet, loosing so much mass that she wasn't considered human anymore... It was rare, it only happened to about 1/5 of the affected, but if you lost more than 90% of your body mass, the government considered you a "class B citizen", so if you died accidentally or if your family couldn't take care of you, there wouldn't be any legal repercussions. It was the result of a big court case that happened when a powerful business owner accidentally killed his wife after she was infected, and his legal team got creative with the manslaughter charges.

If you were killed outright, the law would get involved, but it was basically the same as killing an animal at that point. If *she* was a class B citizen, and I found her... I could do whatever I wanted with her, she'd lose her power, I'd be the school hero, even. I shivered at the idea in excitement, maybe she'd even just... disappear... plenty of the 1-3% had "ideal compression makeup" and just compressed away into nothing, their entire body just vanishing into particles of compression energy.

"Uhm, darling?" Henri's voice jolted me out of my fantasy. "You have been... in the clouds for quite a while, what is up?"

I grinned, sheepishly. "Well, I was just imagining if Marissa was a genetic match for the compression particles, and... how things would change for us if she was..."

Henri's eyes widened. "Ohhh no, no, no, do NOT wish evil on someone, Amber, even if it is *her*, and please do not say such things out loud! It is far too dangerous..."

"Well, it's not EVIL, per say, it happens to a lot of people..."

"It is pretty evil... It is like saying... you wish her to get cancer, it's not even as common as that, and it can be much much worse..."

I blushed and nodded, feeling icky inside. "Oh, yeah... When you put it like that, my grandfather died of cancer. I hadn't thought of it that way, I guess."

"Ja, well, I understand you're just feeling hurt, we will ignore it from now. But now... I think it is time for smoothies, do you agree?"

I glanced down at my machine and realize I had been running at the base setting for the full session. I looked over at Henri's, and saw she was jogging along at quite a brisk pace. I sighed.

"Yeah, ok. I'll buy today, my treat."

She clapped in victory and squeezed my shoulder as we turned off our treadmills and headed to the showers. "I think I will get... blueberry and banana today!" She thought out loud, in a teasing voice "I really earned the extra sugar today!"

I smiled lightly, the mild ribbing was nice, it made me feel closer to her, like we really could trust each other against the world.

~~~

I walked into my apartment, and found my parents sitting on the sofa watching the news. My mother looked over at me and pointed over at the TV.

"Look, did you see that virus got here? It'll be all over town soon."

"Yeah, I was talking about it with Henri, it's kinda scary, but interesting, too, isn't it? We could lose neighbors and stuff..."

My dad cut in "Well, I'm just saying, we need to be proactive about this, I heard you can turn in class Bs to the government for a lot of money, if we can find one... Just keep an eye out at school, ok?"

"Oh, uhh, ok Appa, sure." I said. I highly doubted I'd actually sell any I found, if I found one... I was keeping them. Even if it wasn't Marissa, the status bump, the class of having your own class B... I'd be upgraded from "Rat" to Amber in no time. My dad could get over it. I fixed myself a plate of rice and mandu in the kitchen, and headed upstairs to study.

I munched on the dumplings, the crunchy veggies mixing with the soft tofu and mushrooms and doughy outside to make a delicious, healthy snack. I appreciated my parents being willing to make concessions to my diet, even if they weren't vegetarians themselves, they still made an effort to cook the same meals they always had, but without meat, just for me. My parents were a bit rough and a bit pushy when it came to my schoolwork, but they made sure I had what I needed to succeed. My studies were going pretty well tonight, I had made very decent progress on my paper for my world religions class, and I think my flash card drills were starting to stick for my physics test next weekend.

I finished my dinner and cracked open a sparking water. It was a low chance that'd I'd catch the compression particles, but from now on, canned or bottled water only, just to be safe. I switched off my computer and flopped down on my bed, scrolling my phone and watching old black and white shows until I fell asleep. Tomorrow, I would be on the hunt for anyone affected with the virus, but for now, I just wanted to be cozy.

~~~

I woke up to my alarm going off and I groaned. I picked up my phone from under my pillow and looked at it through crusty, bleary eyes. I had a text from Henri, asking if I wanted to meet her at the park for a jog, and a notification that my religion paper was due soon. I could respond to Henri later, and I knew when my paper was due. I noticed with confusion that my phone was at 75%. Had my charger stopped working? Did I set it on the charging pad crooked? I picked up the charger, and noticed that the cord looked torn, ripped apart, as if by a wild animal. I looked to where it should have been plugged into the wall, and saw... nothing. Not even the wall.

With a cold chill, I looked around. Most of my bed was laying on the floor, and around me was towering massive chunks of dust, giant socks, random junk, and a storage container. I looked up, and saw the ceiling miles above me, fading into a fog and I choked out a scream. *I* had caught the compression virus, and it had taken most of my bed with me, I must have had a *lot* of usable genetic material. But how? I didn't even drink the water...

I looked back at my phone and went to go text Henri, and then I remembered... The showers at school... I moaned, and flopped back onto what was left of my bed, looking at the jagged, half eaten bed frame towering around me. I needed help, and I needed it soon. I wasn't feeling sick or tingly, so I was guessing the infection had run its course, but I had to know if my parents were ok, or if they had gotten away unscathed. I sent my mom a message quickly.

*'mom, plz help, i got infected, I need u 2 help me, im n what's left of my bed, b careful'*

After that, I sent one to Henri as well.

*'omg, grl, i got the virus, im so small, i need u to come over rn, emergency'*

I lay back down and waited. If my parents were ok, they'd be here any minute. If not, I'd need to start the long trek to their room to check on them... After a few seconds, my bedroom door burst open, and my mom was suddenly standing in the doorway with a bathrobe over her pajamas. She looked around the room, her gaze falling on me after a second of looking, and her face crumpled into tears. She fell to her knees, wailing with sobs that I swear must have woken the neighbors.

"Oh gods, oh my dear daughter, why? Why could this happen?"

She moaned, tears pouring out of her face. My dad walked up behind her, looking confused. He saw me though, after a moment, in the wreckage of my bed, and his face fell too, folding up as he knelt next to my mom, hugging her. He didn't cry, he was too stoic for that, but I could see his heart breaking as he rubbed her back.

I shifted in my bed, looking around awkwardly. I wasn't dead, I was just small... I could still be their daughter, I might even be able to have a job, right? By my estimate, I had lost... a lot more than 90% of my height. 90% would put me at about 7 inches, and I was about half that, maybe a little more if my measure against the 'special toy' I kept under my bed was any indication. I flushed red, oh *gods*, my parents were going to see my special toy, uuugh... This morning just kept getting worse... I felt a jolt, and looked up to see my mother, tears still pouring, holding me carefully in her hands, bed and all. I waved at her, and smile nervously.

"Hey, mom... I'm still ok, I'm just, you know, smaller! It's ok, no problem, swear to god, you'll hardly notice I got smaller, I-"

Her renewed crying cut me off.

"I can barely understand you... My own daughter, I can't even hear her..."

"W-well, mom, you know you need hearing aids, we've been saying that for ages, and-"

She kept crying, and carried me down the hall, ignoring my words. Dad followed behind, solemn and quiet. She set me on the kitchen counter, and patted my head, her giant finger pressing just a bit too hard into my head. I shiver, I was so fragile now... I could be smashed flat by complete accident, or injured by a 1 foot drop. Chills went through me as I processed it. I was *stuck* like this... I wasn't a human, I was a class B citizen, I was just and object, a thing to be-

My phone pinged, and I checked it automatically. It was a message from Henri.

*'Holy no! Oh darling sweetie baby I will help you, I promise... You are my precious friend, no matter what. How did it work? Are you missing body parts?'*

I smiled sadly, and texted back

*'no, im in one piece, it was a stable infection, im just small, about like, 4 inches ig? I'm deff a class B now fr'*

*'Oh no... I am going to help, please be safe.'*

I looked up from my phone and see my father on the home phone, nodding to the receiver.

"Yes, that's right, the whole bed.... I don't know, hand sized? About as long as my palm... Ok, I understand... Yes, of course. I'll see you then."

He hung up and looked at my mother sadly.

"They say she needs to be registered as a class B so she can be insured and legally protected, otherwise, she could be taken or hurt by anyone, with no recourse available... They'll be here soon to do it, we should get dressed..."

My mother nodded, and walked to her room sniffling and rubbing her eyes. My father looked down at me with a great sadness on his face.

"I am so sorry this happened to you, Kkoma... I hope you know we still love you, I wish I knew what we could do, but I don't know what the future looks like right now..."

He leaned in and carefully kissed the top of my head like he did when I was little. Or, I guess younger, at least.

"I love you, darling, and we want the best for you, ok?"

I smiled back up at him.

"Ok, Appa, I love you too... Henri is coming over, I think, she said she'd be able to help?"

He nodded and gave a small smile. "I think that she would do anything to help you, Amber, I hope she can..."

He left me on the counter and went to his room to get dressed as well. Maybe I should get dressed, if I'm going to be registered, I wanted to look nice, right? I thought about my outfit, and then realized that none of my clothes could fit me anymore. All my nice dresses, my band tees, my cozy sweaters... Oh *gods*, my boots... I'd never wear them again. I moaned and flopped backwards onto the pillow. This really *was* the worst... I'd have to get custom everything, clothes, shoes, even makeup. I couldn't afford all that... I wondered if there was a common doll about my size, maybe I could borrow clothes from one of them? I did some searching online. It looked like some 'little sister' styled fashion dolls' clothes might fit, but most dolls my size wore plastic clothes, or didn't have replaceable clothes at all...

A knock on the door made me look up from my phone. Henri? My dad rushed out of the bedroom pulling on his tie and swung open the door. A tall man in a green uniform stood in front of him. Not Henri... He looked my dad up and down.

"Mr Park?"

My father nodded.

"Very good, where is the infected individual?"

"Ah, she's on the counter, in here..." He led the man into the kitchen and pointed at me. The man sat at the counter and pulled out a tablet.

"You are... Miss Amber Park, correct?"

"Yeah, that's me..." I replied, tucking my phone into my waistband.

"You're 20 years old?"

"Well, 21 in a couple months, but... yeah..."

"Ok, so of legal age... And your social security number?"

He asked me question after question, measuring me, waving a scanner over me, filling in boxes on his tablet, his face expressionless. My mother joined us after a while, and her and my father stood in silence as the man grilled me. Once he was done, he set the tablet down and looked at me.

"Miss Park, I have determined that you have lost about 94% of your mass, and therefore have been classified as a class B citizen. From this moment on, you will require guardianship of a qualified individual, and do not have rights such as voting, driving, or owning property."

My father cleared his throat. "Ah, sir, we are her guardians, we'll be taking care of her from now on, of course."

The man coldly looked at my father, pulling out paperwork from his jacket. "She is of adult age, so your guardianship does not apply."

"Well, we'll be taking guardianship, then..."

"Then I take it you've passed the class B citizen care and treatment test? And you have the money to pay the processing fees for the transfer, insurance, and required care items for her?"

My fathers eyes widened. "Ah, I can... I can get the license, and I'll pay whatever I need, I just need to get to the bank to get a loan, and-"

"Mr Park, it takes 12 hours at least to be qualified for ownership and guardianship of a class B, and the fees, insurance, and required deposits total about $25,000. I doubt a bank would give you a loan for that amount on short notice, so I recommend looking for other methods of getting the money. I would also advise you to move quickly. The government will, of course, give you a $10,000 finders fee, you can put that towards the $25,000 total. Now if you'll excuse me, I have to bring her to the station to be tagged and processed."

He snapped a glove onto his hand and picked me up off the bed, dropping me in a small mesh bag. I screamed, I was being taken away from my parents? This was unfair, *unthinkable*. The horror of my situation set in, I was being 'tagged'? 'Processed'? Put up for SALE? I clawed against the mesh, trying to get free, trying to get my parents to grab me, to *save* me, please, please...

The door swung open, and a very red faced, very out of breath Henri ran in.

"Wait! Please!" She wheezed. I hadn't seen her this winded in... ever, even at the gym. She must have ran all the way here...

The man looked at her and pursed his lips.

"And you are?..."

"Her... Her best friend, I want to help, let me help..."

My father's eyes lit up "Yes! Henri, you can help! You have money, you can pay the $15,000! We can get her back!"

"Oh, oh my..." She said. "I have... $6000, is that not enough?..."

The man shook his head "No, you are still $9000 short, and you'd still need the license, too. And before all that, I need to process and tag her. Good day."

He turned and stepped quickly out of the doorway, my bag swinging wildly in his hand. I heard my mother start wailing again, and I heard Henri start to comfort her.

"No, it is fine, we will do a crowd fund! We will get the money very fast, it will be ok, you-"

The door slammed, and cut them off. I fell back into the mesh and cried, feeling like the world was slipping away from me.

~~~

I sat in the plexiglass box, shivering. I was still only in my pajamas; a pair of shorts and a big t-shirt, and the 'blanket' they had provided for me was nothing more than a microfiber cloth that my hair got caught in and that pulled at my skin uncomfortably. I reached down and twisted the ankle bracelet with the tracker in it around, trying to get used to the feeling of it on my leg, but it was just slightly too big and too clunky to be a fashion accessory. I understood, of course. Class Bs were as small as a half inch, and as tall as 7-8 inches, usually. The tags needed to be "one size fits a range". But... I seemed to be on the small side of this range, and the chunky piece of plastic on my leg was getting frustrating.

I had been processed hours ago, and I had been on display in this high end boutique for about 6 hours. It was the only place in town that was licensed in the maintenance, sale of, and care for class Bs. That said, I was the only one here, and I would be surprised if they had ever seen someone come through here before like me... I stood up and walked around the container. It was clean, and spotless, with a small "bed" and opaque area for using the bathroom, but it was far too small to be an apartment, even a studio. I hoped that my parents didn't keep me in here when they got me back. I'd love to live in my old dollhouse, actually. I think I still had it, in the back of my closet somewhere...

The door dinged open, and Henri walked into the shop, looking around before seeing me in the display case. She walked over to the clerk, and spoke for a few minutes before stepping over to me. The clerk pulled my little plastic container out of the case, and set it on the counter, leaving his hand on top of it as Henri leaned in to speak to me, her blonde hair and blue eyes filling the wall of the container.

"Amber! Your father applied for the license, and I have started a crowd fund! See? Here is what it looks like!"

Her voice was muffled, but I could still hear her, and I leaned in to see her phone screen as she held it up to the plastic. It was a crowdfunding campaign for $10,000, and it looked like about $3000 of it had been funded already. Maybe I wouldn't be here long after all, then...

"See?" She said, pointing to the numbers "I shared it all over the internet and went around school all day, and people are helping you! We got over $3000 in just a few hours, at this rate, we'll have the money by the time the shop opens tomorrow!"

"That's wonderful, Henri, thank you so much!" I yell, trying to be heard through the glass. She looked at me for a second, and nodded.

"Well, I can't hear you, love, but... I think you're saying you are happy!"

I nodded, and made a heart with my hands. She smiled, and made one back. She snapped a picture of me with her phone and showed it to me.

"This is ok? I want a picture of you to put on the page so people will donate more!"

The picture was... Not flattering. My hair was a mess and I was still in pajamas from last night, but... if it helped. I gave her a thumbs up.

"Well, Kleine Fee, I will see you on tomorrow! I will go and spread the word and get you lots more help! Please, sleep well, and I will do my best!"

I waved goodbye to her as the clerk put me back in the display case, and sat down on my bed. I wasn't really tired, but I was bored and I felt drained. If I was home I'd turn on something old and simple to watch, maybe *I Dream of Jeannie*, or *The Dick Van Dyke* show, but here, all there was to watch was the clerk as he cleaned up the store, locking up, and turning out the lights. I stared out the store window at the empty street through three layers of plastic or glass, and wondered if my parents would be able to make mandu for my size or if I'd just have to eat massive dumplings instead. I lay down and tried and get comfortable on the mattress they gave me. I wish they'd just have let me keep what was left of my bed. I pulled out my phone and checked the battery. 46%... Wireless charging *should* still work, so that's not a problem, but... I didn't have a wireless charger on me, obviously. I sent goodnight texts to my mom and dad, and a thank you message to Henri, then powered it off for the night. I rolled over, and tried to get to sleep.

~~~

I awoke to the sound of thumping in the room, and I looked around to see the same clerk unlocking the shop, tallying the register, pulling out display jewelry, and preparing for the day. I popped my back and leaned against the wall, powering on my phone. 40%... how did it lose 5% while powered fully off?. I checked my messages. A heart from my mother, of course. My father had sent a picture of the certificate of guardianship approval for a class B, and my heart soared, thank *goodness*... Henri had let me know that they had hit the $10,000 goal, and that they were waiting on the money to transfer to the account, then they'd go to the bank at 9:00 to let them know to expect a big transaction so the account wouldn't be locked, then they'd come right over. I looked at the time. 9:05, so they *should* be here in less than twenty or thirty minutes.

I powered my phone off again, and did my best to fold up the microfiber cloth and put it on my bed. I caught my reflection on the wall and ran my fingers through my hair to smooth it out, but it was still frazzled and static-y from the microfiber. I paced my little chamber, glancing at the door every so often to see if I could see them yet, but nothing so far. I took a breath, and focused on my breathing, trying to calm down, then the door jingled. I spun around, looking for them, but my heart stopped instantly as soon as I turned. I whipped out my phone and started powering it up, shaking like a leaf. It *couldn't* be, it was just a coincidence, right?

Marissa stood there, a few feet away, looking at her phone, scanning the room. Suddenly, she saw me, her eyes widening a fraction and flicking back and forth from her phone to me a couple times before she slipped it into her purse and walked up to the counter. My heart had started again and it was thrumming in my chest like a rainstorm. My phone finally turned on, and my fingers flew as I texted Henri

*'GET HERE NOW EMERGENCY'*

A second passed, and then her response popped up

*'On our way. What happened?'*

*'shes here shes trying to get me please get here please'*

*'Who is?'*

Then after a second, she understood.

*'Oh, oh gods, please be calm kleine fee, I am coming fast. the counter man said he would hold you'*

I stared up at the two giants above me. The clerk was shaking his head, and pointing at me, and Marissa was staring at him with her half lidded stare, showing him a document and her credit card. He shook his head again, and pointed to me one more time. She glared at him for a moment, then pulled off her jacket, and tossed it on the counter, on top of her purse. From under the glass, I could see her sliding out a stack of money from her purse. She grabbed the young man's hand and slid it under the coat, pushing the stack of money into his hand. He froze. Then he looked at me. Then back to her, and nodded, and slid the money off the counter and into his pocket out of view of the cameras. I screamed and fell to my knees, this wasn't fair, this was *cheating*, this was my *life* he was bartering away. I banged on the sides of my plexiglass, screaming that my family would pay double if he'd only wait, but my voice wasn't reaching.

Marissa signed the paperwork quickly, and filled out some sort of order sheet, checking boxes down the line in rapid succession as she tapped her foot on the floor, looking bored. She handed over her card and he swiped it. A second later, she pulled out her phone, tapped away for a moment, and then nodded at him. He swiped again, and the green checkmark popped up on the screen. Even rich people could get transaction alerts, it seemed...

He pointed at me, then at the list, and she shook her head, pointing at the door. I didn't know what they were discussing, but I didn't care. I felt sick, I gagged, and I slid to my knees in the enclosure. This couldn't be real, right? No one could be *this* cruel... She *had* to know it was me, she must have seen the crowd funding link and rushed here to snag me up early. I curled up into a ball as the man opened the display case and pulled out my tiny prison by the handle, passing it over the counter to her.

"Well, I don't feel great about this, but if she's that important to you, I'm sure the family will understand." I heard him say.

She ignored his comment.

"You said around three, right?"

"Huh? Oh, yeah, should be about then, yes."

"Ok, tell them to bring it all up when they get there, our man will show them the way."

She grabbed my case, and without looking at me, turned, and walked out of the building. I gagged again, the little room shaking and rocking not helping my feeling of sickness. Marissa turned the corner to where her car was still idling, and came face to face with Henri and my parents. Henri looked at me with a mixture of horror and disbelief, her face going white, her eyes wide, the paleness making her look like a ghost, even in the sunlight. Marissa flexed the hand holding me slightly and I stood up and slammed against the wall.

"Mamma, Appa, please, help me!" My voice, already small, was drown out by the noise from the car and the walls of my prison. Marissa opened the back door and started to get in. Henri lunged for me at the last second, her hands slamming into the car door as it closed. She smacked the window with her palms, her muffled shouts and my parent's sobs barely audible as Marissa set me on the seat beside her.

"Drew, home." She said, calmly. The driver nodded, and pulled off. I lay in the seat, shaking. I had just lost my whole family, I had just been sold to the worst person I knew, I wasn't a human anymore, just a glorified lap dog for this stuck up, violent rich kid. I lay unmoving, letting the chills of despair and realization wash over me. I heard a buzzing and I jumped. It was coming from her pocket, she dug out her phone and checked the screen. She sighed and answered.

"Hello, mother....

"Yes, that was me.

"...

"No, mother, it's *my* money, I can do-

"Ok. right, of course...

"Right. Yes ma'am.

"I bought a new pet. A class B.

"I told you this spring, mother, when I got my license.

"...Ok, yes. No, it should be reasonable after this, it's just a one time cost.

"Yes, mother, it's very trendy. Every girl in school will be jealous of me.

"No, a girl. Someone I knew from school.

"...A bit, yes. She's too small to tell, now, though.

"Ok, mother, I'll do that. You'll be back next Friday, not this coming one, right?

"Ok, I'll see you then."

She hung up and shoved her phone under her leg. A 'new pet'... She really did see me as less than human... Her eyes flicked to me for a split second, and I saw the hint of a smile flicker across her resting bitch face, and I felt cold.

She faced forward, and didn't speak or look at me for the rest of the ride.

# Chapter Two

Once we got to her house, the driver, 'Drew', pulled up directly to the front door. Marissa grabbed my handle and climbed out of the car, letting me swing in an arc as she did. Her house was *huge*, the kind of building that you see as you drive past and think "I could throw the best parties there..." except, you'd never drive past it, because it's hidden away from the rest of the world in an area that only houses like that are in. Obviously, I'd never been to her house before, but it was pretty much what I expected. It was very modern, with several stories, and an overall grey look to it. Not quite... I think it was called 'brutal' or something? But kinda close? I couldn't see much of it from my place in the case, but it was easily the size of the entire apartment complex my family lived in.

The car door slammed, making me jump, and I looked around to see the car pulling off again, to some garage out of sight, I presumed. Marissa walked to the door, deliberately bouncing my case off her thigh with every step. One she got to the door, she knocked, and it swung open to reveal an older man in a light grey suit, but... one of the old ones, not a business suit. She held me up to eye level and pointed at me with her free hand.

"Parker, this is my new pet. You are not to interact with it in any way, not to feed it, clean it, or in any other way acknowledge its existence, unless you find it loose, in which case you will return it to my room. I have supplies for it coming later today, bring them directly up to my room, and knock. I'll let you in, do not enter without knocking."

The gentleman's eyes widened at her first statement, staring at me with mild surprise, but he almost as quickly returned to a neutral gaze, and nodded as she spoke.

"Of course, Miss Marissa, I will be sure to follow your instructions perfectly."

She spun away from him, dropping me back down by her side, jolting me and causing me to fall over, and then she marched off to an elevator.

In the elevator, I looked up at her. She looked pensive, like she was thinking something over as she waited, but I couldn't tell what. She still wasn't looking at me, and at *this* point I had realized that she didn't just 'not value' me, but rather, she was trying to *show* me she didn't value me. Even a regular rich person would be at least slightly interested in the new pet they spent *$25,000* plus bribe on, right? She had to be trying to fuck with me, that's all there was to it. I considered trying to get her attention, maybe knocking on the side or calling out, but then I remembered that her attention was very much a bad thing to have... I lay down and stared up, seeing her knuckles whiten as she squeezed, seeing her arm vanish into her coat, seeing her stretched out away from me like a cartoon character. Being small really made perspectives difficult...

The doors slid open, and she walked out and across the hall, into what I assumed was her room. It was big, it had an open floor plan, and there were a few pillars here and there, but overall, it looked fairly normal, no torture devices or paintings of serial killer victims like I'd half expected. There was a giant bed with a low sofa on one side, a few shelves along the wall, one of the walls was just a big window, and one wall was taken up by a big TV, a computer desk, and between them, a large empty standing desk. The desk was where she put me, she set me right in the middle, and walked away, to one of two doors other than the one we can in from. A bathroom maybe? A closet? I tried to get a sense of what kind of person she was by her decorations, but the posters on the wall were art prints from surrealistic artists I'd never heard of, of things I couldn't quite identify, and her shelves seemed to be full of classics, school books, and the occasional generic fiction novel.

The door opened again and she stepped out. From where I was, it did look like a bathroom after all. She pulled her coat off, and tossed it on the bed, then stood there, taking careful breaths as she looked at the floor. What was she doing? Was she ok? I leaned against the bed, and hoped she had forgotten about me for now... With one last deep breath, she looked my way. She walked over to me slowly, and grabbed the case.

With a twist, she pulled the front wall off, exposing me to the world. I stared at her. For the first time since the store, she was looking at me, full on, her green eyes shining as they bore into mine. Her face filled the entire wall, and her breath was close enough to feel warm. It was minty, like she had just brushed it, and it stung my eyes. I felt dizzy. Was I supposed to say something? I couldn't think of anything safe to say, I didn't know exactly how she saw me yet. I sat there, unmoving, eyes locked on hers. She licked her lips to wet them, then spoke to me.

"Hello, Rat."

So she *DID* know who I was... I knew she knew, but... Now I *really* knew, there was no 'oh, maybe she didn't realize it was me' whispering in my head. She knew, she'd known, and she'd bought me on purpose. I sat forward, and gave her a nervous smile.

"H-hey, Marissa. I see we're going to be... living together, huh?"

Her face finally broke into a cruel sneer, and I felt a sense of relief. I didn't know why, but somehow her dead stare was even worse than her usual face.

"No, there's no 'living together', Rat. You're my *pet*, and you'll be living in my room, under *my* control. Living together implies that we're somehow equals, and *you* aren't my equal. You never were, and now the government agrees, and now I get to do whatever I want to you."

I shuddered and shrink back. Her expression was still just a bit off, either that, or being small made faces look weird somehow. I could see her pores, filled in with foundation but still there, I could tell where her mascara had clumped her eyelashes together, I could see the slight cracks in her lipstick. I could see every detail of her face at once. Maybe that's why she looked off... I was confused why she had lipstick on though, I hadn't seen her wear it at school, even in college, was it something new she was trying? It looked like she wasn't quite used to putting it on yet; it wasn't quite even. Back to the matter at hand, though...

"Are- are you going to kill me?" I asked, needing to get the obvious fear out of the way.

She laughed, a bark of genuine surprise, before she leaned back in and spoke quietly, deliberately hissing the words between her teeth.

"Kill? No, Rat. I need you to be *alive*. I need you to sit nice and pretty where I can show you off to all the other girls, I need them to watch me *own* you. I need them to see you, trapped and owned by me, and I want them to be jealous of me, I need them to desperately want to *BE* me, to own a little you. I need them to see me for the superior godsdamn goddess I've always been. I need them to respect me for owning someone they all looked down on, and respect me for fucking *doing* something about it. But most importantly? I need them to see you and to fucking *fear* me. I need them to look at you and to feel pity for you, then to feel relieved that it wasn't THEM that I bought as a pet. They'll look at you as a symbol of my power, as a threat, and as a buffer between me and them.

"For all that, I need you alive. I might need you to be fucking HEALTHY even, I don't want them to think 'oh, she's just going to play with her for a few months then she'll be too broken to enjoy', I need them to think 'that is a position for LIFE. She'll be eighty years old, still bringing the rat around with her like a toy' and I need them to imagine an entire life being owned by ME."

She leaned back. I was sobbing, hugging my knees to my chest, but she wasn't done yet.

"I'm not going to kill you. Hurt you, maybe. Starve you? You need it anyway. Use you like a fashion accessory? Of course, that's the fun of it, but *kill* you? Hurt you beyond repair? No..." She leaned in close enough for her breath to fog the plexiglass around me and snarled. "Rat, I'm going to treat you like a fucking princess."

I curled against the side of the cage sniffling as she leaned back, my back shaking against my bed. She huffed out of her nose and looked around her room, her face slightly flushed.

"Your stuff will be here in a while, until then... I guess we'll just go over the rules."

I nodded quickly, whatever it took to keep her off of me.

"Ok, well... first off, I need you to call me... Let's see... Miss M? Or... Lady M, or Mistress, or maybe "My Lady"... that sounds pretty nice..."

I cringed compulsively at 'My Lady', but stayed quiet as she thought for a moment more.

"Second, I don't want you to talk to me unless we're already having a conversation. In other words, only speak when spoken to... Unless it's an emergency, I guess.

"Third, don't leave this room without me. This isn't so much a rule to keep you here, as it is a rule to keep you 'safe'. Not that I *care*, but I need you alive long enough to let my ownership of you sink in with the other girls, at least. There's a lot of people working here, and we have a high turnover, so if you wander the house you'll get crushed or vacuumed or something in no time.

"Number four, I don't want you eating without my permission. I think we can do something about that... tummy of yours, and I want to make sure you're on diet while I'm working on it."

I gasped indignantly, I wasn't overweight by any means, a bit of a tummy was *healthy*, and I kept my exercises up, I was in shape as well as anyone, Marissa was just unnaturally thin... This was going to be *hell*, I could tell.

"Fifthly, you'll wear what I say when we go out, and you'll be nice and polite. I doubt anyone will speak to you, but if they do, just pretend you're a kid at a family reunion and your aunt is gushing over you. Something like that, that vibe.

"Six, I don't want you to be talking to people all the time about me, I think one of the bundles I got you has one of those mini tablets for class Bs, so I *guess* you can use the internet but I'll have your password, obviously, and if I find you've been talking bad about me, or even just not talking well about me, I'll take it away and smash it, understand?"

I nodded, feeling my phone digging into my butt in my waistband. It seemed she hadn't noticed I had it yet... Hopefully the stuff she got included a wireless charger I could use.

She leaned back in to squint at me, thinking hard.

"Well... There's more, but I don't know of them yet. It's a living list, so be prepared to have me make rules on the spot at any time. For now..."

She reached in and slid her hand around my torso. My heart lunged as I felt her fingers effortlessly lift me into the air and out of the cage, my legs hanging over the floor. I clung to her thumb as she squeezed me, the air being pushed out of my lungs. I coughed and kicked, trying to get a different position so her middle finger wasn't directly on my sternum. She squeezed harder, watching me closely, then relaxed her grip. I gasped and panted for air, curling up in her hand and she swung me around and walked over to her bed. She tossed me, and I shrieked as I fell, spinning in free fall head over heels onto her pillow.

I hit the plush surface with all my weight, which wasn't much at the moment, but it was enough to click my teeth and stun me for a moment. She hit the bed a moment later, lying down hard next to me, causing me to bounce up into the air before coming back down onto the comforter in a heap. I moaned and felt myself. I was in one piece, and while my teeth hurt, they weren't chipped, and my phone had stayed stuck to my skin under my waistband during that, so it was still hidden.

I sat up and got my bearings. I was on the right side of the bed, and she was on the left side, lying on her side facing me, her body creating a wall along the whole surface. She was lookin down at me with her half lidded stare, watching me try and fail to stand up on the soft surface.

"So... Rat. do you have any useful skills I should know about? Anything that might come in handy for me as your new owner?"

I gave up trying to stand and resigned myself to sitting cross legged instead.

"Well... I know we're in different classes, mostly, but I'm pretty good with homework? I kept up the scholarship for years after all..."

She snorted.

"Homework? I haven't done that since middle school. I buy my way through classes with the administration. Most of us do. You're one of the unlucky few that actually has to *try*. That's not helpful to me at all."

"Oh... Well, I'm good at art? I don't know if that's super helpful, but I can draw pretty good, if that tablet you ordered can support a drawing app..."

"Maybe. Anything else? Anything like, connections? Useful friends? Inside knowledge of... whatever your parents do for a living?"

"U-uh, well, I know the people at the Pad Thai place pretty well, they keep tofu on hand for me, and they don't charge me for the extra sauce I like... Um, other than that, I know Henri, she's pretty good at talking to people and writing? And... my dad is just the manager at an appliance store, so I don't think anything *there* would be useful to you..."

I looked up at her unamused face. The expression spoke for itself.

"So you're pretty much useless as a tool, huh?" She mused, poking me in the forehead, knocking me over backwards. I stayed down and squeezed my eyes shut. I felt her finger run across my face and down to my torso. When it reached my chest, it flinched back for a moment, before pressing into my stomach. I opened my eyes to see her leaning over me with a strange expression on her face, an intensity that I hadn't noticed before. Her eyes flicked back and forth over my face, looking for something, before she drove her finger down into my gut, causing me to spasm, dry heaving to the side as she twisted her finger, her thick nail driving into my skin.

She pulled her finger away, the look on her face still strange and unplaceable. She sat up and crossed her legs, looking down at me as I stopped gagging and caught my breath. Her fingers slipped under me and she lifted me up to her face, to her slightly open lips, and I felt a wash of cold go over me as I stared into her mouth. She wouldn't, right? She wanted me alive and well, and-

Her painted lips parted, and she blew, her minty breath blasting me, the air sucking out of my own lungs. I gasped for air, but only got her secondhand breath, no oxygen. I flopped in her palm, and in a desperate attempt to breathe, I dove off her hand to the bed. As soon as I was out of the path of her icy jet stream, I filled my lungs. I hit the bed hard, and the air left me, but I could breathe.

I heard her laugh as I gulped air heavily.

"I guess I take your breath away, huh, Rat?" She mocked.

I grimaced, and lifted a single finger up to her to show her what I really thought, and her laughing cut short.

"Listen, RAT." She growled. "We're having *fun* here, ok? We're just playing, I don't need you being rude to me, do you understand?"

She pinned me to the bed with her hand and glared down at me.

"Do. You. Fucking. *Understand*, Rat?"

I nodded, begrudgingly.

"I understand, yeah." I panted.

"Say it right, say my name, Rat."

I thought back, what was the least humiliating thing she had told me I could call her?...

"I understand... Lady M."

She smiled, and positioned her other hand next to my side.

"Ok, well, just to make sure..."

She flicked me, and I screamed as my side exploded into pain. She must have hit my kidney, or just had a lucky shot, because the pain was so much I couldn't see straight. I started crying again, and I felt her hand move away from me.

"Oh... W-well... It looks like you learned your lesson..." She said nervously.

She still sounded haughty and cruel, but there was a layer of uncertainty now. She scooped me up and I cringed at the movement, sobbing in pain. She walked back to the desk placed me in my bed, a lot more gently than she'd put me on her own bed, and closed my cage up.

"You just sit in there and think about... stuff, like how you're going to... Make it up to me, until your stuff gets here."

I moaned and curled up. I could hardly see through my tears, but she looked at me for a long minute, reaching out once like she was going to open the cage again, before lowering her hand and walking away. My side still hurt like crazy, I'd never been hit that hard before, not by bullies, not the time I was beaned by a softball, never. I focused on trying to calm down, and before long, I had settled myself down enough to stop crying. It still hurt, but it was more of a throb than a scream.

I peeked out over my shoulder, and saw Marissa on her bed, watching me from across the room. At my look, she jumped slightly, then got up and stalked out of the room, slamming the door behind her. I sat up gingerly and pulled up my shirt. There was no mark yet, but it'd be an ugly bruise before long...

I pulled out my phone and opened it. 35%... There were a lot of new messages from Henri, and a few from my mother. It seemed like they were trying to find a legal way to get me back, but so far they couldn't find anything. I sent my mother and "I love you, I'm safe", and started texting with Henri.

*'im down to 35%, ns if ill b able to charge up, im in her room, she doesnt know i have my phone'*

A second later, Henri was online, responding fast.

*'Is she hurting you???'*

*'a bit yea, but i think ill just bruise. nothing brokn... i hope.'*

*'If you get pics, we can report her?'*

*'it's not bruised yet, but mby. shes saying shes going to use me as a accessory...'*

*'Ugh that bitch, I'll come by and see if I can bargain, do you know your address? or you can drop a pin'*

*'no, dont, she probs would just refuse 2 let u in then take my phone'*

*'Then what shall I do?'*

*'just keep looking 4 a way 2 get me out, legal smth idk, just keep trying, u got this'*

I put my phone back away, powering it down to be safe, and lay down. There was something odd about the way Marissa was acting. It wasn't quite herself, like, she was being cruel and mean, but she seemed to be focused too; not on *hurting* me, on something else. I couldn't tell what she was thinking, but it made me nervous either way. My body was sore all over, especially my side, and I was worn out from being tossed around and crushed, so in a few minutes, I was asleep.

~~~

My cage jolted, and I fell out of bed, hissing in pain as I landed on my side. I looked around, and saw Marissa holding the handle, with two men carrying a large pair of boxes into her room. She jabbed a finger at the desk I had been on.

"There, set it up there. There's a plug to the left, I'll do the furniture myself, just get it set up and working."

"Ok, can do, she's going to love this, it'll be like a castle, just you wait!" The taller of the two men said, cheerfully. Marissa ignored him and crossed her arms, bouncing me against her hip impatiently.

The men pulled parts of a small square house out of the boxes and began snapping them together. It looked like the house was styled after one of those old dollhouses from the early 2000s, where you could open one side and look in. It was three stories, with the lower floor being a kitchen and dining room, the middle floor being an open floor, and the top floor having a bedroom, with a section blocked off that wasn't open to the outside, the bathroom, I assumed. There was a tank on top, right above the bathroom, and a tank below on the floor as well. Presumably that was the water for the plumbing in the home. There was a standard cord that plugged into the wall behind the desk, and when it was plugged in, the house lit up, with small LEDs in each room coming on.

Once it was all connected and set up the shorter man pulled a case out of the bottom of one of the boxes.

"This here is all your extras, the cushions for the bed, a sofa, a little TV, a tablet, the kitchen set, all that stuff. Usually the class B will want to set this stuff up themselves, but the furniture is kinda unwieldy, so you may want to give her a hand. They're stronger than they look, but not *that* strong."

Marissa glared at him and took the case with her free hand. "And the clothes? Where are those?"

The man shook his head. "There's a few basic sets of clothes provided here, but most of what you ordered is going to take a few days. We have her measurements from the government scan, and we're using that to make sure the clothes actually fit."

"Seriously? There's no... one size fits all?"

"Well, there *is*, that's what the temporary clothing is, but the people who dress up their class Bs in the kind of expensive clothes you ordered prefer them to look, you know, nice, and if their clothes are all giant and sloppy, it ruins the effect..."

"Ugh, I suppose. Is that all?"

"Well, here's the manual for the house..." He handed her a small book. "And it'll also come installed on the tablet, too, so your new friend can read up on how to use the stove or wash her clothes or whatever."

Marissa walked to the door and opened it. "Well, if that's all, then..."

Once the men had left, she closed the door and set me down on the desk. "Well, Rat. I told you I'd treat you like a fucking princess, this is the proof. I bet your old shithole house had nothing on this, huh?"

As much as I hated to admit it, she was right. It was really nice. The kitchen was shiny and clean, the countertops looked like real stone, even the stairs had fancy real wood hand rails. She opened the cage, and I walked over, stepping up into the house. As soon as I did, I looked down in shock.

"Are- are the floors heated?!"

"You sub humans have a hard time keeping in body heat, so yeah, heated floors help maintain your temperature. Otherwise, you'll get sick way more often, and you can develop brain damage over time." She replied, automatically.

I looked up in surprise, I hadn't expected her to actually *know* about the care of class Bs. She noticed my look, and frowned.

"I *did* have to take a class, you know. They don't just give the licenses away, you have to earn it or whatever."

I thought about that, it did make me feel... a little bit better, at least. She knew *how* to care for me. Whether she did or not was another question. She pulled out a table and a few chairs from the box and slid them into the dining room, then did the same with a sofa on the floor above me.

"I'm not setting all this up, it's your house you know. I'm just getting stuff out, you need to get it all into place. And another thing, consider it another rule, you see how clean my room is? Your whole house needs to stay that clean, at all times. Got it?"

Upstairs, there was a rug, a boxy TV, the tablet (which was roughly as big as my whole torso), a short table, a flat treadmill, and some blankets. I decided to leave setting the electronics up for later, and went upstairs to make the bed and put the bathroom supplies away. The soaps were all grainy and thick, and instead of toilet paper, the toilet was equip with a bidet, which was nice, and it made sense, I supposed. There was a toothbrush that was weird, it was more of a felt strip than bristles, and there was a hairbrush that seemed much too big to be any use. I found the feminine supplies, and the pads were way too thick to be comfortable, but the *other* option they had provided was... not going to work, to say the least, so I would just have to get used to the pads.

I finished up, and looked around. The house was mostly in order, I just had to get the TV and tablet set up, and it should be fine. I was actually pretty happy with the bed, it was very soft, and the sheets were satin, or something like it, and felt much better than the microfiber I'd been using. I went down to the middle floor, and turned on the TV. It was just a basic streaming box, and the only thing to do was to plug in the wi-fi. I looked over out the open side of the house and saw Marissa sitting on her bed, reading the manual for the house. Huh, it looked like she really did have an interest in this stuff...

"Excuse me, what's the wifi password?" I called out, politely.

"It's Lemoncrush55, capital L." She said, not paying attention. Then she blinked and glared at me. "*Hey*, no speaking unless spoken to, Rat. Do you want me to flick you again?"

I shuddered "No, sorry! I just need it to set up the TV, I'm just minding my own business, I swear..."

She glared at me for another moment, then went back to reading. I calmed myself down and tried to stop shaking. I didn't think she'd really flick me again, she almost seemed to regret it the first time, but... it was still not something I wanted to risk. The whole "don't speak unless spoken to" rule was going to be hard to get used to. I was always a very outspoken girl, and my parents didn't mind me talking except at dinner, so I was used to just saying whatever, whenever.

I finished setting up the TV, and turned my phone on. I sent Henri a message.

*'im gonna set up a tablet 2 text u and stuff, dont mention i have a phone when txting that contact, let my parents kno 2'*

I got a reply instantly.

*'Ok, got it. Stay safe, kleine fee,'*

I'd need to look that up eventually. She kept calling me that, so it must be a term of endearment or something. I put in my info to the tablet, using a different email than usual so it wouldn't synch up my phone's messages, and I messaged her again.

*'hey henri, got a tablet, settling in to my new home. it's amber btw'*

*'Hello, I'm so sorry I missed you at the shop, we love you so much and we will be here for you, I am with your parents, is there anything we can do to help?'*

A shadow fell over me, and I looked up to see Marissa peeking into the house.

"You're texting your friend, huh? Remember, nothing bad about me or you lose the tablet."

I nodded and reply to Henri as Marissa dug through the rest of the box the movers had left.

*'idk, ill think about it, just plz make sure 2 stay in touch, ly2 bbgrl'*

I set the tablet down on the stand, and the charger icon popped up. Wireless... Hopefully it'd work on my phone too, and the shrinking hadn't made the... electronic bits not work right or something. I turned around to see Marissa holding a semi flat bottle up to the house, measuring it against me. I stepped back, was she going to?...

"Hey, does this look like you'll fit?" She asked, holding it sideways. It looked like I'd fit, yeah, but not enough to even take a step, I'd barely have room to sit down...

"Not... Not well? I think I might, but it'd be really close quarters..." I reply reluctantly. She threaded a silver chain through the neck of the bottle and held it up to her chest.

"Well, *this* is going to be your home, while I'm out and about. It's a necklace, and you'll be on display for all the world to see, so you'll need to be on your best behavior, got it?"

"Oh, *gods*. I'll be in THAT all day? I don't think I can-"

"HEY." She snapped, cutting me off. "It's this, or... I safety pin you to my shirt or something, so suck it up. It's cute, these bottles are like, designer. It even has an intercom so you can talk to me through an earpiece if it's too loud." She smirked "IF I decide to wear it, of course. I can't imagine I'd have much need to talk to a Rat like you."

She clasped the chain and takes a few steps around the room, leaning forwards to test out the necklace.

"Yeah, this is nice, I like this. It'll be good. We can do a test run for it tomorrow, I have a class in the morning, I'll wear you then." Her mouth split open in a smile "Gods, I'll *wear* you, that's just... It's so... gah..." She shivered, grinning.

She composed herself, and pulled the necklace off. "Well, take some time to get used to your new place. I have to go get food for you apparently, I thought it was included in all this, but that shop doesn't offer it. Don't break anything, read the manual, and I'll be back any second so don't get sneaky." She grabbed her phone, and walked away.

"Wait, the food, I'm a veg-" I called out. The door slammed, cutting me off. I slumped. Just perfect. Well, as long as she was gone... I slid my phone onto the tablet stand, and... The screen lit up. I sighed in relief. I'd have to stay close while it charged in case Marissa snooped, but at least it wasn't going to be a brick. In the meantime though, I needed a shower... There were a couple of the "one size fits all" clothes in my closet, and the ones I'd been wearing for almost 48 hours needed cleaning badly... I headed up the stairs, and got to work.

A few hours later, I was sitting on my couch watching videos on the tv. I had looked up videos by other class Bs to see if anyone had any tips for living life like this, but most of the channels I found were run by the class B's caretakers, and they seemed to be 'managing' the whole thing, with the class Bs practically reading off a script. It reminded me too much of the 'family channels' that were popular a couple years back and gave me the ick. I couldn't find any genuine vlogs or videos by class Bs, but I wasn't sure if that was because of the algorithm, or if they just didn't really exist. Either way, I had resorted to watching videos *about* class Bs, by caretakers. There was one lady who really seemed to care for hers, and her videos were full of helpful tips on how to make sure we didn't get hurt or die.

I was learning a lot, Some stuff I really should have already figured out, like that we were more susceptible to cold, or getting sick, or that we couldn't eat too much 'people food' or we'd throw up because our stomach acids couldn't break down the proteins and stuff, but other stuff, like the fact that we could lift much more than our body weight, in some cases even a few pounds, really surprised me. I hadn't *felt* any stronger, much less being able to lift a whole other me, but it made sense the way she described it. She was just going into detail about how I'd need to start taking supplements for calcium and fibers eventually when the door opened, and Marissa came in, holding a small bag from an upscale grocery store.

"GODS, your food is expensive. You're lucky you got bought by me, your parents would have had to just buy you the shitty food pellets and call it a day. This is 2 week of meals and it was almost $600. *I* don't even spend that much on food in two weeks, and I'm full sized, with actual taste."

She dropped the bag on my kitchen table and I headed downstairs to see what she'd bought. Hopefully there was something without meat, I didn't want to start anything right now, and she sounded annoyed already...

"Thank you..." I offered, opening the bag.

It was full of small, frozen or refrigeratable cardboard containers. They had a logo of a cartoon person surrounded by shining lines of light, I think, and they were branded as "Micro Power Ready Meals". They had a little list of facts on them, talking about how they were formulated for compressed individuals, how they were heavily processed so we could digest them, and how they were full of all the vitamins we'd need to be healthy. Yeah, it sounded expensive alright. The servings were pretty big too, bigger than I'd have thought.

I pulled out the first box and flipped it over. It was listed as "R'ce and Been Burrito". Well, *that* didn't have meat. It looked like they weren't legally allowed to call the rice and beans 'rice and beans' though, which was... concerning. The next box was labeled "Tofu BBQ Salad".... Not sure what that meant, but it looked like tofu was ok to say at least. I pulled out another one. It was called "Plant Derived Burger Meal, with Fried Carbs". It looked like a fast food meal, burger and fries, they even came in little cardboard fast food boxes too... I could eat all this, actually... I dug through the bag, and started putting it in the fridge, it was all veggie friendly. Was that the norm for class Bs?

I glanced over at Marissa, who was watching me with a strange expression on her face; nervous but slightly confrontational, like she expected me to start something. She stepped closer to her and started putting on lotion when she noticed me staring. I cleared my throat.

"Thank you," I said again "I'm really glad you got these for me, and it's lucky they're all vegetarian too, I was hoping I wouldn't have to eat meat."

She snorted, and shook her head. "Lucky nothing, I paid extra for that stupid meat free shit. It's *way* harder to get plant proteins compressed for a class B, apparently."

I looked at her in surprise. "Wait, you knew I was vegetarian? How? I didn't even get a chance to tell you..."

She glared down at me. "I'm not *stupid*, Rat. We've been going to the same schools for like 6 years, I *do* notice stuff, you know."

"I... didn't know you thought of me enough to notice anything like that, thank you, I really appreciate it..." I said, feeling awkward. I'd never noticed any of *her* eating habits, was I just oblivious?

"Whatever, Rat. You get one of those meals a day, some in the morning, the rest when we get home. Each meal is just under the calories you need in a day each, based on your height, so hopefully you'll get into better shape over time this way."

There it was. I subtly sucked in my stomach and stepped around the table to face her. It wasn't easy to see my body in the oversized bodysuit I'd put on after my shower, but hopefully being small would help me out.

"I really like to work out, I saw there was a treadmill, and I plan on using that every day. I usually go to the gym at least three days a week with Henri, so I do burn more calories than most people, I'm pretty healthy. I just think I might not be... as healthy if I just eat one meal a day..."

Her face loomed in front of me, her half lidded glare bearing down on me.

"Rat. I say you need to get in shape. You fucking say 'Yes Mistress, I'll do my best.' not try and tell me why you don't have to obey me. Now, I say you need to get in shape, Rat, so..."

She looked at me expectantly. I grimaced and fold my arms, looking back at her. She raised an eyebrow, and lifted her hand up to my face, her finger behind her thumb, ready to flick. My side spiked with anticipatory pain and I cringed back. I opened my mouth and forced the words out.

"Y-yes, mistress, I'll try my best..."

She smirked, and poked my face with her finger. "That's good Rat, that sounds lovely. You can eat a whole meal tonight, since it's been a couple days since you ate."

Thank the gods, I was hollow by now. I rubbed my nose and closed the fridge.

"It was the night before last, yeah. I had mandu..."

"Mandu? I don't even know what that is, it sounds like an alien."

"It's... dumplings, it's a food my parents make me. Or... I guess used to make..."

I look at the fridge and slump. I'd never eat that again, I guess. Marissa clicked her tongue and shook her head.

"Better forget about all that Rat, you couldn't even eat it even if they did make it for you. A few bites in and you'd be puking your guts up."

"Yeah, I know. I was watching videos about it before you got here."

She crinkled her nose. "You were watching videos of class Bs puking?"

"No, the- ew, like the videos of people telling how to take care of class Bs. I'm new to all this, I didn't even know about the food issues, or the heat problem, and like, did you know that class Bs have to use special microphones to be heard on the phone?"

"Yeah, Rat. I took the stupid class, I told you. I know all that shit. Anyway, *you* don't need to know all that, I'm in charge, I'll be the one taking care of all that."

"That's a weird thought... Being... 'taken care of' by someone. You, especially."

She reached in and knocked me on my ass with a finger. "Hey, I'm not 'taking care' of you like that. I'm your fucking *owner*. I'm protecting my investment."

My side throbbed from the sudden jarring, and I slowly stood up, rubbing it. Her eyes watched me, going to my side, then my face, and she got that odd look on her face again.

"Anyway, look. Just make your fucking dinner and mind your own business for tonight, I'm taking you out tomorrow, so you need to be well rested, or I'll shake the jar constantly to keep you alert, understand?"

I shuddered and nodded. "I understand... 'Mistress'" I say, injecting sarcasm into the last word. She narrowed her eyes at me, but turned away, and left the room.

I sighed and pulled out the burger meal. This was still going to be hell, but she was somehow a lot more human than I thought she'd be...

# Chapter Three

I lay in my new bed and stared at the ceiling. I had tried to get a full night's sleep, but I had tossed and turned all night. My side still hurt a lot, and while I was tired, my mind just couldn't stop racing, thinking about all the stuff that could happen. I wasn't looking forward to being stuck in a jar all day for one thing, and for another, I was dreading seeing the other girls at school with my new condition. They already made my life terrible before, now it would be almost justified. I turned over and looked at the wall. Marissa had closed the house up before she went to bed, either to give me privacy, or to give her privacy, but the wall that opened to the outside was made of plastic instead of... house stuff, like the rest of my new home to make it easer to open and close, so it had an uncanny, fake look to it. It just made me feel even more like a doll than being small already did.

I sighed and sat up. I needed to do something, at least. I went downstairs, and pulled my phone from the spot behind the tablet and turned it on. I had a new message from Henri, wishing me a good night, and asking if anything else had happened. I decided to message her on the tablet instead, just to make sure Marissa saw that I was sending messages if she decided to check.

*"hey bbgrl, I'm up early. I got my food last nite, it was p good, its veggie stuff 2, i finally can eat again lol, been a while"*

There was no reply, so she must still have been sleeping. I sent another anyway.

*"the floors r heated in this bitch 2, rlly nice, got a big tv and a private treadmill, gonna break ur distance record soon"*

Still no reply, so I slid the phone under the sofa cushion and put the tablet on the charger. I may as well get dressed at least. My pajamas were clean now that I'd figured out the washer and dryer (which took less than 5 minutes from start to end, which was nice), but I wanted something nicer if I was going to be on display all day. My options were limited though, I had either the pink bodysuit I had worn last night, some overalls that I'd need to roll up the legs on, or a light blue sash that kind of wrapped around my body to look like a dress and was kind of adjustable. I went with the dress-sash. I wrapped it in a way that made it look almost like a toga, and used one of the long ropes from the curtain as a belt.

I stood in front of the mirror and turned. It wasn't great, but it was ok, I looked normal enough, if sort of dressed up for just going to school. I needed to brush my teeth and figure out what meal I was going to eat half of next. I chose a poke bowl that had... different colored shapes in it, but I couldn't really tell what they were supposed to be based on texture or taste. I ate about a third of it, and put it away. It wasn't filling, but... I had something in my stomach at least. I was trying to decide if it would be a good idea to have a glass of water if I was going to be trapped in a jar all day when I heard footsteps outside. I walked to my front door and peeked out just in time to see a very groggy Marissa slip into the bathroom and slam the door.

I wasn't exactly happy she was up, but it was good to know that the day had started, and I wasn't up TOO early at least. I headed back to the couch to check my messages (nothing yet), and sent off another one.

*"im going 2 school 2day with 'lady m' keep an eye out, ill b her new accessory lol"*

I flipped the tv on, and continued watching some care tip videos about class Bs. They were kinda helpful, these said we needed less sleep now, but got tired throughout the day and might need an afternoon rest. We're sensitive to bright lights and loud noises, and we have a hard time dealing with multiple people at once or we get overwhelmed. So... nothing new there, that was all stuff that could have been said about me before I was infected. There might be new stuff in a later video, but I still felt like I'd wasted 30 minutes on that for no reason.

My tablet pinged, and I quickly opened the messages.

*"Oh, klein fee... I'm happy you are settling in, but my heart goes out to you for the day you will have... I will be at the school as well, I will come see you as best as I can, and I will hopefully get time to spend with you myself. I do not know if she will let us though..."*

I felt the couch buzz, and I pulled out my phone, listening for footsteps as I checked it. It was Henri again.

*"I will try and steal you, anything to get you away. I can keep you safe, and be on a plane to Germany by tonight with you hidden with me."*

Alarm bells went off in my head and I quickly responded.

*"no no no!!! if u do that youll b arrested and locked up and sent away w out me and m will just flick me again or worse, pls dont steal me"*

*"But my little sweet, I need to know you're safe..."*

*"i wish i knew i was safe 2, but like just chill 4 now we cn figure it out or smth"*

*"Ok, I still want to try and see you..."*

I heard the bathroom door open, and I quickly shut my phone off, hiding it again. The wall of the house swung away, exposing me to the larger world again. I shivered as I was reminded how small I really was, and looked out to see Marissa, dressed and smirking, the bottle in her hand.

"Well, Rat. Are you ready to be *worn?*"

Her smirk got wider at the last word, and I stood slowly, shaking.

"I'm r-ready, I ate, and I put on my nicest thing, and... I'm ready."

Her smirk twisted, as if she'd been wanting me to argue, but she reached in and plucked me out of the house anyway. I lay in her hand as she sat on her bed. Her grip was much lighter than yesterday, and I was grateful for that, I would have screamed if she squeezed my side right now. She unscrewed the top of the bottle, and held me over the opening.

"Have fun in there!~" She said in a singsong voice.

I slid out of her hand as she tipped me, my toga dress flaring up as I dropped into the little jar feet first. I smoothed it down and assessed my new container. It was small, just barely big enough to sit in, and the neck was just over the top of my head if I was standing. Marissa screwed on the lid, and I heard a slight hum, and cool air blew down onto me from the top. Looking up, I could see there were a few buttons on the underside of the lid. One to turn the mic on and off, one to make the fan blow more or less, and one for heat. That would be handy if I really was as susceptible to the cold as they said...

Marissa's slightly warped face loomed in front of me as she looked at me inside the bottle.

"Well, Rat, do you like it?"

I brace myself against the walls as she tipped the bottle back and forth.

"It's- I think I might get seasick in here, but it's not too bad, could I get a pillow to sit on or something?" I called out.

She grinned at me, and held up a small ear bud to the glass before slipping it into her blouse pocket.

"Ohh, sorry Rat, I can't hear you through the glass without this little guy, and it doesn't go with my outfit. I'll just assume you're fine, ok?"

"Careful! I could seriously get concussed in here!" I yelled.

Ignoring me, or just not hearing me, she put the bottle necklace on, letting me bounce against her sternum. I could see the lower part of her face, but not much. the top of the bottle blocked most of my view. I could see in front of me pretty well though; it was warped because of the slightly curved glass, but I could still make everything out. Marissa walked out of her room, and I bounced with every step. She was... flouncing? If that was the right word? Walking with her body and shoulders, to make me shake more. I got on my knees and braced against the walls with my arms. I was already feeling sick, this was going to be a rough day.

~~~

We arrived at the college in her car, Drew pulling away as soon as Marissa got out. She squared her shoulders and took a deep breath.

"Don't embarrass me, Rat. We're going to make an impression, and you're going to look good, and make the others jealous, got it?"

I didn't say anything. She wouldn't have heard me anyway. She shook her head, fluffing her hair, and started toward the front door of the school. I bounced slightly as she walked, and I swallowed hard, trying to fight off the slight nausea I was getting. Hopefully she didn't have a full day of classes, if my schedule was- or, had been I suppose, anything to go by, since she was off yesterday, she'd most likely have at least 2 classes today... She stepped into the main building, and slowed down. I felt her chest puff out as she subtly tried to show me off. It wasn't as subtle as she was going for from where I sat, but I did have a front row seat, so it might have been more classy from the outside.

There weren't many students here yet, and those that were seemed busy with their own stuff; on their phones, or walking to class. Marissa huffed under her breath, and picked up her pace again, practically stalking her way to the school's food hall. I guess she hadn't eaten at home after all. I wondered if she usually ate at home, if maybe she just chose to eat here to get a chance to show me off? Her comment about having "actual taste" implied she ate fancy foods, but the food in the school's cafe was pretty pricy too, I never got much more than a coffee or tea, I much preferred to eat in town.

She got in the back of the line at the cafe and folded her arms under me, framing me with them, and leaned back slightly. As the person in the front of the line got her food and turned, her eyes locked onto Marissa and she flinched slightly. I couldn't see Marissa's expression, but seeing the way the student's eyes flicked down to me, then widened, I could guess she was looking pretty smug. The other student lowered her head and walked past quickly, keeping her eyes forward. I recognized her as she passed. She was one of the students that had actively caused me trouble in the past, she'd even shown up to one of my birthday parties in high school, just to laugh at my family's apartment and leave after a few minutes. It was even worse than if she'd just not shown up, honestly.

To this day, she still smirked at me or made comments about me whenever I was around. She wasn't as bad as Marissa, of course, but... The way she was too afraid to even look at me? The way she just looked down and moved past? It almost gave me a sense of power... I knew it was really Marissa's power. The power to get away with anything, the power to get her mother to ruin anyone's reputation or job, the power that came with being cruel, but... it did feel good to get some of that power for myself.

Marissa got to the front of the line, and ordered a dirty chai and a chicken and lettuce wrap, and moved to stand by the other counter to wait. Her vibe was different now, the lady taking her order had watched me the entire time, her eyes wide, and the other customers kept glancing over when they thought she couldn't see. She was eating this up, and pretended not to notice the others looking at her as she collected her food and stepped out of the cafe into the food hall. She put her stuff on a table in the center of the room, and pulled me off her neck. She looked at me, and I could see the excitement and energy in her eyes as she whispered, her voice barely audible over the sound of my fan.

"Ok, Rat, just sit there and look pretty, maybe look kinda sad or something, got it?"

She set my bottle across from her, and opened her wrap, taking a bite that was bigger than me. I shuddered and hugged myself. That was... not a good train of thought I was going down. I looked around the room, and saw a a couple other students in a group looking back at me. I waved to them, and they jumped, and turned away. I heard Marissa giggle through her mouthful, and I sighed. As much as I wanted her happy, I felt bad feeding her need for power like this, but I didn't have many options, just *existing* fed her need for power.

Marissa stood halfway out of her seat and waved to a girl that had just walked in. She swallowed hard, and called out.

"Tracy! Come here, come sit, let's catch up!"

I watched as Tracy stopped in her tracks like a deer in the headlights, before waving and pointing to the cafe.

"Of course, after, after!" Marissa called out in her singsong.

She sat back down, and grinned at me.

"She's my bitch, but she hates me. She'll tell the whole school about you, and how awful it is that I have you, it'll be great." She said, quietly. I nodded. I didn't know Tracy well, but I did know that she was in Marissa's orbit of people who stayed just close enough to not be a target, but not close enough to be real friends. After she got her food, she sat down across from me and Marissa, a coffee and a muffin in hand.

"So... Marissa, I see you got a new... toy...?" She said, not sure what to call me.

Marissa laughed, and flicked my jar, I flinched and covered my head instinctively, but aside from a sharp pinging noise, I was fine.

"Yeah, it's the Rat! I got it at that boutique in the shops, it was NOT cheap. I saw that Bludsauger was trying to buy it, and was trying to raise money, so I snagged it up before it went out of stock. We can't have HER landing a fun toy like this, right?"

Tracy forced a smile, looking down at me with wide eyes. "Oh, ah, yeah, of course! It wouldn't make sense for her to have something this nice, it'd be- it'd be a joke!"

I watched Tracy take a sip of her coffee, her eyes locked onto mine. I waved at her, and she started, spilling her coffee on her fingers. It seemed people didn't like being reminded I was real...

"But... I did want to ask..." Marissa started, casually. "You see, that little fundraiser that she did, it had a list of people who donated on it, right?"

Tracy leaned back, in full defense mode instantly.

"Oh! Oh, that? No, no, see, she cornered me, and was super pushy- you know how tactless she can be, and I didn't think she'd ever get enough money anyway, and-"

Marissa's fingers drummed on the table. "Well, be that as it may, I only managed to get this new toy because I showed up early. In fact, I ran into its parents and Bludsauger on my way out. I saw you donated, what, $500? That's a lot of money to buy someone else a pet, you know..."

Tracy laughed, high pitched and forced. "That's- well it's a write off, you know! It's a charity! I was just trying to hit my deductions this year, and it seemed harmless, of course I knew you would want her- ah, it, but I knew that even *if* Bludsauger did get the money, you could still buy... it, if you wanted, and you did! Yay..."

She trailed off, her fake smile not reaching her eyes. She wasn't looking at me anymore, and her muffin lay forgotten on the table. Marissa took another bite of her wrap, and I watched her teeth tear through a strip of chicken almost as wide as my torso. I felt the tension in the air as Marissa ate, letting Tracy's 'Yay' hang in the air for too long, no doubt giving Tracy time to pick over every wrong thing she had said, enough time to start planning her next move.

Marissa put her wrap down and picked me up. She unscrewed the top, and dumped me out into her hand. I tumbled, and landed in a heap. Her hand smelled like her wrap and the slight lotion smell she usually had. I straightened myself out, and tried to be still. I couldn't tell if Marissa was actually angry, or having the time of her life, and I didn't want to risk anything until I knew for sure.

"I did buy it, didn't I? It's right here in my hand. It's mine, and no one can ever do anything about that. I own it." She mused. She looked up at Tracy, and held me out to her. "Would you like to hold it?"

Tracy gasped, and looked around. She nodded slowly, and I could tell she didn't really want to, but she knew she had to. Marissa tipped me into Tracy's hand, and this time I managed to slide rather than tumble, staying upright and on my knees. Tracy's hand was shaking, and smelled strongly of coffee. Her fingers were longer than Marissa's, and where Marissa held me like you would a hamster, with her fingers curled up, her thumb over my head to cover me, Tracy held me like you would an insect, with her fingers splayed, and her palm flat. If I wasn't careful, I could tip straight off and onto the table, or even the floor... I wasn't sure I'd survive either of those, so I stayed very still, my hands on her palm, off to my sides.

"Hello, Tracy, it's nice to see you!" I called out.

It wasn't, not really.

She stiffened and made a small noise of... terror? Was she afraid of me? Or was she afraid of Marissa and she was afraid me talking would set her off?

"I hope you're having a nice day!" I said, waving. I didn't care of she was or not, but doing this was upsetting her, and it was pretty obvious that Marissa was trying to upset her. I wasn't about to ruin Marissa's day by messing up the first impression the school had of me.

"N-nice to s-see you, R-rat..." Tracy mumbled, reminding me why I hated her. I doubted she even knew my name at this point, she just simpered along to whatever the more popular girls wanted, spreading rumors and lies about people for attention.

"M-marissa, t-thank you for letting me hold her- hold it, but I need to go to class, I have- stuff, thank you, but I have to go, thank you, sorry, I'll see you?" Tracy stumbled through her words, her hand shaking more and more and she shoved me back into Marissa's hands. She stood, and collected her coffee and muffin, and dipped her head in almost a bow before walking quickly away across the food hall. Marissa watched her go, not saying a word until she had left the room. Once Tracy was gone, she turned to me and closed her hand around me, squeezing, but not enough to take the air out of my lungs.

"*Gods*, did you see that? That was PERFECT. She was horrified, she's going to tell the whole college, it's going to be amazing..." She rubbed the top of my head with her thumb. "And that part where you called her by name and tried to talk to her? I mean, I know I said you shouldn't speak unless spoken to, but *that* rattled her, I swear she thought you were contagious or something, gods..."

She was in a really good mood now, and she sipped her chai with her free hand, her expression smug and satisfied. She kept absently rubbing my head, messing my hair as she sipped her tea, almost happy to just sit and bask in the knowledge that she was about to get a bump in status and fear, and she wasn't even done with breakfast. I wasn't too uncomfortable in her hand, her fingers were cold, and the tortilla and lotion smell was kind of odd, but it somehow felt better than being in the bottle, so I stayed quiet as she sat and finished her tea. She glanced down at me, and then pinched off a corner of her wrap, just the tortilla part, and handed it to me as she put me back in the bottle.

"You did good, Rat, I wasn't expecting to see you play along like that. Have some carbs, on me. You shouldn't get sick off that much, I think."

I took the bit of tortilla, and nodded as I dropped back into my jar. The doughy, fluffy texture felt nice, and I was still hungry from breakfast. From what I'd seen, a couple mouthfuls shouldn't make me too sick, I think.

"Thank you, I thought it'd be a nice touch, she really seemed to get the picture." I said. If I could get points here... I doubted she'd let me see Henri, but I had to try.

"Yeah, gods, her face when I dumped you into her hand? It was like I just handed her a used tissue or something. Anyway, I've got class in ten minutes, and I still want to walk the halls, so I'm putting you back on."

She capped the bottle, and slipped me around her neck again. She tossed the remaining half of her wrap and her cup in the trash on her way out of the food hall, and headed out to show me off to as many people as she could.

~~~

We sat in class, Marissa slumped forward enough to let my bottle rest on the table. We had gotten a few stares, and the professor kept looking at me, but other than that, there was nothing as dramatic as what had happened over breakfast. It was a long class, at least 2 hours, and I had already taken it last year, so I was bored out of my mind. Marissa apparently had to show up to classes to get credit for the class, even if she didn't really do the work, so she was zoned out and bored too, not paying attention because she had no reason to. I kind of wished she'd put in the earbud so at least we could chat, or I could chat to her, but her moods were as of yet a mystery to me, and I wouldn't want to risk saying anything that would upset her.

For a while, she'd tilted my jar onto one corner, and spun it, making me dizzy and plastering me against the floor and wall of the jar, but once she realized she couldn't make fun of me in class or hear me screaming, she'd given up. For now, she just sat, rocking me back and forth as the class dragged on. I had finished my snack, and while I did feel queazy, that easily could have been from the bouncing when she walked, or the spinning from earlier. I wasn't willing to rule out it just being me not being able to digest regular sized food though.

I turned up the fan and tried to lay down. The bottle wasn't big enough to really lay down all the way in, but if I curled my knees and put my feet on the wall, I could kinda lay down. The cool air helped. The rocking did not. I tried to watch the other students, but aside from the occasional glance in my direction, they were eyes forward, focused on the lesson. I suppose not everyone had enough money and power to coast, I know I didn't.

As the lesson drew to a close, Marissa stretched and popped her back, looping my chain around her neck. As she went to leave, the professor called her name.

"Marissa, may I speak to you?"

Marissa turned, and sighed. "Yes, Miss Arkel?" she said, walking down to the front of the classroom.

"I... see you have one of my former students around your neck, what's the story there?"

Marissa crossed her arms. I couldn't see her face, but I guessed she was rolling her eyes.

"She got infected, she got registered, she got put up for adoption, I'm her guardian. All above board, all legal. I have her paperwork if you need to see." Her voice was hard and cold. She'd been expecting this... She was using 'she' instead of 'it' now, which was nice at least. I guess it had something to do with who she was talking to though.

"Well, Marissa, I will need you to submit the paperwork to the head office, and we'll need to get your certification checked out too, I find it suspect that you managed to take and pass a 12 hour class when you can't even seem to stay focused on my two hour class."

Marissa spoke haughtily and icily. "The difference *is*, I actually cared about getting my class B care license. I could not care less about you going on and on about business ethics. If your class interested me, Miss Arkel, I might actually pay attention."

Miss Arkel's mouth compressed into a thin line. "I think it would be best if I took Miss Park off your hands until we get the paperwork we need from you. As it is, as far as the school is concerned, you have an unregistered person in your care, and that's against school policy." She reached for me, and Marissa jumped back, her hand clamping around my jar.

Her voice was a snarl "Don't you *FUCKING* touch her, I will sue you so hard you'll lose your car, I'll get you so blacklisted you'll have to teach at a *community* college. If you so much as *look* at her the wrong way, you will be in so much trouble the courts will be on a first name basis with you."

I got chills. That was the Marissa I knew, the cold fury. I couldn't see Miss Arkel's face with Marissa's hands clenched over me, but her silence was enough to know she'd been 'put in her place'.

Marissa continued "I will get the office the documents. I can *prove* that I own this bitch. I don't need you and your grabby hands trying to take my legally owned and legally *registered* property. Do you understand?"

"...I think it would be best if you got those documents filed by the end of the day, Miss Lund." the professor said, in a formal tone, using Marissa's last name stiffly.

Marissa spun, her hands still clasped around me, my jar dark, with bits of fog between her fingers.

"I'll get you your documents, just don't ever try that again." She spat back over her shoulder as she stormed out.

My heart was racing. She was in a terrible mood now, and it was all because of me. Kind of. Just being around her when she got like this was traumatic. I thought back to the teachers that were fired after bad interactions with her in high school, the students who had to drop out because their parent's companies went under seemingly overnight. Miss Arkel should have known better, but the fact that she used my name, and called me a person... It made me feel odd. I'd almost gotten used to being a 'thing' over the past few days. Something to be owned, used even. I'd played into her games in the food hall, I was being who- WHAT she wanted me to be. I hadn't really had time to process it aside from crying when I was taken away from my home, but somehow being reminded that I was a person, a real person with a real name, Amber Park, made my feelings twist up and tie into knots.

I'd been sliding into a trap. A trick by my own mind to make me feel better. If I was an object, I couldn't be too surprised when I was treated like one, right? I had to refocus, to try and maintain myself.

Marissa's hands fell away from me, and I looked out through the glass to see why. Waiting outside the classroom for Marissa to exit, was Henri.

~~~

## The Feeling of Being Valued    51

It had to be right *then* that she confronted her, didn't it? Right when she was mad, right after she got done chewing out a teacher... I looked across the library table at Henri, the glare on her face uncharacteristic and a little scary. My bottle was halfway between her and Marissa, and I felt caught between two titans, each ready to fight to the finish. I just hoped Henri wouldn't try to grab me and dash off... After seeing what happened when Miss Arkel did the same, I knew it wouldn't end well. I tapped on the glass to get Henri's attention. She glanced away from Marissa for a second, her eyes filled with sadness, before her look hardened and she glared up at Marissa again.

"You are keeping my best friend in a bottle? That is inhumane, you know, I could report you for this." Henri said, low and steady.

"I bet you could, and you know what? I'd just tell them that per guardianship law, I'm allowed to keep my ward in any container with sufficient protections and comfort levels."

"Oh, and a *bottle* meets those requirements? Really?"

"This one does, it has heating, air, and a little microphone so I can communicate, it meets the legal requirements."

Henri looked down at me again, focusing on the top of the bottle and winced. She knew Marissa was right, I'm sure of it. Knowing her, she'd most likely taken the class too yesterday after she realized I had been bought, just to know what Marissa could lose custody over.

"I would like to see her, in private, out of the bottle, please." Henri said in a curt tone.

"Hm, you know, I'm thinking you may be a threat to her wellbeing... If I let you see her privately, any harmful action you take is ultimately on me legally after all..." Marissa droned, almost bored.

I looked at Henri, surprised, had she planned on *hurting* me to get me away from Marissa? That... didn't seem like her, but she was desperate...

"I suppose..." Marissa continued "I suppose I could let her out of her bottle for a few minutes, a supervised visit, of course."

"Ja, ok, that works, just... Please let her out of there."

Marissa unscrewed my top and flipped the bottle over, once more dumping me out. I mostly caught myself with my arms, but still ended up in a heap. I stood, just as Henri's hand closed around me and lifted me up to her face.

"Oh, klein fee, I am so happy to see you... Are you well?" She asked in a hushed tone, her face inches from mine, although it seemed like a few feet to me. Her breath smelled like fruity candy. She must have been binging again... She always overindulged when she was stressed, and chewy, fruity candy was her weakness.

"I'm well enough, I guess..." I replied, wiggling in her grip. She was holding me like a handful of nuts, my limbs at odd angles as she tried to figure out how to let me support myself and to hold tight enough so I wouldn't fall at the same time.

"She is not hurting you?" She asked, tilting her head, her look one of utter pity.

"W-well..." I looked back at Marissa, who had stood and was looming over us. "Well, I'm fragile now, I'm sure once we're used to it, I'll be safe, it's just a learning curve..." I trailed off, hoping Henri understood the words between the lines.

She did, and her eyes filled with tears as she clutched me to her chest. "Oh, Klein Fee, we will save you from this horrible fate, I assure you…"

"Hey." growled Marissa. "I'm still right here, I'm not *that* terrible a fate. I'll keep her fed and alive."

Henri kissed the top of my head gently and I blushed. I guess people didn't see personal space and boundaries the same way once you were a class B... I guess I didn't mind too much though in this case, it was just Henri, after all.

"Ok, too far, visit's over." Marissa cut in, putting her hand on Henri's wrist.

"Please..." Henri said, suddenly squeezing me tight enough to hurt. "She is my best friend, I want to-"

I made a small noise as her ring finger pressed into my side, close to my bruise, and she quickly looked down, shocked.

"See? You're hurting her with your big clumsy hands, *this* is why we didn't want you on the tennis team."

Henri's hand shot open, and she examined me, worried and upset. "No, Amber, I am careful, I promise, I did not..."

I give her a thumbs up as I stood up on her palm and shook my head. I opened my mouth to speak, but Marissa took the opportunity to snatch me back, stuffing me in my bottle and leaning away from Henri.

"She's safest with me, don't you think?" Marissa said, her sharp tone with a hint of cruel playfulness to it.

"No, no, no!" Henri cried, then stopped, looking around at the mostly empty library. "I just want to get to see my friend, I want to spend time with her, we spent every day together..." She finished in a quieter voice.

"Well, until I know you're safe to let around her, I don't know if I can grant that request." Marissa said, mockingly.

Henri's eyes filled with tears again, and she looked at me with longing as Marissa screwed the top back on.

"When can I see her again? I'm free after school, tonight I can come over and-"

"No, I'm busy, we can talk again on Friday, maybe you can see her then." Marissa said, cutting her off.

"Friday?! That is two days, you cannot keep her from me!"

"Well... I *can*, I'm her guardian, I own her. She's mine. I could stop you from seeing her forever if I wanted, take away her tablet so she can't talk to you, it's all within my rights..." Marissa stood to leave. "But... I'm not gonna lie, I like the idea of having *two* new pets, so... I'm sure you can *earn* the right to see her."

Henri frowned through her tears "Earn? Doing what? You have servants and-"

"Oh, trust me. There's a lot of stuff I'd like from you, Bludsauger. Like I said, we'll talk Friday."

Marissa stood up, and dangled my jar in front of Henri's face. For a split second, I thought she was going to grab me, but the look left as soon as it'd come.

"I've got one more class today, then I'm going home. I'll see you Friday, Bludsauger..." Marissa said as Henri's eyes followed my swaying container.

Marissa spun and walked, my bottle swinging in her hand. I could see her face from here, and she was beaming in her horrible, cruel, half lidded way.

## Chapter Four

I sat on her knee, the TV in front of us looking like a movie screen stretched off to each side of me. It would still be massive at my regular size too, but as it was, it felt hard to absorb what was going on on-screen without physically looking around at it. I didn't much care what was on screen though, it was just some docu-drama series about people with more money than I'd ever have, doing dumb things in places I could never afford to go. Although... If Marissa went, I suppose I'd come along by default, and she had more than enough money to do go to the fancy places in the show...

She shifted under me, and I toppled, tumbling off her knee and onto her thigh as she lowered her leg. I gripped the edge of her shorts to steady myself, and she scooped me up into her hand, still slightly damp from her lotion.

"I'm getting a blanket, do you want a tissue or something, Rat?"

"Uh, that's- Yeah, actually, a tissue would be nice, I'm getting really cold..."

Marissa snorted, amused "I was kidding. Have some self respect, don't wear tissues. I'll just hold you or something."

I sighed. Marissa's hands were cold too, so it wouldn't help much. Earlier today when I was in the bottle, I was against her upper chest all day, right under her neck, so the heat from her body kept me warm, and the few minutes I was let out of the bottle were short enough that I didn't have time to get cold. We'd been watching TV since she got home and changed into her lazy clothes though, and knees weren't known for being warm. I hugged myself and rubbed my arms. Hopefully the clothes that she ordered me had some long sleeves... I should have worn my pink jumpsuit while we watched TV, but she'd told me to put on my PJs to 'get cozy', so...

After grabbing a blanket from a wall cubby I couldn't even see until she opened it, she flopped back onto the couch alongside her bed. She had a good grip on me, but I still felt the world shift and my stomach drop as she fell, and my teeth clicked when she landed. I needed to get my hands on a tiny mouth guard, I swear.

She picked up her glass of water and sipped, the ice cubes clinking as she set it down, and folded her hands on her stomach, pinning me to the fuzzy blanket. It was warmer than I thought it'd be and I wiggled into a laying-down position to see the TV while I warmed up.

"So... do you watch this show a lot?" I asked, hoping she'd help explain the appeal.

"You're talking without being talked to again, Rat." she said, but without too much bite. "No, I just watch whatever. I used to like to watch videos about people cooking, especially the tv shows where they had to compete, but these days I just don't really care what I watch."

"That makes sense... There's not a lot of good stuff on. I really like old shows, black and white ones, like... Bewitched, or Twilight Zone and stuff. It's kinda cozy."

"Huh... I never watched much black and white stuff, actually. Just what my dad would have on sometimes. Maybe we can give it a try some time." She said, absently.

I lay there for a few minutes, rising and falling with her breath. She seemed tired, almost peaceful right now. It'd been hard for her to get the paperwork needed to get me approved by the school, and she'd argued the whole time she was filing. It'd taken over an hour for Drew to show up with the purchase proof after she'd found out she needed that too, so she was stuck there waiting on him, complaining until he showed up.

I was tired, not because of the longer that usual day at college, but because I'd been on display the entire time on the desk in the college offices waiting on the paperwork, and the faculty had much less shame in staring at me and making comments about me than the students, so I had to stand and look polite the whole time, no sitting or resting. One or two had tried to talk to me, but once they realized I couldn't talk through the glass, they just stared.

I thought very carefully about what I was going to say next before opening my mouth. Something had bugged me, and I wanted to clarify while she wasn't in her scary mood.

"Hey, Marissa? Why did you cut our visit with Henri short earlier? I understand that it's your right, but I just was wondering why you proposed a supervised visit, then bottled me again so fast..."

She was quiet for a second, her breathing slowing down.

"She went too far, it was supposed to be a visit, not... that."

"What do you mean? Because she kissed my head?"

Marissa's hands closed over me.

"Yeah, she shouldn't have done that. It made me mad."

I thought for a moment. "What about it made you mad? She's my best friend after all..."

"Do 'best friends' usually kiss each other, Rat?" Marissa said, an edge to her voice.

"Well, I think people subconsciously don't think of me as a person now, it's like, you know, I'm small, too small to remember I have personal space? I'm sure she didn't mean anything by it, and she's European, so like they kiss people, right?"

"Well, she's not in Germany anymore. And you being small is no excuse."

I was surprised, did that mean *she* still saw me as a person? I didn't think she'd ever admit it even if she did. That said, she was taking a weird interest in my boundaries for someone who regularly picked me up without asking and manhandled me like a doll constantly.

"Well, thanks, but if it's Henri, I don't really care, she was just being sweet..." I said softly.

Marissa's hand closed around me.

"I didn't *ask* if you cared, Rat, I cared, and you're *my* fucking pet. Does she make a *habit* of kissing you? Have you two ever made out? Do the two of you have that 'special bond between girls'?"

She was firmly gripping me now, and I wiggled, confused and concerned at the hardness in her voice. Was she homophobic or something?

"No! She's my friend, she doesn't usually kiss me, we only did it once, in high school, I swear, like, as a test, we're just friends!"

"A test? A test to see what she tasted like?" Marissa said sarcastically

"No, gods, just a test, to see if we were like, you know, I don't know, like, gay or something."

"And were you?" Marissa asked, her voice quiet.

I coughed, and tried to respond.

"I don't- not then, I was like, I just wanted *someone* to love me, I didn't care who, but kissing her felt like if I kept going, it'd end with me losing her, so I told her I didn't like it..."

"And?" Marissa followed up in the same quiet voice "Did you like it?"

"I- I didn't care, it was fine, it wasn't world changing or something." My ribs ached and my side was flaring up again "I don't think I care about gender or stuff when I kiss people, I don't know what that makes me, but like, I just- I like whoever, I don't care."

I was struggling to keep my arms braced against her tightening grip, the air slowly but surely leaving my lungs. Why did she care? What was this? She lifted me to her face and stared me down, an emotionless glare that cut through me.

"So what do you look for, if gender doesn't matter?" She said, just as emotionless.

I took a deep breath and tried to squirm up higher in her hand "I look for- gods, you're starting to squeeze too tight, I can't-"

"Answer me, Rat."

"I- I like- I look for people who I get along with, common interests, humor, with- oh, gods, please this hurts..." I coughed more and felt my insides twist as she held me, my bruise starting to spike in pain with the pressure.

"It seems like you're getting worked up thinking about it, why don't you cool off and get me an answer later?" she said, opening her hand a crack. I sucked in air and shuddered, I'd felt like I was going to pass out, I don't think I could have lasted much-

She tipped her hand, and I fell, screaming. My knees hit the ice in her glass first, knocking them out of the way as I plunged into the freezing water. The air I had fought for so hard suddenly gone, replaced with liquid in my lungs. The water hurt my eyes, my muscles felt tight, and I spasmed, unable to stop shaking. I twisted and looked up, the ice cubes were above me now, blocking me from the air. I needed to get past them if I wanted to breathe, to live. I kicked frantically and slammed into them head first, knocking them around me as I fought my way to the surface. I hit air and gushed water out of my lungs, coughing and gasping as the ice around me made it harder and harder to keep swimming.

I felt the water level slosh, and saw through the glass that Marissa had lifted the cup. I screamed out to her, but she just took a sip, ignoring me. As she held the glass to her mouth, drinking deeply, I felt the water pull me to her lips and I crashed into them, the ice cubes hitting me in the back as she tipped the glass up further. Her mouth was barely open, just enough to drink the water, not enough to pull me in, but the suction was strong anyway. The last of the ice fell on top of me and I screamed in pain from the impact, hugging and clinging to Marissa for warmth and for any kind of protection.

She took deeper gulps, my leg slipping into her mouth, my tracker bracelet getting caught between her upper and lower teeth. I felt the heat from her tongue and I gripped her lips harder, my body shaking and shuddering as the rushing water drained my strength. The last of the water rushed over me and trickled away into her mouth, and she lowered the glass, leaving me clinging to her face, teeth chattering and head spinning. I felt her fingers gently pinch under my arms, pulling me away from her mouth, making a kissy noise as she did so, and she looked at me, hair in my face, body jerking with shakes, soaking wet, and she smiled.

"Huh, well. I guess it's not that weird to kiss your friends after all, Rat. I thought that was fun, we should do it again sometime..."

~~~

I lay in bed, my blankets, a washcloth, a handkerchief and my microfiber cloth all on top of me. I was in my jumpsuit, and the temperature in my house was turned up to max, and I still couldn't stop shaking. It was the next morning, and Marissa had made a very big deal about me going to class with her anyway, but once she'd made me get out of bed and seen me collapse in a shaky heap on the floor, she'd stopped talking and put me back in bed herself. She'd put the extra 'blankets' on me, and had left my tablet propped against the bed.

I had been a strange mix of too hot, and feeling like I'd never be warm again, and I kept sweating despite feeling like I was freezing. That was much earlier though, and while I was still feeling bad, I was much better than I was when Marissa left to go to class. I slid up in my bed enough to pick up my tablet, and opened my messages. I'd prefer to be using my phone, but it was still under the couch cushion downstairs, and I didn't think I could make it there and back. I pulled my legs up to make a platform for the tablet and winced at the pain in my knees. They were bruised now too, as well as my back, from the ice falling on me.

I opened the messages, and found one from my mother's phone, asking for an update. I realized with a pang of guilt that I hadn't texted them in quite a while, and spent some time giving them a full update on my living situation. Leaving out the parts about Marissa hurting me, of course. My father would do... something even dumber than trying to smuggle me to Germany if he found out, and I wanted to make sure I could still talk to them for now. Once it was sent, I opened Henri's texts, and sent her an explanation.

*'hey bbgrl, srry im not at college, fell in water, got super sick, ill be better soon tho'*

She responded almost instantly

*"Oh, lovely, I have been following your new caretaker all over campus, I had thought she had stowed you in a pocket or somewhere. I was quite worried she was suffocating you. I'm happy to hear you are home, but sorry to hear you are sick. Will you be ready be tomorrow?"*

I frown. What?

*'whats then?'*

*'Oh, that is when I get to talk to Marissa about seeing you again, remember? How could you forget?'*

*'oh, yea, srry, times all run together now'*

*"I understand, I have been trying to find a way to present my case, I think I can convince her to let me see you regularly, but I'm worried about what she said; that I must earn seeing you. I will fight for you, klein fee."*

I was worried about that too. The way Marissa had mentioned 'having two new pets' called to mind Henri on all fours with a collar on, and... while I knew Henri wouldn't mind that in a slightly *different* setting, I was sure she'd hate it in this particular one. Marissa hadn't said anything about it since we'd met Henri, but... I *had* been asleep or in bed for almost 16 hours total now, so there wasn't much opportunity for us to have talked about it. What we had talked about concerning Henri's actions though... I thought about if it was ok to talk about it on the tablet, or if I should wait until I could get out of bed. In the end I decided it'd be pretty suspicious if I *didn't* talk about it to her, so I bit the bullet.

*'hey, tho. the kiss... dont do that, ok?'*

*'Oh, no no, I was just so happy to see you, it was nothing more than me being overjoyed to have my lovely friend back in my arms, nothing more, I'm sorry I caused you to be upset.'*

*'no, i wasn't upset, i get it, but lady m was like 'thats inaprops' so not again plz'*

*'Oh. Interesting. I see, I'm so sorry, I hope nothing bad happened because of me..."*

I thought about the squeezing, the ice water, being stuck in bed, and I tried to think about her potential reaction. Either she's very careful around me forever, and I don't get hurt, or... she gets mad, and she really *does* kidnap me. If she was super careful, I'd miss getting to see her be silly or tease me like she did, I'd lose out on her bluntness and candor, she wouldn't be herself. If she tried to kidnap me, bad things could happen. An image of Henri and Marissa playing tug of war with my whole body flashed in my head, and I quickly typed out a response.

*'no bad stuff, just a comment, ur good bbgrl'*

*'I'm happy to hear that, I shall keep my lips to myself from now on, then, my sweet.'*

I powered off the tablet and slid it back to where it was. I was getting tired again, and I really wanted to see her tomorrow, so hopefully if I went back to sleep for a couple hours, my body would be well rested enough by the morning to go to school again, I was looking forward to it.

...Then I remembered the jar. Fuck. I was looking forward to it a lot less, now.

~~~

I woke up the next morning to Marissa poking me gently with her finger. I moaned and sat up, my back popping with the effort. I pushed the blankets off, and looked over at Marissa, her face practically inside my house. She looked worried, and almost scared, but she started to relax when she saw me moving.

"So... you feeling better?" She said, trying to sound casual.

I thought about it. My knees hurt from the impact, my side was still bruised, my back was sore from the ice, my mouth was a desert, and I was stiff as a board from laying in bed for over a day. But if it was Friday, I got to see Henri if I was ok, so I must be fine, right? I nodded and stepped out of bed, falling onto the floor instantly as my knees gave out.

"I'm fine, I just- I need to get my legs..." I stood shakily, and leaned against the bed.

"You don't look fine... Are you still cold?" Marissa asked.

I checked myself "Nnnno? I'm really hungry, and I really need a shower, but other than the bruises, I think I'm ok."

She reached into my room with the finger that woke me and pressed it onto my face. It was cold, again, and I fell back onto the bed.

"Well, you don't have a fever or anything I think... You should be fine, I'm guessing. Anyway, get dressed and stuff, eat your food or whatever, I gotta get to school. I can eat here today, but in the future, I need you ready when I'm ready, Rat." Her tone had turned haughtier once she'd made sure I wasn't dying, but her heart wasn't in it.

"Um, I was wondering, it kinda hurts to stand, and the bottle is hard, and I'm bruised, so..."

"You want to ride in a pocket?" She interrupted, her eyebrows going up in surprise. "Yeah, if you approve it, we can absolutely do that! I'll have to change, but-"

No, sorry..." I said, cutting her off. "I was just wondering if I could get a pillow for the bottom of the jar this time. I asked yesterday- or, I guess two days ago, but you didn't hear me, and I really need it today or my bruises are going to get worse..."

Her expression fell, and she snorted in disappointment. "Yeah, yeah, you can put a sofa cushion in there for today, if you can fit it through the lid."

She picked the bottle up off the desk and set it next to the couch in the middle floor.

"Anyway," She said "I'm going to eat some eggs benedict or something else you'd never be able to afford, I'll be back in like, forty minutes."

"I- I've had eggs benedict before, I've *made* it before, it's not THAT fancy." I said, confused.

She looked back at me. "You know how to poach an egg? I'm actually impressed, I didn't know you cooked. I've seen full on chefs fuck up a poached egg on TV."

"Well, we cooked all our meals, we only ate out like, once a month, so if I wanted fancy food, I had to learn to make it. It's not too hard, poached eggs take like 5 minutes, I can teach you sometime, if you want?"

She looked at me, and tilted her head. "Like, you'd teach me how to cook? That sounds... yeah, I'd love that. I like watching people cook, but like, when you have a live in cook, it's hard to learn for yourself. It's always made for you."

I nod. There was her human side again, the side with interests and goals, the side that could talk to me like a normal person. I could tell she genuinely enjoyed being a bitch, but every time I was reminded that there was more to her than that, I felt a little bit more hopeful about living together with her.

"I can teach you to make mandu, too, I know you didn't like the name, but it's really good, and we can make them steamed if you have the right stuff, that's my favorite way to eat them, and I'd love to get to have them again."

"Well, you won't be eating much of it unless you want to spend the day making out with a toilet, remember?" Marissa pointed out, smirking.

I held up my hand and shook my head "Listen, if it's for mandu, I'll deal with the consequences."

She laughed and poked me "Yeah, ok. We'll do that sometime, it'll be fun, I'm looking forward to it, Rat."

She left and I lie there on my bed sideways for a moment. It was... jarring, to have a conversation like that with the girl who almost drown me and chilled me so bad I had to stay in bed for a whole day. I almost wanted to *like* her, the her that was open and genuine and had her guard down, but... I knew that as soon as her guard went up, I was in danger of being hurt badly. I needed to get my place here figured out. I had a feeling I could keep her in 'human mode' most of the time if I knew her better, but it was hard to want to know her better when a lot of our conversations ended in me getting hurt.

I needed to get ready, I'd think about it more later. I still hadn't really processed the whole thing, I was just going with it and letting time wash over me. Some time soon, I needed to sit and meditate on how I felt, how I needed to move forward, and what I wanted from life now that I was disabled. I still wanted to have goals, even if my old plan of getting a logistics degree and starting a company to sell print-on-demand items for online artists wasn't a possibility, there had to be something I could do with my life still...

I got my phone and hid it under my mattress while the cushions were off the couch, and crammed the couch cushions into the bottle. They filled the bottom of the jar, and if I put one cushion on the ground, one on a wall, and the two back pillows on the two sides I could kind of have a little throne to sit curled up on. I wouldn't be able to stand up without hitting my head, and it'd be a very tight fit, but only one wall would be open for me to knock up against, so I'd be way safer too.

I headed downstairs and re-heated and finished the poke bowl from Wednesday, but I was still hungry. It was a new day, and I had skipped eating yesterday due to being sick, so it *should* ok if I had more. I heated up a 'Deluxe Chinese Meal", and ate about half the rice and a couple pieces of breaded... somethings before heading upstairs to shower. The shower was frustrating, I'd had issues with it last time too, but I was just quickly getting clean then, now I wanted to fully soap up. The water was hot, but it was more of a steam than a shower, so it was annoying to rinse, but I got the soap off once I found the option to turn the shower into a faucet, dumping water out on my head at what felt like a gallon a second.

Toweling off, I went to get dressed, and realized I had no clothes. I had been wearing my PJs when I 'went swimming', and I had been sweating in my jumpsuit under a pile of blankets for a full day, and as a result it was NOT in a condition to wear in an enclosed space. My toga from before was on the bathroom floor, and I had dumped my wet clothes right on top of it when I'd gotten undressed, so it was soaked.

"Damnit..." I muttered

I wrapped the towel up around me, and put all three sets of clothes in the washer. One of the perks of being small was that clothes washed faster, and dried way faster, because there was less water to dry, I guess? I set the washer to quick dry, and put in a grain of soap starting it up. I had like, 10 minutes to wait for the washer and dryer to be done, I could only hope Marissa was taking her time with those eggs. I sat down in front of my TV and turned on a video about a guardian training his class B to jump through hoops and run obstacle courses. He claimed the class B loved it, but the little guy just looked exhausted to me. I heard the buzz, swapped the clothes to the dryer, and went back downstairs. Just a few more minutes and I could put on my dress... I heard the door and turned to see Marissa walk up to me.

"Hey, Rat, ready to get bottled?" She said, reaching for me. she stopped shy of grabbing me and her eyes got slightly wider.

"Uh, you're not wearing clothes?" She asked, her cheeks coloring lightly.

"Oh, I'm so sorry, I have like, 5 minutes left on the dryer, is that ok?"

She looked at me, her expression strange, and seemed to be thinking about it.

"Well... The other option is you're in the bottle all day in just a towel..." She said, her hand still reached out for me. She pursed her lips. "Damnit, we have to meet your stupid friend... She'd report me for 'improper dress' or something..."

I frowned. "Do you *want* me in a towel all day?"

Her cheeks turn more pink and she glares at me. "You're my property, if I wanted to dress you in a bunny suit and make you follow me around in a hamster ball, I'm allowed to do it."

I cross my arms, slightly self conscious. "You didn't answer the question, you just kinda made it sound like you wanted me in a bunny suit..."

She threw up her hands "Whatever! Just get dressed as soon as you can, Drew is already waiting in the car, and if I get marked absent because of you, I'm going to... to..." She trailed off, unable to think of a fitting punishment.

"...to make you sorry!" She finished, weakly. She turned and walked over to her bed, sitting down and pointedly looking away from me.

...That was... strange. And maybe a little enlightening, but I couldn't tell. I heard the ding from upstairs, and went up to change. A few minutes later, I sat by the bottle, the toga dress wrapped more in a long, dress-like formation, across one shoulder.

"Ok, *'Lady M'*," I called out, making sure my tone showed my distain for the title "I'm ready to go."

She glanced up, glaring slightly, and came over.

"I don't like the way you said my name, Rat. Try again."

I rolled my eyes and spoke in a saccharine voice "Ohhhh Mistress, I'd like to be bottled now..."

I fluttered my eyes at her, fanning my face with my hand.

"Ugh, whatever, good enough." She griped, picking me up and dumping me in the bottle headfirst. The cushions caught me, and I righted myself, getting cozy against the pillows. Marissa held the bottle up and lifted an eyebrow.

"That's a lot more than one cushion, Rat." She observed.

"Well, I wanted to-"

"Yeah, I don't care." She said, rudely. She capped the bottle and clasp me around her neck. "We need to get going, seriously, you'd better not have made me late."

~~~

After her first class, we were once again sitting in the library. Henri was finishing up her class, and would be here soon. We- or, I guess Marissa, had another class this evening, but it was a lab, so she was planning on dropping me off at home and coming back, so I wouldn't be exposed to the fumes. I lay back on the pile of cushions and pillows on the table and stared at the tiles on the ceiling.

"Thanks for thinking of me, I really appreciate that. I hadn't even thought about the chemicals and stuff being stronger to me." I said, to break the silence.

She looked up from her phone "Hm? Oh, yeah, it's in the class I took. It's like, I could lose custody over it, so I'm not risking it. Hey, smile for me"

She held up her phone, and I quickly sat up and put my hands in my lap and smiled. I heard the click, and relaxed.

"Why did you need a picture of me?" I asked, trying to remember if she'd taken one before.

"I'm finally making a social media announcement about you, I figure Tracy's got the nasty rumors going around by now, I wanted to make it official and post something bubbly and happy, really get people's attention."

She tapped away for a few minutes, then asked "Hey, does it sound like I'm being a bitch if I say 'I couldn't risk our beloved charity case getting taken away from us by someone who isn't equip to take care of her, so I knew I had to step up and be there for her when she needed it most' with a heart emoji after it?"

"Yeah? I mean, it does to me, you're calling a disabled person a charity case, and flaunting how you bought me out from under my family without saying it outright..."

"But the heart emoji makes it look like I'm trying to be sweet, right?"

"I mean, I guess? Are you trying to sound like a bitch? I'm confused."

"I'm trying to sound like I'm being a bitch without *meaning* to. That's the whole point."

I shook my head "I'm sorry, I still don't understand, but I think that message is fine."

She knocked me back into the cushions with a knuckle. "Whatever, you'll get it one day."

She posted the picture, and muted her phone, putting it her jeans pocket.

"And now, we let the drama fester. I'll get on tomorrow to see the comments and arguments and posts by people who think I don't know who they are in real life saying what they really think and I'll play the victim and blow up at them. It'll be like fireworks." She said, smiling to herself and rubbing my head.

"Truly you are the queen of bitchy-ness, Marissa... Actually... Can I just call you Queen Bitch? I like that song, and like-"

"Nope, I like the name, but no, I don't like that guy overall, sorry."

"Ah, damn... Ok, that's fair."

We sit for a while, and I rubbed my bruises. My side was feeling almost better, it was still a weird yellow color, but my knees still hurt to move too quickly. I could walk more easily, walking around my house had helped, but it still hurt. I moved the pillows into a throne shape again, and sat up on them. It didn't really work without the sofa frame, but it was still pretty cozy. I reached out with my foot and flicked the heater button on the bottle topper laying near my feet, and felt the rush of warm air blow up into my throne. This was pretty nice, I'd have to remember this next time Marissa wanted to watch TV with me.

"Hello, Amber..." Henri said from behind me.

I look up to see her looking down at me, her hands behind her back.

Marissa pointed to the seat across the table where she'd sat last time.

"Sit down. Stop looming over her, you're going to freak her out."

Henri sat, and stared at me, her mouth moving like she was about to start talking, but her words fell short of her tongue each time.

"Well? You wanted to meet, I could already be on my way to drop the Rat back at the house if I wasn't meeting you, you know." Marissa said

Henri looked up at her and swallowed. "Marissa... I am so sorry I kissed Amber on the head, she was so small, and I care about her a lot, and I just got carried away, it will not happen again, I promise."

Marissa looked at Henri for a few moments, then nodded. "Yeah, I know. If it does, I'll have to do something about it."

Henri looked down at me and I waved at her. She gave me a half hearted smile and waved back.

"So how is this going to work? Are we just going to keep meeting in the library all the time? Me and Henri practically lived together, I want more than just a quick meeting a couple times a week." I said, emboldened by Henri's company.

"You have a tablet, Rat, you can still talk to her you know." Marissa said, glaring down at me.

"If- well... I would like to see Amber in a less formal setting, if we can work it out, I miss her lots, this week is the longest we have spent apart in years, other than when I went home to see my parents." Henri said.

Marissa's glare deepened. "Yeah? You two are really joined at the hip, huh?"

I took a chance, she wouldn't do anything in front of Henri, and she'd be calmed down before we got someplace private anyway, hopefully.

"Yeah, Marissa, we were." I said, plainly. "We had to be, otherwise people like you could have torn us to shreds."

To my surprise, her glare broke into a smile. "Yeah, I would have *eviscerated* you, I wouldn't have needed to wait until you were a class B to make you my bitch. You two were such easy targets, gods, it's like you *wanted* to be bullied the way you just sat and took it. I swear you're secretly both subs."

I perked up and point to Henri "Well, I'm not, but she-"

"I WANT TO VISIT YOUR HOUSE." Henri said, far too loud for the library.

Marissa looked at her, then back to me, and slowly took on her signature smug look. "Ok, yeah. We can do that. Tonight, you come over about 6:30."

"Wait," I said "You won't be home until like 7 something, right? How will that work?"

"Mmm, she'll get like an hour to spend with you by herself, then she gets to spend the rest of the night doing whatever I want her to do. That sounds fair, doesn't it?"

Henri tensed up. "What do you mean 'whatever you want me to do'? That does not sound nice at all..."

"I'm sure it won't be nice for you, but I'll have fun. Tell you what, bring an overnight bag, and a couple changes of clothes, let's make it a real party, ok?"

I looked back and forth between Henri and Marissa. This was... Honestly great for me, as long as Henri was around, I was practically untouchable by Marissa. I'd feel bad for Henri doing whatever it was Marissa had in mind, but she was full sized, she could take it a lot better than I could.

"I like this plan Henri, let's do it, I'll be at the sleepover too, right? So it's like way more time with me, it'll be like before!" I said cheerfully.

Henri looked down at me, scared and anxious "But klein fee, what about-" She looked up at Marissa and closed her mouth.

"I'm part of the deal, pet number 2. Take it or don't, it doesn't matter to me." Marissa plucked me out of the pile of cushions and started stuffing them into the jar. "Either show up, or don't. I'll tell the help to expect you."

Marissa stood, slipping me into the bottle, and smiled at Henri. "I'm off to drop her off at home, I hope to see you later. If not, I guess you don't *really* care about your little friend here, huh?"

Henri sat in her seat, not moving, looking small. She looked at me, and slumped, lowering her gaze, not saying anything as Marissa once more left her alone in the library.

## Chapter Five

I rolled over and fell off the couch onto the floor. I grunted and sat up. Had I fallen asleep watching videos? I guess I really did need an afternoon nap since the infection... I reached for my tablet, but it wasn't there, it was still upstairs by my bed. I sighed and trudged up to get it, and pulled my phone out from under the mattress while I was up there. It was just after 6... If Henri was going to show up, it'd be soon. I checked my messages on my phone, but there was nothing new. I checked my tablet, and saw that my mom and Appa had apparently joined a class action lawsuit against the government to get me back in the past day or so. My mom said if they won, parents would be allowed custody of their class B children despite their ages. I was pretty sure that wasn't how those lawsuits worked, but I told her good luck anyway.

I straightened my dress and wet my hair down to look a little nicer, and consider texting asking Henri to see if she was coming, but... if she was, she'd already be in the car on her way over, so it wouldn't make much sense to message. I tidied the house up as much as I could while I waited; I put the trash from my food in the bin under the cabinet, I wiped down the surfaces, I put my clothes from the dryer into the closet in my bedroom and I sat at the dining room table to wait. It was now 6:36. I sighed, and considered making the rest of my food from this morning while I waited, but... if Henri did show up, and it was a sleepover, her and Marissa would eat later, and I wanted to be able to eat with them.

I kicked back in the chair, thinking as the minutes tick by. Was the idea of dealing with Marissa too much for Henri? Was this the end of our friendship? Sure, we could chat on the tablet when I was home, but our relationship had never been one where we really texted much, it was usually us making plans, and then doing stuff, going to a cafe or a park, or to see a movie, or just to study. Half the time she'd even eaten dinner with us, as she lived alone in the dorms, and her own family was half a world away. I imagined her sitting at the table in her tiny room with a paper cup of noodles in front of her and I felt bad, selfish, in a way. This was hard on her too, and I kept forgetting that. I made a mental note to text my mom and make sure Henri was still eating with them regularly.

I heard a click, and I rocked forward and out of my chair, running to the front of the house to see Marissa's bedroom door. It swung open, and Henri stood in the opening with the Lund family butler by her side. His name was... Brantley? Broofus? Something with a B... She looked like she'd been crying, and she held a mid sized duffle under one arm, the same one that she'd always bring over to my house when she slept over.

"Thank you, Mister Parker." she said. Damnit, not a B name then. "Is there anything else I need to know?"

"No ma'am, just what I mentioned on the way up. I hope you have a lovely evening."

With that he stepped back and gently closed the door behind her. She looked around the room nervously. I waved to her from my kitchen.

"Henri! Here! Over here!"

She looked over at me, and dropped her bag, rushing over to me.

"Klein Fee! I almost did not come, I was so scared of what she may do, of what *I* might do... I am sorry I am late..."

"No no, I'm just happy you're here! It's good to see you like, one on one. We haven't had that since, like, the gym."

She nodded and grimaced. "Ah, yes... I admit, it is... much harder to go to the gym now, Amber... I kept seeing the TVs, and remembering the news report we saw, and- well..."

"...The stuff I said about wanting her to get infected, yeah. I'm trying not to process that yet. I'm not sure if it's karma or coincidence, but I really don't want to think about it."

She reached out for me then blinked and lowered her hand. "Oh, is it- is it ok if I pick you up? I am supposed to ask before touching you."

I tilted my head "You're supposed to? Says who, the class you took? I didn't think that was a rule, the government guy and the shop guy didn't ask..."

"No, it- I have a list of rules I have to follow while I am here, Mister Parker gave them to me."

"Wait, so Marissa told you not to pick me up unless I said it was ok? She grabs me constantly, I don't... Yeah, just be careful, but sure, pick me up."

Henri nodded and slowly reached out, putting her hand around me awkwardly and pulling forward. Her hand was vertical, like she was holding a joystick, and her fingertips dug into me as I hung in her grip.

"Uh, hey, um." I said, clinging to her fingers "If you tilt your hand a bit, I can just rest on your palm mostly? It's less pressure and it's safer, it's what Marissa does."

Henri tilted her hand back, her fingers and thumb still wrapped around me in a weird position, but at least my whole weight wasn't on my ribcage now.

"Thanks, it's tricky to hold us I think, I saw an entire video on how to do it recently, it went in depth. Marissa is pretty good at it though, I think she's practiced."

Henri looked dejected. "Well, I would have practiced too, little one, if I had ever known I would have to hold one of you..."

I tried not to be bothered by the 'little one' comment and gave her a small smile "Marissa has wanted a class B for a while from what she's said. She got her license months and months ago, and she seems like the kind of person to put a lot of effort into the things she's interested in. I'm like, an expensive status symbol, and you're on an allowance, you shouldn't feel bad that you weren't ready for this one in a million thing to happen..."

She rubbed my head and sadly smiled. "Yes, but... I cannot help but feel that I am losing because I was not well prepared..."

"Losing? Oh, babygirl, you're not losing, you're just in a rough spot. She just had more resources is all. Anyway, what are the other 'rules' she gave you? What are we looking at here?"

"Well, I am not allowed on the bed. If I break anything, she will make me pay for it 'by the end of the night', I am supposed to stay off her computer, and I cannot touch you without asking. I am also not allowed to take you out of the room, I cannot hurt you in any way, and if I order food from the kitchen you are not allowed to eat any of it."

"Those are pretty good rules, nothing crazy, nothing I wouldn't say myself if I had a guest over, I suppose."

She walked over to Marissa's couch and sat down. "Ja, I do not like being told what to do though..."

I giggled "Uhh, yeah you do, that's like, half your personality."

She gently set me on the couch and lay down around me, her body on the outside, shielding me from the edge.

"Hey, only sometimes! Also, I cannot *believe* you almost told Marissa about that! What were you thinking?"

"I mean, maybe if she thinks you enjoy it, it'll get awkward and she'll stop?"

"Ja, or what if she takes it as a sign to really ramp it up? Do you think she heard you?..."

I sat and leaned against her hand "Honestly, yeah, I'm guessing she did, or figured it out. She's pretty clever. Or at least, like, she's not stupid."

"Ja. She is getting good grades in everything, a B average."

"Well, I mean. She's not *earning* those Bs, but I think she could, if she actually did the work."

"...oh. I hate her more, now, actually."

"She's a stuck up rich kid who likes seeing other people suffer, and will do anything to have power over others, but other than that... She's actually not that bad."

Henri scoffed "Oh, other than that? Wow, I cannot believe I missed it all these years."

"No, I mean...There's a real human under all her bullshit. I see her sometimes. She's got fears and desires and, like, interests and stuff. It's weird almost. I'm not saying that the cruelty is *fake*, she REALLY enjoys being cruel, but... I think I'm starting to get to know her more and more, and she's getting softer."

"Klein Fee, she *bought* you, she flicked you, she keeps you in a bottle, I am betting she was the one that put you in the water, too. How are you possibly seeing any softness in her?"

I looked across the couch at her, her face full of care and love, and I tried to find the words.

"Well, it's like. That face, the one you're making? I see it sometimes in her, not on the surface, but... Like she's fighting it off. And she does care, I don't know if it's really because she wants to scare people with me and wants me healthy, but like, she got me vegetarian meals, she stops playing if she saw she went too far, she got me extra blankets when I was sick yesterday, she makes jokes and- I don't know. I don't think I can excuse her actions, but I do want to at least learn to be her friend. It'll make the days easier at least..."

"So... you are just going to try and accept things?" Henri said, rubbing my back

"I think I'm going to try and direct them. Direct them to a future where I can co-exist with the human under the bitch. I just have to do my best to find her."

"If that is your path..." she said, wistfully. "But if you want, I think I can get to the airport with you tonight, it is risky, but... my parents would love to have you stay with us. I can transfer to a German school, and we can be happy, just us. I might even be able to get your dad a job working for my dad, so our whole family could be together!"

'Our whole family'. The words hung in my brain for a few minutes as I thought it over. I'd never gotten to travel, I'd always had to get a summer job when Henri flew back home for the few weeks in the summer each year, so seeing far off lands would be nice. Henri would be a much better guardian than Marissa, even if she couldn't buy as much fancy equipment for me, and I'd see my parents... I didn't miss them as much as I'd thought, but I missed them being there, being in the home, being a presence in my day to day.

"Well... How would you get me through TSA? Aren't they looking for people smuggling class Bs?" I asked.

"They mostly are looking for weapons and drugs, but they are looking for class Bs as well, yes. Anything that gets x-rayed will show you, so no carry-on, and the cargo hold gets very cold, so luggage is out. You would have to hide on my person, which I think I could do. It might be awkward, but if I use a private jet I could go through the metal detector instead of the body heat thingy, which would make it hard to find you if we hid you well enough on me."

I thought about it. "What, like, tape me into the small of your back or something?"

She didn't make eye contact "Or something..."

"I don't like this plan. It involves my best friend almost for sure going to jail forever as an international human traffic-er. They will NOT be kind to you in prison, Henri."

"I just want you *safe*, Amber."

I stood up and walked over to her face, giving her a hug around her eyes area. "I'll be ok. I highly doubt I'll be actually hurt for good, and with you here, it's not like she's going to do anything right away anyway, right?"

"I suppose. Amber?"

"Yeah?"

"May I rub you on my face?"

"...What?"

"Oh. Never mind, sorry."

I took a step back, breaking the hug. "You mean like you rub a cat on your face when you snuggle it?"

She nodded "I am sorry, that was a strange request, I know."

"Um, fuck it, go for it, I guess I don't mind."

Her face split open into a smile, and she rose to a sitting position, carefully picking me up and lifting me to her cheek. She cooed as she rubbed me across her face, her skin fairly dry and very warm. I tried to hug her back, but I couldn't quite get my arms untangled. Her breath once again smelled like fruity candy. I imagined she'd been stress eating them in handfuls on the drive over. She pulled me in front of her mouth and let me rest there, against her lips. She sat still, her head lowered as her grip tightened ever so slightly, and she pulled away slowly.

I was overstimulated and flushed, but I managed to get out a small laugh anyway.

"That- that last bit was kinda close to a kiss, Henri. I don't know if there's cameras in here, but Marissa..."

I trailed off as I saw a tear streak down her face, where I'd been moments before.

"I-I just want to have you, all day, every day." she said. I look at her, surprised. She was holding back her tears as best she could, but some were still slipping out and filling her eyes.

"It is not fair, you are my favorite person in the *world*, my precious one, and I could have *had* you, I could have been your savior, I could have gotten to spend every moment with you forever and ever. I could hold you and keep you safe and let you ride with me in my pocket so we would never be apart, and I w-would be the one who fought the world for you, and instead... Instead, I let you get captured by the enemy. You are in a hell of my failings.

If I had more money, if I had g-gone straight to the store instead of to the bank with your parents, I could- I could be the one who has you forever right now."

She was openly sobbing now, her tears dripping down onto the floor as she bent over, holding me in front of her face but not looking at me.

"I want to take you, to hide you away, to *murder* the person who took you from me. I want to burn this whole place to the ground to get to you, I want to make you mine in any way, at any costs, I need you, Amber."

I stay silent, my heart racing. Her emotions were... Strong, filling her up and overflowing. I hadn't noticed she'd felt like that at all... Or, rather, I'd tried to ignore it when I did. I felt her hands shaking around me, and she slid off the couch to the floor, lowering me to the carpet. Her tears fell around me as she sat slumped, her short straight blonde hair hanging around her face like a hood. I sat down and looked up at her. I didn't know what to say, how to react. I had the feeling this speech, or one like it, had been a long time coming, before I was infected even, but now that there was nothing to be done, nothing to fix, her feelings had just come welling up and overflowed. I did the only thing I could think to do, and I pulled her index finger into a hug, squeezing it as tight as I could.

"I am sorry little one..." she whispered. "I have ruined what little time we have with each other."

I shook my head "No, it's ok. You needed to get that out. I'm glad you said it."

I stood next to her limp hand, unsure if I was doing the right thing.

"Listen, I'll do whatever it takes to see you, you're my best friend."

"Ha, 'best friend'?" she said wryly.

I winced. That obviously hadn't been what she'd wanted to hear. I was guessing my next line of 'you're family to me' wouldn't go over well either. I didn't want to hurt her, but I didn't see any way to move forward the way she was obviously wanting to without pain and loss. And an extremely angry Marissa.

"I just want you to know, I'll do whatever I can to keep you in my life, and the fact that you're here shows that you will too. It'll work out, we won't lose each other, I promise." I offered.

She looked up, a slight glimmer of hope "Then, can we try my plan?" she asked, her voice cracking.

"N-no, Henri, if we do, you'll end up in jail. You will never see me again, we can't risk that. YOU can't risk that."

She lowered her head again and breathed out a shaky breath. She reached out both hands to me and I nodded. She picked me up and sat back up on the couch. She put me in the hammock made by her skirt on her thighs and leaned back.

"I am sorry, Klein Fee. I need to think about things, and I don't know if I am ready to talk more, may we please just enjoy each other's company for a while?"

I lean against the back of her hand in her lap.

"Yeah, thats sounds nice, I understand. Do you want to see if we can find out if Marissa pays for whatever service has *The Donna Reed Show*?"

Henri sniffled and let out a half laugh.

"Ja, that sounds lovely, Amber"

~~~

A while later, Marissa's door banged open, causing Henri to jump, almost knocking me off her lap. I clung to her skirt and braced myself, but she stopped herself from standing in time to stop me from tumbling.

Marissa walked in with several things, a couple brown paper bags, and a couple plastic sacks that looked like they were from a gas station and slammed the door behind her.

"Ok, pets, who's ready to fucking worship me?" she said loudly, holding her arms out to the side.

I was a little scared, she was intense, and so full of energy, her eyes were all the way open, and she almost never did that. She looked almost manic, and younger somehow? I thought she was angry at first, but looking closer, she seemed to be more... Excited? She kicked Henri's bag out of the way and pulled a cubby open in the wall next to her door. A refrigerator? I hadn't seen *this* hide-y hole either, I was wondering if her whole room was a series of hidden storage areas. She tossed the bags in and marched over to us on the couch. Henri was shaking, and her hand was hovering over me, in her lap, her fingers in the air just around me. Marissa reached down and plucked me off her lap before she could move.

"Ah, ah, ah, I didn't hear you ask permission, Bludsauger, I'm here for less than a minute and you're already breaking rules?"

Henri looked stricken "No, I was- I was protecting her, I did not touch her, I swear!"

Marissa held me up to her face and looked at me with exaggerated concern. "Oh my pet, did she handle you without asking? Did she use her big clumsy hands to squeeze you without your consent?"

"No no no, she asked!" I say quickly. "Even after I told her it was fine and I didn't care, she still asked, she followed the rules!"

She had followed the rules, technically. I don't think that face rubbing thing counted as a kiss, and... the rules for tonight didn't explicitly say no kissing anyway.

Marissa smiled at me, a strange joy behind her eyes. "Well, we'll just see how she does for the rest of the night then!"

She turned to Henri "Hey, your birthday was a couple months ago, right?"

Henri frowned. "How did you know? It was, yes, I had a chocolate cake with dark chocolate sea salt ganache on top, with strawberries, at Amber's house."

"It was in the school records, dumbass. I just wanted to make sure, because I bought, like, a ton of drinks on the way over, and YOU are going to drink with me."

"Drink? I- I would really prefer to be my usual self tonight, I am already not doing well, and we should not drink around Amber, she could get hurt..."

Marissa leaned over the couch into Henri's face and her smile got bigger.

"Well, I say you're going to drink, and you agreed to do what I wanted, right? I mean, if you didn't, you'd never get to see the Rat again, and we wouldn't want that, would we little Rattie?" She said, holding me up to face Henri, wiggling me back and forth.

"Henri, it's ok, you don't have to do it, we can figure out-" I start.

"Ok, I will play your game, I *will* drink with you." Henri said, suddenly hard and cold. "But I do it under one condition, got it?"

Marissa laughed. "The 'condition' was that you got to sit there and have fun with your friend for an hour, but ok, I'll hear you out."

Henri squared up, and took a breath. "Her name is Amber. Amber. *Fucking. Park.* I want you to start using her name, not 'rat'. She is a full person, and she is just trying to get along with you, she deserves a name."

Marissa frowned. "No, see, the name is part of the fun. It lets her know that I see her as less than human, that's the *point*, Bludsauger."

Henri stood and stomped her foot. "And *that*. That has been bothering me since I moved to this stupid town, it's not even correct, you are not even *saying* it right."

Marissa looked confused "What? Like, Bludsauger?"

"Yes." Hissed Henri. I knew what she was going to say, she'd been complaining to me about this for years.

"It is *Blut*" she spat, emphasizing the 't' harshly. "*saugerin*. Not 'blood sawger' like you and your little minions have been saying. You are not even using a real word, did you even look it up? It is not even in the right *gender* the way you say it. If you are going to insult me, *do it right*." She huffed, her face red and her hands balled into fists. The heightened emotions from earlier were giving her strength, for all the times she'd brought it up to me, I never imagined her actually confronting anyone over it.

Marissa looked at her, taken aback at the outburst. "Uh, wow, yeah, ok. I don't actually know German, and-"

"*Obviously*" interrupted Henri

"...I don't know German, so I was just going off what one of the other girls said. I didn't even come up with it."

"So you have been calling me that all the time without ever looking it up? Without ever getting creative with your insults? Never thinking outside the box past what some... hanger-on said?" Henri said, still hot.

Marissa held up her hands in a calming motion, me dangling from one as she spoke.

"Listen, I don't really care that much anymore. The name calling thing has kinda worn off on you two anyway, it's like the R- uh, Am-amber, doesn't even notice I call her that, and you- I mean, I'd feel stupid calling you something wrong, and I'm NOT about to explain to the girls at college that I'd been using the wrong term all this time, so yeah. I'll use your names, it's not a big deal."

I was stunned, Henri was too, she deflated and stared, unable what to do next. I try to think if I'd ever heard Marissa say my name before, and I couldn't think of a single instance. It sounded... wrong coming from her, like I didn't want her to dirty my name by saying it, but also like she was embarrassed to say it too. Henri swallowed, her anger mostly gone, looking for something to say.

"Well, that was my condition, so... I guess I will drink with you, Marissa."

"Hold on, nope, I said I'd use *your* names. I never said you could use mine. I go by Lady M, Mistress, whatever, both are good, but you can get creative as long as it glorifies me as above you, got it?"

Henri wrinkled her nose. "Ja, I got it."

"Yeah you got it what, *Henri?*"

"...Ja I got it, 'Lady M'."

I nodded. "That's my preferred too. It makes me feel more like a noble person on a lower social tier instead of a slave."

Marissa glanced at me, then set me on her shoulder. I gripped her loose knit coat and lay down for safety.

"You aren't a noble woman or a slave, Ra- Amber, you're a pet. If it wasn't so weird and gross to have someone call me master, I might have you call me that. It's what dog's owners are called after all."

"Wait, isn't mistress just the same thing but feminine?" I said.

"Uh, no? I mean. It's not the same, it's like, a mistress is like, a dom, or like, a woman so desirable that someone will cheat for her. A master... That's just wrong on a lot of levels. You know what I'm saying, right?"

Henri shook her head. "I am confused as well, I don't see the difference, but I will call you Lady M to avoid any sort of unpleasant notions."

Marissa looked frustrated. "No, mistress is sexy, it's different, it's got a different social connotation, it's- ugh. Whatever, I'm so done with the names thing, just shut up, call me Lady M, it's fine."

She sat on her bed.

"I want to get some stuff cleared up here, before you start drinking. I don't want any kind of mess where you don't know what's going on and you end up doing stuff while drunk you wouldn't usually have agreed to."

"Like, consent stuff? Gods, Marissa, what are you planning?" I say, incredulously.

"Oh, hush. I'm not going to- I'm just covering my ass here, it's not like that, I'm not going to do that kind of thing with a drunk girl, just, like, play around a little."

"That's still shady, Lady M." I said "I don't think you can agree to stuff before you get drunk, right?"

"It's not shady, it's- Just hush, you." She pulled me off her shoulder and shoved me under her pillow. I could still hear, but it was muffled. I had air, but it smelled like Marissa and sweat, so I started army crawling out as I listened.

"I can agree to stuff ahead of time I guess, as long as it is not... sexual." Henri said, and I groaned. What was sexual to a normal person and what was sexual to Henri *or* Marissa were two different things.

"Yeah yeah yeah, clothes on, no swimsuit areas, nothing like that. I'm not a monster. I just want to play with my new toy without being worried you'll freak out tomorrow and sue me."

"Ok, so... nothing sexual. What do you want me to consent to?"

"Stop calling it consent, it makes it sound gross. I need you to agree to non sexual physical contact, consuming non toxic food or beverages intended for human consumption, mild infliction of pain without any lasting marks, and lastly, I need you to consent to wearing non sexualized clothing of my choosing. Oh, and you still have to follow all the rules I set up, of course."

"That sounds like a lot of red flags, Lady M." Henri said, unsure. "I cannot think of anything you could feed me that would be too bad though, I already tried durian at the Park's house, and Casu Martzu is banned here, so..."

"I have no idea what those things are. You're not a veggie person too, are you?"

"Me? Oh, no, Amber is, but I am only vegetarian around her, I eat meat at home or when she's not around. She knows, she does not mind." Henri said.

"If she minded, I think she'd be an asshole to be entirely honest." Marissa said, unimpressed.

Truth be told, I did mind, it hurt to see people killing things for food when they didn't need to, but I'd learned early on that actually *saying* that led to angry people and arguments.

"So, do you agree to those things, Henri?" Marissa made sure to use her name, to drive the deal in further.

"I... Yes, I agree to those terms. It sounds good to me. But if I wake up and you've done something bad to me..."

"Gods, I'm not going to do anything like that, ask- ask Amber, I've had her for days, nothing like that."

"She tried to get me to ride in the bottle in nothing but a towel!" I shouted, my voice muffled by the pillow.

"What- NO. That was just- I did not! You weren't ready, and I fucking waited on you to get dressed, you're re-framing it!" She smacked the pillow, smushing me against her sheets for a second.

"And the part about the bunny outfit?~" I said, taunting. This felt good, I was protected by a wall of fluff, and by Henri, who would instantly report any abuse.

"Shut UP, I swear I'll lock you in your house for the night, it was just an example, a hypothetical bunny suit at best." She growled.

"Did she or did she not sexually assault you, Amber?" Henri asked, her voice on the edge of a knife.

"...No, I'm just being a dick, she was just sort of rude." I said. Taking it further could result in Henri making false allegations, or Marissa getting actually mad.

"Ok then, please let me know if anything changes, Amber..." Henri said, still tense.

"Alright, enough with the stupid stuff, Henri, I have an outfit I want you in before the night starts, you can change in the bathroom."

I saw Henri's face fall at that. I had the feeling despite the promise of it being non sexual, it still wouldn't be something Henri would appreciate...

~~~

Henri stood in the bathroom door, the maid dress puffing out just over her knees, the headband keeping her hair out of her face, and the tall white socks ending just under the knees. She was blushing, and had an angry glower on her face as she looked at the floor.

"For the record, I think maid outfits *are* pretty sexualized in today's culture..." I said to Marissa.

"I think it's subjective, really." She replied.

"Well *I* think it is objectifying." Henri muttered.

"I mean, yeah, you're mine for the night, so... that's as objectified as you can get, right? So the costume fits." Marissa said, pulling her phone out.

"Wh- no, no pictures! That is horrible!" Henri said, covering her face.

Marissa rolled her eyes. "Calm down, this is just for my own records, it's not going to be posted anywhere."

"What records?" I asked from atop her shoulder "Why do you need a picture of maid Henri on record?"

"I'm not going to ask you to shut up again, Rat." Marissa said, holding up her fingers as if to flick me.

"AMBER." Henri said angrily pointing at Marissa. "You promised, it was part of the deal."

Marissa sighed. "Ok, sorry, yeah, *Amber*, I won't tell you to shut up again. Got it?"

I shuddered at the idea of being flicked off the shoulder I was on. I must be 5 feet off the ground, I'd never survive that. I kept my mouth shut.

"...Good. So, Henri, your first task... is to do a shot with me." Marissa said, going over to the hidden fridge.

She pulled out a bottle of vodka, and pulled a couple shot glasses out of yet another cubby on the same wall.

"I swear you could have a whole body chopped up in your hide-y holes and detectives would never be able to find them..." I mused.

Marissa grinned. "Yeah, right? These are in the house blueprints and building permits though, so they're not as secret as you'd think."

Henri wrinkled her nose. "I will never understand the way you think, Amber.

You see a hidden door and think 'oh, I could hide bodies in it!', it is just unsettling..."

"Well, *I* appreciate her out of the box thinking, Henri. I guess that means I'm a better friend to her than you, hm?" Marissa shot back smugly.

"I guess it'd be more inside the wall thinking instead of outside the box thinking..." I said, mostly to myself.

Henri and Marissa both giggled slightly at that, before stopping to glare at each other. They weren't playing tug of war with my body yet, but I could tell they were trying to play tug of war with my emotions. It wasn't much of a contest though, one was my best friend, and the other was someone abusing me to get clout. So why did it still feel like I was being pulled in two directions?

"I take it you've done shots before, Henri?" Marissa said, putting the little glasses on the table in front of the TV and pouring the liquid into them.

"Ah, no, I have only had fancy mixed drinks mostly, and Mister Park gave me a bottle of soju as my first 'official' drink. I think it is like wine? It was strawberry flavored..." She said, unsure.

"I have no idea what that is, but shots are super easy, I've been doing them since high school. You just dump it in the back of your throat, and open your neck hole like you're gulping, don't even let yourself taste it."

She handed Henri one of the glasses. I noticed Henri's glass was only about half full, and wondered if Marissa had done that intentionally.

"Ok, ready? Go."

She tossed the drink into her mouth and gulped, the sound loud in her throat next to me. Henri tried to do the same, but ended up with her cheeks puffed out, and her eyes watering instead.

"Ok, just, get the air out of your mouth, keep your head back, try to keep it off your tongue, and swallow." Marissa said gently.

Henri tried, and with a lot of effort, managed to swallow, gagging and her chest heaving in the process.

"Mein götter..." She choked out. "You do that for fun?!"

Marissa laughed and patted her on the shoulder. "It gets easier, trust me, we'll have a lot more practice by the end of the night. But now that you've got a shot in you, it's time for you to start earning that little visit you and Amber got..."

I hug Marissa's shoulder tighter. I wasn't looking forward to seeing what she had in mind, but I was so, so glad it wasn't me this time.

# Chapter Six

H enri stared down at the shot glass of red-brown liquid and grimaced.

"What is this again? It stinks..."

"It's called 'tiet canh', it's... I don't know, I heard of it on a tv show and got our chef to make you some. It... made a lot more sense before you made me stop calling you Bludsauger." Marissa said sheepishly.

"Wait, is that like, just a glass of blood?!" I asked.

"Oh, götter..." muttered Henri. "This is why you asked if I was veggie, wasn't it?"

"In my defense-" Marissa started

"I don't think there's a defense for this, this is fucked..." I said, shaking my head.

"*In my defense*. People eat it all the time in... somewhere else, and it fit, ok?" she finished.

"I- is this cooked? What even is it? Just blood? It looks like a sticky jello..."

"Ah, I'm not reaaaally sure, I think it's just blood and spices, maybe salt or something? Listen, I had the chef make it, and it's just one shot, just take it so we can move on with the night."

"Um," I cut in. "I really don't think this fits the stuff you said, I mean, blood? That's hardly 'intended for human consumption' or whatever you said, it's just, like, *blood*. Where did your chef even get random blood on short notice?"

"I didn't ask, he had an hour or two, I texted him on the way home when I dropped you off. Maybe he sent someone to wherever they sell blood?" Marissa said.

"Ok, ok... I can do this... It is just like blutwurst, just uncooked, I *love* blutwurst, I can do this..." Henri said, rocking back and forth slightly.

"Henri, please don't do this, it's gotta be ille-" I started, but she ignored me.

She reached her hand out and grabbed the glass, and tossed it back. Like the vodka, it hit the back of her throat and she gagged, shuddering. Her eyes streamed, and she huffed through her nose before squeezing her eyes closed and gulping. She stood there, head tilted back, not moving for a full three seconds before she opened her eyes and looked at me and Marissa defiantly.

"Ha! I did it, it was not-" Her eyes clenched shut and her cheeks puffed out. She shoved past us, almost knocking me off of Marissa on the way, and slammed through the bathroom door. The sounds that followed were not pretty.

"Damn, I didn't expect her to be able to swallow if I'm being honest, I'm really impressed with her." Marissa said.

"That was horrible and mean, just because of a dumb name joke? I can't believe you'd make her eat that..." I said, glaring at the side of her face.

She reached up and plucked me off her shoulder.

"This is the cost, R- Amber. She got to spend time with you, and see you alone, and whisper her little secrets to you, and I'm *guessing* cuddle the *fuck* out of you, knowing her. In return, I get to make her drink blood and wear a cute outfit."

"So you DO see the maid outfit as sexual then." I said.

"*No*, cute and sexy are two different things, I'm not making her wear a 'sexy' thing, it's a 'cute' thing, so it's not sexual."

The bathroom door opened and a frazzled Henri stepped out.

"Ugh... I can still taste it... It was still in one piece coming out, just a blob of-" She covered her mouth and shuddered.

"That's disgusting, I don't want to hear about that. Here, take another shot, you didn't keep the first one down and it'll get the taste out too." Marissa stood from her spot on the bed and walked over to the coffee table, setting me down next to the shot glasses. "I'll make you one nice, with lime and triple sec so it goes down easy."

"You could have made the first one nice too you know..." Henri said, slowly walking over.

"Actually... No. You gotta taste the vodka by itself first, so you know how much is in whatever else you're drinking. My dad taught me that, at my 16th birthday."

"You had vodka at your sixteenth birthday party?" I asked. "I didn't know your parents were... cool, I always assumed they were super strict or something because... you know. You."

She bapped me on the head with a finger as she handed the shot to Henri.

"Oh hush. But yeah, my mom is a nightmare. My dad *was* cool, until he left my mom for some bitch who graduated the year before me. I still see him every couple weeks, but... I always wonder how he sees me now, knowing what age range he's into..."

"That's... really rough, and pretty gross. I didn't know you still had contact, I thought you'd have cut him off after all the teasing." I said.

"Yeah. I went to his house every other Sunday because of custody agreements. I don't *have* to anymore because I'm an adult, but I still do. Half my allowance comes from him, and getting paid $2000 every two weeks to sit at his house and listen to him and his 'wife' complain about their friends is a pretty good deal."

Henri threw back her drink. "Oh... that shot was much better, I kind of liked it... And wait, does that mean you get an allowance of..." She thought for a moment. "$104,000?! A year?"

Marissa's smirk slid back onto her face and she tilted her head back proudly. "Yup, since I was 17."

Her face turned to a sneer. "But it's in a joint account with my mother, and she watches it like a hawk, so I can't do anything without her knowing."

"Oh, yeah, she called like, ten minutes after you bought me, that's right..." I said, thinking back.

"Anyway, enough about my stupid family, Henri, want another shot? We're about to do a punishment game, so you'll probably want at least a bit." Marissa changed the subject.

Henri narrowed her eyes. "...Ok, but only if you do one too. I do not want to be drunker than you."

They did their shots, and Marissa pulled a box with some cards in it from under her bed. She set them on the table next to me, and moved the drinks to one side. I tried to climb up to see what the cards said, but Marissa pulled me off the box and bapped me on the head again. It didn't hurt, but if she kept doing it, it'd get pretty annoying. I sat cross-legged, fixing my dress so it flared out around me, and waited on the other two to finish getting ready. Before long, they both sat on the couch across from me and the box, and I waited for Marissa to explain what we were going to do.

"Ok, so, this is a box of punishment cards and tasks. I'll be the game master, and you two will be going against each other. If you fail a task, you get punished. Obviously the ones that make you take a shot won't count if Amber gets them, but other than that, anything goes. I'll draw the cards, and I'll tell you the tasks. Any questions?" Marissa said.

"Uhh, yeah, won't I be at a huge disadvantage for like, all the tasks?" I said. "I'm like, four inches tall, I can't even get off the table."

"Yeah, some. Sucks to be you I guess. Any questions, Henri?" Marissa blew me off.

"Nnno? I am a bit worried that you have a whole box of handwritten punishments ready to go though..."

"High school parties, it was in some show one of the girls liked, so I made a more mean version for us. We'd play this shit all night, it was great. Anyway, this is just warmup stuff. The blood would go bad or I'd have saved it for later, but once we're done with this stuff, I'll get into the *real* stuff I have planned." Marissa said, snickering.

"Gods, that doesn't sound good..." I said, mostly to myself.

"Ok, ladies, the first challenge is..." Marissa dug in the box. "Oh. Lame. Staring contest. Whatever, the punishments are the fun part."

Staring contest? I could do that, my size had nothing to do with how often I blinked, I think. I closed my eyes and leaned forwards, feeling the heat from Henri's face radiating onto me as she leaned in too.

"Ok, and... go!" Marissa said.

I opened my eyes and saw nothing but Henri. Her face blocked everything else, and her light blue eyes stared into mine like holes through her mind, connecting us through eye contact. I felt my face flush, and I felt the light puffs of air as she breathed. She looked focused, but worried and careful at the same time. Her lips were tightly pressed together and she was starting to turn pink. My eyes stung with every one of her lightly alcoholic breaths, they watered, and I felt the need to blink getting closer and closer. Finally, the stinging was too much, and I blinked, drips of tears splashing onto my dress as my eyes finally stopped watering.

I shook my head. "Yeah, ok, she wins. I lose, what's the punishment?"

"Awwww, poor thiiing, losing the first game... Let's see what you have to do, poor baby." Marissa said, her voice taunting and haughty.

Henri rubbed her eyes. "Ugh, you almost had me, klein fee, I was so close myself..."

"Ok but you won so shut up, the punishment is... Oh, hm. Uhhh, I don't know if this will work..." Marissa said, confused.

"What is it?" I asked. "You said we could swap out stuff with drinking for me, right?"

"Well, yeah, but this is... I'll just read it. It says 'The loser of the game must carry the winner around the room twice on their back without falling over.'... So... yeah."

"Oh... oh *no*, I would squash her!" Henri said appalled.

"Yeah, I don't even want to think about that, I don't think I could lift one of her fingers, much less all of her. That's stupid, can we do a different one?" I said.

"Nope, we already set the rules, the whole point of a punishment game is that there's no backing out, we have to do it." Marissa said, thinking hard.

"Ok, ok, let's see if... Uhhh, put me on the floor Henri?" I asked.

"I'm not climbing on top of you, my sweet, you would explode..." she said, but she put me on the floor anyway.

"Ok, so like, maybe if you got on your knees, and I'm between your knees, I could pull, and you could scoot?" I offered.

"Hey, try it at least, let's see how it goes!" Marissa said, looking smug as ever.

"I... suppose we could try it..." Henri said.

We got in position, with me between her knees and her siting behind me. I put my hands behind her knees where her thigh and her shin met, and leaned forward, pulling forward with all my might. She didn't move an inch, but she kicked herself forward with her feet anyway. The lurch forward caused me to slip, and I fell face down on the carpet, buried under her shins. She jumped up and way from me and gasped.

"Oh! Oh! Oh, are you ok? I was trying so hard to be careful..." Henri said, wringing her hands.

I stood up and brushed myself down, smoothing my dress. "Yeah, I'm fine, I just couldn't keep up I guess... So.. What's the punishment for failing a punishment, Lady M?"

"The punishment is usually two more punishments before the next round starts, but I really want to see Henri get punished too, so we'll save yours for later. Let's just move on to the next game."

She dug in the box. "Ok, the next game is... handstand contest! That'll be fun."

"We're both wearing dresses, Lady M, that's hardly fair." I said, flapping mine.

"Well *I* am wearing bloomers, and the waist is pretty tight, I think I am fine to do a handstand, actually." Henri said, smiling confidently.

"Ok, no, we need to fix this, come here." Marissa said, snagging me off the floor. She carried me to her computer desk and pulled open a drawer, pulling out a roll of tape.

"Oh- uhh, that's- I can just change, we don't have to do this..." I protested, but she tore off a few pieces anyway and stuck my dress to my legs on the front, bunching it up tight. I flexed my legs and grumbled. It wasn't great quality tape, but it'd been a week since I'd shaved my legs, and I knew it'd hurt coming off later if I wasn't careful. Marissa brought me over to the window wall on the far side of the room and waved Henri over.

"Come on, do it against the window, it's reinforced, you won't fall." She said.

"Yes, but it is *glass*." Henri said. "Anyone outside will see my butt against the window."

"It faces the woods, and anyway, *you're* wearing bloomers, remember? Now get over here and get started, I want to get to the fun parts."

Marissa set me down on the metal brace the window was attached to, and stepped back. Henri walked over, and took her position, making sure to stay far enough away so even if she fell, she wouldn't hit me. Marissa counted down, then we both stood up on our hands, leaning against the window to brace ourselves. I felt my bruise sting as I clenched my stomach muscles. The injuries from the ice were still sore too, but oddly enough, I barely felt like I was holding myself up. I looked over at Henri, and saw her face was already turning red. She and I mostly focused on cardio, so it made sense that she'd be bad at handstands, but I was surprised I wasn't having any trouble. The blood wasn't pooling in my head, my arms weren't getting tired, and aside from my side, I felt like I could just... keep going. I knew I was a lot smaller now, so I was a lot lighter so that explained some. I remembered the video, and about how I could lift more now, I didn't expect that to come in handy for a dumb party game.

Henri gasped, and tumbled forward, her knees hitting the ground with a thud, knocking me over too with the impact. She held her arms to her chest and moaned as her face returned to its normal pale tone. I stood up, and awkwardly waited for her to get back up herself.

"Aww, I knew you could do it, Amber." Crooned Marissa. "I knew you'd come through for mommy, and you *did*!"

"Ew, can we not do the 'mommy' thing? That feels weird, I can't explain it, but it feels super wrong..." I said, walking over to Henri.

"Yeah, it felt wrong as soon as I said it, I'll stick with mistress." She agreed.

"Still weird, but whatever. Hey, Henri, you good?" I asked, poking her in the face.

"I am fine, I am just dizzy, and my arms hurt... You won fair and square, little one, you did good..."

"Nnnnno, I won because I'm lighter now and compression made me stronger, you're way more in shape than me." I assure her.

"Yeah, we *know*, we have eyes." Jabbed Marissa.

"Hey, I know I'm not like, 'thin' or anything, but I am NOT overweight, and I'd like you to shut up about that, I'm like, normal fucking sized, or I was before I got small, at least." I snapped.

Marissa pushed me into the carpet and rubbed, rolling me around into the high pile fibers.

"I didn't ask you to sass me. I haven't seen you use your little treadmill once since I got you, you're supposed to be losing weight, remember?"

I tried to argue, but only got a mouthful of carpet lint for my troubles.

"Hey, stop that! You are going to hurt her!" Henri said, finally sitting up. She grabbed Marissa's arm and pulled it away enough for me to dash out from under her hand.

"She's not *that* fragile. She's weak, but I'm figuring out what she can take, being rolled around won't hurt her, so stop trying to tell me how to take care of *my* pet." Marissa said, jerking her hand away.

"She does *not* need to lose weight, she is lovely, and she is plenty in shape, that is just rude of you and honestly you are going to give her mental problems!" Henri said. She tried to scoop me up herself, but Marissa slapped her hand.

"Hey, NO. No touching without asking, remember?" Marissa grabbed me herself. "I was super fucking clear about that. And I'm her guardian, it's my job to keep her healthy, and *I* decide what that is. She'll lose the weight in no time, she won't even notice."

"I think I'd use the treadmill more if I was alone more often... I haven't had much time to myself aside from when I was sick, and it's only been a few days. I'll use it, I *like* cardio, I just haven't had a chance." I said, squirming so I could stand on her pinkie as she gripped me.

"Whatever, speaking of, we need to get food. Henri, if you can do this punishment, AND take one of the two that Amber has lined up, I'll let you call our chef and order anything you want for us to eat, otherwise, I pick. Got it?"

Henri crossed her arms. "I would take Amber's punishments anyway, just because I am a GOOD FRIEND, unlike other people, so I'll gladly take you up on that."

Marissa ignored her and set me on the table again. She pulled out a card. "Oh, perfect, this one fits the game you lost, too. You have to do a shot, while hanging upside down off the couch."

"More upside down? Ugh, alright, if I have to..." Henri walked over and lay down, her head hanging off the couch. "You'll have to give it to me, though..."

Marissa mixed another shot, and crouched in front of Henri. Henri opened her mouth, and Marissa poured the drink into it. Henri swallowed, and snorted, then gagged and gasped.

"Ok, I did that, not hard at all, it went into my nose a bit, but not bad, I am getting good at shots, I think." She sat up and wiped her mouth.

"Yeah, that one was a softball. Tell you what, after the next challenge, we'll both do a shot so you're not the only one drinking, ok?" Marissa offered, patting her shoulder.

"Wait, that doesn't wor-" I started, but Marissa's finger found my face before I could finish, knocking me on my ass yet again.

"Ja, ok, I could do that. I am starting to feel them a bit, it is kinda nice, another one would not hurt!" Henri smiled and pointed at the box. "What's my next punishment?"

Marissa grabbed a card out and read it. She smiled and started to laugh. "Oh, wow, gods, it's good *you're* doing this, as funny as it'd be, if Amber got this we'd be cleaning her guts off the floor."

"That sounds horrible, what is it?" Henri peeked at the card over Marissa's shoulder.

"Here, read it yourself, then, you know, do it." She handed her the card.

I watched as Henri's face scrunched, then she frowned. "Wait. Is this a punishment for you or me? Who is on the ground?"

"You're on the ground, obviously, it says. That's the point?" Marissa said, pointing at the ground.

"What is it? I can't see the card..." I asked.

"Marissa has to give me a back massage, apparently." Henri placed the card next to me and I read it.

'The loser must lay on the floor. The game master will then step or stand on the loser for no less than 2 minutes'

"I'm guessing you're the game master a lot when you play this, huh Lady M?" I asked.

"Usually, yeah, but it's not a massage, it's *humiliation*, it's being *stepped on*. It's a *punishment*."

Henri lay down on the ground face down, crossing her arms under her chin.

"Sure, ja, ok, it is a 'punishment'. Go ahead, I will be down here..." she sang.

"Yeah, I hate to break it to you Marissa, but like, my Appa used to get me to do this to him all the time, it's not a really a humiliation thing as much as it is just kinda nice." I said.

She shook her head. "Then your 'appa' was a pervert, and don't call me that, this is- ugh, this is just because *you*" She pointed to Henri. "actually *like* this stuff, isn't it?"

"I'll never telllllll" Henri giggled. I'd seen her like this when we slept over before, but usually only after 2 am, and it was barely 8:30.

"Whatever, fine, just- ugh. Ra- Amber, set a timer. Two minutes." She unlocked her phone and tossed it onto the table, dangerously close to me. I flipped it over, and set the timer.

"And the massage starts.... nnnow." I said.

I watched as Marissa stepped up onto Henri's back and started to step around, on her shoulders and spine. Henri giggled again and rocked slightly as she did so.

"Hey, you're gonna make me fall!" snapped Marissa

"Oh noooo the great 'Lady M', bested by wiggles." snickered Henri.

"You're doing pretty well having a whole ass person on you, huh?" I said. "I was like 12 when my dad decided I was getting too heavy, but you're just tanking it."

"She is all of 125, tops, I think less... I barely feel it, she should try harder..." Henri said wiggling more.

"Damnit, this is a *punishment*, fucking be *punished* already." Marissa growled, stomping on Henri's back. There was a popping sound, and Henri let out a satisfied sigh.

"Ohhhh there it was, keep it up Marissa, you might get your chiropracty license...."

"Uh, thirty seconds on the clock..." I said. Henri was laying it on thick, it might end up making Marissa mad, and...

"Fuck it, I'm done..." Marissa said, and got off. "Just lay there until it's over. That was one of my favorites, and you two ruined it with your 'massage' stuff."

"Well, I had a great time, maybe I should take Amber's *other* punishment too, I am fine with it if you are~." Henri said, grinning up at Marissa.

The alarm went off, and Henri sat up, stretching. "That was fantastic... I believe I get to pick dinner now, yes?"

Marissa crossed her arms. "Whatever. Order what you want, I'm making our shots, just don't give *her* any." She jerked a thumb at me.

"I can't tell if you're being an ass about my weight again, or if you're reminding her that I can't eat 'people food' anymore..." I said.

"I can multitask. Anyway, did you eat yet?" she asked me.

"Ah, no, I have half my daily meal left, maybe a bit more. I wanted to eat with you guys actually." I admitted.

"Aww that is so sweet of you Klein Fee!" Henri said, clapping. "I will order... Ummm... what are you eating Amber?"

"Oh, just a poke bowl. I don't know what it is *exactly*, but it's lumps of stuff that *looks* like a poke bowl?"

"Ok, we shall all eat bowls of stuff! I want pho!" Henri cheered loudly.

"So *order already*." Marissa said, handing her a shot.

"I actually think Henri should slow down on the shots, she's getting kinda silly..." I said as I eye the almost half empty bottle of vodka.

"Oh hush, she's ordering." Marissa flipped a cup over on me, closing me off from the outside world. I reached down to pull it off, but my fingers couldn't get a good grip on the plastic, and the cup was taller than I was, so I couldn't push it off from the top. I heard Henri ordering from the chef over the phone, her voice louder and more excited than usual, and I shook my head. Things were going to get out of hand soon if she didn't watch herself. I pushed the cup along the table as I walked, trying to find an edge so I could reach under the lip of the cup to pull it off of me, and after a few steps, I found one.

As I reached down to grip the bottom of the cup, I heard a shriek, and with a crash, the cup I was under flipped over, scooping me up in it. I lay at the bottom in a heap, my dress flared out over me as I lay on my upper back with my legs up. Henri's face filled the top of the opening, and I frowned up at her.

"What the heck was that?" I asked.

"You did not see? You almost fell off the table! I had to save you, one more step, and you would have broken something!" she said. Her breath was pure alcohol now, and the smell of it filled my cup. I gagged and covered my mouth and nose.

"Put me down, I'm fine, and you need a mint or something, gods..."

She tipped me out and huffed into her hand. "I do? I do not smell anything..."

"They're *way* more sensitive to smells and stuff, I brush my teeth like, four times a day now, and lotion *everything* at least every few hours. Even if the smell isn't enough to bother *you*, it's much stronger for *her*. But... you do have booze breath, yeah." Marissa said, pulling glass bottles of water out of the fridge wall cubby.

"Here, drink this, and eat some of those cherry gummies I know you have hidden in your bag, it'll be fine."

I felt surprised and a little dumb, She'd been putting lotion on constantly for my sake? I had thought it was for a skin care routine. I wondered if she'd even used lotion before she got me, or if it was all for me... Plus, the fact that Henri didn't know that meant that it wasn't covered in the class, so Marissa *was* doing research on class Bs to take care of me better, for certain this time.

"How did you know I had sweets in my bag?" Henri asked, taking a bottle of water.

"I heard it crinkle when I kicked it earlier, and you always had a bag of the same kind with you at school, every day. I assumed you'd have some here. And I was right, obviously." retorted Marissa.

Again, there she was noticing someone's eating habits, just casually noticing that she ate candy at school, and knowing the type, and connecting that with the crinkle of the wrapper. Was she just weird like that? Or did the other girls talk about me and Henri that much, that our lunch habits were a topic of discussion?

Henri chugged the water, and unzipped her bag, pulling out her candy.

"I will just have one piece, we're about to eat, you know..." she said, pushing a cherry into her mouth.

"You know... if we do this again, we can actually plan ahead and we can make vodka gummies with those. We'll need to soak them for like a day, but they're a great way to get drunk, fun." Marissa said.

"Mmm, that *does* sounds fun." mumbled Henri through her gummy. "These are my favorite thing, and I am really liking the feeling I have right now, it is like... a hug, but from the inside, and it makes me not care or something."

"Henri, I think that's called drunk, you should not have any more." I called out, still on the table.

"No, that's called *buzzed*." Marissa interjected. "Drunk would be if she had maybe one or two more."

"Are we suuure we cannot let Amber have some too? I am sure she would be fine, it is not that big a deal, she has got, what, two months? Six weeks?" Henri said, coming back over and sloshing the bottle at me.

"If I let her drink, especially in front of YOU, who'd report it in a heartbeat, I could lose custody. So no, I won't be letting her drink." Marissa pulled the bottle out of Henri's hand. "Drink your water, the food will be here soon."

"Actually, vodka is uhhh, potatoes and stuff, right? I can't eat anything that's not processed to hell and back, could I even drink vodka at all?" I asked.

"It's a moot point, so I don't care. We'll figure it out on your birthday party or something." she said as she put the bottle back in the fridge.

"Ohhh she gets a party? Can I come?" Henri said, lighting up.

"Well, I was planning on using her as a cake topper, on a cake she couldn't even eat without getting sick, so I don't know if you'd *want* to come, but we'll see."

"You were already planning my birthday party? Over a month out? I can't tell if that's sweet or terrible, what the heck." I said.

"It's terrible, I'm using you as a prop to make myself look nice, and all your worst enemies will be there getting drunk, and you won't be able to do anything but sit there on the cake getting sticky and looking pretty." Marissa said casually.

"Awwww you think she is pretty?" Henri said, leaning on Marissa and fluttering her eyelashes. "You cannot tell anyone, but I do tooooo."

Marissa shoved Henri off of her onto the couch where she landed with a squeak and a laugh.

"I can't tell if you're actually drunk, or if you're playing it up for my sake, but don't touch *me* without asking either, got it?" she said coldly.

"I think it's a bit of both, I've seen her get silly before, I think she's just having fun with it to be honest." I said, watching Henri giggle and fluff her maid dress.

There was a knock on the door, and Marissa looked up.

"Oh, shit, that's the food already. Uhh, Here, you cook yours while I get the table set."

She picked me up with both hands and walked over to my house. I could tell she was a bit unsteady herself, but was doing her best to hide it. She put me in my kitchen, and jogged over to the door for the food.

With her gone and me in my home... I put my meal in the microwave and wet a rag in the sink. I rubbed at the tape on my legs with it, but it didn't want to come off. I sighed, and fixed a cup of water, pouring it on the hem of my dress where the tape met it, and peeled the tape off the dress itself, leaving it attached to my leg. I used the rag to rub against the place where the tape met my skin, and had one leg fully un-taped when the microwave beeped. Marissa's face popped into view at the beeping, and she saw me working on my other leg to get the tape off.

She grinned and narrowed her eyes. "Oh, yeah, I forgot about that, let me get that for you..." She reached in and grabbed the tape.

"Oh, no no, stop, no AAAGH, GODS WHY" I screamed as the hair on my left thigh was all yanked out at once, leaving my leg burning and sensitive. I clutched my leg, expecting to see it bleeding, but it was just slightly pinker than usual.

"...Huh, yeah, looks like you had it, sorry." Marissa said, a smirk on her face.

I stood up shakily and winced as my dress brushed my leg. "Just- Let's go eat, whatever..."

I got my bowl out of the microwave, and sat in her hand as she carried me to the table.

"Heyyyy girls, I heard a loud thing, what was that?" Henri said, beaming.

"It was me, getting my leg waxed, apparently." I said, sitting in front of her. "You could have tried to help, if you heard me screaming, you know."

She frowned. "I did not know, I just wanted to eat. I want a wax too..."

She was definitely getting drunk. I scooted away from her, and started eating. Marissa poked at her food, leaving it on the table and looking uninterested in it, but Henri practically gulped hers down, holding the bowl to her face and scooping the noodles and veggies into her mouth. It was getting late, she and I usually ate much earlier than this, so that could have been it, but she seemed downright voracious for some reason. I ate my own food quickly, it looked like Marissa was impatient to get to the next activity, and I didn't want her waiting on me. I ate the last 'something' lump as Henri slurped the rest of her broth and smacked her lips.

"Ahhh, that was wonderful!" she said, and picked me up off the table. "How was yours, Klein Fee?"

"HEY. DROP HER." barked Marissa standing up sharply.

Henri squeaked and let go of me instantly, tossing me away from her.

As I fell, I wondered what it'd be like to be paralyzed; if I'd break my spine when I hit the floor or if I'd catch myself and break my limbs instead. Time flowed slowly, and as I tipped backwards, I realized I'd be hitting head first. In my hyperaware state, I almost felt relived, it'd be a quick death, then.

The back of my head hit, and a sensation of heat rushed through me, and I closed my eyes. I felt myself sinking, and the hot sensation spread across my whole body. I lay there, not feeling the table below me, feeling the heat, feeling my heartbeat, the stinging tingle around me, and I realized I wasn't dead. I opened my eyes, and instantly regretted it. A burning pierced them the second they split open, and my hands rushed to rub them, and I realized, I *could* move, I was fine. I had... just been tossed into Marissa's pho bowl.

I kicked to the surface and gasped for air, swimming through the broth to the side, pushing noodles out of the way to get there. I hung onto the side of the bowl and panted, it was hot, but I wasn't hurt. I looked up to see Marissa looking down on me with a stricken look on her face, her hands out like she'd tried to catch me. I coughed, and shook the oily, salty broth out of my face.

"*Gods* Henri, I could have died, what the fuck?!" I yelled, once my senses came back enough to think straight.

"I- I- Oh, götter, I did not- She said to drop you, I-" Henri stuttered, her hands shaking.

Marissa took a step forward and slapped Henri across the face, knocking her back onto the couch.

"Listen, you fucking *ditz*." she said, her voice deep and hard. "You're here in my house as a *fucking* guest, you follow my *fucking* rules, and you do not. DO NOT. Touch my pet without permission. You need to get a fucking grip, or I will call the fucking pigs and tell them you tried to steal my pet, do you understand?"

Henri's eyes welled up, and she shook, crying as she looked up at Marissa standing over her.

"I- I just wanted to hold my f-friend, I love her, I- I did not want to hurt her, I-"

"Well you damn well near fucking killed her, if she'd hit the table, she'd be dead right now, all because you can't keep a few little rules in your head, do you understand that? That you almost killed her?"

Henri was curled up in a ball now, holding her head and crying hard. I felt bad for her, and I wanted to say something to comfort her, to take the sting away from Marissa's tirade, but as angry and mean as what Marissa said was, she wasn't entirely wrong. I'd find a way to make it up to her later, once she'd calmed down. For now though...

"Hey, um, Lady M? I'm still in the soup, it's kinda hot and I can't get out... I think it ruined this dress, too..."

Marissa stopped glaring at Henri and looked over at me with a look that bordered on concern, before she smirked.

"Ok, let me help, but first... I never finished my dinner..."

She sat down on the couch again and lifted her chopsticks over me and I shuddered.

"Seriously, just pull me out, it really stings..."

"Hmm, I think it'd be easier to just finish the soup, then it wouldn't be stinging you, right?" she teased, twirling up a bite and slurping it up. The level dropped as she did so, and the lip of the bowl got that much farther away. I sighed, and resigned myself to waiting as she finished her meal, bite by bite. The chopsticks speared down around me over and over, plucking veggies, little bites of protein, and noodles on the way up. I floated in the broth, seeing the bowl around me, and I felt a little funny, almost like I could get used to this, like it felt... right, cozy, even. Marissa finished the last of the chunks, and lifted the bowl, my stomach sloshing along with the broth as gravity wobbled, and held it up to her mouth.

"Ready for another kiss, Amber?" She whispered, before tipping the bowl, sending me sliding against her lips once more.

She drank the broth quickly, and pulled away with her lips puckered against me as I slid back into the bowl, and smiled at me. "Mmm, Amber flavored soup... I'll have to make this again sometime."

"Please don't..." I groaned. She just laughed, and used the chopsticks under my arms to lift me out of the bowl.

"I'll put you in your bathroom, wash up and get changed into your pajamas, Henri should be done crying by then and we can keep the night going." She said, walking me to my house.

"I'm still upset about this dress though, it's the only thing I had that was remotely cute..." I said, looking at the stained and oily scrap of fabric.

"Oh, we can throw that out, I got an email this morning, your wardrobe is getting here tomorrow, you'll have way better options soon, and *I'll* be picking your outfits from now on too, so you'll *always* look cute."

I start to pull off the dress as she set me down and she jumped.

"W-wait, close your door at least, geez, ugh. I'm going to change too, just sit on your front step when you're cleaned up."

She closed the walls of my house, and I closed the door to my bathroom. For someone who'd just used me to flavor her dinner, she had a weird level of care about my modesty...

# Chapter Seven

The oil seemed like it'd never wash off. I used so much soap, and had the shower on full blast mode, but I still lightly smelled like broth after nearly 15 minutes of washing. I gave up trying, and got out, drying myself off. It'd fade eventually I guessed, and until then, maybe I could get Marissa to use some perfume or lotion on me to cover the smell. I put on my pajamas, the ones I'd been wearing when I was compressed, and headed downstairs. I considered taking a few moments to rest and relax before going out, but... I couldn't be sure when I'd see Henri again after tonight, and I wanted the time we had to count. Thinking on it, I wasn't sure *if* I'd see Henri again, after that fight she and Marissa had.

I opened my front door and sat on the step like requested. The 'party' hadn't started up again, and Marissa was still in her bathroom for now. Henri was drying her eyes and sniffling, but didn't seem to be too upset anymore, just a bit out of it. She looked over at my house, and her eyes lit up when she saw me. She stood, and quickly crossed the floor.

"Oh, I hope you are not too angry with me, I was just so happy to spend more time with you..." she said, leaning in.

I looked at her hopeful face looming down at me, open and wide eyed, and I felt odd inside. I wasn't angry, more... scared, in a weird way.

"I'm not angry, Henri..." I said, folding my arms. "but you have to remember, being this small is fucking terrifying, all the time. The only reason I'm not constantly having a mental breakdown is because I'm just... refusing to process any of it. When you do stuff like grab me without asking, or throw me because you get scared, it makes it very, very hard to not think about the situation I'm in..."

"Oh... I see... But, Marissa grabs you, and she is *very* mean to you, doesn't that make you think about the situation?" her breath smelled like vodka again, and she was swaying. I didn't even know if she'd remember this, but I may as well explain myself...

"I- Yeah, kinda, but it's *Marissa*. She *never* saw me as a person. She isn't a person treating me like an object, she's like... a force of nature, something to be respected and feared. She's not 'real', if that makes sense..."

I tried to explain myself further. "I don't know, it's- it's different when it's you, she has this sort of carefulness to her, where she's mean, but she'd never willingly put me in danger, I think. You did put me in danger, and didn't even think about it? It just hits different."

I considered what I just said. I had never put it to thought before now, but... that was how I was staying so calm, wasn't it? Just the idea that I *can't* stop my situation, so why try? The idea that she's *not* human, so don't treat her like she is, just try to manage her. That was going to stop working soon, especially since I just said it out loud. I *could* change my situation, or at least, it could be changed. Marissa was calling me Amber for the first time in my life, so change could happen. Marissa *was* a human, and she could be talked to, reasoned with. She saw *me* as a human, or at least as something valuable enough to care about. She tried to protect me, in her own way, she did things to make me comfortable, like the lotion, or making sure I got veggie foods, or even just making sure I was warm. She was mean, but *why* was she mean? Why was she so intent on treating me like I was a pet or a toy if she obviously didn't see me like that?

While I was pondering my new outlook on my condition, Henri's eyes had gotten misty again. "Does that mean you do not want to spend time with me anymore? Because I remind you how small you are?"

"No! No, of course not! You're my favorite person, I wish it'd been you to be my guardian, if you were, I'd be over this weird phase already."

She put her hands on the desk and leaned in closer. "I wish I was your guardian too..." she whispered "Things would be wonderful if I was..."

"Well..." I said, a bit nervous. She was almost touching me with her face now. "I just want you to focus, treat me like your friend and not like a toy, and maybe lay off the alcohol, you're getting weird."

"Well, about that..." Marissa said from behind Henri. "For what I have planned, she's gonna need more alcohol, *and* to treat you like a toy, so good speech, set those boundaries, but I do have to make her break them instantly, sorry."

Henri stiffened, and slowly moved away from me. "I wasn't kissing her! I was just talking!"

Marissa frowned. "I didn't think you *were*, until you said that..." she looked over at me. "Was she?... I guess you wouldn't say anyway if she was, huh?"

I shook my head. "Her breath is too boozy, if she kissed me I swear I'd get drunk from the contact, she was just really close."

Henri nodded, and I stepped off the counter into Marissa's hand.

"Anyway," I said "What do you have in mind that involves me being a toy, and Henri drinking?"

Marissa smiled. "I made this game up myself earlier, I call it 'doll party'. I'm kinda proud of it."

"I suppose Amber is the doll in question?..." Henri asked.

"Of course, yeah. So, the rules are easy, we have a tea party with Amber, right? It would have been better if she was still in her dress, but we have a tea party, and like, we have shots instead of tea? And Amber is the one 'hosting' the party tonight, because she's the doll."

"What does the hostess do?" I asked.

"She gets snacks for the guests, she pours drinks, and she picks conversation topics. We have to all follow proper tea party rules or take a shot each time we break one, and we have to discuss the conversation topics honestly, but if we insult someone, lie and get called out on it, or say something rude, we drink."

"Doesn't that make it so I have control over who drinks the most? I just pick topics that will make one person upset, right?" I asked.

Marissa smirked, "You can tryyyyy" She said, rubbing my head.

"Ok, how will she pour the drinks?" Henri asked. "She cannot lift the bottle..."

"I got a spout with a rubber stopper. I'll prop the bottle up, and she just lifts the stopper after putting the shot glass under it, I thought of everything."

"This just sounds like more complicated truth or dare, without the dares..." I said as Marissa put me back on the coffee table once again. "When you said we'd get to the 'fun stuff' after dinner, I assumed we'd be doing knife throwing or something."

"No, this carpet is really hard to get blood out of..." Marissa said, sounding slightly sad. "And this will be fun, I think it'll be better than you realize."

"Ok, well... let us get the table set up, what are tea party rules, anyway?" Henri asked, taking the bowls and cups off the table.

"Oh, like, pinkies up, no swearing, talk with a fancy voice, napkin on your lap, just, tea party stuff." Marissa said.

Henri frowned, and I hoped that she understood. I knew what Marissa meant, and I couldn't really pretend I didn't. If Henri fucked up, I wouldn't be able to claim whatever rule she broke wasn't a 'real tea party rule' or something. As the two larger girls got the table set, I thought about what topics I'd bring up. I could ask about politics, but I hadn't heard Marissa mention anything political so far, so I didn't know how that would pan out. I could ask about something boring, like the weather, but that sounded boring. Relationships were right out, I was almost scared to ask about that. I could always go with favorite music or something similar? But I got the feeling the game was supposed to be emotionally charged, and I did want to keep Marissa happy, so...

"Is everyone set up?" I asked. They nodded, and Marissa lifted her shot glass up in a toast, and we began.

"So." I said in a fancy voice, thinking of how to word my topic. "I wish to know you all better, tell me, how were your childhood years?"

Marissa's smirk grew, and she tried to hide a snort. "Ohh, such a lllllllovely topic Miss Park, how utttttterrrrlly *therapeutic* of you..." she rolled her words, and raised her voice a notch as she spoke, selling the 'fancy' voice.

"Ah, yessss, Miss Park, yes, I would too llllike to talk about this, it is verrrrry quaint how you ask it of us, such a ladyyy." Henri said, trying and failing to copy Marissa's voice.

"Myyy childhood was *quite* pleasant," Marissa said. "I had suuuuch a llllovely time spending alllll my family's money on such *wonderful* things, I traveled to far off places and had such beautiful experiences, why, I had no worries in the world..." She sipped her shot lightly, pinky up.

"I too had a pleasant childhood, I- helped my father with the business, and learned ever so much!" Henri said, sounding more like a victorian orphan than anything. I supposed accents were hard to fake for someone who already had an accent herself... She took a sip of her drink too and I shook my head, knowing what was coming before it was said.

"Ahhh, it would seem you forgot to lift your pinky, Miss-" Marissa stopped, and blinked. I realized that she didn't actually know Henri's last name and suppressed a grin. "-Miss Henrietta..."She said, her confidence dropping.

Henri smiled smugly, and took her shot, pinky raised this time. "Why Miss Lund, how *forward* of you to call me by my first name... It is almost *improper*."

"Oh, how... rude of me, I shall have to be very careful in the future, won't I?" Marissa said, staring at me, asking with her eyes for me to tell her Henri's last name. I pretended I didn't see. It'd be funny seeing her try to avoid using any name for Henri the rest of the game. She rolled her eyes, and took her shot.

They both passed me their glasses, and I pushed Henri's under the nozzle of the bottle that was propped up on a couple books, and popped off the rubber cap. The vodka came out faster and farther than I expected, and splashed me in the chest before I moved the shot glass to the right spot. The smell burned my nose, and my pajamas dripped, my skin tingled, and I briefly wondered if

I could pause the game to go change, but I knew I'd just spill more on myself later.

I pushed Henri's glass out of the way and slid Marissa's in its place, spilling a little more vodka on myself and the table in the process. I wrinkled my nose and shook my head, the fumes were still burning my senses, I really wanted to hurry up and finish the game...

"Oh, Miss Park, when you're done with that, we'd like some snacks, please." Marissa said, taking her glass and corking the flow before it dripped too much.

I looked around, and saw that there was a bag of Henri's gummies and a small package of cookies on the table. I walked over, and drug the gummies out of the bag and onto one of the plates Marissa had put next to the bag, my hands sticking to the red and green gloss, forcing me to stop and unstick every time I moved one. After, I went to the package of cookies. They were the ones with the hole in the middle, with the buttery taste. I used to really like them but I hadn't seen them in years, although I supposed I couldn't have any now. The package was still sealed though, and no matter how hard I tried, I couldn't get it open.

"Ohhh, Miss Park, let me get that, I know things can be 'difficult' with your 'condition'." Marissa said, after watching me struggle for far too long.

I panted, and stood back as she effortlessly tore it open, dumping cookies onto the other plate. I drug the plates between Henri and Marissa, and sat down hard, tired from the work, and a bit dizzy. I looked up at them. Henri was looking glassier than before, and Marissa looked like she was having a little bit too much fun as well, and was giggling to herself under her breath.

"Alright ladies, next topic of discussion..." I said tiredly. "We shall discuss..." I was drawing a blank, fuck it, ice breaker time. "What is the best thing that happened to you in the last week?"

Marissa smiled "Why Miss Park, *you* are, of course! I got such a lovely obedient pet, and you've been a pleasure to play with!"

I should have seen that coming, I supposed. I shivered at being called an 'obedient pet', and looked to Henri.

"And you?" I asked.

She shook her head. "Why, I *do* believe this week has been absolute shit so far, I cannot think of one good thing." her accent had changed again, this time into a more southern one.

"Ah, I do believe your tongue slipped, please refrain from harsh language, Miss Park does have such *sensitive* ears..." Marissa said, pointing to Henri's glass.

"It doesn't have to be a *good* thing, per se." I clarified, as Henri took her shot. "Just... the best thing that happened?"

"Ugh." Henri shuddered and handed her shot glass down to me. "I suppose I had a phone call with Mama on Monday that went well, she did not mention me finding a boyfriend once, and she heard from my big brother, he is doing quite well."

I filled the shot glass, not spilling as much this time, but still getting a good amount sloshed on me.

"Ah, good to hear, I suppose he's still traveling across the world with a backpack?" I asked.

"Ja, but he said he will be coming home in a few months, hopefully he will be there when I go home for the fall break!" she said, smiling for real.

"Well I'm glad to hear it." I said. I was, she hadn't mentioned it to me before, and I was surprised she hadn't, her brother was her second favorite person aside from me, and she almost never got to see or talk to him, the chance of getting to spend the summer with her must have been very exciting for her.

"How *lovely* it is to hear you have such a *lovely* family, I just *love* to hear about how much you *love* each other." bit Marissa, coldly. She took her shot for lying without being reminded, adding more emphasis to her sarcasm, and slammed it down in front of me.

I stood, and stumbled on my way to fill her up again. I wasn't feeling well; I was itchy and my skin was tingly. I felt dry, like I needed a glass of water, but I ignored it and asked the next question. I was ready to end this game move on already, so I asked the one question I knew would start something, anything, just to get this all over with.

## The Feeling of Being Valued   117

"So, ladies..." I started "How do you feel about *me*? Like, as a person, and in general."

Marissa laughed. "Well, I don't think of you as a *person*, but in general, you're a pretty fun *toy*. I like owning you."

I frowned. "Actually... I've been thinking about it. I think you *do* think of me as a person. I think you care about me a lot more than you're letting on. You try to act like I'm this worthless thing you just want to play with, but you also seem to want me to be, I don't know, happy?"

Marissa narrowed her eyes at me, but took a shot without saying a word. She put it in front of me, and stared me down as I filled it.

"W-well, I think you are the most wonderful person in the world," Henri said, her words slurring slightly "and I want to be with you forever, and I want you to be safe, and to love on you and get you all to myself, and- and- I want to kiss you, every day, I just *love* you, Amber..."

I flushed. She'd just come out and *said* it, I hadn't expected that, I'd expected her to dance around the issue, and Marissa to call her out on it, draw it out into an argument. I stared up at her sitting there defiantly, swaying in place, her cheeks flushed and she looked back at me boldly.

"We can't lie in this game, so I will not lie." she said. "I said what I said, and I loved you for a long time, since we were teenagers, I do not even care anymore. Ich liebe dich, Klein Fee."

I avoided looking at Marissa and tried to think of what to say. "I... know, I kinda figured you did, I've been avoiding thinking about it, I thought if I acknowledged it, it'd ruin our relationship. I just- I don't know what to do about it. I-"

"Well, you don't have to worry about that now, Miss Park." Marissa said, her fingers encircling me. "There's no more relationship there anymore, just the relationships between me, my pet, and my slave."

She looked at Henri as she lifted me to her face. She was swaying too, her eyes were even more lidded than usual, and she was shaking slightly.

"I'm the one in charge of *both* of you, and there's nothing she or you can do, even if she *does* love you back."

She lifted me up and stared at me, hesitating, then her eyes flicked to Henri. She was standing up now, her hand outreached towards me with a hurt expression, and Marissa's face hardened. She pulled me in, and pressed my face to her puckered lips, holding me there as she hummed. I felt my face flushing, this wasn't teasing or me falling onto her mouth, this was an intentional, deliberate kiss. Her lips were soft and slightly wet, I couldn't breathe, and the warmth spread through my whole body, and the vibrations made it hard to concentrate on anything. When she pulled away at last, I gasped for air and wiped my face on my shoulder, getting the damp off. It was... a lot more interesting than the 'test kiss' that I'd had with Henri all those years ago; this one made me feel like I was electrocuted, like I had chugged an energy drink, and like I was falling, all at once. It was breathtaking and dizzying in more ways than one.

She pushed me into her cheek, and rubbed me up and down much like Henri had earlier, and maintained eye contact with her. I knew she was doing this to hurt Henri, to punish her for confessing to me, but her hands were shaking so much, and her breathing was coming in fast pants, and I wondered how comfortable she really was with this too.

"Aww Amber," She said in a sticky sweet voice. "*I* love you too, you know. I love you soooo much, and unlike that *other* girl, I can actually kiss you and snuggle you, and I get to see you *every day*."

I turned my head and saw that Henri was clutching her head and shaking with sobs, her face pink and broken.

"N-no, please, I just told her I- I held it in for so long, I need her to- I- We are still playing the game, please, I need to talk to her about it, please..." she choked out.

"Henri, I-" I said, before Marissa moved me to her chest, hugging me tight with both hands as she stood up and backed away from Henri, muffling my words against her flannel pajama top. I could hear her heartbeat from where I was; it was racing, and her body was very warm, much warmer than I was used to.

"Oh, but Henri, *I* confessed to her too just now, and *I* actually have her, so... I don't think the two of you need to do any more talking tonight. The game is over, and I think it's time for bed, don't you?"

Henri took a few steps forward, following Marissa around the edge of the couch. "Nein, nein, nein yours was just a mean trick, I want to take mine back, I want to do it again, please, that was the wrong time, I *ruined* it, please, *please*, I need to talk to her again..."

Marissa backed up further until she was against her bed, still holding me tight. "Listen, just shut up and fuck off, Henri. You're drunk, and she's *mine* now, if you don't stop pushing it, you'll never see her again, except hanging around my neck as we walk past each other in the halls."

"Nnnnno, it does not matter if she is yours now, I *like* her. You can still have her, I just want to- I do not know, I want to date her, or just hold her, just to be close to her, please." Henri sobbed.

I stayed still, Marissa's heartbeat hadn't slowed, and she was keeping me pressed against her, probably to stop me from speaking. I tried to imagine a world where I was dating Henri, and it wasn't much different from our regular relationship before I was infected, just with kisses goodbye at the end of the day. I tried to then think of a relationship with Henri with my life as it was *now*, and I couldn't. The dates in my mind had Marissa with us making fun of everything we did, the sleepovers were like *this* one, and every kiss started an argument and ended with me getting hurt.

"I like her too, I like her a *lot* actually, in fact, I think I like her *more* than you. You know how I know?" Marissa asked. "Because I actually got to the fucking store on time and fucking *bought her*."

"I WAS AT THE *BANK*, MISTSTÜCK." Henri screamed, shoving her onto the bed. Marissa threw one hand back to catch herself, and held me away from Henri with the other.

"Stop, please, you're both drunk, I don't want to get hurt..." I pleaded, the image of them playing tug-of-war with me popping back into my head.

Marissa glared at me. "I'm not drunk, it would take way, way more than that to get me drunk." She climbed up onto the bed fully and held me to her again, this time her stomach.

"Please, I ruined everything, I need to fix it, let me hold her, let me talk to her, she did not even get to answer, please..." Henri moaned.

"If you don't stop, I'm- I'm calling Parker and Drew to come throw your ass out of here, and- HEY!" Marissa shouted as Henri climbed up after her.

"OFF. OFF MY BED." she yelled. "That was a *fucking* rule, get... OFF." she pushed Henri hard, and she tumbled backwards off the bed into a heap, still crying.

I gasped. "Oh, gods, is she ok? She just went right over..."

"Uhh, damnit..." Marissa muttered, crawling to the edge of the bed. Henri was curled up in the fetal position, her sobs small and quiet, but she seemed to be fine, if way too drunk.

"Whatever. She pushed me first. It's whatever." Marissa said, more to herself than to me. "We need to go to bed anyway, she can sleep there."

"But shouldn't we like, make her sleep on the couch? She'll be sore down there..." I asked.

"If she wants the couch, she's a big girl, she can just go get on the fucking couch." Marissa growled. "She's on her side and she's breathing, that's all that matters. I need to brush my teeth, then you brush yours. I'm not trusting her not to try and grab you out of your house and sneak off with you tonight."

"So where will *I* sleep?" I asked, almost dreading the answer.

She looked at me, and bit her lip nervously. "As- as your legal guardian, I'm making a decision that for your safety and protection, you'll be sleeping with me. In- in my bed I mean, like, we'll both sleep in- fuck, you know what I mean."

"How will you make sure you won't roll on me and squish me?" I asked nervously.

"I'll put pillows around me, and lay on my side. I should have enough plushies in the closet to make a 'fort', and I'll lay around you, so she'd have to either touch me, or move stuff to get you."

I wanted to protest, but there was actually a *very* real chance that Henri really would try to kidnap me tonight, especially after all this. I didn't know if I trusted a drunk Henri to hold me, much less a drunk, hurt, *angry* Henri.

"Ok, yeah, that's a good plan." I said, nodding.

Marissa side eyed me. "So you consent to it?"

"Consent to what?" I asked, confused.

"To- damnit, to being in the bed with me. It could count as 'unnecessary contact', and you need to technically give your permission." she said

"Oh, ok... Yeah, I consent then." I realized something. "Hey, why is sleeping in the same bed... whatever you said, but kissing me isn't?"

She flushed. "It's- well, Henri kissed you before me, so she can't report on me without *me* reporting on *her*, and then she'd *never* get you. Anyway, we'll... we'll talk about the kiss tomorrow, I don't want to think about it tonight."

"Ok... And about Henri's confession... We'll talk about that tomorrow too?"

She didn't respond for a moment, sitting on the edge of the bed with her feet over the side, looking down at Henri, who'd fallen asleep. Her thumb absently rubbed my back as she held me. Finally, she sighed.

"I need to think about that, Amber. I don't want to talk about it *at all*, it doesn't matter one way or another if she 'loves' you or whatever, you belong to *me*. But." she squeezed me gently. "...but... I need to seriously think about this. I knew it, everyone did, but I didn't expect her to ever say it. It makes some stuff harder for me."

I crane my neck to see her face behind me. "What sort of stuff?"

Her grip tightened, and I winced at the familiar pain.

"Nothing *you* need to worry about" she said. "I don't want to talk about it any more tonight, and if I want to talk about it later, *I'll* bring it up, got it?"

"G-got it, yeah." I grunted, trying to pry her fingers off me.

She looked at me for a long second, then relaxed her fingers, and put me on her shoulder again. I held on tight as she shook her head.

"Let's just get ready for bed..."

We each brushed our teeth, and tidied up the room a little (or Marissa did at least) before setting up the bed with the plushies and pillows, stepping over Henri's now passed out form to do so. Marissa held me close as she climbed into her nest, and curled up, gently putting me in the center of her self, with her limbs, head, and torso making a protective place for me to lie down. She tucked the blankets around us, and lowered her head.

"Good night, Amber." she said. It sounded genuine, an actual 'good night', not a taunt or a tease, just someone telling someone else to sleep well. I responded in turn, and we lay there in silence. Her body heat filled the pocket, and her breathing and heartbeats sounded out from all around me. I curled up myself, my back against her thigh, and soon fell asleep, thinking about Henri, dating, Marissa, and finally starting to process my situation.

~~~

I woke up to movement, the bed under me was shifting, and I sat up, stretching. I looked around, and saw that I was still surrounded by Marissa, her sleeping face under the blanket with me. I pressed myself against Marissa's thigh as the bed continued to shift, before it went still. My body itched and stung for some reason, and Marissa's flannel pants felt rough and irritating as I leaned against her, but I stayed close anyway. There was no telling how sober Henri was, and if she blind grabbed for me under the covers, she could snap a limb, or worse. I heard soft thumping noises, the crinkling of a wrapper, and the unmistakable sound of someone crying. I listened for a while longer, and heard the door open and close, and I knew Henri had left. My own eyes welled up, and I lay back down. I knew *why* she'd left, her heart must be shattered right now, but I'd wanted to talk to her about it at least, to work through how I felt, to at least be able to give a full response. As it was, she didn't even wait until morning to leave so she could say goodbye.

I lay there crying softly to myself, wondering if I'd lost her until sleep took me again.

~~~

I woke up a second time as the word shifted around me, and I opened my eyes to see Marissa sitting up, cooler air rushing into the pocket she'd made with around us as the blanket fell away. I shivered, and hugged myself, only to hiss in pain as my limbs rubbed my body. It felt like my body was raw, like my skin had been peeled off. I pulled up my shirt to check as Marissa carefully got up from around me and headed into the bathroom, her eyes still puffy from sleep and her hair frazzled.

Under my clothes, I was a pink and red mess. My body was cracked and bleeding lightly around all my joints, and my hands were cracked to the point where just flexing my fingers caused small drops of blood to appear on the backs. I dropped my shirt, and hissed again when it hit my skin. What had happened? Was this because of the soup? I pulled my shirt off, and slid my shorts off too to have as little fabric touching me as possible, leaving me in my sports bra and panties. I stood as well as I could on the soft bed, and held my limbs away from my body. I was still on fire, and tears escaped my eyes as I tried to think of what could have happened. I felt so, so thirsty, and I could barely swallow.

"M-aa-riss-aa" I called out, but with the water running in the bathroom, my voice was far too small to hear. I looked around for anything that could help my cracked and bleeding skin, and saw the patch of drool from where Marissa's head had been laying and for a *brief* second, I considered it, but I knew even with this pain, slathering myself in someone's sleep drool was just too much.

On Marissa's desk across the room sat her lotion, lotion I knew was safe for me because she handled me with lotion-y fingers constantly, if I could just get there... I started across the bed, I didn't know what I'd do once I got to the couch, or how I'd get down to the floor and up to the desk, but I needed to try, my whole body felt like I'd been massaged with a cheese grater.

I instantly tripped, and fell into a heap, the pain splashing through me and I shrieked. I lay still for a while, letting my body stop throbbing, then I stood up, and stumbled into a plush bunny that Marissa had set on the bed. The microfiber material clung to my ragged and split skin, and I moaned in pain, pushing it away and standing in one place. I couldn't do it, it hurt too bad, I couldn't-

The door swung open, and Marissa stepped out of the bathroom wearing a robe, her hair wrapped up in a towel and a toothbrush in her mouth.

"Hey, le's ge' you into yo'r hou'e so y' can-" She saw me standing on the bed, frowned and ducked her head back into the bathroom to spit.

"Amber, why are you half naked? I leave for ten minutes, and... Oh... Oh, gods, uhh, are you ok?" She rushed over to the bed and picked me up. I writhed and gasped with her touch, and I flapped my hands to get her to stop holding me.

"M-y-y-y s-s-s-ki-i-in, it-s...." I croak out.

"Oh, oh gods, you're so dry, your skin is like paper, how did this happen?" She said, panicked. "Oh, uhh, this wasn't in the class, uhh, here, let's just..."

She rushed me over to my house and opened it up, pushing me into the bathroom. "Get in the shower, I'll try and look on my computer about this, it's gonna be ok."

I stumbled to the shower, turning it on to the mist and stepping inside. The cool spray hit my skin and burned and soothed at the same time, and I rubbed my body with my hands, opening my mouth to swallow some of the liquid. Once the spray had stopped feeling better and had started to feel irritating, I stepped out, and put my undergarments in the dryer, letting them tumble for a minute or two to dry before carefully putting them back on. I considered getting dressed, but my skin was still burning, and I really hoped Marissa would give me some of her lotion, and clothes would just get in the way...

I opened the bathroom door, and stepped out to a grim looking Marissa looking in. She reached out to me, and I flinched away, and she stopped shy.

"Amber..." She said. "I need to pick you up to help you, I promise I'll be careful."

I took a breath, and stepped towards her. I didn't expect her to be mean right now, she seemed too worried about me for that, but I knew it'd hurt anyway. She gently picked me up and let me stand on her palm, my hands on her fingers, and she carried me to her computer desk, her other hand hovering over me, ready to grab at any moment. I stepped off her hand, and onto the desk, and looked up at the bottle of moisturizer next to her monitor. I pointed at it.

"Could I ple-e-ease ha-a-a-ve some of tha-a-at?" I said, my throat still creaking with the effort.

She nodded, and pumped some out onto her fingers. She brought her finger close to me, the lotion in a drop on her fingertip.

"Would you like me to put in on you? Or can you?" She asked. I thought about it. I couldn't reach my back, but my back wasn't as bad. I should be ok.

"I-i-i'll do it." I said, taking it into my hand. I rubbed it in and gasped in relief as the cracks and splits were filled, and I relaxed as I spread it over every inch of myself.

"So... I figured out what happened..." Marissa said quietly. I looked up, waiting on her to continue. "I... I didn't realize that 'ethanol' was the same as vodka. That's one of the chemicals I was supposed to keep you away from. When you spilled it on yourself, it stripped the oils from your skin and evaporated the liquids. It took a while, but it dehydrated you and stopped you from retaining water."

I looked down at my body and thought of all the booze I'd splashed onto myself while filling shots. I'd been getting splashed every few minutes just as I'd started to dry for the whole game. I looked back up at Marissa.

"It's o-o-ok, I- I sho-o-ould have mentioned when it sta-a-arted burning..."

She frowned. "Yeah, no shit. Still. I should have known better, I should have looked into if it was safe."

She wasn't saying she was sorry, but she was still apologizing in her own way. I finished rubbing in the lotion and waved my arms to dry them. Hopefully I'd go back to normal soon. Even with the lotion, my body still hurt, and there were still little dots of blood on the backs of my hands.

"I'm going to finish my morning routine and get dressed." Marissa said, turning away. "After that, I'll give you more lotion, and we'll head out."

I frowned. I did *not* feel up to going anywhere today, was she really going to make me leave the house like this?

"Where a-a-a-re we go-o-o-ing?" I asked, trying to plan a way to stay home and soak in lotion instead.

She glanced over her shoulder at me. "Well, obviously we need to get you taken care of, duh. We're going to the vet."

# Chapter Eight

I lay on the floor of my plexiglass carrying case and looked up at Marissa in the car seat next to me. I was still in my underthings, and the lotion was caked on thick. We'd brought the bottle of it with us in case I needed more, but it wasn't helping as much as it had at first, and my skin was starting to burn under it anyway. I had drank glass after glass of water at the request of Marissa, but I still felt 'dry' somehow... I just hoped the doctor we were going to would have a way to help me.

It turned out that vets don't actually work on class Bs, at least not usually. Marissa had called our town vet, and he said that while he *could* help if it was life or death, we *actually* needed to go to a specialist. The closest one was over an hour and a half away, which frustrated Marissa, but she agreed to take me there instead. I was honestly glad that I wasn't going to a regular vet. I hadn't been around animals at all since I was compressed, and I'd heard stories about cats or even dogs killing class Bs they came across. I knew Marissa wouldn't have let me out of the case or put me in danger, but... I still didn't want to be around animals in general.

"How much longer, Drew?" Marissa asked, pulling me out of my thoughts.

"About an hour, ma'am." He responded automatically.

"Thank you, please raise the privacy curtain until we arrive." she said.

The black wall rose, blocking us from the front seat and blocking out most of the light. Marissa dug in her pocket and pulled something out. She popped open the front of the case, and slid it in. I recognized it as the cap to the bottle she usually kept me in. She pulled out the matching earbud, and put it in, pointing to the cap, and waving her hand. I sat up and flicked the cap on, the heater kicking in and the microphone turning on.

"Ok, Ra- ah, damnit, Amber. You wanted to talk, right? We have a while, so let's talk." she said, leaning to the side to be able to see me better.

I felt nervous and shy, and I didn't know what I *could* say without making her mad. That said, I was in my case, and I was already injured, so what would she really do to me?

"Well... I wanted to ask about, you know... Henri?" I said, testing the waters.

"Yeah, *Henri*." Marissa said, coldly. "She went way way too far. She ruined the game, and she made things just... so much less fun overall."

"Well... be that as it may," I said "She really did mean what she said, I think."

"Yeah, I'm sure she did." Marissa replied. "The whole school has know she's had a crush on you since she got in the country, and they've been making bets on how long it'd be before she comes out."

"That's horrible. I know the girls at our school are cruel," I pointed to Marissa "...case in point, but like, making bets on someone's sexuality feels, I don't know, wrong-er."

"Yeah, them and their little betting pool is the whole reason I never came out." Marissa said causally, ignoring my comment about her.

I looked up at her, trying to see if she was joking or teasing, but she seemed to be as annoyed with them as I was.

"Wait, you're gay?" I asked "Like, for real?"

She nodded. "Mhm, or I guess bi, same thing."

"I think that's what I am, I don't know, I've never really thought about it..." I said.

"You're pan. It's a type of bi. You said you don't care about gender and shit, right? That's pan. I do care, so I'm just bi."

"Uhh, ok... I didn't know." I said. I hadn't expected to be taught about queer stuff by *her* of all people...

"Anyway, I really *do* think she loves you, and that makes her dangerous. It was one thing when she just wanted to be around you, to be your friend, but now that *you* know she's crushing on you, she'll want to take you for herself. I'm not sure it's safe for you to be around her, if I'm being honest."

"Oh..." I said. "I don't think she's really dangerous, she was just drunk, I've pretty much *never* seen her get that upset before, I think she'll calm down enough to be around me in a day or so..."

"Mmmmno. She's not getting to be around you for a *lot* longer than that. If for no other reason than to punish her for ruining the night. I was having a lot of fun until she started causing problems."

"Ok, well... what do we do about her confession?" I asked.

"I don't think we have to do a damn thing about it, Amber. It does not matter one ounce if she loves you, I said that last night, and I meant it."

"But..." I said "What if I wanted to give it a chance?"

Marissa glared at me. "What, do you love her too?"

I shook my head. "No, I don't think so? I think I'm open to it though, I don't know. I've never had a relationship..."

"Parents were that strict, huh?" she said, smirking.

"No, I- I was in an all girl's school since I was like 14, I didn't have a chance..."

"Didn't stop me, I've had..." She thought about it "...5? Boyfriends?"

"I thought you were bi, what about girlfriends?"

"Too risky, if I got outed, I'd have lost my place as the queen of the school, and my mom would... do unkind things, I'm sure."

"Oh. That's fair..." I said. "Well, was there any girls you were interested in then?"

She raised an eyebrow. "Uh, yeah, there *definitely* were, Amber."

I nodded, that was kind of sad to think about, but romantic too. A forbidden love...

"So..." I said "about me and Henri..."

"I'm not comfortable with her being around you, so while, like, I legally can't say you can't 'date' her or whatever, I can say she's not going to be *around* you, so there's no chance *to* date her."

I lay back down, hissing at the floor touching my skin. "Hhhh... She's my best friend, Marissa, can't we work something out? Please?"

"Hey, don't call me that, and I don't know. I don't want to think about it. Like I said last night, I don't really want to think about this topic, just... Let's leave it at 'we'll re-visit it later', ok?"

I wasn't happy with that, why had she brought it up just to shut it down? I couldn't imagine a situation where it'd be possible to date Henri, and seeing her last night, it was almost like she saw me as less of a person than Marissa did. Her touchy-ness, her comments, the way she treated me... Marissa did what she did *because* I was a person, and it made her excited or something to do that stuff to a living human being. Henri... She seemed to see me 'softer' than a human, and that made me wonder how she really thought of me now.

There was still one thing I needed to ask about though...

"So, to change the topic, what was that kiss last night?" I asked

"Ugh..." she groaned "I was just trying to fuck with Henri. Yeah it wasn't *technically* ok to do it without asking, but whatever, it'd be a slap on the wrist at best, and *only* if you complain. It's fine."

"Oh, well... I know you were trying to make Henri mad, but... it felt more.. um, like, your hands were shaking, and you were really warm, and-"

She smacked the top of the case, making me jump.

"Gods, shut up already, ok?" she growled. "A kiss is a kiss, even if it's just to make someone mad, of course I'd be... worked up."

It didn't seem like that, but I shouldn't push it...

"Ok, yeah, sorry." I said. I went quiet, and looked at the ceiling of the car. I was starting to get a suspicion, but I didn't want to jump the gun. I lay there, quiet and thinking for a few minutes until Marissa spoke again.

"Did you like the party at least? The sleepover, I mean."

"Oh, uh, yeah, it was- it was kinda hard to enjoy at times, but I think I had fun overall, I was surprised."

"Surprised?" Marissa said "You didn't expect to have fun at a sleepover?"

"Well, I didn't want to be tortured all night, but really, other than the soup, and I guess that time you smushed me, I wasn't tortured that much at all, so yeah, surprised."

"I'm not- I don't- No, Amber, I don't want to like, *torture* you..." she said, sounding hurt.

I sat back up. "What? You've been torturing me since you *got* me, the water, the bottle, even you 'playing' with me the first day. My side is *still* bruised from that time you flicked me."

"...well, it's- it's not like that..." she muttered. "I play with you yeah, but I don't want to torture you, just play, have some fun I guess."

"It- It's not fun for me, I'd prefer you didn't..." I said quietly.

"Well- fuck, damnit!" she barked, getting frustrated "I shouldn't have to care about what *you* think, I got you because I wanted to have *fun* with you, and *I'm* going to do what's fun for *me*."

I lay there, thinking about what she'd said. I couldn't do anything about it if she *did* dunk me in ice water again, or got too rough and hurt me. Maybe I shouldn't have said anything... I felt small, smaller than I'd felt since I was compressed, and I felt the grip I had on my situation start to slip. I really *was* just a fucking toy, wasn't I? Whether it was her or Henri, or anyone, really, I was just a toy for them to play with. I couldn't hold it back any more, between the pain and the stress and the feelings of hopelessness, I started to cry.

I could never live a normal life again, and it was finally starting to sink in. I was like this, a second class citizen, forever. I'd never be able to date or live on my own, have human rights... She wasn't doing anything a million other people wouldn't do, hell, if I'd found *her* I would have been *much* meaner to her than she'd been to me, I'd have stepped on her and made her-... well, I didn't want to think about it now, I didn't want to manifest it happening to *me*. The tears ran down my face, and I sniffled, thinking about how it was lucky the vodka mostly missed my face, or this would hurt a lot right now.

I felt the case lift, and I looked over. I was eye level with Marissa now, and she had a strange, annoyed and concerned look on her face. I wiped my eyes and looked away from her. I wasn't asking for an apology, or trying to get attention, I just really wanted to feel human again. Seeing her face as large as it was, it just highlighted and reminded me that I *wasn't* human, not legally. I couldn't see her as a force of nature anymore, she was just a girl like me, just a human. I doubted there was any difference between us other than her having money, really.

"Hey... Amber..." she said gently.

"..."

I stayed quiet. It didn't matter anyway, I was just a fucking class B, it wasn't like anything I said could do anything.

"Amber, listen, stop crying, look..." she said. 'Stop crying', wow, that was helpful.

"I'm going to get better at playing with you, I'm learning, I'm trying not to hurt you, ok?"

Then why 'play' with me like that in the first place, bitch? I still didn't answer, but it felt good to think it.

"Amber, really, I'm trying to talk to you..." she said, sounding sad. I looked back over, still crying. She looked hurt, for some reason.

"You don't understand," I said, breaking my silence. "I'm not even fucking human anymore, and the one person who's licensed to take care of me plays so rough I'm scared for my life."

I wasn't, exactly, but I was feeling bitter, and I knew it'd sound tough.

"No, hey, that's not fair, I would *never* endanger your life." she said, not responding to my main point. I guess I set the bar too high, time to dial it back.

"It's more than that, it's not about me being dead, it's about me not being *alive*." I said.

"I really don't understand, what the fuck are you talking about?" she asked, wrinkling her nose.

I sat up. "I'm just a toy, right? Not a human, closer to a pet than an object, sure, but still not really human. I'm not *alive*, 'Lady M'. And everything you do to me just reminds me of that."

"...Oh, yeah, ok." she said. She lowered me to her lap. "Well, I do want to keep playing with you, of course. I really like it, but I guess we can work out a few ways for you to feel like a real person again. I know I haven't been helping with that."

"It was mostly Henri that made me feel the worst." I admitted. "I *knew* her, so it hurt more. You weren't a real person to me until last night."

"I- what?!" she said "What does that even mean?"

"Well, you were like the boogyman or something, not a person, just a figurehead of the bullies at school. You were a symbol, so it made sense for *you* to hurt me, I guess."

She was quiet for a moment. "...A symbol, huh? I almost like that, it makes me feel like a dictator or something. But." She raised me up again. "I *am* a real person, Amber."

I nodded "Yeah, I know, that's why I started crying. Because you're real to me now, and that means what you did actually *counts*. It wasn't just an unstoppable force, it was *you*."

She took a deep breath. "I *thought* you were being weirdly accepting of me owning you. I guess the brain like, preserves itself or something. Look, you can drop the whole 'Lady M' thing if that helps, and... I'll try to remember to, I don't know, ask your opinions on stuff, would that help?"

"Yeah, I think so... And I really would prefer it if you didn't hurt me, too."

It was a small concession from her, but not having to treat her like a higher being would help me a lot. It'd help her see me as a person, too, especially now that she was calling me Amber.

"...Well, I think I can promise not to *hurt* you. I still hold the right to play with you as I see fit, but I won't *hurt* you."

That didn't give me a lot of confidence, but it was better than nothing.

"...Thank you, Marissa."

"No problem, Amber."

~~~

I sat on the large table and shivered. It was cold in here, colder than I'd thought doctor's offices usually were. Didn't they know we were super susceptible to cold? One star review, endangered the patients. I looked around the room. It was big, and there were a lot of drawers on the walls, and a large, low chair, presumably for the doctor to sit in while they worked on me, and a large sitting chair for the guardian. Marissa was sitting in that one, on her phone. It'd been a day since her picture of me, if I had to guess, she was checking the comments and starting drama.

The door swung open and a middle aged man stepped in. I frowned, I'd have preferred a woman doctor, especially since I was already in my underthings, but if he was the only one within an hour and a half's drive...

"Hello, Miss Lund?" he said, addressing Marissa "What seems to be the issue?"

She looked up and pointed to me. "She's- uh, she's there, she had vodka spilled on her, she can tell you more than me."

He turned to me and looked me up and down, wincing at my red and pink skin and cracked joints.

"Ok, and what's *your* name?" he asked in a voice usually reserved for dogs and children under 5.

"My name is Amber, Amber Park." I said. "I got splashed with vodka by mistake, and we didn't know it was dangerous."

He glanced at the sheet he was holding. "Hmm... ok, and did you ingest the vodka?"

"No, I'm too young, I didn't have any."

He frowned. "It's not a matter of age, alcohol is essentially poison, and to someone of your size it could be deadly."

Oh... so much for drinking on my 21st after all. "We put lotion on me, but it still hurts really, really bad..."

"Well, that's to be expected. You're suffering what are basically chemical burns and extreme dehydration. Here."

He went to the sink, and came back with a small paper pill cup, the size of a bucket to me.

"Drink this, as much as you can, please."

I did as he asked, my mouth was still dry, and I'd done a lot of talking earlier, so I was grateful for the drink.

"Hey, like, is there anything you can give her?" Marissa asked "I'd really like her to be better as soon as possible."

"That's kind of you! There is, but it's not cheap. This lotion you've been using is *safe* for her, but it's not *ideal* for her." The doctor said, switching back to his normal voice. "I can get you a bottle of lotion that's medicated and has gone through compression so her body can actually absorb and process it."

"Great, cool, I'll get it, yeah." she said, nodding.

"I recommend getting some gauze too, I sell that as well in her size. I'd say to soak it in the lotion, then wrap her up, and then put a layer of dry gauze on top, that way it'll hold it in."

"I'll look like a mummy..." I complained.

"Yes! It's very cute!" The doctor said, patting my head. This motherfucker...

"Ok, so like, do you need to do a check on her vitals or anything? Or are we really spending three hours in the car and twenty minutes in the waiting room to buy a bottle of lotion?" Marissa said, shaking her head.

"Ah, yes, I need to give her a physical! But I do need to ask you to leave, for privacy reasons. It'll just be a bit, ok?" he said.

Marissa huffed, but stood and left, closing the door behind her. The doctor sat down in front of me and looked at me seriously.

"Now, as your doctor..." he said in that stupid childish tone. "I have to ask, has she been hurting you? Is she putting you in danger? It's not uncommon for new guardians to mistreat their little friends..."

I thought about my answer. I could rat her out, tell him everything she'd done, but... would it be enough to do anything? If a kiss was just a slap on the wrist, would anything come of the other stuff? I could end up just getting her in trouble, and then still have to stay with her, but then she'd know I'd told. I *might* get to go live with Henri if the consequences were serious, but I didn't know if I wanted that right now based on her actions last night.

That said, I'd also have to tell on Henri too if I was being honest. Her grabbing me, the kiss, her throwing me into the soup... I could stay quiet, but Marissa would say how unsafe she was either way, and that could invalidate my own testimony if they found out I'd withheld information. In the end, I'd absolutely not be allowed to be around Henri anymore no matter what.

I could live with my parents, my dad had his guardian license, but if Henri wasn't allowed around me, I'd just be with the two of them, and once they got older and couldn't pass recertification, I'd get shuffled off into the adoption process again. My mom already could hardly hear, and my dad's eyes were going, who's to say it'd be more than a couple years before I got removed from their care anyway? It'd be decades sooner than I would if Marissa was watching me either way, if she ever even failed re-cert. Would never seeing my friend again and risking being put back on the market in a few years be worth getting away from Marissa?

"...No, she hasn't. She was drinking with her friend, and I tried to fix them drinks, that's how I got splashed."

"...I see," he said, not sounding convinced. "and the bruise?"

I looked down at the yellow blotch on my side, visible even through the lotion and red skin.

"...That was an accident. She was playing with me the day she got me, and didn't realize how fragile I was. She knows better now."

I felt gross saying that, making excuses for her, but... I didn't *think* she'd do it again. She'd promised to try at least...

"Ok, Amber, I just want you to know, if there's ever a problem, you need to tell us right away, ok?" he said sadly, patting my head with his finger. His hand smelled like hand sanitizer and old people.

"Yeah, ok. So, the check up... What do I need to do?..."

"Oh? No no, there's no check up, you just got one earlier this week when you were registered, you'll be ok. I just wanted to make sure you weren't being abused, and if you *say* you're not, there's nothing I can do."

"...Ok, yeah. Let's just- I want to get home, so thanks, but let's move it along." I said.

I couldn't tell if I'd made a mistake just now, but he seemed to think I did. He dug in one of the drawers and pulled out a bottle full of grey cream, and bandages from another. He opened the door and called for Marissa to come back in.

"So, what, is she ok?" she asked, stepping in.

"She is! A bit banged up, but that's normal for new class Bs, still finding out how their new bodies work." he said. "Here's the lotion, and the bandages. Soak the bandages for at least ten minutes before putting them on her, then remember to put a dry layer on top, ok?"

"Yeah, ok, no problem." she said, putting my case next to me on the table. I stepped inside and sat down as she collected the items and closed the front of the case.

"You can pay at the front desk, I hope she heals well!" the doctor said, beaming.

Marissa paid at the desk, wincing at the $600 bill, and we headed out to where Drew was waiting for us in the parking lot.

She climbed in, and looked over the lotion. "This stuff had better work." she said "I can't believe it's so fucking expensive."

"I think it was the doctor's time, too. If he's the only one in an eighty mile radius, he can name his price." I offered.

She looked down at me and bit her lip. "Hey, while I was out of the room, what happened?"

Yeah, I though she'd ask that. "...He asked if you were abusive."

She looked at me, almost scared to ask, but trying to work up the courage.

"...I said you weren't." I told her, not giving her the chance to ask it herself. "You told me you wouldn't hurt me, and that you'd be better about 'playing' with me, I'm choosing to trust that."

I didn't trust her, not as far as I could throw her, but if she knew I didn't see tattling on her as a viable option right now... I hated to think of what she'd feel comfortable doing to me.

She looked down guiltily. "Yeah, ok. You didn't say... anything?"

I shook my head. "No, nothing. Like I said, I'm trusting you."

She swallowed and pursed her lips. "That's... kinda a lot of pressure on me all of the sudden, you know?"

I looked up. "Why is that?"

"Well... I don't know, it's like, now there's stakes to everything. I have your trust or whatever, and I know it shouldn't matter, you're a fucking pet, but for some reason, I don't want to lose that."

I lay back down. I felt guilty now too, but I couldn't let that get in the way. I finally had some kind of power, some bargaining tool. Why Marissa of all people cared that I "trusted" her, I couldn't guess, but I needed to use it while I had it. I could *guess* about why she gave a flying fuck, and... it tied back into my earlier suspicions, but I almost didn't want that to be the case, as helpful as it'd be. My life was already getting too complicated.

"Hey, once we get home, I'll show you something cool, ok?" She said, trying to sound chipper. "No playing with you, no tricks, just like, something fun and cool we can do together, ok?"

"...Ok. Just don't forget I need the bandages on me first."

"Oh, yeah, I won't." She said.

The rest of the ride home, we sat in awkward silence. I didn't want to talk and ruin the balance I had, and she stayed quiet, on her phone typing furiously, glancing up at me from time to time before going back to her phone.

~~~

I stood on Marissa's desk with my arms and legs out as she carefully wrapped me up in the sticky gauze. I'd refused to remove the rest of the clothing I had on, and she didn't push the issue past a comment that it'd work better if it touched my skin directly, most likely to her odd modesty hangup. I'd smeared the lotion under my underthings though, so that should help out some at least. Her fingers carefully weaved in and out as she wrapped. I had to brace myself as the tight wrappings rubbed against my skin, but the lotion felt so, so good... It numbed and soothed at the same time, a few minutes after it hit my skin, I couldn't feel anything.

"Thanks for helping me with this." I said, bending so she could wrap better.

"Yeah. It's like, one of my jobs or whatever, I guess." she said. "Seriously though, I can't help but feel responsible, and I need you to look good by tomorrow anyway."

"Tomorrow?" I asked "Is that when your mom gets home?"

"My mom? No, that's like, next weekend." she said, shaking her head "I have to go to my dad's house, and I was going to bring you so at least I'd have something interesting to talk about instead of who's cheating on their golf scores, or who's wearing the same dress twice."

I looked down at the still-exposed part of my body. "Well, I look pretty bad now, but I can't even feel my lower body, so that's a good sign."

She frowned. "Or it means I wrapped you too tight and your circulation got cut off. Are you sure you're ok?"

"Yeah, it's not tight, it's just numb..."

"Ok. I'll re-do this before you go to bed, and I'll check it in the morning when we get up. Or you can check it, I don't know. I'm responsible for you, maybe I *should* check it?"

"Ugh," I said "It doesn't matter, I'll check to see what it looks like and you can watch, geez."

She finished wrapping me up, stopping at my neck, and started on the dry top layer. It was thick and made me feel bigger, clumsier somehow, even though I was barely the size of Marissa's finger. My fingers were especially hard to move, but with how dry my hands were, they needed it most. Before long, I was wrapped up tight, looking like a mummy just like I'd thought I would.

"Ok, thanks again. Hey, before you show me the cool thing, could I get some food? I didn't eat this morning, and I'm kinda hungry."

"Huh? Oh, hm, yeah, I guess I forgot too. I'll get you in your house and order myself a smoothie too. Good thinking." She said, carefully lifting me up.

She seemed to be pushing herself to be nice, the 'good thinking' had seemed like an afterthought, like she'd tacked it on after the fact, to try and make me feel like I had valuable thoughts. Maybe she *did* think it was a good idea, and just didn't know how to praise others? Either way, it felt awkward and fake.

I made a microwave meal, a bowl of mac and che'ze, and ate half of it quickly, standing at my counter. I had been wondering what the 'something cool' could be, it'd *sounded* like a project, maybe we'd do crafts? I tried to think of what crafts she'd need/want my help with; something that required a fine touch, and the only thing that came to mind was dioramas, but that was stupid, that's a boring person hobby.

I swallowed a mouthful of gooey, vaguely cheesy lumps, and shoved the bowl in the fridge. I guess I'd find out soon. I walked outside and sat on the front step to wait for Marissa to get her smoothie from the kitchen. The lotion was *really* helping, not only was I numb, but there was a slight cooling sensation under my skin. If it wasn't so expensive and didn't smell kind of funny, I'd use this all the time. Marissa's door opened and she stepped in, holding a large glass full of purple slush, and walked over to me.

"Ok, this is gonna be fun, I've never gotten to do this with someone in real life before, but like, you're smart, so it'll be cool."

I stepped into her hand and she brought me over to her desk. Smart? What did she mean by *that*?

"So what are we going to do?" I asked.

She wiggled the mouse on her computer and the screen lit up. She clicked on an icon that looked like a globe, and almost instantly a loading screen popped up. It read "The Life and Times Of The Gods", and had a globe spinning with explosions and monuments popping up on the surface as it turned.

"We're gonna play this!" she said, pointing "It's my favorite game, you get to play as a god, and there's like, rival gods? And you have to make your kingdom strong enough to wipe them out. We can do two player and I can take your turn if you tell me what you want to do. We can team up and form an alliance!"

I stared at the screen. Of all the things for Marissa to do in her free time, playing RTS god simulators was the last thing I'd ever have guessed.

...Although, it *did* make a lot of sense, now that I thought about it.

"I'm betting the other girls weren't fans of this?" I asked.

"Oh, gods no, I never even brought it up. I think the only game they ever played was those candy match ones on their phones." she said, clicking through the menus. "You, though, you strike me as a gamer."

"Well," I said, thinking "I haven't had a modern game system in almost ten years, but I *do* have over fifteen hundred hours on Last Legend 28, the one that's an MMO? So, yeah, I guess you could say I'm a gamer."

Marissa's eyebrows raised and her eyes opened all the way for once "Holy *shit*... I have like six hundred in this, and it's my most played game, you seriously have me beat."

"I haven't played many RTS games to be honest." I said "I usually stick to like, games where I can run around and hit stuff, but I know a lot of them are super in depth!"

I should butter her up a bit...

"I would love for you to teach me this one!"

"Oh, yeah! I got into these kinds because my dad was into the simulator games from way back when, like the ones where you simulated bugs or a planet's evolution. He said it helped him see the business world in a new light, so he wanted me to have the same experience. I don't like the ones he liked, but... I like the ones where I get to be god."

Of course she did.

"So... Where do we start?"

She pointed to the screen. "We'll play on easy, because it's your first time, but we start way back 12,000 years go, when humans first really started doing anything interesting, and we go until... Well, usually it's like, modern day, but I have an expansion, so we can play until we have like, moon bases and stuff, as long as there's still other gods playing, of course."

She was... really into this, I had never seen her get this interested in *any*thing before, and there was no hint of irony to her tone, she really, actually just wanted to show me her favorite game because none of her friends would be interested. Despite myself, I felt sorry for her. I thought about the times I'd gushed about the catboy NPCs I was flirting with in LL28, and the times Henri had excitedly shown me a rare monster she'd caught in one of her games. Even if you didn't have the same exact interests, just being able to talk about something you love to someone is... really important.

*The Feeling of Being Valued*  143

"I can't see the screen from here, and I'd like to sit, can I ride on your shoulder while we play?" I asked.

"Yeah, ok!" She picked me up and set me on her shoulder, and I lay against her neck "I'll walk you through the first few turns, they're super important. If we don't kill the atheist tribes before they level up, they end up being really strong, so I'll help you, but after that I'll just let you do your own thing."

"Mm, that sounds good to me."

"Ok, so first off, we need to pick a god or goddess for you... I personally like Artemis, but she's weak late game. Shiva is good the whole time, but complicated to build out her religion tree? Elmaem is the meta, but they are *super* hard to use right. I'd say just... pick the coolest one for now, and I'll pick someone else to support you."

I looked at the screen of dozens of gods and blinked. I'd never even heard of almost any of these, and I didn't really know about *any* of them.

"Uhh, how about Buddha?" I asked, pointing.

"Oooh. Hhh..." She hissed through her teeth. "Not that one, it's not a god, it's a religious system, you influence followers through a reincarnating holy person, it's tricky and hard to get used to."

Well, so much for picking something I had a cultural attachment to then, what about... "Oh, hey, that bunny man is pretty cute, how about him?"

"Oh, yeah, Tu'er Shen. He's a god of like, gay men. He's hard to use, but I can use my main, Artemis, and focus on her lesbian religion tree, and we can have a sort of 'men in one city, women in the other' thing going on."

"Oh, uhh ok, yeah that works for me." This game was complicated, it seemed.

"Alright," she said "so here's my first turn, I have a tribe of about ten people right now..."

As she explained her moves and showed me the mechanics, I started to get an odd feeling inside me. Hearing her gush about her game, talking about the meta, showing off the things she knew, it felt like I was just spending the afternoon with a friend, not living life as her pet. Could this be sustainable? Would I be able to keep her like this, guard down, treating me like a friend? I still didn't really trust her, but if she could be like this all the time, I really wouldn't mind living with her.

I dictated my moves to her as the afternoon passed, and she stayed happy and engaged, showing me tricks and laughing as we smote non believers and conquered the other religions, converting everyone to our joint belief system. It was sort of fun, I wasn't used to this kind of game, but if this became a regular thing, I wouldn't mind. It's not like I could really play other games anyway now. As the afternoon turned to evening, we won through annihilating the last god's city with a holy rain of burning arrows. She cheered, pumping one fist in the air while plucking me off her shoulder with the other hand.

"We did it! That was on easy mode though, next time we'll play on normal, and eventually we'll work up to *my* preferred difficulty, online mode."

"Ok, yeah, I think I want to try a different god next time, one with more attacks instead of just culture, but I had fun!"

"Yeah, for sure!" She set me on the desk. "So, it's getting later, I was going to go out to dinner with my friend Darcy in an hour or so, did you want to come?"

She was asking? "Uh, well..." I said. "I'm still feeling kinda rough, would it be ok if I rested up for tomorrow?"

She frowned, but nodded. "That- ok, yeah. I can show you to her any time, but I need you to make a good impression on daddy."

She picked me up and moved me to my house. "So I guess I'll get ready, and... I'll see you before bed to put more medicine on you?"

"Mhm, that's-"

I was cut off by a knock on the door.

"Yes?" Marissa called out

"A package, ma'am." Parker called through the door.

"Oh! It's- Ok!" She said, running to the door. She swung it open and Parker handed her a package the size of a shoebox, covered in brown paper. She slammed the door and tore into it, revealing a wooden box with two rows of doors on it. She turned a knob, and a platform slid out from between the two rows, and another knob exposed stairs on the other side. She walked it to the desk and set it next to my house.

"It's your clothes! I forgot they were coming today!"

I looked at the wardrobe in shock, there were a good ten closets there, were they all full of clothes for me?

"I... whoah..." I said stupidly.

"Yeah, they're all designer stuff, or like, whatever designer for a subhuman is I guess." she bragged "You can look through them while I'm gone! I have a catalogue of what all is in there, I picked stuff that should go with my outfits, but like, you can look and see what you like, even if I'm going to be picking what you wear, you can still have an opinion."

There it was; 'subhuman', picking my clothes for me, based on what *she* was wearing... A designer doll wearing designer clothes, as soon as her new toy got a fun new accessory, I was back to being a doll. As human as I'd felt today, she just couldn't let it stick. She didn't even know she was doing it, she'd just fallen back into treating me like a pet as soon as we were done 'bonding'. She wasn't 'making' me feel like this, to her, it was just what it was. I looked down at my body, wrapped in bandages, and thought about how long it'd take for her to backslide fully, back to 'playing' with me too rough.

Still, I could try to keep her happy. I looked up and beamed at her.

"Thank you *so* much Marissa! I can't wait to look through them! I really appreciate this!"

# Chapter Nine

I stood in front of the multi story wardrobe, fresh bandages wrapped onto me. I had *not* been healed when I woke up this morning, which was about what I expected, but I *was* looking and feeling much better. I'd washed up, gotten re-wrapped up, and now I was waiting for Marissa to pick out an outfit that would cover as much of the bandages as possible. She had three outfits out on the desk; a kimono, a long sleeve jacket with a lace blouse and dress slacks, and a black track suit with a white floral pattern on the ankles and wrists, but she was still digging.

"Hey, are we sure I can't stay home today? I'm still really sore..." I said. I wasn't actually that sore, but I was slightly achy, and I really didn't want to meet her dad anyway...

"No, you're moving around fine, and you looked way better, we're going." she said absently.

"I'm just worried the bottle will be too rough for me, even with cushions..." I complained.

She turned to look at me, a smile spreading across her face. "Oh, yeah?... you're right... Hm, you know, there's a solution for that..."

I frowned. "What solution?"

She opened her jacket and pointed at her silk blouse. There was a breast pocket hidden under where her jacket lay, on the left side.

"It's nice and silky and soft, no hard edges, and you'd be niiiiice and safe up against me the whole time..."

I thought about it for a second, it was tempting... I almost refused; it was what she wanted after all, for me to be her little 'pocket pet'. She'd leapt at the chance to keep me in her pocket before, so agreeing to it would be like giving her exactly what she wanted. But it did seem like it'd be a *lot* more comfortable than being in that bottle, and I really, really hated the bottle. I wasn't getting out of going to her dad's either way, so...

"Sure, ok." I said

Her eyes lit up. "Really?! Oh, ok! That's- fucking finally, gods, yeah, this is great!"

I winced at her enthusiasm. Was having a person in your pocket really that great? "Just be careful with me in there, ok?"

"Yeah yeah, I know." she said dismissively. "Uhh, let's see, the tracksuit would be the most comfortable for me if you're in my pocket. The kimono would be too bulky, and the business wear would get wrinkled, and *this*" she held up what she'd been looking at a moment before; a blue and yellow harlequin outfit, "would be too much for your first visit with my dad. I'm remembering it though, it's cute as fuck."

I winced "Why did you buy that?"

"So you'd look like a little clown doll." she said, hanging it back up and pushing the tracksuit towards me.

"Oh, of course, yeah." I said sarcastically "Just what every girl wants, to be a clown doll."

"It'll be cute, hush." she quipped as I got dressed.

"So when are we leaving?" I asked

"Uhh, about thirty minutes, give or take." she replied "I don't have an exact time to get there, just a ballpark."

"Ok, yeah..." I said as I zipped up the tracksuit "Can I hang out in my house for a bit until we go then? I want to get some time to myself if that's ok."

She made a face, but nodded. "Yeah, I guess that's fair. You'll be in my pocket all day, right up against me, the whole time, so get your 'alone time' while you can."

Her voice wavered as she mentioned me being 'right up against her', and I wondered if there was an aspect I hadn't thought of about being in her pocket, something less 'appropriate'. The pocket was over her left breast, but she didn't really *have* breasts, not really. Well, she kind of did, but I didn't think I'd be able to tell if I was leaning against them. Maybe that mattered to her anyway? On a conceptual level?

As she flopped onto her bed to look at her phone, I went into my house to check *my* phone. I went to the couch first, and turned on my tablet, slipping the phone out from behind it and into my pocket as I took it off the charger. There was a message from my mom about missing me, and how my dad had tried to drive over to Marissa's house after Henri showed up at our apartment crying early yesterday morning. I assured her that I was safe, and that Henri had just been upset because of some 'party games'. I told her I loved her, and that I'd see if I could video call sometime soon if I could get it set up on the tablet, and then I checked my messages from Henri.

Nothing.

Absolutely nothing.

That meant either she was scared to reach out to me, or... she was so upset she didn't think to fake-text me on the tablet and only messaged my main phone instead. Either way, I was about to find out. I eyed Marissa, still on her own phone, to make sure she wasn't watching, and pressed the power button as I headed upstairs into the bathroom. I shut the door, and locked it behind me. I was pretty sure Marissa could still get in through the lock, but I didn't expect her to. My phone finished powering up, and I looked at the lock-screen nervously. There was a bunch of garbage messages from spammers and tracking info for stuff I ordered I'd never get to use, but... there was one notification from Henri.

I took a breath and opened it, my gauze covered hands barely registering on the glass. It was a brick of a message, and while it'd obviously been *sent* as one message, my cheap phone had to break it up into fifteen smaller messages to get it across.

*'Oh my dearest darling klein fee, I am so terribly sorry that the evening went as it did last night, I know I needed to tell you my truest feelings, to let my love shine for you, but there, in that place, was the wrong time. I wished my love to be conveyed to you gently, like a soft whisper on the wind, like a gentle caress. I know you don't have a preference for your partner, so I was sure you would return my affections and we would live in bliss. I've thought about our first kiss, the 'test' kiss, every day since, and I'd hoped to get to shower you with more kisses every day sometime soon. The curse on your body ruined and destroyed my plans. I know it is a horrible thing to say, but I was selfishly hurt for myself when you told me that you were compressed, I knew my chances at a normal relationship were now none. But I soon chippered, as I realized that I had a unique position. If I could help your family adopt you, I could help them care for you, I could move out of the dorms and into your old room where we would live together! I became invigored with the energy I needed to fulfill this goal, and once you were taken away, I doggedly tracked down and demanded money from all the girls I knew could spare any. I WOULD get you for myself, I would share my love with you fully, and you would be my little sweet forever. That horrid bitch that got you instead is the bane of my existence, if you'd only say the word, her life would be forfeit. I need you in my life, klein fee, you are my everything, you're the only person I know here, and you're the object of my undying love. When we spent every day together it wasn't as hurtful, it was a wonderful life, but now that you're away from me, there's an empty hole where you used to be and I don't know how to stop the pain. I love you, Amber. I will always love you, and I want to do anything I can to help you get free from that terrible prison you're in. I know it's hard to trust me, I know it's scary to think about, you're so, so fragile, but I will rescue you in any way I can, in any way that's safe for you. Be aware, and be prepared my lovely beautiful klein fee, I am coming for you.'*

I lay in the tub, my mouth dry, my head spinning. This wasn't an apology for getting too carried away while drinking, or even just her trying to smooth things over, this was... this was terrifying. I loved her, although *how* I loved her I wasn't sure yet, but the love was there. This, though, made me fear for my safety. It made me fear for *Marissa's* safety. It made me feel like an object, a thing to be won or a trinket to steal away. I didn't know how to respond. I wanted to be around Henri, but not like this, not while she was practically begging me to give her permission to kill my guardian...

Should I warn Marissa? That Henri might actually be a threat to her and her safety? I kicked myself for opening the message without going into offline mode first, now Henri knew I'd read it, there was no way to pretend I hadn't, but I didn't know what to say in response. If I didn't say anything... She could just show up and try to take me by force. Henri wasn't strong, not really, but she *was* heavier than Marissa, and if she wanted to, she could beat her in an all out fight from what I could tell. The only thing I could think of to say sounded lame and like a non-response, but I had to say *some*thing. I typed out my message and sent it, hoping it was enough to curb her energy.

*'hey bbgrl. dont do anything ur my best friend and i luv u ofc but i need time to think. im staying in m's pocket from now on so if u hurt her she could fall and squish me so leave her alone 4 now'*

The read notification popped up almost as soon as I pressed send and I bit my lip. I couldn't deal with this right now, I really did need time to think about it. I powered my phone off as I saw the 'Henri is typing' pop up and slid it under the stack of towels. I'd deal with it later, tonight. Or maybe tomorrow. I got out of the tub and walked to the couch, flopping down. I really, really didn't want to deal with anything today. Maybe me being in Marissa's pocket would calm her down and make her leave me alone, at least until we got to her dad's house.

~~~

Marissa rubbed me through the fabric of her pocket as she crossed the driveway to her dad's front door. She'd been touching me and petting me and peeking into the pocket constantly since I got into her pocket almost an hour ago. She was being oddly affectionate about the whole thing. She'd whispered 'you belong in there...' under her breath when she dropped me in, but hadn't really spoken to me since, except to ask if I was ok once or twice. If I stood up, I could just see over the top of the pocket, with my nose barely clearing it, but every movement caused me to shake and tip over, so I'd spent most of my time curled up at the bottom. It was... boring, but very comfortable. I'd almost dozed off a couple times, until her finger dipped in to rub my head or she patted her pocket, jarring me awake.

I was warm, her body heat radiated into the silk and the jacket over pinned it in. The pocket smelled like she did; that odd, hard to describe 'human' smell that everyone had their own variation of. I'd never given it much thought before I was small, but now that my senses were heightened, I was much more in tune with the scents and sounds of the people around me. Speaking of sounds, her heartbeat thumped steadily, a deep, almost wet noise just behind the fleshy wall I was laying against. It was soothing, but sounded a little gross this close up. Sloshy, with the rush of blood through the veins audible too.

"We're heeeere~" she whispered to me as I curled up tighter.

I heard the door open, and a man's voice sounded out loud and bold.

"Heyyy little Missy! How've you been!"

I felt her lean, angling her body as he hugged her, his body pressing into her right side, missing me. I scooched further left, just in case.

"I've been fine daddy, how are you?"

Her words were said casually, with a sense of amiability, but I noticed a stiffness to it, a manufactured appearance of having her guard down.

"Oh honey bun, I'm just fine, come in, come in! I'll send my man out with some raspberry tea for Drew, it's good to see you, sweetie."

He seemed nice enough at least. He'd actually *cared* about the driver, Marissa usually just left him in the car and ignored him while she was out. Marissa walked in, and her hand slipped under her jacket and cupped me as she pulled it off. I felt the cool air from the house hit me and I shivered. It wasn't any colder than 68 or so, but at this size it was a lot chillier. I'd been at 98 degrees the whole way here give or take, so it'd take a few minutes to get used to the temperature. I stayed still as she kept her hand over me, I got the feeling she didn't want to show me off just yet. I could see lights and shapes through the silk though, and I noticed we'd entered a room that seemed to have quite a lot of windows in it, shining light towards the center. Looking up, I could only see Marissa's face and a slightly industrial looking ceiling, not much to go on. She sat down, and leaned back, tilting me against her, keeping her hand lightly over me.

"Ohh, Missy!" a female voice called out "I hadn't heard you come in, would you like a drink?"

"Oh, hello Raquel." Marissa said, barely keeping the edge out of her voice.

"Please, call me mom!" Raquel said lightly.

Marissa laughed politely, but didn't respond. I shifted, trying to stand to peek out at the woman that caused her so much trouble. but Marissa pressed down harder on me to keep me still.

"My man is going out to give Drew that drink. Knowing them they'll be out there a while!" Marissa's dad said, his voice getting louder as he got closer. He must have stepped away and I didn't realize.

"So, Missy, you want a raspberry tea as well? I'll go fix one, and, ah, add a little something to it, if you like."

"That sounds lovely, daddy. Thank you so much!" Marissa said. I could feel her nodding, her head movements ever so slightly shifting her torso.

After a moment, Raquel spoke up again. "So, Missy... I heard the school will be expanding the tennis program to include budget for three more courts, I bet you're happy about that, right? With 6 courts, you'll be on the bench a lot less!"

"We should have *12* courts, honestly. I don't understand why we don't." Marissa said coldly. "I know we're a small school, but it's just restrictive to only have 3 courts, even 6 is just the bare minimum required for reasonable tournament play."

"Well with this addition, maybe the school will let the team join the ITA, right?" Raquel said, trying to bring up the conversation.

"Doubtful. You know how our school is, they'll never let us play in anything with a ranking, so there's no way for us to lose face."

I had never tried out for sports at college, but Henri did. She'd tried hard to join the tennis team despite me telling her it was a bad idea. She'd *thought* it'd be the perfect chance to get to know the other girls better, and maybe even get Marissa to stop harassing her. In short, it hadn't worked, and we'd spent the entire weekend under a blanket together watching kid's anime, eating candy and sharing sorbet while she cried about being 'not good enough' for them.

Thinking about back on it, it'd been Marissa who'd made the call to not let her join the team in the end. Henri wasn't the *best*, but she was better than several of the other girls, and even won half of her matches during the interview, so her exclusion was almost entirely due to her social status.

"Annnnd here's that drink!" Marissa's dad said. I heard the glass clink on the table and Marissa finally pulled her hand away from me to pick it up.

"Aw, thanks daddy." she said. I heard her take a sip "Gods, is this half vodka? It's strong."

"Hahaha, I made it like I made mine! You're my girl, you can handle it."

"Handle it, sure, but this is a casual daddy-daughter day." Marissa said, laughing.

"Well, and your mother's here, don't forget her!" her dad pointed out.

Marissa took another sip of her drink and didn't respond.

"...So, anything new with you then kiddo?" He asked after a moment.

"Mm, yes, actually," She said, swallowing and lowering the glass. "I got a new toy. I bought it with my own money, too, it's very fancy."

"Oh?" Raquel said, curious "What is it?"

I could hear the grin on Marissa's face as she spoke. "Amber? Wanna come out and say hi?"

I uncurled myself, and stood, lying against Marissa and peaking my head out of her pocket, pulling the top down to show my whole face.

John was across from me sitting forward with his hands steepled, elbows on his knees. He had grey slicked back hair, a blue button up with a bola tie around the neck, and thin grey rimmed glasses. Raquel was to our left, and she looked... very familiar. I'd known Marissa's dad had married someone from our school, but I didn't remember who. I could almost place her in one of my music classes from high school though, if I thought about it. She was wearing a short red dress with red shorts peaking out from under them and matching flats. Her hair was blonde, and it was piled on top of her head in a sort of bun, with short stick things poking through to keep it in place. I absently wondered if she meant for it to be messy, or if it was just a true lack of care...

Raquel let out a shriek "Oh OH. John she's got a thing in there, an alive thing, John!"

She pulled her feet up onto her couch as I looked around at the room, ignoring her outburst. It was all glass on one side overlooking a river, and had a lot of natural lighting as a result. We were sitting around a triangular coffee table on three couches, all with slightly different designs. Marissa, her dad, and Raquel were each on their own couch, with me and Marissa's having a high back on one side, and almost no back on the other. Judging by the tones of grey, grey, and more grey, I assumed that John had been the one to design Marissa's *current* house as well as this one.

"What in- Oh, wow, Marissa, is that one of those tiny humans that've been going around?" John said, peering at me.

Marissa reached in and gently picked me up, tenderly holding me so she didn't put too much pressure on my skin.

"Well, not *technically* a human anymore, but yes! She's a class B, her name is Amber, and I knew her from school before she got compressed."

John whistled, looking at me intently. "Well little lady, is *my* little lady taking good care of you?"

I looked back at Marissa before realizing he was talking to me.

"Ah? Oh! Y-yes, she's taking care of me well enough, she got me a big house and lots of clothes, and ah, she's... good."

I wasn't really sure how to respond to him, I wasn't going to tell him she bullied me or anything, but he knew her better than anyone, so if *anyone* could tell that she'd play rough with her 'toys', it'd be him.

"Now that is just amazing... You talk and act just like a full sized one of us, that is just downright *amazing*." he said, shaking his head.

"They usually don't lose any cognitive functions, they're still people, they're just too small to be *legal* people." Marissa said.

"You- you just bought it?" Raquel asked, putting her feet back on the rug. "Like, just as a pet?"

"Yep!" Marissa said proudly. "I heard she'd been compressed, so I went straight over to the shop and bought her."

"Did they need to do a background check or any such thing?" John asked, holding out a finger to me. I shook it like I would a hand, and he grinned widely.

"Oh, well, yeah. I had to take a twelve hour long class to get my license. And I'll need to take tests to make sure I know my stuff every so often to keep that license." Marissa said dismissively.

"Well, I'm proud of you, honey." John said "I never took you for the type to take in someone, to care for them like this, it's a side of you I never saw before."

Marissa shook her head "To be honest, it's not *just* that, I kinda really like the idea of having a tiny human as a pet too..."

John laughed. "Well, long as you're not hurting nothing, it's all fine, right, uhhh, Amy?" he said, directing the last part at me.

"Amber, and yeah. She had to learn to be gentle, but yeah." I said. Raquel was still staring at me, enraptured.

"Um..." I said, turning to her "do you have any questions?"

"How... Mm, how hard is it to clean the cage for one of these?" she asked Marissa, ignoring me.

"Oh, well, she's like, a person, so like, she cleans her own space?" Marissa responded "And like, her house has plumbing with a water filtration system, so I'll just throw the tank with the used filter and trash away when it's full and add special compressed water as needed. With one class B, the filter should last about two weeks?"

"Oh, ok... Is there anything hard about taking care of them?" She asked, looking up at Marissa

"Nnnot really?" she replied. "You just have to be aware they're super fragile, that's all."

Raquel reached a hand out to me to pick me up, and Marissa blocked it with her own, glaring at her before putting on a fake smile. "Ah, no. She's actually *extra* fragile today, so I'll be the only one touching her for now."

"Well why's she so fragile today?" John said, peering at me "Is it to do with her hands being all wrapped up?"

"I got in a small accident, nothing serious, no one's fault, just me being 'fragile', I'll be fine soon." I told him, giving him a thumbs up.

"Are accidents very common for these... 'class B's?" Raquel asked

"Oh *yes* most new owners manage to hurt their class Bs very badly within the first week of owning them because they don't realize how easy it is to hurt them. It's why the class is so important." Marissa said, her voice taking on a know-it-all tone. "I was very good at the class and Amber here *still* ended up getting hurt."

"So, you do *own* her then?" John said, stirring his drink with a straw

"Well..." Marissa said sheepishly. "I own her in a *way*, because she's mine, like a pet. But legally, no. I'm just her legal guardian and caretaker."

"Caretaker..." murmured Raquel "That sounds nice..."

John drew his straw out of his glass and held it out to me with his finger on the top. A drop of raspberry tea was on the end, about to drip.

"Here you go little lady, take you a sip of this, get something good in you."

I threw up my hands and backed away "Ah, no, sorry, I can't- I'm not supposed to-"

"Aw it's just a drop, it'll be fine, won't it?" He said, smiling at me disarmingly. He was very handsome, in an older man kind of way, but I could have guessed he *would* be just from looking at Marissa. I wondered if this subtly charming behavior was how he'd gotten his current wife interested in him...

"Daddy, no, no vodka. She could die, it'll dry her out and make her very sick." Marissa said sternly, picking me up and cradling me in her fingers.

He whistled again. "Gah-lee, being stuck that small and not even alcohol to get your mind off it... My heart goes out to you, little miss Amber."

I gave a polite smile and withdrew into Marissa's fingers. I *really* didn't like being the center of attention. Being the center of attention was why she'd *brought* me, but I felt like I was on a stage and I didn't know my lines. Marissa noticed me pulling away, and lifted me up to her shoulder. I'd still be seen, but I wouldn't be in everyone's direct line of sight, which was better. I climbed out of her hand, clinging to the collar of the shirt she was wearing to stop from falling. The silk was a lot slipperier than the other tops she'd had on when I had ridden her shoulder, so I had to lean against her and hold tight to stop from sliding down her front.

"That's so cute..." Raquel breathed, her eyes locked onto me. "They don't mind being carried around on you?"

"Well, you have to ask them for anything *fun*, like putting them in pockets, or using them as jewelry or keeping them in your cleavage."

I glanced down at her front, alarmed. Hopefully she wouldn't be asking permission to carry me like *that* any time soon. I'm not sure I'd be comfortable with it, even if she *wasn't* weird about it...

"*Usually* you need an approved container to carry them in, I have a bottle with heating and air that I keep her in sometimes, and I hang it around my neck." Marissa explained "Hands, shoulders, and knees, you're allowed to use to carry them without asking though."

"But if they say it's ok then anywhere is fine?" Raquel asked.

"Well, yeah, they just have to say it's ok. Like, I keep her in my pocket, but I have permission to do that." Marissa said.

Psh, 'I keep her in my pocket'. This was the first time she'd done that, she was just trying to pass it off like she did it all the time to sound more impressive. It sounded like it'd be a regular occurrence from now on though, and she'd really *really* enjoyed it.

"So, how much did it run you to, ah, I suppose 'adopt' Amber here?" John asked, sipping his drink.

Marissa frowned and shrugged. "Well, it's more than just the cost of adoption, it's the adoption, the house, the clothes, the furniture, the food, it adds up. I'd say from walking in the door to the shop earlier this week to sitting in front of you right now, it cost me, oh,$37,000?"

I shook my head, that was as much as a full time job's pay for a whole year for some people, and she'd blown it in less than a week...

"Oh, that's not too bad!" Raquel said "I was expecting it to be much more!"

"They can't make it too high, a lot of the times the families of the class Bs want to adopt them themselves, so it needs to be attainable for the average person, to 'keep families together'." Marissa said.

"Well, I suppose your family didn't want you then, Amber?" John asked "Sorry if that's a sore subject, family didn't want me either, ha!"

"Uh, well they *did* want me, they tried to adopt me, but-" I started to explain

"Unfortunately her family was unfit to care for her, and they were unable to meet the needs she required." Marissa interrupted.

I looked at her incredulously. Really? 'Unfit'? They did their best, they *tried* to get me, they *wanted* to take care of me until this bitch-

"So Amber, Missy said she knew you from school, were the two of you friends?" John asked.

"Ah, we... ran across each other's paths." I said, trying not to think of what had happened to me the times our paths *had* crossed.

"You'd think I'd know who it was..." Raquel said, frowning at me "I was at the school at the same time you were until high school graduation, but I don't remember an 'Amber'..."

"Well, I guess you just didn't pay attent-" Marissa said, her hand slipping up to hold me again.

"Oh! Oh, it's the rat!" Raquel said, perking up with recognition. "That's the rat, isn't it?"

"She- yeah, she goes by Amber now, though." Marissa said, sounding embarrassed.

"Ohhhh, that makes so much sense. I was wondering why someone's family from *our* school wouldn't be fit to adopt" Raquel said, nodding to herself.

"I'm out of the loop here, girls, 'the rat'?" John asked.

"She was some charity case who got in because of test scores or something." Raquel explained "She was a lower grade than me, so *I* mostly ignored her, but she was the 'rat' of the school! No one took her seriously or even talked to her until that weird girl with the accent showed up."

"That sounds a mite cruel of you girls..." John said, frowning "I'm just glad you've grown, Missy, and you're taking care of her now despite her past, that shows true character. You're going to be a wonderful boss one day."

I curled up into Marissa's palm as she gripped me, cringing. I wanted to say something, to call Marissa out to her dad, to tell him that no, she would make a *terrible* boss, actually, but her hand was closing over me, holding me into a ball, her fingers wrapped around me, telling me "if you say anything, I squeeze' without saying a word. I tried to wiggle free, or free-er, at least so I could see the others, but she put her thumb on my face and pushed me back down.

"I just knew what I had to do, daddy." she said "I couldn't *stand* the thought of someone like her suffering in a tiny apartment, her caretakers unable to afford even the most basic of needs... I just wanted her to be safe."

She held me up to her face and I poked my head out of her hand, finally free from her thumb. She rubbed me on her cheek, smiling.

"Plus, she's just so cute! Who *wouldn't* want to take care of a lil baby like this?"

I blushed hard. *Baby?* Really? Way to take away my autonomy, 'Missy'. She booped me on the face with her free hand, smushing my nose. I'm sure it *looked* like a playful tap to the outside, but it stung, and made my nose smell coppery. I looked over my shoulder at John, who had a large smile on his face watching his daughter play at being a loving caretaker. I turned back and looked at Marissa, who was grinning at me, her face genuinely happy, but her eyes betraying a hint of cruelty. I felt like I was going to scream, to fight and yell and cry, I was so, so sick of not being treated like a person, even John, who'd actually addressed me, was now using that stupid child voice to talk to me. I felt like I could explode with frustration, I felt like I was going to bite Marissa, I felt-

A small trickle of something hot on my lip.

I wrestled my hand free and rubbed my nose, revealing a smear of blood in my fingers. I held my hand up to Marissa, pointing at the blood. Her eyes widened slightly, and she squeezed me, choking the air out of me and hurting my skin. She looked around for something, but couldn't find what she was looking for. She stood up abruptly, holding me against her neckline to hide the blood from her dad and Raquel.

"Um- I have to go... give Amber some medicine!" she said "That accident she got in, you know. I'll be back in a sec!"

Without waiting for a response, she turned and walked off down a hall, opening and closing a door with a bang. She set me down on the counter of a lavish bathroom with black tiles and black porcelain furnishings. She crouched down and narrowed her eyes at me looking me up and down.

"Ok, talk. What happened?" she said sternly.

"You hit me in the face!" I said, throwing my hands up "It really hurt, I'm surprised you didn't break my nose."

She sighed "So that's all? Just a bloody nose?"

I crossed my arms. "You said you wouldn't hurt me, Marissa. You've squeezed me and trapped me and given me a bloody nose just since we've been here."

"That's not 'hurting you'." she said "It's at *best* being too rough. The bloody nose was an accident, I've poked you harder than that before, lots of times."

"On the *head*. Not in my *face*." I said.

"Ugh, whatever. I can't go back out with you all bloody like that, here." She pulled a tissue out of a fancy box and tore off a chunk for me.

"Clean yourself up. Once you stop bleeding, we'll go out there, you'll do some tricks or something, and I'll say we need to get you home to change your bandages or something. It'll be a short visit, but at least I have an excuse this time."

"Do tricks...?" I asked "I don't- I'm not a dog, Marissa, I don't know 'tricks', much less any I can do on the spot."

"You're still my *pet* even if you're not a dog, and pets do tricks, so think of something fast, because we're going back out there."

I wiped the blood off my nose, and cleaned up with the wet scrap of tissue she prepared for me. I wracked my brain for anything I could do that would impress them. I was mostly learning logistics and management in school, but John would already know the tips they taught me, I could play piano, kind of, but finding a tiny piano is way too much to ask on the fly, I could draw? Ok, that was something, maybe I could work with that...

"Ok, hurry up, we're in a rush here, we gotta get back out there, are you done bleeding?" Marissa said, tapping the counter.

I sniffed. There was a bit of blood, but nothing that would start dripping if I sniffed every few minutes.

"I should be good, yeah..."

"Ok, great." She grabbed me, and walked out, swinging her arm as she did so. My stomach lurched as her arm rocketed forward, the world streaking around me. She ended the arc by pressing me into her neckline once again as she walked, uncaring as I tried not to vomit from the movement. She strode into the living room once again and set me on the table.

"Ok, she's all better and back to her usual self!" she said in a cheerful voice. "She said she has a trick to show us too, don't you Amber?"

I look around at the waiting faces, John looked pleased and interested, Raquel looked confused, and Marissa looked like she would smack me if I tried to get out of it. I took a deep breath.

"Ok, so I'll need the smallest writing utensil you have, and an unlined notepad. I'll be doing caricatures!"

~~~

I sat in Marissa's pocket on the ride home. She hadn't spoken to me or even touched me since we'd left, and I was starting to get nervous. As we reached our hometown, I poked my head up out of the pocket and looked up at her face. She was looking ahead, bored and slightly grumpy, her usual face.

"Well... I think your dad liked his, at least?" I offered

Her eyes flicked down to me, and her steel gaze seized me. She didn't say anything while I met her stare, and looked back up to the partition between us and Drew. Damnit, so she *was* upset. I'd tried to be fair, but... the point of caricature was to exaggerate. I didn't think I was *too* harsh with her drawing, but the evil expression and sharp teeth were maybe a little much.

"Well." she finally said "I liked how stupid you made Raquel look. I appreciated that."

I sighed with relief, if she wasn't too upset to praise me for making fun of her step-mom, she wouldn't be upset enough to punish me, or as least that's what I hoped. Crisis averted.

...Now all I had to deal with was the crisis waiting for me under a stack of towels at home...

# Chapter Ten

I held the phone in my hand and stared at it. I'd slept on the way home, so even though it was after 1 am, I was still wide awake. Marissa had fallen asleep hours earlier to be rested for her early class on Monday, so I should be good to do what I needed to... I was in between my bed and my wall, on the far side from wall that opened up, with pillows and cushions over and around me to muffle the sounds I'd be making. My tablet was propped up against the bed, and I'd figured out how to do video calls, so if she was still up...

I opened my phone, and cringed at the notifications... 4 missed calls, 10 new texts, one new voicemail. I opened the messages first, and read through them in order.

*'in her pockrt?! no thats illegal, she isn't allowed to do that, it's not allowed, you need to tell her to stop.'*

*'Did you LET her do it? Please tell me you didn't...'*

'Amber, I need you to get video of her putting you in her pocket, can you do that?'

'I'm coming over, I'll be there in 30 minutes, I'll be recording, we're going to get the evidence we need to get you out of there'

'Amber, I need you to respond, I'm out front and Parker won't let me in'

'I'm going to call'

'is your phone off?'

'Amber, please'

'ok, I take it your really are not at home, I climbed a tree behind the house, and Marissa's room looked empty.'

'please call me when you get the chance, I need to talk to you.'

I sighed and played the voicemail. The compression had made the speaker almost impossible to understand, and after listening to her garbled yells for a few seconds I turned it off. I looked at the tablet. If I was going to talk to her, it needed to be on this, my phone couldn't pick up my voice anymore, and I really did want to talk things out with her and not struggle with texting with bandaged fingers. I yanked my new pajamas up higher to hide the bandages on my neck, and pulled up her contact information. I pressed the video call button, making sure the volume was down as low as it could go. It rang twice, then her blurry face popped up on my screen. I could barely see her, but she seemed to have been crying, or sleeping, or both.

"Amber?..." she mumbled

"Hey Henri. We gotta talk."

She rubbed her face and clicked on a lamp, lighting up the room. With a start, I recognized it as *my* room, and what's *more*, she was wearing one of my sweatshirts.

"Ok, yeah, I want to talk about her keeping you in her pocket, you DO know that's-"

"Henri, why are you in my room?" I said, looking around her at all my stuff, half of it pulled out of drawers or on the floor.

"Oh... I am renting it, your dad said it was ok, I can pay them money and help with food, and I get to stay here..." she said, looking around.

"But- all my *stuff* is still in there, and you're wearing my clothes, that feels... I don't know, it's my space, you can't just take it over..." I said. I couldn't put my finger on why, but the idea of her sliding into my old life, into my room and clothes and space and just... picking up where I left off was unsettling.

"No, I am- it's ok! I am just doing this for now, once we get you away from *her*, we will share the room and you can have it back once again!"

That was still concerning, but I didn't have the words to talk about it right now. "...Ok, moving on... "Henri, I don't think getting me away is the top priority right now."

She gasped "Oh, my little sweet, how could you *say* that? She put you in her *pocket*, that should only be done with people you love!"

"Henri, I told her she could put me in her pocket. I was comfortable there."

"But..." Henri shook her head "The bottle, with the cushions, that was comfortable, right?"

I was *not* about to tell her the reason I needed to be in the pocket was me getting chemical burned and going to the doctor. She'd blame herself for it, or worse, blame Marissa and go after her even harder...

"I wanted to try it, and it worked very well, I had no complaints." I said matter of a factly. "I really don't like the bottle, Henri."

"You should not have given her permission, Amber!" Henri said, angrily "If you had said no, she would have done it anyway eventually anyway, and then you could report her and be free!"

"I don't WANT to be free of her right now, Henri." I said, getting angry back "It just doesn't make sense, if I 'get free' of her, I go live with my parents and you, but do you really think Marissa won't report you too? For the kiss and the soup and stuff? You won't even be allowed to touch me or anything even if you ARE still there when I get back home, and I don't even know if my parents will be able to pass the recert test for much longer, so... I'll be 'escaping' Marissa to just get sold again to some random person in a few years."

She stared at me and frowned. "...Look, once you get *here*, I can get you out of the country. It will not matter if I am not allowed to hold you or anything, I will just do it anyway, and we can be on that plane to my homeland in no time. Your parents will report you missing, we shall blame Marissa, and after it calms down, they come over too. I just need you away from Marissa first."

"No... I..." I rubbed my eyes "I don't want to be smuggled out unless I *have* to be, I looked into what class B smuggling involves, and that's *disgusting*, that's worse than anything Marissa would ever do to me."

"It will be just until we get onto the plane, customs in Germany are easier, you you will not have to do it twice, it is-"

"No, Henri, you're not doing that to me, ok?" I snapped, shuddering.

"...I need you back, Klein Fee. I will do whatever it takes to do that. Smuggling you, kidnapping you, if I need to get rid of the person who could stop me, I shall do it."

"Stop! That's- just stop being so *'much'* all the time and you can at least *see* me. We were having fun on Friday, until you went nuts, I think Marissa would have invited you over again even."

"It was not *fun* to see you in that position like that, not for me."

I groaned "It wasn't that bad, the only thing that was even slightly harmful is when YOU threw me in Marissa's soup."

"That was an *accident*," she hissed "and if *she* had not yelled at me, it would not have happened."

"I'm just saying Marissa was having *fun* until you confessed your love to me as part of a *party game*."

Her eyes welled up with tears and she leaned away from the camera. "Amber, I could not hold it in anymore... I just love you so much..."

"..." I didn't know what to say, I still hadn't decided how I felt about her, or if I was even interested, but I did know I wasn't ready to deal with it right now. The compression, Marissa, my new life, if I though about any of it for too long a cold wave of horror rushed over me with a sinking despair. Having to decide if I wanted to risk my best friend by dating her, even if she *wasn't* scaring me? It was just too much.

"Amber..." She whispered "Talk to me..."

"Henri, I called you tonight to tell you to stop trying to find a way to get me back. At least for now. I don't want you trying to kidnap me, *gods* know I don't want you 'smuggling' me, and I don't want you hurting Marissa."

"Why the fuck do you care what happens to Marissa?!" She said throwing her hands up.

"Oh I don't know, maybe because she's the one *taking care of me*? She's the one feeding me and making sure I'm not *killed*, and if you kill or injure *her*, then *I'm* fucked." I snarled. I rarely got angry at Henri, this was unlike me, but THIS was unlike *her* too.

"I can't even imagine what will happen to you if you really do hurt her to get me. You'll be blacklisted from keeping class Bs forever, and if you're living with my parents, THEY could be blacklisted too, do you want that?"

"I just want you to get away from her..." Henri said sadly.

"And get me thrown back into the system?" I said "I've been watching videos from people who have their own class Bs constantly since I was compressed. Marissa bullies me, sure, but do you know what happens to *other* class Bs?"

"...The test very clearly lays out how you need to treat-"

"We're used as living anime waifu figures by creeps, we're given to children as if we were dolls, we're forced to do physical challenges for social media views, we're used as jewelry, we're kept in people's cleavage, we're kept in clear plastic terrariums with no privacy, we're forced to play with whatever pets the guardian owns... I've seen a class B *batted across a room* by a cat, and it was posted on the internet as a cute video of the cat 'playing with him'."

I took a breath "Do you realize that you could be dooming me to any one of those fates if you hurt her? If you take things too far? She is NOT perfect and she scares the *shit* out of me, but at least she's not letting a 6 year old cut all my hair off or making me dance to pop music in embarrassing outfits for an audience."

Henri was crying more clearly now, her hands over her face, and her shoulders shaking "B-but if I can g-get you out of t-there, I would just...*leave* with you, no c-cats or cleavage..."

"Henri, get the idea out of your head. I'm not going to talk to you again until you promise me you won't try to kidnap me OR hurt Marissa." I said firmly.

"But Amber, no you-"

I hung up the call, and powered off the tablet. I was *angry*. Her stupid selfish obsession was going to get me hurt or *worse*, and she couldn't just fucking chill. I couldn't remember the last time I'd been this angry with her, or I'd *ever* been this angry with her. I turned my phone off too to make sure she couldn't contact me until I was ready to talk again, and shoved it under my mattress, and stood up, pulling the pillow fort apart so I could re-make my bed and get some sleep. I turned to go the the bathroom to brush my teeth, and I froze. In the window was a large green eye, watching me.

"...Hi Marissa..." I whimpered as my knees went out from under me.

~~~

We sat in her kitchen. Her chef was long asleep, and while she could have woken him up, she had opted to make the tea herself, and was sitting in front of me slowly drinking it. I was hugging my knees as I sat on the teapot, too afraid to speak up once since she plucked me out of my room without a word. After a long sip, she set the teacup down and tilted her head at me, her expressionless face not telling me anything about her mood.

"So, a little late night girl's talk?" she said, finally breaking the silence.

I swallowed and took a breath "Um, just clearing some things up, just. Girl talk."

She nodded and took another sip of her tea. "...I could hear you, you know. Your house is well made, but it's still a dollhouse, and my room is very quiet."

"I'm sorry, I wasn't trying to wake you up, I had it quiet..." I said, praying that she didn't hear what was said.

She took a deep breath. "That's not the issue here, is it?"

"...I'm not sure what you mean..."

"From what I heard, you had to talk your psycho girlfriend down from literally killing me." she said, still just as calm and emotionless.

"She's not- it was- no, see, she wouldn't-" I stammered

"Oh, but she *would*." Marissa said cooly. "I have no doubt that if she thought she could get away with it, she'd kill me."

"She's not like that, she'd *never*-"

"You know she came to the house today? Tried to force her way in, shouted at Parker and attempted to push past him and get in so she could come find you."

"... she did mention that..." I felt ashamed, embarrassed by her behavior

"I think she's dangerous, and I think you're starting to see it too, Amber."

"*I* think she just needs time to calm down..." I said "She's just worked up, it'll be ok in the long run."

"Mm. Well, she's banned from my house, and I'm planning on telling her I'll get a restraining order if she tries to come near me tomorrow at school."

I looked up alarmed "You can't do that! She'll have to work her whole school schedule around you, she could flunk out of the classes you share!"

"Either she flunks the classes, or I have to sit next to someone who actually wants to kill me, it's not a hard choice for me."

"Ok, ok... It shouldn't come to that... Just keep me in your pocket, and she can't attack you without risking me being crushed when you fall."

A smile spread across Marissa's face despite her attempts to keep it neutral. "Oh wow, that's such a good plan, Amber" She said dramatically "I can't *believe* the only way to keep you safe is for you to hide in my *pocket*, what a twist. Oh well, I guess I have no choice..."

"Don't make it weird, it's just an easy way to make sure you're not in danger." I grumbled.

"Uh huh." She said. "Because you care soooo much about my wellbeing."

I lowered my head and rested my chin on my knees. "A bit, you're supposed to take care of me. You can't do that if she stabs you or something."

"Mhhm. Anyway, next topic... From what you told her, you really are stuck with me, huh? There's no way out for you, you're doomed to like, be my toy for as long as I'll have you, is that right?"

I felt a chill go through my whole body "Oh, fucking hell, you heard that?"

"I woke up at the ringtone, I was listening in when you were still arguing about me keeping you in my pocket."

"No, it-" I tried to think of a way out "I was just saying that to make Henri stop trying to get me. My mother and Appa aren't that bad, I'd be able to stay with them for a long time, and I'm sure they could contact someone back home to take care of me when they can't..."

"Oh, sure, the government's just going to let them transfer ownership to some rando overseas when they're too blind and stupid to keep you safe? No, that's not how it works." She took another sip "I didn't think about the *logistics* of losing you, of what would happen *to* you. I just didn't want my toy getting taken away. Now that I have *your* perspective though..."

"If you just start hurting me, I will straight up report you still." I said coldly "I don't care if I am stuck back on a store shelf, if you're going to be horrible, I'll take my chances."

She laughed and picked me up off the bowl, holding me in front of her face. "I like you, Amber, I won't break you. I like talking to you even, as a... mm, well, not an equal, but someone who can be honest with me, and I don't want to lose that."

She lowered me so my face was just above her steaming cup of tea and I pulled back, the heat making me sweat and the strong chamomile scent making my head swim.

"That said... I now know I can get away with a *lot* more fun without risking you telling."

"I *trusted* you, I lied to a *doctor* for you, Marissa, we're building a relationship, you can't-"

She squeezed me and pulled me back up to her face "We can still build a relationship. Like I said, I like you. That trust stuff though, it's not like you have a choice or anything, you HAVE to trust me, and that feels... very nice."

"No, Marissa, we can just be friends, wouldn't *that* be nice?" I protested, my arms at my sides. I was getting better at bracing myself so she felt like she was squeezing me, but it wasn't too bad. "Just like, a best friend in your pocket, someone always there for you, someone to play games with and who trusts you, wouldn't that be amazing?"

"I'm still going to have all that, Amber. I'll just be able to have the fun the way I wanted to as well." She smiled at me "I feel good! I feel like we really got somewhere tonight, really truly."

"I don't want to be your friend if you're going to hurt me, I won't *trust* you if you don't give me a reason to, do you want to throw that away?"

"Mmm, noooo..." She said "Buuut... it's me or no one as far as friends go, and like, trust aside, you'll have to rely on me for food and stuff, so there's going to be trust there, right?"

I shook my head "Look, can we talk about it in the morning? It's too late to be making these kinds of life-changing decisions, right?"

"This sleepy tea is working pretty well, so sure, we can go to bed. But I'm taking your tablet before bed from now on, and don't expect me to change my mind about stuff, we're going right back to you being a toy, ok?"

I felt lost and hopeless, all the trust I'd shown her, the games we played, her promise to be better, as soon as she found out I was powerless, she threw it all away, and for what? Just to bully me more? She'd forgotten about the threat on her life as soon as we brought up me not being able to tattle on her, so even her own LIFE was second to the idea of treating me as less that human.

At least she hadn't seen my phone...

...Not that I had anyone to talk to on it anyway.

~~~

I woke up and rolled out of bed. I popped my back and stepped into the bathroom to get ready. Hopefully Marissa had calmed down since we spoke last night, and she wouldn't be treating me as poorly as she had before... I spat out the toothpaste, rinsed my mouth, and headed downstairs to find breakfast. As I opened the fridge, the wall of my house swung open, and Marissa's giant hand reached out and grabbed me, her finger closing the refrigerator on the way out.

"Wh- hey! I haven't eaten, and I'm still in my pajamas, what the heck?" I yelled as she swung me around to see her.

She was already dressed, and had a pair of skinny jeans and a yellow sleeveless top on, with a grey ball cap on her head. She smiled, and wiggled me in the air as she walked over to her handbag sitting on her desk.

"Oh, you can just eat when we get home from school, and as for clothes... No one will see you today, so it's fiiine." she said proudly.

"Am-am I going in your purse?" I asked "I don't like that, what if-"

"No no no, little Amber, you'll be going in my pocket, just like we discussed! Alllll day long."

I looked at her outfit, confused, before I realized with a start that she was talking about her jeans pockets.

"Wh- no! I'll suffocate! That doesn't count!"

"I'm sure it'll be ok, *I'm* not worried at least!" she said, slinging the bag over her shoulder. "So, front or back? Your pick."

I gaped at her. This was unrealistic, there was no way I could willingly let her do that to me, I wouldn't be able to *move* for as long as I was in there.

"No preference, huh?" she said "Oh well, I guess I'll pick for youuuuu..." She slowly moved me around to her backside.

"FRONT!" I yelled "Gods, front, fuck..."

"Aw, ok, maybe next time then." she said, grinning wide.

"This isn't what I signed up for, I'll be-"

"Going in nooow!" She sang, and pulled her pocket open, sliding me into the darkness.

The warmth was the first thing I noticed, my face and front were right up against her, so I was directly absorbing her body heat, but my back part was against the jeans themselves, and I could feel the cool air of the room. The top of the pocket snapped closed, and I struggled to move, my arms and legs spread uncomfortably out to the sides, my face pinned to her thigh. I strained against the fabric, and could move it just enough to turn my head if I needed to, but not enough to move my body. I took a deep breath to test my breathing ability, and found that while the air was hot, stale, and smelled like Marissa's skin, I could breathe in light, short breaths.

"Marissa, let me OUT!" I yelled "I can't fucking *move*."

I felt her hand touch me through the fabric, cupping me to her thigh and petting me. She laughed and tapped my butt with one of her fingers and I flushed.

"Aww I can't even understand you!" She said, her voice barely audible "I can see your outline so well though, and I can tell you *have* been working out after all! I'm so proud!"

I boiled inside and clenched my teeth, I was going to spend the day like this? Just an outline on her jeans? This *had* to be against the rules somehow, 'pocket' couldn't really mean *this* could it? Suddenly my stomach lurched and I clamped to her leg hard, my head spinning. She was moving, walking out of her room, every step rocking my world back and forth like a carnival ride. I couldn't stop it, I couldn't stop my stomach from knotting, and I couldn't gather my bearings with all this movement.

She took the stairs down to the first floor, she *never* took the stairs, but every step down felt like I was dropping off a cliff, and then as jarring as a car crash when her foot hit the stair. Her thigh flexed between hard and uncomfortable and soft and relaxed, her feet pounding into the ground as she jogged downwards. The flexing drove air out of my lungs in a pattern, and I panted and gasped as I tried to catch my breath.

Suddenly, I was weightless, and everything around me felt like it was being pulled up. I realized she must have jumped off the last few stairs, and bit hard on the soft material inside her pocket. She hit the ground with a slam, driving my organs back and up with the impact. My mouth popped open and snapped back shut, softened by the mouthful of fabric. My head was throbbing, and I struggled to re-fill my lungs, but she was already moving again, each step still jarring, every movement making me dizzier and dizzier.

I heard the car door and sighed in relief; at least I'd get a break while she was sitting down. I strained to get into a more comfortable position, but I still couldn't move. I felt her climb up, and sit down and I screamed as the jeans bunched and folded over me, pulling and twisting at my skin through the fabric. I was twisted at an angle, and the fabric was rubbing directly onto my already injured skin. I absently realized I hadn't gotten a chance to put more cream on my body this morning, and wondered how that would affect my healing. Not that it'd matter, I couldn't breathe at all now, it felt like I was dying. The new angle pulled my prison too tight and my chest could no longer fight against the pressure.

She pinched the denim next to me and pulled it up, getting the rough folded parts off my back and I gasped for air, breathing in as much as I could. The stretchy fabric popped back down on me, stinging my whole back half and forcing the air out of me again, but at least she'd smoothed out the kinks that were hurting me and making it impossible to breathe. I panted and pushed with my arms to get lift so I could breathe more freely, but my efforts barely got my elbows off her thigh and I soon gave up in the interest of preserving strength.

She traced her fingers over my body from the other side of the pocket and I heard her laugh lightly, poking me and pinching my limbs as she watched me. Could she feel me struggling? Did she have any idea of how painful and horrible this was? I heard the snapping noise of a digital camera and got angrier. Was she posting about me on her fucking socials again? She'd at least let me *know* the first time, but to take a picture of me like this, it felt like a violation.

I breathed slow and deep, I just needed to focus, she couldn't keep me here *all* day, right? She had tennis practice Mondays, so she'd have to change for that, and her tennis uniform didn't have pockets, so I'd at least be able to breathe for a while then, right? Monday... I'd compressed Sunday night, I remembered because Marissa had been changing in the gym locker rooms that afternoon, and she was usually was only in there Mondays and Thursdays after her practices, so it'd been weird to see her. I usually tried to work my schedule around avoiding her, but that day she'd shown up anyway for some reason... It felt like far, far longer than a week, almost like it'd been months. It *felt* like I was almost used to my new life, or I could be if the situation didn't keep changing so much.

I swallowed and tried to pull my limbs in, if I could roll over, maybe I could breathe better... It wasn't easy to move, but I tried and strained and eventually got my arms a little more together, and kicked with one foot. It was tight, but I managed to roll onto my side, at least partially. My arm was pinned and my legs were twisted, but I could breathe like normal, and I lay there, exhausted and worn out until the car stopped moving, my vision returning and my body regaining feeling.

I felt her get out of the car, and the steps started up again, making me sick and causing my stomach to drop. I clenched my body tightly and tried to curl up, but I still couldn't. I felt her going up the stairs to the front doors, and every lift of her leg squeezed me and shot pains through my body as the jeans constricted and pulled at me. I screamed at her to stop, to let me out. I thrashed as much as I could and yelled at the top of my lungs, but she just slapped me lightly and laughed.

"Hey now, be quiet or I really *will* move you to my back pocket, 'k? And here, you got turned all sideways, let me fix that!"

I fought agains the fingers that moved in around me, laying me out flat, face down with my arms and legs out, but it was like trying to wrestle trees, and soon I was in the same position I was in before, unable to move. I breathed heavily, my air feeling like it was running out, the small gap of air I had to breathe from in front of my face getting warmer and warmer and more and more stale as I tried to stay calm. I felt her going to class, her strut obvious and exaggerated. I heard the other students chatting, I swear I heard my name- or at least 'rat'- twice, but Marissa never interacted with them. She took a seat at a seat in the classroom, and once again I lost all my breath as the angle of her leg crushed it out of me. As the teacher started the lesson, I felt myself passing out, my head pounding, my lungs burning, and my skin still stinging, black spots overwhelming me.

~~~

I woke to myself being pulled out of the pocket, it was loose and floppy now, and I could breathe a lot more easily, but my vision was blurred, my body was numb, and my head was throbbing. I could vaguely see someone holding me, and hear laughter. A locker banged open, and some large bundle went past me into it, and then I followed. I tried to see where I was going but I was still too far gone to think straight. I felt myself being shoved into something soft, but not tight, and laid on the cold metal floor. It was quiet for a minute until someone, most likely Marissa, said something, and the locker banged shut on me.

I took breaths as deeply as I could and tried to clear my head. I was still alive, but my head hurt so, so bad. I couldn't lift it, I could only suck down air. As my vision cleared, I saw that I was lying in the front half of a locker, with Marissa's pumps towards the back, her top and those cursed jeans folded up on top of them. I looked down at my body, and saw she had put me into a sock like it was a sleeping bag. Did she think I was just sleeping when she pulled me out? Was this supposed to be a kindness or a humiliation? I tried to pull myself out of it, but my chest hurt, like when you spent too long under water and you can feel the ache for hours after if you try to breathe deeply, but this was a constant throb.

I didn't even care enough to try and get out, it was just a sock, anyway, and I was kind of cold. I lifted a shaky hand to my forehead and let my cool fingers take some of the pulsing pain away, laying there for what seemed like hours. I was still bleary and groggy, and I felt slow and stupid, but I was starting to think again. I couldn't go back in the jeans, I just couldn't. She could put me anywhere else, carry me, do whatever she needed to, but the thought of being that trapped again...

I started to cry. This was all my fault, if I hadn't told Henri about my stupid ideas and fears, Marissa wouldn't have gone this far, she wouldn't have hurt me like this because she'd be too scared of losing me. All I had to do was tell Henri 'no'. It didn't matter WHY I said no, she should have respected that. There was nothing I could do now though, this was my life, and I couldn't imagine it getting any better. Fear struck me, and I kicked my feet in frustration, my tears dripping down to my ears. I could have had a nice, soft life with her if *Henri* hadn't- actually, this WAS Henri's fault. If she wasn't so... clingy, I could just be transferred to HER, but nooo, she had to be obsessive and take things too far. I felt my sadness and fear being replaced with frustration and anger. Why couldn't she just let things be? Why-

A sharp clanging echoed through the locker and I screamed, the noise killing my head and making my headache worse. A pair of blue eyes peeked through the vent, squinting but not seeing.

"Klein fee? I'm getting you out, I have a fire extinguisher, I will break this open and we can get out!" Henri's familiar voice sounded out.

I groaned and squeezed my eyes closed, flinching as the next clanging sounded out, then the next. I peeked, and saw the locker was buckled inwards slightly, and I started thinking about it caving in, crushing me or slamming me into the interior wall. Had she even thought about that?

"Henri, cut it OUT!" I yelled, my voice hoarse and rough from the lack of air. Either she didn't hear me, or she didn't care, because a second later, another slam sounded out.

"HEY. What do you think you're doing young lady?!" I heard a gruff voice say. It sounded like Miss Eloise, the lacrosse coach.

"O-oh, no, it is a misunderstanding, see, I am actually trying to free-"

"You are destroying school property and attempting to steal someone's belongings!" roared Miss Eloise

"No! No, ahh, mein liebhaber ist da drin!" Henri said, her voice shaking.

I heard a clanging of the fire extinguisher hitting the ground, and an exclamation from Henri

"No, please, let go, I need to-"

"We're going to the dean's office, we'll see what SHE has to say about this, I wouldn't be surprised if she calls the cops on you, you know."

Henri, protesting, was dragged out of the locker room, and I couldn't feel the slightest bit sorry for her. It was a crime, and she knew what she was getting into. I felt bad for not feeling bad, but... I told her to stop, and she didn't. It felt almost good to feel this upset with her, like it was justified, but almost in a selfish way. I looked at the door again. It was banged in pretty bad, but it should still open... Not that I really wanted it to, I was more than fine to just lay down and rest here for as long as I could. I felt the tears start back up thinking about going back to my prison, and I had to try and hold back the shakes; the pain it gave my chest was just too much.

After a long, long while, I heard footsteps, and a groan. The lock on the door jiggled, and opened up, and the metal screeched as the bent up door was pried open. Marissa stood there, smug as ever, her lidded grin looking just as confident on her sweaty, pink face as it did on her composed one. She fanned her tennis dress and pointed at the door.

"I guess we had a visitor, huh? Looks like I'll have grounds for a restraining order after all." She peered at me, confused at whatever she saw "Wait... were you...? Hm."

She gathered her things from behind me "Well, I'm going to go change back, and then..." She leaned in and smiled wider "Pocket tiiiiime!~"

I couldn't stand it, my chest seized my face crumpled yet again, and I started sobbing, laying limply as I shook my head

"No no no no no... please..." I said, my voice rough and dry "Please, please, please..."

I was begging, but I didn't care, I couldn't do it, I couldn't go back into that hellish place. Marissa's face was frozen in her smile, her eyes wide. She leaned out of the locker and looked around, then back at me. She swallowed hard and looked at her pile of clothes.

"Uhh... I'll- uh, I-" she said, and her voice caught too. I cried harder, was she trying to make excuses for it? "It's just until we get home, it's no big deal, I was thinking we could like, sit on the couch and watch one of your old lady shows or something?"

"No... please, no..." I whispered. Even just going home was too much, not being able to move, to breathe, I couldn't do it.

She reached out for me, and gently picked me up and I cringed away from her touch, my crying wracking my body as I tried to get out of her grasp.

"...Fuck..." she muttered. "Damnit... Come here..."

She pulled me out of the locker and closer to her. The smell of sweat hung around her, and her body was hot, far hotter than before. I thought about being against her skin, the extra heat, the sweat smell and I shuddered, shaking my head and curling up into a ball. If I was curled up, she couldn't splay me, right? She sighed, and I peeked up at her, she looked almost sad, or scared, and her mouth was moving as if she was trying to say something, but she couldn't.

She frowned and set me on her pile of clothes, pulling her phone out from under the pile and dialing. It rang once, and she started talking, not even waiting for a 'hello'

"Hey, meet me by the side, the gym entrance, pull right up to the door."

She hung up without waiting for a response, and tucked her phone into the strap of her sports bra under her arm and reached out for me. I ducked inside the sock and covered my head with my hands, hoping she'd get the message. I felt her fingers stroke me through the sock and I shivered. Did she think a gentle pat like that could make up for the hours and hours of torture? She carried me outside to her car, and got in, setting me and her pile of stuff on the seat next to her. I felt a wave of relief that she wasn't going to change or put me back in *there*, but I was still shaking. How long would it be before she tried to do it again?

This was becoming a familiar scene, me, hurt and upset on the car seat next to her, her aloof or uncommunicative next to me. I stayed in the sock until we got home, and when she finally put me, sock and all into my house, I went straight upstairs, legs shaking, vision narrow, and flopped into bed, too depressed, hurt, and exhausted to even do anything else. My stomach was empty, but I still felt too nauseous to even *think* about eating microwaved 'po'-ta'tos and sa'usage' or whatever I had. Marissa closed the walls behind me, despite it only being late afternoon, and I heard her flop onto her own bed outside and moan.

Neither of us moved for a long time.

# Chapter Eleven

I got up in the middle of the night and made myself food. I sat at the kitchen table with the lights off eating it, a sick, scared feeling in my stomach. I ate whatever it was I'd made, I hadn't looked at the package, and breathed in and out slowly, enjoying the cool, clear, unscented air. I felt my skin under the dry, uncomfortable bandages and winced. Leaving the bandages on for over 24 hours without changing them hadn't helped the healing at all, and I was sure I stank under them all. I shuffled up the stairs to my bathroom and slowly unwound them, piling them on the floor in a heap, the tan cloth stained pink here and there from where my joints had split back open.

I turned the water on, and stepped in wincing, but trying to stay quiet and calm. I rubbed the dried lotion off and worked my muscles under my skin. I ached all over, my skin stung, my joints creaked, I was sore down to my bones. I looked at my shaking hands and clenched them, watching my fists shake too. If this kept up, I'd fall apart. I scrubbed myself down, washing as well as I could with the shower being either 'soft mist' or 'torrential downpour'. As I gingerly toweled myself off, I heard the door open and close. Marissa must have left to go somewhere, I was just glad she didn't take me with her. I walked to the living room and sat down on the sofa, turning on the television.

I may as well do some more research while she was gone, I didn't want to sit and re-live what had happened, and I wanted to take my mind off it.

After a few hours, the door opened again, and I crept away from a horrifying video about how to free class Bs caught in glue traps (with the camera person putting an actual class B in a glue trap to illustrate it) to peek out the window. I wasn't sure I wanted to see her, but I was curious where she'd gone at past 11 at night without changing from her tennis practice clothes. She flicked the light on, then glanced over at my house and grimaced, turning it off again. She was disheveled and looked exhausted, with her hair far more frazzled than it had been. She tucked a small black bag into another hidden cubby and walked into the bathroom, her bare feet making slapping noises as she stepped inside. The door closed gently, and I heard the shower go on a second later. I breathed a sigh of relief, and realized my heart had been beating like a drum the whole time I watched her.

I went back to the video, watching the person pour oil on their terrified class B for a few minutes before I shut it off. I had this feeling of unrest inside me, something that begged me to take action, to do *something* to fix whatever I could. Instead, I got on my treadmill, my aching legs burning, my chest throbbing, my breaths gasps just moments after getting on. I really *was* falling apart, I could go for hours before this, now... It was just one more reminder of how much it hurt to exist like this, I needed something to fill my brain.

I got my tablet, and poked around on it. I hadn't explored it much, but there were some apps that had come pre-installed that I wanted to check out. One was a nanny app, and while it was off now, it could be set up to send random screenshots or message history to my guardian. I hoped Marissa didn't know about it, but at this point, I was too tired to even care if she *did* know, it wouldn't even make my life any worse than it already was. The next app was a glorified safety manual, something to go over to see how best to stay safe, with quizzes and flashcards. Living with Marissa it wouldn't matter. She was weirdly well versed in class B safety, usually, but ignored it when it suited her. The last app though, sparked an interest in me.

It was an app for class Bs called "AntMound", a social media and news site of sorts, and it could only be installed on devices with a compressed identifier in them, so it was populated only by other class Bs. I set up an account and started browsing the news section. I saw articles about the best brands of compressed food, what restaurants offered compressed alternatives, how to tell if your new guardian is suffering from anxiety about the stresses of taking care of you, and how to fix it... There was even a quiz about "what your day to day life says about your relationship with your guardian!" I took it, out of curiosity, and checked my result. Instead of a fun quip or generic line like I was supposed to get, I got "If you need to contact emergency re-homing services, please press the button below, and we'll connect you with an assessor at once." I snorted. I could have guessed *that*, I supposed. It was tempting, far more than it would have been yesterday... I opened the tab labeled "Science news" and poked around on the articles. A new star was discovered, somehow? How did they not notice a star until now? A new type of protein that compressed more easily had been developed that could provide more nutritious meals for class Bs, which would be nice for me, and...

My eyes widened, and I opened the article I'd seen and read it in more depth.

*"We have discovered that the compression particles, in addition to reproducing themselves during the compression process, have recently begun dumping the excess genetic material that acts as a catalyst for the compressions into the air around them. This has led to individuals re-triggering compression shortly after the initial infection due to the genetic materials re-entering their system, as well as multiple cases of individuals who were previously immune contracting the compression virus simply by being in close proximity to someone with a high compression makeup while they were compressing."*

So... did that mean my parents could be at a higher risk now? How close did they have to be? The article included photos of a man who'd been exposed to high doses of compression particles before and had no adverse effects, but after his child compressed in front of him, the arm he had used to hold him post compression had been fully annihilated along with parts of his left side and thigh the next time he'd drank a glass of water. The photos were... not pretty. I'd forgotten that the most common result of compression was just people missing chunks of their bodies. If he'd picked up his son while the compression was *happening* I could understand, everyone knew to stay away from people who were going through that, in case the particles with the genetic fuel already in them got on you too, but just to hold him *after* the process was done?... I felt so bad for him, he'd just wanted to be there for his kid in a scary time... I didn't know how long it'd taken for my own infection to set in, as it'd happened while I was sleeping, but surely my mom would have mentioned if she'd lost her hand from picking me up, right?

I sent her a link to the article, I didn't know if she'd be able to read it since it was hosted on AntMound, but I was curious if she'd seen any side effects. I also didn't know how recently the particles had changed their behavior, if it was just within the past week, then that's one thing, but if it was an existing issue... That said, were the particles evolving? From my understanding they were just self replicating bits of matter, not living organisms, but if they could grow and change, this could turn from a minor issue to a global panic. It wouldn't affect *me* either way though, I was already as compressed as I was going to get, there wasn't much to worry about there as far as my future was concerned.

The bathroom door opened again, and I looked out the window to see Marissa's shape walk past, and I heard her sit at her computer. I guessed she was going to be playing her game for a while, so I went back to browsing the tablet, trying to stay calm and ignore her. I got my profile looking nice for the social media part of AntMound, and went about trying to find people to chat with. It looked like *most* of the app was political discussion, with arguments about if we deserved full rights, or if spouses should be allowed automatic guardianship, or even if underage class Bs needed to be schooled, with people getting very heated very quickly.

I was impressed with how much some of the class Bs seemed to hate themselves, what with the way they were arguing against their best interests, but I almost understood. They didn't *ask* to be like this, they resented it, and it hurt, so they were lashing out, trying to make themselves feel better by appealing to the class A people's opinions and views, even if the class As didn't care about them either way.

After hours of reading other people's arguments, I checked the clock. It was past 2:30... I was getting tired again, and it was Tuesday tomorrow. Marissa had class with Henri on Tuesdays in the afternoons, so she most likely was going to want to bring me with her. I headed to bed and lay on top of the covers, looking at the ceiling. I really wanted to get more of that cream put on me, with the gauze, but I couldn't bring myself to go outside and get Marissa's attention, and the bottle was much too big for me to squeeze myself. I was more itchy than anything now, which was good, but the air hitting my joints did sting. I closed my eyes, and tried not to flash back to being in her pocket as I dozed off.

~~~

I flinched as the walls of my house swung open around lunchtime the next day, but I stood up from the couch and walked over the front anyway. If she wanted to see me, playing coy or being rude wouldn't help. She stood there, in her sports bra and small shorts and sighed.

"Come on, we're going to my closet to find something to wear." she said, holding her hand out to me.

I was shaking as I climbed in, and I could feel the blood in my ears as I fought back tears. She held me up to her face and stared at me, but I couldn't make eye contact. She clicked her tongue and shook her head.

"I take it you're claustrophobic, then?" she asked gently

I waved my hand in a vague way. I wasn't, usually, but yesterday was something else...

"Ok, so if you're not really claustrophobic, then why are you so mad at me?" she asked, sounding frustrated.

I hugged my chest and tried to talk but the words didn't come out. She huffed and walked over to her bed, sitting down in front of the closet door.

"Amber. Talk to me or I won't know what's wrong." she said sternly. "Why are you angry?"

I looked up at her with tears in my eyes, how could she *not* know? I breathed in and out quickly a few times, and tried again.

"I'm n-not angry, I'm s-scared." my voice sounded small and hollow even to myself.

"Scared? Of a pocket? Or of being left alone? You need to explain better than that."

I struggled, and worked up the courage to let it all out.

"Of YOU." I said, louder than I meant to, but the cork was out now, and the words spewed out

"You put me in that horrible tight place, I couldn't breathe, I was crushed, I was *dying*, I couldn't move, I was *screaming* and you didn't care, you made it *worse* just because you could, I almost *died*, I passed out, and you didn't even *NOTICE*. You put me in the most painful, horrible situation of my entire life and you *didn't even register you were doing it*, and you could do it again at any time, or do something *even worse*. I am *TERRIFIED* of you, Marissa."

I panted for air, my heart racing.

"I can't imagine being ok around you right now, I *dread* the next thing you do to me, I can't even *think* straight I'm so worked up. Honestly?"

I looked her in the eyes, my own wide and wild. I felt a hot, burning anger and fear in my chest and pulled it out, throwing it at her with my words.

"I just wish you'd go ahead and skip to the inevitable end and fucking *kill me*, because after what you said Sunday night, what you did yesterday, I don't even want to *live* like this anymore. This is fucking *hell*. You. Are. My. Hell. It's bad enough not even being a fucking *human* anymore, but compared to spending time around you? I'd be more ok being a fucking hamster than a class B if it meant you'd *leave me the fuck alone*."

She stared at me, her eyes filling with tears, her breathing coming out in puffs. She opened her mouth and shuddered, unable to say what she wanted without overflowing. Her hand shook and she set me down on the bed like I was made of bubbles, and turned away. She obviously didn't want me to see how I had effected her, how *my* words had power this time, but I didn't care, I'd said it, and I still felt full of terror and fire, mixing together into a blue flame in my chest. Tears went down my cheeks but I didn't feel like I was crying, I felt powerful and insignificant at the same time, like I could kill or be killed and not know the difference. I watched her back as it shook slightly, and she stepped into the bathroom, not turning around as she shut the door behind her. The fan cut on, but under the buzzing noise, I heard her finally break into sobs.

I fell over, the energy going out of me as I felt the victory, the small feeling of winning. I could feel the tears now, inside me and out, and I let myself cry. Did I really hate her that much? I couldn't tell. I'd spoken from the heart, and my heart was on fire, so there's no telling how much I meant of it. I didn't *really* want to die, I knew that much, but it'd felt good to say I did. Making her feel like *she's* the reason I felt this way felt like some kind of justice. I did feel mildly bad about it, but it also felt so, so good to see her cry, to know that I somehow did something cruel to *her* for once.

The bathroom door opened and Marissa stepped out, still red eyed and breathing heavy. She got on her knees in front of the bed and stared at me with an intensity I had never seen from her. She was alert, her eyes were open, and she looked like she was scared and hurt all at once. She put her hands on either side of me and my chest locked up, and I sat back up, scrambling away from her. She shook her head.

"No, look, stop. I'm not good at this, and I don't know how to deal with my thoughts," she said "but I need to get this shit out now while I'm feeling real emotions for once, or I'll never let myself say anything."

I watched her as her eyes flicked over me, looking for a sign of... something. She continued. "You are *important* to me. I really do care about you, Amber. I have a shitty way of showing it, I know, but you are my favorite thing in life, and not just because you're my new toy. I *value* you. I value you *as Amber*, and it's really really hard for me to admit that, but I do. I'm not going to kill you, I'm not trying to break you, I don't want to traumatize you."

Her face shifted to a more embarrassed one

"I need you to be here, Amber, and I'm so, so glad I was able to get to you first, because... The only way I could ever have gotten to even be around you was if something like *this* happened." She waved at my tiny body vaguely.

I felt a chill. It almost sounded like she'd been wanting me even *before* I was compressed when she said it like that. Like she'd tracked me down last week not because she wanted a new pet, but because she'd wanted *me*.

She brushed her hair out of her face. "That said... I have... needs. Urges, I have cravings and wants, and it feels better to... indulge myself in those needs when it's someone I care about. Someone like my 'friends', or... you."

Was she talking about the past week? Or the past 6 years? Was she saying she'd bullied me, pushed me around, gotten the other girls to hurt me or ruin my clothes and homework and keep me out of after school clubs because she *cared* about me?

"I'm sorry, I don't understand..." I said, my teeth clicking together as I shivered

She groaned. "I'm not going to *say* it Amber, I can't say it, not for real. I don't know *how*. Just know that I *care* about you, that's as close as I can come to saying what I mean. I'm... I don't- ...I really... regret what you went through yesterday, I had no idea, and I was so busy tending to my cravings, I didn't think about things like air or you being crushed. I want to be able to care for you and *protect* you, Amber. But I also want to be able to... do things to you..."

"W-what if I don't like that?..." I asked, trying to collect my thoughts

"I- I have other outlets." she admitted. "That computer game we played was one, just not a very satisfying one, and... I have an agreement with someone who has the 'opposite' interests as me that I use from time to time."

"Is that where you went last night?" I asked

Her cheeks tinted pink and she shook her head dismissively "That's not important, what *is* important is that I need you, and I can't stand it if you don't like me, or at least tolerate me. I want you to like being here. I know I told you I'd treat you like a princess, and I really meant it, Amber. Not in the mean way like when I said it earlier, I can treat you like a princess for real, you just have to be ok with a little bit of roughness too. I want you to have a good time, I want you to love me." Her face got pinker at the last part, and I felt my cheeks flushing to match.

I couldn't imagine loving her, but...

"I really had fun at the sleepover..." I said tentatively "I thought that was the most normal our relationship had ever been, aside from a couple moments. You were rude and you had fun, but you never hurt me."

"Yeah, I had fun too, mostly." she agreed. "Let's, I don't know, I feel all sick and hopeless right now, and I hate the thought of losing all connections to you, I don't want you to be scared of me, let's find a way, ok?"

"I'm still *four inches tall*." I reminded her "You're a mountain to me either way, I don't think I can ever be *not* scared of you, especially if you're getting 'cravings' to hurt me."

"No, no, not- not to *hurt* you, never to hurt you." she said, her hand slipping around me softly "Just... to feel powerful, to feel control. I need to feel that sometimes..."

"I just don't know, you hurt me really bad, you messed me up, I passed out. And it's been like a day and a half since you helped me with my bandages, my skin is still raw. I'm not blaming you for the vodka, but you're supposed to help me with stuff when I need it." I said swallowing against the lump in my throat.

"Ok, ok, I'll help you with your bandages, we can do that right away. I didn't know you passed out yesterday, ok? I was just trying to flex my power, I flexed too hard. It won't happen again." she said soothingly.

It felt off, like she was telling me what I wanted to hear, but still, she *was* telling me what I wanted to hear, mostly.

"I still don't think I can relax around you." I admitted "I think I'll need time, but we can re-build that trust we had, and it'll be like before in no time, ok?"

She smiled, and sniffed, wiping her eyes with her free hand. "Thanks, I guess that's all I can ask for. I wanted to try a few new things though..."

I locked up and braced myself against her hand with my arms shaking my head "No no no no, please, I can't-"

"Hey, no, hey." she interrupted "Good things. First up, you pick my clothes, or at least, you pick a pocket you're ok with, and I build an outfit around it."

I thought about it. It could be a trap, but it could also be a peace offering... I'd have to test her with it, and I already had an idea as to how.

"Ok, I- I can do that." I said

"And next... Tonight at a community center a few cities away, there's a support group for class Bs and their guardians. I found it last night, they meet twice a week. I thought that'd be... good for us. If we leave my second class and head straight there, we can even get dinner on the way."

She thought for a second and shook her head

"Oh... Well, hm. I'm not sure how dinner would work actually..."

"There's a place called Cecarina, it's a chain, they offer compressed foods..." I said, thinking about the article I'd read "If it's a few towns over, there may be one on the way?"

"Ah, ok, yeah, we- we can try it!" she said, nodding encouragingly. "So... I think we can do this, I think we'll be ok..."

"It's worth a shot..." I said. It didn't feel like it was worth anything, but I would much prefer to be around a Marissa who's trying to win me back than one who thinks I'm a lost cause.

"Thank you so much, Amber." She picked me up and opened her closet. "Let's figure out what we're going to wear, ok?"

~~~

I tugged at the kimono to loosen it a bit and lay against Marissa's stomach as she walked, swinging and bouncing slightly as she headed to class. Her compromise for wearing what I picked was that she got to pick what *I* wore, and I needed to be on the table in the classroom the whole time to show off *my* outfit. I didn't mind too much, the kimono was light but warm, and the soft leggings I had on under it reminded me of long underwear. The stupid band around my waist though didn't want to stay flat, and kept bending, making it too tight on my stomach. Nothing as bad as yesterday, but still annoying.

"Oh, um... Are you feeling ok, Marissa?" I heard a familiar voice say, Tracy maybe?

"I don't think I've ever seen you in a hoodie before, M." Another voice said. It sounded like Quince, another of Marissa's hangers on.

"I look good in anything, I can wear what I want." snapped Marissa from above me.

"No, no! I'm so sorry, I wasn't saying- you look great, comfortable and cute!" Tracy said, quickly correcting herself.

"I wear hoodies all the time, I just didn't know you had one is all." Quince said, her voice still slightly judgy

What absolute bitches... Let a girl wear a hoodie now and then, for fuck's sake. Then again, this reaction was *exactly* why I had picked out the hoodie in the first place. That and it was the biggest, softest pocket in anything she owned.

"I got it during orientation, everyone got one. *You two* got one." Marissa said grumpily. "It's within dress code, I'm wearing real pants, not leggings after all."

"Yeah, of course." Tracy said "Like I said, you look cute. So, um, is your new toy here too?"

Marissa's hand plunged into my pocket and I quickly fixed the loosened kimono as she drug me out. I sat on her palm on my knees and tried to look neutral, she was being nice for now, I should be nice too.

"Ohhhh..." gushed Quince, leaning in to see me better "She's so, so cute! I can't believe it's the Rat, she could never be this adorable!"

"I'm not calling her that anymore." corrected Marissa. "I don't like thinking about keeping a rat in my pocket, that's unsanitary. I just call her Amber now, so it's not as gross."

"Amber?" Quince said, looking up "Did you pick that out for her?"

"Uh, I think that's her real name, Q." Tracy said politely, watching me

"Yeah, I'm no good with names, I just used her old one." Marissa said, nodding. "I have a few minutes before class, do either of you want to hold her?"

"Oh gosh, no..." Tracy said "My dad works with them at his job, and the things he's said, I'd prefer not to..."

"What kind of things?" Quince asked

"He- he said it can be *contagious*" Tracy said, looking around nervously.

"Only if you come in physical contact with us within a few minutes of compression" I said "I heard about that too, I'm way past that point by now."

Tracy flinched at me talking, and Quince cooed and reached out with a finger like she was going to poke me. I didn't want to be held by Tracy again, last time I'd felt like she was going to drop me, but I didn't want her ignorance to make other people ignorant too. Call it class pride, or something.

"She's not fucking contagious," Marissa snapped "if she was I'd be an inch tall- look, do either one of you want to hold her? She's going back away if not."

"Oh I would *love* to!" Quince said "I want one of them so, so bad, I already have a down payment at the boutique for the next one that comes in."

That seemed like cheating, what if it was someone whose family wanted to get them back? Or someone who she didn't want? I grimaced at the thought as Marissa handed me over to her. Like with every new person to touch me, the smell of her hand stood out to me. It was a vaguely floral scent, with... pretzels? Maybe? Some kind of carb at least. She made kissy noises and rubbed my face with her finger, bringing me close enough to her face to smell her breath. Yup, that was pretzels. I pushed her finger away and cleared my throat.

"So, Quince, you mentioned a down payment, that means you've taken the class and stuff?" I asked her

"Awww, of course!~ She said smiling at me, doing that same, horrible baby voice people kept doing to me. "I worked real hard after I saw that cute picture of you last week!"

"The one in the dress?" I asked "Marissa said she'd post it, I didn't hear if anyone liked it though."

"Oh, they liked it." Marissa said "You got lots of attention, trust me."

"Attention is right..." Tracy murmured

"I liked the second picture too, you know, the one from yesterday?" Quince said. "I loved how helpless and silly you looked!"

I winced. I'd really, really hoped that hadn't gone up... "That was, uh, not fun, I didn't like that."

"Yeah, it didn't work out, too dangerous, as cute as it was." Marissa said dismissively, like it hadn't almost killed me.

"Aw, that's too bad. I'd have liked to carry mine around like that when I get them, all flat..." Quince said, pouting.

"You should talk to your class B to make sure they're ok with you doing anything like that." I reminded her

"I'm super persuasive, I'm sure they won't mind." she said, patting my head "Besides, I have an even *cuter* idea for how to carry them around!"

"Oh?" Tracy said "Like, a kind of accessory or something?"

"I really liked the bottle I have, with the heating and air built in? It's very fashionable." Marissa offered.

"No no, I'm going to do something I've been talking about for years..." Quince said "I'm gonna lose the double afro puffs, and just have a regular afro! And then I'll be able to keep them on my head, I'll make a hole in the front, and they can just ride on top of me! I'm thinking I can even decorate it with flowers and stuff!"

"I don't know, Quince..." Tracy said "I don't think hair is strong enough to hold them in place, they'll fall out, and plus, you've had afro puffs since we were kids, it's like, part of you."

"It sounds gross to be like, in someone's hair, too." I pointed out "I'd be grossed out, at least. Hair is gross."

"I'll remember that..." Marissa said, taking me back from Quince. I shuddered, thinking of the hair related torture she could be planning.

"Anyway, I've got to get to class..." Marissa said "But... why don't the two of you come over Friday for a sleepover? I had one last week with Henri, so she could see Amber, and I was missing how fun ours used to be."

"Who's Henry?" Quince asked "Does Amber have a brother?"

"No, uhh, Henri-etta?" Marissa said, glancing at me and faking ignorance. "I think. Bludsauger."

"Why are you calling her Henri?" Tracy asked "Are you two friends?"

"No, she's like, my servant, kinda." Marissa said, bragging. "I just wanted to be more professional towards her."

"Oooh, servant?" Quince said wiggling her eyebrows "I wanna play with her too, invite her over Friday?"

Marissa blanched for a split second, and put on a sneer. "Psh, we'll see. She's a psycho, but maybe."

"Well... I'll see you two there if I don't see you before then!" Tracy said, waving and walking towards her class.

"Yeah, I'm SO looking forward to getting to spend time with lil Amber!~" Quince said, patting me on the head one more time. "Byeee!"

As they walked away, I looked up at Marissa, concerned.

"Another sleepover?"

She rolled her eyes. "You said you liked it, whatever. We won't do the punishments and stuff, it'll be like, movies and board games or something, fuck I don't know. You said you had fun, I want you to have fun."

I nodded. I didn't know how 'fun' it'd be to hang out with those two... Tracy was a gossipy bitch with no backbone, and Quince was... usually a lot meaner than today, I guess she really liked class Bs? It may not be so bad. That said...

"And... Henri?" I asked "She did threaten to kill you, and smashed up your locker, I don't know if it's safe for her to be around me..."

Marissa growled. "I know, right? Ugh, I shouldn't have fucking mentioned her, I'm better than that... I don't want to lose face to those two peons though, I just- ugh..."

"Maybe we could say she's busy?" I suggested.

"No, that's obvious. Maybe... Hm..." Marissa said, thinking as we walked to her classroom. "I think I have an idea, but it'll be risky. Do you trust Henri enough to behave in a group setting if she thinks you're in potential danger?"

My eyes widened. "Danger? Oh, uhhh"

"Not real danger. Just- you know that ankle bracelet of yours?"

I looked down at the annoying, chunky reminder I was a class B. "...Yeah, I do."

"Ok, I'm going to tell her I wired the tracker in it to explode if you get too far from my phone, taking your leg and most of you with it."

I looked at her, shocked. "She's just going to steal your phone at that point."

Marissa nodded, and slowed down, digging in her purse for something.

"Right, ok, so what if..."

She pulled out a small knife and drug it on her wrist, making a line of blood. I shrieked and backed up against her fingers, watching the blood seep out slowly. She unwrapped a bandage out of her purse with her teeth and slapped it over the cut, and another to hide the blood.

"...I had a tracker *inside* me, that works even if I'm dead? Then she can't take you without taking my whole arm with her, right?"

I look between her and her arm. She hadn't even *flinched*, what was wrong with this lady? I rubbed my own arm in sympathy and shook my head. If she'd gone this far already, we may as well give it a shot.

"Ok, ok yeah, we can try it. If she saws off your arm though, it's on you." I said.

Marissa grinned and tossed the trash from the bandages in the can next to the classroom door. "Perfect, now, let's go manipulate the fuck out of her."

She stepped inside and walked straight to where Henri was sitting, flopping down in the seat next to her and putting me on the table in front of her. She leaned over and smiled smugly, staring into Henri's scared and confused face.

"Sup, bitch? Wanna go to another fucking sleepover?"

# Chapter Twelve

I sat at the tiny table and rocked back and forth in my chair, it was nice to be out and in the world again, and feel like I belonged. It was *also* nice to see Marissa this embarrassed.

"I wasn't thinking about dinner when I let you dress me..." She muttered, looking around at all the other diners in their nice clothes.

"Well I feel right at home!" I said chipperly, looking over the compressed menu. I was so looking forward to having real, non microwaved food... There were a lot of options, I was having trouble trying to pick just one thing...

"So, support group, huh?" Marissa asked, swirling her wine, looking bored

"Yeah. I've never been to something like that, do we like, stand up and say 'hi, my name is Amber Park and I'm a class B' or something?" I said, trying to imagine the setup for a multi-size support group.

"I have no clue, I just hope it's not full of sad weirdos." Marissa said, rolling her eyes "Oh, my life is so hard, food is expensive, I'm tired of being so small waahhh..."

I glared at her "Hey, it's actually really hard and scary being this size, you can't make fun of me like that."

She blushed. "No- not you, I- damnit, no, Amber, I wasn't saying that..."

I looked back at my menu, still frustrated.

"Look, I get it, yeah." she said "I know it's hard, I shouldn't have said that."

I glanced over at her "I'm just saying, even if you weren't having 'urges' it's really hard. You know we have 38% more heart attacks? Over 60% of us have anxiety, and statistically speaking, almost all of us will get a major life changing injury within the ten years of being compressed. I watched a video essay about it yesterday."

"Compression particles have only existed for like, seven years or something, at least outside of a lab. How would they even know?" she complained.

"They do math and see how much we get hurt at what rate over the course of the sample timeline and extrapolate." I said

"...I forgot you were smart to be honest." Marissa said "You never talk like that."

"Well..." I looked at my hands "I'm not actually smart, I was smart as a kid, but nowadays I've really gotten dumber, I don't know why."

"Could it be the compression?" she asked, curious

"No- I mean, like, starting senior year, school was harder, I had to work more, and it was a struggle to get As, and now... I'm just an average student. If I didn't have the scholarship program, I wouldn't have even been allowed into the school with my current test scores, I can't buy my way in like most of the girls."

"Oh, that sucks." Marissa said. "I feel like I've been getting smarter lately myself, like I've been able to plan things out and think faster, and really get what I want more easily."

"In that case, you should do your own schoolwork then." I pointed out.

"Hey, I have money, I'll use the money." She said, sticking her tongue out at me slightly.

"Are you two ready to order?" The waiter asked, and I jumped

"Oh, yup, I'll have the bruschetta, with a caprese salad please." Marissa said politely.

"And... I'd like the e'egplant lasagna!" I said, finally deciding

"Very good, and what compression rate will that lasagna be at?" he asked

I looked at the menu, compression rate? What? "Uhhhh..."

"She'll have it at 95%, please." Marissa said for me.

"I'll be back shortly, thank you very much." the waiter said, bowing and walking away.

I looked at Marissa "What's compression rate?"

She sighed and pointed at me "You compressed 94.22%, that's *your* compression rate. That means you need food that's as close 94.22% compression rate as possible or you won't be able to digest it. Generally speaking, compressed food comes in 50%, 75%, 85%, 90%, 95%, 97%, and 99%. I buy you the 95% kind."

"What about people who only compressed like, 20%?" I asked "And why do the numbers get closer together the further it goes?"

She shook her head "See, under 50%, there's so little difference in your body that you can mostly just eat human food, or just stick to 50% stuff, no problem, so there's no market for anything under 50%. As for the larger numbers, as you compress smaller, even if the percents don't go down as much, the relative scale does. Say there's someone with... 99% compression, ok? Only less than 5% more than you, right? But *you're* 4 inches, and that person would be closer to... a half inch? They'd come up to *your* shin, so like. 12% or something the height of you, so relative to you, they're 88% smaller, even though they're only 5% smaller to everyone else, so the difference in the food is super important, you have to be very, very careful to feed class Bs the right compression."

I stared at her in shock. "You, like, just knew all that? Off the top of your head? Was that in the class?"

She looked away. "Some. Some I learned on my own, the companies selling the food I buy you put out a lot of documentation about it. I care about you, and this stuff is the difference between you being healthy and your bones shattering from lack of nutrients or something."

"Yeah, I guess so..." I said, feeling weird inside again. It felt special, almost safe or cozy to have her know this much about me and care, but it felt wrong to feel good about her at all...

"Anyway, I think this meeting thing will be good for us, honestly." Marissa said "It'll give us a better perspective, and maybe help us to like, I don't know, understand stuff from other people's point of view?"

Well yeah," I said "I think that's the point of these things... How open should we be, by the way?"

"Uh, yeah, uhhh... Don't mention like, the kisses, or like, I don't know?" she said, frowning "It's hard to know, just, like, feel it out. I don't think they can take you away from me there? But like, we can't get help if we pretend everything's ok."

"Hm, ok." I said. I'd have to be careful, I guessed. I wondered if the meeting would actually offer help, or if it'd just be another way to let Marissa brag about owning me.

~~~

"Hi, we're here for the thing?" Marissa said awkwardly to the lady at the front desk.

"You mean the support group?" she asked "Of course! It's down the hall, you'll drop off your little friend with the person in the room with a green door, and you'll be in the room across from it!"

"Wait, we're doing the support group together, why are we in different rooms?" Marissa asked, alarmed

"Yeah, shouldn't we be together so we can get support?" I asked.

The lady shook her head "Oh, no, see they found that by separating the class

Bs from their guardians, both parties can speak more freely and get some things off their chests they wouldn't be able to otherwise!"

"I really don't know if I'm comfortable giving up Amber like that though..." Marissa said, holding me a little closer to her

"She'll be perfectly safe, I promise!" the lady assured her "They've got lots of precautions, I assure you, none of the class Bs have been hurt while here!"

Marissa looked at me and sighed, nodding. "Ok, but if she even has a chipped nail, I'm bringing the full legal force of LundCorp down on this place."

The woman looked confused and concerned, but nodded anyway. I patted Marissa's finger and pointed down the hall, pushing her to go ahead and go. She looked at me for a long moment, then nodded and started down towards the rooms.

"I feel weird and nervous about this..." she muttered as she passed me over to the guy at the green door "I really don't like it..."

"She'll be juuust fine, I promise!" The man said, gently taking me from her. "I'll put her with the others, it'll be nice!"

Marissa watched as he brought me over to a wide, shallow box on a table, setting me inside. I could still see the shelves and colorful posters on the walls from the after-school program this room usually housed, but the door was blocked. Me and Marissa were officially separated. I looked around at the other class Bs in the box with me, surprised at the variety. There were around 5 or so of them, and the tallest was twice my height, and the smallest came just up to my knee. I took a seat in one of the dollhouse chairs sitting around, finding one that was mostly my size, and I looked around as I fixed my kimono.

"Hello, newcomer, are you freshly compressed?" asked a lady about a third bigger than me

"I mean, uhh, just over a week, I guess." I said, unsure

"Oh wow, that's really new, you're already having problems?" The knee high girl said "Usually there's a honeymoon period of at least most of a month before the class B and the guardian realize how hard it is."

"Mm, well, we thought this was going to be different." I explained "We thought we'd be in the group at the same time?"

"That doesn't work, no." A man who barely fit into his chair said "The class Bs get talked over, and the guardians just dominate the whole time, it's not productive."

"Alright then, tell us a bit why you're here, hun." The first lady said "I'm Nada, we all see each other twice a week, we usually just chat, but if you're here, looking like a doll on a shelf, I'm guessing you've got some serious issues, huh?"

I looked down at my outfit. "Oh, no- this is- me and Marissa picked out each other's outfits today. She wanted to make sure the pocket I rode in was comfortable this time."

"You ride in her *pocket*?" A young man about my size asked "That's SO dangerous, you need to stop that."

I shook my head "No, it's usually fine and cozy, but, ah, yesterday she was wearing skinny jeans, and..."

The smallest girl hissed and shuddered "Oh gods, that sounds horrible..."

"Hun, if you need any of us to contact someone..." Nada said, concerned

"No, no, that's why we're here, to work things out. She was just being a little rough, she didn't know it was as bad as it was, I swear." I said. I felt odd defending her, but I couldn't risk being taken away.

"So you mentioned she was being rough," A shorter man with glasses said "does she have a *habit* of being rough?"

"Um..." I said, thinking.

"That's a yes then." Nada said for me. I nodded slowly.

"I see you're wearing bandages under that lovely dress," The tallest man said "was that her as well?"

"Oh... no, this was an accident." I said "I was getting drinks for her and my friend and I spilled it on myself, it was my fault."

"It was her fault for making you GET the drinks in the first place, obviously." The tiny one said crossing her arms "We're not slaves, we're supposed to be cared for, not ordered around."

"Babae, not everyone has guardians like yours, your situation is very rare." Nada said gently.

I looked over at her "What situation?"

Nada laughed "Babae's guardian treats her like a queen, lets her run her entire life. She's our resident princess, the only well-to-do class B in the group, really."

I blushed. "Uh, well, my guardian is the heiress to the LundCorp company, she's *very* well off. She literally bought me with her allowance."

"We don't say 'bought' here." The glasses man said "We prefer to say 'paid the adoption fees'."

"Still, that's very impressive!" the boy my size said "I bet you have one of those fancy houses, huh?"

"Markus, that's rude." Nada said admonishingly. "Just because her guardian has money doesn't mean she spends it on- What's your name, hun?"

I realize I'd never introduced myself and stood up. "Oh, uhh, Amber, Amber Park. And yeah, she does spend money on me. A LOT of money actually. She bought everything the shop had when she picked me up, including a three story house."

I sat back down. Was I supposed to stand when I introduced myself? No one else was, I may have missed that part...

"Whoah, holy shit..." Babae whispered "Even *I* just have an apartment suite."

"So she's rough and thoughtless, but she also fawns over you?" The tall man said "I'm Arnold, by the way, it's nice to meet you, Amber."

"Likewise." I said "Um, no? She really wants me to like her, like, I think she has a crush on me, from what she said, but she really likes the feeling of being mean to me too, it's hard."

"The feeling of being mean?" Nada asked "What do you mean?"

I shrugged helplessly "I don't know, she just... likes playing rough with me, but she doesn't want to hurt me hurt me I guess."

"That sounds dangerous." the glasses man said "Especially if she really does have a crush on you, class Bs and class As are not good fits romantically. My wife, she had to give me up after 6 months, just having me, being that close to me, but not being able to express her love or be with me in any meaningful way, it tore our relationship apart..."

"Paul here has had three guardians in the past three years." Nada explained to me. "His second one lost her license for using him illegally in films, he's had a rough experience with 'love' at this size."

"Huh, I don't know if that'll be an issue for me?" I said "Marissa seems to just want to like, toss me around and smush me a bit, she doesn't seem to want anything more. My friend Henri on the other hand though...."

"Henry?" Babae asked "Ooh, drama, do tell, please!"

"I guess..." I thought of how to describe her "She's been my best friend since the beginning of high school, but ever since I compressed she's gotten super clingy and obsessive. She tried to kidnap me from Marissa a couple times even, and she confessed her love for me and everything."

"Ooooh," Markus said "two girls fighting over another girl..."

I wrinkled my nose. "It sounds gross when you say it like that."

"Yeah, don't be a creep, that's her life you're talking about." said Paul in a hard tone.

"And how do *you* feel about the situation?" Nada asked. I got the feeling she was the de-facto leader of the group.

"Well, Henri is my best friend, but I almost feel safer around Marissa at this point. Then again, Marissa is a wildcard, she could just decide to squeeze me or play with me too hard, or put me in a tight pocket for hours, and she wouldn't even care. I... I really don't know."

"Would you say you trust Marissa more?" Arnold asked "I have two guardians, one is very sweet, she dotes on me and brings me with her everywhere, and loves me very much, but she'll forget I'm on her shoulder, or forget to feed me, or even just leave me places by mistake. My other guardian, her sister, couldn't care less about me, and never interacts with me past a few words, but when she's responsible for me, I always feel safe and secure. She never forgets anything or puts me in danger, and always remains aware of me the whole time. I love my primary guardian, but if I had to pick, her sister is the *better* guardian."

"I- yeah, I understand that." I said. "Marissa *is* the better guardian. Henri is scaring me, and she dropped me in soup once. Marissa has never dropped me ever, unless it was on purpose."

"It's extra not good if she's dropping you on purpose, you know." Babae pointed out.

"What kind of soup was it?" Markus asked

"Uhh, like, pho?" I said

"Nice, I love pho." he said "Did you eat any of it? Like, try to eat your way out?"

I shook my head "What? No, it was uncompressed, I'd get sick."

He shrugged "I eat regular food all the time, I don't get sick."

"No, it's- it's on the news, and I ate like two bites of a tortilla and got a stomachache, how are you eating regular food?" I asked, confused

"That's not entirely accurate," Paul said "I eat regular food too, from time to time, in doses. I haven't gotten sick from it in a long while."

"I *only* eat regular food." announced Babae "on that super compressed junk, I was wasting away, there's no nutrients in it. My guardian gave me some broth on my deathbed and I perked right up, now its all broth, cream, honey, and juice."

"She's on an all liquid diet, because of her size." explained Nada "We think it's because she's not eating solids that she's not being hurt by an exclusively uncompressed diet, but we don't know."

"That shouldn't be possible..." I muttered, thinking about all the articles and videos I'd seen about class B digestion, about the conversation I'd just had with Marissa.

"We're still being understood, you see" Paul explained "in a way, we're all lab rats. We won't really know anything about our new biology for years and years."

"Anyway, more about your problem, Amber, you mentioned you and Marissa wanted to come here to work through something together?" Nada asked, probingly.

"Right." I said. "We wanted to talk about her urges, and her feelings about me, but it feels weird to talk about that without her."

"It's good to talk about it," Paul said " but I think that both her urges and her feelings are both red flags, to be honest."

"I don't want to be taken away though, I can't risk being bo- uhh 'adopted' by someone worse." I said

"That might be a risk you have to take, Amber." Nada said sadly.

"I've heard horror stories..." I said "But you all sound like you have ok guardians, is it really that bad?"

"You have to understand," Arnold pointed out "bad guardians don't usually take their class Bs to a support group. We're a poor sample to pull from."

I looked at my feet. The weird white socks with the one toe hole in them was bugging me, but I knew that was only a distraction from what was *really* bugging me. "Well... Marissa took me here, so she's got to be at least some good, right?"

"She said she likes being mean to you?" Babae pointed out "That's like, classic bad guardian right there."

"It's a game, like, she'll put me under her pillow when I sass, or she'll uhh, smush me on the carpet when I talk back..." I said, downplaying the severity.

"That sounds *mostly* playful." Paul admitted "Has she ever gone farther than that?"

I thought about the ice water, the constant squeezing, the threats. "No, once she flicked me, and it hurt, but once she realized it actually hurt, she hasn't done it again."

"At least she can learn." Arnold pointed out "I think that's a good sign that she might not be as bad as she seems."

"Now, I want to call back to something you mentioned earlier, the jeans pocket?" Paul pointed out "That seems like a big deal if that's why you're here, was that just her being mean too?"

I made a face "Yeah, she wanted to be mean and keep me smushed. Posted a picture on her social media of my outline in her pants and stuff, it wasn't cool."

"Ok, and it hurt you badly enough to warrant coming here?" he asked

"I passed out, yeah, and I had a meltdown and-" I thought about the argument, I couldn't tell them I'd said *that*... "I ended up chewing her out and telling her I was scared of her."

"That's so fair, I'm scared of my guardians." Markus said "I legit never know if they're gonna blow up at me or buy me a treat."

"Markus, your guardians are your mom and dad." pointed out Babae "That's pretty normal, it's nothing to do with you being compressed."

He laughed "Yeah, and I don't exactly make it easy on them."

"I miss my parents..." I said, thinking of my mom's cooking, my dad's kind attitude, the feeling of safety...

"They couldn't afford you?" Nada asked gently

"They- they could, they were on their way to the store with the money, but- but Marissa got there first, and..."

"Oh, wow, that's rough, she must have *really* wanted a class B if she swooped in and grabbed you out from under their noses like that." Markus said, raising his eyebrows.

"No- well, yeah, she really wanted a class B, but..." I remember her phrasing

"...I think she made sure to get there first more because it was me, like, specifically me."

"You knew her before she adopted you?" asked Nada

I nodded. "Yeah, she went to the school I did. She, um... bullied me, for most of my teenage life."

"Oh, that's not good." Arnold said, his eyebrows raised "She wanted to adopt you to bully you more?"

"...She bullied me because she wanted to be close to me, I think." I said, blushing.

"That sounds kinda nice, actually..." said Markus.

"Markus, please stop talking for now, ok?" Nada said firmly, shaking her head at him. "Now, Amber, We're all pretty good at understanding problems, but yours seems a little more complicated. I think we can work out the best way to move forward though, and I don't think it sounds like you *need* to get away from Marissa, but you do need to be very, very careful. Now, what I recommend is-"

The door to the room banged open and I heard stomping sounds.

"Miss, you can't get her yourself, there's-" the man who'd carried me in started

"Shut the FUCK up, she's mine, I'll get her if I *fucking* want." I heard Marissa growl.

Everyone in the box braced themselves, and Babae clutched her chair in fear. Marissa peeked over the box, looking around at the little people, a deep glare on her face.

"Amber, say goodbye, we're getting the fuck out of here." her eyes fell on Babae "Holy shit, I didn't know you guys came that small... I mean, I *did*, but seeing you, gods, Amber got lucky..."

I stood up "Marissa, we're in the middle of the meeting, what's going on?"

"Ma'am, please, allow me to-" the man said, but Marissa shoved him back.

"Those people couldn't support a tent, they're fucking stupid. *I* know I care about you, I don't need their stupid fucking name calling and shit. Come on, we can watch those old people shows you like, and you can tell me what's so great about them."

I looked at the others, slightly embarrassed "Uhhh. I think I have to go, it was nice meeting you?"

"Here, take this, it's my messaging info." Nada said, passing me a card out from a bag under her chair "I'd love to talk more, later, ok?"

I nodded and took it, climbing into Marissa's waiting hand. She glanced down at the other 5 class Bs, and let her gaze rest on each one individually.

"Sorry for interrupting your meeting, your guardians suck. Maybe get new ones or something." she said, in an almost-polite tone.

"I'm... guessing we're having another car talk?" I asked as she walked down the hallway, pushing past the worried guardians outside the door.

"Yeah, whatever. We're getting to make a habit of it, why break that habit now?" she snarked, steel in her voice.

I shivered and leaned against her stomach as she held me to herself.

As we left the building, she looked down. "Hey, I'm mad, but not at you, ok? Me and you are cool, nothing weird."

I looked up, surprised. I'd assumed that was the case, but to have her make sure I knew showed a genuine care to build trust. Maybe this meeting wasn't as bad for her as she'd thought. She climbed into the car, and flopped over, laying down across all three seats, and dropped me in front of her face.

"Take us home, Drew. Close the thingy." she said, popping a breath mint from her purse into her mouth. "So... you wanna go first?"

"Well, I didn't get far, we just talked about me and you a bit, they didn't say much I didn't already know."

"Yeah? Like what?"

"Just, like," I thought about keeping it to myself, but I could tell she wanted to hear, and if she was willing to work on it... "they said I needed to be careful around you, and that you had a lot of red flags."

She snorted and blew her now-icy breath at me "Well *I* could have told you *that*."

I tipped over as the car hit a bump, and her hand snapped forward to cup me, holding me in place. Her expression didn't change, and she didn't make any indication she'd moved other than her hand.

"You gonna contact that lady?" she asked, referring to the card in my kimono

"Her name is Nada, and yeah, I think so, she was very sweet."

Marissa hummed "Well... Just remember I can see what you talk about and stuff, if I want."

"Yeah. I'm aware." I said, mildly insulted she'd reminded me.

She noticed my tone. "It's not like that, come on. It's a safety thing, she could be part of a class B liberation group or something."

"I really don't think she is." I said.

"Yeah, well. I don't know. Let me feel powerful in this little way, ok?" she said, her thumb rubbing my back.

I leaned into it. "Yeah, the urges or whatever, I got it. So I'm guessing your meeting went a lot worse than mine?"

"Oh *gods*. One lady told me I was a 'monster', and another tried to tell me to give you up to the state, and this couple were so fucking mad that I 'took you from your family' that they told me to leave, and to leave you here with *them*."

"What did you tell them?!" I asked incredulously

"Everything, really. The urges, my feelings towards you, the thing with the pocket, Henri, all of it. I wanted them to give me a fix for it, so I said it all."

Her feelings towards me... When she wasn't confessing, the words slipped out so easily, like they didn't carry any weight, like they were assumed. I looked at her face, covered in shadows in the dim car, and tried to see her the way she saw me. I could see so much more of her now, emotionally. I could see her depth, I'd seen her tears, her struggles. It was an alien feeling, but I was starting to feel like I wanted to be around her, despite her flaws, if she could only stop *hurting* me. Every time I felt like I could get close to her, she...

"You're doing that thing you do." she said, jarring me out of my thought.

"What thing?" I asked

"You get all worried looking and go quiet, and your face kind of freezes. You've done it for years."

I shook my head "No, sorry. I just get lost in thought."

"It's fine. What were you thinking about this time?" she asked softly

"..." I was scared to say it, but if she was aware of it, hopefully she'd stop. "I was thinking how I'm starting to get you more. Like, as a person. And how every time I think we can be cool and just exist together, you... get urges, and it ruins it."

She hissed, her breath sharp "Oh, ow, yeah..."

"It's just, I think we could be really close, you're like, my guardian, you're providing for me, you keep me safe, most of the time. It'd be so, so easy to like you, if you didn't scare me so bad every time my guard was down."

Her grip tightened for a split second, and relaxed. "I know, but- gods, you're just so- I need you to understand, I want that too, I need you to be close to me, ok? I need that. But... When I see you being all adorable and soft, or just weak in general, I just want to *squeeze* you, I don't know why..."

"I don't like being squeezed, Marissa." I said firmly.

"Ok, ok, it's not all bad, right? The feeling of being overpowered by me? That's gotta be kinda fun, right? I'm sure a lot of people would love it." she said hopefully.

I thought about it. "I don't know, I'm so scared of you it's mostly just scary when you do that?"

She groaned "Ok but I won't really *hurt* you. Knowing that?..."

"But you *did* hurt me, you bruised me, you got me sick, you suffocated me, you did actually, actively hurt me."

"Granted, but I won't *now*." she said exasperated "I'm like, trying to win you over or something."

"I don't know. I'd have to see. I'd need to be in the right setting, and it'd have to be in a very safe place, and I really would prefer it have rules and stuff like in the books."

"Wait, what books?" she asked

"The romance books, like with the-" I realized who'd recommended those books to me "...oh, well, I guess the S and M books..."

Marissa sat up slightly, her white teeth shining in the darkness. "No *way*, you read that shit?"

I shook my head "No! Henri told me about her favorite books, I read some, it's not my thing."

She lay back down, giggling at me "Interesting, tell you what, let's get home, get the school and judgement washed off of us, and before we watch those shows of yours, we test and see if maybe you can't have fun while I'm having fun too."

I jolted "Tonight?! No, I'm not ready for that, I can't, I'm not that kind of person, I just-"

She stroked me softly. "Hey, hey, no no no, just playing, just a little game, nothing like what you're imagining, just a fun game, and you'll be in full control ok? Just to see if you like it"

I was shaking, the stuff I'd read in Henri's books were *not* things I was comfortable doing with Marissa, I imagined how it could work, and I couldn't picture it, it ended in disaster in my imagination every time. My heart was pounding and I felt a panic attack coming on, but I bit my lip to focus myself. If I let her do this, if we 'played' and I pretended to like it, then she could be a normal fucking person the rest of the time, and I could feel safer overall. Just let her get her urges out every so often in a special scenario that she claimed I'd have some control over, and be able to relax in my day to day. I felt dread at agreeing to anything like this, but I almost didn't have an option. I *could* say no, and I knew she'd respect it, she wasn't actually a monster, but I had so much to gain from saying yes, and she didn't even realize it.

I swallowed hard, tasting metal from my bitten lip. "Ok, yeah, let's do it, I'm interested too, I want to see how it goes."

Her eyes widened, and her smile grew wider, and she drew me in, rubbing me on her face.

"Oh, gods, Amber, you're going to love this, I'm *really* good at it!" she said, her hands shaking slightly.

As excited as she was, it was nice to see I wasn't the only one who was nervous.

~~~

I stood in front of my mirror, trying to calm myself down. I was wearing a loose sweater and a pair of soft pants, a casual, comfortable outfit. I had no idea what Marissa wanted to do, or what kind of playing she had in mind, but I was determined to get through this in any way I could. I wanted so, so badly to be able to be able to let my guard down and not be punished for it... I thought about what she'd said, that I was going to 'love it', and I sighed. I could *try*, but I'd never even thought about that sort of thing before, and the stuff in Henri's books always seemed so alien, like they had a language that I didn't speak.

I walked out of the bathroom and into my bedroom, facing Marissa's room. She was on her bed, in a t shirt and leggings, poking on her phone. I looked around her on the bed, looking for anything she might want to 'use' on me. They always had 'tools' in those books, spiky things, or flat things for smacking, whips, if the story was risqué enough, but the only thing on her bed was her. I coughed, but she didn't look up. I sighed, and whistled, and her head snapped up at me.

"Don't fucking whistle to me, I'm not a horse or a dog or something." she said as she came over, but there was no real annoyance in her voice.

"I didn't want to yell and make you think I was in danger or something." I said defensively "My voice goes all of like, 4 feet if I'm not screaming."

"Whatever, ok, so, are you ready?" she said, grinning

"Nnnnot really? I don't understand what we're doing exactly..."

She grabbed me around the torso and walked back over to her bed. "Well, let's go over it, shall we?~"

She dropped me onto the bed, and I let myself go limp, flopping onto the plush comforter. I rolled over and flinched as I saw her whole body looming over me, an excited smile on her face.

"I'm gonna have a little fun, and if you're having a bad time, you say 'red light', ok? And if you need a moment, you say 'yellow light'."

"What's green light for?" I asked

"It means keep going, but I'll assume if you don't use the other two, we're in the green, 'k?"

"That doesn't sound right, but ok. And if I can't talk?"

"Uhh, two taps or bites or something, and that's 'stop'."

"Wait." I said, alarmed "Bites? What situation would involve me having to bite you?!"

"Um, we'll have to see... Anyway, are you ok with that?" She said leaning in, her smile wide and her face taking up my whole range of vision.

I took a long, steady breath. "Ok, yeah, let's do it."

# Chapter 12.5
## A City of Plexiglass and Filament

Nada glanced up at her brother, sitting in the driver's seat and wondered how his part of the meeting had gone. On her end, she'd really wanted to talk to the new girl, Amber, more, but when her guardian burst in like that to grab her, all she could do was give her a card and hope for the best. The guardian wasn't the worst she'd ever seen, she'd met some class Bs with scars or missing fingers due to careless guardians, or even ones who'd stopped coming altogether, and she'd later heard through mutuals on AntMound that they'd died via accident. Amber wasn't in danger of dying, at least she didn't think she was, but the red flag of her guardian wanting to *date* her, mixed with the sadism... It wouldn't end well.

"So, I'm guessing Marissa busting in there like that scared you guys, huh?" Adil said, glancing down at her

"Well, it wasn't *too* bad." Nada replied "She was just upset, she was still careful."

"Yeah, that's good." Adil said "I feel bad for her class B, it can't be easy to live with her."

"I gave Amber my contact info, I'm sure she'll contact me if she's ok."

"Nada, you're not trying to get her on board with your ideas, are you?" Adil said tiredly

"I didn't discuss my ideas one time to her, no."

"Good, that's not the solution to everyone's problems, you know."

"If she seems like she's in danger, it could be an alternative, and her guardian is very well off, she could help bankroll if I get her on board too."

He laughed without humor "You really think a guardian who's in love with her class B will *pay you money* to found an apartment complex for class Bs? She'd never see Amber again, it's counter intuitive."

"If she really loves her, she'd see that being in a community of like-sized people would be the safest, best thing for her. If it takes off, we might not even *need* guardians anymore!"

Adil pulled into the driveway and shut the car off "You think anyone with power will agree?"

"I think we still have a voice, powerful people are being compressed, celebrities, it's- we have more power every day."

"May I carry you inside?" Adil asked automatically as he reached for the cupholder she was in. She nodded and he continued "The powerful people are stripped of their powers, the celebrities are either used by the companies they worked for to keep selling albums and movies, or auctioned off to fans for millions. The power you're talking about doesn't exist."

"I still think people will care..." she said "I can get support, I need to, for our sake."

"And what about your daughter, huh?" he snapped, unlocking the door "*She* can't live in your tiny utopia, you're just going to abandon her?"

"No, I-" she clenched her fists "She can visit, or- if she gets proper training, she could check me out for a couple hours, to do activities."

"Nada, you're describing *prison*." he said as the door opened "No one is going to want to willingly check themselves into prison."

"Adil, just *being* like this is a prison! At least this place would be *safe*."

"Ummi? Why are you talking about prison?" a voice asked from around the corner.

Nada flinched "It's nothing, sweetie, just- I was just discussing something with your uncle."

Adil brought her around the corner and set her on the short table her daughter Layla was sitting at.

"Well... you two should talk about it quieter, if you're not going to tell me what it was about." Layla said

"Sorry, we should have kept it at the support group." Nada said, nodding "What are you working on over there?"

Layla pointed at the small clunky electric car on the table, half apart with wires and broken plastic on the table around it "I'm trying to fix your car. I think I can get it working again, the board is in one piece, it's just the wiring and frame that got messed up..."

"That's- I'm proud of you for trying, sweetie," Nada said "But I'm not sure it's safe for me to be driving around on the floor. If you already stepped on it once while it was parked, what's stopping you from accidentally doing it again when I'm in it?"

Layla's face screwed up slightly and she bit her lip "I just feel bad for breaking it, I know it wasn't cheap..."

"Honey, we all make mistakes." Adil said, patting her on the back "We know you didn't mean to."

"I would just feel better if I could get it working again." she said. "Maybe we could have times that she's allowed to use it, so we don't accidentally kick it or something?"

'Allowed to use it'. A weight settled on Nada's heart. Her daughter, barely 14, was talking about what *she* was going to let *her* do. As much as Nada loved Layla, this wasn't motherhood. This was a bastardization of it. She'd gotten lucky her brother had been able to get custody of her and her daughter, but living here like this, with her daughter treating her like this, it almost made her wish they'd been separated, to preserve herself in her daughter's mind as a tall, protective mother figure, not a tiny non-human who needed to be 'allowed' to do things.

Layla had nothing but respect for her mother, which was a good thing in and of itself. She loved her and was gentle and quiet around her, and always made sure to do what she was told, but there was a layer of pity to it, and a feeling that *maybe*, if Nada was still her full sized self, Layla would be more willing to talk back, to break the rules, to let her room get messy now and again. Normal kid stuff, things everyone did growing up. In a way, Nada just existing was holding her daughter back from developing as a person, at least as far as Nada was concerned.

The class B apartment complex would fix all that. It could be built in a single unit in a strip mall and fit hundreds of class Bs, it could be heated and cooled easily, water would be cheap, all that would need to be done would be to pest-proof the area, fabricate the apartments- Nada was already working on interlocking 3D printable walls for that- and find class Bs to wire and plumb it out. It could be done in under six months, if she could get the right funding. She'd be founder of a new community, everyone would be safe, and her daughter would see her as a successful civil rights leader instead of a doll sized, fragile, former person.

"Well, if you think you can fix it, I say go ahead and try!" Nada said "Even if I only use it sometimes, it'll be a good project for you!"

"I borrowed the soldering iron from my after school club, so I can get most of it done tonight, I think." Layla said

"Uhh, let's put down a wet towel, if you're going to be soldering stuff." Adil said, slightly concerned

"I have a mat I can use, Uncle, it's ok." she said, pulling a rolled rubber tube out of her bag.

She unfurled it, and lay it out on the table, air puffing out from under it and blowing Nada's hair back, threatening to knock her over. Nada's stomach curled, a simple mat, a silicone placemat, and she'd almost been blown away. This wasn't any way to live, to exist. This world wasn't made for her, she *needed* to have an environment she could thrive in, not just one where she had people taking care of her all the time. She closed her eyes and tried to calm down, this wasn't productive, this wasn't helpful, she needed to stay here for now, build up a network and find support.

"Adil?" She asked "Could you bring me to my desk for a while? I'd like to check my tablet and see if Amber texted me yet or not."

He held out his hand and she stepped into it, and he lifted her up, walking over to the little desk she'd made into a makeshift home.

"I could have brought you, Ummi..." Layla said "I like getting to hold you."

Nada tried to hide her cringe, and stepped off Adil's hand next to my chair and waved over at her "Next time, love!"

Nada hated her daughter holding her. It wasn't as bad when it was Adil, they'd grown up together, he'd seen her as an equal her whole life, even looked down on her a little as older brothers are wont to do, so him carrying her, holding her, taking care of her, it wasn't painful, it felt almost normal. When *Layla* did it, it made her feel so, so much more useless than usual. She couldn't care for her daughter outside encouragements and kind words, but here she was lifting her up and bringing her miles worth of distance just to sit with her while she made a sandwich or watched a movie. It was nice to still be included in her life, but it still made Nada feel worthless, disgusting, even. She wasn't a mother, she was a parasite.

She picked up her tablet and powered it on. It was older, she needed a new one, but they were so much money, and even now that she could eat larger amounts of uncompressed food, Adil still insisted on getting her the expensive, high vitamin compressed stuff too. A new tablet just wasn't in the picture right now, so slow loading times and a fuzzy screen would have to be put up with for now.

After what felt like forever, her screen lit up, and she pulled up her messaging app. A couple of messages from her AntMound friends, but none from any accounts she didn't already know. Amber would message when she was ready, she was sure. Really though, she wanted to check her posts and listings on the social media side of things... So far she had around a hundred and fifty class Bs interested in her apartment complex, and at least twenty of them were fairly local. The threads she'd started weren't 'popular' like the ones about compressed celebs or new bills being passed, but she had regular posters who gave ideas and were helping her nail down details.

One person had suggested that they have their own currency, and have shops and spas and things, and while she liked the idea of replicating a real- *a class A city*, that clashed with her plan of having the residents working as a remote tech company for hire to pay for the costs. She admitted that maybe not everyone had a degree in computer science like *she* did, but they could learn, she'd taught low level classes at the community college before- in the past, she could help these people too, she was sure. Still, some of the older members might be hard to teach, maybe having some non-tech positions around the complex would be good too. Just to make sure everyone was doing her part.

She started a new message, and uploaded the STL files for the walls she'd been working on this afternoon before group. They weren't perfect, but she'd added channels for the pipes on one side, and wire on the other, and was trying to find a way to make snap-on covers for the channels so people weren't seeing pipes and wires in their home, but it looked like anything with clips small enough for a class B to pop on and off themselves would break too easily. Hopefully someone would have a solution, but she was drawing a blank.

One member had asked if there would be a 'state religion' in the complex, but she brushed it aside, there was no place for that discussion in her utopia, people could do what they wanted, of course, but anyone who tried to push their religion would be politely asked to leave. Or not so politely, if they refused. Maybe one of the jobs people could have in the complex would be security? She'd be a fool to think that there'd be no crime, of course, and with some residents up to six times bigger than each other, it could be useful to have some of the more meaty residents keep the peace...

Fuck, this really *was* becoming a prison, wasn't it?... Still, as long as everyone was safe, and she wasn't forcing them to do anything, it'd be ok. She could live with security guards.

"Ummi?" Layla asked from in front of her

Nada looked up, she hadn't even heard her come over, she was so careful and quiet these days...

"Yes, love?"

"Uh, I haven't fixed the frame and plastic parts, but I think I got the motor working again? I put all the wires back, and it's getting power, but my fingers won't fit into the car to push the pedals, can you help me test it?"

Nada looked around for Adil, but he'd gone, up to his room, she'd guessed, or to the shower. She steeled herself, and smiled "Of course! Let's do it on the floor, though, just in case."

She could just imagine the car lurching the wrong way, sending her over the edge of the desk to her death...

"Ok, may I lift you to put you on the ground?" Layla asked

"Yes, sweetie, be gentle."

There was no need to say that, not really. Layla was *always* careful, but it still gave her a feeling of power. *She* was telling Layla to do that, and that proved she was still the mother.

That clashed with the idea that Layla only obeyed out of pity, but Nada didn't care, she took her victories where her mind would let her. She touched the floor lightly, and opened her car door, the cracked and bent frame above her making her wince. The top of the car had crushed in right above where her head would have been... She was lucky she'd been out of the car by then, climbing the stairs behind her desk to get some reading done. The crunch and Layla's resulting scream still made her nauseous though, and she couldn't see herself driving much anymore aside from this test run.

She slid into the seat, and flicked the power on, the light hum letting her know the power was working. She lightly tapped the gas, and the car jumped forward, startling her slightly as it always did. She drove forward, going past Layla's legs, under the table, and back around in front of her. She parked, and powered the car off, got out, and walked over to Layla's knee, giving her a big smile and thumbs up.

"It works wonderfully, honey! I'm proud of you!"

Layla's face lit up, and she grinned, showing her teeth. "I guess my after school club is paying off!"

Nada climbed into her hand and let her take her back to her 'home', and climbed off her, turning to look at her. Praising was a motherly thing to do, and she was happy about it, so that was good, that's *two* small victories. Whether or not those victories outweighed being carried by her though... that was a different matter.

"It really is, you'll be building robots in no time!" Nada said encouragingly.

"Or..." Layla looked nervous "Or- maybe if I'm good enough at it, I can be the one to wire your apartments?"

Nada stopped on her way to her chair and turned to look at her "...Oh?..."

"Yeah, like- I thought- I know it's important, I thought I could help, and maybe, I don't know, I can't help with money, but I can do the work, maybe?"

"Well..." This was sweet of her, but the point of it was to prove to Layla that she was still just as important and capable as anyone, if Layla was doing parts of it herself... "Honey, I think you have to be licensed for that, but if you do get licensed, I'd love for you to help!"

"I can be a licensed apprentice in less than two years, as long as I have someone I'm working under, I think I can do it for you..."

"That's amazing!" Nada's heart sank. Two years, that was her deadline now, she'd need to push hard to get it done by then. "I look forward to seeing you work toward that!"

Layla smiled again and picked up the car "I'll fix the frame and stuff now, it should just be pliers and glue, I'll be done tonight or tomorrow!"

Nada watched as she walked back to the table to work, and sank back in her chair. She checked her tablet, still no message from Amber, maybe later. She *really* wanted to try and get some kind of funding, and this really could be the break she needed, if Marissa was generous with her money. Maybe Amber didn't even need to *live* in the complex, just visit now and then, maybe get a space away from Marissa, like a vacation home? That was good, that's how she'd sell it to them, it'd all work out, and she'd be the strong, independent mother she used to be.

In the meantime, she could still find people on AntMound to support her too, and this past evening had given her just the idea she needed to get more people on her side. She opened the documents tab, and started typing, she'd have it done by tomorrow, and include a link to her thread. She wrote the name of her new article; "The Dangers of Transit: The Necessity of Walkable Spaces for Class Bs"

This would be *perfect*, she'd get so many new readers from this, she could already tell. In the background, Layla was hard at work herself, just as focused, just as desperate for support and connection. The two of them worked into the night, neither interacting with the other, but each of their minds full of thoughts of each other all the same.

## Chapter Thirteen

My heart was pounding in my chest as Marissa slowly lifted her hand over me, her fingers over my face, with gaps for me to see her above me. Why had I agreed to this? I knew *why*, but gods, was I stupid? Her hand pressed into me, and I felt her adding pressure, pushing the air out of me with her palm. I clenched my stomach and braced against it, my body tense and hard as she pushed harder and harder. It didn't *hurt*, but it was making it hard to breathe, and I was shoved deep into the comforter, the soft fluff making a wall around me. I pushed against her with my hands, struggling to keep her off, but her palm was too strong. How could something so soft be this hard to budge?

"Remember, if you need a break, you have the power~" she said, tauntingly.

I realized I was holding my breath, and tried to suck in more air and she rocked more of her weight over onto her arm, pressing me even harder. I didn't think I could talk at this point without losing what little air I had, so I wrestled a hand free and smacked the side of her hand. She had to stop now, right? That was the rule, she had to get off, why wasn't she- The hand pulled off me and I gasped, coughing and rolling over. I had thought she wouldn't, she took so long, I just- I closed my eyes and focused. It'd been less than a second after I patted, it wasn't that long, she'd listened, it was ok, I was ok.

"You good?" she asked

I flipped over and looked up at her. She had that mean, smug look on her face, and was walking her hands towards me with her fingers, her towering body still a wall between me and the rest of the world.

"I'm- yeah..." I said, still out of breath "I just- I need to breathe."

"Fiiiine~" she said, fake annoyed "You're fun to crush, you know that? You strain so hard but you're still so small and soft, it feels *so* good..."

"I'm glad you're having fun then." I said, giving her a look.

"But are *you* having fun yet?" she asked

I shook my head "I-I still need to get used to it for now..."

"Ok, well... try to see me as an unstoppable force, and just let the feeling of helplessness fill you up." she said "I want you to try and *enjoy* the feeling of being unable to stop me, but remember, you *can* stop me, so... it's ok to have fun, ok?"

That sounded... backwards, and wrong, but I nodded. She smiled and scooted more forward on the bed, her fingers 'walking' up to me again. Her fingernails were short and unpainted, but they were just long enough to poke over the edge of her finger. Using that edge, she pushed me to the comforter again, and 'walked' across my legs, up to my torso with her nails. I felt the hardness, the slight pain, and watched them make lines on my skin. If she wanted, she could press just a *little* too hard, and my literally paper-thin skin would tear open.

My heart rate was going up again, and I lay back as the fingernails made it to my ribcage. I tried to control my breathing, watching her as she slowly, slowly worked up to my chest, pushing my sweater up. I tried to find the enjoyment in it, the feeling of being overpowered in the good way, but I was still so, scared. Her nail touched my left breast and I flinched, I couldn't, not yet, I-

"Yellow! Yellow light, yellow, sorry...." I yelled.

She pulled her hand back and pursed her lips.

"Can- can I flip over?" I asked

"I love watching your little face though..." she complained "Fine, flip over, we'll start again."

I rolled over onto my stomach, and gripped the bed, her nails walked up my body, pressing into me and making me shudder. I closed my eyes and thought about her, so much bigger, so much more powerful, the ability to smear me across the bed like a crushed grape if she wanted... It wasn't working, it was still too scary. Her fingers crawled up to my head, and rubbed me, smushing my face into the comforter. I rolled away, and stood up, feeling the pricks and tingles of all the places her nails had dug into me.

"Look at you, like a little tiger with all your stripes..." she cooed

I glanced down, and saw that she'd pressed and drug her nails hard enough to leave marks on my skin.

"Will- Am I going to bruise?" I asked, rubbing the marks. Maybe I should have put my bandages back on...

"Who knows!" she said "I don't think so..."

She leaned in closer "But how does it make you feel? All those marks on you? Knowing they're from me? They mean you're mine, you know..."

I thought about it "I mean, I already have this anklet that shows I'm yours, so I'm kinda used to the idea?"

She rolled her eyes "That's no fun, like, I want you to feel *intimidated* and like, *into* it."

"I get what you're trying to do..." I said "...but it's hard to feel any different when you really *do* own me, all the time."

She huffed. "Yeah, ok. Let's try..." She thought for a moment, then smiled. "Let's try role-play."

I frowned "Like, with dice and stuff?"

"What?" she asked "Why would we need dice? No, I'll be a mean hungry cat, and you'll be..."

I fought to keep the grimace off my face "...the rat, yeah, ok."

She giggled and got up on all fours. "I know my bed is pretty big, but there's still not much room to run and hide, you'll have to work hard!~"

Joke's on her, I do *cardio*. I took off at a dead sprint, and she laughed, snapping her hand out to slap at me. I tried to jump over it, but it hit my legs, tumbling me head over heels. I scrambled up and dashed forward again, I just had to make it to the pillows, I could get lost in them and she'd never-

Her hand slammed into the bed behind me, knocking me up into the air, her other hand snatching me as I fell. I braced myself for the squeeze, but it didn't come, instead, she rolled over onto her back and held me over her.

"You know... cats play with their food..." she said in a low, growly voice.

I hung there, looking down at her as her grin got bigger and bigger, her eyes sparking, her hair spread around her, and my heart caught.

She was... so cute like that, her face open, relaxed, no walls up, nothing between her and me... The feeling of being held, the knowledge that she was *using* me for her own pleasure mixed the feeling of safety, knowing she was trying very hard not to hurt me but still scare me. It felt... nice, almost.

I rubbed her soft hands around me and I started to get it. I wasn't supposed to like being bullied because it was *fun*, I was supposed to like it because it was *her*. She was horrible, she was scary, but she'd never hurt me if she could help it, this was a game, and as long as I played along, we could *both* have fun.

I swallowed hard and opened my mouth to tell her I understood, but her hand twitched and flicked upwards, launching me into the air.

I flailed for a split second before I felt her hands close around me again, pulling me down and tossing me up, over and over. My head spun, I was weightless, I felt myself fly up and drop into her soft hands over and over. It was like a roller coaster, and while I wasn't a big fan of coasters, this felt safer, because there was someone in control. I tumbled past her hand on the last throw and I jolted, had she missed me? I went limp and anticipated the impact, but found myself dropping into her other hand, on her chest.

I panted for air, and started to get up, when her hand flipped over, pressing me to her chest, right along her lower sternum. I felt her skin through her thin t-shirt and her warmth mixed with mine. I knew I was blushing, but I couldn't even feel it because her body heat was so strong. It felt right, being here, her hand over me. It felt much warmer and more secure than when she'd had me on her knee, or on her shoulder. A rumbling sound filled the air, and the surface under me shook. I realized she was *purring*, or at least, purring as well as a human could. Her voice was low, but it didn't quite get as low as it needed to be for a realistic purr, but the vibrations still felt good on my battered, tired body. I lay my head down and let the warmth and rumble soothe me. I could melt here, if she'd let me, just melt into a gooey puddle and fall asleep.

I felt the world shift and turn, and I rolled, falling to the side, dropping to the bed through the gap between her arm and chest. The bed shifted, and suddenly she was towering over me again, on her elbows with her face lowering down. Still purring, she pushed me into the bed with her face, rubbing against me with her cheek. I pushed back and stood up, holding myself steady with my hands on her face. She pushed into me with her nose and forehead, and I went over backwards again, on my butt with my hands behind me.

Her ever-present grin softened, and her lips pressed together, puckering lightly. I gasped, realizing what she was trying. She watched me carefully, waiting on me to say anything as she slowly drew closer. I almost wanted to, I was only doing this game to get her to stop hurting me, right? But as much as I *wanted* to want to tell her no, I just didn't, I craved this, in a way. I leaned onto my arms, and waited for her.

Even if she was horrible to me sometimes, she really did care about me. She made me feel *special*, in her own way, and I needed that feeling, I needed it to counteract the feeling of being a tiny, valueless subhuman. Even her *hurting* me was because she loved me. She could hurt anyone, but she cared enough about me to hurt *me*, to care for me in the only way she knew how. I wanted her to *stop* hurting me, of course. At least, I thought I did. In this light though, feeling her heat, her care and tenderness, seeing her in front of me trying her hardest to get me to care about her the way she cared about me, I couldn't help but feel a pang of something for her. Maybe not love, maybe not even trust, but something that made me want to be close to her all the same.

I closed my eyes as her lips touched me, they covered my face and chest, soft and so, so warm. I lifted my arms and held her cheeks as she held the kiss, letting her know I was returning it, even if she couldn't feel it. My chest fluttered, my head swam, and a million feelings at once buzzed around me. She was so much, everything around me, taking up my whole sensory scope with her being. I understood everything now, I wanted her to overwhelm me, to make me *love* her, to make me feel like I *belonged* there, with her. The smell of her cinnamon toothpaste mixed with her body scent, her skin, smooth and covered in tiny silky hairs, her blood, rushing through her veins, she was filling me up, and I couldn't stand it.

I broke away, and fell to the bed, my breaths heavy and slow. She hung there, her lips still pursed, for just a moment longer, then her grin returned. Her look was one of triumph, a look of victory. She knew she had me, she could see it in my face, she could feel it in my touch. She licked her lips, and bared her teeth, crouching over me, looking like she was about to-

Oh, right, cat.

I barely rolled out of the way as her teeth snapped closed where I was, or right above where I was? It couldn't tell. I went back to my original plan, make for the pillows. I didn't think I'd mind being caught now, but... I didn't want to just *give* myself to her. I dashed left and rolled under her next swipe, smiling to myself. It made me think of those video games with the big bosses, run, dodge, and roll to survive. I broke to the right as she slapped the bed again, and landed crooked, falling over in a heap. I pushed myself up, ready to run again when her fingers found my legs. I kicked, but she was holding me down for real, not letting me go. The chase was over.

She pulled in close again and breathed on me, the hot, humid air ruffling my clothes, and got her mouth right up next to me. I was panting, half from effort, half from anticipation, was she about to kiss me again? I closed my eyes and waited for the touch of her lips, but my shin twitched in surprise as something hot and wet touched it. My eyes opened, and I watched her lick up my leg, the tip of her tongue leaving a cold trail behind it, reminding me where it'd been. She reached my waistline, and used her tongue to slide up my sweater, licking my stomach gently. Her breathing was short and fast, her tongue felt firm and unyielding against my soft stomach and I felt dizzy from the contact. Just as she reached my ribcage, she stopped, and pulled away. Even though I hadn't said anything, she had remembered and respected my boundaries. Part of me was grateful. The other part of me wished she hadn't.

Her tongue flicked my cheek, and her right hand slid under me, sitting me up. Her face was so close I could see every detail, every single thing I was experiencing was her. Her mouth opened, her lips splitting apart and pulling back to show her teeth. She lowered herself over me, and my upper body went into her mouth. It was dark, and exceedingly humid, and her breaths in and out lifted and pushed my hair and clothes, but I didn't care, it felt right, to be like this, this kind of closeness felt like something I'd craved for *years*, and never even noticed it was missing. This level of human contact, this full-body hug, it felt so, so good, and so, so right, like the first rain after a drought. I pulled my arms inside her lips and let her close her mouth around me, my legs still on the bed.

The light was blotted out as her lips met around my stomach, and her tongue pressed me into the roof of her mouth. For a frozen moment in time, I felt a twinge of annoyance that I'd need another shower after this, but as I felt the pressure and texture around me, I stopped caring. Her jaw closed around my chest, her teeth closing on my ribcage, and my feet curled up in a mix of horror and satisfaction as her bite tightened. The air was growing thin, and the teeth were digging into my body. I tried to squirm, but she was clenched too tight. I could feel her shaking as her purring started up again, and I felt the bed under me shift as she clawed at the comforter. I felt something push too tight in my chest, and realized she was biting me so hard I couldn't breathe. I gasped as much as a could, and flailed, but my arms just met hard teeth and soft flesh, nothing gave.

I coughed out with what little air I had, not ready to end it, but unable to keep going

"R-red light! Red! Red!"

The teeth tightened ever so slightly, and held for just a moment, just long enough to worry Marissa couldn't hear me outside of my cage, then her mouth opened, and cool, fresh air rushed in. She lifted her head, and I fell over to the side, coughing and gasping as my lungs re-inflated. She flopped down beside me, looking at me with a soft, lazy look.

"So..." she whispered "did you like it?"

I took one last deep breath, and slowly nodded. I'd planned to lie either way, but... I really, actually understood it now.

"I get it," I said, panting "I get what you were saying, about trusting you, and having fun with it."

She giggled, and reached over, pulling my damp sweater up. I looked down, and saw a row of teeth marks on my chest, deep enough to leave a bruise.

"See that?" she asked, pointing

I nodded

She gently picked me up in her hand and I curled against her fingers, enjoying the contact. "*That* means you're mine~"

~~~

I lay on her chest, re-showered and clean after our little experiment. The TV was on low, playing an episode of Andy Griffith playing in the background. Marissa's dad had watched it with her when she was a kid, so she'd wanted to start there. I'd tried to talk to her about the long-reaching negative effects of this show as copaganga, but she didn't want to talk about that right now, so we just sat, relaxing. Her chest rose and fell under me, and her hand cupped me gently. We'd had a long day, and I for one was exhausted, but I wanted to stay up with her a while longer.

She rubbed me gently and laughed under her breath at the antics of the deputy, her hand stroking me like you would a cat. I listened to her heartbeat, slow and gentle, and I wonder if she really had gotten it all out of her system, if we could be normal for once. I thought about school tomorrow; we didn't share a class with Henri, but we might run into her. She'd gotten *very* scared at the idea of me having my leg blown off, so I couldn't imagine she'd try anything. Marissa's arm was still scratched, but it was healing pretty well, Henri might see that and get suspicious that there *was* no tracker, but would she risk it?

Speaking of Henri, I supposed I had an answer for her now. Or at least something of an answer? I couldn't imagine her taking it laying down, she'd make a fuss over it, but I had to trust that she'd respect me and my decisions. I shifted to look up at Marissa, and wondered how *she* saw our relationship, was it as owner and pet? Girlfriends? Friends with Benefits? Or did she just assume she'd get what she wanted, no labels needed?

"Hey, M?" I asked

"Mm, what's up?" she said, her voice thick with tiredness.

"What are we?"

Her breathing hitched, and she sat up slightly, moving me to sit in her palm so she could look at me. Her eyes traced over me with a curious fixation.

"...Why don't you tell me?"

I shook my head "I don't really know. I know you're in charge, and for now I'm ok with that, but I wasn't sure what we looked like past that."

She rubbed her face with her free hand and looked at the TV. "Fuck, Amber, isn't just knowing I'm in charge enough?"

"I guess I just-" I said "I was thinking about Henri."

She glared at me "What, like, while we were playing?"

I shook my head "No no no! Sorry, just- just now. I was thinking about her confession, and if I had an answer for her or not. I thought tonight might have given me that answer."

Marissa sighed. "Well we *did* go on a date to a fancy restaurant earlier, if *that* helps you figure it out."

I gasped "Holy *shit* that was a date, wasn't it?"

Marissa snickered "Yeah, it was pretty obviously a date. I took you to a fancy restaurant and bought you food directly after admitting I liked you. And *you* made me wear a fucking school pride hoodie to our first date, remember that."

"But..." I said "I was still scared of you then, does it even count?"

"You're not scared of me now?" she asked, tipping her hand like she was going to drop me

I clung to her fingers "Stop that, no, I'm- I don't know, I'm scared of you like I'm scared of roller coasters, I guess."

"Are you calling me mentally unstable?" she teased

"No, but you *are*?" I said "I was more saying that I'm scared of you, but... if it's going to be like it was tonight, it's a thrilling fear, not a bad one. I don't know..."

She set me on her stomach and started petting me. "So, all that in mind, what are we?" she prompted

"We- We're dating, kinda, I think? But it's like, I'm dating *you*, and you're *keeping* me?" I tried to puzzle it out "I think we're together because we need each other, but maybe it's not quite dating, more like..."

"Like?" she asked

"Ugh, I don't have a word for it..." I muttered. "I still don't know what we are."

"I'll tell you what I think then." Marissa said. "I think you're the girl I've had a crush on for years, the person I would kill for, my favorite toy, my brand new pet, my stress relief, and my new best friend, all in one tiny package. What that makes us? That's up to you, but that's what you are to me."

I sat quietly, thinking it over "In that case... You're my jailer, my protector, my provider, the girl I'm scared of more than anyone else, my favorite place to lay down on, and right now? You're my closest friend."

"Aww, I'm glad you like lying on me at least." She smushed my cheeks, and I flushed pink

"Yeah, you're warm. I am constantly *freezing* cold, your body heat feels like heaven, lying on you is one of the most comfortable things in the world."

"Well, even if being a glorified heated mattress is the best I have going for me right now, I'm glad you think of me as your closest friend."

"It's between you and Henri..." I muttered "and Henri is kind of scaring me."

"Yeah, she could have crushed you by trying to smash open the locker like that, and the whole wanting to kill me thing? Gods."

"Mm, that too, but-" I hadn't told Marissa about this, I wasn't sure if I should. It couldn't *hurt* though... "-she's moved into my old room, she's using my old stuff, wearing my old clothes, all that, trying to feel close to me or something. It's scary of a different level."

"Oh, shit, that's like, actually obsessed kinda shit." Marissa said sitting up further, making me hug her stomach to stay on "Your parents are ok with it?"

"I haven't talked to them." I admitted "They're not great with tech stuff, so I don't have a chance to talk past a few sentences, and I just found out about this Sunday night. I miss them, though."

"Hm, I'd say maybe we could go see them, but if Henri's living there..." Marissa trailed off

"Maybe we still could?" I said hopefully "You could go over there after practice on Thursday, you get off early, and we could go there straight from school. Henri usually goes to the gym after you go home, so there might be a couple hour gap?"

"You know my practice schedule?" Marissa asked, confused "I never saw you around, how do you know it off the top of your head?

"...Me and Henri liked to wait until after you finished to go to the gym, so we didn't run into you in the lockers. It paid to know when you'd be there"

"Oh, hm. I was wondering why I stopped seeing you down there..." she said sadly "I looked forward to it."

"Sorry... You tended to get up close and violent."

"I had to get up close somehow."

"...Oh."

She sighed "We have two days, we'll see about going to visit your family later."

"Thanks, just, I want to give them a heads up, so, um, by tomorrow night?"

"Yeah, I'll let you know." she said, turning back to the TV and settling down, putting me on her chest "Ugh, meeting the parents, that's always awkward."

I lay down, and rested against her as the show droned on in the background, my eyes feeling heavy, and my body still aching from the past week of non-stop excitement. I closed my eyes and let myself slip away into the night.

~~~

I woke to Marissa putting me on the sofa in my house. I yawned and rolled up to a siting position.

"Ugh, is it morning already?" I asked.

"Yup, just about." she said, looking at her phone. "I figure we'll eat in the dining hall again today. I've only got a couple classes, so we get to come home early, and we can do something fun?"

Her voice tilted up, like she was asking permission, but I wasn't sure if she wanted to 'play', or if she wanted to do something else. I pulled up my shirt to check my bruises, and saw that the teethmarks were still there, plain as day. I winced, and lowered my shirt.

"I think I'll need a while to recover before we have any more 'fun'." I said. I found myself almost feeling bad, I was sore and exhausted, but I wanted that connection and thrill from last night too.

"No, no, that's ok." Marissa said "Uh, I was thinking like, playing that one game I like? Or I could dress you up in different outfits and take pictures?"

"Oh, yeah." Being treated like a doll again... I *was*, in a way, and that didn't make me feel as gross as it would have a couple days ago, but I still got a strange, wrong feeling deep down when I thought about it.

"Anyway... get dressed, I picked out a nice blouse and skirt for you today, here." She set the items in question down on the couch. The skirt was long and pleated, and the blouse was fluffy and a rich blue color, with a low cut and short sleeves. "I remember you looking good in that blue thing you wore a while ago, so... blue."

"Do I get to pick your clothes again?" I asked, hopefully.

She stuck out her tongue "The hoodie's in the wash, no. You can make a request though, or you can go in the bottle, up to you."

"Ok, uhh..." I thought about it "I want to nap, actually, so anything that's good for napping."

Marissa thought about it "Let's see... it's a little early in the year for it, but I can make an exception, I have a nice wool cardigan with one of those pockets that's on the inside and the outside, you can go on the inside."

I thought about curling up in a soft wool sleeping bag that smelled like Marissa and my insides buzzed again. I was *not* used to feeling this way, especially not about *her*. "That sounds great, actually, sure."

"Perfect! I'll be back in a few minutes to pick you up."

I got dressed, and pondered my life. I'd gone through so, so much upset in such a short amount of time, it's like Marissa was a different person now, relaxed, happy, discussing things with me... I felt like I was betraying my past self by allowing myself to *like* her, but I just needed something safe, and if she could be that for me, I'd do whatever she wanted, even if she was the one I needed safety *from*. Today though, it'd give me a chance to see what life was like day to day, nothing weird, no plans, just school and home. I was looking forward to experiencing a normal day for once.

After getting to the school, Marissa made her way to the food hall, and ordered herself a salad and smoothie, and took her food to a table in the middle of the room, pulling me out of my soft, warm, cozy heaven and putting me on the cold, hard, bright table next to her food. I looked around, and didn't notice any faces I recognized, so I sat down and watched Marissa sip her drink. I remembered something I'd wanted to ask about, and scooted closer to her.

"You know, it's weird," I said "some of the class Bs in that group we went to said they could eat regular food without getting sick, one even had an all uncompressed diet."

Marissa frowned and shook her head "That's not possible, I've read up on it. Your guts can't break down the stuff in the food anymore."

"Yeah, and that tortilla you gave me made be sick too, but Babae said she almost *died* on compressed foods, and she only lived because her guardian fed her regular food."

"Hey, if you want to test it, be my guest, but not here. The school doesn't have bathrooms for class Bs, and I do *not* want to figure out how you can use a full sized one."

"No, uh ew." I shuddered thinking of all the things that could go wrong "I wasn't going to try, I was just making conversation I guess."

"Maybe you *should* try once we get home, it could be- Oh, hello Quince." Marissa's attitude and mood snapped back to her usual self in an instant.

"Don't 'hello Quince' me, I heard you having a perfectly good conversation until I walked up, that's just rude." Quince quipped, dropping a meat patty on the table and unwrapping it.

"I was talking to my pet, not you." Marissa said bluntly.

"Aww, I'd prefer to talk to her over you too, M, it's ok!" Quince said, poking me with her finger. "Heyyyy Amber, I love your little outfit, you look like a little artist!"

"Don't fucking touch her with your meat-hands, just let her sit, ugh." Marissa snapped.

"My 'meat hands'? As opposed to the ones I have made of stone?" Quince jabbed. It seemed she was used to Marissa's demeanor, and wasn't particularly bothered by it.

"I think she means because you're eating a pastry with meat in it." I offered, pointing.

"Oh, yeah, whatever, it's not *that* greasy." Quince dismissed

"I still don't want you touching her, the oil from our hands is *already*-"

"Oh hushhhhh..." Quince said, taking a bite "Ah too' th' sa'am cla'ss 'u di'."

Marissa looked around, annoyed. "Where the fuck are Tracy and Darcy today?"

Quince flapped her hand, swallowing. "Mm, Tracy is at her dad's work, he has her doing 'intern work' there for class credits now, and Darcy left for Europe a couple days ago."

"What the fuck?" Marissa said "I just saw Darcy for dinner Saturday and she didn't say *shit* about a European trip."

"No shit, maybe she didn't want you ruining it like you ruined her last one?"

"I didn't *ruin* it, I just happened to decide to go to the same hotel as her, she made it sound fun, fuck."

"You followed her on vacation?" I asked "That's wild. I thought *Henri* was bad."

"Oh, shut up, it wasn't like that." she said pushing me against the side of the cup her smoothie was in. The chill cut through my body and I gasped, scooting forward again, shaking slightly. Ok, so she wasn't all *that* different.

"Still, Tracy is doing intern work?" Marissa said "She can't even do her classwork, or afford to pay for it, like me, what's she even doing there?"

"Same old, you know, her dad wants her to take over when he retires in a couple years, so she's learning all his job stuff. Boring stuff for a boring bitch. Today is her first day, she was *terrified* when we talked earlier."

"I'm taking over *both* my parent's companies when I turn 26." bragged Marissa "Getting to run her dad's rinky dink bio studies lab isn't that impressive."

"Why 26?" I asked, fanning my damp shirt to dry it faster "That seems arbitrary."

"It's something to do with my graduation plan. I graduate, work under them, then they both give their companies to me after a set amount of time, and the two LundCorps become one again, and they make more money."

"Why do *they* make more money?" I asked "You'll be the owner, right?"

"They'll still be majority shareholders." Marissa explained

"Oh, ok." I said. I still didn't understand, but at that point I didn't care anymore.

"Gosh, she's so cute when she's all inquisitive..." Quince breathed, looking at me longingly

I wrinkled my nose at her breakfast breath and leaned back.

"Stop breathing on her, Quince." Marissa said "If you keep messing with her, I'm putting her away."

I *wished* she would put me away, I missed my pocket.

"Why do *you* care?" Quince sneered "You probably bully the fuck out of her yourself anyway. I can just see you putting her in your shoes, or like, taping her to a ceiling fan blade, or- I don't know, making her clean your bathroom or something."

I looked up at Marissa in alarm, she'd *better* not be planning on using any of those ideas...

"I *care*." Marissa said flatly "Because she's a $25,000 piece of property that gets sick extremely easily, broken at the slightest touch, or crushed by almost anything that falls on her, and I don't want to have fucking *wasted* all that money just to have you get her sick and die by breathing germs all over her."

"I really don't think they're that fragile." Quince said, but she lifted her head anyway.

"No, we really, really are." I assured her "I could be killed by a falling textbook or just falling from the table to the chair, please remember that when you adopt your class B..."

Quince looked at me, her face a mixture of boredom and 'd'aww', and pushed the rest of her breakfast into her mouth.

"I'll re'ember tha'." she mumbled around the food, standing up. She swallowed and glanced at Marissa "I've gotta go. We're still on for Friday night?"

"Yup, you, me, Tracy, Amber, and Henri." Marissa said. "Although I'm debating on if I'll actually have Henri over..."

"Oh you *got* to!" Quince said "An actual servant instead of one of those boring people in grey dresses that won't talk to you? It'll be so much fun!"

"I'm worried about a couple things..." admitted Marissa "But we'll see."

"You should see sooner than later." Quince said, jutting her jaw at something behind us. "She's been right behind you since I sat down."

Marissa and I both turned and looked. Sure enough, at the table behind us, wearing one of my sweaters and my favorite hat, was Henri, her phone out, recording us without any shame in her face.

I sighed and slumped. It just couldn't be a normal fucking school-day, could it?

## Chapter Fourteen

"*Gods**damnit* Henri, what the fuck are you doing?" Marissa growled at her

Henri held the camera up higher and calmly walked over to the table we were at, sitting at the seat Quince had just left.

"I am documenting you, I am gathering evidence, obviously." she said, lifting her chin defiantly

I stood and walked across the table to her "Henri, you need to stop, I don't want this. We talked about it."

She looked down at me, and her eyes were full of hurt and pain. She lowered the camera to point at me before responding

"Klein fee, she is terrible, she hurts you... We need to rescue you, and this is the only way we can do it, we need to show how horrible she is..."

"I'm right here, you know." Marissa said angrily

"She's not *that* bad." I said "She's- we- I mean, I think it's going to be ok. I don't want to leave her anymore."

With mild surprise, I realized I wasn't lying. After what she'd done to me, the pain, the suffocation, was one day of tenderness and playing enough to fix it? I felt a pang of fear and dread at the thought of her getting angry at me, or deciding I wasn't worth it, and I knew it *wasn't* enough. Still, I wanted to be worth it to *her*, despite myself, and I *did* like the feeling of being close to her. It was like having a raging angry dragon, and you're underneath it, protected from the flames and destruction by the very thing causing them.

Henri's eyes filled with tears, but she held them back "No, Amber, you don't mean it..."

I reached out and met the finger she extended to me with my hands "Henri, look. I think we have things figured out now, I think she's ok, and I think I can live with her more easily now."

She slumped, and set her phone on the table, looking at me despondently "...It's because I went too far, wasn't it?"

"With the lockers? Absolutely." Marissa said "I'm shocked you're not suspended right now."

Henri winced "I convinced them I did it because I thought Amber couldn't breathe in there..."

I shuddered, oh, the irony. Marissa made a slight hissing noise, and I could tell she was thinking the same thing.

"That's stupid, there's vents and stuff."

"...I was having a panic attack when they brought me in, I told them I wasn't thinking clearly. They recommended a therapist, and I am on a kind of 'probation'."

"I think the lockers was too far, yeah." I said "But you know what else is too far?"

I waved at her outfit

"All this. I don't even understand, are you trying to simulate being me? It's so creepy, wear your own clothes, we're not even the same size."

"Yeah, if you were just like, borrowing them, ok, whatever." Marissa said "But, like, taking her parents? And her room? It's like if you can't have her or whatever, you'll just become her."

Henri hugged herself "I just miss her... the clothes smell like her, *my* parents are an ocean away, and my dorm room is so small and lonely...."

"Stop it, you're scaring her." Marissa said bluntly

"You're just a *lot* right now, and you're really going overboard with a lot of the stuff you're doing." I said "I'm not trying to say we can't be friends, I care about you, but this isn't the you I know."

Henri looked between me and Marissa "So- so... If I can go back to how I was, if I can just be normal, you will be ok with me and maybe we can-"

I kept my face neutral, but I felt my heart drop

"You never gave me a real answer, Amber..." she said sadly "...about my confession, I mean. You changed the subject each time. If I work hard to be 'normal', will you and Marissa give me a chance to date you?"

"What like both of us at once?" Marissa said, sarcastically

"No, just Amber, why would I date-" Henri's face flushed, then paled. She looked at me, horrified, then up to Marissa

"No..." she whispered

"It's not quite like that, Henri, we-" I said

"It's kinda like that." Marissa said "In a sub-dom kinda way."

Henri stood up, tears dripping to the table "I am your *best friend*, klein fee, your first kiss, I confessed my love, and you go with this fucking *bitch*?!"

"Again, I'm right. Fucking. Here." Marissa said, her voice hard

"No, look, I live with her, she explained things, we're just trying out-" I tried to explain

"You could have lived with *me*, Amber!" Henri said, her voice raised "Why couldn't *we* try it out?"

"I'm a lot more persuasive than you, I guess." Marissa said, the grin in her voice ill fitting to the conversation

Henri looked at me, her eyes wide and confused, not comprehending "I *love* you, Amber, this person... this bitch, she does *not*. She will not even care about your *safety*."

"*Hey*, no." Marissa said, standing up herself "Her safety is my number one priority, don't you *ever* accuse me of not caring about that."

"Marissa loves me in her own way, I think." I said quietly, lowering my head "And she does kind of protect me, I guess."

"You have hurt her, haven't you?" Henri said tauntingly "That does not sound like caring to me."

"She's had *accidents*." Marissa clarified "And I learned, each time, that's normal. And YOU had an accident with her too, the first time I let you spend time with her."

They weren't *all* accidents... But I was pretty sure the phone was still recording, so I wasn't going to say anything. Not that they were listening to me anyway.

"Was kissing her an accident?" Henri taunted "*I* did not know that was not ok when I did it, you *did*, and you did it anyway."

"Amber *likes* kisses from me, I made sure of that." Marissa said haughtily

"And she does not like kisses from me?" Henri said, smacking the table "I was kissing her years ago, before you even laid eyes on her."

"It was only the once..." I muttered

"I *highly* doubt that." Marissa said "I had eyes for Amber as soon as I saw her awkward, shitty scholarship acceptance speech at the high school. Everything about her, from the way her clothes didn't quite fit, to how she used words she thought would make her sound smart, to her little pauses for laughter and clapping that never came; all of it. You weren't even *there* for that speech."

"If I was I would have at least *clapped*." Henri said. "If you really fell for her then, you would have too, I heard no one even acknowledged she had *said* anything, and she walked off the stage in tears."

It wasn't 'in tears'. I was fighting *back* tears, but I didn't cry until I got backstage.

"That made me like her *even more*." Marissa crooned, drumming her fingers. "No attempt to get the assembly to care once she finished, not a word of apology, just a quick, defeated, stiff walk offstage, and the faint sounds of crying after she thought no one could hear. That made me *crazy* for her, I could just *see* myself owning her and making her my little lackey. She'd do anything I wanted, because she knew I'd be the only one to treat her right when no one else was around."

"That is *sick*, you are disgusting." Henri said, venom in her voice

"You're the only fucking reason I couldn't have her back then, you know." Marissa said, her tone scarily calm "Once she had a friend, she stopped trying to get along with me, and just let all the stuff I did to her happen. In a way, you made her life path go from being the right hand woman and girlfriend of the most powerful girl in school, to being a bullied loser who everyone saw as an easy target."

Marissa leaned in and picked me up, carefully and gently holding me up to her face.

"You ruined her life, Henri. I'm just finally getting it back to where she *should* have been all those years ago, by my side, being mine."

I imagined life with Marissa, if *I'd* been her sidekick instead of the three she ended up with. I didn't *think* I could have bullied people like she did, but I was ashamed to say that I might have tried, if it'd meant not being bullied myself. I'd never realized I'd had a shot at being anything but 'the rat', I thought I'd blown it on that first day. I wasn't sure how to feel about this information, but I *did* know that the warmth from Marissa's cheek was doing wonders for my still-chilly back. I leaned into her to warm up more.

"See that?" Marissa pointed out "She heard all that, and cuddled in closer to me. She's mine, and she *likes* it."

Henri was openly sobbing now, tears making small stains on the sweater. I should say something, this was *wrong*. Marissa wasn't lying, but she was still *destroying* my friend right in front of me, and I couldn't think of anything smart to say. In the end, I just said the first thing in my head without thinking.

"Henri, you made life have value. You gave me a friend when I needed one, and you were always there for me. I love you, but maybe not the same way you love me? I don't know right now... Marissa is scary and mean, and she likes to hurt people, but she's wrong about *one* thing at least, you didn't *ruin* my life, you just changed it, and I liked getting to know you, more than I would have liked being Marissa's bitch, at least."

Marissa pet me gently, letting me know she wasn't going to stop me, so I kept going.

"Right now though, more than a friend, I need someone to care for me and to protect me. I think right *now*, that's Marissa. You're a really great friend, and I really hope you can work all this out, but I don't think in your current state you could care for me correctly."

"I could!" she said "I really, really could. I would be so, so gentle, and I would be so terribly careful, too."

"I think you could *learn* to be a good caretaker..." I admitted "But right now, you're too unstable. Marissa is cruel, but her cruelty is measured and careful, she'd never willingly hurt me. I don't think you would willingly hurt me, but you've almost killed me *twice* because you did something without thinking. Marissa did that, like, once, and we've been together over a week, compared to the few hours I spent with you. I'm just saying, you've got a much worse track record than she does so far."

Henri sniffled "Ok, so... if I get a better track record, you will let me date you and you will break up with Marissa?"

Marissa's hands tightened on me slightly, and I quickly shook my head

"No no no, no. If you get a better track record, you'll be able to hang out with me more often. I don't even know if me and Marissa have the kind of relationship that you break up from, anyway. It's kind of unclear."

"Oh, wait," Henri said "you mean I could maybe still date you?"

"I don-" I started

"*No*." Marissa said, with finality. "Whatever relationship we have, she's mine, and I'm not sharing her."

Henri sank back down in her seat and dropped her head on the table.

"I really do not understand..." she whispered

I sighed "Henri, all that happened is that I want you to go back to your old self, no more threatening to kill people, no property damage, no stealing my identity, and no more planning to do horrible things to me to get me out of the country."

"It's not *that* horrible..." she muttered "You'd be safe, at least."

"That's not the point." I said "I live with Marissa now, accept that, and accept that we've got some kind of relationship, and we'll be fine."

"I don't even know what the relationship *is*, how am I supposed to accept it?" She said, glaring up at Marissa

"We don't need to call it anything." Marissa said "Me and Amber know how it works, and all you need to know is that she's taken."

Henri stood up again, and wiped her eyes. Her makeup was smeared, and her cheeks and nose were pink.

"...I am going to skip class, today." she said "I am going to move my own stuff from the dorms into my new room. I will stop wearing your stuff, Amber."

I looked at her sadly "...You can borrow some of the clothes, I guess. Just don't be weird about it. Don't wear them just to smell them or whatever you're doing..."

She nodded, and looked at Marissa "I looked into that thing you told me, by the way. There is no bomb on Amber's leg. They do not make those, or anything like it. You were lying to me about that."

Marissa nodded back. "Yup, you're a psycho, I lied to keep Amber safe."

"Am I still invited to the party?" she asked, her voice small

"...Do you even want to go?" Marissa said, confused

"...Ja, I want to see Amber, and get a chance to be a normal person, to prove I can be ok around her."

I glanced over at Marissa, she'd lowered me from her face and was gently rubbing my back with a thinking look on her face.

"For Amber's sake, you can come. But make sure to show up late, and you have to play along with the servant thing. If you do anything to endanger Amber, me and the girls will 'hold you accountable' for it."

"Like, beat me up?" Henri asked

"Just don't do anything stupid, got it?" Marissa said quietly.

Henri nodded, and collected her phone.

"...I will be there. Bye Amber, I love you..."

Without waiting for a response, she walked away.

~~~

I sighed and shifted on my couch, I wasn't sure if she'd even know how to answer, but... I set the tablet on the stand, pressed the 'call' button, and waited. After a few minutes, the screen flashed, and I was looking at a partially blurred image of the ceiling in my old apartment.

"Amber?" my mom asked "Are you there? I saw it said you were calling, are you there?"

"I'm here, mom." I said "Point the screen at your face, is anyone else there?"

She moved the camera until it showed her face, and smiled as she saw me on the screen "Ohh, Amber! There you are! That's a nice dress, why didn't you wear things like that when you lived here?"

"I didn't pick this, I- mom, are you alone right now?"

"Oh, your Appa is at work, and Henri is in her room. Did you hear she moved in? It's like having a daughter again!"

I sighed and gave my mom a half smile "Mom, I've been gone for less than two weeks, did you really need a replacement daughter?"

She waved her hand at me "Oh, it's not a replacement, it's helping with the mourning!"

"I'm not dead, I'm still alive and still in the same town, even."

"But can we really expect to see you? It's terrible to know you are stuck being a... I think Henri said 'stress toy'? for that horrible girl."

"It's not that bad, look, mom, don't tell Henri, but-"

"You want me to get Henri? I can call her, I-"

"MOM, no. *Don't* tell Henri, ugh. Marissa wants to come over tomorrow and meet you two, and maybe have dinner."

"We've met her at school events, I didn't like her, she was rotten." My mom said, dismissively

"Well I miss you and Appa, and this is the only way I'll get to see you, so..."

"Not if the lawsuit goes through, we'll get you back and get big money too!" she said, nodding like she knew what she was doing

"I'm not banking on that lawsuit going anywhere, look, can we come over? It'll be around 5 or so, is that ok?"

She nodded "Of course, if that rotten girl behaves herself. I'll make your favorite, and we can all try and make her give you back!"

"No, I can't- don't-" I gave up "Just... be polite. If you're too rude, she won't bring me back over anymore, ok?.."

My mom sighed and rolled her eyes "Ok, ok, I can 'play nice' for a bit. I'll tell your Appa tonight. Why can't I tell Henri?"

"I want it to just be us this time." I lied "I don't want to hurt her feelings, but I want to just spend time with the two of you."

She put her hand over her heart "Oh, Amber, That is so kind of you, I will do my best to hide it from the replacement daughter."

"She's not- ugh." I dropped my protests at her smirk, and shook my head "I'll see you tomorrow, mom. I love you."

"I love you too, Amber, stay safe, dumpling."

I watched as she fiddled with her phone, trying to turn it off. I heard a door open, and Henri's voice behind her, she'd been crying again

"Miss Park? I heard Amber's name, was she-"

The phone hung up, and my screen went back to the contacts page. I bit my lip, and wondered how my mother was taking all this so well. Her and my dad were strict, but loving and caring. I hadn't seen my mother much lately, but aside from her reaction to finding me, my interactions with her; the texts and that call, were very relaxed, like she wasn't bothered at all. Was she unbothered? Or was she just pretending, for my sake? I walked to my front door and called out for Marissa. She glanced over from her PC, and held out her hand, letting me drop into it. She pulled me in and set me in front of her keyboard, still playing her game.

"Are we on for tomorrow?" she asked

"Affirmative, Lady M. We'll get there about 5." I said "She's making mandu, I couldn't break the news that I wouldn't be able to eat any."

Marissa nodded "Hm, well, maybe you can have a bite or two, do a test, like you said."

"Yeah, it'd just be bites of dough or tofu or something though." I said "I can't really get a mouthful like this. I'll most likely just eat until I'm full though, I miss my mom's cooking."

"Maybe we make lil Amber sized ones?" Marissa suggested "If she starts the cooking while we're there, maybe you could even help show me how to cook!"

I laughed "Yeah, I can *try*. A tiny person in a small room of splashing oil and sharp knives though, that's an accident waiting to happen."

"Oh, I'm sure we can work something out..." she hummed, petting me with her mouse hand as her opponents took their turns. "After this one, want to play a round with me? We can bump up the difficulty, and try different gods?"

I glanced at the screen and shrugged "Yeah, that sounds like fun! I wanted to try out someone with more combat stuff anyway."

She lit up "Oooh, you should try Lord Kartikeya! Craaazy good at military stuff, I'll show you some of the tricks, and with *that* religion, if your troops die, there's a chance the next time you make a new one of that kind of troop, they'll keep the experience and training as the one that died!"

I let her explain the ins and outs of her game, and smiled. She was cute, all chatty and excited to share her information. I think I'd made the right decision, seeing her here like this, relaxing with her. Henri would baby me and treat me like I couldn't stand on my own two feet, Marissa at least could see me as an equal, even if seeing me as an equal made her 'urges' even stronger. I lay my head on her wrist and she flinched.

"Oh, sorry, was I talking you to sleep?" she asked

"Nah." I said "I just wanted to touch you, I guess."

She didn't respond, but I could see a soft, slightly proud smile flickering on her face as she kept playing.

~~~

I leaned against the water bottle marking my seat and watched Marissa do her thing. Her leaps and swings, her thighs flexing, the snap of the ball hitting her racquet as she drove it over the net. It was like she was dancing, or like she was fighting someone with all her might. Either way, seeing her move with this amount of power in her frail looking body put her into perspective for me. She was *strong*. I'd assumed Henri would win in a fight, but *gods*, the way she flexed and twisted, Henri wouldn't stand a chance. I enjoyed the sun on me as I admired her movements, and was grateful the water bottle wasn't chilled, the warmth was nice, and I was *finally* a good temperature outside of Marissa's pocket or my house. A shadow passed in front of me, and a figure dropped onto the seat next to me, making my heart leap and almost knocking over the water bottle.

"Ooh…" a familiar voice said "I take it you're into the female form?"

I looked up at Quince, who was coyly grinning down at me

"W-what?" I asked

"You've been oogling Marissa's ass for the last two matches, it's *so* obvious you're into her."

"N-no, I just was impressed, she's very good, and I wanted to watch her closely so we'd have something to talk about later…"

Quince snorted and put on an impression of my voice "Oh, Marissa, I loooved watching you playyy, you were soooo hot, I just staaared and staaared"

"I mean… She'd probably like that…" I said, embarrassed

"She might. It's a tossup if she'd be creeped out to have a lesbian spying on her 24/7 or thrilled to have someone who appreciated her body forced to watch it."

"I'm not a- I don't- I'm not anything, I just- There's nothing wrong with being open…"

"So you WERE creeping on her." Quince said, patting my head

"I really wasn't, but even if I was, she'd be ok with it, I promise you."

Quince looked at me and raised an eyebrow "Do you know something I don't know?"

Alarm bells went off in my head, I was one wrong word away from outing Marissa by accident "She… really, really wants me to be a devoted pet. If I was into her, it'd be me playing right into her wishes."

Was that enough?

"Ohhhh" Quince said, nodding "I got it, a secret crush. You don't want her to know because it'd make it even *harder* to deal with her.

She looked at me appraisingly "You're more bold than I thought, Rat. I'm impressed you're even trying to play her like that, she'll find out, you know, one way or another."

I looked up at her. I didn't *think* Quince suspected anything, so I'd done an ok job on the save, from what I could tell.

"Are you going to tell her?"

Quince held her hand out to me "It depends, do I get snuggles?"

I frowned "Snuggles?"

"Oh come on, you thought I came over just to make fun of you? I wanna playyy lil baybee!~"

I winced "Ok, just... be gentle, please."

She squee'd and snatched me up, in a very un-gentle way, her fingers playing across my body like I was a controller

"I'm just so blown away by your tiny limbs and hands!" She said, pulling on me "They're so, so small and they still work!"

"Not if you pull them off, please be- OW!" I yelped as she turned my arm the wrong way "Seriously Quince, that hurts..."

She held me up to her face and wiggled me back and forth, her thumb and forefinger under her my ribs. "It's ok baybe, I'll kiss it allll better..."

"No you won't, seriously, Marissa will beat you the fuck up, please don't." I said coldly

Her eyes went to Marissa still on the court and her forehead creased in worry "...Yeah, ok. that's fair..."

She held me up to the top of her head "Wanna ride between my puffs?"

"No, that's dangerous!" I said, kicking my feet "Just hold me, gods, how did you pass the class?"

"The test is easy, the class is just long. The test is like 'Did you pay attention? Can you force your new pet to do stuff? Can you give them as a gift?' Blah blah blah, obvious stuff. Practically anyone could pass it."

"That's concerning." I said "Marissa made it sound super important."

"Oh, she *would*." Quince said "But yeah, she took it very seriously. I think she knew she was at a higher risk of having her class B taken away, so like, she studied extra hard to know what she could get away with."

"That *sounds* like her." I said

Quince turned me over, hanging me by my feet "I can't wait to have my own little one of you..."

"Just promise you'll be more careful with them, ok?" I asked, my stomach doing flips

"I don't have to promise you shit, Rat." She said, narrowing her eyes at me

"Amber." A voice from behind said

Quince flinched, and carefully set me down on my seat "Well, she's not going in *my* pocket, I can call her whatever I want, right?"

"No." Marissa said, sitting on the other side of me. She was sweaty and looked tired, her face pink and her dress wet around the armpits and neckline.

"Why the fuck were you playing with my pet?" she asked, catching her breath and cracking open the water bottle I'd been leaning against

"She said I could?" Quince offered, sounding like she wasn't sure if that was the right answer

Marissa looked at me and raised an eyebrow.

"Well, I said she could hold me, if she was gentle..." I admitted

"Hanging her upside down isn't gentle, Quince." Marissa said bluntly "Respect her like you would me, she's *my* fucking pet, and you're just my friend."

"Hold on, pets are more important than friends?!" Quince said, taken aback

"Yup." Marissa said, not elaborating.

Quince sat there, thinking. Finally she spoke "Your 'pet' was staring at your ass, like, the whole time."

I'd figured she'd 'tell' eventually, but I was surprised she'd done it so fast. She must *really* not like being put lower than me on the social ladder.

Marissa eyed me, her mouth fighting a smile "...It's a nice ass."

Quince shook her head "It's really not. You barely *have* an ass, but she was still staring at it, that's the takeaway here."

Marissa shrugged "She can look at my ass if she wants, She's mine, so it's like, it's not weird. She's my property or whatever."

Quince frowned "It doesn't bother you that there's a lesbo watching your every move, constantly?"

"I'm not a- Ugh, no, I'm not NOT a lesbian, I just-" I tried to correct her, but I didn't quite know how 'pan' and 'lesbian' interacted. Could I be both? Did one cancel out the other? I needed to figure this out eventually...

Marissa picked me up in her hand and I basked in her body heat, she was so, so warm, even warmer than the sunlight, her face was still flushed, and her blood was still pumping. I fell back into her fingers, feeling the slightly harder bits where her skin rubbed the racquet and stopped trying to talk.

"Think about it this way" Marissa said "If there was a hot guy watching you all the time, appreciating you and admiring you, but respectfully, like, you're still a person to him, would you mind?"

"Nnno? I mean, yeah, sometimes, but,I don't know, I guess not, if he was cool about it." Quince said

"Same thing here." Marissa said wiggling me "I don't mind if she looks. She'd be cool about it, and we've talked over stuff, and she respects me, I guess."

Something about that argument felt... wrong, somehow. Sexist, to say the least, but I didn't know enough about that stuff to figure out what exactly *was* wrong...

"...Whatever, it's your body, I guess." Quince said, looking at me with a curious, almost contemplative look.

"And that's all that really matters." Marissa said, standing up and arching her back "Come on, Amber, let's go take a shower."

I stiffened, and looked up at her wide eyed as she walked away. Once we were out of earshot of Quince, I hissed up to her "Are you seriously taking me in the shower with you?!"

Marissa's face finally broke into an easy smile and she snorted "I could, I guess. Do you think our relationship is that far yet?"

I shook my head furiously "No! I haven't even seen you naked, showers are like, 5 steps past that!"

"Well, maybe this is how you *get* to see me naked?" She said innocently

I punched her finger and frowned "You're messing with me, right?"

"Noooo." she said "I was messing with Quince, but this is fun too."

I sighed. "I think Quince is homophobic or something..."

"Yeah, for sure, that's why it's *funny*." Marissa said "Less phobic, more. repressed. She's straight as an arrow, but I think if she could get past her upbringing she'd be ok with me and you at least, she's just been around the assholes at school her whole life telling her how to think."

"I guess that's fair..." I said as we entered the locker room. "She was just saying some stuff that sounded... eh."

"She's the main reason I haven't come out. I think Tracy would be more ok with it?" Marissa pulled her bag out of the smashed up locker and headed to the showers "But she'd tell *everyone*, of course, and *most* people in this school wouldn't be ok with it at all."

"Tracy seems like the kind of person who would act like she was offended just to fit in." I said thoughtfully as Marissa set me on the bench in her shower cubby

"She totally would, I swear she'll do anything to feel like she fits." Marissa laughed "I think she only dated people because she felt she'd be an outcast if she didn't."

"That's- hey, *I* never dated, what are you saying?" I asked indignantly

"That you're a loser outcast with no friends or social standing. Obviously." Marissa retorted and she stepped behind the curtain and started putting her clothes next to me on the bench "But hey, that's why I love you, that pathetic vibe you give off just *does* something for me."

I got up and walked to the end of the bench, looking through the cracks in the swinging doors on the cubby at the rest of the showers to see if anyone was around

"You're pretty comfortable saying 'I love you' to me in a public place like this."

"I canceled my last match, we're alone for at least half an hour while the other girls finish up, maybe longer." She said over the water "No one's around, and if they are, fuck 'em. People tell their pets they love them all the time."

"I think that's the first time you said it, right?" I said, thinking back

She poked her head out of the shower "No, I totally said it at the sleepover, you just didn't know I meant it then."

"But you *do* mean it?" I said "You couldn't even get the words out a couple days ago."

"I still couldn't tell it to you straight to your face if I *tried*, but yeah, I mean it. Take it where you can get it, I guess." She ducked back in "I don't think *you've* said it yet though, not that you have to or anything, but I *have* noticed."

I stayed quiet. I didn't love her, not yet at least, but I did care about her. I tried to think of how to express that, but it all sounded so fake and sad.

The water shut off and Marissa grabbed a towel off the bar across from me. I could see her through the clouded plastic sheet, and I watched as she rubbed herself down. Did *this* count as creeping? She was my... something, owner or partner or something, so it couldn't be *that* bad, but if I couldn't even say I loved her...

The curtain opened to Marissa in a towel, and I felt myself flush. I was *absolutely* feeling creepy now.

"Hey, look, I've had, like, half a decade to fall head over heels with you." Marissa said "If you haven't gotten there in a week, I get it. As long as we're good."

I nodded "That's a very mature way of looking at it. I don't know what love feels like, so I don't know if I'll be able to tell when I *do* love you..."

"*If* you love me." she said, picking some things out of her bag "Relationships, especially ones like ours, don't always need to have both parties love each other."

"That feels like an unfair power dynamic..." I said.

She stopped halfway into the shower and looked back "...Amber. I fucking OWN you. You're small enough for me to crush with a single hand. You're wearing an anklet that tells the world you're mine, and you're not a legal human anymore. What fucking possible way could a power dynamic get more imbalanced than that already? You're my fucking *pet*."

I blinked. Somehow, I'd forgotten how starkly different our situations were. With her guard down, it almost felt like we were equals, but... She *could* do whatever she wanted to me, and I needed to keep that in mind, even if she was treating me more and more like a person.

"Uh, yeah. that's a good point."

"Yeah, no shit." she said, snapping the shower closed "Now shut up, I need to get ready and you're distracting me."

~~~

We stood in front of my old apartment door and I waited on Marissa to knock. She shifted her feet and looked ahead, not moving, and I climbed up out of her palm to see her face. She had her usual public face on, the bitchy one with the narrow stare and the thin, tight lips. I tugged on her thumb and waved to get her attention. She glanced down, her eyes focusing and her face softening slightly.

"What is it?" she asked quietly

"Is everything good? We're supposed to be getting here, like, right now. My parents admire promptness..."

She looked at me and curled her lips "We're- We- Look. I'm the monster that stole their daughter away from them, I'm the reason you're not still living there, and who *knows* what Henri has told them?"

She looked back up at the door

"Plus... ugh, power dynamics aside, we are in some kind of relationship..."

"Were- oh, um, are we telling them that?" I asked, suddenly nervous myself

"I'm guessing Henri already *did*, so... I don't want to tip off my master lying skills by pretending we're not if they already know." She sighed "I'll save those for when I have to pretend to like whatever gifts they give me for our anniversary."

"Uh, I don't think we can legally marry?" I said

"Huh? They legalized it like, 20 years ago."

"No, I mean, I'm not... human anymore." I shifted in her hand nervously

"Oh. Yeah. Well, the anniversary thing was a joke anyway, it's whatever."

We sat there for a few moments longer. I was getting anxious just waiting like this...

"I really think it'll be ok, my mom seemed fine when I talked to her yesterday."

"Does your dad have a gun? Is he going to do the whole 'cleaning his gun' thing to scare me?"

"I think he has one? But he'll just be aggressively disappointed in you more than likely."

Marissa groaned "Gods, I get that from my own parents..."

"Ok, so are you going to-"

The door swung open, and my mom stepped out, a frown on her face.

"Are you going to come in or just stand out here and whine?" She said, pointing into the apartment "You have my daughter, get inside so we can see her too."

Marissa threw up her hand in apology and scooched past her into the familiar space of my old living room. As she passed by, I heard my mom whisper "Rotten girl..." under her breath. If Marissa had heard, she didn't even flinch.

## Chapter Fifteen

I squirmed in Marissa's hand, my Appa looking at me with sad eyes, my mother standing up straight, her arms crossed. Marissa squirmed too, shifting in the couch as she looked for something to say. I could feel her heartbeat in the palm of her hand through my leg, and while her face was placid and calm, the heartbeat was picking up pace the longer we sat here. I couldn't sit here much longer, I knew my parents wanted her to break the ice, but if she didn't do it soon, I would. Marissa cleared her throat slightly, and I tensed up, waiting to see her first words to them.

"I- *ehm*- I just wanted to thank you for the opportunity to meet you, and I wanted to say that I have enjoyed getting to know your daughter over the past couple weeks, she's been an absolute delight."

Marissa's words hung in the air, heavy and clunky, and my parents didn't move an inch.

"She- we, I mean, she and I, we're getting pretty close," Marissa clarified "and we've learned to get along, and I just wanted to tell you- to let you know, that we- I'm not- I think we, uh, get along very well now, we're... good."

The air was still, and I saw my mother's barely contained fire rising to the surface.

"Uh, Appa," I said, trying to keep things going, and to give my mother time to calm down "Has- has Henri talked to you about- things? Between me and Marissa?"

My mother snorted, and my Appa sighed "Henri told us last night at dinner that you were being used as a 'toy' for this girl, and that you thought that meant you two were... together."

"I taught you better than that, Amber." my mom snapped at me "Love is more than someone liking you for what you give them."

"You- you didn't teach me anything!" I said, suddenly frustrated "I've never *dated* before, you told me *nothing* about dating except to find someone to marry before I was 25, this is *not* on me."

I turned to my dad "And Appa, we *are* together, it's not the way Henri said. Marissa doesn't *use* me, we play games and stuff, she's- she's learning. She cares for me, she just likes to play rough..."

"So you two *are* together? As far as you're concerned?" he asked, looking between me and her

"..." Marissa swallowed hard "...Yes, we are."

"I can't believe my daughter gets caught up with a girl like *you*, after *all* we did to make sure she'd end up with someone who would treat her right..." my mother muttered

"I- I'm- I do my best to take care of her, Miss Park." Marissa said, her hand shaking slightly

"You *took* her from me." she said, glaring at her.

"M-mom, I told Marissa that maybe we could all learn to make mandu together?" I said, trying to change the subject

She clicked her tongue "You want me to teach her to cook? This girl is not my daughter, why should I teach her *my* recipes?"

"Because she's taking care of our daughter." My father said tiredly "And I'd like our daughter to at least be able to think of us while she's there without us. Having our recipes cooked for her will help."

*The Feeling of Being Valued* 263

I looked at him, shocked. I hadn't expected him to be so quick to support Marissa, he always seemed so protective of me, I'd thought he'd-

"If you could let Hye-jin hold Amber, I would like to talk to you in my room for a moment..." my father said to Marissa

...There it was, that made more sense.

Marissa frowned, and looked at me, confused. I nodded, and pointed to my mom. Marissa grimaced, and stood, passing me gently to my mother, who carefully cupped me with two hands. I watched as Marissa followed my dad into his and mom's room and shut the door behind them.

I looked up at my mother, whose stern, hard face had softened into a sad, mournful one. "Mom... It's ok, really. She's- like, we're learning to get along, I actually *like* her, now, mostly."

"Amber..." she said, walking slowly to the kitchen and setting me on the table in front of her as she sat down "I talked to Henri, she said that rotten girl is doing horrible, horrible things to you."

"She's not, she's- she likes to be rough, being in charge is important to her, but it's not as bad as Henri says, I promise."

It might *have* been as bad, to tell the truth, I was assuming Henri was exaggerating, but *she* didn't know about the jeans pocket.

"Henri just wants you to be safe, Amber." she said, petting my head softly, far more carefully than any other person had.

"Henri *loves* me, mom. She's desperate to get me back."

"We *all* love you, dumpling, we *all* want you back." She leaned away and her brow wrinkled "I've been calling that man running the lawsuit almost every day, hoping for news..."

"I don't think the lawsuit will go anywhere, mom." I muttered "But you misunderstand, Henri *loves* me. She wants to date me, and keep me, and kiss me and stuff."

My mom frowned "That explains why I found her crying into a pile of dirty clothes in your room earlier this week..."

I winced and shook my head "Please make sure all my stuff has been washed... and throw out my toothbrush and stuff, please."

She nodded and sighed "Why couldn't you have gotten girlfriends when you were regular sized? Why is it only when you're too small to get married that you have people interested?"

"They were interested before, me being compressed- well, it just made it more urgent." I explained

Her eyes widened in shock "The rotten girl liked you before? She was so horrible to you though."

"Yeah, go figure" I muttered "Turns out, being horrible to people is how she gets close to them."

"That's awful, I don't understand this generation." she said sadly

"I don't either." I admitted "But she really, really, actually cares about me, and she just wants to be close to me and keep me safe, so please, can you at least pretend you're ok with it?"

She looked at me for a few long seconds, then blinked slowly, a tear falling out of her eye. "I always imagined you bringing home your first love differently. This way... it feels like my dreams for you were all washed away, and you're asking me to just forget it?"

"It's no one's fault, except those people who made the compression particles, I guess." I said "It's just how it is, it sucks, but... it's what I have. I'm, like, I don't know, lucky to have her? It could be much, much worse. I'd rather have a guardian who hurts me a little on purpose than one who hurts me by mistake."

"Lucky..." she said, wiping her eyes "lucky would be you *here*, with us. Being our daughter, not being hidden away from us by a girl that tried to ruin your life."

The door to my parent's bedroom opened, and my mom glanced up over the bar, and back down at me "I'll be polite, I'll be kind, and I'll pretend to support her, for you." she said in a whisper "But I will *never* forgive her from taking you away from me when you needed me most."

*The Feeling of Being Valued* 265

I nodded, and climbed back into her hand as she brought me over to the bar, setting me on it as Marissa took a seat across from us. Marissa looked worried, and mildly angry, but she gave me a tiny smile when I waved at her.

"So. Amber wants you to learn to make mandu, hm?" my mom asked Marissa "I'd prefer to teach you something more unique, like bulgogi or tteokbokki. Everyone in the world makes dumplings, but only *Korea* has yook hwei."

"I *like* dumplings, mom." I said, blushing

"And *I* like passing my culture down to the next generation, but *no*, we're making dumplings, apparently." she snapped back

Marissa swallowed "Uh, we can make whatever you like, I don't know what bulogi or the others are, but I would be more than happy to learn any of them."

"Absolutely not." she said "My daughter wants mandu, we make mandu."

"Honey," my father said "Amber might not be able to eat very much of anything you make, just so you know. They have digestion problems."

"I'll eat it anyway." I said "I need this."

My mom's eyes softened and she looked at me, almost hurt, but locked back in the next moment.

"We need to start if we're going to eat before the replacement daughter gets home. I gave her a shopping list, so she'll be late, but she'll still be home before long."

"Yeah, we- replacement?" Marissa asked, looking at me sharply.

"Let's- I'll ride on your shoulder, Marissa, if that's ok." I said, pushing past it "So you have both hands free."

She scooped me up and dropped me on her shoulder, and I hooked one arm under her bra strap to hold on as she walked into the kitchen.

"Well, let's get started." my mom said "We'll make two batches, real ones, and a small batch with tofu, for Amber."

She looked Marissa up and down

"You eat meat, right?"

Marissa gave a thumbs up "Yup, gotta get that protein for tennis."

My mom nodded approvingly. "I thought so, you have strong arms."

"You can still get protein without meat." I said "There's beans, eggs, nuts, tofu..."

"I'm gonna keep eating meat, Amber." Marissa said "I have a figure to watch."

"Amber's been watching her figure too," my mom cut in "watching it grow."

"Mom, I work out, I'm healthy!" I said, indignant. She'd been rough about my tummy before, but in front of *Marissa?* I got it bad enough from her already.

"I kinda like Amber's shape..." Marissa said softly "She's- I don't know, she's soft. I like the way she feels in my hand."

My mom looked at Marissa hard, then turned back to the cabinets she was pulling the ingredients out of "Well, if *you* like it, then."

I felt myself relax, and I hugged Marissa's shoulder. She'd backed me up, and my mom had kept her word and been supporting.

"Do you two need anything?" my Appa asked "Or should I just watch?"

I leaned up to Marissa's ear "Get him one of the green bottles from the fridge, he'll love that."

She eyed the fridge as my mom opened it, and stepped over, pulling out a lychee soju, and passed it over the bar to my dad "I think you can just hang out and watch." she said

My dad let out a laugh, and cracked open the bottle "You're already doing better than replacement daughter. Jinie, can we keep this one instead?"

My mom huffed and rolled her eyes, ignoring him.

"Here, you're an adult, right?" he asked Marissa "Get one for yourself, they're very good."

"Uh, yeah, ok." Marissa said "I'm not driving or anything."

"*Can* you drive?" I asked and she pulled one with a peach on it out of the fridge and closed it

"I got my license when I was 16, yeah." she said "I wrecked my fucking spider after two weeks though."

"Spider?" my dad asked

"That's what my dad called it. I don't know the make or whatever, some two seater convertible thing." she said dismissively, opening her soju and taking a sip. Her face crinkled, then she pulled away from the bottle "Oh, shit, it's like, juice or something..."

"Are you going to talk about cars and booze all afternoon or help me cook?" my mom asked, pointing to the veggies, meat, tofu, and dumpling wraps she'd laid out.

"Oh, sorry, let's get started, sorry..." Marissa gulped some more of the soju, and set it to the side, stepping up beside my mother to help chop up the cabbage.

I watched them work, pointing out how to cut the mushrooms and zucchini, while my mom prepared the tofu for my batch. I unhooked my arm and nestled against Marissa's neck feeling the blood rushing past me and her neck pulse as she drank her soju. I knew this feeling of peace was fabricated, Marissa was on her best behavior and trying to impress them, and my parents were uncomfortable with her but playing along for me, but it almost felt like it could be *real* some day, if we just tried a little harder. That made me feel a sense of hope for the future, one that I hadn't felt in weeks...

Marissa began chopping the pork, and I tried to avert my eyes. It was just meat, yeah, but it was still a *dead* thing, that she was just chopping up to eat. It was gross and weird, even if it was 'normal'. She laughed under her breath, and I looked up to see a hidden smile on her face as she watched me. I tensed up, nothing good happened when she smiled like that... She bent forward slightly, and rolled her shoulder, and I felt myself slipping. I shrieked, and tumbled through the air, falling a full foot at least before I hit the counter with a squish-

Squish? No, not the counter, then... I felt my heart catch, and I pushed my face off the sticky wet sucking surface I was laying on and screamed, the grey meat and blood clinging to my face, hair, and tracksuit. I struggled to stand, my feet slipping on the fleshy surface, falling back to my knees with a squelch. I felt my eyes tear up and my breathing quickened. I lifted my hands up away from my body and stared up at Marissa giggling down at me, her cheeks pink and her eyes sparkling. I felt the tears go down my face and I sobbed once, shaking my head as she reached down for me.

"Aw, Amber, you gotta be careful!" she said "You could have hurt yourself, you need to remember to hold on!"

I flinched at her touch, and shook as she picked me up off the slab of dead flesh, dead parts hanging on me, dead blood in my hair, dead bits, dead dead dead, I was covered in animal, in dead, it filled my nose, it was on my skin, in my clothes, I couldn't think, I couldn't breathe, the meat was going into my lungs, it was too much, I was covered in death I wanted-

"Miss Park, Amber got some pork on her, I'd like to clean her up, where's the bathroom?"

I head the voice, but I couldn't understand it, the world was foggy and distant, and I let myself be carried around the corner to the small dimly lit bathroom. I felt myself get set on the counter and the water turned on.

"Wow, that sound was great, you just fucking splatted, I was impressed." Marissa snickered "Hey, get your tracksuit off, I'll get water on it and clean it up, hope you don't mind being a little dressed down for dinner."

I sat still, arms to my sides, breathing out of my mouth, afraid to move and remember that I was practically dripping with death.

"Amber?" Marissa said "You gotta undress, I don't want to waterboard you, I can't wash them with you in them..."

I let out a whimper and tried to stand, but went back to my knees. I was covered in a dead thing, all the bits of it, all over me. Marissa lowered herself to the counter level, and stared at me from behind. She let out a low sigh, and picked me up, unzipping my top and pulling it off.

"Amber, it's just pork, it's fine, you'll be ok."

"D-dead thing..." I said, shaking as she pulled my sweatpants off, leaving me in an undershirt and boy shorts.

"I mean, I *guess* it's a dead thing, it's meat, it's- I don't know, that's a gross way to describe it."

"It- it's a gross thing..." I said, my teeth chattering

She dunked my clothes in the water, scrubbing them gently "Ok, fine, whatever. It was just like, a dumb prank."

I felt myself sharpen and I turned to her "You can't just slather someone in dead thing and call it a *prank*, Marissa, I have dead thing in my *hair*."

She glared at me "Oh- it's- ugh look, you're fine, you'll be a little awkward now, being around your parents in your underthings, that's the point of it, not the 'dead thing' or whatever."

"I just- I can't believe you let your urges get the best of you *here*." I said "You know this is important."

"I blame that juice your dad gave me. I just had one, but *gods*, I'm actually feeling it, I'll have to remember that stuff."

"You can't just blame alcohol." I snipped "You need to take responsibility."

She looked at me, and hummed thoughtfully "Alright, whatever. Let's wash your hair, then I'll take 'responsibility', ok?"

She looked in the shower and got some shampoo, Henri's, I noticed, the cherry scented kind, and put a dab in my hair. She held me in one hand as she pushed my head into the trickle of water. Her fingers rubbed my hair, pulling slightly but foaming up the soap and cleaning my hair all the same. Her fingers moved to my face, pushing against it, clearing the blood, then to my hands, her fingertips bigger than both of them together, as she cleaned me off. Once the blood was gone, she plucked a tissue out of a box next to the sink and dabbed me dry, being careful not to rub too hard against me. Once she was done, she sat on the edge of the tub and looked at me, shivering but clean, and smiled.

"Gods, you're so fucking cute." she said, her smile implying that wasn't as much of a good thing as it sounded

"Ok, so can we find something for me to wear?" I said, hugging myself

"Oh," she said softly "are you cold because I took your clothes? I guess I need to *take responsibility* and warm you up..."

"Marissa, we are at my *parent's* house." I said, incredulously "What are you thinking?"

"Well, I hate seeing my little girl all cold like this," she said, grinning her stupid, adorable lazy grin "I can warm you up so, so easily..."

I thought about protesting more, but I *was* pretty cold, and I was still upset at her for covering me in dead animal. If this was an apology, I should accept it, for now. She pulled me in towards her mouth and pressed her lips into my torso, kissing my chest, and moving down to my arms, letting her alcohol-warmed skin do the work for her. I closed my eyes as her mouth kissed my cold, cold hands, and her fingers rubbed my legs. It was nice, it made me feel like I was her whole focus, the sole person in her life. I felt a tingle of power, a feeling that *I* was in control here, she was doing this for *me*.

She pulled me away "Oh... you're not warming up, Amber..." she said in a fake sad voice

"Y- you can keep trying." I said "I'll warm up soon, I'm sure.

"Let's try something else..." she said, pulling up her shirt and moving me under it.

I found myself pressing into her chest, right where her ribcage met. Her bone was hard, but covered by a layer of warm, soft skin that took me into it. I pushed my cold body against her, my legs drawing heat, my hands rubbing, the tops of my feet flat against her upper stomach. I felt so, so good. It was one thing laying on her stomach through her shirts, or in a pocket, it was another thing to be pressed against her bare skin itself. I looked up at the cavern I was in, her chest curving slightly over me, her face peeking through the neck hole of her shirt, the shirt itself flared out like a tent making her body look like the centerpiece of a cathedral. I wasn't going to forgive her for the meat just yet, I was still upset, but this was a very, very good way for her to make it up to me.

A loud banging on the door make Marissa jerk, smushing me against her even tighter.

"Hey, hurry up! I'm trying to teach you!" My mom yelled "You've been in there too long!"

"S-sorry!" Marissa said, her face flushing "I was trying to make sure her hair was dry and stuff."

She pulled me out and set me on the counter, pulling another tissue out of the box and wrapping it around my waist. I tucked it along my side to make a skirt, and tried not to laugh at how flustered Marissa looked. She'd get in someone's face and make them feel like trash, but almost getting caught cuddling me sent her into a tizzy. It reminded me of how overly modest and concerned for my privacy she'd been when I first moved in. I stepped into her hand, the tissue skirt doing well enough to cover me and provide warmth, and we headed back to the kitchen.

"Sorry Miss Park," Marissa said "she was really concerned about the meat juice on her, so I wanted to help her feel clean again."

"And that involved taking her clothes off?" my mom eyed me

"I had meat juice on the clothes." I said "They had to be washed, but they're too wet to wear now."

My dad leveled a look at Marissa "I'm sure that was the only reason your clothes are off, Amber"

Marissa nodded quickly "Yeah, that's the only reason."

"Come help me make Amber's mandu." My mom said "We have to chop it up very very small, and I'm using eggroll wraps instead of regular wraps for hers, so it's not just dough."

"Oh, uh, that's clever." Marissa said, putting me back on her shoulder and stepping back over.

I made sure to hold on very tightly to her strap this time as she moved through the kitchen, learning how the steamer worked, how to crimp the mandu, and how to tell if the dumplings were done. By the time she was finished, the kitchen was warm and cozy, and full of wonderful smells.

I tugged at Marissa "Hey, I'm getting kinda hungry, and it's getting late, let's get Appa and eat, ok?"

My mom pointed her finger at me "No, we need rice and kimchi, I have the kimchi in the fridge, but we need to cook the rice. Marissa, do you cook rice at home?"

"No, I don't." Marissa said, politely neglecting to mention she didn't cook *any*thing at her home, due to her live in cook. "This-" my mother pointed at the rice cooker "is a rice cooker. You put rice in it up to the line." She pointed "Then water up to this line. Then you turn it on, ten minutes later, you have rice."

Marissa nodded "Well, even if I forget the rest, I'll know how to make rice."

"You want 'sticky rice'. The ones that aren't sticky are no good." my mother explained, setting up the cooker and turning it on. "Now we wait."

"Should we warm up the kimchi?" Marissa asked

"We eat it cold, here." my dad said "I grew up with it cold, so I prefer it that way."

Marissa nodded slowly "Ok, yeah. That makes sense. I think I've had it before, but it would have been hot."

"I like it hot." I said "But I'll just be eating the mandu."

"You need to eat slowly, Amber." my dad reminded me "You aren't supposed to eat people food at all, much less make a meal of it."

Marissa's mouth twitched "...People food?" she asked, innocently

I kicked her in the neck, but she just smiled wider

"Oh, oh no, Not- Amber, *Kkoma*, no." he said, stricken "I wasn't- oh, I'm so sorry, it was a slip of the tongue..."

"I get it, Appa." I said. It stung more than it should, but I understood what he'd meant. It still felt hurtful to have my dad remind me that I wasn't human anymore.

"Marissa." my mother said sternly "Go sit on the couch until the rice is done."

Marissa looked around, and then walked out of the kitchen, and sat in front of the tv, pulling me into her hand and holding me around the waist. She looked up at my mom and dad, my dad was still drinking soju, and my mom had started setting the table. She bit her lip and looked down at me nervously. She shrugged, in a 'what happened?' way, and I shook my head. She hadn't *said* anything bad, but I knew my mom had picked up on her trying to make my dad feel bad. I knew she couldn't resist it, it's who she was, but my mom was *sharp*, and she didn't stand for anyone hurting her people.

We sat quietly, Marissa playing with me, moving my limbs and 'dancing' with me on her knees. It was nerve wracking to be spinning and twirling next to the drop off, it was just her knee to the floor, but it would still be enough to hurt me badly, or kill me. Still, her ring finger seemed to stay behind me the whole time, as her other fingers pulled me along the makeshift dance floor.

"Ok, dinner is ready, you two." my mom called out.

We made our way to the table, and sat down, me and Marissa across from my parents. The air was still tense, but it was less oppressive than it had been. The dumplings, rice, and kimchi were in nice serving dishes, and a fresh bottle of soju sat in from of both my dad and Marissa. She really didn't need any more, but as long as her tipsy urges were cuddly instead of bullying, I didn't care.

"This smells *really* good." Marissa said

"Fix your plate, get what you want." my dad said, putting the tiny, tofu filled dumplings on his bottle cap and setting them in front of me. As Marissa fixed her plate and my parents followed suit, I picked up one of the mandu. It was still lots of dough despite the thinner wraps, and the veggies were *huge* compared to what I was used to, but if I stretched my mouth, I should be able to fit it in. I looked down at my stomach. Was this a good idea? I really, *really* didn't want to get sick, and my parents didn't have a bathroom my size, so I'd have to ask Marissa to bring up my travel box from the car, and... it would just be honestly humiliating. Still, if the others at group ate people food with no issue, I *could* end up being ok...

"How is it, Amber?" Marissa asked, holding one of her own

"Uh, let me check..." I said. These would get cold fast, so I needed to eat up, stomach issues be damned. I took a large bite, and chewed slowly. The texture was... wrong and weird, nothing like the dumplings I'd grown up with, but the *flavor* was everything I remembered it was, and that's what counted. I gave a thumbs up and a smile as I took another bite.

"Wow, too busy eating to talk, huh." Marissa said "I guess we did a good job?"

"Eat your dinner, try it for yourself." my mom said, pointing.

I swallowed and looked up at Marissa "We usually don't talk and eat much, it's like, disrespectful. It's food time, not talking time."

"Ah, ok, got it." Marissa took a bite of mandu, and chewed thoughtfully.

"Well," she said "it's pretty good, I see why you like it."

My mom just pointed to the plate, and waved her hand. Marissa nodded, and we ate in silence. It usually wasn't *this* quiet, we almost always talked a *little*, especially when we had company over, traditions aside. It felt more like my mom was testing Marissa, or possibly trying to show she's still in charge here, even if Marissa owns me. I ate my last dumpling, and sighed in contentment. Even if I got super sick, the feeling I had right now was worth it, the family meal, the people I loved, the full tummy, the food I grew up with, all shared with my new partner, who was doing her absolute best to be good tonight, nothing could ruin this...

The door to our apartment jiggled and swung open, and I flinched, cursing myself for tempting fate. My head darted to the opening to the living room to see how she'd react.

"Sorry Miss Park, I forgot to get your card for the groceries when I left this morning, I will just pick it up and-" Henri's voice trailed off as she rounded the corner and stood at the bar, her mouth hanging open at the four of us eating dinner.

"Hi, Henri." Marissa said smoothly "I wasn't expecting you here, what a pleasant surprise."

Henri's eyes flicked from me to Marissa to my parents, and she worked her mouth, trying to come up with words to say

"I- we, ah, yes, such a lovely surprise..." she said "I *really* did not expect to see *you* here..."

"Wouldn't you like some mandu?" Marissa crooned "I made it myself, even Amber had some, I'm trying to learn how to make her more comfortable, and knowing how to make her favorite food goes a *long* way."

"I- Th- Amber cannot *eat* mandu..." Henri said "She- she is going to get sick, you- you cannot just give her whatever she wants, you need to take *care* of her."

"My daughter is a grown woman." my mom said firmly "If she wants to eat my cooking and get sick, I'll cook anything she wants."

"But- no, you cannot just- Marissa, you have a *duty* to keep her safe."

"Henri, maybe possibly being a little sick later isn't unsafe." I said "It's no different than me and you going to that one taco place you like."

Henri was breathing heavily, and her head was turning to look at each of us in turn, her words on the verge of coming out.

Finally, she stamped her foot and shouted, her voice cracking as she pointed at Marissa

"She is not supposed to be here!" she yelled "She is worming her way in, she is trying to trick you, to make you *like* her so she can do whatever she wants, she is fucking *evil*!"

My father stood up "Henri, Marissa is here as a favor to Amber. Not because she wants to be."

"That's what she *wants* you to think, she is making you think she is willing to do what Amber wants, to bend over backwards for her, to learn to cook for some reason, but really she is just trying to get you to like her, she is manipulating all of you!"

I stood up too "Look, I *asked* her to be here, we talked it out, like adults, we talked to my parents about it. We're doing the family thing, we're getting along, and they're getting to know each other, because I *asked* them to."

Henri glared at me "You are only doing this because Marissa had so much time to worm into *your* brain, to influence you to 'choose' this. If you *really* wanted to have everyone get to know each other, why did you hide it from *me*? Because you knew I would expose her game?"

"Because I knew you'd do *this*." I snapped "You act like I can't make my own fucking choices, like I can't *talk to people* or decide stuff, but this was *my fucking idea*, whether you believe it or not. I'm not being manipulated, I can think for myself, and if I want to eat my favorite food, I can deal with the fucking consequences my fucking self, godsdamnit."

Henri shook her hands "But-"

"But nothing, go to your room!" my mom cut her off "You're ruining dinner, and you're being disrespectful!"

Henri's eyes shone and her face crumpled, but she spun and stomped off to my- *her* room and slammed the door behind her. My dad shook his head slowly and took a drink.

"You know..." he said "Sometimes when people want something enough, they have a hard time seeing *other* people's needs as important..."

I stared at the greasy bottle cap I'd been eating off of. She wasn't *bad*, but she'd just proved that she didn't see me as a 'real person' anymore, not deep down. I missed her anyway though, the Henri that had movie nights with me, and that worked out with me, or who helped me study. I pulled on Marissa's hand, and she looked down.

"You good?" she asked

"I think we should go talk to her." I said "We won't have a chance tomorrow if she's getting there after everyone, and we need to get some stuff settled."

"It might do you some good to have privacy with her." my dad agreed

My mom picked up the serving dishes and started putting them away "Just make sure she won't be crying all night again." she said "I'm tired of having to keep the TV up to drown her out."

Me and Marissa made out way to my old room and pushed through the door. Henri was on the bed, a new one, since mine had mostly compressed, and was crying, with an episode of *Mister Ed* on my old TV. She glanced over at us, and huffed, throwing her pillow at Marissa's head. Marissa cupped my body with her fingers as the pillow hit her and she kicked the door shut behind her.

"That's one more time you could have killed Amber, you know." Marissa said neutrally.

"What?" Henri said, sitting up

"The pillow, it could have knocked her out of my hands, she could have hit her neck on the floor, instant death." Marissa said, looking at the posters of video game and anime characters on my walls.

"That- no, you were holding her." Henri said

"I'm just saying, you're very quick to judge me for just wanting to eat dinner with her family, while you're seemingly on a mission to end her life. Or *someone*'s life, at least."

"I would not *ever* hurt her!" Henri said shooting out of bed "I love her! You know that!"

"You love her like a doll, Henri." Marissa said, staring into her eyes "You don't see her as a human."

"I- I do, I promise, I just know we are supposed to protect class Bs, it is not about her being 'human' or anything, I just- I have to make sure she is safe..."

"You're sure you see her as a full person?" Marissa asked, tilting her head

"I do, and I know I do."

"Then it's interesting how you haven't addressed *her* once since I came in, and didn't say anything to her earlier until *she* said something to *you*" Marissa said softly "Almost like you forget she's real..."

"That- no, you are lying!" Henri said "I did *too* talk to her."

"You didn't, actually." I said, thinking about it "And you ignored me when I tried to talk the first time, and the second time I tried to talk to you, you dismissed it as me not being able to make my own decisions."

Henri glanced down, and her face crumpled for a split second, then flared, then changed to an expression of shock. She backed up and sat back on the bed.

"Oh no..." she whispered "Oh, oh no..."

"Yes, Henri?" Marissa asked in a sweet voice

"I cannot-" she looked at Marissa and her face turned into a snarl "You are trying to trick me again."

"Nope, it was Amber who said that last part." Marissa said "I'm just standing here."

"I don't understand, what happened?" I asked

"Henri just realized that she *doesn't* see you as a real person anymore after all." Marissa said smugly.

My heart fell. I'd *hoped* it wasn't true, that I was overreacting, but...

"I- Amber, I can be better, you are just so small and fragile, I just-" Henri said "I love you, I just- I want to care for you, I value you so much, I can still see you as a person, I promise."

"Tell you what." Marissa said "Tomorrow night, I'll tell everyone you're *Amber's* servant. You'll follow her every order, you'll do what she says, you'll call her mistress. Treating her like your better for a while should help re-wire your brain into remembering she's a person, right?"

"Oh, wait, um," I said "I'm not good at giving orders."

"I'll coach you, it's fine." Marissa said, smiling

"I will do it, anything she says, I will do." Henri said, her eyes fierce and cold "But not because *you* told me to, but because I fucking love her and I want to fucking prove I see her as a fucking human."

"Well don't tell me, tell *her*." reminded Marissa "You're still talking past her, even now."

Henri flinched, and looked at me, her eyes meeting mine. "I love you Klein Fee, and I would do anything you ask, forever, and to the ends of time."

"Ok, well, don't kill Marissa, don't act like a creep, and stop letting your emotions run away, to start." I said

She looked at her hands, and didn't respond.

"Well I think this has been very productive!" Marissa said, smiling "I gotta get Amber back home, but hey, this was a good talk, see you tomorrow?"

Henri still didn't respond, so Marissa nodded and turned, heading back to the living room. As we said goodbye to my parents and got ready to leave, I couldn't help but wonder how much Henri could really change, and if I'd ever get my friend back again...

# Chapter Sixteen

I *had* gotten sick after all. Not as bad as the labels on my compressed foods would have you believe, but I shouldn't have eaten as much as I did. Either way, it was worth it to get to see my mom and Appa again, and to get to bond with Marissa more. I'd stayed up a little late playing on my tablet, I still hadn't messaged Nada yet, but I wanted to have time to really sit down and talk to her when I did, so I figured it could wait a little more. I tried making friends on AntMound to talk about my living situation with, but I was having trouble finding people who I 'matched' with, size, guardian type, etc. I'd gone to bed, thoughts of the next day's sleepover in my head, dreading it and almost looking forward to it at the same time.

The next morning, a knock on my wall woke me up, and I climbed out of bed, walking over the edge as Marissa opened it up.

"Hey, uhh, I need you to wear this today, and I gotta pick my own clothes..." she said, handing me a pair of tan flared slacks and a white frilled blouse

"This is kind of formal for a school day, what's the occasion?" I asked, taking the clothes

Marissa gave me a pained, nervous smile "...My mom got back into town last night after we came upstairs, she wants to eat breakfast together, and... you know, first impressions and all."

"I guess we're *both* having a 'meet the parents' moment this week, huh?" I said jokingly

"Yeahhhh, uh, ok. so." Marissa said awkwardly "I need to set up some rules for this, it's not me being a bitch this time, it's actually important."

"I mean, I don't mind if you're a *little* bit of a bitch." I said lightly "Why rules?"

"This is serious, Amber. My mom is... mmm, ok, so if *she* talks to *you*, you can say something, but otherwise, please just sit quietly? And like, try to be as graceful as possible, and please, please, don't mention us being together, even if she *does* talk to you..."

"Wait," I said "wait, you're- you're really going to try and convince her I'm nothing but a pet, aren't you?"

I was hurt, I knew I shouldn't be, she'd done the same with her friends, but to not even be allowed to *talk*? I felt like she was ashamed of me, or that she valued her 'dignity' over mine. With her friends, it was easy to say it was an act, her manipulating them the way she always did, but with her mother, it was more *personal*. I felt the emotions swirling inside me, and I tried to push them down, but they still made it up to my face and I fought off tears.

"Oh, fuck, Amber..." Marissa said, taking me into her hand, the clothes left on the floor behind me "My mom isn't happy I got you at *all*, she'd hate if she knew we were even *friends*, even if you were still your old size. If she realized we were a *thing*? She could kick me out, or- I don't know, stop paying for school until I got rid of you."

"I'm- I'm not an *item* to get rid of like a shirt or an old sock." I said, my voice cracking. "I'm a person, I'm *your* person."

Why was I feeling this *now*? Was it because I'd finally let myself feel like we were ok together?

"Amber, no matter what she did, I wouldn't get rid of you" she said. She kissed the top of my head and squeezed me tightly "I'll never ever give you up, ever."

A week ago, that would have been a threat. It might still be, in the right setting.

"I just- I want to feel like a person, I felt like a person all day yesterday, and now I'm supposed to be your new toy again?"

"I know, I know." she cooed "I understand, but if you can do this and just hold out, she'll be gone again in a week or so, and we'll have the run of the house. We don't even have to see her much, just a dinner here or there, a breakfast, maybe going shopping once, it'll be fine."

"It feels like I'm only your 'whatever we are' when it's convenient for you..."

"It's not forever, when I graduate I get the company, remember?" she said "And then I'll be able to do what I want, including telling everyone how much you mean to me."

I sniff, I hadn't cried, but I'd come very close. "Please, just... make sure you don't de-humanize me to her."

She frowned, but nodded "I can do that, yeah. And hey, tonight is the sleep-over party! You'll be the star of the show, bossing Henri around, Quince will want to play with you, Tracy will be scared of touching you, you'll have *all* the power, I'll even take a backseat, if you like."

"...Fine." I said "Let's just get breakfast over with and get to school..."

"It'll be ok, Amber." Marissa said setting me down "I'm sure once you get dressed up and downstairs, you'll feel much better about it."

~~~

I sat on the table, my knees primly folded under me as I looked up at Ms Lund. Her eyes were the same green as Marissa's and her half-lidded stare was uncomfortably familiar. She wasn't an exact match, her nose was sharper, her cheeks more defined, surgery maybe? And her style was severe. Her tight, light grey suit hugged her body, making angles and sharp corners where there shouldn't be, making her feel unapproachable or even 'spiky'.

Her eyes drilled into me, and I kept my face neutral as Marissa ate her breakfast beside me, a fancy egg dish with spinach and tofu, something her mom had ordered for the two of them. I wondered if it was any good, it didn't have anything I *couldn't* eat as a vegetarian, and I'd proven uncompressed food wasn't *too* bad for me. If it'd been just me and Marissa, I might have asked for a bite, but with the frosty giant across from me, I was unable to even tease her about eating tofu the day after bragging to *my* mom about how she only ate meat.

"Marissa, this... class B, you got." Ms Lund said, her eyes flicking up to her daughter

"Yes?" Marissa replied in a polite tone, even more polite than the one she'd used with my family

"It is legally considered a less than human entity, is it not?"

"They're legally considered to be *less* human than us due to the percent of compressed non-human material making up their bodies, but they are still technically within the Homo genus, so, it's a grey area." Marissa said, a waver in her voice

"I see. So they can be considered sub-human primates, then, by the same logic?"

"I- well, the law and science is still catching up to them, and-"

"Marissa." Ms Lund said, her voice sharp. Marissa shut up and stared at her "We discussed you owning *animals* before. It's not becoming of you."

"I'm her guardian, it's not the same as if I got a dog, I'm a government licensed-" Marissa started in vain

"It is not a human, therefore it is an animal." Ms Lund said firmly.

My heart was pounding, and I was struggling to hold back my breakfast. Having someone that big call me an animal to my face, to talk over me like I wasn't even aware of the words she was saying, it was almost too much. I kept my composure, somehow, almost. My head floated away, and I listened to the conversation through a cloud.

"I- I- There's-" Marissa said, sounding upset, but trying to hide it

"I don't want *animals* in my house, Marissa."

"She's- I'll make sure she's with me, I'll-"

"You didn't ask if you could spend that money, you didn't ask if you could get a pet, and you couldn't even get one that took *care* of itself."

"She does cardio..." Marissa said weakly

"I *want* to tell you to throw it out, to get rid of it." Ms Lund said

My heart seized, and I involuntarily jolted. *Thrown out*? Not even put up for adoption? My breathing felt shallow, and I was on the edge of passing out.

"Those things are a drain on society. The people in charge pull resources and researchers that could be doing *helpful* things away, just to keep these parasites alive longer."

"..." Marissa didn't answer, but I could feel the table shaking slightly from her trembling

"You know that one friend of yours? Tracy Millon? Her father owns a company doing studies on these things."

"Sh-she mentioned."

"Well, the company is purely run off of government grants and charity. Terrible business model. I'm planning a hostile takeover in a couple weeks, and I'm going to put those resources to actual good use."

"You're a majority shareholder in the company?" Marissa asked "Tracy never said..."

"No, I own a lot, but I'm working with the other shareholders who are fed up of the way it's being run to buy their shares. LundCorp will be the new majority shareholder by the end of the month."

"I thought- Tracy just started an internship there, management track, and-" Marissa said, obviously trying to steer the conversation away from me

"She'll keep her job, her father will have the 'ownership' of the company, and the titles to go along with that, but the voting power and upper management will all be LundCorp"

"That's- So I'll be her boss eventually?"

"In a way, yes. As you should be. You're a Lund, you need to *act* like it, you're not like the others around you, they only exist to support *you*, you're forgetting that again."

"Ah. Ok, yes, of course." Marissa said

I understood why Marissa was like this a little more now. You can't blame *everything* on a parent, of course, but so much of her behavior was apparent in her mother, it was a little concerning. The way she spoke, the superiority, the veiled insecurities, everything subtle in Marissa was apparent in Ms Lund, and vice versa.

"Which is why I'm so frustrated at you for buying that *thing*." Ms Lund said, jabbing a finger towards me "You're putting yourself on a lower level, a tier of servanthood, just to look after a *pet*. Pets aren't for truly better people, Marissa. Getting a pet just makes you that pet's slave, working to keep it alive, with no regard to your own value."

"..." Marissa's breath got slightly faster. Part of me wanted to be upset at her for not defending me here, but the rest of me was terrified that one wrong move would end with me getting 'disposed of'.

"I won't kill your new pet, Marissa. I'm not cruel." Ms Lund said "But I won't entertain it, either. Take it off the table, and I don't want to see it again. Keep it hidden around me. When I look at that thing next to you, I don't see you as a strong, confident business woman who can take on the world, I see you as a fucking caretaker."

She took a bite of her eggs

"I won't have a caretaker for a daughter, Marissa."

"...ok..." Marissa said, her voice small and hoarse. She reached out, and carefully picked me up off the table, moving me to her lap, putting me in the hammock of her pleated skirt. I curled up against her left hand as she stroked me, and I started to cry. I'd never felt more worthless or hurt, I didn't even *know* this woman, and she'd reduced me to tears without ever talking to me. I couldn't imagine Marissa having to *live* with her. I gripped Marissa's thumb tightly, and rubbed my cheek against her, it felt like we were somehow closer now, we had a common threat, a shared 'enemy', and even though my chest hurt and I felt like shit, it was nice to know I had her with me.

~~~

Marissa cried in the car after breakfast. She sobbed tears that ran down her cheeks and onto my clothes as she rubbed me into her face, her whole body shaking.

"I don't know why she can't just leave me alone..." she said, her voice thick

"She's horrible, Marissa, you don't have to listen to her..." I said

"I d-do though..."

"Well, you don't have to respect her, I guess."

She looked at me and smoothed down my tear-stained hair, her eyes puffy and watery. "I'm sorry she said all those things. You're *not* an animal, Amber."

"She kinda didn't say anything *you* haven't already said, though, aside from straight up using the word 'animal'." I pointed out. I shouldn't have, it was petty, but I was hurting, and Marissa *had* called me 'not human' and 'pet' before.

Marissa's face broke again and she choked "But I didn't *mean* it, I was *fucking* with you, it's a game, it's-"

She took a breath "She really *actually* thinks that, and I'm so so sorry you have to deal with that."

I changed the subject slightly "I guess I'm not allowed to like, be out and in sight when she's around, huh?"

"We mostly stay in my room anyway. I was going to use the theater tonight, but if she comes in while we're there, I'll put you under my shirt or something."

"You have a theater?!" I asked "I just realized, I've only seen like, your room, the front entrance, and the hall leading to the kitchen and dining room, out of the whole giant house."

"...It's too big."

"What is, the theater?"

"Nnno." Marissa said, wiping her eyes "The house. When my dad lived there, we'd have parties, we'd have people from far away countries staying over in the floor below mine for weeks at a time, some even brought their kids for me to boss around. The garage was full of cool cars, the kitchen had more than one chef because we always had guests, and even the servants were more present."

She dug in her purse and pulled out a small ice mask, slightly melted, and applied it to her eyes.

"Ever since the divorce, the house has been too big. No one comes over, no one uses the guest rooms, the smoking room is empty and doesn't smell like him anymore, and all the fun decor is gone. The only place that feels 'safe' anymore is the kitchen and my room."

"I didn't realize." I said "I just thought that's how rich people's houses were."

She sniffled and shook her head "No, that's all my mother. She sucked the life out of him, and threw him out when he found someone who 'cared' about him. His new wife fucking sucks, so I can't even go live with *him*. It's better to just stay with my mom, at least she's gone ten months out of the year."

"Maybe- if you ask, he could get you a place of your own?" I suggested "He really seemed to love you, he hugged you, asked about you, and he was all smiles, and- I don't know..."

"Maybe." Marissa said, rubbing the icepack into her eye sockets "I think it'd jeopardize my mom's willingness to give up her half of LundCorp to me, though. She'd know I was escaping her and take it personally."

"Did you *plan* on crying in the car?" I asked "Or do you just always have an ice pack in your bag?

"I knew I probably would." she said "I learned in high school, always prepare to cry as soon as you're out of sight of mom, even if it doesn't happen, it pays to be prepared."

"That really sucks..." I said

"Yeah, whatever. I'll be rich and powerful soon enough, and my mom can go blow a pig."

"Won't she be majority something though?" I asked

"She'll have like, I don't know, forty percent or something, and my dad will too, and I'll have the rest, I'll just do puppy dog eyes at my dad to get him to vote my way. Once the companies are merged, I'll actually have the *real* power."

"Oh, you really thought it all out." I said, mildly impressed

"It's the only thing that kept me sane these past few years." Marissa said "That and fantasizing about you, of course."

I flushed "Uh huh, yeah, fantasizing about *bullying* me, I'm sure"

She pulled the eye mask off and smiled at me smugly "Maybe. Speaking of..."

She lifted me up to her face, closing her right eye and pushing me against it "Does this feel puffy to you?"

I squirmed against her cold skin, the ice pack having made her face much too chilly for my thin blouse to be pressed against "It's fine, it's fine! Take me off, you're too cold!"

She lowered me and shook her head "Mmm, see *you* cried a lot too, your eyes must be puffy, right? Gotta make sure to get you school ready, here, let's get the ice pack..."

"No- stop!" I said, if she put me on the ice pack, I'd be chattering all day trying to get warm "If I look like I was crying, people will just think *you* did it to me, which is good, right?"

She stopped, and thought about it for a second "Welllll... I *guess* so. Of course, I could just make you cry for *real*, and it'd feel even better~"

"Don't you have makeup to put on?" I asked, punching her index finger

"Yeah, yeah..." she said, and set me in her lap, digging through her purse for her makeup bag.

I lay in her lap, looking up at her upside down, my head pointed towards her stomach. She was simple, in a way, she'd been crying and opening up about her family troubles just moments before, and switched to her usual, teasing self as soon as she was reminded to bully me. Was that my effect on her? She'd mentioned she wasn't close to her friends before, was I the only one she'd talked to about this stuff? The car hit a bump, jolting us, causing her to wipe a smear of mascara on her nose. At the same time, her thighs clamped together around me, smushing me and holding me in place firmly. I pressed into her meat, and felt her warmth, and put my head to one side, rubbing my face against her thigh through her skirt. It was scratchy through the fabric, but I didn't care, it was soft, and warm, and her, and that was enough.

She looked down at me as she was wiping the makeup off with a towelette and frowned "You ok?" Her thighs loosened their grip again and I fell away into the fabric of her skirt. "You were wiggling."

"Yeah, I'm ok." I said "Sometimes I just like touching you, I guess. It's like, comforting, in a weird way."

"I just threatened to make you cry, and then you're snuggling my legs?" she asked "Do you *want* me to make you cry?"

"Not- I don't know." I said "I don't think you *would*, now."

"Oh, trust me, I really would." she said, rolling her eyes. "Just wait until next time we 'play', I'll have you *begging* for mercy."

"Whatever." I said "I liked the first time, it was fun. I'd like to do it again, to be honest."

"Well good, because we absolutely will. That was the deal." she reminded me

"Hey, where are you going to carry me today?" I asked, realizing her top didn't have pockets

"I was thinking my purse, but, like, it's up to you." she said, packing her makeup away and tucking it into the bag in question

"I'd prefer to be in physical contact with you, honestly." I said, disappointed "Like, through clothes or whatever, somehow."

"Uhh, I could tuck you into my waistband?" she said "I dressed for my mom, not for you, so I don't have pockets. I could always just hold you in my hand all day, I could squeeze and pet you constantly, which sounds nice."

"How tight is the waistband?" I asked, looking at where it hugged her tummy. Her black top hung just over it, the sheer fabric light and silky.

She stuck a finger in "Hm, stretchy? So, I could maybe fit my hand in there if I tried."

"Ok, I'll ride there." I said

"Are you sure?" Marissa asked "It'd be safer in the purse, I have a zip area I cleaned out and put a glasses cloth in for you for padding..."

"I wanna try this, and I want to feel you." I said "We're together, so like, it's normal for me to want to be close to you, right?"

"Hm, yeah, fine. But if you want out, let me know ok? Same as before, two taps, seriously, communicate."

"Aww, you're all *worried* about me now, that's cute!" I teased, trying to keep the blush off my face and the tingles out of my chest. It felt *good* to be cared for, I wasn't quite used to it yet.

"Oh, fuck you, tiny." Marissa said, pulling her seatbelt off "Let's just get to class before we're late."

"Nice of you to include me in that 'we', like I haven't already finished this course already."

"Oh, great, then *you* can do my homework!"

"...*You* don't even do homework."

She grinned at me as she got out, scooping me up in the process "That makes it even more evil of me to make *you* do it."

She pulled her waistband out, and slid me into the front of her skirt, my legs against her shorts, my torso pinned by the elastic, and my upper body against her tummy. My arms hung over the waistband, and I could kick my feet and make the skirt flare a little under me. I giggled, it was kinda like we were both wearing the same skirt, in a way. I looked up at Marissa, but only saw the darkness of the inside of her top above me, her torso fading away into shadows.

"I can feel you wiggling again..." Marissa said, poking me as she got her bag "You're not in any danger of falling or anything, right?"

I pushed at the waistband, finding it tight "I don't think so, no, and I'm holding on."

"Ok, because if you *do* fall, there's like, a one hundred percent chance I accidentally kick you down the hall as you fall and you get stepped on."

"Please don't say that." I said, shivering "This is cozy, I can breathe."

"Yeah, breathing is important, huh?" Marissa said, walking carefully into the school "*Gods*, I can't believe I was so oblivious..."

"..." I wanted to tell her it was fine, but it really, really wasn't, and I was still having trouble accepting that whole experience.

"No, yeah, I get it." Marissa said, her hand finding me and making sure I was secure "Let's not talk about that anymore."

I pressed my face up against her, *this* was better, no rough denim, no passing out, just me, and the beautiful, wonderful warmth. I could hear her stomach digesting too, slightly. It was odd, and the noises were gross in a way, but in another way, it reminded me that she was human, too. I felt her soft meat against my cheek and for a second, I thought about how lucky I was it was *living* meat, instead of the dead stuff.

...A weird thought for anyone to have, but a valid one for me after yesterday.

I opened my mouth and got a mouthful of Marissa, biting down as hard as I could, just to see what would happen. I heard her hiss, and her hand swung down, lightly smacking me, her palm knocking the air out of me and slightly stunning me. I laughed, and went to bite her again. If she could bite *me* to claim me, I could bite *her* too. She was mine after all, right?

"I swear, if you do that again, you're going in the purse whether you like it or not." Marissa growled "*And* I'm zipping your pocket closed."

...Right, the power imbalance, yeah. Still, I could see my teethmarks on her skin, and that was enough to satisfy my 'marking' desires for now. I pulled her top aside and felt the *thud thud thud* of her footsteps as she walked, and looked out at the world around me. There were a lot of students who glanced at Marissa, and quickly turned away, or flinched, and a couple whose eyes followed her as she confidently walked past them. I wondered what their stories were, did they think they could out play her? Had they just not been targeted and only knew her by reputation?

...Did they have a thing for her?

I wasn't sure how I'd feel about that. *We* were a thing, but if I was still a class B, was that thing exclusive? Would she, given the chance, get a full sized partner too? I'd heard of that before, on AntMound, where someone's spouse got guardianship, and because the marriage is nullified with the class B classification, they re-married. It sounded shitty, to have to watch your loved one marry someone else right in front of you, and still have to rely on them for everything. I really hoped it wouldn't come to that for me and her...

She slipped into the classroom, and sat down, her legs making a 'bench' of sorts for me to sit on. I dug my heels into her thigh and looked around at the underside of the lecture hall desks. They were clean, as was to be expected from our college, but they were also very boring. I couldn't even see the professor from down here. Well, there was more than one place to sit, so I kicked my feet, and shimmied out of the waistband, standing on her leg and surveying my next move. Marissa looked down at me, confused, but didn't move to put me back, and kept watching me as the lecture started

I'd need a way to climb up... Her shirt was sheer, and offered little in the way of handholds, so that left going under. Marissa was slouching, so even with her muscles she was so proud of, she had *some* rolls of skin and fat over her belly area. It wasn't much, but I had literally nothing better to do, and no reason not to try. I ducked under her shirt, and started up.

I fit my hands onto the folds and turns of skin, pulling myself up, looking down to the 'ground' below me. Marissa shifted, making her skirt a little looser between her thighs, I guessed in case I fell, but I couldn't see her face, so her reaction was a mystery to me. I worked my way up, feeling her shirt brush against me, feeling the tiny, almost invisible hairs on her stomach, and pulled myself up to her bra. It was a fancy one, underwired, black like her shirt, and fitted well, a perk of being 'normal' sized. All mine had to be elastic these days, and were all slightly loose. It bugged me to the point I'd go without if I could get away with it. As it was though, the bra was not an obstacle, it was more of a help than anything, giving me a good grip and foothold to climb from. I looked at the 'canyon' I was in and snorted. As hard as she'd try, she'd never be able to hold me in place *here*. I climbed up without resistance, getting to her neckline by pulling myself up her collarbone.

I pushed against her collar, and poked my head out, proud of myself, I'd gotten all the way up! I pushed myself the rest of the way through, and after some wiggling, I was free and able to crawl over to my spot on Marissa's shoulder. I grinned up at her, expecting to see an exasperated glare or a bored eye roll, but instead, her whole face was bright red. I held back laughter as she eyed me pointedly, widening her eyes to send me a message. Whatever it was, I wasn't getting it, but seeing how out of sorts she was, I felt like I'd beaten her somehow. I lay on her shoulder, stomach down, and kicked my legs as I watched the lecture, feeling Marissa shift uncomfortably under me. It was one I'd attended last year, but it was still better than staring at the underside of a desk.

~~~

"I can't *believe* you chose a fucking lecture as the perfect time to explore my body." Marissa said, her face still red

I climbed on top of a stack of library books and sat down on them like a staircase "I'm getting more comfortable with you, and I wanted to get to your shoulder to see."

"Then do 'upsies' or something, don't just clamber across my body like a tiny monkey. Do you know how hard it is to keep still with a tiny person crawling up you?"

"*I* think you did pretty good, at least." I said, smiling

"Look, I enjoyed that, it was fun, but- just, not in public, please." Marissa muttered

"Too worried someone will see?" I said

"*Yes*. Exactly that, gods." Marissa said in a hushed shout

"Ok, fine." I said "I won't explore your body in public in front of your peers again."

Her face flushed harder and she lowered her head. For once, I had an upper hand. Marissa, as it turned out, had a bad case of modesty, as weird as it was. I, on the other hand, had been unbothered by changing rooms, shower rooms, and sleeping in a bra at sleepovers since I was a teen. I didn't have anything anyone would be interested in those places, I'd assumed, so I was immune to the embarrassment. It did make me wonder how Marissa dealt with the whole tennis team going in for showers at once... I'd have to ask her about that later, once she didn't look like she was about to swat me.

"Anyway, are we staying here until your labs? Or like, are we going to go home and you drop me off?" I asked

"I'm blowing off labs today." she said "I... don't want you out of my sight while my mom is here, not that she'd do anything, but... still."

"Ok, so home then?"

"Nope, I wanted to head out to the big mall in the next town over if it's ok." she said "There's a class B store, and I wanted to see if there's anything cool I can get you, as like a 'hey we're an item' gift."

"Oh, wow, really?" I said, flattered "I- yeah, that sounds amazing. I don't think you're supposed to tell me that though, if it's a gift."

"Yeah, yeah, whatever." she said, standing and slipping me into her skirt again "You'll be there with me, so there won't be any secret, plus you need to tell me what you want. Come on, let's get Drew, we still need to hit a liquor store before tonight too."

"Didn't you have stuff left over from last time?" I asked

"Not enough, and I want that Korean stuff your dad gave me, that was great, it was a weird buzz, but it's nice."

"Just be aware that stuff is strong, you got cuddly off one bottle last time." I reminded her

"Ohhh nooo I might *snuggle* you, gosh, whatever shall we do..." she said sarcastically, pushing open the doors leading out of the school

"If you want to come out as bi to your friends and give me kisses all night, I won't complain." I said "But I kinda thought you were trying to keep up the 'aloof straight girl' thing."

"Whatever." she said, waving to Drew to come over "We'll see how it goes. If it comes down to it, I can blame the alcohol or something."

I kicked my legs again, feeling her skirt flutter. I was in a weirdly good mood for someone who'd been crying her eyes out a few hours ago because she'd been called an animal who needed to be thrown away. I couldn't put my finger on it exactly, but I was pretty sure it was because the feeling of 'holy *shit* I have a girlfriend who cares about me' was finally kicking in, even if said girlfriend would probably enjoy kicking *me* a little too.

~~~

I sat in Marissa's hand in front of the store; "*Tiny Toys for Tiny Treasures*". I felt insulted, somehow. Being called a 'treasure' wasn't insulting itself, but it just felt like it was objectifying me, somehow. I looked around at the displays in the windows; tiny cars in several sizes, portable kitchens that ran on batteries, accessory pieces like the one Marissa had, anything you could think of.

I glanced up at her, and pointed at the bottles "Hey, you have that one!"

"Uh huh" she murmured, half paying attention to me "This place doesn't feel like the ad..."

"I mean," I said "we don't *have* to go in here, we can just go look at movies and figures, that's what me and Henri usually did at the mall."

"No, I wanted to get you something. This place just feels like it's a luxury pet store or something, not a store offering services for disabled people."

"I *am* a pet, Marissa." I pointed out "You say that all the time."

"You're a pet, sure, but- gods, I don't know. I've been seeing you differently the past couple days, and like, *yeah*, you're my pet, I own you, but like, I don't know..."

"Guess you shouldn't have tried dating a pet, huh?" I snarked "If you'd gotten a dog instead of me, would you have pulled a classic white woman with it?"

"What?" She frowned at me "...I don't get it."

"...Never mind. Let's just go in..."

We went up to the front of the store, and an employee appeared as if by magic. Or as if by retail manager, which was more likely.

"Well hello ladies!" he said in a high, soft voice "May I interest you in a complementary relaxation and socialization event for class Bs happening right now?"

"Like, you want to take Amber?" Marissa asked, her voice hard

"No, no no no, of course not, we simply have a fun, relaxing area set up for her to stay in, make some friends, and try out the products while you're free to shop all you want! You can even leave and come back to pick her up later if you have other shopping to do too!" he assured her

Marissa pushed past him "No, fuck off, you're not getting her."

"Oh, won't you please just look at the area?" he asked "It's very safe, and designed by our top class B specialists, to ensure the most comfortable experience."

Marissa growled, but let him drag her over to a large open topped box in one corner of the store. I held onto her finger and looked over into the 'relaxation and socialization' center and shuddered. The stuff was all there, mismatched sizes and all on at once, making the whole box drone with tv noise, the hum of motors, and the buzz of the bright sunlamps built into the the walls. The class Bs inside were all exhausted and disheveled, some laying on chairs, one in a hot tub, threatening to slip in, one was laying prone on a piece of workout equipment soaked in sweat, but it didn't look it was because she'd been using the machine. She looked up and made eye contact with me, subtly shaking her head.

"Uhh, Marissa, didn't you say *I* was getting to pick something out today?" I asked loudly "I can't do that from here."

She looked at me, and glared back up at the employee "Yeah, guy, how the fuck is she supposed to pick shit out from a fucking box?"

He wilted a little and shook his head "If she stays here, she can test our most popular items and let you know which ones she wants!"

"Stop trying to push your weird box on us so you can sell me crap she doesn't want." Marissa said "Just leave us alone, I want to shop."

The employee frowned, but nodded. "Alright, please let me know if you have any questions." he said, and walked back to the front of the store

"That guy was pushy, but you were kind of a dick too." I said "They say how your partner treats employees is a sign of how the relationship will go, you know."

Marissa squeezed me "He wanted you in there so I wouldn't know what you wanted and get you the wrong thing, and so you'd want stuff in there that isn't on shelves, it's a trick or something. I won't be tricked. It's not about him being an employee or whatever."

"Fair enough, I guess." I said "I didn't want a hot tub or anything anyway."

"Darn, there goes my birthday idea for you." she said, rolling her eyes. "What *do* you want?"

"Uh, I have no idea." I said "I don't know the budget, or what all is here."

"My credit card has a $2000 limit, anything over that, I'll need to use my debit, which alerts my mom. So under $2000 total."

"Oh, fuck." I said "I was thinking like, $25 or something, I could get one of those *cars* for $2000..."

"You want a car, then?" Marissa said, stopping to look at them, holding me up to measure my size against the different models

"No, I don't know when I'd drive it." I said. Not much use for a car when I could just ride the Marissa express "Oh, actually-"

"Yeah?"

"...It's stupid, but could we check the electronics?"

"You want a better TV or something?" She asked, walking to the aisle "Your tablet is already top of the line. It has cellular, by the way, I haven't seen you bring it anywhere, but it works everywhere."

"Oh, wow! I didn't realize that." I said. I didn't know if I'd bring it many places with me, but that was good to know I could "I'm actually looking for two things, headphones so I can watch stuff at night while you sleep, and... something kinda dumb..."

"Mm, I forget, you only need like five or six hours of sleep, right?" Marissa said, pulling a pair of 95% compression headphones off the shelf

"Mhhm, which leads to my next thing I wanted to ask about..." I said. I knew she wouldn't make fun, but still, it felt silly to ask for it...

"Spit it out, Amber." she said, annoyed

I pointed "That. I heard about it on AntMound. It's a games console with controllers that are almost my size, and... it can play Last Legend 28, too."

Marissa picked one up and flipped it over, looking at the stats "I mean, I *guess* this counts as a 'console'?" she said "It's not much better than my phone."

"The version of LL28 on it *was* built from an abandoned mobile port." I admitted "But that's my favorite game, and I thought I couldn't ever play it again, until I saw people on AntMound talking about it."

"It's like, less than $300, yeah, you can get this." Marissa said, nodding "Is it crossplay with PC?"

"LL28 is crossplay with everything, sure." I said

"Cool..." she said "I don't like that kind of game usually, but I'll give it a shot, we can play together sometime."

"Oh!" I said "I hadn't thought of that! Yeah, I'd love that! I'll show you the ropes, I'll smurf so we can do the starter missions together. I'll see if it has Life and Times on this console, and we can do that one too, on different screens!"

"Nnnnno, I like holding you while we play that." Marissa said "Let's just play that like usual. But yeah, I'll get you this console thing."

"Thank you, Missy!~" I said, hugging her fingers

"That's what my *dad* calls me..." she said, a funny look on her face as she pet me

I broke the hug "Should I not?..."

"It- it's just weird, but I don't hate it. I'll let you know if you need to stop." she said

We checked out, and Marissa flipped off the employee on the way out, her bag in one hand, and me in the other. I felt odd, like I had a pit in my stomach from this morning, but like I was also on top of the world from the good day I'd spent with my *girlfriend~*... or... something, whatever she was to me. It didn't matter, we were together, labels were a fuck. I was very excited to try my new console, I'd missed playing LL28 every day or two, and I'd missed so, so many dailys by now, and I think at least two catwalk shows? Maybe three, it was hard to remember, but assuming my account worked on this console, I'd be flirting with catboys again in no time...

As soon as the sleepover was finished, of course. I got a growing sense of trepidation as we drove to the alcohol store to stock up. I'd had a fun enough time at the last one, but I'd had a close call too, and we'd be playing 5D chess trying to keep our relationship a secret and to manage Henri at the same time. If *anyone* could manipulate people that well though, it was Marissa, I just had to hope she didn't get too drunk on soju to work her magic...

## Chapter Seventeen

I sat on the sofa next to Marissa, we'd run into her mom on the way up with the alcohol and my new gifts, but the exchange had been quick. She'd seemed apathetic to Marissa having people over, and let her know she'd be having dinner out tonight, so she shouldn't expect to eat with her. I had heard the entire thing from Marissa's waistband, her shirt pulled in front of me to hide me, and I had been on the edge of my seat the whole time, terrified Ms Lund would notice me.

Now though, it was almost time for the others to show up, and Marissa had already opened her first bottle of Soju, sipping it as her leg bounced, making the couch move slightly under me. I lay back and looked up at the ceiling. Marissa had said she'd focus the party on just hanging out, watching a movie or two in the theater and drinking, no punishments like last time, but *I* was still expected to bully Henri, and I wasn't really sure how I was supposed to do that.

"Hey, M?" I said, glancing over

"Yeah?" she said, putting her drink down

"You mentioned you'd coach me on how to, uh, boss Henri around?" I glanced at the door "We have a few minutes, and I have *no* idea about how to do that kind of thing..."

She hummed thoughtfully "It's not hard, see, you gotta think of *why* you're doing it, and the how will follow. You being her boss tonight is serving two purposes, the first is to make sure she stops seeing you as less than human, the second is to humiliate her."

"Why does me being her boss help her see me as a person?" I asked "I think I missed that part."

"Because if *she's* a person, and you're better than her- or, more important or something, then that means you must be human too, right?"

"Um, I don't follow exactly, but I think I understand the logic." I said "What kinds of things should I have her do, though?"

"Oh, like, dancing, barking, being a footrest, that kind of thing." Marissa said dismissively

"I don't know how I'd use her as a footrest if I'm being honest." I said "I can't thing of a single situation that would work in at this size."

"Oh yeah? Here, let me show you, it's simple~" Marissa said, scooting to the edge of the couch "You just put your feet on her like thiiis..."

She lifted her socked feet up and onto the couch, and I rolled out of the way, dashing to the other end of the couch from her before she could pin me.

"No examples, please." I said, smiling at her "I get the picture."

Marissa giggled and reached out, poking me with her toe "What's the matter? Don't like feet? They're clean, and fresh socks tooo~"

I shook my head, backing up "No, I don't really like feet, I don't understand people who *do*, to be honest."

Marissa swung her legs off the couch and spun herself so her face was next to me now "Yeah, I don't get it either, but it's pretty fun to use them on people, stepping on them, making them kiss them, kicking..."

"I bet, but could we maybe make a rule that you don't do that to me?" I asked "Like, when we're playing."

She frowned, but nodded "Yeah, I guess so. Anything else off limits?"

I thought about it "Well, I really don't want broken bones..."

She snorted and bapped me with a finger, on the head instead of the face "Yeah, no shit, dumbass, I meant like, stuff you don't want me to do."

"Ah, right. Hm, suffocation wasn't fun, but being in your mouth *was*, and I couldn't breathe *then*, so I don't really know>" I said thoughtfully "I guess I'll just have to see how stuff goes, and let you know what I liked?"

"That's totally fair." Marissa said "I'll try to get creative."

She grinned at me smugly "Still, you said you liked being in my mouth?"

I flushed, and nodded "Y-yeah, no, it was- I enjoyed that."

"I *thought* so, but you should have said something sooner!~" Marissa said, using her best teasing voice

"W-why is that?" I asked, already knowing what was coming and bracing for it with anticipation

"Because if I had known, I'd have done *this* more..." She leaned forward, her mouth encircling me, her hot, cinnamon breath washing over me, feeling so, so good and warming me to my bone. Her teeth find the familiar spot on my ribs, digging into the still-bruised teethmarks from before, and her tongue flicked forward to lick my cheek. I shuddered, I felt helpless, useful, powerful. I knew I was making her feel nice and in charge, and that made *me* feel nice. The pressure, the warmth, the smells of her saliva and toothpaste, the smooth wetness of her tongue on my neck, knowing I was *hers*, knowing she could flex and bite and *end* me, but she *loved* me, so she never would. I reach back with my arms to pull her lips closed around me, I wanted to be sealed in, to be-

The door opened with a bang and Marissa jerked up, me still in her mouth, and I screamed at the sudden movement. To her credit, she didn't bite down, but I was still laying ribs first on her bottom row of teeth, holding myself off her tongue with my hands.

"Heyy-ooo!" Quince yelled "We're here to partyyy- What the *fuck*?"

Marissa's hand closed around my waist and gently pulled me out of her mouth, and I took a deep breath and rubbed my ribs gingerly. It had been fun, but... I was frustrated that it ended so unsatisfactorily.

"Uh, was A-Amber in your *mouth*?" Tracy asked, sounding grossed out. I twisted in Marissa's grip to see, and sure enough, she had a disgusted look on her face, opposing Quince's sly grin.

"I, uhh..." Marissa said, and I knew her face was bright red with shame.

"I'm sorry!" I yelled, thinking quickly "I won't try to get out of wearing it anymore, just please, don't do that again!"

Marissa blinked, and then re-applied her signature grin "Fuck *yeah* you'll wear it, and don't fucking forget it!"

She stood and brought me over to my house, setting me in front of my bathroom door. "Sorry, girls, I just got carried away punishing her when she started talking back, you know I'm a biter."

"That is *so* fun though!" Quince said "Jesus, just fucking *chomping* on her? I'll have to remember that."

"It's so, so unsanitary..." Tracy said "And pretty dangerous too."

"Whatever, it worked." Marissa said, putting the clown costume from my wardrobe in my hands "She's wearing it now, and she'll think twice about giving me lip."

I stared at the costume. I'd done this to myself, but it looked so *stupid*. The neck frill, the bobbles down the front, the vivid blues and yellows, *and* it was some kind of knock off silk, so it was super thin. I waved Marissa down to talk to her, holding up the costume. She bent over, listening as the other two set their bags down.

"I'll wear this, but it's thin as all get out, you'll need to remember to hold me often enough to keep me warm, got it?" I said quietly, knowing the others most likely couldn't hear me, but still being careful.

"I would have anyway, whatever, just get changed." she said, nodding.

"What was she saying? More lip?" Quince said, perking up

"Uh, no, it's a back zip, she wanted me to zip her up." Marissa said

"Oh, ok." Quince said "Tell her to hurry up, I wanna show you guys something!"

I stepped in the bathroom, quickly changing out of the fancy clothes I was wearing and slipping into the garish clown outfit. I stepped outside and let Marissa zip me up. She pursed her lips in a way that made it obvious she was holding back an "awww", and picked me up, moving over to the coffee table, sitting on the floor across from the couch where the other two were. She set me on the table, and I waved at Quince and Tracy, the big sleeves flapping as I did so. Tracy got a small smile on her face, and Quince's eyes widened.

"Ok, I can *kinda* see the appeal, seeing her like that." Tracy said, looking at me like I was a cute cat

"Oh my ghaaads I wanna *snuggle* her!" Quince muttered "That's adorable~"

"She really didn't wanna wear it, but I'm pretty damn persuasive." Marissa bragged

"Ok, ok, ok, I got this though." Quince said "I can *finally* one up you, here, look! at!" She dug in her bag and pulled out a small black rectangular plastic box, about 10 inches long and set it on the table

"...this!" she said, popping the front off.

From the box, a woman about 7 inches tall stumbled out, coughing and stumbling, gasping for air. She was slightly tan, almost twice as tall as me with sandy hair and a thin frame. She was older than us, in her 30s if I had to guess, and she was dressed in off white scrubs. I gasped, and ran over to her as she coughed and tried to breathe. That box was *not* an approved carrying container, I could tell that much, and she was having trouble catching her breath. I patted her on the back, and she took deep breaths, trying to calm down as the others talked over us.

"I picked her up this morning!" Quince said "Skipped class and everything to go get her. She was found a couple days ago, but apparently there was some debate about if she was really a class B or not."

"What?" Tracy asked "She very obviously is."

"Maybe not." Marissa said "Only if she's less than 90% of her former height, she could have been short, so she would still be a full class A."

"Yup!" Quince said "They said she was literally 9.84% of her old size after all the tests and looking at records, another quarter inch and she'd still be human!"

"Holy shit, that's horrible..." Tracy said "That's- I can't imagine..."

"Yeah." Marissa said, eyeing me as I hugged the crying woman "Hey, that box you had her in though, it's not safe, she looks pretty shook up. You really need a real container for her."

"I know, I know, whatever." Quince said "I already had this one, and the lid doesn't seal all the way, it's fine. I'll be getting her supplies and stuff tomorrow or Sunday or something."

"What's her name?" Marissa asked

"Uhhh, it's- damnit, hey, what was your name again?" Quince asked the woman.

She took a deep breath "It- I'm Kensey." she said standing up and finally looking around. I came up roughly to the bottom of her ribs, and I was surprised at how small that made me feel. I was used to being just under ankle high, but having someone who was effectively 9 feet tall compared to me made me feel even smaller...

"Yeah, Kensey." Quince said "I might change it though, I haven't decided."

"So, Kensey, tell me about yourself." Marissa said, looking at her cooly

She looked at me, bewildered and confused "I... uh... I don't... I'm just-"

She shook her hands, and bent down and looked at me "What's going on? Are we safe here?" she whispered, her eyes wide

"Debatable..." I whispered back, unsure how to answer that "We're at a party, with a bunch of rich girls who get what they want. Play along and you should be ok."

She stared at me for a couple seconds, then nodded, and straightened up looking back at the others.

"I'm 36, I have a job as an assistant manager at a dry goods distribution center, I like to read books about romance and fantasy, and I have three cats." she said, her voice wavering

"You *had* a job and cats." Quince said "You can't hold a job now, and your cats would eat you if they saw you."

"They... they tried..." Kensey said sadly, her eyes getting wet.

"I- I'm Amber!" I said, trying to distract her "I like to draw, I play video games, I was in college for a business degree so I could open a print-on-demand store for online artists, and I love watching old tv shows."

She looked down at me, her gaze slightly unfixed, and nodded "Uh, it's nice to meet you, Amber. Have you been... like this for long?"

"Kinda, a couple weeks, I guess." I said "About."

"Aww they're bonding!" Tracy whispered. I saw Quince shoot Marissa a smug look, but I didn't understand the context.

"Uh, is- is that your dollhouse?" Kensey asked, pointing to my house

"It's a regular house, actually, but yeah!" I said "Wanna get a closer look?"

I glanced over at Marissa, who looked up at Quince.

"May I?" she asked

"Oh yeah, I have some questions I need to ask you about concerning class Bs anyway." Quince said to Marissa proudly

Marissa lifted us up, one of us in each hand, and brought us over to the house. She gave me a quick squeeze and placed us in front of the kitchen area, giving me a small smile before she went back down to the coffee table.

"Can- can they hear us?" Kensey asked, looking at them, not going into the house

"If we talk low, they can't." I said "Our voices usually only carry about 4 feet. Yours might go a bit further though, so like I said, talk low."

She nodded and stepped up into my house, her head bent over by the ceiling.

"Alright," she said quietly "please tell me there's something I'm missing, what is this?"

I glanced up at her, and frowned "What do you mean?"

"I mean-" She waved helplessly around her, ducking into my dining room and taking a seat "am I really some college girl's pet now? How do I get my old life back?"

"Ah, that... Yeah, you're a pet now. Like, for life." I said sadly "Not legally, legally you're a ward or something, and Quince is your guardian, but yeah, you're her pet until she gives you up or something."

"No, there- I have to have *rights*, plus I wasn't quite five ten like my driver's license said, I was rounding, I can appeal this, right?"

"I would hope so? I can ask on AntMound?" I said "I haven't heard about that... You do have rights though, you have *lots* of them, no excessive contact, you have to be carried in approved containers, no physical abuse, no kisses or anything, lots of stuff."

"What's AntMound?" she asked "What- I was just roughly scanned and tested, held in a glass tank for three days, then given directly to that brat outside, without any explanation of *anything*."

"That's pretty much how it goes." I said "here, let's go upstairs, I'll show you my tablet."

We headed upstairs, her crawling through the staircase with a little difficulty, and sat on my couch, her taking up most of it and me on one end.

"Look, this is AntMound." I said, showing her the app "It's like, social media for us class Bs."

"Class fucking B." Kensey muttered "I can't believe that I'm not even considered 'human' anymore."

"Well, you know, that's a whole debate." I said, waving my hand "Here, I know someone who will most likely know the answer to your question..."

I pulled the card Nada had given me out of the shelf under the tablet stand,

and poked in the address on it. She should know, she seemed pretty well versed in this stuff...

*'hey, its amberrrrr hiiii, got a friend who was tested and she ws like just under 10% but she said shes was actually shortr than her drivers lisense and she wants to fight the class b lable, how does she do that?'*

I pressed send and glanced over at Kensey "She'll reply soon, I bet. I met her in group. To swap topics though, anything you want to know about being a class B?"

She took a deep breath "How do you do it?"

I shook my head "Do what exactly?"

"I heard through the bag, your... 'owner' was *biting* you when we got in. That *can't* be safe, and you're just totally fine with it? Does she usually hurt you? How do you just deal with it? I swear, I'm on the verge of just throwing myself out your house onto the floor and being done with it and that 'Quince' girl has only had me for less than half a day."

"Right for the hard question, right off the bat..." I sighed "Uh, don't think too hard about the biting thing, it's- it's a game, I'm ok with it. But she *does* hurt me from time to time. I don't mind, if there's communication. We have an understanding, it's a type of playing, it's consensual."

"I-" she looked at me, her face wrinkling in disbelief as she got what I was implying "An *understanding*? No, I'm not- no, I don't *do* that stuff, especially with someone as young as *her*. That's *horrible*, it's not safe or even *moral*."

"To be fair, our relationship got a *lot* better once we started playing and doing two-way communication about it, I finally feel safe around her..." I said, slightly hurt and defensive. It wasn't *that* bad. I was consenting to it after all, and it was fun.

Kensey looked out at the girls and shuddered "No, seriously I have, what, fifteen years on them? That won't work at all, that's not ok, I'd feel sick."

"I didn't say you *should*, I was just saying what worked for me, Quince is more likely to like, snuggle you and accidentally hurt you than be outright mean like Marissa."

"What if I don't *want* snuggles?" she said "I'm not a touchy person when it comes to strangers, I need to be friends before I start hugging people even."

"That sucks for you, because Quince very much wants to cuddle you." I said "Look, I went to high school with her, and I was in college with her when I was compressed. She is vicious and cruel to her peers, just because she thinks it's funny or it'll get her points with her friends. If you don't play along and let her play with you, she might start seeing you as a *target* rather than a toy."

Kensey looked horrified "And- no, I have to put up with this? I'm a full grown adult, I can't-"

"Nnno, you're a class B." I said, cutting her off. "And yeah. You think that's bad? Marissa bought me *to be mean* to me, not because she thinks it's funny, but because she craves the feeling of power and control."

"You- you said you had an understanding with her?" Kensey asked, looking hopeful "I could do what you did, how did you get her to stop hurting you without consent?"

"It's complicated..." I wasn't about to out Marissa as queer to this random woman who could tell Quince, but I could give her tips "It turned out that Marissa has a soft side, a more human side than what she shows most people. Because I wasn't *real* to her in the same way, she opened up to me, and we built trust, and I became real again after we got close."

That wasn't really what happened, but it was close enough.

"She didn't see you as 'real'?" she shook her head "This whole this is sickening. What's stopping Quince from just- I don't know, tossing me in a bag and forgetting about me all day?"

"The bag needs to be an approved container, for one." I said "It needs to be approved by the government as a suitable carrying case, or you need to explicitly consent to it. Other than that, nothing, really."

"So I'm fucked then?" she asked, waving her hands "I'm in hell, and the devil has a Chanel handbag and Balenciaga sneakers?"

"Well..." I felt helpless, I couldn't really give her much hope here... "...Yeah, I guess so."

She flopped back on the couch, making it rock back dangerously. I looked at her, trying to think of something to say, but... I couldn't come up with anything useful. Luckily, the tablet dinged, and I didn't have to.

"Oh, we got a reply!" I said, opening Nada's message and showing it to Kensey

*'Hello, Amber! It is so good to hear from you, I trust you're doing well? I'm happy to hear you've made another class B friend, we need to stick together in these trying times. Please feel free to give her my contact information as well! Unfortunately due to the process, once you lose your status as a class A citizen, you can't get it back without a court order, and we as class Bs don't have the legal right to go to court ourselves, we need a liaison, usually the legal guardian. If your friend's guardian is willing to take the case to court, then she does have a shot at a re-evaluation, but if her guardian is anything like yours, I doubt that you would have much luck.'*

"So no, it's not an option." Kensey said, her body collapsing "I- fuck, a quarter of an *inch*..."

"Hey, it's not too bad?" I said "If she talks to Marissa, she'll get to know all kinds of useful stuff about taking care of you, it might be ok."

"She already took a stupid class..." she murmured "And she *still* put me in that box."

"...yeah..." I agreed "It's not looking good. I'll ask Marissa if you can come over though, like, regularly? Maybe get a break from it all."

"That'd be nice, thank you, Amber." Kensey said gently "So, you and Marissa, do you-"

A knock on the door to Marissa's room cut her off and she looked up, alarmed "Oh gods, more of them?" she hissed

"No no, this is- well, she's my best friend, or was, but she's going through something." I said, standing and walking to the edge of the desk "If she can behave tonight, she's a great person. If not, uh, just be careful around her."

"That- no, that's not- what?" she said, looking from me to the door.

Marissa got up, and crossed over to the door, opening it up to show Henri, already in her maid costume. "Heyyyy Henri..." Marissa crooned "Ready to serve us?"

"I am ready to serve *Amber*." she said, looking around and seeing me on the desk "I am her maid after all."

"Wait, you're *Amber's* maid?" Tracy asked, confused

"Aw, I wanted to boss her around..." Quince said pouting

"Yeah, I figured 'what's more humiliating than *being* a pet? Having to do whatever a pet tells you to, obviously' so I made her Amber's maid instead." Marissa said, waving Henri in.

"Hi Henri!" I called out as she walked up to the desk, slowly.

"Nuh uh, what did we talk about?" Marissa said, wiggling her finger

"Ummm..." we hadn't talked about anything like that, what was she talking about? I took a wild guess "...I mean, hey, bitch!"

Marissa grinned and clapped "There it is, ok, you kids have fun, I'm ordering pizza, any requests?"

"Can I just get cheese?" Tracy asked

"I want Hawaiian" Quince said

"Uh, ok, so one meat lover's, one cheese, one Hawaiian, got it." Marissa said, picking up the phone and stepping to the side "I'll let the chef know."

As she made the order and the other two girls talked with each other, Henri leaned in to look at me and Kensey "Did she get another one?" she asked "One was not enough!?"

"No, this is Kensey, she's here with Quince." I explained, wording it in a way that shouldn't hurt Kensey's feelings

"Oh. That is not as bad as Marissa, but it is still rough." Henri said. Marissa looked up from the phone and glared at her, giving her the middle finger as she kept ordering.

Henri ignored her looking me up and down "What are you wearing? It is cute, but..."

"Don't ask." I said, shaking my head

"Hold on- if she is forcing you to wear something, it could be a fetish, and that would count as-"

"SO." I said, changing the subject "I guess I'm your boss tonight?"

"Yeah, what's that all about?" Kensey asked "This whole thing is making me uncomfortable."

"It's an elaborate social game." I said "These girls treat their lives like a soap opera, we just need to play along with their drama, it's not that bad. Tonight's drama is me being in charge of Henri, because they think that's humiliating."

"What kinds of things will you want me to do?" Henri said, her hand reaching out close to me, almost touching but not quite

"Oh, uh, I'll figure it out as I go." I said "I'll make up stuff."

"It has got to be believable you know." Henri said, her face flushing slightly "You will need to tell me to do things that are at least a little embarrassing..."

I looked up at her sharply and remembered with slight panic that the girl in front of me was not only *in love with me*, but also a hopeless sub, and I had the leash in my hand tonight. This was kind of a problem, or it *could* be if I wasn't careful. I needed something to get her away, so I could collect my thoughts... I looked her over, she'd showered before she came, so her face was clean, I could use that.

"Ok, uh, well first off, I want you looking your best, go put on makeup for me, bitch!" I said loudly enough for the others to hear.

Henri flushed again, but stood and grabbed her bag, heading into Marissa's bathroom.

"Amber, I think this is a kink thing." Kensey whispered to me as she left "I think she *wants* this."

"Yup." I said "I know, I'm... trying to figure out how ok I am with it right now."

"Damn, Amber, you really called her ugly and sent her off, huh?" Quince said, grinning at me from over on the couch "I'm impressed, Marissa is really rubbing off on you!"

"She's doing *what* with her!?" Tracy said, looking up from her phone in alarm

I gave Quince a thumbs up, and glanced over at Marissa as she hung up the phone and came back over to us.

"Alright, let's all go to the table now." she said, picking us both up and bringing us with her.

She set us down and Kensey dropped to her knees in a ball instantly.

"I don't think I can do this..." she said, shaking

"Do what?" I asked, confused

"Just- I got picked up in a split second and carried across a *canyon*, and dropped again, all with no warning or safety precautions..."

"Yeah, duh, you're a class B." Quince said "You gotta get used to it, baby."

"It's just how it goes." Marissa said, rolling her eyes "You can't freak out just from being picked up, you're literally doll sized, people pick up dolls."

"I'm not a DOLL!" yelled Kensey "I'm a full grown woman with needs and wants and hopes and dreams and..." she fell over, crying into her hands.

"Oh, that's- that's rough..." said Tracy sadly "I get it, I'm terrified of being one of those things, I understand her fear."

"Ugh." Quince said "She's nowhere near as fun as Amber..."

She picked me up and swung me by the frilled neck of my clown costume "You're a regular team player, huh gay girl? You're always talking back, making jokes, you probably loooooove this, getting to be played with all the time, getting to see Marissa naked. I wish *mine* was gay..."

"Shut the fuck up." Me and Marissa said at the same time

I looked at her, and she narrowed her eyes, reaching over and pulling me out of Quince's hand

"Look." she said, putting me on her shoulder "You need to be nice to yours or she'll *always* be a wet blanket. It's got nothing to do with if she's 'gay' or not. I'm just nice to Amber most of the time, I treat her well enough, and I respect her, kinda. I absolutely don't make fun of her sexuality or keep her in a little box she can't move in or forget her name."

"You don't need to get hostile" Quince said "I just know that if she *was* into us, she'd be a lot happier about being here."

"That's not how that works." I pointed out "Being gay doesn't mean you're automatically into *all* girls or whatever."

"I think Amber's only into Marissa, Quince." Tracy said "I've never gotten gay vibes from her before you told me about her spying on Marissa."

"I wasn't *spying*!" I yelled, frustrated "I was watching my friend play tennis, she put me on the bench to *watch her play tennis*. I was doing what she asked!"

"But you *are* gay, right?" Tracy asked, slightly confused

"I'm- I'm something, yeah, gay, a little, I guess..." I said, defeated. I hadn't even figured it all out for myself yet, and here they were giving me the third degree.

Kensey sat up and looked at Quince, sniffing back her tears "If I was gay, would you be nice to me?"

"Babydoll, I haven't been *mean* to you." Quince said, sounding hurt

"You put her in a coffin, put the coffin buried under designer pajamas and swung her around, banging her against walls and throwing her on the floor." Marissa said "Mean isn't just the stuff you mean to do."

"I didn't bang her on walls!" Quince said, glaring at Marissa

"I did see you toss your bag on the floor though." Tracy pointed out "That's like, torture or something, all trapped and thrown around? I'd be upset too."

"Ok, gods, ugh *fine*." Quince said "I'll do whatever it is you're all telling me to do." she looked down at Kensey "And I don't care, maybe pretend to be gay or something, see if I like it."

Kensey looked up at me and back to her "Um, I don't know how to 'act gay' without offending the gay people here."

"Gay less-than-a-person, really." Tracy pointed out.

"No, she was right. Gay *people*." Henri said, sitting down at the table.

I looked at her from across Marissa's shoulder and waved. She was wearing a full face of makeup, and had worked hard to make the glossy lipstick give the appearance of slightly puckered lips. Her eyeliner was drawn to make her eyes look wider, with pink eyeshadow that made her pale blue eyes pop. She looked... better than she had on prom night, and that was saying something. Her eyes slid over to me, and she bowed slightly.

"Lady Amber, how may I serve you this evening?" she asked in a cool, rehearsed tone.

I felt a weird feeling inside, like I wanted to call it off, but only because I was feeling guilty for how much I was anticipating it.

I lifted my head and called out in a clear voice "Henri, I believe our guests need refreshments?"

"Ooh, yeah, hang on." Marissa drank the rest of her soju in a gulp "I'll have another one of these, the one with a watermelon on it this time."

I kicked her in the back, out of sight of the other girls. If she kept this pace up, she'd have me in her mouth again in no time, or start kissing me again like last sleepover. She ignored my kick, and patted me on the head, her smug smile spreading across her face.

"I'd like a tonic and vodka?" Tracy said "With a splash of lemon."

"Oh, do you have seltzer?" Quince asked "I'd love a pineapple one. In a fluted glass, of course."

"I have seltzer, yeah, but drink it out of the can or a cup, I'm not calling the kitchen again for a special glass." Marissa said shaking her head

"Uh, can I have- Would it be ok if I had some wine?" Kensey said from down on the table

"Awww drunk lil babies!" said Quince, kicking her feet "Amber, you get something too! It's legal if your guardian says it's ok!"

"No, no, uh, that's a bad idea Kensey." I called to her, sitting up crosslegged "I had to go to the hospital when I got vodka on myself, *drinking* alcohol would be a death sentence."

"I can't even *drink*?!" Kensey wailed, falling back over into a heap

"You had to *what*." Henri growled me, slamming the fresh soju on the table in front of Marissa and glaring

Oh, shit, we hadn't told her about that...

"It was- I just needed some lotion, it's fine..." I said "I'm right as rain now!"

"You spilled it all down your front, you soaked yourself, I need to see." Henri said, leaning in closer

"No, it was mostly just dry skin, really, I-"

"Amber." she hissed.

I looked around at the other girls, they were watching with interest, but not getting involved, and Marissa was still just sitting there, not doing *anything* helpful. I sighed and shimmied, pulling the zipper best I could and lowering the clown outfit so she could see my front. I was blazing with pink as she examined me closely, her eyes going over every inch of me.

"Well, I do not see any rashes or burns, I guess- Wait, are those *teeth marks*?!" She said, her voice pitching up at the end

I quickly put the clown outfit back on, struggling with the zipper "It's- we have fun here, you know?"

Henri stared at me, her mouth working open and closed slightly as she tried to think of what to say or how to explode.

I cleared my throat "Uh, you've got two more drinks on the way, right? Better get those..."

Her mouth snapped shut and she hissed out a breath "...Fine, but we are talking about this."

As she got up and went back to get the other drinks, Marissa looked down at me

"You always let the help talk to you like that?" she asked in a faux snooty voice

"It raises morale." I said, matching her tone.

"Wow, I gotta say, I'm impressed Marissa." Tracy said "Usually you would have slapped her or gotten her mom taken off the PTA or something, what happened?"

"This is Amber's night to be the boss." Marissa said "If she wants Henri slapped, she's gotta do it herself."

"Can she even slap anyone?" Quince said "I doubt they could feel it."

"Come over here and let's find out." I taunted her.

She thought about it, then shrugged, a small slime on her face "Yeah, ok, whatever."

She slid off the couch, and walked over to Marissa on her knees, leaning in so her cheek was almost resting on Marissa's shoulder.

"Slap away, lil bitch." she said

"Ok, uhhh close your eyes?" I asked "I don't want to hit you in the eyeball or something."

She complied. I turned to Marissa, and made motions with my hand to her. She grinned, and reached up with her free hand, flicking Quince hard in the cheek with her middle finger.

"Ow! Fuck..." Quince rubbed her cheek and made her way back to the sofa "Ok, yeah I guess you can hit kinda hard..."

Tracy giggled to herself, but didn't say anything as Henri made her way over with the other drinks, and a small glass for herself. She sat down, and picked up her glass, raising it to her mouth to take a sip when there was a knock on the door.

"Oh, Henri, be a dear and get the pizza, would you?" I asked sweetly

She looked at me, her face unreadable, and stood up without a word, going to the door to fetch the pizza from Parker. She came back, setting two of the pizzas down and going back for the third. Kensey stood and backed up away from the piping hot dishes, looking at the food hungrily.

"Hey, Quince, did you bring food for Kensey?" I asked

She frowned and dug in her bag, pulling out a pouch of small green pellets "This is what they gave me when I bought her, I figured she could eat this?"

"Oh, ew." Marissa said, shaking her head "Come on, it's not ideal, but you can eat one of Amber's dinners tonight, Kensey."

"But-" Kensey said, looking between the pellets and the steaming hot pizza "Why can't I just eat pizza?"

"It could make you sick." I said "We can try a little bit, but we're supposed to eat compressed food."

"So like, gerbil food?" her voice wavered

"No, it's- well, maybe. Henri, move us back to my house, I want to show her the good stuff."

"Yes, Lady Amber." Henri said, picking us up and bringing us to the desk "Let me know when you wish to re-join the group."

She stiffly walked away, and I waved Kensey over to the fridge. "These are the meals I eat, they're 95% compression, so... they're not great for you, you need 90% compression. Here, pick one out, and I'll finish the other half of my burrito from breakfast."

"Fuck, I need special food?" she muttered "I wish I'd found out about this stuff before I got found by my landlord, I'd have just let my cats eat me."

"Because of... food?" I asked putting mine in the microwave

"Because of a loss of *rights*, plus no drinking, no food, being treated like shit. I just... I don't think I can do this, I really don't." she sat down with her back against the counters, her choice in her hand, a r'ce, ch'ckn, and p'ea dinner.

I took it from her and put it in the microwave after mine beeped and set it. I didn't really know what to say to her, yeah it sucked, but there was nothing to do about it. We just weren't people anymore. I could at least try and help one way though, I'd been mostly fine with the mandu, if I hadn't gorged myself I'd have absolutely been fine. I waved at the others, and Tracy noticed, pointing Henri my way. She stood quickly and rushed over.

"Yes Lady Amber?" she said, sounding almost excited

"Uh, I wanted you to get me and my friend here a small bit of pizza each. Just a scrap, of the cheese kind. I was fine after the mandu, kinda, so I wanted to at least let her try a little."

Henri winced "They make compressed food for a reason, you cannot-"

"That's an order, Henri." I said firmly. Her face flushed, and her breath caught for a split second.

"...Of course, Lady Amber."

She came back a second later with two tiny cuts of pizza. She put them on the kitchen table, and I waved her away, putting my and Kensey's food on the table next to them. She watched for a second longer, then went back to sit by Marissa at the coffee table. Was I doing good? I think she was enjoying herself, it was so hard to tell though...

I looked down at Kensey "Hey, silverware is in the drawer by the dining room entrance or you can use the plastic one attached to the packaging, get some and come eat, ok? No sense in letting it get cold."

She did as I asked, and sat down across from me, eating small bites of her dinner and grimacing. It didn't *look* great, that's for sure, and it was one of the weirder ones I'd been avoiding. How do you make fake peas? I tried the pizza and moaned, it was perfect, the sweet, light sauce, the buttery undertone, the massive amount of cheese... That last one was a benefit of being small, I supposed.

I pointed at Kensey's pizza "You don't have to try it, but I'll have it if you don't."

She sighed and picked it up, taking a bite. Her eyes widened, and she nodded slowly

"Mm, you said we can still eat a little bit of regular food?" she asked

"Yeah, I ate a plate of mandu the size of my head and barely got sick at all." I said, taking another bite.

"That's not so bad, then..." she said "I can live with that."

We ate in silence, enjoying the food, and thinking about the evening ahead of us. Things were going well I was feeling pretty good about the evening so far. It was a little tense, but I was feeling comfortable and relaxed, this was going well.

Fifteen minutes later, Kensey was bent over the toilet upstairs, losing her dinner. I, on the other hand, felt fine. Maybe not all class Bs can eat uncompressed foods after all...

# Chapter Eighteen

I sat in Marissa's hand, her fingers gently curled around me to keep me warm as she and her friends drank and chatted about school drama. I watched Kensey as she lay on the table, looking at the pizza with a bitter look on her face. The three small pizzas had been hit hard, and all of them had been combined into one tray with the other two stacked up under it, freeing most of the coffee table for drinks. I'd very much enjoyed my slice, but I felt terrible that it'd hurt Kensey so much and so quickly. I needed to distract myself...

I hugged Marissa's middle finger to my chest and lightly bit her fingertip, feeling her jerk her hand. I looked up to see her glaring down at me. I smiled and waved, and she rolled her eyes, squeezing me lightly. I'd started to enjoy the squeezes, now that she wasn't forcing the air out of my lungs and making me feel like my ribs were about to snap. It was like a hug of sorts, my sized and safe. It let me push my guilt over Kensey's stomachache out of my mind for the time, and draw my attention back to the conversation at hand.

"...and after that, she just kept glaring at me, like, she *knew* I'd done it, but she couldn't prove anything, it was *so* funny..." Quince said, laughing.

"I can't believe you got away with it, that's crazy..." Tracy said

"What about you, Trace?" Marissa asked "You been spreading any good rumors lately?"

"No, they've all been about you- Ah! Not that *I'm* spreading rumors about you, I just- you and Amber are a hot topic..." Tracy smiled nervously.

Marissa's thumb rubbed my back "Well, we *are* the most interesting thing to happen at school lately..."

"If- if it helps, next week, I was going to start pointing out how Dana has been wearing a lot of tops cinched under the boobs, like she's hiding her stomach for some reason? I'm thinking I'll try and get a pregnancy rumor going..." Tracy offered

"Dana is like, 22, who cares if she's pregnant?" Quince said

"Well, *actually*, I heard from Maurine that her boyfriend is in seminary?" Tracy said, perking up "So either this could get him kicked out, *or* it could get them broken up if it turns out she's sleeping around."

"You- fuck, you all actually *plan* all this?" Henri asked "You have *strategy meetings* about whose life you are going to ruin?"

"Well, not *ruin*." Quince said "Just add some drama to."

"It's not really that bad, in my opinion." Tracy said "I like to think of it as like, a hobby or something. I can't target people long term as well as Marissa can, I don't have the political sway Darcy does, and I can't just casually ruin someone's day like Quince, so I just like to add a little drama, like Quince said."

"It's- you are treating other people's lives like it's a *game!*" Henri said, her temper flaring "You four ruined my teenage years with your name calling, and keeping me out of school clubs, and slamming me into walls as you walked past, and telling my mom I had died of AIDS, and getting me taken off the guest list for homecoming, and everything, and the *rumors* just made everything worse! You are all terrible...."

"...Well, it's only for a couple more years." Tracy said "Honestly, once we graduate, we'll all be living our separate lives, and we'll forget all about this, we just want to have a little fun while we're all still here."

"Yeah I guess we'll all be scattered," Quince said to Tracy, slightly sad "Marissa will have one of the biggest companies in the country, you'll be working at your dad's bio lab, Darcy will have her family fortune, and I'm too nouveau riche to even be invited to the same *parties* as the rest of you."

"Well, we won't *all* be separate." Marissa said, drinking deeply from her third soju "My mom is buying Tracy's dad's company, I'll be her boss in a few years."

Tracy's face flushed, then turned white "What? No, that's- *no*! My dad didn't tell me that... He said *I* was going to be in charge, I'd finally be the one in charge!"

"Well, your dad made the mistake of selling the majority of the shares during one of his fundraisers, and my mom is collecting them all up. You'll be in charge all right, but you'll do what *I* tell you." Marissa said casually

Tracy was fighting off tears, and I could feel the smug satisfaction radiating off of Marissa as she soaked up Tracy's panic.

"*No*, that's not right, I'm supposed to take over for him in less than two years, this is all we have, we need it!" she said, hand against her chest

"Aw, it's ok." Marissa crooned "You'll still get paid, and you'll still have a place in the company, there's just going to be some minor changes, for profit's sake. You'll be making more money than before, I bet! We'll be stripping out the charity and non-profit side of things, and changing the focus to something a little more profitable, it'll be great!"

Tracy was crying at this point, and her hands were shaking "Marissa, no- that's- it's my dad's *legacy*, the charity side of it is his *passion*, he's just trying to help people, why would you do this?"

"It's not *me*, it's my mother, and as for why... the stakeholders are upset with him, simple as that." she replied with a soft edge, still stroking my back.

This was... electric. It felt *so* good to see Tracy crying like this, the girl who'd lied to everyone that I had lice and gotten the nurse to shave my head in junior year, the girl who convinced the other girls to send my name and address to a prison pen-pal program, the girl who'd sweetly asked if I needed a ride home after I'd 'had so much to drink' within earshot of the chaperone on prom night. It was *good* to see her like this, it was odd, feeling good seeing someone else hurt, but... I could feel the slight tremble in Marissa's hand, the edge to her voice, how she was holding in her power and cruelty, just letting enough out at once to let it *burn*, to hurt and singe Tracy.

I lay against her palm and pulled her fingers over me, this was her, this was her *power*, and as much as I hated to admit it, I wanted to see more of it. I wanted her to *hurt* someone, and I wanted to watch. My chest was full of butterflies as she gave me a gentle squeeze, and I shivered. She could do that to me, make *me* cry, take me to bits, ruin my future, but she wasn't, I was safe in her hand, the eye of the storm, and I loved her for it.

"It does not feel so good, huh?" Henri taunted "Being bullied yourself? I bet you never thought you would be the *target*, soak it up, bitch, and get over yourself."

"She's been bullied lots, actually." Quince said "She's only friends with us because she's good at getting the word out about drama, we lay into her a ton. She's never *cried* about it though, Jesus."

"Well *excuse me*!" Tracy shouted "My whole future just fucking *crumbled*, so sorry if I *cry about it*!"

"...Gods, Trace, it's not *that* bad." Marissa said "It's just a hostile takeover, it's not going to change anything for *you*."

Tracy buried her face in her knees and kept crying, ignoring Marissa. I frowned, this *did* seem like a big reaction to being told upper management was being changed around in your dad's company, even if you *were* supposed to run it someday. She must have had other stuff going on too, under the surface or whatever.

"Tracy, just drink your vodka..." Quince said, pushing it towards her "And seriously, can I get another seltzer? Service is *awful* around here."

"Oh, sorry." I said "Henri, could you get everyone fresh drinks?"

She looked at me in a way that said 'Really? Now?' but she stood up anyway "Of course, Lady Amber."

"Actually, if you could bring the drinks to the theater in a few minutes instead? And I'll have two more Soju, if that's ok." Marissa said, standing up. "I'm going to go set up the movie, meet me there in like, ten minutes, ok?"

"Fiiiine" Quince said "I wanna pick the next movie, though."

"We'll see." Marissa said "Maybe we can get Kensey to pick? The screen would be the size of a blimp to her, might be cool to let her watch her favorite movie on the biggest screen she's ever seen."

Kensey looked up, and stood "Uh, can- can I just stay on Amber's couch for now? I'm still feeling sick..."

"Laaaame." grumbled Quince "Swear to god, you're never eating pizza again."

Kensey's face crumpled, and she dropped down to her knees. I felt a pang of sadness for her, it wasn't really about not getting any more pizza, it was how Quince had *said* it, the casual flexing of power without even noticing. I watched her shake as Marissa dropped her off in my house on our way out the door. She'd need to toughen up soon, I couldn't imagine life with Quince would be easy, but if she could manage to play along a bit, it'd be way better... Otherwise Quince really *would* treat her like a target, and her life would be a living hell. I'd need to talk to her about that, give her some pointers.

Marissa moved down the hall to a set of double doors and swung them open, revealing a wide, darkly colored theater with three tiered rows of 5 seater sofas. It was a full two story affair, with a projector high up on the wall and a mini concession booth with a popcorn machine and fancy candies and chips laid out across it. The popcorn booth was lit up with a dull yellow glow, and the smell of butter and oil hit me as we drew closer.

"Holy shit, this really *is* a theater." I said "I was half expecting like, a big room with a big tv or something."

"No, my dad really liked entertaining," Marissa said, opening a cabinet on the far wall "so he built this for all his work friends to come over and watch... whatever it is guys get together and watch. He also used it to show off for the visiting diplomats or foreign business owners that stayed here, as a flex."

"I guess the cook made the popcorn and brought all the snacks and stuff in?" I asked "What is there for you to do?"

"I have to set up the movie." she said, putting a disk into a reader "I picked first, because it's my house, so we're watching Harold and Maude."

"I haven't seen that one." I said. I'd heard of it, but I'd never looked into it

"You'll like it, it's funny. Kinda gross, but fun, in a weird way." she assured me

"Ok, I'll trust you, I guess." I said, glancing over at the screen as it lit up with a DVD menu of the movie in question, a young man and an old lady framed in boxes lighting up the room.

"So, the movie is set up, the snacks are already here, why did you tell everyone to wait ten minutes to come here?" I asked

Marissa looked at me, her eyes slowly crinkling and her grin slowly creeping across her face "Hm, I guess I just wanted some alone time with you, away from everyone else~"

I flushed "I- yeah, that's- fair, yeah." I feel her fingers grip me, my silken outfit so thin I swear I could feel her fingerprints "But what if someone walks in early and sees us?"

She rolled over the top of the sofa nearest to us, sending my stomach spinning as she flopped on her tummy, holding me in front of her face. Her fingers played along my sides, like she couldn't decide if she wanted to crush me, tickle me, or squeeze me. She pulled me in close, her fruity soju breath washing over me as she whispered.

"I kinda like that idea, getting walked in on again..."

I bury my face in my hands and shudder with energy, I couldn't tell if I liked the idea too, it scared me, but I was learning to like *that* feeling too.

"Was that why you got caught with me in your mouth earlier?" I asked

"Nnnno, that was just a nice accident~" she said.

Her fingers finally decided what they wanted to do, and I writhed and gasped and they dug in, under my ribs, into my tummy, my back, my legs, jabbing, poking, stroking, like a five legged octopus trying to give a hug. It was so much, so much to keep track of and think about. Her fingers were strong, each enough to punch a hole through me if she wanted. This was *good*, but I could feel the need to be in danger growing, or to at least *feel* like I was in danger.

"H-hh-hh" I let slip out "squeeze me, Missy, please..."

She hissed through her teeth, and her hand gripped me, forcing my breath out in one go. I saw stars, and I wriggled against her hand, feeling the unmoving flesh, her body heat, *her*. I felt my back popping, and she let go quickly, looking me up and down to make sure nothing had broken. I gasped for air and my vision came back slowly. She cupped her hands, and I lay spread out on them, looking up at her, at my world. I smiled a ragged smile, and waved at my body, letting her know she was free to do what she wanted.

She looked at me for a moment, her face in a strange expression "Gods, you really are fucking adorable in that outfit..."

I laughed, I'd almost forgotten what I looked like, I'd been enjoying the feeling of her skin through the thin material, I'd forgotten that I was dressed up as a clown.

"What's the matter, Missy? Do you have a thing for clowns?" I taunted

"I have a thing for *you*." she growled "You could be dressed like a fucking *hobo* and I'd still think you look great."

I cringed inside at the classist statement, but brushed past it. Like I'd found before with the Andy Griffith show, cuddling time was never a good time to bring up someone's problematic internalized ideas. I could always work on that stuff *later*, we did have the rest of our lives together, after all.

The rest of our lives... I grinned at the thought of that, she *owned* me, we couldn't break up if we *wanted* to, that meant that forever and ever, I'd always have someone to love, to love *me*. I hadn't ever noticed how badly I'd wanted that until recently. With Henri, there was always a danger edge to it, like if I accepted love from her, I'd lose *her* overall.

"You look all weird, what's up?" Marissa asked, poking me with her thumb

"Just thinking about how I'm all yours and everything." I said, letting the smile into my voice "Forever and ever..."

"Forever until I get bored and squash you, of course." she teased

"Oh, I'm sure you'd *never* do something like that." I said "You'd be down your favorite victim, after all."

"Well, I could find a new one." she said "In the meantime, I'm not bored of you *yet*, I've got *lots* of ideas of how to torture you."

"I don't believe you," I said "prove it."

"Ok, how abooooout...." she said, drawing out the last word "pressure *and* humiliation?"

She dropped her face down, pressing her lips into me, smushing me with kisses, deep and hard across my whole body, her lips pressing me hard into her hand. The firmness of her lips surprised me, usually they were soft and cozy, but she'd tightened them to more effectively push me into her hands. I wiggled as the sensation of lips worked all over my body, not stoping for more than a split second to kiss before moving on. My limbs, my stomach, chest, face, all were targets in her furious, rough attack.

Finally, she pulled her head back, her face flushed pink, and her hair making a curtain around us. She laughed once under her breath.

"Proof enough?" she whispered

"It- hah..." I ran my hands over my body, feeling her phantom touch still lingering. "It was d-derivative, but I can forgive that..."

She snorted, and kissed me on the face one last time, her lips soft and gentle like normal. "Ok, ok. I'll think up some more torture methods soon I promise."

I looked up at her as she rose into a sitting position, still holding me and I felt a pang of guilt mixed with the love. I'd felt fantastic the whole time we played just now, and I was still glowing, but...

"Hey..." I started, not sure how to continue

She looked down at me lazily and frowned slightly at my expression "What? You good?"

"Yeah, yeah, I just- You spent the whole mini cuddle session just now making me feel great, what can I do to make *you* feel like that?"

Her eyes widened, and she held back a laugh "Amber, I just like getting to make you *squirm*. Knowing you can't stop me, knowing I'm doing whatever the fuck I want to you, it's, I don't know, it fills me up, refreshes me, like pouring water over my face on a hot day."

"Mmm.." I said "I get that, I have a similar feeling, but the *physical* side of things is really nice too, I just wish I could help you out there too."

"You're 4 inches tall, I could barely feel you if you tried to do what I do to you to me." Marissa said, sounding almost sad "I appreciate it, and maybe we'll try letting you 'explore' me a little again- in *private* this time- but honestly, I think the most I get out of playing with you is the feeling of power."

I sighed and nodded "Yeah, ok. I'll try to think of something."

I felt sad, selfish even, but if she didn't have too much of a problem with it, I shouldn't feel *too* bad. The double doors swung open, and the other three girls walked in, Quince holding her seltzer, and Henri trying to hold the other four drinks.

"Marissa, here, take your bottles, they are going to fall." she said, waving at the green bottles under her arms

"Nice, what flavors?" Marissa asked, standing and setting me on her shoulder.

"Uhhh, dragonfruit and yogurt?" Henri said "I've never heard of yogurt flavored alcohol."

"That sounds so gross, Marissa." Quince said "Just because you're trying to impress your Korean class B doesn't mean you have to drink the weird Korean drinks."

"I don't give a shit if she's 'impressed', I just like the flavor of this stuff, shut up." Marissa said, frowning "I'm sure the yogurt one will be just as good as the rest."

"How did you even find out about this stuff?" Tracy asked, her eyes still slightly puffy "You're usually a vodka and tequila girl."

"I tried it at Amber's house, her dad gave me some." Marissa said, setting the dragonfruit bottle on the couch as she sat in the corner seat and cracked open the other one

"You went to her *house*?" Quince said "Ewww it was probably full of bugs and stuff, I heard she lived in an *apartment*. Not even a condo."

"I didn't *see* any bugs." Marissa said carefully "I wanted to flex on her parents, show off that I owned their daughter. I even tortured her a little in front of them, and made her wear tissues instead of clothes most of the time we were there."

"That's... holy *shit*." Tracy said, her eyes wide "You're like, an actual *monster*, that's so impressive..."

"I paid enough for her, I wanna get my money's worth out of her." Marissa said, grinning.

Henri's face was set in a confused frown, looking back and forth between me and Marissa. She'd *been* there for the dinner, she'd seen us just casually eating, and *she'd* gotten yelled at for trying to cause problems. She'd most likely gotten the whole story from my parents after, and as wary as they were of Marissa, whatever they told her wasn't lining up with what Marissa was telling her friends. I hoped this helped her start to separate the two sides of Marissa, instead of seeing her as *just* the bitch who puts on a show and tried to hurt people.

"So, what are we watching?" Quince said "Romance, right?"

"Uh, kinda." Marissa said "It's romance, but... not normal romance. Let's just start the movie and start getting popcorn and stuff."

She took a swig of her drink, and pulled away "Oh, wow, that's not yogurt, that's- I don't even know."

"It's based on a fermented milk drink." I explained "Not western yogurt."

"Yeah, it's different, kinda creamy and citrusy or something..." she said "I like it, I'd have it again."

"It's like, *so* obvious that you're sucking up right now." Quince said "Is the opinion of your little lesbian pet that important to you?"

"I thought we weren't making fun of queer people anymore, right?" Tracy said "I could swear we talked about that earlier."

"Whatever, I'm just saying, sucking up to a pet isn't a good look either way." Quince said rudely

"I'm not sucking up, gods." Marissa snapped "I just like this stuff, it's good, fuck off."

"I had it before too," Henri said "it was strawberry, it was pretty good. Better than just plain vodka."

"Oh, wow, the *blood drinker* likes it, well I guess I stand corrected then!" Quince said, sipping her seltzer

"We do not *drink* it," Henri said, glaring at Quince "it is put in fertilizer, and in candy bars, and made into supplements, and made into sausages, and animal food, and we even use some to do blood transfusions in humans, it is not just raw 'blood', we deal in so much stuff..."

"Buuuut you did drink it, that one time." Marissa reminded her

"That- you said it was a common dish!" she snapped back

"Yeah, it's a fucking delicacy in Asia someplace, and you puked it all over my fucking bathroom." Marissa snarked

"Oh, *gods*, you actually got her to drink blood?" Tracy asked "You're such a fucking bitch, you *terrify* me, Marissa."

Marissa looked at her cooly and smiled "As I should. Know your place."

I gripped her shoulder, holding back the shivers, I wanted to crawl into her mouth and let her bite me in half, I felt so pent up and tense, but I couldn't do anything about it with people around...

"Let's just start the movie." grumbled Henri, taking a seat on the couch.

Marissa glanced at her, then at me, jerking her head towards her, telling me to do... something? I guessed what she was suggesting, and called out to her.

"Oh, Henri? If you wouldn't mind, the couch is quite crowded, could you sit on the floor? Over by me, if you please."

Henri looked at the wide couch, easily big enough for everyone there and then some, and glared at me, her cheeks tinting.

"I could just move forward a row." she said, pointing

"No no, I wouldn't want you to miss out on this lovely female bonding time, you can stay up here with us." I told her in my most gracious voice

"..." Henri got up, and walked stiffly over to the side of the couch me and Marissa were on, sitting cross legged on the floor next to us.

"Ah, actually Henri, would you mind sitting on your legs? Tuck them under you, if you don't mind. It's more ladylike." I told her, waving a hand.

She made a noise in her throat, something between indignation and a gasp, and did as I asked, staring straight ahead. Marissa turned her head to look at her, quickly planting a kiss on my head as she did so. I bit my lip and glanced over at Tracy and Quince, who were getting snacks from the table. I giggled, and hugged her shoulder as hard as I could. I heard a strained noise, and I looked at Henri who'd seen out of the corner of her eye and now had an expression like a kicked puppy. I sighed, we'd talk later, I supposed, but for now, she should enjoy that I'm bossing her around like I am.

"Here ya go, bitch." Quince said, flopping down next to us, handing Marissa a box of chocolate raisins and a paper sack of popcorn

"Aw, thanks, how'd you know I wanted raisins?" Marissa said

"Well, you're the only one who eats those weird, gross lumps, and there was a stack of them on the table, so..." Quince said rolling her eyes

I looked around Marissa's neck at the other two, they both had popcorn, and Quince was eating gumdrops, Tracy was eating red licorice, and they had a box of peanut butter chocolate between them too. *My* go to had always been chocolate covered mints, but I'd mix it up with some cookie dough bites now and then too. It was interesting to see who picked what. Henri didn't have any snacks, she'd sat down without visiting the booth first, but *her* choice was obvious; fruity gummies, the cherry ones if they had them.

I scooched closer to Marissa's neck to better absorb her body heat, and the movie began. I was feeling so, so cozy; I had a friend on either side of me, I was in control of my situation, I was full of good food, the other girls weren't messing with me... As weird as it was, for the first time since I'd compressed, surrounded almost entirely by people I'd hated half my life, I was content. Marissa lifted a single piece of popcorn up to me and I took it, biting a chunk out of it and kicking my feet, this was a great evening, I was *very* happy with the way things were going.

~~~

"That made me, um, kind of uncomfortable..." Tracy said as the movie ended

"I thought it was pretty funny, not gonna lie." Quince said, snickering

"It made me feel all, I'm not sure, mopey, I guess?" Henri murmured

It'd been a weird movie, there were some parts I didn't know how to feel about, but it was... sweet? In a fucked up way? I liked the darker humor mixed in, but I didn't see myself watching it a second time. I was curious why Marissa picked that one, though, was she comparing me and her to the two main characters? It wasn't really the same kind of power imbalance as ours, but there was an almost similar feeling at least.

"Yeah, it's one of a k-kind, kinda a w-weird one, but hey, I like it at least." Marissa said "Anyway, who's picking next?"

"I wanna watch Freaky Friday, I pick that." Quince said

"The old one or the new one?" Tracy asked

"There's actually like, 4 of them, not including sequels, buuut I was thinking the one like, twenty or thirty years ago? With that one girl from Mean Girls" Quince said

"Why can't we just watch Mean Girls?" Tracy asked "That's one's better."

"It is a little on the nose, don't you think?" Henri pointed out

"Whatever, I think we have Freaky Friday, it might be in the closet. If not, I'm sure it's on streaming s-somewhere." Marissa said, pulling out her phone and flipping through her notifications

"Hey, I wanna check on Kensey, ok?" I said, sitting up

"I'm not moving, get your maid to take you." Marissa said. She'd gone through her two drinks during the movie, and her face was hot and her eyes sleepy. I didn't *think* she was drunk, but it was really hard to tell with her.

I turned to Henri "Hey, can you bring me back to my house real quick?"

She looked up at me and nodded, reaching out her hands. I frowned, thinking to myself. I hadn't really gotten to enjoy her being under my control tonight, maybe I could play with her a bit...

"No, I want to ride you." I said "Bend over"

Her eyes widened, and she looked askance "Uhhh..." she said, looking confused

I sighed "No, look, like, I want to ride on your back, like a horse or something, get on your hands and knees."

She blushed and bent over, pressing her side against the couch. I shimmied down Marissa's arm and onto the armrest, and slid off that onto the white and black fabric of Henri's maid costume. I crawled over to the middle, and realized that unless I could do the splits, which I didn't think I could, I wouldn't be able to ride her horseback. I rolled down to the small of her back and lay down, face up, her spine dipping in and giving me a divot to lay in.

"Away, steed!" I called out

"Y-yes Lady Amber." Henri said, her voice wobbling.

She carefully crawled forward, Quince jeering as she headed for the movie closet, Marissa snickering, and Tracy watching wide eyed as I waved to them. Henri's back muscles flexed as she moved, rocking me back and forth, and I tucked my arms behind my head, enjoying the ride as she left the theater. Henri pushed through the doors and started her way down the hall quietly, her breathing was short and shallow, I could feel it through her spine.

I watched the doors pass me by, idly wondering what was in all of those rooms, it had to be something, but what did rich people fill all their space with? I saw the elevator ding, and the light lit up, and a cold feeling shot down my own spine. I dashed up to Henri's shoulder and slapped her neck.

"Quick, stand up and hide me! I think that's Marissa's mom coming, she hates me!" I hissed "She said if she saw me again, she'd make Missy kill me!"

Henri jolted, and snatched me off her shoulder, standing upright so quickly my whole body felt like I was on a rollercoaster. She patted herself down with one hand, looking for a place to stash me, she patted her chest and glanced at me, but winced and kept looking. As the elevator doors slid open, she stuck me under her fluffy skirt, tucking me into the puffy part of her bloomers, snapping them closed under me as her skirts fell around me like a mushroom cap. I tumbled against her thigh, her tights smooth and tight against her, the ruffles around me soft, the space warm and dimly lit, the elastic under me strong enough to hold me inside, the material digging into her thigh. I flushed red, and tried to stay still while I leaned on the bloomer's fabric, trying not to touch her thigh or look up as she turned to greet whoever had just exited the elevator.

"You, who are you?" Miss Lund's harsh voice cut to my bones as she walked up to Henri "I don't think I've seen you before."

"I am Henrietta, ma'am." Henri said in her most polite voice

"Are you a new maid? You should know we have a uniform for that, not this 'frill' that you have on."

"No, ma'am, I am one of Marissa's friends, from college. I lost a game, and I am wearing this as a punishment." Henri's voice wavered slightly at the word 'friend', but she kept her tone steady.

Miss Lund's voice took a slightly softer tone, but was still full of that same cold energy she always had around her "A punishment? Ah, her games, she's told me about those. I didn't know Marissa had made a new 'friend'. Henrietta, you said?"

"Yes, ma'am. We have known each other for quite a while, but this is only my third time coming over."

Third?... Oh, right, when she tried to force her way in to kidnap me. Bold of her to include that as 'coming over'. I slipped on the smooth fabric and went sideways, my body leaning against her thigh. I kept my eyes down, then thought better and closed them altogether. There was just enough light in here to make looking up a violation of privacy, and even if *she's* the one who put me here and most likely wouldn't mind, I wasn't about to do that to someone.

"I see, and where are you off to? I assume the others are in the theater by now."

"I am on drink duty, ma'am. I am getting new drinks for everyone." she said, and I felt her body move as she waved towards Marissa's room at the end of the hall.

"Oh, of course." Miss Lund's voice was the same sharp, cold spike of fear it always was, but it was oddly disarming to hear her have a normal conversation, instead of one laced with disappointment and thinly veiled disgust.

"Tell me," she continued "what does your family do? I'm catching a hint of an accent, I assume you're in the European market?"

"Yes, ma'am, but we export all over the planet. My family owns the world's largest animal byproduct harvesting and processing company, and we are the main source for many, many useful items, including fertilizers, medical materials, and even food products."

"Oh, I see, that's very impressive." Miss Lund sounded slightly less impressed than she claimed to be, but she went on "Here, take my card. I'm in the tech industry right now, but I'm going to be acquiring a bio lab soon, if you could have your people call my people in six to eight months, we may be able to work out some joint ventures."

"Thank you, ma'am, I will get this to our people, I look forward to working with you."

"Thank *you*, I'm here to see my daughter before I head to bed, she's in the theater? And drunk already, I'm guessing?"

"She is in the theater, ma'am, I couldn't speak for her state of inebriation though, she has a very strong constitution." Henri said as she shifted slightly, causing her other thigh to brush into me from the other side of the bloomers

"She gets that from her father." Miss Lund muttered "Hopeless hedonists the two of them. With any luck she'll get it out of her system by the end of her schooling."

"With any luck, ma'am." Henri agreed.

There was a moment of silence, then a sigh "Well, Henrietta, I must say I prefer you to Marissa's other friends. Other than Darcy, you are the most polite, and *you* don't seem to have the propensity for 'alternative inebriation' she does. I look forward to seeing you in the future, have a lovely night."

"And you as well, ma'am." Henri said, a slight smile in her voice.

She turned, and walked the rest of the way to Marissa's room, stepping inside and almost instantly dropping to the floor, smushing my arm between her calf and thigh. I yelped, and she dug me out of her bloomers and held me up to her face.

"Mein götter, Klein Fee, that was *terrifying*..." she gasped "I felt like she was going to tear into me at any moment."

"She reduced me to tears the first time I met her..." I admitted "Marissa too, but don't tell her I told you that."

"It was so much!" she said, shaking me slightly "You said she was going to have Marissa *kill* you?"

"She *said* she wouldn't, but she implied if she saw me again, she'd change her mind." I said, my brains slightly rattled

Henri slumped against the wall "I felt like I was going to crack any moment, she is worse than my great aunt on my mother's side..."

She looked at me sharply "Did I hear you call Marissa 'Missy' earlier?"

"It's something I'm trying out." I admitted "I think it sounds cute, and her dad calls her that, and she likes *him*, so I figure she likes the nickname, I don't know, please don't use it yourself, though."

"'Missy'." Henri mused "It makes her sound so much less dangerous than 'Marissa'."

"Well, she's still the same person as always, really." I said

"Is she though?" Henri asked "Is she *really*? I am starting to understand her, it is all an act, is it not?"

I thought about it "What parts, exactly?"

"You know, the whole evil bitch thing." Henri said, waving her free hand "She is putting it on to impress people, right?"

"Uhh, no, that's not an act, that's who she really is." I clarified "She's just also *more* than that, like, she's complex. She's a sweet girl, she just likes hurting people sometimes, and has mommy issues."

"Is she still a bitch to *you*, though?" Henri asked "I saw how she treats you now, she is careful and sweet, and she- she kissed you, like it was no big deal."

"Well..." I thought about how to word it "She's a bitch to me, yeah, but I *like* it. She's also sweet to me, and I like that too. Unless she's angry, I think we have a good balance most of the time right now."

"So you really *are* dating her?"

"I have no idea. We're some kind of partners, that's all I know. But I consider her my girlfriend, if that's what you mean."

Henri's face crumpled for a split second before straightening out "If *I* was a bitch to you, would you have dated me?"

I winced "Nnno. I was too scared of losing you to ever consider dating you."

"...At least you care more about me than her in *that* way at least."

I didn't mention that there wasn't a risk of me losing Marissa since we were stuck together by law. Henri needed this.

"You have bruises shaped like teeth marks on your chest, was *that* something you wanted?" she asked "If there is anything she is doing that is hurting you, or that she is taking too far, I can help. I will get evidence and blackmail her with it."

"No, we play rough, and, mm, I like it when she bites me. I like biting her too, but she doesn't like being bitten, it's fun."

Henri pursed her lips for a moment "Would you like to bite *me*?"

I shook my head "No, that's- I think that's like cheating on her?"

She nodded slowly "What about a kiss? A chaste kiss between best friends?"

"Do best friends usually kiss each other?" I asked

"They do where I am from, ja." she said. I didn't believe her

"Ok, then yeah, one quick, chaste kiss." I agreed, patting her hand. She was still being weird, but... she wasn't as dangerous as she was a few days ago.

She pulled me to her lips and kissed me. I turned my head to catch it on the cheek, and it felt... nice. It wasn't as scary or fun as when Missy kissed me, but it felt important, like I needed it from her, to feel ok about something I'd been ignoring. She pulled away and sighed sadly.

"You ok?" I asked

"Just- ja, I just wish things ended differently." she said. "Gods, I miss you, I cannot believe how fucked up all my plans for our future went..."

"Things change," I said "we just have to adapt to it."

"That is stupid, but whatever." she muttered "You said you wanted to check on the other one?"

"Kensey, yeah, I wanted to see if she's ok." I said, pointing at the house on the desk.

"Ok, Klein Fee, I will put you up there..." Henri said gently, petting my shoulder. I got the feeling she wanted to keep talking to me, but was risking saying something that would ruin the moment, and needed a way to end it. I didn't mind, I needed a way out too, she had a lot to think about, and I wanted her to dwell on the things we'd talked about for a while without a fight tainting the conversation like it always seemed to these days.

Henri lifted me up and moved me over to the dollhouse, and set me on the second story next to Kensey's curled up form. I sighed, this would be a hard conversation, and I was getting tired of those, but she needed to hear what I had to say...

# Chapter Nineteen

I walked over to the couch and patted Kensey on the shoulder, waking her up. She sat up slowly, towering over me and rubbing her eyes. Popping her back, she slid over, making room for me on the couch next to her.

"Hey, what's up?" she asked, sounding defeated

"I wanted to talk, give you some tips on things." I said "I've been compressed for a while now, and I think I have some insight on how to help you not get treated like trash."

"Like trash?" she said quietly "I don't even care, I just want this to be over, I want to make it end..."

"What, like, suicide?" I asked, giving her a look

"Something like that, yeah. I don't see how anyone can live like this, to not be a *person* anymore, forever and ever..."

"Well, you *have* to." I said "I don't want the suicide statistics for class Bs to go up any higher than they already are, so you need to stick it out and suck it up."

"Telling someone to 'suck it up' is never good advice, Amber." Kensey sighed "I just don't think I can do this, you know?"

"I assure you, you can." I said "Look, I got *bought* by my high school bully, I was absolutely sure my life was over, right?"

"She knew you before?" she asked, shocked

"She did, we've known each other for like, six years or something. When she walked into the store and made eye contact with me, I felt everything breaking around me, I felt like I was going to drop dead right there."

"I'm so sorry to hear that..." she said sympathetically

"I'm not going to lie, it was rough at first." I continued "She was mean, I was hit, I was dropped in ice water, I was suffocated, thrown, treated like nothing, I felt like I wasn't even human."

"You're not really making it sound worth it to me." she complained

"No, look, I stuck it out. I talked to her, I communicated, I built up a relationship with her, and while we had some problems, eventually, we figured out what worked for us, and now? She's my best friend."

"Ach!" Henri barked from the floor behind us, indignant. I hadn't realized she was listening in...

"Henri, wait, like, not like *that*, you know, the way we talked about." I said over my shoulder to her, trying not to *imply* that I was dating Marissa to Kensey while still letting Henri know what I meant.

"So- so if I just let her hurt me, and then just talk to her, she'll get better?" Kensey asked "That sounds like a coping mechanism or a syndrome or something, that's not healthy."

"No, it's- mm." I said "It's more like, you have to build a relationship with her somehow, and she'll value you."

"I don't need her *value*." she snapped "I need her to treat me like a normal fucking person."

"Well *that's* not going to happen, so you need to figure out how to play up what she *likes* about you so she at *least* treats you like a pet, in a good way instead of an abusive way." I said, getting fed up with her.

"What does that even *mean*?" she said, exasperated

"Quince likes class Bs because she thinks they're cute, because she sees them as a high class symbol of money, and because she likes bossing people around." I explained "You need to feed that. You need to act cuter, you need to make her feel fancy and impress her friends and peers, and when she says 'jump', you say 'of course!' in a happy voice."

"That sounds *humiliating*." Kensey muttered

"Yeah, a little bit." I said "But I've know Quince as long as I've known Marissa, and longer than I've known Henri, and if you want her to value you, you need to *work* for it."

"Um, Amber," Henri said, poking her head up, looking into my house "this does not sound like healthy advice, I think it might be more helpful to try and get Quince to see class Bs differently, not play into her ideas."

I frowned at her "No, *you* saw me as less than human, you still kind of do, and we were besties for over five years. Quince isn't going to just magically see her new toy as a person just through conversations."

"I do too see you as human!" Henri said, stamping her foot "You- you are just small, and you need more care and oversight than you did before."

"Were you giving me care and oversight before?" I asked

"Ja, and you gave me some too, we were there for each other, but now you need *more*, you are fragile."

"You talked over me like I wasn't there, several times." I reminded her "You ignored my opinions and feelings."

"Oh for- no!" she snapped "I did not, I just wanted to keep you safe, and I was addressing the *reason* you were not safe!"

"You didn't *ask* if I was safe." I said

"You are with *Marissa*, you're never safe." she argued.

"And *now* you're deciding that because I'm small, I can't make my own decisions or assess situations." I crossed my arms "Henri, I appreciate that you're protective, but it's coming off as you not respecting me as a person, and you're proving my point."

She leveled a look at me and took a breath, letting it out slowly in a hiss "I can tell you are not going to listen to me. Amber, I *do* respect you, and I *do* see you as a person, that is all I can say."

She glanced to Kensey "Do not let yourself be taken advantage of, if Quince hurts you or does anything that breaks the rules, let someone know as soon as possible, me ideally, if you can. If you let us, we can get you taken away from her."

"Taken away?" she asked "I- would a different person really be any different?"

"That's the risk." I said "It could be someone who cares for you and tries to help you, or it could be someone who makes you dress up in cute outfits and wait on them or something."

"Ja, that would be so terrible." Henri said dryly.

"Are you still here?" I asked "Go get everyone new drinks, I'll be done here in a moment."

"And you say I do not treat *you* like a person." she said, her cheeks flushing, but she stepped away anyway

I turned back to Kensey "Anyway, just try and be cute, and play up the small and helpless side of things. She might be rough with you, but she's not going to physically hurt you on purpose. By accident? Absolutely, but just help her understand what can and can't hurt you, I guess."

"This conversation didn't help much..." Kensey said "Thanks for talking to me, but I just feel even more conflicted than before."

"If you're conflicted instead of about to kill yourself, then I'd say I did pretty good, right?" I said

"I guess so." she conceded. "You're going to go back to the movie?"

"Yeah, I wanna get back to Marissa. You want to come? We're watching Freaky Friday!"

"No, I'll stay here." she said, shaking her head "I need to think."

"Well if you want, the remote is there, maybe use the TV to watch some videos about class Bs to understand more? it helped me a lot." I recommended "Just use the guest account, I don't want my algorithm getting weird."

Kensey snorted "Ok, yeah, I'll try that. Enjoy the movie."

I waved to her, and turned to Henri, who was carefully holding new drinks, two cocktails for her and Tracy, a seltzer for Quince, and the last soju Marissa had bought earlier.

"I don't have hands, you gotta climb on." she said, and leaned towards the house, back to me. I carefully stepped out of the living room onto her shoulder, grabbing on to the shoulder frills to stop myself from falling.

"Be prepared to slide down into my dress if we see Miss Lund." she pushed her shoulders together, making a gap in her neckline in front of me

I bit my lip, and lay low, sticking close to her collarbone. I didn't really want to go in *there*, partly because the logistics of getting me out again in front of a group of people was concerning, but also because it'd be awkward as hell. I needed to be ready anyway, though, and I braced myself. Henri opened the door, turning the knob with the back of her hand, and stepped out, her foot hooking the door as she walked, pulling it closed again behind her.

I looked ahead to see Miss Lund standing in the doorway to the theater down the hall, her back to us as she spoke to the other girls. Henri hissed at me, and I froze. I still didn't want to do *that*, plus Marissa would be mad, it'd be a mess, I just-

Fuck it.

I slid back and around the back of Henri's head instead, and shimmied into the back of her dress. She tensed up, and leaned forward to give me better traction, and I crawled backwards down her back until I came to her bra strap, and slid into it, letting the band go across my chest, holding on with my arms. This was *much* better than the other option, and I was even more hidden than before, right? Henri stiffened, and then relaxed, and I heard a sound like a sigh, but she kept walking, carefully moving forward so I didn't fall.

As she got to the door, she stopped "Hello Miss Lund" she said calmly "Did you get to chat with Marissa?"

"Hello Henrietta, I did, yes." she said coldly "Tell me- do you have any pets?"

"My family keeps racehorses back home," she replied "but I've only seen them once or twice. They are more of an investment."

"Good, good." Miss Lund said "And do you have any plans to get pets in the future?"

"No, ma'am, I do not think I will ever get a pet. I think having an animal around would only hinder my plans for the future."

Her plans? What plans? Was she *still* trying to figure out a way to get me? I folded my arms and held back a huff, she was trying harder, but if that comment meant what I thought, she was still scheming under the surface.

"You have a good head on your shoulders, Henrietta." Miss Lund said "My daughter recently got a pet, as did one of her friends, it seems. I expected it from her friend, her family is 'inexperienced' in our world, but to see my daughter parade her new toy around like a status symbol? It pains me. If you can, convince her to dispose of it, would you?"

For a split second Henri's breath faltered, and I felt a chill. She was exactly the person to stand up to Miss Lund, but in the worst way possible.

"Oh, of course, I will speak to her about it, do not worry." Henri said smoothly

"Thank you, I'm happy Marissa has a friend like you, you're the influence she needs in her life." Miss Lund said "I'm off to bed, I have a full day of appointments and meetings tomorrow, please, stay as long as you like, and you're always welcome here."

"Thank you, rest well." Henri said easily, and I felt her move forward into the theater, the door closing behind her.

"Where's Amber?" hissed Marissa almost as soon as the door was shut

"She is safe, here, everyone get their stuff, I will get her out..." Henri said, passing the drinks out

"Get h-her out?" Marissa said dangerously "Out of where, exactly?"

I heard the clanking of drinks moving from hand to hand, and Henri moved her arms "She is in my bra, she-"

"She's f-fucking *what*." Marissa said, grabbing Henri by the shoulders, her voice cold and heavy

"No! No! No, in the back, hanging onto the strap, she-" Henri jumped to explain, but Marissa was already spinning her around. The dress bunched up around me, and Henri muffled a shriek as Marissa's hand came into view under me. I pulled my arms out of the strap and dropped into the hand as Marissa hunted for me, and she pulled me out just a little too quickly for comfort. I clutched Marissa's fingers as she stared at me, her face hard and angry. After a second she pressed me against her chest, just below her neck, rocking back and forth on her feet. Her heartbeat was loud enough to hear through her bones, and her hand was shaking slightly.

"Jesus Christ, Marissa, calm down." Quince said "No need to flip up her dress, she was trying to get her out."

"I- No, you don't understand." Marissa said, her voice slightly thick. "My mother said she'd *k-kill* Amber if she s-saw her again, then *yyyou* had to go and brag to her about *your* new toy to her, and Henri was outside with mom, and she came in without Amber-"

I realized with a mild shock that Marissa was holding back tears, desperately trying to save face and not cry in front of her minions. Five drinks and an emotionally charged night weren't helping though, and her hand started shaking even harder. I squeezed her fingers tightly, giving her the best hug I could, and she pressed me into her chest hard, her hand still trembling.

"Oh, that's- gods, that's sick." Tracy said, her voice shaking too "I don't blame you, do you need a hug?"

"No, w-what the fuck?" Marissa snapped, her voice hard again, the tears covered by the faked anger "I just want to make sure my new t-toy is safe, and- and, nnnot being put places she shouldn't be."

"Full disclosure, I met your mom on the way *to* the room too." Henri said. I couldn't tell if she was enjoying this, or just being honest, but either way, I cringed.

"She did not see Amber, but that was because I stuck her in my bloomers. I would have done it again just now, but my hands were full."

"That's- That's gotta be against the law, right?" Tracy asked "That feels like a violation or something, right?"

"It *is* illegal." Marissa said, her hand shaking again "If I *ever* hear of you p-putting Amber in your clothes again, I will personally ensure you are incapable of d-doing it a third time."

"Is that a threat of physical violence?" Henri asked, sounding almost happy

"It was vague enough that it could just mean you being banned from her house, I think." Quince said "It wouldn't hold up in court, so don't try, trust me, I know."

"I just- I want- you-" Marissa struggled to get the words out, her words slightly slurred, still shaken up "Just, please, no more touching Amber at all unless I'm right- right there."

Henri sighed "Ja, whatever, ok. You are *way* over-reacting, she was over my tights and against my leg, and the bra-strap thing was nothing."

I climbed up to Marissa's neck and hugged it, sitting on her collarbone and leaning carefully to make sure I didn't slip. Her hand moved up to cup me and she took a deep breath.

"My mother is a dangerous person, even to people she c-cares about. *Especially* to people she cares about." Marissa explained "She'd *love* it if Amber was killed-"

"She asked me to convince you to 'dispose' of her, ja..." Henri murmured

"...yeah." Marissa said, stroking my back "So w-with *that* threat over my head, and having you act inappropriately towards her, it makes me v-very angry, and I'm having a hard time c-calming down."

"Ok. I will not hide Amber in my clothes ever again." Henri said, her voice a little subdued

"You really care about her, huh?" Quince said to Marissa "You treat her like she's made of glass or something, I swear you were about to cr-"

"She is a fucking *human being*." snarled Marissa, just before Quince said something that'd ruin the night "She's *my* human being, but she-she's still a human being, and part of her being *mine* is that I have to protect her and care for her. In fact, t-t-that's the *whole main point* of me *hav-having* her, not that *yyyou'd* know with how you treat *yours*. You're a *joke* of a guardian, you'll kill yours in a week, she'll snap like a fucking c-c-cookie, and you won't even *care*. You'll be a fucking *murderer* and you won't even n-notice, you'll just get a new one and move on like the fucking *brat* you are."

I glanced back at Quince, her eyes were wide and her mouth was open slightly, and she took a step back, blinking furiously. "I won't! I'll be careful!" she said, half arguing, half insisting "I won't murder her, even by accident!"

"I don't *f-f-fffucking* believe you." growled Marissa "But fine, whatever. Just don't try and make fun of *mmme* when I try to do my job and take care of *my* human being."

I held tighter to her neck, feeling the blood rushing through the thick vein I was against, her heartbeat loud and fast. I looked out at the other girls, Quince was standing still, her seltzer by her side, biting her lip, Tracy was looking at Marissa with a look that seemed hostile and concerned at the same time, and Henri was looking at the ground, not saying anything. It looked like Marissa had re-asserted herself as the queen of the group, while still defending me and upholding me as a person. I was impressed, and more than a little flushed myself at her display, and I let myself melt into her skin, going soft as she pet me.

"Whatever." Marissa said "Let's just watch the f-fucking movie. Just like, veg out and forget about all this, ok?"

"Can I sit on the couch this time?" Henri said, her voice small "My legs still hurt from the last movie."

"F-fine, sure, yeah, I don't care." Marissa said, stumbling to her spot on the couch and flopping down, pressing me into her neck as she fell so I wouldn't be jarred. Henri looked at the other two girls, then walked over, sitting next to Marissa, their thighs touching. Marissa stared at her, and opened her mouth to tell her to move, but let her breath out in a sigh, and cracked open her last drink of the evening. Six sojus was a *ton* of alcohol, I was surprised she was still standing, but I got the impression she was a lot more drunk than she was letting on, even *with* the slurring and stuttering.

As Quince started the movie, Henri leaned in to Marissa's ear and whispered loud enough for me to hear.

"Can we both hold her?"

"What? Like p-pass her back and ffforth? Nnno, that's st-stupid."

"I mean like, we put our hands together and she sits between them, like, here."

Henri pulled at Marissa's left hand and I let myself fall into it, and she dropped it down where their thighs met. Then, Henri looped her right hand under Marissa's arm, and clasped her fingers with Marissa's hand, pinning me between their hands, my head poking up in front of their thumbs.

"Is this ok?" Henri whispered "I want to hold her, but I know you need to be close to her right now, and I do not want you thinking I am doing anything bad, I just want to hold her."

Marissa glared at Henri, and looked down at her hand, wiggling her fingers between Henri's and scrunched up her face.

"Yeah. I'm only llletting you do th-this so I don't have to worry about k-keeping track of her."

"She's getting kinda drunk." I told Henri

"Fuck you, I'm n-not drunk on fucking 5 bottles." Marissa muttered

"Each bottle is three or four drinks, Marissa." I said "You had the equivalent of like, eighteen shots."

"Oh, f-fuck." she said, blinking. She glanced at her last bottle, open but mostly un-drunk "I guess I'll just s-s-stop here..."

"It is weird that you stutter when you're dunk, usually people slur their words..." Henri mused

Quince giggled from the other side of her and Tracy gasped dramatically. Marissa's grip on us tightened and she growled.

"Shut th-th-the fuck up, Henri." she hissed

"Marissa used to have a *huge* stuttering problem, she couldn't say two sentences without tripping up, it took *years* of speech therapy to fix it." Tracy said quietly "She's *very* insecure about it, she used to attack people who'd bring it up."

"Th-that's not your s-s-s-story to fucking t-t-tell, you dumb b-bitch." Marissa said, her hand shaking. Henri squeezed her hand at the same time as I hugged her thumb, and we looked at each other, our eyes meeting each others for a moment.

"That's why she started being a bitch to people, really." Quince said "I heard she was almost normal until she found out that being terrible to others made them too scared to tease her."

"I s-swear to the gods, Quince, I will f-fucking murder you. It's not like that." Marissa said, her breath getting quicker

"Mm, bullying people who made fun of her gave her a taste of power, but mommy issues made her go all in. Then of course, the divorce-" Tracy said matter-of-factly, like she was reciting a history book

Marissa stood, cutting her off, and pushed me into Henri's lap

"Hold this." she muttered, and walked over to the other girls. She was swaying, but she reached out with her hands and braced herself on their heads, looking back and forth between them.

"I'm gonna say th-this once." she said, her voice dark but shaking, sounding angry and terrified at the same time "If y-you ever talk ab-about m-my past again, I'll f-f-fucking ruin your lives. Quince, I have en-enough dirt f-from Darcy to make your d-d-dad's p-practice close down *instantly*, and Tracy, I can f-fucking *ruin* your n-new company w-with j-just a w-word to m-mom. I'll f-fucking bury you b-both."

She jolted, and slammed their heads together with a smacking noise, and they both screamed. I jumped and Henri curled up on the couch and gasped, clutching me tightly. The other two girls whimpered and held their heads, I saw a trickle of blood on Tracy's cheek, from Quince's earring hitting her, maybe? My heart was pounding, and I held myself tightly. This... wasn't the

Missy I'd come to love, this was the Marissa who would lash out and hurt people rather than being hurt herself, the one who bought me in the first place...

She turned and took a breath. "Alright then. Let's watch the fucking movie now, all of you shut the fuck up."

I had just enough time to realize she hadn't stuttered once that sentence before she collapsed to the ground in a heap, face down.

"Stay down, fucking bitch." hissed Quince "Fucking asshole..."

"What happened?" I asked, clambering out of Henri's grip to look at her "Is she ok?"

"Yeah, your fucking *girlfriend* is fine, she's the kind of drunk who goes hard until she passes out." Quince snapped "I, on the other hand, might have a concussion."

"She's not my girlfriend, I- I don't know why she did that, does she usually get violent when she drinks?" I asked

"It's *pretty* obvious there's something between you two, Amber, you can give up the act while she's out." Tracy said, rubbing her head, one eye closed. She hadn't noticed the blood yet "We've just been playing along because we don't want to tick her off."

"You failed at that." Henri said "She seemed pretty ticked off."

"No kidding." Quince stood up and paused the movie, giving Marissa a light kick. She moaned, but didn't move

"She usually gets more *relaxed* when she drinks, her need to be the boss bitch wears off. Guess she just cared that much about her stupid fucking villain backstory to fight through the drunken haze."

She walked over to the snack table and brought back ice from a small bucket, wrapping them in napkins

"Fuuuck, she hasn't physically hurt any of us in *years*." Tracy moaned "I thought she grew out of that."

"I- you say you 'know' that there's something between us, what are you talking about?" I asked. I wanted to make sure of what they knew before I said anything that would cause problems.

"Seriously?" Quince asked "I knew before the tennis game. She treats you like a little queen, she's never shown this much care for any*one* or any*thing* before. She asked us to stop calling you the Rat, *and* she asked us to call your minion by her real name, in the same conversation? Super obvi she was trying to get on your good side."

"She was *making out with you* when we walked in earlier, Amber. I almost said something then, but I wasn't sure how she'd take it." Tracy said

"We- it wasn't quite making out..." I said weakly

"Then she was straight up getting kinky with you, and as horrible as she is, she's not about to do *that* with someone who doesn't want it." Quince flopped back on the couch, propping her feet up on Marissa's butt and wiping the blood off Tracy's face with an icy napkin

"They are not girlfriends." Henri said ""They are something else. I do not understand it, but they have a romantic relationship that involves being physical, but they somehow aren't girlfriends, apparently."

"Gods, I can't believe she's so homophobic that she won't even admit she has a girlfriend." Quince sighed, rubbing her head with the ice

"She's not homophobic though?" I said, confused "I thought *you* were homophobic, what? You said shitty things about me being queer."

"Nah, I'm homo-apathetic, at best." Quince said "It's a good tool to use against people, but I don't *actually* care. It's a power move."

"I think most people are like that." Tracy said "I noticed people seem to just go with whatever the majority thinks, if they don't have a horse in the race themselves. I think if Marissa had been more open about liking girls instead of poorly hiding it, there'd be a lot more openly queer people in school, and *way* more allies."

"Back in high school I was *kind* of open about it." Henri said "I had one of those cute bacon colored pins to show I liked girls, but it got pulled off my bag within a week."

"Uh huh, because you're a *loser*." Quince said "If a loser is gay, they get picked on, if the school queen was gay, she'd make it cool to be gay or tear everyone else down with her."

"*Is* Marissa gay?" Henri asked "I wondered if she just liked having power over Amber instead of like, being *gay* gay."

"If you're a woman that likes women, you're gay, even if you only like doming them, Henri." I said

"She's absolutely just regular gay." Quince said "Or- I don't know, Bi, I guess, with a lean towards girls?"

"How are you so sure?" Henri asked

"There were tells. She'd never look at us in the showers, like, ever. Everyone looks a little, but she never did, eyes down, glare on her face." Tracy said "And she'd go quiet when we talked about our bodies and stuff, and she'd always make sure we alllll knew when she had a crush on a guy. Over the top, talking about them like she didn't quite know what she liked about them. Oh, and it was *always* these little subby twink boys too, I think one is even a girl now?"

"Hm..." Henri said, eyeing Marissa's sleeping form "Part of me wonders if *I* would have had a shot if I'd tried to go after her. After Amber turned me down, I gave up hope finding love in high school, but if I had been dating *her*..."

"No, she would have shredded you." Quince said "At best, you'd have been someone she strung along and pretended to like so you'd do stuff for her."

"She said if *I* wasn't around, she would have gone after Amber, and claimed her." Henri mused "I wonder if she would have come out or if it'd have been an open secret."

"Can we please not talk about her like this?" I asked "I feel really shitty about this, you guys are acting like she's this 'idea' instead of a person and talking about her like she's not here."

"Oh I'm sure you know allll about not being a person, huh lil baybe?" Quince said in a mocking tone

I sighed and let myself fall back into Henri's lap. They were being less guarded and more open now that Marissa was out of the picture, but they were still terrible.

"Whatever." I said "Look, I like Marissa, she likes me, I'm fed up talking about queer this and gay that, it's not a big deal. It sounds like no one here cares, so can we just drop it?"

"*I* like talking about queer stuff." Tracy said "It's great gossip material."

"What time is it, anyway?" Henri said "We've been arguing and stuff all night, all we did was watch one movie and eat pizza, the rest of the time we just argued."

"It's uhh, just after eleven." Tracy said, checking her phone

"Wait, it's only *eleven*? I thought it was like, two at least." I asked sitting up "You guys got here after seven thirty. That means... Marissa drank eighteen fucking drinks in four hours?"

"Uhh yeah, I guess?" Quince said

"That's- that could be lethal!" I said, alarmed. I thought back to the mandatory drugs and alcohol class I'd taken in college and felt my heart rate rise "Henri, pull out your phone, we need to check this..."

Henri pulled her phone out from under her skirt, unlocked it and handed it to me. I typed quickly, using my palms to get the touchscreen to read my taps, and entered her stats into a BAC calculator website and shrieked when the results popped up.

"What? What happened?" Tracy asked

"This said her blood is like, oh point forty six!" I said, panicking "It says she'll go into a coma and *die*!"

I shook my head "Oh gods, *fuck*, we need an ambulance!"

"An ambulance?" Tracy asked "She's passed out drunk before, I'm pretty sure she'll be fine."

"I'm *not* calling an ambulance because of *this* bitch." Quince said "Let's just make sure she's face down for the night and play a game or something."

"No, it- it says she could just stop breathing, we need to get her help!" I shouted "She's not used to this kind of alcohol, she had way too much!"

"Are you sure?" Henri said, looking worried "It did not look like that much. She was kind of staggering though."

"It's like, a ton, gods, please, can you call?" I asked, pulling on her arm "Please, I can't have her dying on me, we *just* got together..."

Henri looked at me, and I felt my heart go into my mouth. Quince and Tracy didn't care or thought it was no big deal, and Henri... I watched as her eyes flicked back and forth between me and Marissa, and her breathing slowed. If Marissa was dying, like *actually* dying, then *I* was back on the table, and Henri wouldn't even have to get her hands dirty to do it. She watched Marissa's unmoving form on the carpet, and huffed. I was shaking, she was taking too long, she'd decided to let her go into a coma and die, she-

She picked up her phone and pressed the side buttons, opening the emergency menu and tapped the call button. I fell back onto her thigh with a sigh of relief.

The next few minutes were a blur, me and Kensey were collected and put into Henri's purse, wrapped in a silk handkerchief for the time being. Miss Lund was woken up by Tracy, and Marissa had carefully been moved to the front hall by Parker and Drew. Everyone stood quietly as we waited for the ambulance to arrive, me and Kensey still hiding in the purse, out of sight of Miss Lund. My heart was pounding, and I hugged Kensey without thinking. She stiffened for a second, then returned the hug reluctantly.

Miss Lund broke the silence

"I can't believe she's so stupid she'd give herself alcohol poisoning." she muttered "I raised her *better* than that. Her gluttony and hedonism will kill her, eventually."

No one answered, and Miss Lund sighed loudly "I suppose I'll need to go to the hospital with her. I won't be getting much sleep tonight, it seems. Drew, get the car ready."

"I would like to go as well, Miss Lund." Henri said as Drew left the room to pull the car around to the front "I want to be there when she wakes up."

"Alright, you may ride with me, Henrietta." Miss Lund said "Have you had much to drink?"

"I had one and a half drinks, ma'am." Henri replied

"Good, good." she said "You other two, you'll remain here until morning, do you understand? I don't want you driving while drunk."

"Ok..." Tracy squeaked

"But Henri's got my-" Quince started, then thought better of it "-my number, in case she needs to get in touch..." she finished, trailing off.

Sirens filled the air, and I poked my head up to see the ambulance pull around the rotunda in front of the door and two EMS workers climbed out, getting a stretcher out of the back. I glanced around at the others, Quince looked frustrated, Tracy was scared, Miss Lund was angry, but her arms were nervously rubbing against each other, and Marissa was laying face down on a blanket, not moving. I bit my lips and ducked back into the purse as the EMS workers started to load her up.

"Is someone going to ride with her?" one of them asked

"No, we're following in a car." Miss Lund snapped "Get out of here, go pump her stomach or something, quickly."

I heard the other person scoff, but the doors closed and the sirens started up again, and the ambulance pulled out.

"Come on Henrietta, here's Drew with my car."

I heard the crunch of gravel as Henri walked to Miss Lund's car and got in, swinging me and Kensey onto the floor of the car. She climbed in and closed the door, her leg pressing us against the car door, a barrier between us and Miss Lund. Kensey shifted slightly to get into a better position, and I grabbed her arm, shaking my head. If she saw us moving now, we'd be dead...

"I still can't believe she was so, so *stupid*." Miss Lund muttered as the car took off "She's been making poor decisions lately, spending all her money, drinking herself silly, buying that pet, I just don't know what to *do* with her."

"She is still at that age, I suppose." Henri said "I myself have made some foolish choices in the recent past, I like to see them as moments of growth."

She was really laying it on, wasn't she? I didn't know why she wanted to impress Miss Lund so much, but it seemed to be working.

"I can agree with that." she said "As long as the mistakes aren't repeated. Speaking of mistakes, did you get a chance to talk to Marissa about her pet?"

"I did speak with her, ja." Henri said "Although..."

"Although?"

"It was her new pet who demanded we call the ambulance, ma'am." Henri explained "She recognized the signs of alcohol poison, and insisted we get her help before Marissa 'went into a coma and died', as she put it."

"It did?" Miss Lund said, sounding slightly confused "I'd assumed it would hate Marissa, lord knows her friends do."

"I think she sees Marissa as a protector of sorts, and respects her as an owner." Henri offered

Why was she doing this? She was helping me, trying to make Miss Lund see me in a better light, I didn't understand her angle, but I was grateful she was trying at least.

"At least the pet knows her place." Miss Lund said more gently. "Still, I can't stand the things. Pets in general, *or* those subhumans. I'm trying to find a way to eradicate them, you know."

Kensey stiffened, and I had to fight to not react myself, she wanted to- that wording was unfortunate, it didn't do her any favors.

"Eradicate, ma'am?" Henri said, her voice strained

"To be more accurate, at least let them die off." Miss Lund clarified "That new bio-lab I mentioned, I want to use it to produce and sell a vaccine for the compression particles. No new class Bs, if I can help it."

"That- that is very noble of you, ma'am." Henri said, confused

"It's more about the money than the milk of human kindness, but thank you." she said "The only issue is that we need to activate the body's entire supply of the compatible genetic makeup *without* compressing it in order to vaccinate. We need pre-compressed particles to do the research, but testing on class Bs is illegal as of yet, meaning we barely have enough testing materials to work with, just what volunteers who let us inject them with the genetic material can give us, but each time someone volunteers, they lose a bit of their height, of course, so the volunteers are very rare."

"Alright, I- I understand, why are you telling me this?" Henri asked

"This is something I'd like Marissa to understand, so I'm trying to explain myself to you in the hopes you'll explain it to her. I respect you, Henrietta. Once I take over that lab fully, I have people in legislation who can legalize limited testing on class Bs in exchange for a small fee to their families or guardians, we'll frame it as researching a way to *help* the class Bs, and it'll pass with support from both sides."

"I see." Henri said politely

"Earlier this morning, I'd gotten up and gotten to work, I was in the middle of doing all the prep work for this, trying to find subjects, buying up shares, planning the takeover, finding ways to use these pests to make money, and seeing a future of *massive* profits ahead of us, and my daughter comes down to breakfast with one of *them* in a fashion outfit like its an accessory and sits it on the table right in front of me, proud as punch. Do you see the problem?"

"I believe so, yes, it seems like a conflict of interest." Henri said dryly

"Exactly!" Miss Lund said, happily "She's taking over the company in less than four years, and here she is, bonding with one of the things that's going to make us richer than god. She's going to love it, and become attached, and when the time comes for her to take over, she'll shut down all the work and research we'll have been doing, all because she can't look at a test subject without thinking of her little- what was its name again?"

"Amber, ma'am."

"Right, she'll just see her little Amber there in the test tanks getting blood and marrow drawn, and she'll get emotional and shut the whole thing down, losing us *billions* in vaccinations. I heard the particles are *evolving*, too, so we could let people get new ones *yearly*, like flu shots, and we'd have the only patent. We'd be a world power, all by ourselves... And all that crumbles if Marissa is stupid enough to get attached to a glorified lab rat."

"I can see how that would be frustrating." Henri said "If I may ask, why not use actual lab rats? Or cows, or monkeys?"

"The compression particles only target a specific mutation in the human body." Miss Lund said "As far as I've heard, it seems they were made to target one person, or maybe a family, and the creators didn't realize the mutation was so widespread."

"I thought we did not know anything about the creation?" Henri asked, sounding interested

"We don't. But we can study the particles, and they *were* made for a reason, that's for damn sure. They're designed, and they have signs of being coded artificially"

The car rocked and came to a stop. Miss Lund sighed "Well, I need to go sign some things, I presume. Drew, park the car, I'll call for you later. Henrietta, thank you for the stimulating conversation, maybe we can continue it later, while we're waiting on Marissa to wake up?"

"Of course, I look forward to it, ma'am. I will see you in the waiting room."

I felt Henri get out of the car, and it drove off. After a few moments, there was the sound of a door sliding open, and air conditioning. We swung back and forth for a short while, then there was a *flump* as Henri dropped into a chair. There was more movement, and the top of the purse opened up, Henri peeking down at us in her lap.

"Good news, Amber." she said darkly

"What's that?" I asked

"I have found someone I want to kill even more than Marissa."

## Chapter Twenty

The next few hours flew by in a blur, the noise and acrid smells of the hospital were overwhelming, so I stayed in the purse most of the time. Henri's hand would dip in and pet me and Kensey every so often while we tried to nap, but she mostly sat still, waiting. At around three in the morning, Miss Lund made her way over to us from the room where she'd been with Marissa and Henri stood to meet her.

"They say she's mostly fine." Miss Lund said "They have tubes in her nose and an IV in her arm, and they're monitoring her heart rate, if it stops, they'll be able to help her."

"So she is going to be ok?" Henri asked

"Aside from the risk of heart failure for the next few hours, yes, she should be ok." Miss Lund replied "They said there's a risk of brain damage, but I told them if she did *this* to herself, it's already too late for her brain."

"I... see." Henri said "So, is there any chance I can go see her?"

"She's still passed out, they don't think she'll wake up for a while, but I let the doctors know you'll be staying with her until about two this afternoon, if that's ok with you. I have several important meetings and that's the first open time slot I have to come back here. I can pay you for the trouble, of course."

"I would be happy to stay with her, of course." Henri said "And no need to pay me. We are friends, after all."

"Ah, of course, of course." Miss Lund said "I hope I didn't offend, I was just trying to ensure I wasn't wasting your time."

"It is not a waste of time at all, ma'am." she said politely

"I appreciate that..." Miss Lund said "I don't know when I'll have free time, but I'll treat you to dinner this week sometime, assuming I can find a free evening. Maybe Marissa can come along, if she's up to it."

"That sounds like a lovely time, Miss Lund, I look forward to it." Henri said.

I didn't think it sounded lovely at *all*, but Henri was good at being very polite to people she wanted to strangle.

"Oh, and with the new information that's come to light, you can stop trying to get my daughter to dispose of her pet." Miss Lund said "I may not like the fact that it exists, or that she owns it, but it did save her life. I'll end my grudge with it, for her sake."

"That is very kind of you, ma'am." Henri said, surprised "What about the conflict of interest?"

"Don't misunderstand, I still want you to impart the importance of ending the class B plague to her, try and get her to see that the continued existence of them is a detriment to society, but do it gently. If she can understand the greater good, her pet may not hurt her views on class B testing after all."

"I will discuss that with her." Henri said

"Thank you, it'll sound so much better coming from you." Miss Lund sighed

"If I may, ma'am, the class B plague isn't picky about who it targets, what would you do if it evolves to the point where you yourself get infected? Or Marissa?" Henri asked carefully

"That's a *horrible* thought" Miss Lund said, aghast "I don't even want to *think* about that. I suppose... if it were me, I'd find a painless way to end my life. If it were *Marissa*, heaven forbid- I'd..."

She sighed, and went quiet for a moment "...I'd have no choice but to use her as a test subject. My priority would change from *ending* the transformations to *reversing* them, of course, but I wouldn't let her condition influence my morals, I couldn't."

"I understand." Henri said quietly

"Why would you think about that kind of thing, anyway?" Miss Lund asked

"Mm, I saw an article about it, and I have been considering what my own life would look like if I was infected." Henri said "I wanted a more experienced view on the matter, thank you."

"No, thank you, It's a dark topic, but one worth considering. I'm going to go home and get an hour or two of sleep before my breakfast meeting, I'll see you this afternoon?"

"Of course, hopefully she will be awake by then."

Miss Lund gave Henri the room number and left, leaving us alone in the waiting room. Henri sighed and patted the bag, heading for the doors deeper into the hospital. It took a few minutes to reach the room Marissa was staying in, and the lights were all off inside, making it look gloomy and sad. I peeked at her lying there on the bed, hooked up to machines and hoses and I felt my heart break just a little. She had an almost blue pallor to her skin, very pale and very fragile. Henri walked over to the bed slowly and set her purse by Marissa's shins. I stared at my unconscious girlfriend for a few more seconds, taking in her slight frown, listening to the heart rate monitor beep, and feeling a chill go through me.

"Fuck, she looks bad," Kensey said from beside me "you said she got this way off of five drinks?"

"Five bottles of wine, really." I said "It's rice wine, but it's still wine."

"Oh, yeah, that'd do it" she muttered "I remember my alcoholic days, I was drinking a bottle and a half a night at one point. Five is wild."

"She is an idiot." Henri said, pulling a chair over to the bed "She should know better than to have that much."

"It was a new kind of alcohol for her, it was in a bottle like beer, if she'd had 5 beers, she'd have been fine." I defended her "She's just not used to soju."

"She still should have noticed that she was way drunker than she had any right to be." Henri said, sitting down and laying her upper body on the bed "I'm going to try and sleep a little, do you guys need anything first?"

"I'm ok." Kensey said "I'm just happy to not be dealing with Quince for a little bit longer. Wanna put that off as long as possible."

"Yeah, I'm good." I said "I want to stay up in case she wakes up though."

"*I'm* going to get some sleep." Kensey said "I need my rest."

"We need way less sleep than class As, so you'll probably be fine if you want to stay up with me?" I reminded her

"Nah, I want to sleep." she said, and ducked back into the purse.

"Amber, just be careful, ok?" Henri said as I climbed out "Wake me up if you need anything."

I nodded, but doubted I'd be able to. Henri was a very deep sleeper, and even when we were the same size I'd had trouble waking her up.

"Actually-" I said, thinking back

"Hm?" she said, lifting her head to look at me

"What was all that about 'what if you or Marissa were compressed' back there?" I asked "That's a weird thing to ask someone."

Henri sighed "I was trying to see if she would think differently if I forced empathy on her, but it did not work."

She folded her arms under her head "Plus, it's something I've been thinking about a lot myself."

"Her or Marissa catching it?" I asked "You told me not to think like that..."

"No no, *me* catching it." she clarified "If it can spread from direct contact with people who are compressing, and we can test to see if people can compress now, I could compress *myself* by surrounding myself with people who can compress and infecting *them*, right?"

"Why would you *want* that?" I asked "This is horrible, I know I'm in a better place than I was last week, but Henri, you *don't* want this."

"I know, I know, I just- I want to know I see you as an equal, I guess." she muttered "And we could be roomies, if Marissa adopted me too."

"I don't think you'd want her to." I said "She's only as nice as she is to me because she's dating me."

"Ja, 'nice'." Henri huffed "Anyway, it was just a fantasy. The odds of finding a group of people who'd be willing to let me compress them before they do it naturally is slim to none."

"Well don't go looking." I said "Seriously, I know we disagree about a lot right now, but having a full sized friend to defend me from whatever threats come my way is kinda nice. Even if I don't always need defending the way you think I do."

"I will not, it was just a stray thought." she assured me "I need sleep though, I will see you later, Klein Fee."

"Goodnight, Henri." I said, and patted her forehead as I walked past her.

I made my way up to Marissa's face, sitting on the pillow next to her, watching her sleep. I wondered what would have happened if I hadn't said anything, if she'd have woken up in the morning with a massive headache, or if she'd have never woken up at all. There was no way of knowing, but I was glad for that dumb health and safety class they'd made us take our first semester. I didn't think I'd need to know any of that stuff, but it ended up paying off in the end.

I shivered and rubbed my arms through my sleeves. The dumb clown costume was still too thin to be comfortable, and the hospital was even colder than Marissa's house, it felt like about 70, which was far too cold for me. She'd played around the temperature in her room back home, trying to find a spot where I wasn't uncomfortably cold and she wasn't feeling sticky, and we'd found that about 78 degrees was about as hot as she could stand without being too uncomfortable, while I'd be ok in a t-shirt and pjs, maybe my track-suit jacket too. I preferred it to be closer to 83, which is what *my* house was set to, but it didn't stay that warm unless the walls were closed.

I scooted closer to Marissa, nestling into her neck, just above her shoulder. She was warm, very warm, most likely because of the alcohol still in her system making her run hot. I listened to the thumping of her blood, the gentle hiss of the oxygen as she breathed, and I let out a breath. I felt like I'd been trying to fight against the panic all night, and being here with her was finally letting it slip away. I let myself relax as she warmed me, and I lay there, not sleeping, but relaxing in the crook of her neck.

Time passed slowly. While I wanted her to wake up, I also wanted her to rest, and I felt wonderful just being close to her. It was the longest we'd gone like this since she'd slept curled up around me during the first sleepover, and it was the first time I'd been able to appreciate it, really. As the sun started to come in through the window, I heard Henri moan and felt the bed move as she readjusted in her sleep to get the light out of her face. Marissa hummed, and she moved slightly, causing me to slip down slightly as she turned her head. I clambered out of my cozy hole and over to her shoulder, standing so I could see her face.

She turned to me, one eye open and wrinkled her nose, her hand moving like she was going to lift it, but it fell back down and she gave up.

"Whurmi?" she slurred

Her face was bleary, and her eye looked bloodshot and puffy. I winced as she tried to fight through the haze to see me, and sat down, rubbing her shoulder to try and help her focus on me.

"You're in the hospital." I said "You drank too much last night and we had to call an ambulance."

Her one open eye blinked at me and then she looked around the room

"Imminna hobsital?" she asked

"Yeah, they were worried you'd die, you were almost in a coma." I explained

"Hnn... too drunk t' thin' boutall that..." she moaned

"You'll be drunk until Sunday morning, according to the internet." I said "You drank a *lot*, really fast."

"Ss eryonne ok?" she asked

"You knocked Quince and Tracy's heads together pretty hard, but I think they're ok." I told her

"Hhhh... I got tubes inme..." she said wiggling her nose

"That's air, they thought you'd stop breathing." I said "You were really drunk."

"Fffeels more drumnk than I rember being..." she sighed

"You're acting more drunk than you were before you passed out, yeah." I agreed "I guess it hadn't all gotten in your system yet."

"Imgoin t' sleep..." she said "cm gimme kiss..."

I walked my way to her face as she turned it to meet me and pressed myself against her lips. She made a loud 'mwah' noise and turned her head back up to look at the ceiling, and moaned lightly in pain before going still, her breathing growing slow and heavy once again. I returned to my nook in the crook of her neck and curled up. It really was entirely too cold in this room. I felt the time pass as I lie there, the sun soon streaming through the window. It was still early, but it was late enough she'd usually be awake by now, if not for the alcohol. The door to the room swung open and I froze, had Miss Lund swung by before her breakfast meeting after all?

Henri stirred at the sound and lifted her head "I am up, I just- I wanted to lie there a bit more..." she mumbled lazily

"Oh, that's ok, ma'am." the new person said, and I recognized the uniform as she walked into the room. A nurse, checking in on Marissa, of course. "I'm sorry to wake you, I just need to put new bags on the IV, and check to make sure she's still doing ok."

"Ja, I just... I did not get to sleep until after three..." Henri yawned

"Are you her girlfriend?" the nurse asked, moving to the IV to swap them out.

"Oh, *götter*, nein." Henri said, rubbing her face "I am just her... friend, I guess. I am watching her class B for her."

"Oh? She has a class B?" the nurse looked interested "Where are they? I don't see them."

I sat up and waved, and got a small start from the nurse for my troubles. I hid a smile and climbed back onto Marissa's shoulder, sitting down so I'd be more visible.

"I don't know if it's safe for you to be that close to her." the nurse said "She could roll over or vomit in her sleep, and then where would you be?"

"Hey, ja, why is she on her back?" Henri said "I thought she was supposed to be face down if she was drunk."

"We pumped her stomach after we heard she'd had so much within the last couple hours, and we gave her antiemetics as well. There's not much of a vomiting risk, and she's intubated, anyway." the nurse explained

I looked at Marissa, her skin was a better color, and she was still looking slightly pained, but she wasn't as bad as she'd been before. Whatever they'd done, hopefully it helped.

"Why'd you list that as a reason not to sleep next to her, then?" I asked

"I just don't want you getting hurt" the nurse said "I'll be back in a while to check on her again, try not to wake her up, ok?"

Henri nodded, and peeked in her purse as soon as we were alone "You doing ok Kensey?" she asked

"I need to use the bathroom." Kensey said, her voice small and nervous

"Uhhh." Henri said, her face going blank "Um. I do not- we- there is a bathroom in the room here, but it is not- there's not a- Mm, Amber, how do we do this?"

"I don't know, don't look at me," I said, shrugging "I'm always in my carrying case when we're gone for more than a couple hours, I've never had this problem."

"Ok, ok." Henri said "What if you use the sink?"

"The sink?" Kensey said poking her head up "That's- I don't know how that'd work."

"Yeah, Henri could leave the water running a little, you could take your clothes off so they don't get wet, and-" I started

"Ok ok, just shut up." Kensey snapped "We'll do that, just- don't talk about it."

"Alright." Henri said, picking Kensey up and looking uncomfortable "I will just- I will bring you in there and uh, I can set a timer for what, five minutes? So you can get undressed and stuff?"

"Please stop talking about it." Kensey said, her face in her hands.

Henri walked to the bathroom and I heard the water turn on. She closed the door, and came back over to the table, sans Kensey.

"That is..." Henri said, looking mildly uncomfortable "That is humiliating."

"Yeah, no kidding." I agreed "I feel bad for her."

"Do you also need to..?" Henri asked as she set her phone timer

"No, I'm good." I said. I looked over at Marissa and hugged myself again "Thanks, for calling the ambulance."

Henri went still, and looked at me, her expression unreadable.

"...No problem." she said finally

"I was kinda worried for a second there." I admitted "I could see your brain working, and, well..."

She made a noise in the back of her throat and scrunched her face up "I *will* kill for you, Klein Fee, if I think I need to. But I do not know that I need to right now. So I called."

"But you *thought* about letting her die?" I asked

"I mean, ja, of course I did." Henri said "It is like, if she is gone, you are basically mine, still, I knew you would hate me for it."

"You mean her being alive is because you didn't want to upset *me*?" I clarified

"Well it certainly was not because I liked her." Henri admitted

"I don't know how to feel about that." I said, folding my arms "I'm glad you called, but if the only thing between her and death was a fear of me being upset with you, then I'm worried you're still a danger."

"If it makes you feel better, I promise not to kill Marissa, and I promise not to steal you, ok?" Henri said, frustrated "Is that ok with you? Does that make your feeling of being 'in danger' go away?"

"Do you *mean* it?" I asked, glaring at her

"Ja, gods, I mean it." she said, rolling her eyes "It is not like I have done either of those things before."

"You have actively tried, multiple times, to steal me." I pointed out "And you just admitted to wanting to let *her* die due to negligence."

"Ok, but did I?" she asked, shrugging "Amber, I am giving you my word, I am being friendly to her, I am making friends with her bitch of a mom, I am staying at the hospital for hours because I know you want to be with her during this mess, I am being good, and you cannot even fucking let me do that without trying to make me a bad guy?"

"Oh. Fuck, I'm sorry, yeah, ok." I said, ashamed "Thank you, I- I don't know why I started a fight over that."

Henri just pointed at Marissa in response and raised an eyebrow. I sighed, maybe she *was* a bad influence, but weren't all the best relationships? Henri's phone went off, and she stood, walking to the bathroom without a word. She knocked, waited a moment, then opened the door. A few seconds later, a damp and angry Kensey was sitting on the bed, teeth chattering.

"The water splashed all over me." she said, wringing her hair out "That was the *worst*, I hope to god Quince buys me a real bathroom, *today*."

"I will talk to her about it." Henri said "She has the money, I am sure she will get you lots of fancy stuff."

"Just don't let her take you to 'Tiny Toys for Tiny Treasures'," I said "Or if she does, don't let them put you in the little daycare area, it was bad..."

"How bad?" Henri asked, her eyes sharpening

"Like, hot and boring and loud and overstimulating, just a mess put together to try and sell you stuff." I said "I don't know, Marissa wouldn't let them keep me there, she was insistent about it."

"I don't think I'll be able to stop her if I tried." Kensey said "Thanks for the heads up though."

A moan from Marissa shut us all up, and I stood quickly, turning to look at her. Her eyes slid open, and she coughed slightly

"I- water..." she mumbled

"You have an IV, it is-" Henri said

"Shut up, water." Marissa growled.

Henri made a face, but got up and went to the bathroom again, coming back with a paper cup of water. She held it up to Marissa's mouth, and she slurped, swishing it with her teeth before swallowing.

"Amber, you ok?" she asked, licking her lips

""Yeah, just worried about you, are *you* ok?" I asked back

"Mmm, head hurts, body hurts, stomach hurts, I've got stuff up my nose, a hole in my arm, and I'm pretty sure there's a catheter in me. So, no, I'm not great." she winced and closed her eyes again "Gods, I haven't been in this much pain since the car accident..."

"You drank too much." Henri said coldly "Amber made me call an ambulance on you."

"Oh, yeah, I remember drinking a lot, I was all tingly by the end." Marissa said "Those drinks hit hard, huh?"

"Yeah, especially when you have like, no meat on your body." I pointed out

"Was that a dig?" Marissa asked "I get it bad enough from Quince."

"No, I- sorry, I was just- you look good, sorry." I apologized "I like your body."

"I do not appreciate you doing this to yourself when you are supposed to be taking care of my best friend." Henri said, crossing her arms

"It's not like I did this on purpose." Marissa said, slowly sitting up against the headboard and breathing deeply

"Honestly, 5 bottles of wine?" Kensey asked "Really? You *had* to have known."

Marissa glared at her "I don't remember asking *your* opinion. You can't even drink anymore."

Kensey's face threatened to crumple, but she worked it into a glare "I'm still the oldest person here, by like ten years, and I can say from *experience* that you were being *stupid* to try and drink that much."

Marissa shook her head "Oh, Quince is going to break you so hard..."

"Could you get her to, um, not do that?" I asked "I like having a friend almost my size."

"I'm not doing jack shit." Marissa said "I feel like I was run over by a train, and I *really* don't care about the lady, except that she's making a wet spot on my blanket."

"You are still horrible, aren't you?" Henri said "You are just nice to Amber because she gives you what you want."

"I'm not *that* nice to her." Marissa said tauntingly, knocking me off her shoulder onto her pillow and laying her arm on top of me

"Uuugh, just- fucking be normal, ok?" Henri said, pulling me out from under Marissa "We stayed here all night because *she* wanted to see you, and you wake up and just act like this?"

"I'm hungover, I'm still kinda drunk, and I feel like shit, you're lucky I'm not being worse." Marissa snapped "Now give me Amber and the two of you fuck off. Go get breakfast or something."

"I am not giving you Amber while you're like this." Henri said "It is not safe for her."

I felt my temper flare and I smacked her finger, hard.

"Excuse you, Henri?" I said "*I'll* decide if it's safe or not, and I think it's plenty safe. Give me to my girlfriend, and go find food."

"Girlfriend!?" Kensey said, shocked

Henri glared at me, but shoved me into Marissa's lap. She turned, snatching Kensey and her purse off the bed and stormed out, slamming the door behind her.

I righted myself and looked up at Marissa "She's just tired or something." I said "I'm sure she's not really mad."

"She can be mad if she wants to be." Marissa said stubbornly "I'm a bitch, and right now I'm a bitch in pain, so I'll act like even more of a bitch."

"...Your mom is coming by around two." I said, trying to re-direct the conversation

"Awh, fuck." Marissa moaned "I really don't want to see her like this."

"She's getting along with Henri pretty well, weirdly enough." I said "Henri even got her to agree to let you keep me, no pressure to kill me."

"Oh, yeah, so my girlfriend's bestie convinced my mom that I can date her, great." Marissa said sarcastically "I don't know why she wanted me to kill you so bad anyway."

"Mm, I know, actually." I said "She's going to use Tracy's dad's company to experiment on class Bs to make vaccinations, and she wants you to not feel bad for us getting experimented on. She doesn't like the idea of you getting attached to a class B if you're gonna have to torture other class Bs in a few years."

"What the fuck?" Marissa said, sitting up straighter "Is she a cartoon villain or something?"

"I don't know, she used the word 'eradicate' when talking about us." I said "I still don't want her to see me, even if she's 'ok' with me now."

"She's a fucking bitch..." Marissa mumbled "She just wants to ruin and control everything, I hate her so much."

"She's pretty awful." I agreed "She cares about you though, in a weird way. She like, stayed here until three in the morning and made sure you were stable, and like, you're almost all she talked to Henri about."

"I wish she *didn't* care." she said "Honestly, if she didn't care, she wouldn't hurt me so much. If she'd ignore me instead of picking me apart to 'help' me, I'd be so much better off."

"Yeah..." I said "Hey, just as a point of curiosity, you used 'girlfriend' to refer to me earlier, are we putting a label on it?"

"You said it first." Marissa said sullenly

"Uh huh, and you repeated it." I said smugly "So, are we putting a label on it? Are we girlfriends?"

Marissa glared at me for a long moment then slowly nodded "Yeah, whatever. But I still own you, and you're still my pet, and I'm still in charge."

I smiled and flopped over so I could hug her leg through the blanket "Of course, yeah, absolutely, *girlfriend~*"

"Obviously don't talk about it in front of my mom or the girls, but whatever, yeah." she said

"Oh, they already know." I said "Not your mom, but Quince and Tracy."

Marissa's eyes widened, and she sucked in air "*What.*" she hissed "Why do they know?"

"Uh, well, once you passed out, one of them made a comment about it, and I denied it, and um, they both said they knew already, because you're bad at hiding it, and- yeah..."

Marissa dropped back into the bed "Holy fuck, my social life is *over*." she whispered "I just lost all the power I had left after high school, right there."

"Hey, it's not *that* bad." I said, offended "They didn't really care too much, they said they knew you liked girls for ages already anyway, they kinda implied everyone knew."

"Yeah, but if they know I know they knew, it makes me look weak, it'll look like I'm ashamed of myself, which is an insecurity, and my whole persona falls apart, *gods.*"

"I didn't really follow that, but do you *need* a persona?" I asked "Can't you just be like, normal?"

Marissa glanced at me, her face flickering with annoyance before changing to resignation "Yeah, Amber, I do. I need to be feared, because I'm sure as *hell* incapable of being loved. I gotta play the role, be the mean one with no weaknesses."

"I mean, *I* don't think you're incapable of being loved." I said

"I'm not fishing for compliments, Amber." she said "I'm saying I've hurt people, a lot, and they don't forgive you after that. I need them to stay afraid of me or it all crumbles and it's all for nothing, and if it looks like I was insecure about something, it crumbles."

"You were insecure about the divorce, and your stutter, and you still got through that ok." I pointed out

She snarled "The *divorce* was a nightmare, I had to personally hurt everyone I knew to keep them afraid of me, and- the stuttering..."

She looked at me, her expression slightly hurt "just please don't mention that again, ok?"

I nodded and patted her leg. "Sorry, I was trying to be encouraging."

"Whatever." she said "Gods, I'm in so much pain right now... all my stomach muscles are screaming, why the fuck are my stomach muscles sore?"

"I don't know, I've never drank much before." I said "Is that not normal?"

"Maybe it is if you have this much." she said tiredly "Fuck, I'm not going to drink for a while."

"That's a good idea." I said "You really scared me, Missy. The internet said you were dying..."

"I don't think I was *dying*." she said "I think maybe I was like, in danger of dying, but I wasn't dying."

"You were just laying there, I kept having to look and make sure you were breathing..."

"Well, I'm ok now, so don't be all weird about it." she said "I'll be ok soon."

"Yeah, Sunday night, I think." I told her "From what I read, it'll be Sunday night before you're ok again."

"Fuuuck," she said "this sucks ass... I'm still all buzzed and drunk feeling, and I'm already hungover, how is that fair?"

"Maybe they'll give you painkillers?" I said hopefully

"You can't mix painkillers and alcohol, Amber." she said flatly "I doubt they'll slip up there."

I chewed my lip and thought about it for a moment "On the plus side, I'll be here with you, the whole time, that's good, right? I'll need Henri to bring my carrying case though, to sleep in and... stuff."

"'And stuff'." she said, raising her eyebrow

"'And stuff' is why Kensey was all wet earlier, I'd really rather have my case." I explained

Marissa frowned "Oh, huh. That had to suck... sink?"

"Yeah, sink." I said "I want to see if Henri can message Quince to bring some stuff for us, and we can give Kensey back to her."

"I don't want to see her, honestly." Marissa said "I remember fighting or something?"

"Yeah, her and Tracy told your backstory, and you bonked their heads. Tracy bled, even."

"Oh, shit, yeah, that sounds right." Marissa looked sick "Fuck, I- fuck. Now I *have* to see them..."

"To apologize?" I asked, curious. I hadn't known her to say she was sorry yet, and I was interested to see how she did it here.

"To say *some*thing. I don't know what." Marissa said "Fuck, I haven't hurt them in like, five years, I feel like shit now..."

"Well, I'll tell Henri to get them both here. I want my tablet and some clothes that aren't clown clothes, and I need my case."

"Maybe I'll put that off until later." Marissa said "Give myself time to prepare."

"It needs to be sooner than later," I told her "Your mom doesn't know I'm here, and unless you can pull a slight of hand and pretend Quince just brought me whenever she shows up, I'll need to hide the whole time she's here, and I don't want to suffocate under your pillow."

"You could just go under the blanket, that's not hard." Marissa said

"There'd be a lump." I pointed out "She'd see me."

"Not if you hid in the tent between my-" Marissa started to counter, then stopped, remembering she was in a hospital robe "...When Henri gets back, I'll get her to text Quince, yeah."

I lay back on her thigh and looked up at her face. I loved this angle, upside down, her looking down at me, laying and feeling cozy... She lifted her hand onto me and pet my stomach and I held her finger. I was glad she was ok, she was in a rare mood today, snippy and pushing too far, even being rude to me, but there was still that layer of 'I don't quite mean it' or maybe 'I just want to be rude' that helped me not to take it seriously.

The door opened again, and Henri walked in with a tray of food. Eggs, toast, a carton of milk, some jelly, and a bowl of something white and grainy. She sat in her chair, put the tray on Marissa's bed, and pulled Kensey out of her purse, sitting her on the bed next to the tray.

"It was too crowded in the mess hall." Henri said, still sounding angry "I figured we would just come up here. Amber, I got you breakfast too, it is not fancy, but it is something."

She handed me a tiny paper pill cup, the size of a bucket to me, and I looked in. There were small, green pellets in the bottom, the size meatballs would be if they were my sized, and they smelled kind of like grass and falafel.

"Don't do it, it's not worth it." Kensey warned me "They're like grainy balls of sawdust."

"This is what other class Bs eat?" I asked, pulling one out and looking at it

"Yeah, poor ones." Marissa snorted "That shit is the legal definition of 'edible' and that's all."

"Solidarity, then." I said, and braced myself

I took a bite, and instantly regretted it. It was dry, grainy, and somehow doughy, all at once. The flavor was 'plant', with some kind of 'spice' added in, but it wasn't one I could identify. I chewed, and it fell to bits, covering my tongue in powder, drying my mouth out and turning into a sticky, waxy paste. I grimaced, and swallowed, putting the rest of the pellet into the cup and pushing it away.

"Solidarity or not, that tasted awful." I said "That's like, the worst thing I've ever tried to eat, that's meant for *humans*?"

"Wellll...." Marissa said jokingly

"Hey!" Henri snapped "Not funny!"

"I know she's kidding, it's fine." I said "But yeah, no, I'm not eating that. Thank you for thinking of me though."

"We'll need Quince to bring you some food too, then." Marissa said

"Quince is coming?" Kensey asked, suddenly nervous

"Yeah, we, uh, need some stuff." Marissa said "My phone, her case, stuff."

"I really hoped I'd get to stay with you guys longer." Kensey said "I just- that pencil case, her attitude, I'm just not looking forward to seeing her."

"It will be ok." Henri said "Marissa and I will talk to her, right?" she glared at Marissa, who looked nonplussed

"Give me your phone, I'll text her." Marissa said, holding out her hand

"I do not have her number." Henri said, shaking her head

"I'll do it on social media, come on, she has DMs open, she'll see it." Marissa insisted.

"...Fine." Henri said "But only because we are talking to her about treating Kensey well."

"Whatever, cool." Marissa snatched the phone out of Henri's hand and tapped quickly, and was soon typing, her thumbs flying across the screen "Amber, what food do you want? I'm telling her to get your tracksuit and your pajamas for clothes."

"Uh, there's nothing thawed, so anything is ok, but she needs to microwave it first? It might be hard to push the buttons with her fingers, maybe she could use a toothpick?"

"That's a pain." Marissa said "I doubt she'll do it, but I'll ask."

"My heart is beating like a drum," Kensey said "I'm just- ugh, I'm so nervous..."

"Hey, just remember what I told you, it'll be ok." I told her

"Ok, message sent." Marissa said "Now, what food did you get me?"

"I did not get *you* anything." Henri scoffed "I got my food for me, they will bring you food whenever they feel like it."

Marissa frowned "If I give you my toast later, can I have your toast now?"

"I wanted the toast now, so I got the toast now." Henri said, dipping it in the grainy white stuff "You can wait."

"...Fuck it, I'm calling for a nurse." Marissa muttered "My stomach is in knots and I'm starving."

I moved the cup of ick back to Henri's tray and lay against Marissa's thigh next to Kensey, taking her hand in mine. Her fingers were too big to lace with mine at the base, but our fingertips could interlock. I smiled up at her encouragingly, and she looked back down sadly.

"It'll be ok, I promise." I told her

"Easy for you to say, you're sleeping with the enemy." she muttered

"Well, we're not-" I said, then changed my approach "Tell you what, if she'll get you a tablet, we can video call every day, ok? I'll coach you through stuff, right?"

"Ok, yeah, that's fine..." she said "Thanks. I still think there's something wrong with you, your relationship is *not* healthy, but... thanks for being there for me."

I smiled again and wiggled her hand. I knew my relationship wasn't 'normal', but it wasn't unhealthy. We communicated, we cared about each other, we respected each other, most of the time, and that's what counted. I wasn't sure if Kensey'd be able to have the same kind of relationship we did, but I could do my best to coach her into a safe, comfortable owner/pet relationship that worked for her, she... just might have to make a few concessions along the way.

# Chapter Twenty-One

"And here's those microwave meals you wanted, I made two of them. I couldn't tell what they were, though, so... hope they're good?" Quince said, putting a folded up napkin next to my case.

I unwrapped it, and found that one of the meals was a lasagna, and the other was some kind of 'ch'cken' covered in spices. Tandoori maybe? I pulled out the lasagna and unsnapped the fork from the packaging and wrapped the other one back up.

"Thank you, Quince." I said, pulling the wrapper off "I was pretty hungry, and the pellets are pretty much inedible."

She'd shown up a few minutes ago with Tracy, and the two of them were sitting next to Marissa, having brought my stuff and Marissa's phone in and dumped it on the bed. Kensey had 'hidden' behind Henri's purse, and was nervously holding her knees, trying to pretend she wasn't there.

"Yeah, whatever." Quince said "I just wanted my new pet back, otherwise I wouldn't have bothered showing up."

I shrugged and ate the lasagna, the gooey, stringy pulp tasting far better than the pellets did.

"You can have her back..." Henri said "But we would really like to have a talk with you about her first, Marissa and I, I mean."

Quince glanced at Marissa, who was scrolling on her phone with a scowl "...I don't really want to talk to *her* at all, honestly."

"Yeah, my head was bleeding..." Tracy added "That's like, I could sue."

"Then sue, see if I care." Marissa grumbled

"Uh, Marissa said she wanted to talk to you two as well, though..." I said "I think it's a good idea..."

"Shut *up*, Amber." Marissa said, glowering at me

"I'm honestly pretty fed up with you, you know." Quince said to Marissa "You acted like a bitch, you physically hurt me, you ruined the first girl's night we've had in *ages*, and we didn't even get to watch the movie I picked out."

"We've *seen* that one before, like, five times." Marissa said

"Uh, yeah? It was gonna be nostalgic?" Tracy said "Then you put yourself in the hospital and smashed my head up."

"..." Marissa glared at them for a few seconds. I poked her leg, she'd mentioned wanting to make amends, right?

She took a breath and spoke clearly and carefully "...Look, due to inexperience with a new type of drink, I may have misjudged the amount of alcohol I was drinking, and as a result of that, I may have reacted disproportionately to your conversation. It's sad we didn't get to watch the movie, maybe we'll get another chance soon."

I frowned. She... didn't apologize at all, she didn't even *attempt* to. I wasn't expecting her to, really, but she'd addressed the problems Quince brought up, without ever really accepting fault.

"...Whatever." Quince said "I just want my pet, I gotta go."

"Well, wait!" Henri said "I really want to talk to you about her, I think-"

"Are you trying to tell me how to treat my pet?" Quince said, her eyes snapping to Henri

"Uh, I think you should listen to her..." Tracy said "Kensey looked... not great, when you took her out for the first time."

"Marissa and I just think you should hear a few tips from people who know about class Bs..." Henri said

Quince scoffed "Oh, yeah, I can hear Marissa's advice now 'if you want to have fun with your class B, torture them half the time, and fuck them the other half', great advice."

"We're not- ugh, just shut up and listen." Marissa rolled her eyes "You need to get her a case with a bed and bathroom in it, like Amber's. She had to pee in the sink earlier, and that's not ok."

"Don't *tell* people that!" yelped Kensey from her hiding spot

"Yeah, whatever, I'll get one." Quince said dismissively

"I'm surprised you didn't get one at the shop..." I said "I was in one for a whole night before I got bought, and they just gave Marissa the case with me."

"I ordered her express." Quince said "They delivered her to me directly instead of the store, duh."

"Well, peeing in a sink is awful, you really need to go get that thing for her." Tracy said, wrinkling her nose

"And *food*, you have to get her real food, not pellets." Henri said

"The internet and the class said the pellets were fine, I'm not going grocery shopping for a pet." Quince snapped

"I have the rest of my breakfast on Henri's tray, you should try the pellets..." I said, pointing.

She glanced at the paper cup, sighed, and picked it up, tipping the balls of 'food' into her hand

"Ok, fine, I'll try it." she said, and tossed them into her mouth all at once. She looked neutral for a moment as she broke them up with her tongue, then her face scrunched. "...Fuck, yeah, that's like eating a lawn..." she muttered

She looked down at Kensey, who flinched at her glance "...I'll get you the fucking microwave stuff, I guess."

"Which means you need a tiny microwave." Marissa pointed out "And a home to put it in."

"Marissa, that fucking house you got was thousands of dollars, it was almost as much as *Amber*, I can't afford that!" Quince said

"I never thought I'd hear you admit you can't afford something!" Tracy said, impressed

"I just bought a car and a pet, within a couple weeks of each other." she mumbled "I wiped out my savings."

"You didn't tell me you got a car..." Marissa said, sounding mildly hurt

"An electric sports car, yeah. It's gold and black. I figured you wouldn't care since you can just pay Drew to drive you around." she sighed

"Well, even if you're spending money on... gold sports cars," I cut in "I know there's cheaper options. I got a full house, yeah, but I know one girl, uhh, Babae I think? She had an apartment, it sounded like it was way cheaper, the way she said it."

"I just- I imagined her sleeping on a little pillow on my bed..." Quince admitted, looking disappointed

"Maybe if you have sleepovers she can?" Henri said "But that is not comfortable long term. Maybe once a week she can sleep on your pillow or something."

"*Fine*, I'll look into an apartment too." Quince said "Listen, I- I really just wanted her so I could dress her up and show her off and snuggle with her, all the... logistics of it are sucking the fun out of having a cute new pet."

"She's still cute and fun!" I assured her "She'll be super happy if you do this stuff and treat her well, and happy class Bs are cuter, right?"

Kensey looked at me, her expression torn, before plastering a grin on her face and nodding "Yeah, I loooove being treated like a little princess! It makes me feel all special and wanted, I'd love to be your cute new toy, I just get scared easily!"

"It's super scary being this small!" I said, helping her play it up "And we're just lil people, really, so you just have to be super gentle and careful with us. She'll be a great pet, you just have to know how to be extra careful!"

Quince looked at Kensey smiling up at her nervously, and a flicker of pity rushed across her face, before being replaced by her usual know-it-all smirk "Little princess, huh?... I can do that."

Henri relaxed a bit, and Marissa rolled her eyes, not looking up from her phone. I felt slightly relieved, if we could get Quince to think of her in a cute, pitying way, she'd be so much safer... Before I forgot though...

"Oh, um, I wanted to know if she could get a tablet?" I asked "Like the one you brought for me. I don't have many friends, and I'd love to chat!"

"It's got parental controls on it, and it's useful for keeping them busy if you want to go on a date or something." Marissa said, still scrolling "Amber is on hers a lot, when I don't want to play with her."

"..." Quince thought about it " I guess so..."

"Can she message regular people from it?" Tracy said "I'd like to chat with her a little."

"You never asked to chat with *me*..." I said, frowning

"Yeah, but you're the Ra- uhhh, I already know you." Tracy said, catching herself "It'd be weird to text *you*."

"Amber messages me sometimes, you can text anyone." Henri assured her "Quince, if you could get all of us her username once it's all set up?"

Quince huffed "Great, ok, look, it's already almost noon, and I need to go shopping for... a lot, apparently, so come on Tracy, we're leaving."

"Why do *I* have to go?" Tracy asked "I wanted to hang out more..."

Quince pointed at us in turn "Loser, physically hurt you last night, and, you know, *Amber*. do you really want to spend time with *them* over me?"

Tracy looked around at the rest of us before glaring at Quince "...Well it'd be awkward *now*..."

She stood up with Quince, and the latter scooped up Kensey into her hands

"Come on, princess, let's go make you feel special." Quince said in that baby-voice people kept using for me. I winced, but gave Kensey a thumbs up, and watched them leave the room.

"...Hopefully her life will not be *too* bad now..." Henri sighed

"It's gonna be shit either way." Marissa said, finally looking up from her phone "Either she fights back and it turns into an abusive relationship, or she has to 'stepford wife' herself into being the perfect pet."

"...Isn't that what Amber did, though?" Henri asked

"Hey! I'm still me, I'm not brainwashed or anything." I protested "I just experimented and liked what I found."

Henri shuddered "Experiments that involved getting bitten so hard you bruised..."

"Henri, that's private, don't mention it again." Marissa said quietly

"I saw the marks when I was checking for *abuse*, it is a valid thing to be concerned about..." Henri said

"Henri, new rule, if you ever force my girlfriend to strip for you again, for any reason, I *will* kill you." Marissa growled

"Fine! Fine, I just I do not get *that*, it is so dangerous..." Henri said

"It's not as bad as the stuff in those books you told me to read." I pointed out "One of them had the guy use a branding iron, that's way worse."

"Those are just *books*, Amber." Henri said "It is not like, my *friend* being in danger of being snipped in half."

"I wouldn't ever snip her in half." Marissa said "A limb or two, yeah, maybe, but I'd never bite her in half, her organs would taste terrible."

I shivered and pressed against her body. I knew she was kidding, but somehow, even the idea of her biting my leg off, her teeth tearing into me, snapping my bone... It was horrifying, but I still almost wanted to see what it'd feel like.

"You know..." Henri said "That is something that actually happened, recently."

I looked up, surprised "What?"

"Yeah, what?" Marissa echoed, moving my case to her side table

"Well, not *bitten* off, but ja, someone pulled the limbs off their class B recently, it was in the news. They had an argument or something, it was a popular content creator, too." Henri said, her eyes sparkling with interest

"That's *so* fucked up..." Marissa said, making a face

"Was the person jailed or something?" I asked

"No, they just had their rights to be a class B guardian taken away..." Henri said, shaking her head "It was on the news, so people *know* it was fucked up, but the guy just got away with it."

"That's horrifying..." I said, shuddering "I try to stay away from that kind of news, it just makes me paranoid."

Marissa gently picked me up and brought me to her face "I promise I'll never, ever, ever do anything that leaves permanent damage to you." she said sincerely

"That is not as reassuring as you think it is..." Henri said, shaking her head "I gotta go get lunch, you want anything?"

"Yeah, gods, anything." Marissa said "They never brought my fucking breakfast..."

"Ok, I will be back, ok?" Henri said, more to me than to Marissa

"Here, while she's gone, put me in my case, I wanna change out of this clown outfit." I said "Clown-fit. Clow-fit? Clowntfit? Hm..."

"Don't hurt yourself there..." Marissa snarked, but I could see her smile peeking though anyway.

~~~

"Oh, fucking *gods* this is good..." Marissa moaned around a mouthful of burger

"It is really not..." Henri said, frowning at hers "It is made of like, beans and peas and stuff, it is weird..."

"You underestimate how hungry I am..." Marissa mumbled around another bite "And I'm still all hungover and buzzed..."

"Oh, I forgot they pumped your stomach!" I said "You were like, *empty* empty."

"They did what?" Marissa asked "No wonder my throat is all raw, I thought that was just the hangover..."

I lounged on Marissa's chest as she ate, hearing the weird noises of her swallowing through her ribs. It was almost disappointing to be out of my clown outfit. It'd looked stupid and I'd been freezing my butt off, but at least it was thin enough to feel Marissa through. Now, with the track suit on, it felt like I was lying on a warm mattress, not a bed of flesh.

"So, do you think-" Henri started, just as the door swung open

I tensed up and felt my body lock into place as Miss Lund walked in and took one of the seats the girls had pulled up to Marissa's bed. Her eyes fell on me and stayed there, cold and unreadable, before turning up to Marissa.

"I canceled my afternoon meetings, I was able to get here earlier than I anticipated. I see you weren't expecting me..." she said, her voice firm

"I was just... eating lunch." Marissa said carefully

"Your pet is out, and acting like it belongs on you." she snapped back "I thought I told you I never wanted to see it again."

"Well, I wasn't expecting you, so..." Marissa said, sitting up straighter, one of her hands lightly resting over me. It smelled like burgers.

"How did it even get here?" Miss Lund asked, sitting back and crossing her arms

"Quince brought her over!" Henri interjected "She was going to go home, and she did not want to leave Amber alone in the house."

"I don't want you to be distracted by pets while you're supposed to be recovering." Miss Lund said "It will return home, and stay there until you are discharged from the hospital.

I stifled a gasp, did that mean Miss Lund would be bringing me back?! I really didn't want to be handled by her at *all*, ever.

"Oh, I can look after her, it is not a problem." Henri said casually "I imagine you would not be interested in taking care of her yourself, Miss Lund, and I doubt the servants are qualified."

I felt Marissa tense up, her heart rate rising under me "Oh, no, I can just keep her here..." she said "She's really not that distracting, she just sits there, mostly."

"It is no trouble, I can return her to you Monday sometime, assuming you can still make it to school, of course." Henri said "I think it might good for Amber to be... out of the house for a while."

"I agree, I think this is an excellent idea." Miss Lund agreed "I don't have the time to feed or clothe it, and I wouldn't trust most of the help not to steal it."

"I don't think that's the best-" I started, before being cut off

"Perfect! Let me just get out of your hair then!" Henri said chipperly, swiping me off Marissa's chest and picking up my case "I will be on my way, may I borrow Drew to take me back to the house to get my car? I will send him back here after, of course."

"Oh, of course, feel free!" Miss Lund said, nodding

"Wait- no, I can't- this is- you..." Marissa stumbled over her words, too scared of her mother to fight back, but still desperately looking for a way to keep me "I- you can't take her, I'm her guardian, and I don't approve it!"

"Mm, in the case of a medical emergency, another licensed guardian can take temporary custody if the original guardian is comatose or in an altered mental state." Henri recited "And you are still drunk, and I am licensed."

"You know your laws!" Miss Lund said, impressed

"I made it a point to be well informed once people I am close to started getting involved with class Bs, ma'am. I got my license just in case I needed to watch Amber here for Marissa for any reason." Henri said smugly

"You just want to steal her, if you take her, I'll never get her back!" Marissa said, her face panicked and flushed

"I would really rather stay with Marissa, please..." I said

I stared at her, my heart racing. Would I see her again if I left with Henri? What would living with Henri even look like? Marissa's face looked like she was on the verge of tears, but her eyes kept flicking to her mother, and I knew she wasn't going to- *couldn't* fight this, no matter how much she wanted to.

"Sorry, but as the guardian here, I will have to overrule..." Henri said, patting my head "Say goodbye, we will see her again soon enough, ok?"

"Amber, I-" Marissa started, the blankets clenched in her fists, the fight left her body and she slumped, her face hollow "I... I'll see you Monday..."

My heart was racing, would I? I swallowed, and nodded "I'll... see you then, Marissa..."

Henri laughed lightly, and picked up my case, waving goodbye as she left the room.

~~~

I sat in the backseat of the car, feeling weird and alien about being here, where me and Missy had so many heartfelt conversations, with my best friend. My best friend who just essentially kidnapped me, right under Marissa's nose. I hadn't said anything since we'd left the room, and while she'd tried to engage me a few times, she was being awkward about it, and had settled into just watching me sit and squirm. Her face was pensive, and she was humming to herself as she watched me, making me feel self conscious.

"C-can you stop?" I ventured

"Stop the humming?" she asked

"No, just- staring me down... it's making me nervous."

She sighed and shook her head "I am just... thinking about stuff."

"What kinds of stuff?" I asked, afraid of the answer

"I am.. trying to decide what to do with you, honestly." she replied truthfully "I know you do not want to go back to Marissa, but so many things could happen to you while you're with me, it... It is tempting."

"Are you *threatening* me?!" I asked, scooting away. This wasn't like her, I thought she wanted to have me for herself, if she did something to me, she'd lose me too, right?

"No, no, not- well, a little." she admitted "I was just thinking, if you die while I'm watching you, or if you run away to try and get back to Marissa before it's time and no one finds you... Well, I am just saying, it would be a tragedy, but it would stop *her* from having you."

"You're threatening to *kill* me?!" I yelped "You're a monster, what the fuck Henri?! If you can't have me, no one can, is that it?"

"I- no!" she said, shocked "I would never kill you, Amber... I love you far too much for that, I just meant I would fake your death!"

"...What?"

"If you 'die', then I get to keep you forever, all I need to do is to find a way to make it look real... There will be an investigation, sure, and I will loose my license, but once it blows over, you would be a ghost, no one will know you exist! And you will be mine forever!"

I backed all the way up from her "I won't go along with that, I'll fight back, I'll escape for real, I- I won't be your secret toy."

"Not a toy, my partner! My girlfriend! And you *say* you will escape or fight back, but honestly, I'm not doing anything Marissa isn't doing..." she cooed, laying down to get closer to me again, her smile wide and bright "*She* kept you locked up, *she* gets to keep you forever, *she* is dating you, all I am doing is taking her place!"

"But- I don't- No! It's different!" I shouted "Marissa paid for me, she follows the rules, mostly, she's accountable to the law for taking care of me, we're dating, as weird as it is, I *choose* to stay with her, Henri!"

"You do not seem to have much of a choice to me..." she said "The law locks you to her, no way out, ja?"

"I could report her and get away, I don't *want* to get away." I said, pushing away one of her hands "They'd catch you in a heart beat, anyway. I have a tracker on my leg, and it doesn't come off!"

"I am sure I could get it off, with wire cutters or something, it will be fine." she said dismissively

"It's got glass in it, it'd explode, it could shred my leg!" I protested "They don't come off, for exactly this reason!"

"...well, there are *other* ways to get it off." Henri said, frowning

I remembered the news story she'd told us about earlier and shuddered, she wouldn't go that far, would she?

"Please, Henri, I just- please..." I said, not knowing what to say "Just enjoy the time you have with me, it's ok, let's just have fun and relax, please?"

"I *said* I was still thinking about it." Henri said, slightly annoyed "You do not have to beg, it is not happening for sure."

"I don't even want it on the table!" I yelled "I want to have a fun time with my best friend, and get returned to my girlfriend in a couple days, without having to worry about my best friend cutting my foot off with wire cutters!"

"I am just thinking out loud, Amber, götter..." Henri sighed "We will have a lovely, safe time, I assure you."

"So you promise not to fake my death or anything?" I asked

"I promise we will have a good weekend, nothing more, nothing less." Henri said.

She sat back up and picked me up off the seat. I shivered, realizing that in here, with her, there was nowhere I could go that wasn't within arm's reach. As the car pulled up to Marissa's house, Henri's hand squeezed me gently, and her thumb brushed my head. It felt... not right. Not the way Marissa did it. Missy's squeezes were more "You're mine and I want to hurt you, but I love you, too.". Henri's felt more like... "I want to hold you and keep you, no matter what you want.". It made me feel gross, in an objectified way. She'd done so good at the party, she promised she'd get better, why the fuck was she being so scary now?

~~~

Henri stepped into my old apartment and looked around, her arms full of the supplies she'd picked up when we stopped at Marissa's. She peeked around the living area, then nodded and made her way to my- or, her room, closing and locking the door behind her.

"Looks like your family is not home!" she said "That's lucky!"

"Why is that lucky?" I asked sullenly as she put me on the desk and dumped the clothes, blankets, and food on the desk

"We get to have fun now, right?" she asked "Or- actually, I think we should have showers first, *then* have fun."

I sucked in a breath "What kind of fun requires *showers?*"

"Well we both smell like hospital, so, like, all fun would be enhanced by *not* smelling like a hospital, right?" she pointed out "Ah, but... we do not have a shower your size, do we?..."

"Henri, no, I don't want to-" I said, my teeth gritted

"It would be irresponsible of me to let you shower alone though!" she said, her grin widening. I could see her hands shaking as she collected her clothes and stared at me

"It's very unsafe for you to shower with me, though..." I said "There's nowhere good to set me, and one slip or fall from either of us and I'd be dead..."

She stared at me for a moment, then nodded slowly "I suppose... That just means I will go first, then come get you for your shower, and give you my full attention!"

"I'm not comfortable with that either!" I yelped "Just- let me use the sink!"

"Mm, I would really feel safer if I could watch you, though." she said, picking me up and dropping me into my case, and pushed a stack of textbooks agains the door "Here, it will just be a moment, I will be clean in a bit!"

"How is this treating me like a person?!" I yelled at her through the plexiglass "You're being worse than ever!"

"I am doing what you want!" she protested, turning from the door "I am still seeing you as a person that needs love and care, but I am being a bitch about it, that is what you like!"

"When did I say *that*?" I asked, confused

"Last night, at the sleepover. You said you liked Marissa being a bitch to you, and that the only reason you were not dating *me* instead of *her* was because you're scared of losing me. Well, I can be a bitch too, and still care for you, and you never ever have to worry about losing me!" her smile was wide, but she looked nervous "It is the best of both worlds!"

"I don't want *you* to be a bitch, I want *Missy* to be a bitch, you're supposed to be my friend!" I said, shaking my head

She sighed, and the energy slipped from her for a moment, and I felt like I was looking at my old friend again, not the person who kidnapped me and threatened me "...Amber, just... we are doing it this way, ok? Just go along with it, it is ok, I promise."

I stared at her, and leaned against the glass, my mind throbbing. Was it an act? Was she putting it on to get me to like her? Or was she genuinely like that and just had a temporary moment of lucidity? She stared at me for a couple seconds, then gave me an awkward smile and closed the door. I dropped to the floor, not even bothering to try and move the books out of the way. There was nowhere to go, not really. We were a good twenty minute drive from the hospital, at least, so getting back to Missy was impossible without help. My tablet was on the bed, so I couldn't message Nada and ask her for help, but I'd feel guilty, since the only other time I'd messaged her so far was to ask for help, I wanted to actually chat with her too. Maybe if she messaged first...

After what felt like an eternity, the door opened again, and Henri stepped back in, hair wound up in a microfiber towel, wearing one of my tank tops and shorts. I noticed with mild annoyance that she was stretching out the tank top, but... it wasn't like I was ever going to wear it again, I guess. She locked eyes with me, and made her way over to the desk, shoving the books out of the way.

"Ready to get clean?" she said sweetly

"No, I'm not! Stop being like this, you're not going to endear yourself to me, this is like, sexual assault!" I said, backing up to the bed

"There is nothing inherently sexual about a shower, Amber." Henri admonished "It is no different than a nurse giving you a sponge bath at a hospital."

"Except the nurse wouldn't be *in love with me*, I can wash myself, please..."

She sighed "Come on, there is a nice pink dress waiting for you after your shower, won't that be nice?"

I glared at her "You're acting like *Quince*, Henri. Cut it out."

She reached in and pulled me out as I kicked and yelled "You like bitches, I was being a bitch, would you rather I act like Marissa? I can do that too, you know."

She reached up with her other hand and flicked me in the stomach. I gasped for air and curled up, it wasn't as bad as Marissa's flick, but I was still lightly bruised, and she'd hit me directly under my lungs, forcing the air out.

"Come on, Rat, let's go give you a shower." she said, lowering her voice and narrowing her eyes in her best Marissa impression

"Sh-she wouldn't do that!" I yelled, thinking fast "She's super good about sexual stuff, this is out of character for her!"

She turned and walked towards the bathroom, stepping inside and closing the door behind her. She got on her knees and turned the water on with her free hand and set me on the edge of the tub, the water thundering down behind me. She looked at me, her face a mix of placid and upset and pointed at my tracksuit.

"Take it o-" she choked and took a breath "Take it off..." she continued, her voice shaky and quiet

She was having second thoughts, she was nervous... If I could break her act... I curled up in a ball, using my hands to cover my chest and crotch, despite still being fully clothed

"I'm not doing this, Henri, if you want me to be naked, you'll have to tear the clothes off me yourself!" I yelled, pushing fear and pain into my voice

She swallowed again, and reached up, her hand shaking violently, stopping just before it reached me, and she sobbed, tears springing up in her eyes, shoulders and chest shaking, and she fell over, curling up on the rug in front of the toilet. I sat there, shaking, too afraid to move, too afraid to remind her I was here. Whatever she was going through, I didn't want her to drag me into it anymore than she already had. Her wails and sobs filled the small tile bathroom, and she lay and shook until the water turned cold and the fog on the mirror disappeared.

Finally, after what felt like ages, she sat back up, the pattern of the rug pressed into her cheek, her eyes bloodshot, and her breaths coming in short gasps. She tenderly reached over and picked me up off the side of the tub and shut the water off. I trembled in her hand as she stared at me, tears still flowing out of her eyes, but she didn't say anything, just looked at me with a haunted, empty look. She stood up, and brought me back to my old room, setting me gently in front of my case.

She looked at the stack of books she'd used to block me in before, and then at the bed. She stepped over to the bed and moved all of my things to the desk next to me, carefully setting my tablet down by my still-curled-up form and looked at me, her expression hollow. She went back over to the bed and collapsed face down on the mattress, and rolled onto the bed, wrapping the comforter around her as she did, and lay there, still as a stone.

I watched her, her body unmoving. I couldn't even see her breathing, but that could have been from the thick, down comforter. After five minutes, I felt safe enough to stand up. I grabbed my tablet, and made my way to the back of the desk, behind my computer tower, where the fans blew warm air out, and sat down. I powered it on, and muted it as soon as I could. I knew she knew I had it, but was she expecting me to tell Marissa on her? The cops? I didn't know, and I didn't know what I wanted to do, either. I could get her banned from seeing me if I told the authorities what she'd tried to do, but... She might be the only thing keeping Marissa in check. I knew Missy wasn't as bad as she first was, but having the threat of someone taking me away was a good thing to have.

I opened the messages tab and saw a few new messages, one from Kensey's new AntMound account reading

*'Hey friend! I feel like an absolute princess! Quince even got me a little hot tub and a super cute bathing suit, and we're going to have a hot tub party tonight! I'd love for you to come if you can!'*

Quince had obviously set up message forwarding, then... I thought about it for a few minutes. It might be nice to be around a group again, if nothing else it'd stop Henri from trying anything else. There was no assurance that she'd be up for going though, even assuming she wanted to see those people again. Still, I didn't want to be rude.

*'Ill see if henri is up 2 it, shes watching me rn so like its up 2 her. what r the deets'*

I didn't think I had a swimsuit with me anyway, but I'd have to see. I just really didn't want to be alone with Henri longer than I had to be...

The next message was from Marissa, and I winced as soon as I saw it

*'Amber, so help me, if she hurts you at all, if she's creepy, or if she tries to convince you to leave me, let me know and I'll kill her on the spot. STG I can do it from this hospital bed, I know people.'*

I didn't doubt she did, and I doubted even less that she'd go through with it. I typed a response back, telling her that Henri was being a bitch, but she was taking a nap right now, and checked the next message. It was a number I didn't recognize, but it was obvious who it was from the context.

*'Hey, ok, so I know I was super rude about texting you, and I'm sorry about that, friend of my friend is my friend and all that. Anyway, I wanted to know, I heard Henri took you, is she like, being weird about it? I wanna know how she's acting, is she singing you german lullabies or something?'*

I sighed, and sent a short message back

*'Shes just sleeping, actually'*

I opened the last message in my inbox and sighed. It was from Nada, asking for an update about last night. At least I didn't have to feel bad about asking for advice now. I sent her a message too.

*'yea shes not getting 2 go 2 court. we convinced her ownr that shes like a little princess so shes treating her better??? but its still not great. i wnated 2 ask tho, my big friend i mentoned at the group us being weird. she thinks i like bitches so shes acting like one and shes the one watching me rn bc my owner is in the hospital and she tried 2 get me 2 shower wth her then cried a lot when i said no. im scared and upset, but i dont think she was TRYING 2 b bad just maybet liek she was pushing herself 2 b bad or smth idk what do i do she cried herself to sleep and hgave me the tablet i think so i can call the cops but idk if i want 2'*

I sent it, and was surprised to see the typing bubbles pop up almost instantly. Nada must have already been on her tablet... Before long a response popped up on my screen

'Amber, that's less than ideal! I'm glad your class B friend is in a better place, but we need to impart our humanity and equality on our class As, not just adoration for us. As for your class A friend, I cannot recommend you continue to have contact with her. Trying to force you into that situation is highly illegal, and she should have her license taken away. I recommend you using the emergency contact feature on your tablet as soon as you can. Even if she showed remorse for her actions, that's unacceptable. I'm so sorry to hear Marissa is in the hospital! How ever did that happen?'

I groaned and stared at the message. It wasn't what I wanted to see, and I especially didn't want to call the cops on her. I needed to think about this long and hard...

'i dont kno if i want 2 call the cops on her. shes making sure im safe with marissa i dont know if its a good idea for her 2 not b here. marissa was drinking at a party and has 2 much so i called an amulance fro her. shes ok but not safw 2 take care of me rn ig or smth and her mom wants 2 kill me and make me a lab rat so henri is the only other option ig'

I turned the tablet off, and figured I'd check her response later, I needed to just exist for a while right now... I breathed the hot, computer-y air and thought about everything I'd been through. It was non stop, especially the past couple days. I hadn't even set up my new video game yet, and I most likely wouldn't get the chance until Tuesday... I just wanted to play with my catboys, damnit.

I heard a creaking noise, and footsteps, and I froze, she was awake... I carefully lay flat and shimmied under the pc tower, leaving my face out enough to breathe, but hopefully hidden enough to stay away from her for now until I knew she was stable. I heard her walk over to the desk and shift things around, looking for me.

"Amber?..." she said, her voice frail and wobbly "I want to talk, I- I need to talk to you... Amber?"

She moved more stuff, and her movements for more frantic "Amber, did you- are you trying to escape? No- I swear, Amber, I'll give you back, please, it's not safe for you to go by yourself, Amber?"

She dropped to the floor and started sliding things around "No, no, no... Amber, please! Please don't be gone... Fuck, no, Amber..."

Her voice was melting into sobs again, and I felt a twinge of pity, this was my friend, she loved me, she just wanted to know I was ok, that I hadn't tried to leave the apartment, I could give her that, right? I started to slide out, when she screamed, loud and angry at nothing.

"I just want you to love me! I'm doing everything I can! Why can't you just love me?!" she howled, and I heard the sounds of things being pulled out from under the bed, the closet opening, and containers being dumped out.

I slid back under and closed my eyes, praying to as many gods as would listen that she wouldn't find me under the PC, and I listened to her tear my room apart looking for me.

# Chapter Twenty-Two

After a while, I shimmied out from under the computer. I couldn't stay under there forever, I knew that, and I'd need to talk to Henri eventually if I wanted to ever see Missy again instead of just living in the small, hidden places of my former room. I carefully walked around the tower to the front of the desk to see Henri hugging her knees to her chest and staring at my old dollhouse, a single doll in the middle of the floor in front of it. She'd calmed down a little since her meltdown, and was just looking at the doll, rocking back and forth slightly, her breaths uneven and catching from her freakout.

I turned on my tablet, still looking at Henri, and opened the message from Kensey. She'd sent the address and time of the 'hot tub party', and had asked (practically begged) me to come. She really needed more help easing into her new life, and if I could be there for her, I wanted to be. Henri was scaring me a lot, but she had kind of proved that she wouldn't *hurt* me, even if she was trying to convince herself otherwise for some reason, so I just had to trust she'd be stable if I showed myself.

"Uh, H-Henri?" I said, my voice wavering.

Her breath caught and her head snapped around, not looking at me, but still focusing on me. Her breathing quickened and I rushed to keep talking before she decided to grab me or something.

"Kensey w-wanted us to come to a party for her tonight, I- she needs our help, and I'd like to go, please..." I said quickly

Henri slowly rotated until she was looking at me, her face expressionless.

"...I thought you ran away?" she said, unsure

"I was hiding from you." I said "You scared me, Henri."

"I- I- you said- you *like* scary, though..."

"I like it when Missy plays with me, sometimes." I said, sitting down on the edge of the desk "Not when my supposed friend is trying to sexually assault me or throwing my stuff around the room trying to find me."

"I was- it was *not* sexual!" Henri protested

"Then why did you stop?" I asked harshly "If there was nothing wrong with undressing me by force, why did you start crying?"

I was pushing harder than was really wise, but I *really* didn't want that to happen again.

Henri clenched her teeth and her hands balled up into fists.

"You are so *frustrating*!" she said, shaking her head "I try so hard, I do things I do not like, I make myself be who you say you like, and then you say I did it all wrong and you run away and hate me? For doing what I thought you *wanted*?"

"Why would I want you to *strip* me?!" I asked incredulously "When have I ever implied I wanted that?"

"You want a bully!" she yelled back, waving her hands "You just want to be *bullied*! You're so insecure and sad that the only way you can imagine being with someone is if they treat you like trash! I can *do* that, *I* can treat you like trash!"

I hugged the tablet to my chest, her words stinging. Was I really only with

Marissa because I thought I 'deserved' her? I *liked* Marissa, it couldn't just be my insecurities, right? "I'm not *that* insecure..."

"You *are*." she said, sounding exhausted "Please, Klein Fee, just- let me bully you, ok? Let me be the person you need..."

"That's what this all is?" I asked "All the talk of cutting my leg off, making me disappear, faking my death, trying to force me into the shower, it was so I'd see you as a bully because that's what you think I need in a partner?"

"It *is* what you need." she said sadly "You need someone to bite you and to squish you and to be rough and bossy. I have seen how you cuddle up to Marissa whenever she is being horrible to someone, you *like* it."

"I like it when *she* does it." I said "It makes me feel safe, somehow."

"Then let me make you feel safe, ok?" Henri asked, crawling up to me on her knees "I have tried everything I know to get you to love me, this is all I have left."

"Henri, I just don't love you." I said plainly "I thought I maybe could at one point, but after everything, I just don't ever see that being possible."

She stared at me, her eyes dry and her face plain. I swallowed and shifted in place, had she not heard me? Or was she *planning* something?. Her blue eyes watched me, tracing me up and down, soaking me in. I tried not to squirm, why wasn't she *saying* anything? Should *I* say something? Was she waiting on me to keep talking?

"...Well." she said after an eternity "I cannot accept that. I am going to keep trying, Amber."

I groaned, slightly relieved she'd finally answered "Henri, I'm dating someone, You can't just 'not accept' that, it's a fact, and what's more, if I really *do* 'need a bully' like you think, *your* subby ass is the worst possible option."

"I can fake it!" she protested "And you will break up with her eventually, I can wait."

"You can't fucking fake it!" I shouted "You trying to fake it almost made me call the cops on you, and you *know* how much I hate the cops!"

"Ugh, fine!" she said "Then we do it the other way, you are insecure, and I was supposed to help with that by being your maid, right? So *you* bully *me*! Just- bully me and be mean and I will just take it and you'll get more secure and be happy, with me!"

"You were supposed to be my maid because you weren't treating me like a *human*, not because I'm 'insecure', what?"

"That is the same thing." she said, frowning

"You just want me to bully you because of your kinks." I said

"Ja, no, wow, really?" Henri said sarcastically, her eyes widening "You are a tiny psychologin or something, now, huh?"

"Can we just be *normal*? Please?" I begged "I can even ask Missy if she'd be ok doming you or something, and I can be there too to keep you company? But me and you, can we please just be normal?"

Henri fell over with a thump, and my heart jumped as the cheaply made desk rocked at her impact, threatening to knock me off "I am just so tired, Klein Fee, I just- I just want to forget the whole thing... The confession, competing with Marissa for you, trying to find ways for you to love me, I just want it all to be over..."

"Me too." I sighed "Can we just be friends for now? Until you give me back to Marissa at least? Just drop all this, and stop trying?"

"...Ja, that is ok with me." Henri said "I am so tired.. Mm, I- mm... What were you trying to ask me about a minute ago?"

"Ah, um, Kensey wanted to invite us over to Quince's house for a party so it's not just her and the girls..."

"I do not have the energy for *that*." Henri said "When is it?"

"She wanted us to get there in like three hours."

"...Ok, I will get a nap in, and pick up an energy drink on the way. I will bring you."

"Thank you..." I said, feeling like I'd just run a marathon myself "She really needs us there, I appreciate you taking me."

"Ja, whatever, just do not expect me to talk much." Henri said, her voice hollow.

She got up and poked on her phone, setting an alarm, and got onto the bed, rolling up in the blankets once again. I fought off a yawn and glanced at my little case. The bed wasn't the most comfortable, but it'd do for a quick nap. I'd stayed up listening to Missy breathe most of the night, so I should get some rest to.. I grabbed some of my extra clothes to use as blankets, and stepped into the case to get a nap.

~~~

We stood in front of the giant house, looking up. It was the exact opposite of Marissa's house in almost every way but the size. Where hers was a sleek, sharp, grey toned example of modern design, this one spoke of opulence and showmanship. The walls were white with gold accents, there were pillars on either side of the door, and the whole thing was lit up with yellow lights to give it a 'pop' against the night sky. It was borderline garish, but not to the point it looked tacky, it came across as bragging, if anything.

"What is this unholy mix?" Henri whispered, aghast "It is all the worst parts of a temple styled neo-clasical design slapped onto a french renaissance base, this is... an *affront*..."

"I'm guessing they designed it themselves?" I asked "It looks impressive at least."

Henri snorted "Maybe to someone who did not grow up in a beautiful Bavarian gothic revival styled manor. I love big fancy homes, and *this* one is even more disappointing than the Lund home."

"You don't have to make fun of me for being poor, you know." I said, feeling hurt

She glanced at me, her eyes wide "I did not! I- oh. I see, yes. I am sorry, I was not thinking."

"...Ok." I said "Let's just go in."

She pursed her lips, but nodded, and walked the remaining steps up to the front door and pushed the button. A loud, melodic chime sounded out, and a shape moved in front of the frosted glass a few seconds later, before the door swung open. A tall, bald man with a leisure suit was standing in front of us, grinning wide. He nodded at Henri, then his gaze fell on me in her hand and his already wide smile got even bigger.

"I take it you two are Henri and Amber?" he asked in a rich voice "The other girls are out back, the hot tub is behind the pool, and the pool house has a changing room, of course."

"Yes sir, I am Henrietta." Henri said "Are you Quince's father?"

"I am!" he said, nodding and shutting the door behind us "Please, call me Cal, it's nice to meet you! If you'll excuse me though, I have a guest myself, make yourselves at home, there's liquor in the poolside bar!"

"Thank you Cal!" I said "Just make our way to the back then?"

He pointed to the bifurcated staircase that wrapped around the sides of the grand entrance and nodded "Just take the door there, between the stairs. It leads to the kitchen, and the back door is just through the mud room. Have a good evening!"

He waved at us and made his way to a door on the side, smoke curling out as he went through. Henri took a breath, and carefully walked to the door, slipping through it into a long corridor that ended into a brightly lit, yellow toned kitchen. A middle aged woman with Quince's hair texture stood at one of the counters, her tight curls pulled back into a single low bun. She was wearing a yellow dress that matched the walls of the kitchen, with a crisp white apron over it. There were rows of ingredients on the counter in front of her, and she was mixing them into a bowl by hand, humming as she worked. Henri cleared her throat slightly to let her know we were there, and she turned, beaming at us as she did so.

"Ohhh! Quince's new friends!" she exclaimed "I'm so happy you could make it! She hasn't made any new friends in *ages*, it's so nice to see her get out there!"

"Ah, we- yes." Henri said "We just started, um, hanging out on Friday, really."

"Of course, of course." the lady said "My name is Ayana, I'm Quince's mother. Whom do I have the pleasure of speaking to?"

"Henrietta, ma'am, and this is Amber." Henri said, holding me out so Ayana could see

"Aw! It's so nice to meet the both of you! I was worried when Quince brought home her little friend, Kensey? I assumed she'd be lonely by herself, but I'm happy to see *she'll* have a friend too."

"I'm looking forward to being her friend, she's a very kind person, and she's very mature!" I said, nodding

"Mm, not things you could say about my Quince, I'm sure." Ayana said, raising an eyebrow

I blinked "Um- well, I wasn't thinking about-"

"Oh no no, it's ok." Ayana laughed lightly, if a bit forced "I know she's a terror, she always has been. It comes with getting everything she could ever want, I suppose."

She looked at me and Henri appraisingly "It'll be good for her to widen her friend group, hopefully you two can ground her. And hopefully Kensey can help her learn some compassion, while we're at it."

"I think she is already learning to care for her, ma'am." Henri said, nodding "She has improved a lot just since yesterday."

"Well, I'm happy to hear that." she sighed "Amber, I heard Marissa is your... person?"

I held back a wince at how she'd just stopped short of saying 'owner' and nodded "Yes, she's taking care of me, I live in a little house in her room."

"Mm, I'm sorry to hear that." she said, her eyebrows drawing together "If you need anything, or if you need somewhere to stay for a while, please let me or my husband know."

"She's not *that* bad." I said "But thank you, I'll keep that in mind."

Ayana waved towards a wooden door at the back of the room "The pool area is out through there, I'll be out soon with scones for everyone, so don't fill up on the junk food Quince bought, ok?"

Henri smiled and nodded "That sounds lovely, thank you so much Miss Ayana!"

We headed through the door into a strange room with a low to the floor sink and benches along one wall. It had tiled floors and a drain in the center, and what looked like a shower with a basin in the corner. The door to the back was heavy wood, and Henri had to lean against it to get it to open, and she stumbled through as it swung.

The back yard area was paved with wide, flat stones, and there was a large stone pool in the center that looked like it'd been carved out of one giant rock. Off to one side on the porch was a grilling area, on the other side was a conversation pit with a massive TV over it, and on the far side of the pool was a small building with a porch around it, rocking chairs lining the walls. The hot tub was directly across from the back door, and there was a covered path leading from the back of the porch above us to the hot tub itself, making a roof over it.

"Hello Henri!" Tracy called out from the hot tub "Get a drink and get changed, we've got snacks!"

"Hurry up, I wanna see Amber and Kensey in the mini hot tub!" Quince added on "She's been waiting on Amber so we can get the temperature right!"

"Oh- ja! I will change right away, sorry!" Henri said, and jogged over to the pool house.

The inside of the pool house was a lot less opulent than the main house, it was comfortably warm and there were a few changing booths to one side, as well as a wide table in the center of the room. There was another TV in here with a weird plastic couch in front of it, most likely waterproofed in some way in case you wanted to watch TV in here instead of in the pool for some reason. Henri stepped over to one of the changing rooms and set me on the seat, digging in her bag. She pulled out a small plastic bag with my swim stuff in it and passed it to me.

"I will be in the changing room next to you, let me know if you need anything, ok?" she said, and stepped out, closing the door behind her.

I changed quickly, putting on the swimsuit that'd come with the rest of my clothes, and pulling my hair back with a headband that was just ever so slightly too tight to be comfortable. I looked down at myself and sighed, the suit was a two piece, and while it looked *cute*, my tummy did poke out a little. I *preferred* the high waisted kind that went over my belly button, but these were lower, around my hips. It was a light blue and white checkered swimsuit with frills along the edges, with a sports bra styled top. I'd have to see if Marissa would be interested in finding me one with more coverage. I got the feeling she'd jump at the chance to pick out new outfits for me, no matter what they were.

Henri knocked on the door and stepped in, picking me up. I was pleased to see that she was wearing her *own* swimsuit, a red one piece with cherries on it, instead of one of mine. Not that she'd *fit* in one of mine, it'd hang loose in all the wrong places and be tight in even worse ones. She bit her lip and I could see her fighting off an 'aww' at the sight of me. I rolled my eyes and sat down on her palm as she walked outside. She waved to the girls with her free hand and made her way over to the bar under the porch to get a drink. Looking at the bottles lined up along the wall, she frowned and shook her head.

"Let's see... I do not know the ratios, I had my phone last time for the measurements, and there is no shot glass, do I eyeball it? she asked, setting me down on the slightly sticky marble "I do not want to get drunk here."

"I don't know either, just mix stuff that looks good?" I asked "Look, there's an ice box, just put ice in the cup, and do what Missy did, right?"

"Ok, um." she put a lump of ice into a tall glass and picked up a vodka bottle "Ok, so this...."

She poured half the glass of vodka "Then... this?" She added sugar syrup most of the rest of the way "And... lime, I think."

I watched her put the lime in and mix it up with a spoon "That sounds about right. It should be fine, it's only one glass, right?"

She sipped and wrinkled her face slightly "It is strong, but sticky, all at once. It kind of tastes right though?"

She picked me up in her free hand "Anyway, let's get over to the others."

She carefully walked over to the hot tub and stood awkwardly over it, a thin smile on her face. "Hello, we are ready, thank you for inviting me." she said politely

"Yeah, whatever, just get in, ok?" Quince said "You're not as boring as I thought you'd be, and anyway, you had Amber with you."

"You're nicer than *Marissa*, at least." Tracy said, rubbing the side of her head where a small scratch was visible against her pale skin

Henri set me down on the side of the hot tub next to Kensey and carefully lowered herself in, holding her drink over the side in case it spilled. Quince's eyes locked on me and she did *not* stop herself from 'aww'-ing at my outfit.

"Aww! She's so cuuute!" she whined "Her lil tummy and the frills, gaahh, I want to squeeze her!"

She poked me in the stomach with a finger, knocking me on my ass and I flushed, crossing my arms over my midsection in embarrassment.

"It's wild how on a full sized person, a little meat makes them look sloppy, but on a class B, it's just a cuteness enhancer!" Tracy giggled "Gosh Amber, you're making *me* want a class B, even."

I curled up and brought my knees up, even if they were saying 'nice' things, it still felt wrong and gross for them to be talking about my body like that. I tried to come up with a good response, but anything I could think of sounded childish or rude. I felt strong hands under my armpits lifting me up, and I turned to see Kensey giving me a wry smile as she put me on my feet.

"They've been doing the same to me all night, don't take it seriously." she said, patting me.

Looking at her up and down, she had the tan lines of someone who usually wore a one piece, but Quince had put her in a fluffy orange two piece with a big bow on the front and bottoms that looked more like bloomers than a swimsuit. It was loud and vibrant, and not what I'd have expected to see her

*The Feeling of Being Valued* 411

in if she was choosing her own clothes. She stepped over to the little hot tub, the one I'd seen in the store with Marissa, and slapped the side.

"Come on, I wanna try this thing out. I wasn't sure how hot you could stand, with you being as small as you are, so I just set it to 96. We can raise it higher if we're ok with that, sound good?"

I took a breath and smiled "Y-yeah, let's do it! Sorry, I'm just insecure about some things is all."

"You don't *get* to be insecure anymore." Quince said "You're a class B, you just get to be cute and fun, no insecurities."

"She can still be insecure." Henri said "Just because she is small does not mean she lost all her body issues."

"It's like, a proportions thing." Tracy said as she put stuff from the big pile of candies and cheese squares onto a plate "Or, I don't know, my dad was telling me about it. Because class Bs are so small, we don't notice their flaws as much, and they look more proportional to us because they're already a smaller size, so we don't notice the things we'd usually notice about a full sized person."

"Does that mean they see *us* as uglier?." Quince said, frowning

"I didn't notice you guys looking uglier." I said "I just notice people's pores and body hair more, I guess."

"So I need to start waxing *everything*, got it." Quince said nodding

"If you don't want us noticing stuff like peach fuzz, yeah." I said "Everyone has it though, it's not a big deal. What's a bigger deal is smells, especially on your hands? Mis- Marissa uses lotion every half hour to stay smelling clean, and she uses breath mints and stuff constantly too."

"...Have you noticed *me* smelling bad, then?" she asked, looking uncomfortable

"Every time you hold me I can tell what the last thing you ate was, it's not a big deal, but it's something to consider." I said

"Oh... ok, yeah, I'll get more lotion or something. I already use some, I'll just have to use it more." she said, looking at her hands "I *have* been eating cheese tonight, I guess that's something that sticks to your hands."

I felt good about that, *I'd* made *her* insecure now, I'd never imagined being able to do that to her of all people. I climbed over the edge of the little hot tub and slipped in, instantly falling under the water. I burbled and stood up, my face just clearing the water on my tiptoes.

"What?" I croaked, kicking my feet to swim up "How is it so deep?!"

"Oh, whoops, sorry." Kensey said, helping me onto one of the seats "The hot tub is in a cupholder, I thought you'd seen."

I pulled myself up onto the seat and took a breath, the water now just up to my chest "It's fine, I wondered how you'd fit, I just didn't think too hard about it."

A shadow fell over us and I looked up to see Henri staring down at us worriedly "Are you ok Klein Fee?" she asked, reaching out for me

I leaned away "Yeah, geez, just go sit down, I'm fine."

She tightened her mouth, but nodded and went to go back to her seat. I could see all the other girls from where I sat, and Kensey was across from me, on a much lower seat, so we were almost eye level with each other for once. She smiled at me gently.

"Thank you for coming, Amber." she said "It feels so much better to have someone else like me here, it's less scary."

"Aw, I'm not scary, Kay..." Quince said, sounding slightly hurt "Am I?"

"N-no!" Kensey said quickly, doing a poor job of convincing anyone she wasn't scared of Quince "Not at all, you're sweet! I just- it's more like, it feels better socially, you know?"

"I get it." I said "I haven't been around a lot of class Bs, but it always feels nice when it happens. There's a meeting for people like us a couple towns away, that's where I met Nada? The one I was texting? It was very nice to get to chat with them about class B stuff."

"A meeting?" Tracy asked "Like, class Bs anonymous?"

"I mean, kinda, yeah." I said "We sit in a circle and talk about being a class B, and the guardians have a separate room to do the same in."

"That sounds nice, yeah." Kensey said, nodding "Quince, do you think we could go?"

"Uh, fuck, that's a lot." Quince said "I don't know, will Marissa be there?"

I shook my head "She didn't like it, we most likely won't go back."

Quince sighed "At least I'll be the center of attention for once then, I suppose. When is it?"

"Tuesdays and Thursdays, at around six thirty." I said, and gave her the name of the community center it was at

Quince looked at Kensey closely, and her hand drifted to her, rubbing her cheek with a fingernail. "Maybe, I don't know, maybe."

Henri spoke up "If I still have Amber by then, I would be more than happy to meet you there?"

"You won't though." I said defensively "I'm getting back with Marissa on Monday, remember?"

"Unless Miss Lund wants you two to stay separated longer, of course." Henri pointed out "She may make Marissa wait until Wednesday, or even Friday."

I shook my head "No! No, just- I want to get back with her, if she tries to do that, just- just sneak me over there or something, I need to be back with her soon."

"Is Henri really that bad?" Tracy asked, looking between us "I thought you'd *like* staying with her, since you're best friends and everything."

"Henri is-" I started to complain, but thought better of it "I just miss Marissa."

"Why does Miss Lund want you two separated so badly anyway?" Tracy asked "Marissa said she wanted to *kill* you or something, that's pretty extreme."

"Well," I said, thinking how to word it "it's got to do with you, actually."

"Me?!" she asked, her eyes widening "I don't even *have* a class B, what?"

"She thinks if Marissa gets close to Amber, she will not be willing to do what she needs to when she is running your father's company." Henri explained "She thinks Amber will make her soft and cripple her."

Tracy shook her head "That's stupid, we *study* class Bs at the lab, we're helping them get better food and care. If anything, caring for Amber would make Marissa *better* at that."

"Miss Lund is changing the focus of the lab, Tracy." I said "She used the term 'eradicate' when referring to class Bs. She's trying to stop us from existing, either by vaccinations, or by eliminating the virus altogether, and she needs existing class Bs to do that."

"Holy shit, that's like, super villain stuff." Quince said, impressed

"No-I- no! My dad wants to *help* class Bs!" Tracy said, her face stricken "We're trying to help m- I- We- We *need* to, it's important!"

"It might not be up to him." Henri said "Miss Lund wants to use their cells to make vaccines, so you may need to find another way to help them."

Tracy clenched her teeth and glowered "I- she- fucking- *gods*, does the bitch have no *empathy*?"

"Not much." Henri said, rolling her eyes "She said even if *Marissa* was compressed she planned to still use her as a test subject, she would just change her focus from turning class Bs into vaccines to trying to reverse the compressions."

"Calling it now, she's going to have a big evil queen speech the day she takes over the company." Quince said, shaking her head "I'm not letting her do experiments on Kensey, that's for damn sure."

"W-well thank you for that." Kensey said, smiling nervously "I know you wouldn't, but- thank you for saying it."

"I'm not letting her do experiments on *any* of the class Bs, especially not the ones at the lab, I'll fight her before that happens." Tracy said darkly

"How are you going to stop her?" I asked "She's going to own it all outright soon, so unless your dad gets the shareholders to sell him back the shares, I think they're fucked."

"I don't- fuck, I don't know." Tracy said, her usual air headed attitude replaced with a serious one "I- I have to think about this, this is important."

"I didn't know you cared so much about class Bs, Trace." Quince said "You always seemed weirded out by them before."

"They're still *people*." Tracy said, crossing her arms "They- you know, they all mean something to someone, they're all someone's family..."

The group went quiet at that, looking over at Kensey and me solemnly.

"Who cares about *you*, Kensey?" Quince asked gently "Who do you mean something to?"

Kensey looked up at her and her face wavered for a moment before she caught herself and answered in the chipper, happy voice she'd been using since the hospital "W-well, my co-workers and I got along well, we'd go out for drinks sometimes, and, um, I'd visit my dad once a week to eat dinner with him. I have a few old friends, but we hadn't seen each other in a while, we mostly talked online, I want to reconnect though. Oh, and I had a book club I was part of too, every other week, we'd drink wine and chat about romance."

"You had a whole like, network, huh?" Tracy said sadly "It's easy to see class Bs as just little friends who popped up to live with you, but they're all *people*, and that's so, *so* horrifying..."

"What do you mean horrifying?" Henri asked, confused

"Well- I mean, they're people. But, like, not really anymore, right?" Tracy said "It's like, they're not people anymore and they *know* it and they have to live with not being people forever, and there's nothing they can do about it. It's so scary to think about."

"It sounds like you thought about it a lot more than the rest of us have." Quince said, frowning

"My- I work with them." Tracy said, frowning "I have to watch them run on treadmills and eat weird things and get stress tested, and then there's all the psychological tests and interviews. That's where it comes out, how human they are I mean, in the interviews."

She looked over at me and Kensey "I *know* you're humans, but it really is so much easier to pretend you're not sometimes. I don't have that luxury, I guess."

"I understand." I said "It hurts when people don't see me as a person," I glared pointedly at Henri "but I can understand it at least a little."

Quince sank down into the water up to her chin "I just wanted a new pet, not a philosophical debate on the nature of humanity."

She patted Kensey's head with a dripping finger "You're still my pet, just so you know, philosophy aside."

"Y-yeah, I know." Kensey said "I don't mind, I do appreciate this conversation, though, about me still being... human."

"Mm, it's important to keep in mind." Quince said quietly

"You are both so reasonable tonight." Henri said "I am happy to see you two acting so, I am not sure, normal, I suppose?"

"We're not around Marissa." Tracy said "When we're around her, or in her bubble, like at school, it's a big performance. We have to play our roles, and do what she expects, like a stage play."

"It's exhausting" Quince agreed "I feel like my guard is up around her all the time."

"Well- you were still mean to me when she was doing her tennis practice and it was just us." I pointed out "Was *that* an act?"

Quince rolled her eyes "I wasn't being *mean*, I was playing with my friend's new toy, just get over that."

"So you're *still* a bitch, then." I said, raising an eyebrow "Marissa just makes it worse?"

She reached over and knocked me off my seat, plunging me into the hot water. I swam up, but her finger poked me back down, and I spun, trying to find a way up. Kensey's hand grabbed mine, and hauled me up and to the side and I gasped for air and shook the water off my face. I glanced over to see Quince holding Henri off of her with a foot as Henri flailed and tried to get to me. I coughed and squeezed Kensey's hand to thank her and carefully made my way back to my seat.

"Does that answer your question, Amber?" Tracy asked, waving a hand at Quince and Henri, now wrestling in the center of the hot tub, Henri's arm around Quince's neck and Quince yanking on Henri's hair

I coughed again, and took a deep breath "Yeah, I get it." I said

"For the record," Tracy said as Quince dunked Henri "I'm pretty much only a bitch performatively. At least, that's what I tell myself."

"Is that why you were looking forward to getting away from Marissa?" I asked

"Kinda, yeah." she ate a bite of cheese as she thought about it "I just wanted a low social stakes position where I don't have to like, tear everyone to bits all the time. If she's there, I gotta keep it up or I'll be a target myself."

"That's got to be so stressful." Kensey said as Henri drug Quince under the water with her "I don't remember the social game being nearly this cut throat when I was in school, and certainly not in *college*."

"Marissa built an empire of drama." I said "These are her generals, plus one you haven't met yet, but like, there's absolutely a tiered hierarchy, and she sits at the top of it all, making sure the empire stays intact. She'll most likely even bring it into the workplace when she gets her degree."

Henri and Quince burst up out of the water, glaring at each other.

"You got my *hair* wet, bitch." Quince growled

"You tried to drown my friend!" Henri protested "That is far more important."

"I dunked her, that's not drowning. Plus, I bet Kay here knows how to do CPR, even if Amber *did* get a little drowned."

"I- Yes?" Kensey said, surprised "I'm CPR certified, but please don't drown anyone."

"Don't touch my friend again, or I'll do a lot more that get your hair-" Henri started

"Giiiirls!" a voice called out, and I looked at the house to see Quince's mom in the doorway holding a tray of steaming hot triangles

"Ok, stop, truce. We gotta get out while we eat." Quince said to Henri "The candy and stuff I bought is ok in the tub, but crumbly scones aren't."

"I needed a break anyway." Tracy said, standing up and picking up a towel "I was getting a little floaty there."

"Here, I will carry Amber." Henri said firmly, plucking me out of the hot tub and picking up her drink "I do not trust anyone else to handle her."

"Yeah, whatever." Quince said, huffing "It's a truce right now, just go eat the scones, god."

Henri looked at me and took a deep breath, letting it out slowly as she watched me. She stepped away from the hot tub, setting me and her drink on a table as she toweled off.

"Amber, are you enjoying this?" she asked

"I- sure, I think so?" I said "It feels kinda like hanging out with friends, just, you know, a little strained."

"I am enjoying *this* more than the sleepover." Henri admitted "But I do not like Quince and her apparent lack of care."

She handed me a corner of the towel for me to use.

"Hm." I mused "She's learning. It's important for us to be here and talk to her about this stuff. I think she's already seeing Kensey different just since before we got here."

Henri wrinkled her nose "It should not be our job to-" she sighed "...You are right. We need to show her the right way to be."

"It sounds ominous when you say it like that." I said, stepping onto her hand.

She picked up her drink and made her way towards the conversation pit where the other girls and Ayana were already sitting.

"If she keeps taking the safety of class Bs lightly," she muttered "it very well may be ominous..."

# Chapter Twenty-Three

I ate my bit of scone as the girls chatted with Miss Ayana and leaned against Kensey. It felt weird, being here like this, with such low stakes. Even at Missy's house, the sleepovers felt like we were all on the edge of a knife, all trying to outplay each other. I missed Marissa, but there was no denying that she made people nervous. She even made me nervous still, despite how much I wanted to see her. Kensey shifted behind me and the pillow we were on rocked, sending me falling over backwards into her lap. She frowned at me and gently sat me back up.

"I still don't think it's fair that you get to eat regular sized food." she said "I've never felt as sick in my life after that pizza."

"I honestly don't know how I don't get sick..." I said, taking another bite of the warm, crumbly pastry "Maybe you just have to get used to it? Have a little here and there, and you'll get used to it?"

"Is that what you did?" she asked

"I don't think so?" I said "I had a little bit of tortilla, then like a week later I had a whole plate of homemade mandu. I got sick on the mandu, but only a little, a stomachache, really."

She sighed. "I just don't know if I want to risk it."

"That's fair." I said, nodding "So I'm guessing Quince got you the good stuff then?"

"She did, yeah!" Kensey said, smiling "I got to pick them out, too."

"What did I do?" Quince said, leaning over

"Honey, let them be, they were having a conversation." Ayana said with a small frown

"No, it's fine." Kensey said "Uh, we were just talking about food, and the stuff me and Quince got for me earlier."

"Yeah, I got *all* the good stuff." Quince bragged "I even got, like, ice cream and soda and chips and stuff, all tiny sized."

"I'll be eating well, that's for sure!" Kensey said, pushing her smile bigger and putting on her chipper voice

Ayana narrowed her eyes slightly and looked at the rest of the girls. "Are you all going to be getting back in the hot tub after this?"

"Yeah, duh." Quince said "We were barely in it before the scones were done."

"Thank you for the scones, by the way." Henri said "They are very good."

"Mm, yes, thank you!" Tracy said "I love the hint of maple in them, it really works!"

Ayana smiled widely "I'm so glad you girls like them! They're Q's favorite, so I've perfected the recipe over the years. Now, I see Kensey isn't eating, would it be alright if I took her to Quince's room so she can make some food? It's about dinner time, and I'd hate for her to be hungry."

"Oh, uh, well, she had lunch a while ago, um," Quince said "I guess, yeah? Just bring her back after so we can hang out."

"I'll come too, and keep you company." I told Kensey

"I- you should- mm..." Henri started, then looked at Ayana "Just please be careful with Amber, Miss Ayana. She is very fragile."

"Of course, of course!" she said, and held her hands out for us to climb in. She nodded to the girls, and carefully walked back to the house with us in her palms, her steps measured and slow. Once we were in the kitchen she carefully set us down on the countertop of the island and sat on a stool next to us.

"Ok, girls, I wanted to talk to you about what's going on, especially with Quince, is that ok?" she asked politely

"What do you 'mean what's going on'?" Kensey asked "Is something happening?"

"I just know that Quince dove into guardianship quickly, and maybe didn't think through the ramifications of taking care of a person all the way first." Ayana said "I wanted to talk to you two about it and see if there's anything I can do to make the situation easier for you both."

"I mean, Quince is getting better." I said "Like, she's improved a lot over the past few days alone."

"I'm concerned she doesn't see Kensey as a responsibility, but rather as a..." Ayana trailed off, looking uncomfortable

"A toy?" Kensey offered

"That may be accurate, it just feels so hurtful to say." Ayana said, shaking her head

"If it helps, I think Quince sees her more like a pet or a something. She saw her as a toy at first for sure, but she's learning." I said

"I don't think that having her see Kensey as a *pet* is altogether any better than having her see her as a toy, Amber." Ayana sighe

"I'm not too worried about it, Miss Ayana." Kensey said "As long as she takes care of me, I'll be ok, even if I'm a pet. I hated the idea, but seeing her buy stuff for me and find things to dress me in, and seeing how enamored she is with me... I could be doing a lot worse than Quince."

"It's not about if things could be *worse*, it's about if they could be *better*." Ayana said gently "I don't care if Quince is in the top five percent of caretakers, if she's not treating you with respect and care, and as a *person*, she needs to get better."

"How do you propose you do that?" I asked "It took Marissa *dating* me before she really started seeing me as an equal, and even then she's very insistent that she's the one in charge."

"Marissa is *dating you*?" Ayana asked, mildly appalled "I wasn't aware she was a- well, I'm not saying I didn't *suspect*, but I'm shocked Vivian is allowing it."

"Vivian?" I asked

"Miss Lund, Marissa's mother." she explained

"I think they're trying to keep it a secret, ma'am." Kensey said "Miss Lund wants to use us to make vaccines, she'd never approve."

"That sounds like her." Ayana murmured "The woman is colder than a snow cone on Pluto..."

She shook her head "As for how I want to get Q to see you as a person. I'll do my best to gently remind her, but if you don't mind, I'd really like to lead by example."

"What do you mean?" Kensey asked

"I mean I want to spend time with you myself." Ayana explained "You're not *that* much younger than me, if we could be friends and do activities together as equals, I think Quince would start seeing you as less of a 'pet' and more of 'a lady I'm caring for'."

"That could work." I said, nodding "Quince is pretty easily influenced, so I could see that getting through to her."

"I- well, what kinds of things would you want to do together?" Kensey asked "I'm too small to do much."

"I could show you how to bake, or we could use the spa, or even just sit with tea and chat, it doesn't have to be anything special." Ayana said

"I think I'd love that, actually." Kensey said "It sounds like it'd be very humanizing for me..."

"Ok, lovely!" Ayana said with a smile "I'll find some good activities, and I'll start 'borrowing' you from Quince to spend time with me next week, sound good?"

Kensey nodded "I look forward to it, Miss Ayana, thank you for caring about me."

Ayana scooped us up into her hands again carefully as she stood up "Oh, please, just Ayana is fine, now let's get you girls some dinner!"

We made our way through the house, the tall ceilings and wide hallways making me feel even smaller than usual. I looked at the paintings on the walls as we passed; they were nice, more grounded and realistic than the odd looking ones Marissa had in her room, but they lacked something, too. I was an artist at heart, and the art filling Quince's home felt manufactured. Produced by an artist to make a painting, not to make art. I wondered if they'd been picked by an interior designer, or if they'd been selected personally by Ayana or Cal.

Stopping in front of a fancy door, Ayana swung it open, revealing a much fancier room than Marissa's. Where Marissa had a large simple bed with a headboard and nothing else, Quince had a four poster bed with hanging drapes and thick sheets, where Marissa had a large TV in front of a sofa, Quince's took up most of one wall across from a row of recliners, and where Marissa had a couple shelves with personal items on them, Quince's shelves were covered in the oddest collection of vinyl figures and expensive looking statuettes I'd ever seen. Even the desk Ayana carried us over to was a hardwood roll-top with carvings all over it. A box was sitting on the desk, just small enough that the desk could be closed over it, and as Ayana lowered us into it, I saw that it was a tiny studio apartment.

It was nice, I felt the heated floors as soon as I touched the ground, and there was a big fridge and kitchen to one side, with the bed and TV on the other. There was a pathway to get to the front door, with cubbies on either side. The bathroom and the closet, I guessed. Kensey made her way to the fridge and pulled out a couple packs of food, waving them at me.

"Do you want one?" she asked

"Well, we're at different compression rates, so maybe I guess? It'll be fine, I'm sure. I can eat regular food in moderation after all." I said

"It's got to be better to eat a 90% compressed meal than a 0% compressed one, though." she pointed out

"Yeah, true. Hey, can I try some of the chips?" I asked "I was curious about that."

She pulled open a cabinet and got out a bag of barbecue chips and handed them to me "I haven't tried them yet, but it's nice that they still make junk food for us."

I tore the bag open and pulled out a chip. It was giant, and it was a lot thicker than the ones I was used to, but taking a bite proved it was just as crunchy and flavorful as the ones I liked when I was full sized. I crunched on the chips while we waited, and Kensey tried a couple as well, the chips looking much more at home in her larger hands. Finally the 'oven' dinged, and Kensey pulled our meals out. She'd made us both a kind of mushroom soup with a side of bean... things? It was pretty good, the lumps of fake mushroom were chewy and savory, and the bean things were salty and mushy, just the way I liked them. Kensey put our dishes in her sink and folded up the chips to put away and looked around the room, smiling slightly.

"I feel kind of domestic right now, honestly." she said "It's not really too much different than how things were before I compressed, I could get used to living like this."

"I'm glad to hear that!" Ayana said, peering down at us, making me jump. She'd been out of sight, but from how quickly she showed up once we were done, I guessed she'd still been in the room waiting on us.

"Thank you for taking us up here!" I said "Would you mind taking us back to the hot tub? I want to get cozy again."

"I'll bring you two down there, but please remember to wait thirty minutes before getting in, ok?" she said, raising an eyebrow

We agreed, and before long, we were back by the side of the hot tub, the other girls already in the big one.

"Thank you Miss Ayana!" I said to her as she set us down and went to leave

"No problem Amber, be safe!" she called, and waved to us as she walked off.

"Did you eat, Amber?" Henri said, looking at me

"We both did, we had soup." Kensey said "And some chips, too."

Henri nodded and looked pensive "I did not see much food for you in your house when I picked your stuff up, Amber. Just one pack in your freezer. I suppose I will need to go out tomorrow and get you some food."

"It's really expensive, can you afford it?" Quince asked

"I have a little money." she said "We lost most of the money from the crowdfund due to refund requests, and I had to refund it out of my personal accounts while we waited to get the situation resolved, so I'm a little low."

"So I can't stay with you all week, you don't have any food, right?" I said hopefully

"You really want to get back to Marissa, huh?" Tracy said softly

"I just-" I glanced at Henri "I honestly just prefer it when she's taking care of me."

"That is not fair, I want to do a good job of taking care of you, Klein Fee." Henri said, sounding hurt "I so try..."

"You know my problems with you 'taking care of me', Henri." I said, folding my arms

"Is this drama?" Tracy asked "Did she do something bad?"

"We are on a truce right now, I do not want to talk about it." Henri said sadly

"Amber?" Tracy asked, prompting me

"Yeah, no. Truce. If I told you what was going on, it'd be breaking the truce. Just know that I really, really want to get back to Marissa." I said

"I will be better, Amber. I promise." Henri said solemnly

"Jesus, way to ruin the mood." Quince said, rolling her eyes "Just, fuck, we're in a hot tub, just chill."

I nodded and looked at Kensey "Think it's been thirty minutes?"

"It's not that big a deal." she said "I'm getting in, at least."

I climbed in after her, and after a few minutes, the awkward mood had shifted back to a more lighthearted one, and the rest of the night went by smoothly.

~~~

I woke up and popped my back, wishing I had my regular bed. The case was fine, but it really wasn't that comfortable overall, and it left me feeling slightly stiff. Henri was still curled up on her bed, and our stuff was in a pile on the floor where she'd dumped it late last night when we got in. I left my case and went over to the random pile of stuff Henri had brought me, and found my tablet, flopping down on a pile of clothes to use it for a bit. It powered up, and instantly the screen filled with notifications from Marissa. Most were her asking how I was, or asking if there was any way for me to meet up with her today instead of Monday at school, but the further I scrolled the more stressed she sounded. I frowned and skipped messaging her and just started a video call.

"Amber what the fuck?" she said urgently as soon as the call went through

"Hey, I didn't have my-"

"If you're safe, tell me the first god I used when we played Life and Times, if you're in danger, get it wrong." she snapped

I blinked, thinking back to last weekend "Uh, you were Artemis and I was a guy I can't pronounce?"

She visibly relaxed, and lay back onto her hospital bed "Gods, Amber, why didn't you respond?"

"I'm sorry, I was at Quince's house, we had a hot tub party, and I didn't think to bring my tablet..."

"You hung out with Quince without me?" she asked "*Henri* hung out with Quince? Willingly?"

"They fought a little, but yeah, I wanted to see Kensey and her new place."

"Gods, I was freaking out, I thought Henri had taken you to the airport or something. I even sent a team over, but they said there were only two life signatures at your parent's apartment, so I was assuming the worst..."

I winced "I'm so sorry, I should have messaged you about it, me and Henri got in a fight, and we went to the party to get our minds off it."

"A fight?" she asked "About what, me?"

"Not *everything* is about you." I said

She raised an eyebrow at me

"...But yeah, it was kinda about you."

"I'm guessing she still doesn't like me?" Marissa asked

"More like she was trying to *be* you." I explained "She thought if she tried to scare me or bully me, I'd fall in love with her, but she pushed herself too far and had a meltdown or something."

"That's a pretty good plan, if she wasn't so bad at being in charge." Marissa mused "If most other girls started taking charge of you and pushing you around, you'd fall for them instantly."

"That's not- No I wouldn't!" I said, glaring at her and blushing

"I bullied you for six years. It took a week of me playing with you for you to be ok dating me." she pointed out

"...Don't say it like *that*, it sounds toxic or something." I said, not looking at her face

"Oh, it *is*." she crooned "And that's what you love about it. It could have been anyone with a mean streak, I just got lucky~"

"Whatever." I grumbled "I see you're still in the hospital, you doing ok?"

"Yeah, they said I *still* have alcohol in my system somehow, I don't feel anything, and they have me hooked up to an IV so I'll be fine in a few hours I think. I'm getting out tonight though."

"That's good..." I said "I want to get back to you, I'm not enjoying it here."

"You don't like getting to see your parents?" she asked "I'd thought you'd be thrilled about that."

"I haven't seen them yet, we keep missing them. I'll see them today though. It's more just Henri, and not trusting her, and the fact that my old room is a mess now, she's not very tidy, and she made an even bigger mess last night when I was hiding from her, so it's stressful."

"Well, I have bad news." she said "If you were actually missing I was going to call the whole thing off and call in a few more teams to track down Henri, but now that I know you're safe..."

"What? What news?" I asked, alarmed

"Not really sure how to say this, but..." Marissa's face scrunched up "...My mom is setting me up with a clinic to help my 'alcoholism'."

I felt a chill "What- what does that look like for us?"

"It's a rich people clinic. I won't lose my class B guardianship license over it or anything, nothing will be reported, and it's mostly outpatient, but I do need to stay for a few days for observation, starting tonight."

"A few *days*?!" I said, alarmed "Missy, I was supposed to get back together with you tomorrow *morning*!"

"It's just until Wednesday, it's so they can make sure I'm not going to get withdraws or something, it's- it's hardly a problem, right? My mom even said we can all meet up for dinner at Chrysós Wednesday night to get you back to me. I think that means *you'll* be allowed to eat with us, too, that's huge, right? My mom is kinda opening up, that's worth a few days of Henri, isn't it?"

"I miss you though, and- I don't know what she'll do if she has me that long. It could be bad..."

"I know, I don't trust her either, I thought about asking Quince to watch you instead, but that could go even *worse*."

"She's not so bad." I said "Quince, I mean. She's rude and she doesn't think things through, but she's taking pretty good care of Kensey so far. It's only been a couple days though, so I'm not sure..."

"I could try and get her to take you home on Monday?" Marissa said thoughtfully "And give you back to Henri on Wednesday after her classes. That might work, would you be ok with that?"

"If that works with Henri and Quince, I'd like that." I said "I guess Henri would just drop me off at Quince's tennis match on Monday, then they could meet up again Wednesday afternoon, yeah."

"I doubt Henri will go for it, though." Marissa said thoughtfully

"Well, she only has one more meal for me left, and no money for more, from what it sounds like." I said

"Oh, shit, really?" Marissa said "Fuck, I forgot I was supposed to get you more food tomorrow. That might make things go better, yeah. Each of your special meals is like, almost fifty dollars."

I sat bolt upright "What the fuck!?" I asked in shock

"I thought I mentioned that before?" she said "Anyway, yeah, the higher quality vegetarian stuff I get you isn't cheap."

"I wasn't aware I cost so much to feed..." I said, feeling slightly ashamed

"It's literally not a problem." Marissa said "Honestly, I'm thinking about buying you like, candy and juice and stuff next time. I only limited your supply because I wanted you to lose weight."

"W-well, it's a lot harder than you'd think for me to lose weight, and I'm still *fit*, so-"

"I get it, sorry..." she said quietly "I was thinking of you as more of a doll back then. I'm not going to try and dictate your body. That's... more toxic than I'm comfortable with."

"Thanks..." I said, my face still red "Tracy was saying that class Bs look cuter than class As even with the same body shapes, because of, like, they can't see details or something?"

"That's one theory, yeah." Missy said "Another is that when we see a small human, our brain triggers the response we're supposed to get when we see a baby, so we associate class Bs with babies and see them as cuter as a result."

"That *would* explain why every other person I meet uses baby talk with me." I muttered

"Yeah, and why I want to squeeze you so bad." Marissa snorted

"You want to squeeze babies?" I asked "Uh..."

"No- I- You know, like you see a baby and you're like 'aww I wanna poke it and pinch it' and stuff?"

"I don't think so?" I said "That might just be a you thing."

"Whatever." she said rolling her eyes "Anyway, I'm really glad you're ok. I was honestly freaking out over here."

"I'm really sorry." I said "I didn't forget about you, I just- I didn't have my tablet. I was missing you the whole time."

"It's fine." she said "I just have to make a few calls, call off a h- oh, hi Henri."

A shadow fell over me, and I turned to see a groggy Henri looming over me. She mumbled something, and waved at Marissa.

"Hey, I'll give you time to wake up, but call me when you get the chance, ok?" Marissa said "I want to discuss something with you if that's ok."

"Mmm uhgh... me? Me call?" Henri muttered

"Yes, Henri, *you* call, Henri call Marissa." Missy said in caveman speak

Henri flipped her off and shuffled off to the bathroom, leaving me alone again.

"She's not a morning person, huh?" Marissa asked with a grin

"She's never been too keen on waking up, no." I said, shaking my head

"Well, anyway, I gotta go call off... a guy, and I guess talk to Quince too. I'll talk to you soon? I hope?" Marissa said

"Ok, fine, I miss you, Lady M. Hugs and kisses?"

"Mm, squeezes and bites, but same idea, yeah." she said, laughing

"I'll see you soon, Missy." I said, giving her a smile

"And I'll see *you* soon, Stress Toy." she said back, and hung up, still smiling.

I flopped backwards on the pile of clothes I'd been sitting on. Fuck, I had it bad, didn't I? That one fucking tease, 'stress toy', and I was practically curling my toes in anticipation of her brand of 'bullying'.

...Maybe there *was* something to her theory that I'd have fallen for any dom that pursued me after all....

~~~

I sat in the front pocket of Henri's cardigan as she walked through the halls of our college, the slight bouncing and swaying making me slightly nauseous. I didn't have this problem when *Missy* carried me around... It'd been nice to see my parents again, once Henri finished waking up and had taken me out to see them, we'd spent the whole day together, just talking and catching up on all the little life things that had happened over the last two weeks.

It'd been weird to wake up in my room again and get dressed to go to school, just like I had before all this happened, but now that I was here, it wasn't too different from being at college with Marissa. Henri had cried when she called Marissa and heard about the exchange, and she'd begged me to let her keep me the whole time, but in the spirit of the truce, she'd let the matter go.

"Do I have to watch her matches?" Henri asked under her breath as she made her way down the stairs to the tennis courts "Or can I leave?"

"Uh, I mean, if you leave, you have less time with me, I guess." I said

"...Drat. I will stay." she muttered, pushing open the door that lead to the fenced in area the teams played in.

I pointed across the court to the benches "Hey, there's a little umbrella, I bet that's where Kensey is, let's go sit there."

Henri sighed and carefully walked around the court to the benches and set me down next to Kensey. She had a her-sized chair with a small umbrella over it, and a bottle of something blue that she was sipping. I waved to her and made my way under the shade and sat on the bench next to the chair.

"Hey, Kay!" I said "Is Quince winning?"

"Mm, she won the first game, but this one's giving her trouble, they've been fighting over the last point for like four rounds."

"I never liked how the points worked in tennis." Henri complained "It is frustrating. If you get to forty points, you should win, not 'get to forty and win but only if you get one more point and also have two more points than the other person at the same time'. And why do you not count points above forty as points? They call it 'advantage' and you cannot tell how many points you *really* got. And why do the points go fifteen, thirty, forty? Why not forty five? Why not one, two, three? The whole thing is so confusing."

"You're just salty they didn't let you join." I said, taking the bottle of blue stuff Kensey handed me

"I won my matches!" Henri complained "They were just being mean."

"You play too, then, Henri?" Kensey asked

"Ah, no, I learned how to one year, I took lessons, but I did not make the team." she said, glaring at Quince out on the court

"It actually *was* just because the other girls were being mean." I said "They just didn't want her in their special club."

"Their special club being a college tennis team that's not allowed to play against other schools?"

"Worse, a *high school* tennis team that's not allowed to play against other schools." I said, nodding

"Gods, these girls are so petty..." Kensey muttered

"Tell me about it." Henri grumbled "Imagine being so petty and small minded that you try to ruin a girl's life for six years just because she had a slight accent and her dad sells animal products."

"I will say, you trying to *hide* your accent is a lot more noticeable than the accent would be, in my opinion." Kensey said "You enunciate everything so carefully, it's, I don't know, like you're trying to prove you don't have one anymore."

*The Feeling of Being Valued*   433

"Listen, I spent a lot of time learning this language, I will speak it with the care and effort I put into learning it." Henri said, sounding annoyed

"It's not *that* bad." I said, sipping my blue drink "You do sound a little formal sometimes though, nothing wrong with that."

"Miss Lund liked it at least." Kensey said, rolling her eyes

"Do you have a problem with me being polite to the woman who could have my best friend killed, Kensey?" Henri snapped "Or do you think maybe I should be making her angry instead?"

"No, fuck, I just- you really sucked up to her is all." Kensey said "It made me uncomfortable to see you so willing to agree with her saying those horrible things."

"I guess sometimes people just have to do that, though." I said "In lots of ways, like, if a skinhead is saying shit to you about, I don't know, racist stuff, arguing could like, get you stabbed, right? You gotta just be as neutral as you can in that situation."

"I disagree, full stop." Kensey said "If a skinhead is saying shit and you don't argue back, you're just as bad as they are."

"Ok, but- Ok, so here's an example." I said "You and Quince are coming out of the mall, a skinhead starts making comments about her because she's black. He's six foot three, you're, what, seven inches? If you start arguing with him, he's going to smack you out of Q's hand and stomp on you. Do you argue with him?"

"I'd get stomped, yeah." Kensey said "I'm not going to let people talk shit, and again, if you *do* let people talk shit, you're complacent in what they're doing."

"That sounds dangerous..." Henri said "Isn't it better to survive or protect yourself so you can address the problems from a place of security on your own terms?"

"The shit talkers are *already* doing that." Kensey pointed out "*Everywhere* is their place of security, it's all on their terms. You have to be willing to face them on those terms and still stand up for yourself and what you believe."

"I don't know if I agree with that..." I muttered "I'm so, so fragile, I gotta protect myself."

"So if we go to the mall with Quince later and someone says shit, you'll ignore it?" Kensey asked

"It's- they won't do that, we don't have that kind of problem around here." I said "It's not a real example."

"Well it's the one *you* picked." Kensey said, shaking her head "Look, I understand your point of view, but protecting yourself is useless when others who can't protect themselves are still suffering."

"Now I just feel guilty for some reason." Henri said, frowning "I- I do not think I did anything wrong, but- I feel, hm, not good about something."

"Why do you care so much about this anyway?" I asked Kensey

"My ex was a nazi." she said "I didn't know until we were already together, and I told myself I'd be able to change him, but it doesn't work like that, he just drug me down."

"Fuck..." I said "Fuck, that's gotta be rough."

"Worst part of my life. Why do you think I became an alcoholic?" she said, looking at me firmly

Quince jogged up and dropped onto the bench next to us, on the other side of Kensey from Henri and dug a sports drink out of her bag. She gulped a few mouthfuls of it and sighed contentedly.

"Damn, did you see that win? It took so fucking long, but I finally pulled it off." she bragged "I still have at least two more matches though, and I'm already tired after that one."

"We were watching!" I said "You're very good at tennis."

"Yeah, I bet *you* were, ass watcher." Quince said, poking me with her finger "What were you guys talking about, Henri? You look upset."

"Ah, we were discussing if we'd stand up to someone who was being racist to you at the mall later." Henri said "It was a very tough conversation."

"What the fuck?" Quince said "I- fuck, what?"

"It wasn't just about you, it was about if you have an obligation to protect yourself from harm, or if you have the obligation to protect others from harm." Kensey explained "You were just the example."

"Well don't use me as an example anymore, that's weird." Quince said "If someone tries any of that shit, I can take care of myself anyway. I know judo, fuck."

"It was just a debate, we didn't mean anything by it." I said sheepishly

"I don't like to think about you guys having debates." Quince said "Y'all are lil babies, I want to think about you dressing up in cute clothes and riding in my pockets."

"They're still human beings." Henri said roughly

"Human beings that fit in my pocket, yeah." Quince said "They're adorable. Anyway, what was that about going to the mall later?"

"It was just part of the example, it was more like *if* we went to the mall." I said

"We can go to the mall, I don't care." she said "I need to get you food anyway, according to Marissa, and the health food shop has your stuff."

"So we'd be going to the local mall, not the one in Camden?" Kensey asked

"Yeah, I already went to the class B shop in Camden like two days ago, you don't need any more toys." Quince said "I'm down for it after my next matches, Henri, you coming?"

"I, ah, I do not have money for the mall." she said "My savings are still tied up in the crowd funds, and my allowance doesn't come until Friday. That is why you have to take care of Amber for me, remember?"

"So? Just don't buy anything." Quince said

"That is rude, if you go to an establishment, you should buy something there." Henri said firmly

"If they don't have something you want, you shouldn't have to buy anything, that's not a rule, Henri." Kensey said

"But to *plan* on going to a store with the intention of not buying something?" she shook her head "That is just impolite."

"Whatever, we'll have fun without you I guess." Quince said "I'll talk to you girls later, my rest time is over, wish me luck!"

She got up and stretched her back and legs as the other player made her way over to the field. I very carefully looked at Kensey while she warmed up, refusing to give Quince the satisfaction of me admiring her form. Kensey's eyebrow quirked up as she made eye contact, and her mouth pulled into a small grin. I nodded solemnly, still looking at her as Quince finished up. She grabbed the sports drink next to me and Kensey and took a gulp, before patting Kensey on the head and jogging back to the court.

"So, I'm guessing that display has something to do with her nickname for you?" Kensey asked

"Nickname?" Henri leaned in

"Yeah, she called Amber 'ass watcher', there's a story there, I bet."

I frowned and shook my head "Just Quince being rude again. I'm allowed to watch my girlfriend play sports, it's literally not an issue."

"You like watching Marissa play sports?" Henri asked, looking thoughtful

"Yeah, she's really good, and her body is-" I stopped and looked at Henri "If you take up sports again out of the blue, I'll *know* what you're doing, you know."

"Trust me, I did not have any intention of hiding what I was doing, Amber." Henri said "If you can see through my plans, then that simply means you appreciate the dedication I have for you. Now, what sports do you like to watch?"

I glared at her "...Golf."

"Ah, Well. I will do my own research I suppose." Henri said "I do have the computer with your internet history, after all."

I flushed "So help me, Henri, if you so much as check my *bookmarks*, I will tell the whole world about your 'fanfiction' phase."

"Oh, even if you don't tell the world, can you just tell me?" Kensey said "That sounds like a fun bit of lore..."

Henri narrowed her eyes at me and bit her lip. "Ok, Amber. We're still in a truce. I will just find out what sport will win you over the hard way."

She stood up "I will be going now, I have lots of sports to sort through after all, enjoy your time with Quince."

She set the bag with my stuff in it on the bench next to us, and got up, nodding to us, and then she was gone.

"So, do you think we can get her to try log rolling?" Kensey asked "That's a sport."

"I don't want to encourage her." I moaned "I think she forgot the meaning of the truce..."

"I'm sure it'll be fine." Kensey said "There's nothing wrong with her trying a few sports, right?"

I hadn't thought there would be any problems, but hearing it said out loud, I was starting to have my doubts...

## Chapter Twenty-Four

Kensey held my hand as I tried to get a better view out of Quince's pocket. She'd gotten this jacket for the pocket on the front just so she could show off Kensey as she walked around, but with Kensey being a full three inches taller than me, I kept sliding down into the pocket where I couldn't peek out. I wrapped my arms over the lip of the pocket and hung there, looking around at the mall around us. My arms would go to sleep soon, but for now at least, I could see.

"You sure do wiggle a lot more than Kensey does." Quince said, glancing down at me

"I want to see, it's hard to keep my head out of the pocket." I complained

"Well you should have thought about that before being so short." she said

I sighed and dropped back down into the pocket, sitting at Kensey's feet. It wasn't *that* interesting, just the same mall I'd been to dozens of times before, just this time everything loomed around me and people pointed and whispered about me slightly more. Quince's pocket wasn't as cozy as Marissa's; while Marissa usually wore softer clothes, Quince seemed to like the shiny, attention grabbing ones. The jacket in question was made of some kind of plastic or latex, and was glossy all over. It was red with black highlights and yellow under the arms, and it looked like it belonged on a fashion model, not a girl casually walking around her local mall. I wished I'd have brought my tablet, at least then I wouldn't just be stuck down at the bottom of a pocket with nothing to do.

Kensey ducked inside the pocket with me, and poked my shoulder "Hey, you ok?" she asked

"I'm just getting a little tired of not being able to see what's going on when I'm in public, or like, being hidden in people's clothes." I said "I know I was never very flashy before, but I want to be able to be noticed as a person and not just as a pet, I guess."

"Oh, yeah." she sat down and curled her knees up to give us more room "I'm still coming to terms with that myself. I'm one of, what? A percent of a percent of the population who's a class B? The people here are staring at me, but I can't even blame them, I'm probably the only class B they'll ever see."

"Mm, it's just- our community is so small, I've been spending more time on AntMound recently, and it feels like the same names keep coming up in the comments of every post or article I look at, it's isolating, and not being able to be physically *seen* by people even when I'm spending time at the mall with friends just makes me feel so..."

"Small?" she asked with a slight smile

I slumped "Yeah, I guess. I love being around Marissa because I feel like I'm her whole focus, like, I'm taking up space in her mind all the time. I don't feel small, I feel normal, even if she's in charge, she values me."

"I think that's important, but it's unrealistic for most people to have that." Kensey said "If most people had a partner who thought about them that much I'd assume they were being love bombed."

"I don't think she's doing that." I said "She's too mean to me to be love bombing me, but even when she's mean, I'm still like, her focus. It's a safe sort of loved feeling, even when she's hurting me a little."

"I almost feel jealous of you, hearing you describe it like that." she sighed, leaning over on me "I just hope Quince cares about me even a fraction as much. Just, y'know, hopefully she's not as mean. I don't want to be hurt at all."

"You two know I can hear you, right?" Quince asked, fishing her hand into the pocket and pulling us out, smushing us together as she lifted us up

"I'm not going to 'hurt' you, Kay. I just want you to be all cute and sweet for me."

"I *am* cute and sweet!" she said, untangling her limbs from mine "Aren't I?"

"Yeah, you are, but like, we're at the mall, talk about what you want to buy, or like, judge people based on what they're wearing, not politics or philosophy or whatever."

"Welllll," Kensey said "not to get too, um, 'un-cute', but talking about wants and what we need to be happy is technically philosophy, and when you think about it, judging people because of their outfits is political, because we're reinforcing the social classes based on what the masses can afford to buy."

Quince slowed to a stop and frowned at Kensey and me in her hands "I really don't want to think that way. Who cares if I'm reinforcing the social classes? I just want to point at someone wearing a flannel and patterned sweats and laugh, is that too much to ask?"

A woman walking past who'd obviously inspired Quince's example turned and gave her a dirty look.

"No, not you, I meant it in a political sense!" Quince told her as she walked off, and looked back to us "Ugh, see? That, that's why we come to the mall, to find people like *that* who are so obviously below us they're legal, viable targets to make fun of. It's not political at all."

"Seeing people as less than you is pretty political." I said "What about us, do you see us as less than you?"

"Uh, yeah?" she said, turning towards the food court "I *own* one of you and the other I've seen sprawled on the locker room floor covered in beans and weenies. I'd say I'm pretty far above you."

"You're the one who *put* the beans and weenies on me." I pointed out "That doesn't make you better, it just makes you mean."

"Ok, so I'm mean. You *like* mean, right?" she asked, getting in line for Chinese food

"It's not about if I like people who are mean, it's about ranking people based on perceived value." I said "I don't think size or bank accounts can accurately inform us to a person's valu- ow!"

I glared at Kensey "Stop that, why'd you do that?"

"Do you like me more now?" she asked innocently, pinching me again "I'm being mean to you..."

"Ow! Stop it, no!" I said, trying to scoot away from her. Unfortunately Quince's hands were too small, and I ended up rolling back on top of her again "We're on the same side, dumbass."

"Whatever, I just want to get home, I've been going since I got compressed, and I really want to crash." she said

"That's not true, you spent all Friday night on Amber's couch." Quince said "And Sunday we just had that party for my dad's partner, we had like, all morning to chill."

"Friday I was dying of stomach pains, I was throwing up every few minutes." Kensey reminded her "And I think having to be around that many giants from mid afternoon until almost midnight *more* than counters the couple hours we spent playing dress-up."

"Well- oh, yes, may I get a water and an order of-" Quince squinted at the menu as the worker frowned at her "Uhh, Amber, what's good?"

"What?" I asked "I'm Korean, not Chinese."

"Ugh, no, I meant because you're *poor* and you probably ate at low quality places like this a lot." she said, rolling her eyes

I glared up at her "Figure it out."

"Fiiine..." she said "I'll have the walnut shrimp then, god."

"Anyway," Kensey said as Quince went to the other end of the counter to wait "I was just saying I was looking forward to getting home and crashing for a bit."

"Yeah, and I don't have class tomorrow morning because the teacher has jury duty, so I'll be watching videos and drinking seltzer until I fall asleep in my recliner." Quince said, smiling at the thought

"I'd really like to get sleep though, especially if we're going to be going to school together later in the day." Kensey said "Being passed around and shown off all day was really exhausting."

"You can go to sleep whenever." Quince said, dropping us into her pocket so she could grab the food "I'll just close your lid."

I pushed Kensey's shoulder off my face "How will the sleeping arrangements work?"

"I figured you'd just share Kensey's bed." Quince sat down and pulled us back out, setting us on the table next to her tray "Unless Kensey has some hangups about sharing a bed with a lesbian."

"I- uh," Kensey looked at me "I guess not? I wouldn't have thought of it if you hadn't said something."

"I'm not a creep or something." I said, my feelings hurt "I can sleep on the floor if it's a problem."

"No, it's fine." Kensey said "I'm cool with it, you're like, tiny, I'll barely notice you're there."

"I vo'e she hash to slee' on the floor." Quince said though a mouthful of nuts and seafood

"No one is sleeping on the floor, damnit." Kensey sighed "I'm too old for her and she's taken, it's not an issue."

"Yeah, stop making it weird." I said "Henri and I slept in the same bed for years whenever-"

I stopped "Oh. Uh, well that was on her, not me."

"Way to help your case there, shrimp." Quince said sarcastically, punctuating the word 'shrimp' by stabbing a shrimp as big as me and biting it in half.

"...As sickening as it is to see you eat, I'm kinda getting hungry. Don't forget to get me some meals." I said, watching her try and pile honey-covered walnuts on another piece of shrimp

"What the fuck?" she said "I'm literally just eating, what's sicking about it?"

"No no, I get what she means actually." Kensey said "It's like, you see a giant eat something, and they take a bite, and you're hit with a wave of 'oh, fuck, they could do that to *me*, and these things eat *meat*...'. It's like that one old movie with the dinosaurs? On the island?"

"It *is*!" I said "Gosh, I was watching Marissa eat recently, and it reminded me of something but I didn't know what, it's totally that!"

"So I eat like a dinosaur?" Quince asked, setting down her fork. She looked uncomfortable, and once again I felt a sense of power at making her insecure. It seemed she had some kind of hang-ups about looking scary or gross to class Bs, I'd have to see if I could use that again...

"It's all giants, really." Kensey said "It's just scary to be casually hanging out with someone who could chomp you in half like a gingerbread man while they're eating."

"I- I have to eat though, I need my protein for tennis, and I get hungry a lot..." Quince said "I don't know how to fix this..."

I looked at her with surprise, she was actually, legitimately upset about this. She looked at her half-eaten shrimp and made a face, dabbing at her face with a napkin.

"It's ok..." Kensey said "I wasn't trying to hurt your feelings, I just was making an observation. It doesn't bother me, you can finish eating."

"Yeah, it's not a you thing, it's ok." I said, nodding reluctantly. "Sorry we made you uncomfortable."

Quince looked at us with a nervous look, but picked her fork back up to eat again, but she held her napkin in front of her mouth when she took a bite.

"I think after I'm done we'll head to the health food store then go home..." she said "I want to just not think about stuff."

"That sounds good to me." Kensey said quietly.

Quince watched us closely for the rest of her meal, an almost sad look on her face, and she barely spoke to us for the rest of the shopping trip, opting to give nods or gentle 'mh hm's when we tried to engage with her. I hoped I hadn't hurt her and Kensey's relationship somehow, but with her being quieter than I'd ever seen her, there was no way to tell.

~~~

We sat on Kensey's bed watching a movie about some old guy who was re-living his teen years after a weird accident. It was ok, not the greatest movie of all time, but it was watchable. I slurped my noodles and kicked my feet out, it was a nice evening. Quince was on the other side of the room from us watching something that sounded loud and dramatic, but I couldn't make out what was going on from here. Kensey was eating a roast of some kind, and we had made plans to split a 'pint' of ice cream once we finished our meals.

It was turning out to be a good night, I'd chatted with Marissa a little and she was settled into rehab already, doing crafts and making friends. Kensey had been in rehab herself, and was even able to give her some tips to make her short stay a little better. If you'd told me I'd end up being good friends with a lady in her mid thirties a few weeks ago, I'd have been pretty confused, but she was a nice person, and I really liked spending time with her.

I drained the broth from my ramen, and sighed contentedly, full of warm and cozy in the blanket. I could fall asleep right now if I wanted, but the main character had just re-enrolled in high school and I was interested to see how things played out for him. I leaned against Kensey, her upper arm big enough to me to use as a pillow, and tightened the blanket around me. I hoped we could do this more often, she was still much bigger than me, but in a 'big sister' way, not a 'I'm a giant' way. I heard footsteps sound out through the room, and the lid to the desk slid open, Quince peeking down at us almost nervously.

"Uh, I know it's- uh, hey I wanted to like, hang out, is that ok?" she asked

I was impressed with her for asking, I'd expected her to have just grabbed us whenever she wanted to play with us. This was great to see, but I did wonder if it was because of our comments earlier or if she honestly was starting to respect us. I glanced at Kensey, who paused the movie and shrugged.

"Yeah, I'm ok with that. Me and Amber were gonna get some ice cream later, so you might have to bring us back over for that once we're all digested from dinner, if that's ok." she said

"Ok, no, that's not a problem." she said "I was just watching stuff and I was thinking about you two over here hanging out, and, uh, I guess I wanted to hang out too?"

"We can hang out." I said "I guess we'll sit in your lap while you watch videos?"

"Or- I don't know, I have four recliners, you can share a different one if you prefer." she said, looking over her shoulder

"I don't mind sitting in your lap, it's ok." Kensey said, putting down her empty plate "Here, we're ready whenever you are."

Quince carefully picked us up, one in each hand and brought us over to one of the recliners, a pile of corn puffs, chocolates, and seltzer cans in the one next to it. I noticed Quince's hands didn't *smell* like corn puffs, they smelled like, hm, vanilla shea butter? She'd washed her hands and lotion-ed up before coming to see us. She placed us on the recliner next to her, got into hers, crossed her legs, and made a 'tent' with the blanket, tucking it under her knees and butt to make a wide, springy area for us and moved us into it. She cracked open a can and set it in the cupholder of the armrest and turned the giant TV back on.

"I'm not going to have a lot." she said, pointing to the can "Just like, two or three, I'm not going to get tipsy or anything, I promise."

"That's good." I said "I know bad stuff tends to happen when people get drunk around me."

"Yeah, yeah, no, I won't get drunk." she said, looking at Kensey "I just wanted to spend time with you guys. What do you like to watch?"

"Like, on the internet?" Kensey asked "I mostly watch compilations of cat videos and sometimes people talking about current events."

"I like the videos about class Bs." I said "But like, you have to be careful, some of the content creators are horrible to their class Bs, and no one even notices for some reason."

"Horrible how?" Kensey asked

"Like, making them run obstacle courses, or play with animals, or like, making them do trendy challenges like eat way too spicy foods, or like- they make videos about how not to treat class Bs, but they use their own class Bs in the example sections of what not to do? Messed up stuff."

"Personally, I like the videos of people doing stuff like filling a swimming pool with slime, or playing pranks on their friends." Quince said

"I'm down for whatever, really." Kensey said, laying back against Quince's knee

"You guys can pick." I said "I'll watch anything."

"Ok, um, how about..." Quince picked a video from a class B creator I knew, and we settled in as he did a 'room tour' of his class B's room. He'd 'tricked out' the whole place with rock climbing walls, zip-lines, swimming pools, and more. The class B in question looked overwhelmed and out of his element, but was doing his best to do reaction faces and look excited at each new 'upgrade'. We watched in silence for a while before Quince turned it down, and her hands came to wrap around us softly.

"Should I be doing that?" she asked "I don't think my parents would like me taking one of the guest rooms to make into a one tenth scale theme park, but I can section off part of my room and set up like, a pool and stuff."

"I don't need all that." Kensey said "I have a hot tub and a nice apartment, I bet that guy doesn't even *use* all the stuff his guardian built him, it's just for clicks."

"Well- I just feel like I need to be doing *more*." Quince said, sounding frustrated

"As long as you treat us with respect and stuff, that's all we ask, really." I said "You're doing ok so far."

"No, look, you and Marissa? That's my only basis for a relationship like this, and I'm not even coming close to that. Like, I know I'll be able to afford a giant house like yours eventually and give Kensey a mansion, but, like, I can't give her the relationship and safety Marissa gives you."

"You can!" Kensey said "You just need to *be* someone who's safe to be around, and I'll feel safe! you're working on it"

"It's not that simple." Quince said flumping back into the seat "I want you to be all cute and fun for me, and you're so, so perfect and sweet and pretty, and like, in return, I'm- I thought I could do it, I thought I could just be myself and have a tiny lil baby person to take care of and play with, but just being *around* you makes me all... I don't know..."

"Like, responsible?" I asked "No, not like that, like..." Quince's face twisted "I feel disgusting being around you guys. I feel like making you guys be around me is like *torture* or something for you. I'm scary when I eat, my hands smell like cheese or bread or whatever I touch, I have body hair everywhere, all my flaws stand out to you, I'm supposed to be taking care of you but every time I try to be silly or tease you like I do everyone else, the mood shifts and I feel like an asshole because I'm flexing my power or privilege or something and that's scary to you. I just feel so, so *gross*, and you guys keep referring to class As as 'giants' and that just makes me feel even worse and I'm *already* insecure about my height, and-"

She pressed her hands into her face and shivered "This isn't how it was supposed to be, I was supposed to feel special and cute and have a little friend with me all the time, not feel like a monster..."

"You're *not* a monster, Quince." Kensey said "I'm sorry, I didn't know saying those things would hurt your feelings, you seemed so indomitable, and I guess I didn't consider how telling you that stuff would make you feel."

"I'm 'indomitable' when it's the girls, they're *trying* to hurt me, to make me insecure. It rolls off like water." Quince explained "With you, it's like, I actually *care* about how you see me, and I feel like you see me like some gross creature keeping you prisoner."

"I know the size difference is... a big deal." I said "It makes class As much scarier, yeah, and sure we can see lots of details and stuff, but we're not judging you for it. If anything it reminds me how *I* look under a microscope, having cheese hands or not waxing your forearms isn't a flaw, it's just humanity, unfiltered, up close."

"I really don't see you as a monster." Kensey said "When you put me in that pencil case, yeah, ok, I saw you as a monster. But since then? I see you as like, a mix between a weird aunt and a little sister. You've really grown a lot in the past few days, I'm honestly impressed."

Quince took a careful breath, one she probably thought hid how close to tears she was and nodded "I didn't realize how much I cared for your opinion until I really, actually hung out with you at the Camden mall. Seeing you pick stuff out and get excited about the hot tub and be all cute about your new clothes, and seeing how much Amber cared for Marissa, just- head over heels, fuck, I just wanted you to actually *want* to be around me."

"You started to value *her*, instead of valuing *owning* her." I said

"...I guess that's a good way to put it." Quince agreed

"Well I appreciate you caring about me, Q." Kensey said "I won't call you a giant anymore, and please know that I'm not grossed out by you, and I'll get used to you eating, it's not gross, it just reminds me how small I am. You're doing good, and we're getting along really well, there's no problems on my end, ok?"

"...Ok." Quince said "I just kinda feel like shit about it all, and I know I shouldn't, I've been hurting people around me since I was in middle school with no remorse, but like, fuck. I just wanted you so bad, and I wanted you to like me, and I had all these thoughts about what it'd be like, and... fuck, I don't know."

"You honestly should feel more remorse than you do about hurting people." I said "This is normal, caring about what people think about you is normal."

"So I've heard." Quince said "I can't believe I'm actually sitting here thinking about what *you* of all people think of me."

"Maybe it's the start of a new arc for you guys?" I said "Growing up and all that. Marissa is starting to relax more these days, drunken fights not withstanding, you're starting to think about other people, Tracy is just following you two, maybe you guys just let off of your grip on everyone and let yourselves mature?"

"Yeah, that would work, up until Darcy comes back from her vacation." Quince said, rolling her eyes.

"Shit, yeah, that- hm." I said sadly

"Who's Darcy?" Kensey asked "You guys have mentioned her a couple times, I'm guessing she's a part of your friend group?"

"She's more like Marissa's rival." Quince explained "Except *she's* over the whole rivalry thing, and Marissa won't drop it, so she *can't* drop it, and they just end up being super cold and petty to each other. She's good though, her family is in the government, like, *all* of them are in the government somewhere. She's kinda a pothead, and she likes coke a little too much for my tastes, but she's a lot of fun if you want to do something stupid and get away with it."

"She's the main reason the rest of the girls never got in trouble for being terrible people." I said "She's not the worst one to deal with directly, more like, she's the threat over your head. If you go to the teachers, your house might get foreclosed on after the bank starts ignoring the payments, if you try to fight back too hard, your mom might get pulled over and falsely jailed for drunk driving, if you dare to actually try and do something to *her*... well, Marissa has admitted to having access to hitmen, and I'm pretty sure Darcy put her in contact with them."

"That's- I *really* don't want to meet her, do I?" Kensey asked "She sounds like a cross between a mobster and a politician."

"So a politician?" I joked "Yeah, stay away from her. I'll probably have to see her fairly regularly because she's Marissa's best friend, but..."

"Hey, *I'm* Marissa's best friend!" Quince protested "They hate each other!"

"Mm, I think *I'm* actually her best friend." I said "but like, she spends more time with Darcy than you, usually."

"That's only because she's trying to get an edge on her, not because she actually cares about her." Quince muttered

"So now you care what Marissa thinks of you too?" I asked "Wow, you really *are* changing!"

"No, I'm just-" a knock on the door interrupted Quince and she turned to the entrance to her room "Come in?" she called out, confused

Miss Ayana walked in with a tray of scones and a couple mugs of tea in her hand "Do you mind if I join you sweetie? I wanted to get to know our new housemate a little more."

"Uh, we're just watching videos." Quince said, sounding like she *did* mind, but didn't know how to say it

"What kinds of videos?" Ayana asked, carefully sitting in the seat next to Quince and handing her one of the mugs

"This guy made a kind of theme park or something in his house for his class B." Kensey said, pointing "Look, it even has a water slide that's six feet long! That's like, um, I think almost a hundred feet relative to the class B's size?"

"That doesn't sound safe." Ayana said, frowning

"It's not." I said "the class B experiences relative speeds of over three hundred miles an hour. The slide ends in a three foot long foam pool with a crash-pad at the other side"

"And that's legal?" she asked, sipping her tea

"You'd be surprised what's legal when it comes to class Bs, mom." Quince said

Miss Ayana gave her a look "Legality doesn't mean something's ok, Q."

"I know, I know!" she said, rolling her eyes "I wasn't planning on building a water slide for Kensey anyway."

She sipped her own tea and frowned "Is this the honey gingerbread? I thought that was a winter tea."

"Well, I like it, so it's an anytime tea." Ayana said matter of factly

"I like it too, it goes well with the scones." Quince said

"Would you like a bit of scone, Amber? I know you liked it last time. They're a little stale, hence the tea, but I can share my tea as well if you like?" Ayana offered "Kensey, I know you have a sensitive stomach, but if you'd like to risk it, you can have some too!"

"Oh, thank you Miss Ayana, but I'm having ice cream with Kensey in a little bit." I said "I appreciate the offer though!"

Ayana gave me a smile and settled back into her seat, watching the two of us in Quince's lap "So what were all of you doing in here? Just watching the videos?"

"Ugh, *Jesus*, mom, it's like having a boy over. Yes, we were just watching the videos, having a girl talk, nothing bad." Quince said, shaking her head

"Well, with the things I've caught you doing in your room with people, do you blame me for being a little suspicious?" Ayana asked

"Oooh, what sorts of things?" Kensey asked "Dish!"

"Well, one time she'd had her friends over for a sleepover..."she started

"Mom, no!" Quince said, shaking her head, but Ayana kept talking anyway

"It was her turn to host, and they were playing that punishment game they'd made, based on one of Quince's shows? And I open the door because I smelled pot, and I find *Quince* of all people, lying on the floor, stripped down to her bra and covered in lit candles. The little kind you put in jack-o-lanterns?" she laughed

"Darcy made eye contact with me and lit a joint off of Quince's ribcage, *daring* me to say something. I just backed out slowly and closed the door behind me. I know better than to risk my husband's practice over a little weed."

"It was part of the game." Quince said "You *never* go back on a bet."

"The next day, I saw them in the pool, and Quince had little rings all over her front where the metal tins of the candles had burned her..." Ayana sighed "If Darcy didn't have a black eye too, I'd have probably talked to her parents over the whole thing."

"The black eye was from a handless cartwheel she failed." Quince said "And the candles were a Marissa thing, Darcy just thought it was funny to use me as a lighter."

"You lot sure live interesting lives." Kensey said, looking at Quince and smiling "In my days we just hung out behind the video store and drank wine coolers."

"I miss wine coolers..." Ayana sighed "They were not 'good' by any stretch, but they had a flavor the modern stuff just doesn't have, I would pay so much for a six pack..."

"Mm, they really were something else." Kensey agreed "The buzz off of them was different than the seltzers they sell now, it was more dipsy, more cozy, somehow. I also really liked the red wine with the train on it? That was so, so good... got you drunk as hell super fast."

"You know *why*, right?" Miss Ayana said, smirking "They put brandy in it, it wasn't pure wine. I need to find some of that again, re-live my youth."

"This is the problem with old people." I said to Quince "Put them in any situation for too long, and they'll start gushing about how good it was to be our age."

"They can gush all they want, when my mom was my age, she already had me, and I'm *not* ready for that." Quince said, shaking her head

"You were a terror and a half." Ayana shook her head "But I wouldn't trade you for the world."

"That's sweet of you." Kensey said "I never wanted kids, I always wanted to live for myself, but sometimes I still got the urge. I don't think I'd have made a good mother though."

"You still could!" Ayana said "You could find a nice man, you never know!"

"*I* know." I said "The odds of two people compressed at different rates having a kid together is around point zero two percent if the woman is ovulating. The odds of two people being compressed at the exact same rate? It's almost infinitesimally small. The odds of a compressed person surviving giving birth? About twenty percent."

The conversation stopped there for a moment while everyone processed what I'd said.

"So you'll pretty much never have kids?" Quince asked me "That's kinda good to know at least."

"I guess." I said "Not that it matters, I'd basically be a single mom even if I did find a way to have a kid, it's not like Marissa can help care for a baby the size of her fingernail."

"Did you want to be a mom?" Kensey asked me

"I wanted to be able to choose I guess." I said "I'm not too worried about it. If anything, I'll convince Marissa to have a kid, and we'll raise it together."

"I'm sorry about that, it sucks to think about that..." Quince said "I'd never seen a compressed baby before, I didn't think about why."

"They exist from natural compression, just like compressed kids exist." I said "But it's illegal to document them outside a lab because of safety concerns, and it's illegal for anyone to buy a class B under the age of fifteen unless they're directly related, and even then, any class Bs under the age of ten need to be kept in a group home until the age of ten."

"Holy shit, so these kids that compress, they just get shoved in a box and left there until their parents come get them?" Kensey asked, shocked

"Uh, I think the group homes are nice?" I said, unsure "I just know they're state owned and run."

"How do you know all this, Amber?" Miss Ayana asked me "Did you take a class on it?"

"It's all on the app we class Bs use for social media." I said "I just picked it up reading stuff on there I guess, and in videos."

"It's weird to think about lil baybees having babies." Quince said, petting me "I'm kinda glad it's not a common problem."

"Quince, Amber and Kensey are grown women." Ayana said firmly "Please don't call them 'babies'."

"She just means I'm small and cute and she's taking care of me." Kensey said "Quince is working hard to respect me and provide a safe, fulfilling environment for me, right?"

"I guess, yeah." she said, petting Kensey too "I just like thinking of you as little sweeties, I know you're like, an adult or whatever, but it's weird to have the person I'm taking care of be older than me."

"I think it's good for you to have her around." Ayana said "She seems like a very respectable lady, and you could learn a thing or two from her I bet!"

"Mom, you're making it weird." Quince said, making a face "I buy her cute clothes and she rides in my pocket, she doesn't teach me stuff."

Ayana pursed her lips, but nodded "Ok, I understand. I just want to see Kensey live her life as comfortably as possible, we have the means to provide for her after all."

"I'm very happy with my situation, Ayana." Kensey assured her "I miss my cats, and I'll miss my dad and my group meetings, but we're starting a new group meeting tomorrow, so I'm sure I'll make more friends there!"

"Ohhh damnit." Quince groaned "I did agree to go to that, and *Henri* is gonna be there..."

"A group meeting?" Ayana asked "For what?"

"It's a meeting for people've been compressed, and for their guardians." I told her "I've been, it's nice. Good crowd of people too."

"That sounds so helpful!" Miss Ayana said, her face lighting up "Quince, I'm so proud of you for taking this initiative!"

"...Thanks." Quince grumbled, but she looked pleased with herself. She put her hands around us and gave us a light 'hug'

"Can we go get that ice cream now?" I asked "I'm feeling snackish."

"Ooh, yeah, and we should watch a movie, videos are fine, but I prefer movies." Kensey said "I know one about a couple who are trying to see if fate wants them to get together, but they keep missing the signs, it's one of my favorites."

"Alright, alright, let's get the ice cream." Quince said, picking us up "Mom, are you going to watch the movie with us?"

Miss Ayana smiled "Of course! I love romances!"

I knew she was trying to help and guide Quince into being more aware and careful with Kensey, but I could tell Quince wasn't having any of it. She'd already come to the conclusions she needed to on her own, and no one likes to be told something they were already planning on doing, especially by their mother. I just hoped this wouldn't throw a wrench into our plans to get Quince to treat Kensey more like a person...

## Chapter Twenty-Five

"This better at least be interesting..." Quince said, standing outside the community center as we waited on Henri

"It should be, I don't know how the class A side is, but I enjoyed the class B one last week when we went." I said "I think it's pretty good overall, it helped me a little at least."

"I can't believe Henri is late..." Quince muttered "She's like, the responsible one or something, right?"

"I don't know if I'd call her *responsible*." I said "she just comes off like that because she's polite."

A man in his late thirties walked up to the door next to us, his hand cupped in front of him. As he passed, he glanced down, and then over at us, stepping over to where Quince stood. In his hand was Nada, and she peered at us resting in Quince's shirt pocket, then smiled and waved, gesturing for the man to step closer.

"I *thought* that was you, Amber!" Nada said, smiling at me "I messaged you Sunday but never heard back, I was worried!"

"Oh, gosh, I'm sorry, I must have missed that..." I said, wincing "I wasn't checking my messages, I was just talking to Marissa directly."

"It's ok, I'm glad you're safe." Nada said "So, is this Henri?" she asked, looking up at Quince

"Fuck no, I'm Quince." Quince said "I'm watching Amber because Henri's a broke bitch."

"I'm Adil, it's nice to meet you all." the man said dipping his head at us

"I'm Kensey? We talked a little on AntFarm?" Kensey said "I'm the one that was barely short enough to be a class B."

"Ant *Mound*," Nada said "And yes, I remember you! It's just such a terrible situation..."

"It's not *that* terrible." Quince said "I take good care of her..."

"No matter how well you care for a class B, it will always be a struggle." Adil said solemnly

"Uh, b-but Quince really cares about me, so it's like, not even a big deal!" Kensey said, putting on a big smile

"Yeah, she's doing pretty good as a guardian." I said "She's really figuring it out."

"That's good to hear." Nada said, looking between the three of us "Why don't we head in so we can get to the groups?"

"We're waiting on Henri..." Quince grumbled "She's supposed to already be here."

"Maybe she's already inside?" Adil asked "You could always pop in and check."

"Ah, nope, there she is." I said, pointing

Henri jogged up from the parking lot and slowed to a stop next to us, catching her breath "Sorry- it was- too many lights were red..." she said, panting

"*This* is Henri." I said "Henri, this is Nada, and her guardian Adil."

Henri waved and straightened up. "So, we shall go in now?" she asked, still out of breath

"Well hello to you too, Henri." Quince snarked

Henri rolled her eyes at her "I just saw you three hours ago at school, get over it."

"We should go ahead and get in, though." Adil said, opening the door to the community center with his free hand.

We all followed him in, and made our way to the rooms in the back, splitting up at the door. As the helper set us down in the little box for the class B meetings, I noticed that all the same people who'd been here last time were already sitting in the seats they'd been sitting in last time. I didn't know if there was assigned seating, but I made my way over to the chair I'd used and sat down looking around the room as we settled, several people giving me a surprised look. Once we were all situated, with Kensey having drug a chair over to me so we'd be together, Nada clapped her hands.

"Alright! Sorry about the late start," she said "I was greeting our newest visitors in the parking lot and time got away from us. Everyone, you'll remember Amber from last week, and she's brought a friend this time, would you like to introduce yourself?"

Kensey stood "Hi, my name is Kensey, and I'm a class B. Uh, I was compressed a week and a half ago or so, and I've been with my guardian, Quince, for about four or five days, and Amber has been sleeping over for the past two nights. Amber said this group would be helpful for us, since Quince originally got me as a pet instead of with the intent to be an actual guardian."

"I hate people like that..." Paul said darkly, pushing his glasses up "My second guardian was that way, she only got me so she could do certain videos with me that people would pay a premium to see, without caring about *my* feelings at all."

"Ah, well, Quince doesn't have interests in 'videos'." Kensey said "And she's started to see me as a person, actually *having* me helped her to realize I'm still a human. When I was just an idea, she was thinking of me differently, I think."

"So do *you* think your relationship is harmful?" Nada asked her

"I think... she's doing her best." Kensey said "It's a two way street, she wants me to be all cutesy and fun, and to be her little pocket friend, and I want her to care for me and respect me and my boundaries. We're both working on giving the other what they want."

"And you, Amber? You've seen their relationship, do you feel it's harmful?" Nada asked me

"Uh, I'm literally dating my guardian, I'm the *worst* person to ask." I said "But, I mean, yeah, I think they're doing ok. Quince opened up about her needs and stuff last night, and it really sounds like she just wants a friend who's not going to hurt or judge her, and Kensey can totally do that."

"Oh gods it's official!?" Babae said, bouncing "Last week you were just talking about how she liked you, you like her back?"

I blushed "Yeah, I do. We, um, 'played' and found out that I like the same kinds of things she does, kinda, and as long as we communicate, I'm kinda... into it? And she's been really- well, not 'sweet', but protective, and treating me like a person, valuing me more, so yeah, we're girlfriends now."

"Totally hot." Marcus said, grinning

"Marcus, we talked about that behavior." Nada said sternly

"I'm glad you're happy with your relationship, but are you sure it's not creating an unhealthy dynamic between you and her?" Arnold asked, looking down at me

"It is *very* unhealthy." I confirmed "It's unbalanced, it's got an unfair power dynamic, she can and does use her size against me, she's still mean to others the same way she was mean to me before, she threatens to hurt me constantly, and she treats me like she owns me still."

"That sounds horrible, I'm so sorry to hear that, Amber..." Paul said

"Can I be honest?" I asked "I, um, really kinda like it like that..."

"It sounds- wait, you *like* it?!" Nada asked, shocked

"Yeah, I know it sounds bad, but it makes me feel safe." I admitted "Hearing her be mean to someone else makes me feel cozy, like she's protecting me or something, and when she's mean to *me* it feels... I don't know, like she's showing me she loves me, because she's not being *really* mean to me."

"Whoah..." Babae said, her eyes wide "You're like, fucked *up* fucked up."

"Maybe." I said "But like I said, I like it, and I want this relationship. I'm an adult, she's an adult, I understand that she has power over me, and I want that. I don't think there's anything *wrong* with it."

"I think it's very dangerous." Nada said "It sounds like you two moved very quickly based on- ah, to be polite- 'attraction' rather than meaningful connection?"

"Is that really bad though?" Marcus asked "All my relationships were based entirely on 'attraction', if someone's hot, you want to be with them. I saw Marissa, she's hot in like that, scary cute way? I'd totally go for her."

"She's at least five years older than you, Marcus, and that's *still* inappropriate behavior." Nada said "Why is it that whenever there's any talk of anything feminine you turn it around to your own interests?"

"Sorry." he muttered "Look, my dating pool is non-existent and my parents have a copy of my tablet on their phones, I have no 'outlets' for anything."

"That's not an excuse to make it other people's problem, Marcus, this is a very serious topic and you need to respect it."

Marcus looked like he was going to cry, and crossed his arms "So when her problem is having a hot girlfriend that does hot stuff she likes, and new girl's problem is having an owner that treats her like she's a special little flower, it's ok to talk about, but when my problem is being alone forever and not being able to even get off, and my parents treating me like a baby, all of the sudden it's all about me and I need to shut up?"

Nada slumped "Marcus..."

Arnold spoke up "No one is saying your problems aren't important, you just keep turning all of the conversations to how attractive you think the topic is, it's making us uncomfortable."

"...Ok." he said, and looked at the ground

"We'll talk about your personal problem with your parents, Marcus." Nada said "I think we can work out something with them to help you out."

He moaned and put his head in his hands "Just- forget about it, fuck, I'll shut up, gods."

"We can talk after the meeting, don't let this make you too upset, ok?" Nada said "Moving on though, I *do* think that both Amber and Kensey are in fairly toxic relationships with their guardians, does anyone see it differently?"

"I think... If Amber likes it, there's not much we can say about it." Paul said "Honestly, I don't agree with the idea of class A and class B relationships at all due to my past, but I think it's her choice. It's not our job to judge that, we need to be guiding her on how to do it safely."

"I have some thoughts about Kensey." Babae said "Um you mentioned your guardian wants you to be 'cute and fun' or something?"

Kensey nodded "Yeah, she likes me to be chipper and sweet, and she likes it when I like, hug her fingers or neck or something."

"Ok, so is that like, something you would normally do? Act chipper and be touchy?" Babae asked

"I usually have lower energy, and I was kind of known for being serious at work and stuff, but if I'm around friends I usually perk up." Kensey said, thinking about it "I'm not super touchy with strangers, but I don't *mind* hugs, I just didn't usually initiate them."

"Interesting..." Babae said "I was hoping it'd be like 'oh, I'm a huge grump and I hate hugs', but you're just kinda middle of the line. My original point was that if you're changing who you are, you're not really living your own life anymore, but I don't know if that applies."

"I think everyone changes who they are around others to some extent, no matter what kind of relationship they have." Kensey said "Everyone knows the 'you have three faces' thing, I don't think this is really all that different. I'm just putting on a face for Quince that makes us get along better."

"But you shouldn't have to put on a face at all, you should be accepted for who you are. The fact that she isn't accepting *you* is building a harmful foundation for your relationship." Nada said, frowning

"Now, I'm not so sure," Arnold said "I know I put on a face or a mask to come here, and I put one on when I'm around my guardians. I actually have two masks around them, one for each. For my main guardian, I make jokes, I'm loud so she remembers I'm there, I try to give her companionship. For her sister, I'm more reserved, she doesn't appreciate my jokes, and she doesn't tend to forget about me as much, so I'm quiet and respectful of her spending her time to take care of me. That's a very normal thing to do, around guardians or around anyone."

"I tend to agree." Paul said "Kensey's relationship, from what little I know of it, seems to be at least fairly normal."

"Her mom is helping a lot too." I said "Miss Ayana? She's Quince's mom, not Kensey's, but like, she's really nice and she's very sweet to us, and she's always making sure to treat us like people and to call Quince out when she's not."

"That's the kind of relationship I *like* to see, support from the family can make things go so much smoother." Nada said "Without my brother, I don't know where I'd be."

"Your daughter too, right?" Babae asked "You called her a big help too. I'm just with my guardian, I wish I had more support."

"My... daughter, yes." Nada said frowning "Family is important, I think that's the main thing to take away here. Amber, what's the family situation in your home?"

"Me?" I asked "Oh, um, well I've gotten to see my parents a couple times now, and it's always fun. They're getting used to everything, but they're just happy I'm in one piece."

"I meant more of what Marissa's family relationship was like." Nada clarified

I blushed "Oh, duh, yeah. Her dad is great, I've only met him once, but I'll see him again Sunday? I think? His wife refuses to talk to me mostly, but fuck her, I went to high school with her and she's always been a brat."

I winced "Miss Lund though, the parent Marissa lives with, she's tried to get Marissa to get rid of me a few times, and uh, she's like, in charge of a bunch of companies? And she wants to use them to, uh, get rid of the compression virus."

"Amber is sugar coating it." Kensey said flatly "Miss Lund wanted Marissa to kill Amber to sever her emotional attachment to class Bs, and is planning on mass-buying class Bs for her labs so she can turn them into vaccines for class As."

"That- that's possible?!" Babae asked, her jaw dropping

"You can't- we're *people*, you can't 'buy' us." Nada said "Her plans won't go very far, I can assure you."

"It's more like, renting us from guardians and draining our blood and fluids and stuff I think." I clarified "She just needs 'pre-compressed particles' or something."

Nada pulled out her tablet "Do you know the name of the companies involved?" she asked

"Well, LundCorp, for one." I said "Our friend Tracy's dad is running the main lab she'll be using, but I don't know the name."

Nada bit her lip "If you can find out the name, let me know. I'd like to write an article about it."

"I thought nothing in these meetings could leave the meetings?" Kensey said, surprised

"That's other kinds of meetings." Nada said, typing "We don't even have legal rights in court as class Bs, so that wouldn't apply here anyway."

"I don't know if that's a good idea." I said "If it got out, Miss Lund would know it came from me or Henri, and she'd try to take action against us."

"I think it'll be ok, what was your friend's name?" Nada asked me

"Oh, it was Tracy... Millon?" I said, not quite sure if I was remembering it right

"Mm, I'll look into this on my own time." Nada said, putting her tablet away "If I do write an article, I may need to interview you, ok?"

"I- I guess." I said, looking at Kensey.

She shrugged and shook her head "I doubt an article on a class B only app would get back to Miss Lund." she assured me

"That aside," Nada said "does anyone else have anything they'd like to bring up to discuss tonight?"

"I actually had something, yeah." Paul said, raising his hand "I wanted to ask everyone's opinions about the merits of creating a class B only zone in shared spaces, something to give us a sense of security? I've been discussing it with my guardian, I like the idea overall..."

As the rest of the meeting went without incident, I couldn't help but wonder if we should have kept our mouths shut about Miss Lund's plans. if she *did* hear we talked, I didn't doubt that there would be serious consequences.

~~~

"So, I didn't *hate* it." Quince said, putting hot sauce on her burrito

"It was not what I expected, but it was useful anyway." Henri agreed

"I liked getting to meet new class Bs, it was really humanizing for me." Kensey said "And there's one who's my height and kinda cute, his name is Arnold, and I mayyy want to see about getting his number next time."

"Awww!" Quince said, hiding her mouth as she bit her food "I'd I've t' shee tha'!"

"I would personally like to go back, they had some very helpful tips on getting Amber to like me more." Henri nodded

"That's exactly why you *shouldn't* go back." I muttered

"It wasn't anything bad, it's fine." Quince assured me "They just told her to like, try and find common ground that you two can engage in at your new size, and that she needs to be careful to not treat you differently and stuff."

"Well that second one was thrown out of the window almost instantly." I said, rolling my eyes

"I am trying very hard, Amber." Henri said, picking at her taco-pizza "I tried things, I found what did not work, I am respecting you, and I am moving on. I would like it if you moved on too."

"You tried to bathe me, it's gonna be a while before I can trust you again." I pointed out

"Oooh, that sounds so cute!" Quince said "Kensey, do you-"

"Nope, I'll bathe myself thank you very much." Kensey said quickly, shaking her head

"Aw, even if you had your bathing suit on?" Quince pouted

"Even if, Quince. Even if." she said

"I think I messed up, to change the subject." I said "I told Nada about Miss Lund's plans, and now she's trying to write an article about it."

"Why is that a mess up?" Quince asked "Isn't it *good* to tell everyone how crazy she is?"

"If a class B publishes an article about it, Miss Lund will know it was me who leaked it." Henri said "She will turn against me, and most likely make things difficult for me to see Amber."

"I mean, what if she goes to jail, though?" Kensey said "It's gotta be illegal to do what she wants to do, right?"

"I have been looking into it," Henri sighed "it is far more legal than I would like, and there are no protections for the class Bs she uses. If she kills them by accident, it would be a fine, not a shutdown, so there is no reason for her to even try to harvest the particles safely."

"That doesn't sound right, if someone kills a class B, they lose their rights to have them, right?" I asked

"Again, not quite." Henri said "It is... tricky, only sometimes. If it was an accident or if it was a reasonable response to a situation, then it would be ok, no consequence. In the case of Miss Lund, the proposed death would be both an accident, and an attempt to help the class B community by eliminating the virus, so it would not effect her studies at all."

"That's fucked..." Quince said "Think we could get Darcy to ask her family to change the laws?"

"That- ohhhh." Henri's eyes widened "I forgot you had that resource. I would love to ask her, when does she get back?"

"A few weeks, I guess." Quince said "She's coming to Amber's 21st, she responded to the invite, so by then at least."

"There was an invite?" I asked "I knew there was a party planned, Marissa told me she was- mm, I think it's a surprise, but I didn't know she'd invited people."

"Yeah, the day she took the picture of you in the library, she put the invite link in the comments. There's like, twenty people coming." Quince said, putting even more hot sauce on her meal

"I will be there, of course." Henri said, pushing her sauce packs over to Quince

"Can I come?" Kensey asked

"I mean, yeah, obvs." Quince said "You think I'd let Marissa show me up? I'm getting you the most princess-y, fluffiest, sparkliest dress I can find, just to fuck with Marissa."

"Yeah, that's fair." Kensey nodded

"Anyway, tomorrow. I guess we just meet up after class and I give Amber over?" Quince asked

"Yes. I will bring her home and we will get ready for the dinner, and from there she will go home with Marissa." Henri confirmed

"Aw, I'll miss my bed-warmer..." Kensey said "Tonight's the last night, huh?"

"I'm looking forward to my own bed again." I said "You kick in your sleep, and your thighs are the size of my waist."

"We could have a sleepover tomorrow night?" Quince said "You could sleep on my pillow!"

Kensey made a face "I'm concerned I'd get squished if you roll over."

"I'm a light sleeper." Quince said "Just like, bite my face, I'll wake up."

"We can *maybe* try it." Kensey said nervously

"Yeah, and we can wear those matching pajamas I got us!" Quince said, grinning "God, I'm excited... Can I snuggle you?"

"You- you're asking?" Kensey said "Um, just hold your breath so you don't burn my eyes, I saw what you did to that burrito, that thing is practically a war crime..."

Quince rolled her eyes and picked her up, rubbing her against her cheek for a moment before pressing her to her chest, just above her collarbone, and setting her back down. Henri looked at me longingly, but I ignored her. She'd have to earn that, and she hadn't yet.

"This is what I wanted..." Quince said, a smile on her face "Just this. Eating cheap tacos, talking about sleepovers, getting to cuddle you, you being all cute and comfortable around me. I feel like a kid or something, *this* is what I wanted when I b- adopted you."

"Well it's a lot nicer than I expected. Thank you for taking care of me, Q." Kensey said gently

"Yeah, no, like, thanks for letting me be, like, me, you know?" Quince said "All three of you. Like, no one to impress, no one to make fun of, just us, being here. I haven't had this since middle school."

"You could have it all the time." Henri said "You just need to get Marissa to calm down and not be so much all the time, and to stop trying to start fights with Darcy."

"Yeah..." Quince said "I- fuck, I'll try. Whatever, I'm just happy to be here."

I looked around at the table and realized that I was pretty happy to be here too. I was excited to see Marissa again soon, and I was looking forward to hanging out with Kensey in front of the TV later, but... It was nice just hanging out and existing at a late night taco place with people I trusted. Henri not withstanding. I'd have to see if Marissa would be down for this, if she'd be ok with the setting, or be cool about it. Of course, I'd have to convince her to go to the group again...

~~~

Henri walked into my old room and set me on the desk, smiling at me proudly "Ok Amber, pick out your outfit for tonight, and I will go change out of my fussball outfit and into something classy."

She looked down at the soccer uniform she'd dug out of my closet from middle school "Or do you think this would be a good thing to wear to the dinner meeting?"

I tried not to look as she flexed and twisted in the far too small outfit, tugging on it as it slid places it shouldn't and highlighted things I'd never have. The name 'Park' was still on the back, and I didn't doubt she was taking a certain pleasure in wearing my name on her clothes, like a brand or something. I covered my face and shook my head at the embarrassment of the whole thing.

"I can't believe you wore that to *school*." I said

"Our college's dress code allows for clothing intended for sports, I am considering joining the fussball team, so I am wearing the uniform, it is within the rules, Amber."

"Can you at least call it soccer?" I asked, looking up and quickly turning my head as her backside turned towards me "Or if not that then *football*, like the rest of the world?"

"I call it how I called it at home, it is a very popular sport in Germany, so I will use the German term." she said, turning her nose up "How does the uniform look on me, Amber? If I join the team, will you get Marissa to bring you to my games?"

"If you join, you'll be wearing a uniform that *fits*, none of this... exhibitionism. I swear, a deep breath or a toe touch and you'd burst right out of that thing, I grew out of it in like the tenth grade."

"It was the twelfth grade and you know it." she corrected me "You did not grow up, down, or sideways until senior year."

"Yeah, yeah. Then I got the freshman fifteen and never looked the same, you sound like my mom." I grumbled

"It was more than fifteen, and it was very much *needed*, ignore your mother." Henri said, frowning "You looked like a thirteen year old boy all through high school, now you look like a woman."

"I look like a mom." I said, rolling my eyes

"You look like a regular person, Amber." Henri said, crossing her arms "Is my body making you insecure? I did not mean to make you feel bad. I simply wanted you to look at me and think of me like... a sexual person, rather than a sister."

"I'm not insecure!" I said "You *telling* me I'm insecure is making me insecure, fuck. I just know I'm a little bit mom-shaped. I'm fine with it, I'm almost twenty one, everyone turns mom-shaped eventually, I just went early"

"You are not mom-shaped!" Henri said "You have a tummy, ja, but you wear it well. I hear tummies are actually *in* now, they are considered attractive!"

"Just go change..." I said "I need to find an outfit that says 'please don't squash me' and I can't do that when you're over there showing me your ass."

"I am sorry," Henri said "but I still see this as a success. I was attractive enough to distract you, this is a good sign!"

"Just go!" I said, blushing

I didn't want to think about her that way, I didn't like how she was bringing up my body in relation to hers, I didn't like how she was so easily falling into the 'temptress' archetype at the same time she was using her 'protector' mode, but as long as she was around wearing that stupid outfit my eyes would keep finding places they shouldn't, and I *really* needed to think about Marissa right now. Henri was just a distraction, and I was still mad at her, so why couldn't I get her stupid 'fussball' outfit out of my head?

~~~

I adjusted my neckline one more time as Henri prepared to go into Chrysós to meet up with Marissa and her mom. I was wearing a nice light green dress with layers to give it volume, and a v-cut neckline that had fluff built in around the edges to give it a sense of modesty. I was pleased with how I looked in it, and I'd managed to get my hair to smooth down and stay still instead of being the ever-frizzy mess I usually had due to the static that seemed to stick to me at this size. The trick ended up being a little coconut oil and a touch of aloe. It was weird, and I smelled like the beach, but I was happy with it.

Henri was a little more dressed up, she had a blue sleeveless turtleneck accented with a thick black leather belt across her stomach, and a knee-length black skirt. She'd worn her big hoop earrings, and had matching bracelets too. For once, she'd put on lipstick, a dark matte rouge, and she was wearing pantyhose and heels to round the outfit out. She looked a lot more professional than the girl I usually saw in sweats or knit cardigans. For the second time that day, I couldn't help but be slightly surprised at how attracted I was to Henri. It was *Henri*, I'd never thought about her like that before, it was almost unsettling. I just hoped it was a side effect of her having confessed to me, and not me actually growing attached to her like that. I had Marissa, and I was very happy with her thank you very much.

"Well Amber, are you ready to re-enter the lion's den?" Henri asked

"I've *been* ready, hurry up, they'll think we're avoiding them." I said

She picked up the bag containing all my things and walked up to the door. The doorman opened it for her, and she slipped in, walking straight up to the front desk.

*The Feeling of Being Valued* 471

"Yes, Lund, party of four?" she asked the lady politely

The lady looked at her list and frowned, then looked up at Henri, and her eyes fell on me in her hand and she realized the mix up.

"Ah, of course. I'll bring you right there." she said "May we check your bag?"

Henri handed it over to the doorman and tucked the slip in her purse, and followed the lady to the very back where a tall table sat just out of sight of the door and the kitchen. Miss Lund and Marissa were already there, and Henri smiled to them as she took her seat, setting me down on the table in front of her.

"Henrietta, so lovely to see you again, and thank you for talking care of my daughter's... responsibility." Miss Lund said "I think the time apart has helped Marissa greatly."

"Oh, of course, it was no trouble at all." Henri said "Quince was quite keen on helping watch her as well, so I had a full day's respite to myself."

"H-hey Amber." Marissa said, and I looked up at her, my heart pounding. She was still a little pale, and somehow thinner than I remembered, despite it only having been five days since we'd seen each other and her not having the weight to lose in the first place. Her hair was up in twisted loose braids, pinned behind her ears, and she was wearing a black button up that made her look slightly masc, or maybe like a waiter. I smiled up at her, unsure of what I could say or do in front of Miss Lund. In the end, I went for the easiest option; the honest truth.

"Hi, Marissa. I really missed you..."

"I missed you too, I- I wanted- I'm supposed to-" she looked up at her mother, who was impassively looking at her with raised eyebrows.

She tried again "I was immature and selfish, and I didn't do my job as your guardian on Friday. I put myself, and by extension, you, in danger, and I deeply regret it."

"I- w-well, um." I started to say "Amber, let her talk." Miss Lund said sternly

I shut up and my breath caught as I realized that was the first time she'd ever actually spoken to me. I looked down as Marissa kept talking.

"While at the rehab center, I came to understand that I was being a bad friend and a bad guardian by involving you in my addictions, and I'd like to ask for your help to change that."

I looked up, confused. What was this? Was she asking me to- what, sponsor her? I'd barely ever drank, I couldn't do that...

"You'd be responsible for me, like I am with you." Marissa continued "Where I help *you* by giving you food and shelter and protection, you'd help *me* by, uh, making sure I don't engage in my harmful habits. You'd have my rehab therapist's number, and my mom's number, and if I engage in harmful behavior and don't listen to you when you guide me to stop, you'd message them and tell them what happened."

"I'd tattle on you?" I asked

"Is this a healthy way to deal with it?" Henri asked "I would think it would drive the class A and class B apart, if the class B is acting with authority like that."

I tensed up at that, unsure if it was a result of Henri seeing me as a 'less than' again, or if she was sucking up to Miss Lund...

"It's a system the rehab program actually promotes." Miss Lund said to me, her tone sounding for all the world like she was discussing the weather "They have many high end clients like Marissa, so in a lot of cases they'll recommend becoming a guardian with the intent of their ward assisting them in their struggles with their addiction. When I saw that program as an option, I knew it was the best fit for Marissa, and it would give *you* at least *some* amount of value past being an expensive toy."

"I'd be happy to help you, Marissa, in any way I can." I said

My mind was racing, would this change our relationship? Would things get weird? Would I have to actually talk to Miss Lund regularly? I knew Marissa did what she wanted, so I doubted she'd *let* me tell on her if she really wanted to drink, but she didn't seem like an alcoholic to me, she'd drank a few times, at the sleepover, at the other sleepover, at her dad's house, while we gamed a few times, but I didn't think it was hurting anything. I felt a pang of loss, would she stop being rough with me because of this? If she couldn't express herself with me, she'd go back to being *actually* mean to me...

"Thank you, Amber." Marissa said "May I hold you until the food comes?"

"Of course, I would like that." I said, polite and mindful of Miss Lund watching us carefully

Marissa reached over and picked me up, and I smelled the familiar scent of her lotion and practically melted into her hand. I looked up at her tired, nervous face, and hugged her thumb tightly. I was back where I belonged, one way or another, right? I'm sure it'd be ok. Her eyes traced my body and her face flickered for a moment, a look of hunger that flashed so quickly I almost thought I'd imagined it. Her fingers closed around me, and slowly, slowly, slowly they began to squeeze. Too slowly for anyone else to notice, but as the air was forced out of my lungs and her fingers pressed into familiar sore spots where bruises hid just under the surface, I felt safe, and I squeezed her back, feeling my back pop and my limbs tighten. We were ok, it'd still be the same as it was before. The new dynamic wouldn't affect us at all.

As Miss Lund and Henri began talking about business things and Marissa's fingers began tugging and prodding me more pointedly, I closed my eyes and let myself go limp. It didn't matter what was going on around me, I was where I belonged and everything was right in my world.

## Chapter Twenty-Six

Marissa brought me into her bedroom for the first time in days, the familiar space feeling like home. I felt a feeling of safety and relaxation wash over me as she dumped the bag of clothes and food on the desk and flopped over onto the couch, holding me to her chest. Dinner had gone 'interestingly'. Henri had behaved herself, and Marissa had been content to hold me and pet me most of the time, while Miss Lund just talked about business things. I didn't really pay attention, but she'd dominated the conversation. Marissa had gotten some kind of white sauce pasta, and I'd tried a bite. It wasn't great, but she seemed to really like it. I was less than impressed with Miss Lund for ordering a glass of wine at a dinner partially celebrating her daughter getting out of rehab, but that's who she was, I supposed.

I lay on Marissa's chest as her fingers worked me into her flesh, her thin dress shirt providing little barrier between me and her body. I absently wished I was wearing my clown suit, my formal clothes were just getting in the way. I smelled her familiar scent and clenched her shirt in my fists, I wanted her to *be*, to push, to *exist* for me, why was she just lying here? I'd lie on her all night if she wanted me to, but I wanted more of *her*... I dug my fingers into her skin hard to get her to notice me for real instead of just petting me. Her fingers slowed and she stopped stroking me. I growled, this was the opposite of what I wanted...

"Hey, Stress Toy?" she asked, her voice quiet

I curled up into her hand, I loved it when she called me that... I wanted her to play with me, it'd been so long... "Yeah?"

"...Am I an alcoholic?"

I dropped back onto her chest, the mood killed. "...I don't know, I think you get carried away sometimes, but you don't drink every day, so that's good, right?"

"They said getting drunk every week means you're an alcoholic, and I get drunk like, at least twice a week."

I rolled over to look at the ceiling "Well, If they said that, I guess they know, it's their job, right?"

"Yeah, I guess so." she said "I just didn't think about it like that. It's like, fuck, I was just having fun, I'm not dependent or something, not like the people there that were long term patients..."

"I guess it creeps up on you?" I said "I don't know, my dad drinks a soju or two pretty much every night and *he's* not an alcoholic."

"No, they said that's being an alcoholic too." she sighed

"Oh... He didn't seem like one, growing up. Maybe that place is too strict?"

"Maybe. I don't know." she said "Hey, for real though, uh, I'm really sorry about fucking up the sleepover, and the whole weekend, and... most of the week."

"It's ok, I'm just... happy you're safe?" I said, shocked. I hadn't expected to hear the words 'I'm sorry' come out of her mouth over anything. "And I got to hang out with Kensey more, and we went to group, too."

"It's *not* ok, I was selfish, I was putting myself in a position where I was in charge and out of control, I put you in danger, I had to give you up for days... I- Fuck..." her voice cracked

I lay there for a moment, listening to her heart beating below me. They'd really done a number to her at that rehab place. I pulled her finger down to my chest and hugged it "Missy, I think you made a mistake, but no one but you was hurt, and you're ok now, and I forgive you, ok? It's all ok."

"I'm a horrible girlfriend..." she said, her hand shaking "I could have killed you, I'm a horrible owner and the fact that I'm dating you makes the whole thing worse..."

"I *like* you being my girlfriend!" I said "It makes me feel special, I like you *more* as my girlfriend, I think you're doing a fine job."

"I can't even hold you without wanting to squish you, Amber. I made you play weird kink games with me, I *used* you..."

I felt a chill go through me and I sat bold upright "Missy, so help me if you're feeling guilty because you helped a consenting adult figure out she likes playing rough, I'll, I don't know, bite you between your fingers or something."

"I pushed you when I shouldn't have." she said "My therapist told me I shouldn't be playing those kinds of games with you, it's unsafe and selfish, and you can't *really* say no, so your consent is meaningless."

I stood up and stomped on her "Stop! That therapist is stupid, and doesn't see me as a person. I'm twenty fucking years old, I can fucking consent if I fucking want to."

Marissa looked up at me and I saw her eyes were wet "Amber, I don't know what I'm doing, I want to *hurt* you, I want it a lot, but like, I think that means I should give you up, I shouldn't want that for someone I'm supposed to be taking care of."

I stomped harder "Fuck! That! I just got you back! I want you, I like you, I feel *safe* around you, fuck the therapy, fuck what they told you, I'm a fucking adult that can make her own choices. If you being my owner is going to cause problems, let *me* decide that. I love you and I want you to take care of me. You *got* me just to bully me, you're a bitch, it's who you *are*, be a bitch! Bully me! I'm *asking* you to, as an adult, ok?"

"I want to take care of you, but I'm an abusive alcoholic, and I-"

"Ok, whatever, look. Shut up, listen." I said, my feelings flared up "I want you to get up, put me in my room, go get a shower and put on your cozy clothes, then you're going to come get me and bully me until I beg you to stop, do you understand? I'm not consenting, I'm fucking *demanding*."

She stared at me, her eyes wide and her cheeks pink. She sat up slowly and pulled me off her chest and held me tenderly in her hands, looking at me with a strong intensity. She frowned and tightened her mouth, looking like she wanted to punch someone. I watched her, my heart racing, I couldn't risk her giving me up, I couldn't stand to think about losing the only real partner I'd ever had, I didn't want to have to put up with her treating me like a child, she just needed to be her normal, mean, horrible, beautiful, caring self...

"Fuck." she muttered "Gods fuck."

"Did you hear what I said?" I asked, folding my arms

Instead of answering me, she pulled me up to her mouth and kissed me lightly, holding me in front of her face for a second before she stood up and set me in my house.

"Fuck therapy." she said "Fuck the whole thing, fuck rehab, fuck them all getting up in my feelings and making me feel like a piece of shit, I'm fucking amazing and I own the best fucking girlfriend-pet in the whole fucking world and I'll do what I *fucking* want with her."

"Yeah you will!" I said, grinning

"I'm going to get cozy as fuck, I'm gonna come get you, and we're gonna show 'Doctor Michael' that our relationship isn't 'problematic' at all, it's fucking amazing."

"It's not problematic, it's *toxic*." I said "And I *want* it like that."

She grinned at me and rubbed my head "Thanks for that pep talk, I've spent the past few days rethinking everything about my life, I kind of got overwhelmed with their stupid psycho-bullshit. I love you, Stress Toy."

I grinned as she walked off to 'get cozy' and sighed contentedly. Yeah she *might* have gotten better if she'd kept feeling sorry for herself, she *might* have treated me with more care, and she might have even become a better person, but did she really need to? I was already happy with her, she was perfect, and if she tried to change, it might ruin what we had... I turned and stepped inside my house, I needed to get ready too if we were going to play again...

~~~

Marissa lay on the bed, still looking nervous and wired but now in her soft, heavy flannel pajamas. I was in a thin nightgown I'd picked out so I could feel her touch better. I enjoyed her heat as she held me in her hands, cupping me as she breathed lightly. Her thumb traced my back and she took on her usual half lidded stare.

"So, pet, I want to do what I want to you, whenever I want to do it, got it?" she said, pushing herself to sound intimidating

"Of course, Lady M, I'm here for your every want and desire." I said, bowing to her with a smile

"Do you know what I want more than anything, pet?" she asked, looking at me with a bored expression

"Oh, I couldn't hazard a guess..." I leaned against her hands

She sat forward on her bed and reached down, placing me between her feet. "I want a kiss from my girlfriend, right... here." she touched her lips with her finger "But I want *her* to want it too."

"I do want it, Lady M..." I said, putting a hand on her foot. It twitched and I smiled to myself, I'd remember that.

"I want you to prove you want it, to work for it, to build up to it." she lay down on her pile of pillows "I want you to *crawl* all the way up to my lips."

"I would love to..." I said, and got on my hands and knees

"Ah ah ah..." she crooned "You have to make up here... through my pajamas..."

I looked at the opening to her pants leg and my chest pounded in anticipation. I started for the opening, and pulled it open further, seeing the dark path in front of me. I grinned and used her sock to pull myself up onto her ankle and lay down, belly crawling forward, feeling her smooth skin against my nightgown. I clambered on top of her shin and pressed my face into it. I crawled forward steadily, the warmth from her body filling the tunnel as her flannel rubbed against the back of my head. The light from behind me faded and as I got to her knee, the only way I could see was the faint light filtering through the fabric around me.

I sat up on her knee, looking at the expanse in front of me, and I heard her laugh, the sound coming from in front of me, but from all around me too.

"Feeling tired already? Really?" she asked, and I lay down again, I wouldn't let her down.

As my hand sank into the soft flesh of her thigh, I felt a wave of peace wash over me. Soft... I lay down again and let my cheek sink into her skin, the heat pouring off her. She tightened her thigh and I felt the muscles turn hard and springy, and I pressed against the flannel behind me. I crawled forward, arm over arm, up her thigh, feeling the air get warmer and the smell of her body get stronger. As the fabric got tighter and more restrictive, her fingers traced my body, and I wondered what my outline looked like from the outside... She'd liked it a lot last time, it had been horrible for me that time, but *now*, now she had her full attention on me and the material was a lot more breathable, it was a fully different experience.

"Almost halfway there..." she taunted me

I pushed forward, determined to get my kiss, my hands sliding across her sk- My fingers hit cloth and I felt a wave of, what? anticipation? embarrassment? I smiled to myself, under, she said? I could do under. I pulled up the elastic on the boy shorts and wiggled in, feeling her leg twitch in shock as I inched forward, smushed into her closely.

"I- I see *you're* enthusiastic." Marissa said, her voice muffled and nervous "Just be careful you... stay on the path?"

'The path', of course. I wouldn't do *that* to her, not without her permission. We weren't ready for that yet, anyway. Or at least *I* wasn't. I reached the bend in her leg, where her hip started, and rested in the crook, her skin getting softer and thinner to my left. I pressed into her inner thigh with my hand, and she twitched a second time, then her leg tightened up again, and her voice came through the cloth again.

"Keep moving, pet, you've got a lot of distance left to go if you want that kiss..."

I felt her waistbands in front of me, both of them, and I used my head to lift the stretchy material while moving forward, my hands pulling against her skin. She hissed at my fingers digging into her, and shifted under me. I popped out onto her lower stomach, just to the right of her abs, and collapsed, taking a breather. I stared up at the sea of Marissa in front of me and hummed to myself. This was all *mine*, she might own *me*, but I owned this, this view, this *place* was all mine...

I climbed the familiar flesh of her stomach, my hands making small slapping sounds as I traveled up and in. With her laying down, I was having a much easier time getting up to her chest than I had when I made this same journey in class. I savored the trip, making my hands into claws and dragging myself forward, feeling her flinch and twist under me slightly as my little fingernails jabbed in to her. I made my way up to her sports bra and I found myself slightly disappointed she hadn't worn something nicer, then again, I *had* told her to get comfortable. I wouldn't want to try and cram myself past an underwire, so this was for the best. I stopped and tugged on the black cloth, and sat back, waiting on her to say something to let me know it was ok, we still hadn't gotten this close this way before, and I didn't want to rush her.

"Come on pet, in you go." she said, her finger poking me from outside her top

I felt my body shake with excitement, this was a big step! I yanked at the bottom of her bra and pulled myself in, feeling the tight band pressing against my body as I slid in fully. I lay there on my back on her sternum, basking in her body, her smell, the two breasts on either side of me. Laying here in the valley I couldn't help but feel the smallness of my body exemplified, each of the mounds I shared a space with were small in comparison to the rest of her, but they still dwarfed my body, still bigger than me... I reached out and pressed my hand into the soft wall to my left, and Marissa lay still. I used my nails and she twitched, her chest moving and the space I was in getting smaller as her arms moved closer together. I hummed and rolled over, moving forward. We'd go further later, I had a kiss to get to.

I pushed out of the top of her bra and out into the clear air, the smell of Marissa fading slightly into the smells of lotion and light cleaner that her room usually had in it. I looked up, hoping to see her looking back, but her face was turned, seemingly uninterested at me crawling out of her top. I tensed with frustration and moved forward, up her neck, straddling her jugular and feeling the rush of her lifeblood coursing under me. I thought about biting her, feeling the blood under my teeth, even if I was too weak to break the skin, I'd at least get the symbology across. I decided against it, I didn't want to get swatted, at least not yet. I finally pulled myself up to her jaw and onto her cheek, staring at her lips, the lips that belonged to me as much as her, and I slid forward on my knees to fall onto them.

"So, do you really think you earned this kiss?" she asked before I could make my move

"Yes Lady M, I think I worked very hard for this, I did what you asked and I'm finally here for my reward." I said

"Hm... I think you enjoyed it a little too much, Amber. I think you didn't earn it at all, the quest was too easy and you spent too much time exploring and having fun."

"I just wanted to make sure I appreciated every inch of you, Lady M." I said "Worshiping your form can't be a bad thing, because your form is perfect, right?"

"My form is beautiful and well crafted, yes..." she mused "But I still do not like you denying your tasks to spend time selfishly enjoying it."

"Do I not get my kiss..?" I asked sadly, reaching my hand out and touching the corner of her mouth

"I'll give you the kiss." she said "But I'll have to punish you for your actions after."

"Oh, of course Lady M!" I said "Your grace and mercy know no bounds!"

"I know, I'm magnanimous to my pets." she said, looking bored "Now, come and get your kiss, unless you don't want it?"

"Oh, I *do* want it, Lady M!" I said, and fell whole-bodied onto her lips.

They puckered under me, and her fingers found my waist, pulling at me and straightening me out to align me with her mouth better. I kissed back, her damp mouth soft and gentle as her fingers pinched me. She pulled my face away and kissed my upper body, her lips pressing into my chest and neck, then she kissed my stomach, and I hugged her, leaning against her upper lip and just to the side of her nose. I loved this woman, I needed her in my life, and the way her legs curled up as she pressed me firmly into her, kissing me hard, I knew she needed me too. The therapist could never understand this, and I didn't want him to. This was private, just for us.

She finally broke the kiss and rolled onto her side, her dark green eyes looking like mossy pools I was about to fall into. She held me and squeezed me in her hands, my lower ribs shooting with pain and I wrestled with her fingers, my teeth finding hold on her index finger, making her squeeze harder. I coughed and spasmed, trying to hide the reaction. She needed to do this, I was fulfilling my purpose for her, and I needed to take whatever she gave. I wanted to, anyway... Even if I came away bruised, that was just a reminder I could use to feel close to her when she wasn't around.

"Fuck Amber, I don't deserve you..." she said, watching me squirm "I really don't, I was horrible to you half your life and somehow it paid off and I get to play with you whenever I want, I don't deserve that."

"You're not being horrible to me now!" I said, my voice coming out like a gasp "You're being so, so wonderful..."

"Mmm. I'm glad you think so, pet." she said, adding the last part as an afterthought "Right now though, I still need to punish you."

"I'm at your will and your mercy, Lady M." I said, feeling the buzz of excitement

"Ok, hm, on your hands and knees, then." Marissa said, dropping me to the bed

I complied, and wiggled in anticipation at what she might do, it was exciting but a little frightening too, the rollercoaster analogy we'd used the first time still held up.

"Ok, turn around, and clench your teeth." she said

I crawled in a circle, my teeth pressed together tightly, this narrowed down what she was going to do to one or two options. We hadn't done any of *this* yet, at least not since I agreed to it, I didn't know if I'd like-

Her index finger slapped against my thighs and I gasped, the stinging pain shooting me like a lightning bolt. It wasn't as hard as the time she'd flicked me in the stomach, she'd toned it down a lot, but her fingernail still stung. I wasn't sure I liked it, it hurt, and in a stinging way that wasn't the same as the pressure I usually liked, there was a-

Another impact made me let out a small shriek, and I tensed, how many times was she going to do this? She hummed and flicked again, this time her nail hit my butt, making me jump forward slightly. It was starting to really sting, and she put her other hand in front of me, pulling me back to the spot I'd jumped from.

"No, bad pet, stay still while you're being punished, or I'll have to keep doing it." she said, her voice somehow cold and heavy at the same time

I squirmed in place, awaiting the next blow, I could tell she liked this, her free hand was over me, her fingers holding me down as she flicked again, and I shrieked. That one had been harder... She hummed louder and her hand pressed down, forcing my face into the bed and I reached back, grabbing her finger with my hands, holding her to my shoulders for support. She flicked again and I did my best not to writhe in place. I couldn't tell if I liked this, I liked *her* doing this, but the pain itself wasn't like the pain I'd come to know from her, the kind that meant 'trust', this was new, and almost unpleasant, but it was still *her*, pouring herself into me. I was still being the center of her attention... I liked that part more than I disliked the pain, I decided.

She flicked one last time, the sound actually reaching her this time, if her laugh was anything to go by, and I kicked my legs out, twisting under her fingers and wishing I'd worn something other than a nightgown. She cooed at me and drew me closer to her, my hands free to rub at my backside and thighs, my body twitching and moving without my input. She smiled at me, her wonderful, cruel, loving smile and I melted back into her grip. If flicking my butt made her happy, I'd let her do it, the way her expression softened as she looked at me was worth being flicked a hundred times...

My ass ached, and I reconsidered... Maybe it was worth being flicked five times, or at most ten.

A knock on her bedroom door made me jump, and she looked up at it, across the room from us, miles away for me, and her smile grew even more cruel.

"Oh, pet, the snack I ordered is here, how lucky!" she said "What perfect timing!"

"W-wha-what snack?" I asked, still rubbing myself down to get the feeling back in my thighs

"You~!" she said, and rolled out of bed, leaving me there alone as she walked to the door and took a small box from Parker

I sat there, shivering and wishing she'd hurry up and come back, I was cold damnit, I needed her body heat, and I wanted to play more... She went into her closet and came back out with a large blanket, and unfolded it out onto her bed covering me up in it. I pulled at the slightly scratchy material, and finally got my bearings, heading for the pillows at the top of the bed. The bed rocked under me, and a crushing weight slammed into me from above, pressing me down into the comforter and sandwiching me between the covers. I couldn't move, Marissa must be laying on me from above. I heard her giggle lightly, and her hand snaked up to me from under the blanket, grabbing me firmly and sliding me out into the open air again. The box was on the blanket, and she dropped me next to it, her face a mask of anticipation.

"So *I'm* the snack?" I asked, looking at the box "I'm happy to serve you Lady M, but if you eat me, you won't be able to play with me anymore."

"Are you telling me what I can and can't do with my property, pet?" she asked "Do I need to punish you again?"

"No, of course not, Lady M." I said, and pulled at the ribbon tying the box closed

Marissa opened the lid and pulled out a small, clear jar of amber liquid, and then a honey dipper and I realized what her game was. I swallowed hard and quickly took off my nightgown, leaving me in my underthings, and knelt in front of her.

"Lady M, I trust you, please, I'll be your snack, forgive my prior misunderstandings."

"Hhhh...." she hissed "G-get up, pet, hold onto the stick, I have to prepare you..."

She popped the top off the jar of honey, and I clung tightly to the dipper, wrapping my arms around it and fitting my feet into the lowest groove. She held me over the jar, slowly lowering me until my feet touched the viscous liquid and I twitched, the honey unexpectedly hot. Had she had the chef heat it up first? The stick lowered further, up to my knees, then to my hips, clinging to me and soaking me. My breathing sped up as the honey suctioned around my chest and made it harder to inhale and I closed my eyes tightly, focusing on drawing in breath. The honey was thick, but I could still move if I needed to. I gripped the dipper harder as the liquid got up to my neck.

"You ok Amber? You look stressed." Marissa said quietly

I felt a wave of love for her, making sure I was ok even as she tortured me, and I pulled my face into a grin.

"Y-yeah, green light, just a new experience..." I told her

She nodded, and dipped me the rest of the way in, pulling me back out quickly. The honey flooded my mouth, my nose, my ears. I closed my eyes in time to stop it from getting in there, but I was still fully submersed in honey for a full half second. As I felt myself pulled out, I exhaled, trying to push the honey out of my mouth so I could breathe, but it still coated my face, drizzling down, sealing me off from the air. I thrashed, I used a hand to pull at the honey on my face, to wipe it away, but it was much thicker and heavier to me at this size, and I couldn't claw it away in time. Fear shot through my mind and I thrashed, pulling and shaking, trying to get to air, trying to get the honey off my face, I was drowning in a fluid to thick to breathe, I was going to die like this, I needed to breathe, I needed to scream, I couldn't even *scream*.

I felt something hot and firm surround me, and the familiar feeling of a massive tongue roughly slid across my face. I coughed out the last of the honey from my mouth clogging my breath, and Marissa licked it away too. I was in her mouth again, or at least my head and upper shoulders were. I gasped in the stale air inside her mouth, feeling my stress and panic melting away as I filled my lungs. Her mouth sucked at me, her lips and tongue pulling at my hair, my face, every bit of me as she cleaned the honey off. She pulled the stick I was holding on to away and I exited her mouth with a pop, blinking in the light, most of my body still coated in thick, dripping honey.

"You good?" she asked "You freaked out."

"N-not on my face again." I said, shaking "The rest of me is ok though..."

"Alright, yeah." she said "Anyway, I want to enjoy my snack now, pet..."

I held out one of my arms "Please, feel free to partake, Lady M..."

She snapped her head forward, taking my arm up to the shoulder, pulling at it and licking it while looking down her nose at me smugly. Her mouth was warm and slimy, and it was a little gross, but it felt weirdly exciting to have my hand in her like that... Once the 'flavor' was gone, she slid the arm out of her mouth and picked me up by it dangling me over the jar. She put the dipper back in the jar and licked the honey off her lips.

"Wow, pet, you've still got so much honey on you. You're turning into a lovely snack so far, I'll have to remember this~"

"Oh, I feel delicious, Lady M, I'm happy you're enjoying me!" I said, kicking my feet in the air slightly

She laughed, and pulled my other arm into her mouth, giving it the same treatment as the first one. I squirmed, and when she finally finished licking it clean, I held the arm up for her to hold, so I wasn't just hanging by one arm anymore. My new size meant that I could hang by one arm for a while before I got tired, but... It wasn't comfortable. She looked me up and down and bit her bottom lip, her head tilting as she examined me.

"You know, there's a lot of honey on your body... your chest, even..." she said, watching my face

"Green light- I- yes, Lady M, I'm sure it's just as tasty as the rest of me..." I said, my heart pounding

She grinned and she turned me around, licking my back and cleaning most of the honey off in a couple passes. At this point I was more covered in her wet, slightly sticky spit than the honey, and I think I liked that more. She rotated me so I was facing her again, and her face was serious. She swallowed, and took a breath, then dove in, her lips meeting my tummy and kissing the dripping honey off, her tongue snaking out and licking up what she missed with every kiss.

My stomach was soon just as clean at the rest of me, and I braced myself for what was next, controlling my breathing as she moved to kiss my chest, then hung for a split second, before pressing me against her and surrounding my breasts with her mouth. The kiss was every bit worth the wait, the trust I had for her coupled with me willingly giving myself to her made me awash with feelings of care and bliss. Her tongue flickered over the places she'd been interested in for weeks now, slipping under my bra to clean every inch of me, the texture rough against my more sensitive skin.

When she finally moved away with a 'mwah', I was shaking, my face flushed and my head spinning. We'd done it, we'd taken the step, and I loved that I had. I looked up at her face, she was glowing, her mouth sticky with honey and her eyes flashing with love and cruelty in equal measures. I hung there, and looked down at myself. She hadn't gone lower than my hips so far... I took a shaky breath and made eye contact with her.

"Th-there's still some left for you to enjoy, Lady M..." I said "Yellow light? I really hope you enjoy yourself."

I didn't want her to get too enthusiastic, but I wanted her to get the full experience, too. I lifted a leg to her and she smiled, and dangled me over her mouth. I looked down, seeing her teeth, straight and sharp, her throat, deep and dangerous, and I closed my eyes as she lowered me. I knew she'd be careful, but part of me wished she wouldn't. I almost wanted to be in more danger than I was, I wanted the thrill. Her lips closed around my stomach and her teeth instantly dug into my hips and I bucked, the unexpected pain surprising me. I kicked my legs slightly, but let myself go limp as she pulled her hand away. I hung upside down, waiting for her to do her thing, feeling the saliva pool around me, and I saw her grab her phone, typing away on it quickly.

"Are- are you texting?" I asked

She didn't respond, and pulled up the camera, pointing it at us and smiling as she took a picture. I flushed, hopefully she wouldn't sent that to anyone... She tossed the now-slightly sticky phone to the side and began to suck, her lips and mouth pulling the honey off of me as her lower jaw worked in circles, her teeth digging in sharply as she 'chewed' my hips. I'd have teethmarks after this again. I hoped they'd last longer, the ones from last week were already faded to almost nothing. Of course, my ass and thighs still stung, I'd be willing to bet that I'd feel *that* for at least a week. Her tongue slid over my legs, slimy and firm, never reaching up high enough to make me uncomfortable, but getting close enough to make me consider how long we should wait before going that far.

Once I was clean, or at least, mostly clean, she slid me out and lay me on the blanket. I looked at my hips and traced the marks, feeling the twinges of pain as I recovered. She could bite me in half, and these marks proved it. I wondered if I could get them tattooed on at some point, could class Bs even get tattoos? I know if you had them beforehand the compression usually messed them up, but there had to be a market for tiny tattoos, right?

"You're quite the snack, pet..." Marissa said, her smile kind and gentle now

"Thank you, Lady M..." I replied, holding my stomach and letting the bruises keep my buzz going "I had fun tonight..."

"Oh, we're not quite done just yet." she said, and there came another knock at the door

More? I was exhausted, I didn't know if I could go much further, but if she wanted to, I wasn't going to argue. She came back with a teacup on a saucer, the liquid inside smelling like oranges and spices. She carefully lowered it onto the bed so it wouldn't spill, and bent down next to me, her face playful.

"I was going to have a cup of tea, pet, won't you join me?" she asked teasingly

"Of course!" I said "I would love to, Lady M!"

"Hm, I do so love honey in my tea though..." she said, frowning "Could you be a dear and help with that?"

"I'd- I'd love to?" I said, looking at the cup nervously. If she was planning what I thought, I could get scalded... She picked me up around the chest and dipped my lower half into the jar of honey, and slid the tea over next to me. The color in it was very light, and as she lowered me into it, I felt the hot tea wash over me like a warm blanket. I sighed in relief, it wasn't too hot at all.

"This is a bergamot white tea with nutmeg and allspice." Marissa said casually, lifting the cup with me in it "It's brewed at a very low temperature, and I had it chilled slightly with ice before being brought up. It's a blend I made on a website I like- do be a good little pet and stir, won't you?"

"Yes, of course Lady M!" I said, swishing the hot tea with my legs, the honey washing off of them and mixing in.

She lifted the cup to her lips and took a deep sip, pulling the liquid in and making me slide forward in the little teacup. I grinned at her, and she pretended to think for a second.

"Hm, I do believe I'd have preferred if it'd seeped a little longer, the 'Amber' flavor is too mild for my liking."

I dunked under the tea and swished my whole body in it, the liquid doing a surprisingly good job of getting the residual honey off of me. I popped up and bowed to her, or I tried, bowing while sitting was awkward.

"I think that should be more to your liking, Lady M." I said

She raised an eyebrow and took another sip, humming as she tasted it "Hm... yes, I do think that's the flavor I was going for, good pet."

I laughed, and she rolled her eyes and took another drink. I leaned forward and kissed her top lip as she did, and she pulled away, surprised.

"Pet, are you stealing kisses?" she asked "You know you have to earn those!"

Her happy face and sparking eyes let me know I wasn't really in any danger of punishment, and I folded my hands under my chin "Why, I helped with your tea, didn't I? Is that not enough to pay for a kiss?"

She tsked, and sighed "I suppose you did. I'll let it go this time... "

She drained the rest of the cup, tipping me forward onto her mouth and set the cup down. I looked up at her, looking down at me with a smug look, and she reached down and plucked me out of the teacup.

"I believe we're done for the evening, pet." she said "Clean yourself, I'll come get you shortly."

She set me in my house, and I sighed contentedly as she closed the wall behind me. I was so, so tired, but I'd had one of the best times of my life.. I could only hope she enjoyed it as much as I did...

~~~

The wall of my house opened up, and I waved at Marissa, looking tired and pleased with herself. She reached out and carefully picked me up, bringing me over to her couch, and lay down holding me on her stomach. I was wearing my pink, warm jumpsuit, and everything was right with the world.

"You doing ok, Amber?" she asked "I know we went farther that time."

"I'm doing wonderfully, Lady M." I said "Maybe don't flick me quite as hard next time?"

"No- don't- I'm not Lady M right now." Marissa said, looking mildly uncomfortable "I want to have a *real* relationship too, not just that stuff. If you treat me like that all the time, it'll erase 'us'. Just use my name when we're not playing, please. Pet names are fine, but not the ones we use while we're playing."

"...Oh, sorry, that makes sense." I said "That's a far cry from our first day."

"Back then I wanted you as a full time pet." she said "Now. I like you as a person too much to want that all the time."

"Well I like you as a person too, Missy." I said and climbed up her body to lay on her chest.

I heard a click, and I looked up to see she on her phone above me, having just taken a picture. "Another picture?"

"This one's for my therapist, a 'fuck you' for telling me to break up with you." she said, typing out a message and sending it.

"Aww, you love me more than therapy, that's sweet..." I said, curling up

She rested her hand on me and snorted "There's not much I like more than you, Stress Toy."

Her phone dinged and she opened it, her face turning into a frown.

"What'd he say?" I asked

"Blah blah blah, consent, blah blah blah, concerning behavior, blah blah blah, unhealthy attachment." she said "I'll show *him* an unhealthy attachment..." She typed out another message and attached the pic from earlier, with me hanging upside down out of her mouth, and sent it.

"Missy I was in my bra in that one!" I said, punching her

"Eh, he's a therapist, he has confidentiality or something, it doesn't count."

"I hope this doesn't come back and bite you in the ass." I said "I really don't want to be taken away."

"It's fine, like I said, confidentiality." she sighed "Now let's do something brainless for a while, I've been putting up with the stupid therapy for days. Any ideas what to watch? Something dumb."

"Oh, *I Dream of Jeanie*!" I said "I think you'll like it, the main character has to live in a bottle for most of the first season because... reasons."

"Sounds good to me." she said, and opened the streaming app "People in bottles are always great."

As Barbara Eden caused problems for Larry Hagman, Marissa and I dozed off, my bruises and pains bringing me closer to her and making me feel loved. I wondered absently if she'd be down for a genie-in-a-bottle roleplay sometime, and I resolved to ask her when we woke up. I wanted to keep things as interesting as I could between us, so she'd never get bored of me.

## Chapter Twenty-Seven

"Fuck you, I know what I said." Marissa snapped harshly

"And I'm telling *you*, you need to focus on your partner's actual needs more." Dr Michael said, frustrated

"My needs are to be squeezed and held and put in cozy pockets." I said "She does a *great* job at that."

"You really shouldn't be here at her therapy session, she can't speak openly if she's got you in her front pocket." he sighed

"No, see, I'm her accountability partner, I'm supposed to make sure she doesn't drink. If I wasn't here, she might be chugging grain liquor for all I know." I said "I'm just doing my job."

"She's not going to 'chug grain liquor' at therapy, Amber. You could have stayed with the receptionist"

"I might have chugged grain liquor, who knows?" Marissa said, shrugging "Anyway, fuck you, I'll bite her if I want."

"Uh huh, she can bite me if she wants, I'm hers, it's her right to bite me." I said, nodding

"You're not 'hers'. You're her *responsibility*, and her biting you crosses the line between caretaker and lover." he said, writing in his notebook

"I mean, she *is* my lover." Marissa said "As much as anyone can be at four inches tall at least."

"Yeah, I'm her lover, her biting me proves it, you said so yourself." I agreed

"You two aren't *supposed* to be lovers." he sighed "The power difference is too great. Amber, what if you want to break up with her and she doesn't let you?"

"That's kinda hot..." I said, thinking about it "Like, I like her owning me already, so it'd be like, even more of that?"

"If you ever break up with me, I'm stepping on you." Marissa said

"Hey, no!" I said "We agreed no feet, just squish me with your hand instead."

"She doesn't *own* you!" the therapist said, standing up partway out of his chair "She is *caring for you*, you need to re-frame your whole relationship!"

"Ok, but I *do* kinda own her?" Marissa said, crossing her legs. I suppressed an urge to jump out of her shirt pocket and nestle into the thigh-flesh where her legs met... "Honestly though? I bought her, I do what I want with her, I keep her in a box in my room, I feed her, I clothe her, I own the little bitch."

"Yeah, she owns me, it's fine, I like her owning me." I said, smiling to him sweetly

He sighed and sat down, running his hand through his hair and shaking his head "This is... the most problematic relationship between a class B and their guardian I've ever seen, and I once did therapy for a pair who were doing adult videos without the class B's consent."

"Hey, I know him!" I said, perking up "We're friends, Paul, right?"

The therapist looks at me, his face lightly pained "...I... Just- Can I please talk to Amber one on one?"

Marissa cupped me in her hand "Why, so you can trick her into saying something that will get her taken away?"

"My job isn't to get class Bs taken away, it's to help you have better relationships with them." he said tiredly "I'll only try to get the class B removed if there's something illegal or potentially dangerous going on."

"Just to be clear, me being bitten isn't dangerous." I said "It's playing, we're totally safe about it and everything, we use the traffic lights to tell if I need to take a break."

"Traffic lights?" he asked

"Green is keep going, yellow is take it easy or not as hard, red is full on stop playing and re-group." Marissa said "Gods, it's like, basic shit, why don't you know this?"

"I'm... not in the habit of discussing kink play with my clients, I'm a class B relations therapist, why- I don't-" he pulled off his glasses "...Leave Amber on the desk, step outside. This isn't a request, I need to talk to her in private, or I'm not going to be your therapist anymore."

"Fine by me, I don't even want therapy." Marissa snarked

"Oh, uh, actually..." I said "we kinda probably should do what he's asking. Because of your mom?"

"That's right, if I kick you out of the program, how do you think your mother would feel?" Dr Michael asked

Marissa made a noise like a frog having its tongue scraped, and looked away.

"I'm sure it's just a chat like the one the doctor had with me a couple weeks ago." I told her "I'll just tell him what I'm telling him now, and it'll all be over in a flash."

"Ugh, fine, but like, I'm right outside, and if you try to do anything fucky to her, I'll-." Marissa narrowed her eyes, realizing that threatening her therapist was a bad idea "...I'll be angry..."

She slid me into her hand and gave me a squeeze and a little kiss, and then set me on the desk, watching me with her beautiful green eyes. She huffed, annoyed at the situation, but she stood up and stalked out of the room anyway, slamming the door behind her. I watched her go, and folded my arms. I'd been apart from her very little since she got back; Thursday she'd had practice so I was on the bench, this morning she was with her mom and I stayed hidden, bathroom trips and showers of course, but *most* of the time, even while we were sleeping, we were within a few inches of each other at the most. It was odd to be away from her, it felt like I should feel her warmth all the time, like she was an extension of me. Or I was an extension of her, more accurately.

I turned to Dr Michael and raised my chin "Well? You wanted to talk?"

He lowered his chair to be closer to my height and leveled a look at me "Amber, I need you to be honest with me."

"Yup, called it." I said, sitting down on the wooden surface

"There's nothing to 'call', Amber. You're in an abusive relationship."

"Nnnno, I'm in a sub/dom relationship that I consent to and enjoy."

"Whose idea was it to start the relationship?" he asked

"We- I don't know, we just compromised and found ourselves in the middle." I said "No one 'started it'. She said I love you first, but I called her my girlfriend first."

"Ok, but which of you initiated the... play sessions?" he asked

I shuffled "Uh, she wanted the first one, I asked her for the second one, I guess."

"So she used her position of power to play with you?" he asked

"I mean that's what a dom *does*." I said "That's just- it's *normal*."

"I don't think her being your dom is normal at all in the first place, she shouldn't be bullying you like that, you can't say no."

"I can say no, she'd respect it." I said coldly "I'm an adult, Michael. Just because my body isn't the same as yours doesn't change that. It's *more* dehumanizing for you to tell me I can't consent because my body is like this than it is for her to play with me. She loves me, she cares about me, she respects me. You're being an ass about it, and I'm fed up with it."

"I'm not being an 'ass', Amber, I'm concerned about your safety." he sighed and shook his head "I can't help you if you don't let me, you know."

"Good, I'm not letting you. Fuck off and let my cool, loving girlfriend do what she wants to me."

He looked at me for a few minutes and swallowed, his expression tight. After a few minutes of me not responding further, he pressed the button on his desk. "Kandra, send Marissa back in."

Almost at once, she strode in and grabbed me off the deck roughly. I clung to her fingers like a life preserver, snuggling into her palm. She glared down at me, her lip curling "What the fuck did he say?"

"Same old shit." I said, enjoying her "Claims I can't consent because you could force me to do stuff if you wanted."

"I just think that's a stupid fucking argument." she snapped, bringing me up to her face "If someone's like, a body builder and they date a... I don't know, basement dweller or something, is that a problematic relationship? The body builder could bully the basement dweller and stuff after all."

"Any imbalance of power can potentially be problematic, yes." Dr Michael said

"So you're gay, then, right?" Marissa asked

"I- what?" he looked confused

"Well, the patriarchy gives men an unfair power dynamic over women, so if you're dating women, you're flexing your power dynamic over them. Even if you're not using it, it's still there and you could abuse it." Marissa said, giving me a quick peck "If you're talking to *us* this way, you *must* be gay, because fucking other men is the only non-problematic way to date, in your worldview."

"I- no, that's not the same at all!" Dr Michael said angrily "Amber is incapable of consent!"

"Amber is a soon to be twenty one year old woman who can make her own choices, fucker, how many times do I have to say it?" Marissa growled, her voice low and throaty. I hummed and kissed next to her mouth

"...I think our session is over for the week." Dr Michael said, closing his notebook "Marissa, I- please, take it easy, try to focus on her as someone you need to take care of, ok?"

"Oh, I take care of her." Marissa said "I take care of alllll her needs..."

"Just get out, I need to talk to my colleagues about this..." he muttered

"Whatever." Marissa said, picking her purse off of the chair and dropping me in "See you next Friday."

I curled up against the glasses cloth I'd landed on and looked up at her walking out of the office, head held high, not looking down at me once. Fuck therapy, I loved this...

~~~

The download finally finished and I clapped my hands. It'd been hours, the wi-fi on my new console was so, so slow... I plugged in the headphones and picked up the slightly too big controller, opening the game.

"Missy! It's done!" I yelled out the open wall of my house

A moment later, a pinging noise sounded out in my headphones and I tapped the button, connecting the call.

"Alright, let's play this nerd game of yours, how do we start?" Marissa asked

"You gotta make a character!" I said, putting in my log-in info "I'll make a new one too so we can play together right away."

"Ok, let me- Uh... What are these options?" she asked "I was thinking it'd be like, elves and dwarves, what the heck is a Loropie?"

"Those are little bunny characters, they're little and good at being sneaky." I said "I'm going to play whatever helps your character most, so pick whatever you like!"

"This one lady is cool" Marissa said "She's like, really tall, and she had horns, I wanna be her."

"Those are the dragons, that's a Drogernian, if you're one of those, you'll be playing a close range character, so I'll be..." I flipped through the options "...ah, shit."

"What, is something wrong with your game system?" Marissa asked, concerned

"No, it's..." I sighed "The best ranged support class is the Magi-Gauntleteers, and the best race for those is... The Muronites..."

"Muro... huh, oh, here they are..." she murmured "Ahh, ok. Yeah, nope, you *gotta* do it, Stress Toy, you *said* you would!"

"I know, I know..." I said, reluctantly picking the little rodent-person "Just... keep it friendly, 'k?"

"Yeah, yeah, no name calling, I got it." she laughed "Ok, so it's asking me to like, pick stuff on a chart to make my character look like me, how accurate does it need to be?"

"No, just- just make any character you like." I said "It's supposed to be anything you want, really. Just make the person you'd *like* to be, it's fine, that's what I do!"

"Mm, fun, yeah." she said, and went quiet for a while

I finished setting up my character, and joined the starter world, watching the opening scene and loading in to the hub while I waited.

"Ok, ok, so, like, I pick a... you said close range?" she asked

"Yeah, do you like big swords or big hammers more?" I asked her

"Hammers." she said instantly "I wanna squash people".

"Not thinking about *that* too hard." I said "You'll want to be a Mountainsbane then."

"Ok, ok, and it's asking me about a world?"

"The one that says 'starter world', that's where I am." I told her "I'm waiting for you to join, I'm at the spawn location."

"Alright, it's- oh, shit it's a movie?"

"Yeah, watch it, but it's not important to remember all of it, it sets up our world and mission, it's fine."

We waited on her to watch the opening cutscene, and I kicked my feet in excitement. Henri only had handheld consoles, so she'd never been able to play with me before, this would be my first time playing with a friend I didn't meet in-game. Finally, eventually, she popped in next to me, and I did a dance emote at her.

"Oh, fuck, my cool clothes went away, I'm wearing rags..." she said "How do I change back?"

"You gotta *earn* the cool clothes from the character maker." I said "It's late-game stuff, that's just is supposed to show you how badass you *will* be soon."

"Fuck that shit, I want to be badass now..." she muttered "How are you wiggling like that? Is there a button?"

"On keyboard it's... uhhh... spacebar, the type slash-dance, then enter."

"What the fuck?" she asked "Fuck, am I going to have to fucking type everything I want to do? I've played games like that, my dad showed me his favorites from when he was a kid, they aren't for me."

"No no no, sorry, there's a menu too, in the lower right, I- I just use the commands, you can click buttons, or set the dances to a number key or something."

"I have ten number buttons, will I need all of them?" she asked, walking around jerkily, apparently using the click-to-walk instead of wsad

"You'll need more than that." I said "If you hold shift you can swap between like, multiple sets of zero through one hotkeys."

"Shit, fuck Amber, I don't know if I'm up for this." she said "That's a lot to keep track of..."

"You play RTS games, you're not *allowed* to complain about complexity." I pointed out "This is easier, it's just different, it's ok."

"Is there a tutorial?" she asked "I don't have any powers and I can't figure out how to hit you with my hammer."

"There is, we can go get you a hammer. You don't have one yet. Also you can't use it in cities, we'll have to go out into the wastes for that."

"But I *can* hit you with it, right?"

"It'll go through me, but yeah. When we hit level thirty we can do PVP and fight, and you can hit me for real then though."

"Great, let's get to level thirty then, I guess." she said "Hey, just don't rush me on this, ok? I don't play a lot of games other than that one we play, and... this one is a lot."

"I understand." I told her "If you're ok with it I could take charge? Just while we play the game, I could be the... you?"

"...Just for the game?" she asked quietly

"Yeah, just to help you learn stuff, I'll be the one in charge, I'll guide you and walk you through it. You can still choose the quests, but I'll make sure you have support and know what to do."

"...Ok, I guess." she said "Just for the game, I'll let you be in charge. I still plan on squashing you when we get to level thirty though."

I smiled and danced at her again "I'm looking forward to it!"

~~~

I wrapped around Marissa's finger and bit it lightly. She bopped me on the head and squeezed. I laughed and dropped back into her hand, fixing my dress- a nice red one with lots of material in the skirt- and stuck my tongue out at her.

"So, think your dad can keep a secret?" I asked, glancing out the car window at the fancy house we'd just pulled up to

"Yeah, it's Raquel I'm worried about..." Marissa grumbled

"Does she *talk* to your mom?" I asked "I thought she'd hate her."

"They hate each other, yeah, but she's an asshole, she'd make a post about it and how much she supports it and tag mom just to cause drama." Marissa said, slipping me into her pocket

"Damn, so no pda, I guess." I grumbled

"Nope, just regular squeezes and stuff." she sighed.

She opened the door and slowly walked to the door, knocking firmly. I kept my head poked up out of her pocket, it was a flannel over a plain grey shirt, and with the jeans she wore, she looked... so normal, so much less scary... She didn't have a lot of clothes with pockets up on the chest or close to the face, so she was having to dip deep into her wardrobe, outside of her usual style. She crossed her arms and I leaned back against her as we waited, wondering if this visit would go any better than the last...

The door finally opened, and John stood there, grinning widely, waving her in.

"Missy! Great to see you, and, ah, Amber was it? Good to see you too!" he said

"Good to see you too, Daddy!" Marissa said, and hugged him, not bothering to avoid smushing me between them

We all walked into the living room where Raquel is already sitting, looking smug and proud of herself. She was dressed like she was expecting to go to an opera tonight instead of seeing her step-daughter, and her white and blue dress was spread around her on the big sofa, marking her territory.

"Why hello Marissa! It's always so good to see you!" she said, her eyes flicking to my little form peeking at her

"Hello Raquel." Marissa said flatly, and took her seat in the cushioned chair Raquel had been in last time

"I'm going to go get us some lemonade and get some out to Drew, Missy, you want the usual?" John asked

"Ah, I'm not- I'm not drinking right now." Marissa said, and I felt her subtly glance at Raquel "I'm... taking a break for now."

"Oh, it's just one glass, I'll make it half as strong, sound good?" he said genially

"No thank you, just regular lemonade sounds perfect right now." Marissa said more firmly

John threw up his hands and grinned easily "Got, it, just regular lemonade, I'll be right back. I, uh, think your mom has something to show you!"

"Johhnnnn!" Raquel whined "Hush, go on, I'll tell her myself!"

He laughed and stepped away as Marissa reluctantly turned towards Raquel and sighed "Ok, what is it you wanted to show me?"

Raquel preened "Wellll.... I can't say I liked the idea of having the *rat* in my pocket-"

"*Amber*, not 'the rat'." Marissa said coldly

"-fine, I didn't want *her* in my pocket, but I was thinking, what about a little man? I could so get a little guy that was just a little man to love on and to play with, and... well, I did it!" she said proudly

Marissa raised an eyebrow "*You* took a twelve hour class?"

"I found a private testing facility with less strict rules and took the class-thingy there." she said "Then I had the little guy shipped from a place up north!"

"Shipped?!" I asked in alarm

"He had a little water sponge, it was fine." Raquel said. She pulled out her phone and tapped a couple times. A ringing sounded out somewhere deeper in the house, and she smiled "Yes, Joss? Please bring in my little guy!"

As she hung up, the sound of something rolling across hard floors sounded out, and soon a well-dressed woman in a black skirt and a tuxedo style top walked out of the far hallway pushing a cart with a beige box on top. She wheeled it over between Marissa and Raquel and gave a light bow before walking quickly out of the room again. The box was roughly two and a half feet square, and it looked... sad.

There was a little bed, a bowl of water, a pile of those horrible pellets for class Bs, a blanket, a hamster wheel, and in the center, a man in a white t-shirt and black pants, about my height. He was standing with his arms crossed and a glare on his face, and Raquel clapped when she saw him.

"Look, look!" she said "He's so small and fun! I call him Munchkin!"

"What's his real name?" Marissa asked

"I don't know, it's Munchkin now." Raquel said, shrugging.

The man met my gaze, and his eyes widened, his arms uncrossing for a moment before his glare hardened again and he huffed. Raquel reached down and picked him up by his shirt and he instantly started struggling, his arms flailing and legs kicking as she brought him up to her face and gave him a kiss and laughed.

"He's so much fun! I love getting to watch him run around and play..." she crooned

"You're not allowed to kiss him like that unless he gives you permission you know." Marissa said coldly

"Well if I let *him* decide he'd just hide in his blankets all day." Raquel sighed "Besides, he doesn't mind."

I watched the man with a blue lipstick stain on his face and shirt struggling and I shivered, it looked like he minded a lot, actually.

Raquel put him back in the box and pointed at me "I thought our pets could play!" she said "We could see how they get along!"

Marissa slowly pulled me out of her pocket and her fingers danced across my body "I don't know... I don't know if I trust this guy with Amber."

"I see you've met Munchkin!" John said, taking a seat next to Marissa in his chair "He's not as cute as Amber, but he sure is fun to watch!"

"Fun?" Marissa asked, gently rubbing my tummy with her thumb

"Yeah, watching him climb your mom is crazy, she'll put a pellet on her shoulder and he'll have to climb up her dress all the way there, or we'll put him on the floor in a little ball, and he'll just go, bouncing off stuff, running everywhere he can!"

"I'm *so* glad you gave me the idea to get him." Raquel grinned "I've been waiting to show him off for a week!"

"Yeah..." Marissa said, holding me with both hands "He's- you should really get him an actual house or something, this thing is jank."

"I'm ordering a custom one, it'll have a lock on it so he can't get out," she said "All the ones on the market don't lock for some reason, how did *you* fix that issue?"

"I just... actually want to be with her?" I piped up "I don't need a lock, I *like* being with Marissa."

"I guess our little guy will come around in time then!" John smiled, drinking a swig of his lemonade

"Maybe..." Marissa said, eyeing him.

"Here, put Amber in there too!" Raquel said "I want them to play!"

Marissa looked at me, and I looked at the box. It looked... not fun, and the guy was still angry, but if talking to him could help me guide him into having a better life somehow, it was worth putting up with it for a little while. I nodded to Marissa, and she made a face. She carefully set me in front of him, and pulled her hand away slowly. I looked at the guy, he was just a regular guy. Angry, messy looking, balding brown hair and a five o'clock shadow, just... a guy. I stepped forward and put out my hand.

"Hi, I'm Amber. What's your name?" I said

"...Munchkin, apparently." he snapped, but he took my hand "...It's Jasper."

"It's nice to meet you Jasper." I said, trying twice to take my hand back before he glanced down and let go "I, uh, this is your home?"

"It's where I live, I guess." he said, crossing his arms again.

"Yeah, I gathered." I said, trying to think of a conversation topic "Uh, do you have anything you like to do?"

"Look around, do you *see* anything?" he waved one hand around the box

I looked around and pointed at the hamster wheel "There's that, do you like to run? I do a lot of cardio myself, when I have the chance. I like the rush!"

He shook his head "I can't say I'm a fan. You can give it a go, though."

I waved down at my clothes "Yeah, I'm... not really dressed for running right now. My dress would get caught in the spokes."

He shrugged "Ok, so take it off, problem solved."

I frowned at him "I'm- I don't want-" I glanced up at Marissa, but she'd sat back in her seat and we were out of sight of each other. Raquel wasn't looking either, and I bit my tongue "...Maybe we just chat?"

If nothing else this was a chance to pick his brain about how he was being treated.

"How are you enjoying your living situation?" I asked

He sneered at me "How the fuck do you think?"

I sighed "Is she really that bad? If she's hurting you, I can-"

"It's not about getting hurt, I'm not a pussy, it's about *respect*." he said, his voice dripping with hate "She doesn't fucking respect me, I'm like a fucking *dog* to her. She doesn't even see me as a fucking man."

"It can be hard for new guardians to see their new wards as-" I tried

"It's not just that, she sees me as fucking impotent or something." he said "She'll put me in her top to carry me, no shame, because to her I'm not fucking big enough to be a man. I have to spend all day around a hot chick, and she doesn't even see fucking me as a *possibility*. Do you know how fucking much I want to kill her?"

"K-kill?" I said, thinking of Henri "She's a lot bigger than you, I- that's a tall order..."

"Really? You're making *jokes* about it?" he shook his head "Fucking bitches, all of you, I can't even get respect from a chick *my* size, what the *fuck*."

"It wasn't a joke!" I said, waving my hands "No, I was just- I'm kinda stupid, I didn't think about it."

"'*Kinda*' stupid?" he asked, stepping closer to me, and I noticed we *weren't* the same size, he was almost half a head taller and I flinched

He huffed and reached for me "Whatever. Look, I've got nothing to lose here, so why don't you just shut up and take off that dress already?"

I felt disgust, then fear, and I started to step back and scream, but his hand snapped forward and closed over my mouth. I felt a spike of panic set into me and I thrashed, his other hand finding all the same places Marissa's fingers did, but in a way that made my chest hurt and my brain feel sluggish and gross. I twisted and fell, him on top of me, his knee on my stomach, and his hand slipped off my mouth and slammed into the floor next to me. I screamed as loud as I could, and his hand found my face again and I tasted blood as my teeth hit my lips. I blotted out where his body was touching mine, and I tried to look away from his intense, focused, angry glare, but my survival instincts told me not to look away, to keep fighting. I wriggled, and I felt him grab me hard, and I choked, my legs kicking, kneeing him in the ass.

I pushed him up with all my might, and lifted him all of a handbreadth off of me. I steeled myself and tried to get his hand off my, if I could scream, if I could get Missy's attention-

Something large and fast snapped into my line of sight with a crunch and suddenly I wasn't looking at his face anymore, but the side and back of his head. His body spasmed and went limp, falling onto me. His mouth was at my ear, and a stream of gurgles and hisses came out. His hand was off my mouth and I screamed long and loud and hard as I rolled him off me, his head flopping at an unnatural angle. I gasped for air and looked up wildly to see Marissa staring down at me, her horrified face frozen, her hand still poised over us from where she'd flicked him. Jasper let out one last noise, a strangled cough, and then there was silence.

The quiet lasted for moments that felt like years, my eyes spilling tears, Marissa's threatening to, my chest screaming at me that I needed to lie down, my insides threatening to empty themselves, and after an eternity of nothing, the air was finally broken with the sound of Raquel letting out a horrible, keening wail, and reality came back to where it was supposed to be.

~~~

I lay in Marissa's hand as she sat against the wall of the living room. The cops and social workers clustered around the roll-around table, discussing... something, I couldn't imagine what they could *possibly* have to talk about still. I'd finished crying long ago and I was just holding on to Marissa's hand, drinking in and absorbing as much of her as I could before we were-

I didn't want to think about what was going to happen to me next. I kissed her palm and tried not to remember the crunching noise the man- Jasper's neck had made when she flicked him. She could do that to *me*... She could make me make those same sounds he had, twist my neck around like his did. Usually when I thought about her power, it made me feel safe, like I was *special*, but now there was a cold spike in my chest where I couldn't feel anything, that I had to ignore if I wanted to be ok touching her. I needed her, as much of her as I could get, but I was so, so scared. Seeing her do that in an instant, a heartbeat, it didn't matter how much she loved me, I understood the power difference so much more now, I didn't know if I could handle it.

I'd have to, I knew that much. Whoever I ended up with, I'd still have to put up with the power, the threat. I wanted it to be her. Even though she was the one who made me aware of the cold, terrifying void between me and the rest of humanity in the first place, she was the only person I could imagine even feeling slightly safe right now. She'd opened that void for me after all, to *help* me. I kissed her palm again, and she still didn't respond.

A shadow fell over us, and I flinched, Raquel back to scream at us more? John hadn't been able to calm her down, and had practically had to drag her to the kitchen, but I knew she was still furious at Marissa. I carefully looked up to see a man in a green uniform- the same kind the man who'd taken me from my family had worn- stood over us, notepad in hand.

This was it, this was when I got taken away and put back into the system. I lunged for Marissa's fingers, wrapping them around me and willing her to squeeze me, one last time. She blinked, her eyes focusing, and her hand closed on me, sealing me in her flesh. She glanced up at the man and her grip got stronger, forcing the air out of me.

"I'm not giving her up, you'll have to fight me for her." she said without emotion

"Miss Lund, we just need to ask a few questions." he said "We've gotten statements from Mr and Mrs Lund already, we just need you and Amber's statements."

"I saw him... on her, pinning her down, and I flicked him to make him stop hurting her." Marissa said "She was screaming, he was trying to pull at her dress."

"That's the whole statement you want to make?" he asked, frowning

"That's what happed, as far as I know." Marissa mumbled, loosening her grip

I took a deep, steady breath, and went back to hugging her fingers, the ice feeling in my chest still there.

"And Miss Park?" the man asked "Would you like to give a statement?"

I shivered, and sat up, using Marissa's thumb as a handhold "Y-yeah, I would."

I told the whole visit, as best as I could, trying to remember Jasper's exact wording and how he acted, and pushed through the descriptions of him attacking me. I ended with Marissa picking me up out of the box and holding me to her neck, shaking. I watched him write, and he nodded slowly and put the pen back on the notepad.

"Thank you for your cooperation." he said, and walked back over to the other group

I felt my eyes fill up with tears, I didn't want to lose her, I couldn't, I *needed* her at this point. I needed to be touching her, I just wanted to feel safe again, and all these giant people here were doing the opposite of that for me. I shuddered at the thought of any of the people milling around the living room just walking up and flicking me in the head, and I tried not to imagine Marissa doing the same. She'd bruised me a lot on our first day with a flick. What would have happened if she'd aimed for my face instead? Flicked just a little bit harder?

...If we *were* still going to be together, I'd have had to make a rule about no more flicking during playtime...

The man in green walked back over and crouched down in front of us again "At this time, we've determined that-"

"You're not *taking her*." Marissa said firmly

"Please listen closely to what I'm about to say, you may need to remember it in the future if it gets contested." The man said, slightly annoyed "We've determined that in this situation what you did was in service of the protection of your class B, and due to the circumstances, it was purely self-defense."

"Self-defense?" I asked "But *she* wasn't-" I caught myself before I accidentally talked him out of it

"Yes, in this case, Marissa counts as an intervenor. Usually you'd be looking at manslaughter in the case of self-defense ending in death, but because the attacker was a class B, there's no legal form of 'manslaughter' on the books. Since you were protecting your class B and acting in a role as guardian, we've decided you're allowed to keep your license and custody of Miss Park."

"Ohhhh thank the fucking gods." Marissa said, finally relaxing into a pile against the wall "Fuck, just fucking *say* that."

"I take it you have no objections to staying with Miss Lund, Miss Park?" he asked, looking at me

I shook my head furiously "No, none!"

He nodded and stood to leave, making another mark on his notepad, and Marissa tugged at his pants leg

"Hey, uh," she said "what about Raquel? She was pretty mad, is she..?"

The man made a face "Her license has been fully revoked and her access to class Bs restricted. She was found to have a fraudulently earned test result, and she adopted her class B from a government facility that should *not* have been adopting out the inmates. I'm sorry, but I'd recommend keeping Amber away from her, she's legally not allowed to be alone with her, or have a class B living in the house."

"Well. Fuck." Marissa said "That's fine, I don't care about her anyway, I was just hoping she wasn't going to be allowed to get a new one, I'm glad to hear that."

"Marissa?" a masculine voice called out, causing Marissa to let go of the man's leg and look around

I glanced over and saw John walking up to us, a slightly guilty look on his face. I flinched as he looked down at me in her hand with an odd expression "Your, uh, mom is here I had Drew go pick her up from the office. I know women are a lot better at dealing with this kind of emotional stuff, and-"

He looked over his shoulder at the kitchen where Raquel was and his shoulders dropped "...I'm a little busy with your *other* mom right now. If you're done here, it might be better for Raquel if you stepped out, maybe went home and took a nap."

Marissa looked at the man in green and he nodded, so she stood up "Yeah, I'll get out of your hair." she said quietly

"It's not like that, I just- she won't come out of the kitchen because she doesn't want to see you..." John said "She'll be fine soon."

"Yeah, I bet."

"I love you Missy, goodbye hug?" he asked

"...I gotta go." she muttered, and pushed past him, down the hall and out the front door

Miss Lund was standing next to the car, dressed in her business suit, and she nodded to us as we walked up.

"Hello, Marissa, I heard there was an accident?" she asked calmly

"Um, I..." Marissa said, her hand locking up. She looked down at me and back up to her mom "I- I think- I mean I *know*- I... I killed a guy."

Her hands started shaking and I had to brace myself to stop myself from falling over

"Mm, you killed *some*thing alright." Miss Lund said, still just as calm "Why did you do it?"

"He was- he- Amber, he was- I know you don't like me to have her, but he was *on* her, and she was screaming, and-"

"Tell me, do you value Amber?" Miss Lund said, cutting her off

"Mhhm, I really do." Marissa said, her voice cool and hollow

"You know what I think?" Miss Lund said, her finger finding my chin and gently tilting my face up to look at her

It was the first time she'd ever touched me. Her hands were warm, far too warm for someone with a heart as cold as hers

"I think..." she continued, her fingers dancing around my head "...that you did what you *needed* to in order to protect one of your assets."

"Asset?" Marissa asked, pulling me away from her mother's hand slightly

"Investment, asset, however you'd like to think of it." she said, stepping closer

Miss Lund had a smile on her face, it looked alien and wrong, broken in a way that clashed with how genuinely happy she looked.

"You did what you *had* to do to protect what's yours, what you *value*, even if it cost a life, even if others had to fall in front of you or lose the things *they* valued, you did it for *you*." she said softly, reaching her hand behind Marissa's head this time, brushing her hair out of her face "You're finally acting like my daughter again."

She embraced Marissa, and I was sealed between them as she held her daughter tightly and whispered to her, just loud enough for me to hear.

"I'm *proud* of you, Missy."

## Chapter Twenty-Eight

Marissa lay on her bed, arms spread out and staring up at her ceiling. I lay next to her, just far enough away that I wouldn't roll into the divot she was making, and I wrestled with my feelings. She was... scary again. Not because she was going to hurt me, but because I'd watched her kill a man as easily as opening a soda. I knew she had that power before of course, I understood it, that's why playing with her was so important, but to feel it, the crunch, the noises the man had made as he'd realized he was dead, it shook me.

I didn't feel sadness for him, not as much as I felt like I should. I mostly felt relieved about the ordeal; I'd never have to see him again, I'd never have to put up with his scary presence, I'd never have to- well, he'd never get to hurt me. I didn't feel sad over him, no. I did feel a regret over his death though, in a way. A sense that Marissa and I had lost something important, a connection we shared before she'd flicked him. I eyed her form next to me, massive and mind boggling, and I wondered if we'd be able to get it back. If I'd be able to feel at home with her again instead of just slightly safer than if I was alone.

She was *big*, and I didn't appreciate that enough. I could feel it when I touched her, when I experienced her hands or her mouth or even just laying on top of her, but it didn't capture her *size*. She was bigger than any living thing I'd ever seen before I was compressed, or anything I would *ever* have seen even if I traveled the world. Bigger than a whale, I bet, at least. I didn't know how big whales were, but she'd be bigger, if the diver comparisons I'd seen were right. I know it's rude to call your girlfriend a whale, but that's all I could think of that would compare...

There was something else bigger than whales, but it was a fungus or something, right? Like, a whole forest that was one living mushroom? I didn't remember exactly, but that wasn't a fair comparison. Trees would be a more apt comparison if we were leaving the animal kingdom, like... a redwood tree. They were super tall though, she'd be way smaller. What trees would be closer? How tall would she be if she was big, and I was regular? I was 94% compressed, so I'd be 6% of her size, and... hm. Math was hard to do in your head, but I think she'd be... around ninety feet? Maybe a hundred? There were trees that big, but I didn't know which ones. Maybe a better comparison would be the statue of liberty or like, an eight story building, I guess. That made her seem a lot more dangerous, a hundred foot Marissa versus a five and a half foot one. Not that it should *matter*, she was still the same as if she *was* a hundred feet to me.

I watched her breathe, her chest rising and falling, and wondered why I was thinking about her size *now* of all times, I should be coming to terms with the dead guy that'd fallen on me, or the fact that every class A I'd seen since the incident had made my heart jump. Hell, I hadn't even *begun* to process the assault itself, I was still reeling from everything, I couldn't even say I just wanted to lie here and think about it, because I *didn't*, I just wanted to forget the whole thing, pretend it never happened at all.

"Hey, Stre-mm..." Marissa started, then trailed off. She turned over and looked at me, but I kept staring at the ceiling "Amber?"

"What's up?" I asked softly

"You're- I'm..." she struggled to get her words together "Fuck, you know what I'm trying to ask..."

I frowned "I- what?"

I *didn't* know what she wanted to ask, and there were a million options, how could I possibly know which one was correct? Did she want to ask about what happened? Did she want to ask about *details* of what happened? Was she looking for playtime? If so, why pick *now* of all times? Didn't she notice I was in no mood to play? Although, the way I was feeling, if she asked, I'd say yes no matter *how* badly I felt. Knowing she could- *risking* her saying we're playing anyway was too terrifying to think about.

...Fuck, *this* is what that stupid therapist was talking about, wasn't it? Fuck fuck *fuck*, that was so stupid, we were *fine* yesterday, We'd be fine again soon, or at least I hoped we would be. I didn't know what to do, this was awful.

"I mean, like about me..." Marissa said, reminding me she'd been asking a question "You flinch when I touch you, you're not talking to me, you keep looking at me weird, but only when I'm not looking back at you. I know you're thinking about it, I get that, but.. like, are you- are you really scared of *me*?"

She rolled all the way over and curled up, her body and legs circling me on half of my body "I never wanted that, even when I was being cruel, I don't know what I'd do if you were actually scared of me..."

"..." I didn't respond, but I swallowed in case I had something to say

I didn't.

"Fuck, no, Amber, please..." Marissa pleaded "I'm not *really* scary, I did it for you, I was *protecting* you, that's, like, the opposite of scary, it's safe, right?"

I struggled for an anything to say, and settled on the least hurtful thing I could think of without lying "It's not about you, Marissa, it's about the size difference. You're the one who showed me just how easy we are to kill, yeah, but it's *all* class As. I can't look at them without thinking about all the ways they could kill me."

"*I'm* not going to kill you, though." she said, her voice pained

"I- well, I know that, like, in my brain..." I said slowly "But the rest of me keeps imagining you flicking me in the head. What if you'd flicked my head instead of my side on day one? I'm *still* slightly sore there a month later, I don't think I'd be here if you hit my head..."

"I'm not *stupid*, Amber." she said "I know not to hit people in the head."

"I know you're not stupid, but you bop my head all the time, you even hit me in the face hard enough to make my nose bleed once."

"Are you saying I'm doing a bad job?" she asked, her voice torn between insult and injury

"No, I just- it makes me think of stuff is all." I said "I could have died at any point, and I could *still* die at any point, and it'd be so, so easy for you- or anyone- to do it."

"No one's going to kill you, though." she said "I swear to you, I will keep you alive, no matter what."

"I know you'll try, I just- when your mom touched me earlier, all I could imagine is her twitching her finger and sending me tumbling off your hand to my death, and you *know* her, and it took *ages* for you to pull me back to you."

"She's- I don't think she'd kill you, not now." Marissa said "I'm pretty sure she's planning on letting me exempt you from testing, even."

"That's not a comfort, Missy." I said "I still have to think about all the *other* people who have to go through the tests, getting their blood drawn, being exposed to stuff, just one more reminder of how fragile and small we are."

"You *are* fragile and small, and that's why I'm never going to let anyone get close enough to hurt you again" she said firmly

She rolled over top of me and looked down, her face hanging over me, her wavy hair blocking out most of the light "You're *tiny*, Amber, and I love you. I liked you before you were tiny, and I'll love you even if you're scared of me. I'll do whatever it takes to make sure the woman I love is safe and cared for, and whatever that looks like, I'm ok with it."

I looked up at her and swallowed, she wasn't helping me feel any bigger looming over me like this, but being in her hair-curtains like this at least felt somewhat cozy. My stomach fluttered in fear and love, and I relaxed, watching her hover over me, searching my face for any hints or signs I disagreed.

"I do feel safer with you than anyone else..." I said "I love you too, Missy. It's not you, it's really not, it's just everything all hitting me at once..."

"...Can I kiss you?" she asked

I looked up at her, this was a weird time to ask that, I'd just- I looked at her mouth, thinking, then back to her eyes, her deep green eyes, and I melted a little.

"Ok, yeah." I said softly

She leaned down and kissed me softly on the face, her lips going around my head like two warm pillows. I tried to kiss back, but my own lips were lost in hers, and I did little more than press my face into her mouth. She broke away, and I curled up in a ball, tears streaming down my face. Her breath sucked in and she dropped lower to me her cheek pressed into the bed behind me, her breath washing over me as I shook.

"Fuck, I- *no*, you said I could, I was- it was supposed to be loving and *help* you, fuck." she said, her voice cracking "Are you crying because of me? Was it the kiss?"

I rolled over, still crying and I held out a hand to her. She met it with her finger, and I clutched it to my chest, hugging her tightly.

"I'm crying because I *can't* kiss you." I sobbed, rubbing my face on her fingertip "I can't kiss you, I can only *be* kissed, that's *horrible*."

"I- do you *want* to kiss me?" Marissa asked, trying to wipe the tears off my face

"*Obviously* I want to kiss my girlfriend, Missy!" I said in a flash of anger "I want to kiss you and hug you and make you feel nice, and all I can do is wrestle your fingers..."

"Well I want to hug *you* too, you know." Missy said "I want to feel your arms around my neck, or feel our cheeks press together, or have your head in my lap while we watch a movie, it's- I love you so so much, and I want more of you."

She looked at me with a feeling of sadness "Can I be honest? It's going to be a little offensive..."

I nodded, honesty was best right now, even if it hurt...

"I've been... almost *jealous* of you, getting to be held, feeling so much of me, getting to touch my body, you even went in my bra and just lay there, that's... that's so, *so* intimate. I love having power over you, I love getting to bully you and control you, but-"

She blinked and a tear rolled down her nose "I want what you have from me. I know I told you it wasn't a big deal last week, but it hurts, Amber. I want to be able to enjoy my girlfriend the way she enjoys me. I know it's not polite to tell a class B you're jealous of their disability, but I want to be held by you too..."

We were both crying now, and I hugged her finger "I wish I'd never compressed." I said, sniffling

"Yeah, I figured that much." she said "Fuck, I just- I want to melt into a puddle and wash away, I just feel like shit."

"I want to be buried somewhere and forgotten about for a few thousand years, until this feeling goes away." I said "I hate this, I don't know what to do..."

"I don't think there's anything *to* do." Marissa said "We dove into this thing headfirst, we ignored everyone around us, and now... we're just stuck with it."

"Stuck?" I asked "Do you feel stuck with me? It's ok if you do..."

"I *love* you, stupid." she said, mildly annoyed. "I'm not stuck with *you*, I'm stuck in a weird relationship where we can't really get what we want from the other."

"At least we can play, that's always a nice feeling." I said

"That's not a basis for a relationship, that's something you do in *addition* to a relationship." Marissa sighed "Or- with someone you don't have a relationship with at all. We've got the love, so we're doing ok there, but- I want to *show* you I love you."

I rubbed her finger as I thought "I want to show you I love you too. I can't kiss you, or hug you, or put my head in your lap, but we can still share each other's favorite things? We're playing games the other likes, we're showing each other our favorite shows, we're learning how to just sit and talk together, that's love. Those are *all* things that show love."

"You're holding my hand, you sleep in my bed, we share a room, and we functionally have a long distance relationship." Marissa said, her eyes finally dry. She sat up "Amber, I don't know how to fix you being scared, and I don't know how to fix the... physical issues, but..."

"We'll figure it out." I said, sitting up myself "I know we will."

She looked down at me with an expression of pain and pity, but she still smiled and picked me up "Yeah, we'll figure it out. Are you ok to..."

She thought for a moment "...sit in my shirt collar and watch some tv?"

I looked at her plain grey t-shirt and imagined sitting in it with her, using it as a blanket, my head just poking out of the neck hole. It wasn't me putting my head in her lap, it wasn't a hug, but it was something.

"I'd love that." I said "Maybe hug one of your plushies and think of me while we do it?"

She made a face, but nodded "That sounds pathetic and sad, but I need to hug something right now, yeah."

As we watched TV, I rubbed my face against the soft skin under her collar bone and imagined we were face to face; her wrapped around me, her head over mine. She hugged the stuffed bunny hard, and her chest sank in, making me feel like I was going to slip down into a world of Marissa and fabric. It wasn't what we'd wanted, I still wanted to kiss her, she still wanted to hug me for real, but it was what we had, and I felt safe again, so it was all we could really ask for.

~~~

We stood under the awning next to the tennis courts and watched the rain fall hard and heavy. It was too loud for me, and I had my hands clamped over my ears to blot out the noise. Marissa's face was sour and frustrated, but she didn't say anything, just turned and opened the door that led into the lockers, leading our group out of the noisy outdoors. Henri closed the umbrella she'd been holding and handed it back to Tracy, who put it in the drying rack, and we all looked around at the locker room, girls walking in and out of the showers and gyms, changing back out of tennis and swim clothes into more fashionable outfits.

"I can't believe today of all days got rained out." grumbled Marissa "Fuck, I was looking forward to this all season..."

"Aw, I'm sure they'll re-schedule our game, it's whatever." Quince said "I can kick your ass on Thursday instead."

"You- No, I have a better record than you, Quince, I don't think you'd be kicking anything." Marissa said, shaking her head

"I admit, I have been curious to see who is the better player." Henri said "Quince has an eye for weaknesses, but Marissa seems to be anywhere on the field she needs to be, it would have been a good match."

"They played last season, twice." Tracy said "They both won one, so the jury is out."

"Well, we have like, three hours free now." Kensey said from Quince's hand "Want to do something as a group?"

"I'm *not* going to the mall again." Quince said "I'm bored of that, something else. I don't care what."

"We could go skating?" Tracy asked "We haven't been in ages, and it's retro now, so we could get pics of the carpet and stuff to post."

"Yeah, but someone would have to stay at a table and watch the tinies." Quince pointed out "They can't go on the rink."

"I'd watch them!" Henri offered

"Nope, let's do something else." Marissa said "Uhh, I'm pretty good at bowling, we could go do that?"

"You're not 'good' at bowling, you use the bumpers." Tracy said "That doesn't count."

"It makes it more fun, you bounce the ball off them to get the best angles, why would I play if I'm going to get a gutter ball every time?" Marissa rolled her eyes

"I would be up for some karaoke, I know a bar with private rooms, I went there with Amber once!" Henri said

"Absolutely not. I'm not listening to Tracy warble out aughts pop again." Quince said

"Hey, it's part of the fun!" Tracy said, hurt "We can do it, you can suck it up."

"Nah, we'd need to keep the volume low so it doesn't hurt the class B's ears." Marissa said "We'd have to hear our voices while we sing, and no one wants that."

"Why not let *them* decide?" Henri asked "They will be left out of everything we do, why not find what is most interesting to them?"

"Huh, yeah, what do you guys want to do?" Quince asked me and Kensey

"I have no idea, I'm just going to hide in Marissa's pocket most of the time to be honest." I said, leaning against her "I'm not up for dangerous situations right now"

"Oh, *I* have an idea..." Kensey said with a smirk "The *perfect* rainy day activity..."

~~~

We stood in front of the building looking up at it. Marissa was still frustrated, and Kensey's plan hadn't changed her mood much, but Tracy was giggling, and Henri kept looking at me to gauge my reaction. I wasn't looking forward to this, but I'd play along for everyone else's sake.

"You know, if anyone else had suggested this, I'd have said it was offensive." Quince said "But..."

"Look, I've been to more than one company party here, it was one of the first things I thought of when I compressed, let me have this, ok?" Kensey said

"Let's just go inside." Marissa said, rolling her eyes

As we walked in, Kensey threw her hands out, waving them at the plastic grass, the tiny buildings, the wild paintings on the walls and made a trumpet sound with her mouth "Dun da duuun! I give you... The Miniature Village Indoor Mini Golf experience! Or, for me and Amber, The Normal-Sized Village Indoor Regular Golf experience!"

"Did you pick this place just so you could say that?" Tracy asked, shaking her head with a small grin on her face

"Nooo, of course not..." Kensey said "I also chose it so I could run around and explore the little buildings up close. Doesn't that sound like fun, Amber?"

"Uh, we might get stepped on?" I said nervously

"It's one 'o clock in the afternoon on a Monday, there's no one here." Quince said "We're the only people in the building, and none of *us* would step on you."

"..." I looked around, feeling vulnerable and scared. I didn't want to leave Marissa's side yet, I was still feeling fragile, and she was the only thing that helped that feeling, as scary as she was.

"Aw, come on, it could be fun..." Marissa said to me, her expression softening "Kensey seems excited about it, don't you think it's at least a little cool?"

"Yeah, I know it's cool, but like," I looked around "everyone's going to be hitting balls around, what if one goes where we are and crushes us?"

Marissa looked at me then around at the rest of the group "So if there was no risk of you getting hit with a ball, you'd do it?"

"Sure, I just can't be in danger right now, I need to know I'm safe." I said

"Got it." Marissa said, and walked up to the counter "Hey, how much to rent out the whole place for the next two hours?"

The man behind the counter frowned "We usually have to have a reservation for a party, we don't-"

"No, not a party, just us." Marissa said "Two hours, until three thirty. We won't even interfere with the after school rush."

"Huh, well." the man looked around the empty room "Games are fifteen, and you'd spend less than two hours playing through all eighteen holes, if I'm being honest. It would be cheaper to just pay the..." he looked at our group and counted "...sixty dollars and play normally."

Marissa dug in her purse with her free hand and pulled out her wallet, opening it up deftly and dropping two hundreds on the counter.

"Will this get you to lock the doors and stay behind the counter?" she asked, annoyed

"Hm." the man looked at the money and sighed "That's enough, yes. But if you mistreat the course or props, I'll still throw you out."

"Ok, fine, thanks. Lock the doors and go eat a sandwich or something." Marissa said "We're not messing with the props, we just want privacy."

The man shrugged and got up, locking the doors before going back to the counter "The putters are here, balls are in the basket, I'll be in the back, but I *do* have cameras on, so don't give me reason to check them, ok?"

"Yyyyup." Marissa said, tossing her purse onto a chair and grabbing a putter

"I'm confused, what's going on?" I asked her as she walked over to the others

"We're playing up one hole, then you two will get to explore the little town around each hole while we're ahead of you. No people, no danger." she said, passing me to Tracy and picking out a yellow ball

"That's so thoughtful of you!" Kensey said "Thank you, Marissa!"

"Mm, yeah. Come on, bitches, let's just play the first hole so the littles can enjoy themselves too." Marissa said, dropping her ball on the green "They need a break, this will be good for them."

The girls all played the first hole, a simple one where you hit the ball across a field to the outskirts of the town, and I found myself and Kensey placed down at the edge of the course.

"Have fun exploring, ladies!" Quince said "It's like, urban exploration, but tiny, that's so cute!"

"Be careful, and yell if you need anything, please!" Henri reminded us

After a flurry of steps and the sensation of something impossible moving, the girls were over by the next hole, Marissa lining up her next shot down main street.

"Alright, let's look around this little farm!" Kensey said "It looks like the buildings are in between my and your sizes, so we should both be able to explore."

"Yeah." I said, watching the girls and looking around the room nervously

I'd never been on the floor like this when I wasn't everyone's center of attention. It was one of the big rules of being a class B, don't ever be on the floor unless you absolutely *have* to be on the floor, and never, ever *stay* on the floor if you find yourself there. Don't run up to class As while you're on the floor, stay out of open areas on the floor, and try to be as loud and flashy as possible. Not 'wander around a mini golf course with four regular sized girls wandering around too'. That was just stupid behavior. Still, Marissa had paid two hundred dollars for me and Kensey to get this experience, so I'd just have to be extra *extra* careful.

"Come on, let's go look in the barn!" Kensey said, pulling on my arm

I was jerked along and I struggled to keep up as she ran over to the double doors and pulled me in.

"Oooh, little farm animals!" she said, admiring the plastic cows on one side of the room

I glanced over at the fake horses on my side, and raised an eyebrow, they were weirdly detailed, why were the cows just cows, and the horses so lifelike? I patted one on the head and glanced around the barn. Not much here, just regular sized hay and some toys. I wondered if we'd find anything worthwhile in any of the areas...

"Aw I had these when I was little!" Kensey said, coming up beside me "I was a bit of a horse girl, don't judge."

"I'm not, I was a weeb, I have no room to judge." I said, shrugging

"Weeb?" she asked "Huh, anyway, check *this* out."

She grabbed my hand and crouched down, pointing under the horse. I glanced over, then stood up quickly, stepping away from the figure.

"Why the *fuck* does it have a dick?" I asked

She shrugged, laughing "I have *no* idea, I just know that *all* the best quality horse figures had them, it was weird, but I never second guessed it as a kid."

"That's weird as fuck." I muttered, walking out of the barn and leaving the anatomically correct toys behind

"Hey, slow down!" she said "Wanna check out the farmhouse next?"

"Yyyeah, do you think it opens?" I asked, looking at the little house

"Let's see..." she said, walking up and jiggling the handle "Ah, nope. try the windows?"

I pulled on the plastic, and shrugged "It's glued. Looks like there's nothing inside though..."

"Aw... Oh well, come on, the others are ahead now, we can check out the main town area!"

We walked over to the street and walked into the town itself, the small buildings and fake trees giving me a weird sense of... nostalgia? I remembered being able to walk down the street like this...

"Wow, this place is pretty cool up close!" Kensey said "I swear it's based on our actual town."

"I think it is." I said, pointing "See that shop? That's the place Marissa bought me from."

"Ew, don't say 'bought'." she complained "That's not respectful of us."

I snorted "You sound like Nada."

"I've been talking to her a lot lately." Kensey sighed "She's really lonely, and she's really happy to have a lady her age to chat with locally."

"Fair, I guess." I said "Hey- town hall is open, we could look in there?"

"Ok, sure!" she said, walking up the stairs beside me, two steps to my one

We walked into the dark grey building and looked around. It was pretty plain, just grey floors and walls, nothing unique except for a half-counter along the back wall to give the illusion of detail if a class A happened to peek in.

I shrugged and walked around the room "Nothing of note, really."

"Yeah, just- hm, what's that behind the counter?" Kensey asked, pointing

I couldn't see from my angle, so I leaned over the grey foam wall and frowned, picking up a cloth sack "It's a little bag or something?"

I pulled on it, and it opened up. Inside was a button with string on it, half a french fry, a handkerchief, and a roll of cotton. I stepped back, looking around the room with in a new light.

"That's weird stuff to put back there. Is it a prop?" Kensey said

"It's- it's someone's stuff." I said "Food, a blanket, a pillow, and a button. There's someone *living* here, the french fry isn't even crunchy yet."

Kensey was quiet for a minute, then she bundled up the sack again and put it where we'd found it "...Should we tell someone?"

"..." I thought about it. If a class B *was* living here, in the buildings, they were hiding. It couldn't be safe for them to be in here, right? Which meant they were worried they'd be found and, what, returned to someone they didn't like? Be put on the market? I bit my lip. It wasn't our place to decide, to condemn whoever this was to a life they didn't want. There were safe ways for them to be found on their own, if they wanted that.

"No, we should pretend we didn't see anything." I finally said "It's not for us to decide if they get found or not."

"That's fair." Kensey said "We should get going, and, fuck, I guess stop exploring, so we don't accidentally expose them or something?"

"Yeah." I said "Fuck, let's just- let's get somewhere else."

We left the building and followed the other girls, at a distance, staying on the green, close to the edges. My eyes roamed all across the landscape, wondering if the mystery person was here, watching us from just out of sight. Maybe I'd tell Nada about them, in vague terms, to see what she thought. It couldn't be safe for them to be living without a guardian, but if they didn't want to be in the system. She'd be able to help me figure it out, I should absolutely mention it to her.

"So, uh, to change the topic, so we're not just walking around imagining living on scraps and sleeping in empty buildings..." Kensey said "Um, what's up with you and Marissa today?"

I glanced at her as we crested the fourteenth hole, a tiny replica of the mini golf place we were in.

"I *wasn't* thinking about that." I said "But Marissa and me, it's really complicated."

"Are you two in a fight?" she asked gently "Is she bullying you in the bad way again?"

"No, she's not." I said "We still love each other, uh, but this is something for her to tell the whole group, later, ok?"

"Oh..." Kensey said "That sounds serious."

"It is. I'll try to get her to talk about it to everyone, later, after golf. Ok?"

"Yeah, ok, sure." Kensey said, her expression looking protective and slightly scared at once "If she doesn't though, I'll understand. Just message me about it later, k?"

"Mm. We'll see, I guess." I said, sighing

I'd *like* Missy to say something, I was sick of having to feel like this and not be able to talk to anyone about it, but it was her issue too, she'd been the one to *do* it, so I couldn't just blurt it out without being an asshole. The group would probably go to get coffee or something after this, I'd try to initiate the conversation then.

~~~

We sat at a table at another one of the same cheap taco places Quince liked, and everyone took stock to make sure they'd gotten the right food. Henri had another one of the little taco-pizzas, Quince had several burritos stuffed with meat and hot sauce, Marissa had a slushie and some kind of taco salad piled high with chicken strips, and Tracy had a chicken quesadilla. Kensey and I had nothing, although Henri *had* given me a shard of her pizza with some guac on it to munch on. She'd finally admitted it was ok for me to have a little bit of uncompressed food, after having talked to the people about it in group.

"I wish we could go to *my* favorite taco place." Henri said, picking at her food "It has churros."

"It's drive-through only, we're *not* eating in my new car." Quince said, rolling her eyes

"I drove myself and Tracy." Henri said "*We* two could have eaten in my car at least, I have a backseat, even, if the rest of you would have liked to join us."

"Oooh, Henri just asked us all to join her in her backseat!" Tracy said, elbowing her

"I- ugh, no." Henri shook her head "Forget it, I just wanted to get churros."

Everyone was relaxed and looked so easy going. Marissa was the only one who wasn't smiling, and her hand kept finding its way over to me to touch me, like we needed to make sure we were both still there. Henri was watching me closely, her posture relaxed, but her face concerned. I noticed she'd never changed out of the tennis dress she'd put on for the game earlier, was she still trying to win me over with sports? She saw me staring, and opened her mouth to say something, but was cut off by Tracy leaning forward and slapping her hand on the table.

"Ok, I'll bite. What on earth is up with you two today?" she asked, pointing to me and Marissa "I need the goss, you've both been off all day, Marissa has been a *grump* and Amber has been acting like she just compressed, but you're *obviously* not fighting because you've been stuck together like glue, so what's up?"

Marissa glared at her and her fingers settled around me "Amber's just feeling fragile right now, it's none of your business."

"I'm pretty curious too, I wanna know the drama." Quince said, leaning in and smiling conspiratorially

"She is my friend, and she is not a fragile woman." Henri said "What made her so fragile?"

Marissa looked around and huffed, plucking me off the table and holding me to her chest "There was an incident, I'm not going to tell it because it's not just *my* story, you're being rude."

"It's ok." I said quietly "You can tell them, it might be good to have them help us through this..."

She glared at me, but rubbed me against her cheek gently "...Fine, ok, whatever." she said in a harsh, unsure tone

She set me back on the table and looked around the room, making sure we were alone "So, uh, yesterday, I was at my dad's house, and Raquel had adopted a class B since I'd seen her a few weeks ago."

"Oh, ew." Tracy said "She's the *last* person who should have one..."

"Yeah, she cheated on the test and had to adopt from some shady government place selling them under the table, it was stupid." Marissa said, glaring at the table "Anyway, she's manhandling him and not following the rules, and she asks if Amber can play with him, and I'm like 'no, what the fuck', but then she asks again, and Amber is like 'I guess it's ok', and I put her in the box with the guy while I talk to my parents..."

"The box?" Henri asked, a little worried

"Like, a box without a lid, it was his house or something." Marissa clarified "Anyway, they talk, and it seems fine, and then I hear a weird noise, and I look around, and there's nothing, so I check on Am-amber, and sh-she, uh, th-the g-guy is on t-top of her and like, p-pulling at her clothes and she's s-screaming..."

"Oh, *gods*, what the fuck?" Tracy said, shocked

"*Please* tell me you knocked him the fuck out." Quince said with a scowl

"Uh, w-well, I just, I see him, and I'm s-scared, and I just w-want him off her..." Marissa choked out, her hands shaking as she tried to get the words out "And I j-just r-reach over and f-flick him in th-the head, and there's a pop, and h-he s-st-stops m-moving..."

"You... killed him?" Henri asks quietly

"Y-yeah. The cops came, social services came, they investigated, it was a big deal." Marissa said, her body drooping now that the story was out

"I... Jesus, Marissa, I feel sick just *hearing* about that..." Quince said, putting her hand on Marissa's shoulder "That was yesterday? I can't believe you're even up for leaving the house..."

"I wanted to play tennis." Marissa said simply

"So- that's a really serious thing that happened..." Kensey said "I get why you two are shaken up now, but I have to ask, is Amber in danger of getting taken away?"

"No, I'm safe." I said solemnly "She gets to keep me."

"Do you *want* her to keep you?" Tracy asked me "She killed a guy right in front of you."

"Tracy!" Marissa said, her eyes flashing "Seriously?! What the fuck?"

"I want her to!" I said quickly "She's the only person I trust right now, I'm scared, but I still need her..."

"I can take you for a couple days if you need space." Quince offered "I know you feel pretty safe at my house, and I loved watching you."

"Thanks, but... I need Marissa." I said

"Marissa, you did what needed to be done to protect our loved one." Henri said "I cannot fault you for that. I think you did the right thing."

"You sound like my mom." Marissa said, looking at the table "She said something similar."

"Your mom thought you killing a guy was the right thing to do?" Kensey asked "Oh, nope, yeah that tracks."

"She said Missy was 'protecting an asset', and that she was 'proud of her'." I told her "It gave me chills..."

"Asset?" Tracy said, looking at us with a stricken look on her face "She- ugh..."

Her face twisted, and she frowned, resolution written across her features. She looked at Marissa and looked like she wanted to say something, but slumped, and back and shook her head.

"Spit it out, Trace." Marissa sighed "Just say it."

"W-well, I was thinking," Tracy said carefully, the look of determination creeping back in "I was wondering if maybe you could come with me to do a tour of the lab Wednesday afternoon? We've got lots of class Bs there, and, um, I just think if you were *there*, it could help you come to terms with what you did, because you were *helping* a class B, and that's all we do there. And, uh, maybe you being there and experiencing it could help you change your mom's mind about class Bs being... 'assets'?"

"A tour?" Marissa asked "I'll *own* it soon enough, why do I need a tour?"

"I'll take a tour, Trace." Quince said "I'm curious about it, and I want to see all the little baybees."

"Ooh, bring me along too!" Kensey said, perking up "I want to see all the advancements you're making!"

"I will pass." Henri said "I would not take it well, I think, to see them all getting tested on."

"We don't test on them in bad ways, we treat them like *people*." Tracy said "and it wasn't an open invitation, it was just to Marissa."

"Well, I'm not spending the whole afternoon with you alone at a lab while you tell me science stuff, that sounds boring. So Quince is coming too." Marissa said "But fine, I'll go."

"Oh, uh, that's- I don't know if I can get her in, but we'll see." Tracy said nervously "Thank you, I just- I think this will be really helpful. I'm really sorry about what happened."

"Yeah, that's really fucked up, if you need to talk, I've got you." Quince nodded

"I would be willing to talk as well." Henri nodded "I cannot imagine it would easy to have that weighing on you."

Marissa looked around, surprised and touched "Oh, wow, thanks, you guys. I didn't expect you to actually care, I guess."

"I *like* the new Marissa, I care about her a lot." Quince said "The old Marissa *never* would have apologized about getting drunk or opened up like you just did."

"You have grown a lot, ja, I want to see you keep growing, for Amber's sake and for the sake of this friend group I have found myself in." Henri said gently

"We all love you, Marissa." I told her "I know you don't think it's possible, but if you treat people well, and don't use them like tools, they'll be there for you. I'll be there for you no matter what."

Marissa's mouth was tight, and she looked around at the table at each of us there, looking back at her. She stood up and swallowed .

"Thanks, yeah. I appreciate it. I'll be back, I have to go pee." she grabbed her purse off the back of the chair and walked quickly to the bathrooms, not looking back

"Aaand we made her cry, great." Tracy said "At least it was a happy cry this time."

"She was crying?" Henri asked "I never would have guessed..."

"She's a secret cryer, she hides to cry." I said "But yeah, she was crying."

"Crying like a *bitch*." Quince nodded "She'll be back in a few minutes. Fuck, I hope she takes what we said to heart though, I really do like this more recent version of her."

"Aside from her getting drunk and attacking us, the past couple weeks have been pretty great, yeah. Mostly drama-free." Tracy agreed, sighing. She looked sad, almost worried "I just- I hope she'll be... Well, she'll be whoever she is, wherever she is, I guess."

"That's a weird way to put it," Quince said "but yeah, I agree. Henri, you sure you don't want in on the tour?"

"*You're* not even invited on the tour." grumbled Tracy

"I am fine, I would not enjoy it." Henri nodded

"More free samples for the rest of us, then." Kensey shrugged

"Free- What free samples?" Tracy asked incredulously

"You know exactly what free samples." Quince said "I'm walking out of there with at least three new class Bs, all to myself."

As the chatter went on and I waited impatiently for Marissa to return, I was once again amazed at how seamlessly Henri, Kensey, and I had slipped into the friend group. The ease at which they offered support for each other, the care, the quick forgiveness for serious things, it all felt invincible, like nothing could tear the group apart. I crunched a bite of my guac-chip and let the feeling of belonging wash over me. It wasn't the same safe feeling I got with Marissa, but I wasn't scared around these people either, they were a safe place, even if I still wanted Marissa more, and that was very important to have.

# Chapter Twenty-Nine

I sighed and closed the tablet, stuffing it into my bag. Nada had been *no* help with the class B that was living in the mini golf place. She just kept going on and on about "reporting them to the proper authorities", and getting mad at me when I refused to tell her where I'd found them. I'd already decided I wouldn't narc on them, so her acting like this just served to tick me off. I shouldn't have asked for her opinion on it, really. I'd known what she'd most likely have said, so there was no point in even having let her know we'd *found* someone.

I poked my head out of Marissa's hoodie pocket and looked around. We were *still* waiting in the entrance to Millon Labs for Tracy to get back with the guest keycards. It looked like we were the only people here for some reason, even the person behind the desk was gone. Quince was across the room from us playing a game on her phone with Kensey, the sound low enough that I couldn't quite tell what it was, but it looked like it was a two player game. I'd have to ask Kay about it later, it'd be nice to have a phone game to play with Missy every now and then.

I climbed out of the pocket and onto Marissa's tummy, lying on my side as I looked up at her sullen and slightly annoyed face. She'd been complaining about having to come here for the past day and a half already, and now that she was having to sit and wait, she was even more annoyed. She put her hand over me without looking and slid down in her seat, crossing her legs with a sense of frustration, and rubbed my back with her thumb, the gentle movement mismatched to her grumpy attitude.

Finally, after what had seemed like ages, the door to the waiting room opened up and Tracy walked back in holding a couple lanyards with white squares on them. She glanced at us and waved for us to get up, holding the door open with her foot. She looked stressed and annoyed, but I was just happy to finally see her after over half an hour of nothing.

"Ok, I managed to get the passes, the alarms won't go off or anything now." she said "I told everyone to go home until tonight so we'd have the place to ourselves, and I ended up having to figure out how to make these stupid things in the security office myself."

Marissa picked me up and her hand went up to her chest, pressing against her sternum, her warmth radiating into me "It's about time, I was getting ready to leave."

"I wasn't!" Quince said "I want to see all the tinies so bad, I'd have waited for days!"

"She's been talking about this for the past day and a half." Kensey laughed "She's *really* excited."

"Mm, well, I'm not thrilled about you being here, this was just supposed to be a *private* tour, Quince." Tracy said, giving her a look "This is very important to the future of the lab, and you being here might affect that."

"Well, she's here, so let's get on with it." Marissa said, grabbing one of the lanyards "Amber doesn't need one of these?"

"No, she's too small to trip the sensors, just hold her." Tracy said, opening the door all the way "Come on, first step is showing you how we process the new class Bs."

"Wow, *so* exciting." Marissa said, rolling her eyes, but she followed anyway with Quince close behind

The hallway led to a small room with an 'airlock' styled security gate with an empty desk, and Tracy showed Marissa and Quince how to scan their cards at each checkpoint, letting them through into a larger room on the other side. The room was brightly lit and had rows and rows of small baskets on the walls with sizes on them, measured in millimeters. There were a few tables in the center of the room, and a rack of cleansuits on one wall with names above them and small lockers below them. Tracy walked over to a small machine on one of the tables and turned it on, a sound like a faucet filling the air.

"This is where we process new test subjects to get them ready for the treatments." she said "This little box here is one of our creations, it's a class B sterilization chamber! They climb in, and using a mix of water and very gentle chemicals, they get clean and germ-free in less than two minutes, far shorter than if they took a shower themselves."

"I should get that for you, Kay." Quince said "Maybe *then* you'd stop taking forty minute showers."

"I barely use any water, you can't complain about that." Kensey said, rolling her eyes "Plus a long, hot shower is one of life's pleasures, I don't want to give that up."

"It's not about the water, it's that we can't hang out while you're in there." Quince said "But I get it, I like showers too."

"So you made a washing machine for class Bs, cool." Marissa said "Is this what you wanted to show me?"

"I- no, ugh, I'm walking you through the process, you need to understand what we're doing here before we get to the meat." Tracy said "We wash them first, then we get them a kit that's their size, as accurate as we can get it."

She pointed to the baskets "These are kits for class Bs, they have food, clothes, soaps, blankets, lots of stuff, special made for the class Bs, down to the millimeter."

"Can I have one of the kits?" Kensey asked "I'm about, uhh, I *think* 180 millimeters? I'm not great with metric."

"W-well, I can't really give them away." Tracy said "They're all accounted for, we'd have to process you through the system as a test subject."

"Ah, damn..." Quince said, shaking her head "You would have looked cute in a lab coat."

"She wouldn't get a lab coat, it's scrubs." Tracy said "Anyways, once that's done, then a trained professional will bring the class B to the living quarters. Some of them are here for just a while, like volunteers for a couple days, and some are here full time with the lab itself being their legal guardian. Kinda."

"So," I said, speaking up "do the ones who're here full time have a choice to be here?"

"Of course!" Tracy nodded "If they ever want to leave, we'll help re-home them to the best of our ability. We're not forcing *any* of the people here to be here."

She waved us on to the next room, and we filed in after her. The next room, while still brightly lit, was much more cluttered and packed full of things on tables and desks. I examined some of the machines, they looked dangerous... I wasn't sure I really liked the looks of some of them, they were sharp and scary looking. Marissa stopped in front of one of the tables and frowned, poking one of the more intimidating ones with a finger.

"Uh, is there any reason why you need a thingie with needles on it and a place to strap class Bs?" she asked, looking at the multiple syringes sticking out of the top

"Oh, that's to give them their nutrients and to take blood and stuff!" Tracy said "See, their skin is way, *way* too thin to actually let a class A give them shots or take blood, one twitch and they'd be impaled. We made this thing so we can take samples of their cells and inject them with medicines without risking hurting them."

"Do you often need to take blood?" Quince asked, poking her head into a much bigger machine meant for full sized people

"Well, yeah, we need a *lot* of blood." Tracy said "We're trying to find out as much as we can about the compression particles, and pre-compressed particles are important for that."

*The Feeling of Being Valued* 537

"What's to understand?" Marissa said "That's what I don't get, we know how they work; they convert cells with the genetic components into more of themselves and then spread. I don't know why you and my mom are trying to figure out more, it's pretty easy to get."

"It's not that easy." Tracy said "The particles do convert cells into more of themselves, but if it *just* did that, there'd be huge piles of compression particles every time someone compressed, and if it was pure *compression*, the class Bs would weigh almost as much as they did *pre*-compression, they'd just be, well, compressed. They'd most likely suffocate because their bodies would be too heavy for their size."

"Ok, so there's a mix of conversion and compression, got it." Marissa said "It's still not that helpful."

"No- look, there's more to it than that." Tracy sighed "We can track how much something compressed based on weight, and we can check how much is converted to more compression cells by letting people compress in an enclosed environment and checking the compression cell count in the air before and after. Those two things combined make up for roughly thirty five percent of the missing mass."

"You mean there's almost three fifths of the person that just goes missing?" Kensey asked "That doesn't make sense, where did it go?"

"That's a large part of what we're trying to figure out here." Tracy said "It's important, it goes somewhere, but it's not *here*, it's... somewhere else. If we could find out *where*, we might be able to get people their size back, or, at least a few feet of it."

"Ok, ok, I get it." Marissa said "You're trying to cure class Bs, I support that, I'd *love* to have a mostly regular sized girlfriend to boss around and keep as a pet. My mom still isn't going to let you keep doing this research even if I tell her this though."

"So even if she was her normal size, Amber'd *still* be a pet?" Quince asked

"Yes." I said, nodding. Of course I would, what else would I be? I belonged to Marissa now, whatever size I was.

"I'm not trying to convince your mom with *just* this." Tracy said "It- it's complicated."

"You drug me all the way out here, so start talking, bitch." Marissa sighed, putting me on her shoulder and crossing her arms

"I am, or- I'm trying to." Tracy said "We're making better food for them, we're finding what hurts them, we're making medicine to boost their immune systems- did you know there are now viruses that are adapting *just* for class Bs? It's our *job* to help them, to make them safer, to cure them if we can. We *have* to."

"You're pretty passionate about this." Quince said "This passion happened in, what, a month since starting your internship?"

"Yeah, you almost cried when I made you hold Amber the day after I got her." Marissa said "It's just weird you did a full one eighty."

"Uh, uh-huh, yeah, about that..." Tracy said, taking a breath "After that day I held Amber, I was freaked *out*. I went home, and I complained to my dad about it, having to *hold* someone, to feel them in my hands, to be that big and not know what to do with them..."

She brushed her hair out of her face and swiped her keycard at the next door "He got quiet, and the next day he signed me up for the internship. He said it was important."

"You knew he worked with class Bs, and you complained to him about having to touch a class B?" Kensey asked "That's just rude."

"No- I was just venting, really. He listened to me though and wanted to do something about it." Tracy said "Did I ever talk to you guys about my mom?"

"I haven't heard you mention your mom in like, years." Marissa said "I assumed she left your dad and you didn't want to give us fuel to hurt you over it."

"No, there was a car crash." Tracy said, opening the door and propping it open "A head on collision, everyone involved died."

"Oh, *fuck*" Quince gasped "Your mom is dead?!"

"It was a compression accident." Tracy said, not listening as she led us into the next room. "She compressed while driving and lost control."

There were rows and rows of plastic tubs, frosted covers over them, hiding their contents. The lights in the room were dim, but many of the tubs were lit up from the inside, shining out into the walkways as we walked past. I peered at the boxes, and I could see movement in some of them, shadows moving inside, as the inhabitants went about their lives. These must be apartments, homes for the class Bs who lived in the lab. We were passing through a whole town enclosed in plastic bins. The muffled sound of videos and music slipped out of a few of them as we walked past, getting deeper and deeper into the room full of tiny people.

"Fuck..." Marissa said "So the virus killed her, then. That really sucks."

"Yeah, for like, two *years* I mourned the loss of my mother, blamed the virus, hated class Bs, I was so scared of them..." Tracy said, her voice quiet. "The first day of my internship, my dad brought me into this room, and he showed me something that changed all of that..."

We stood in front of an extra large tank, one with more floors and a wider base. There were pipes going in and out and there was a thick wire going into the side. This one was a permanent fixture, not to be moved and replaced like the others. There was a large plaque above it that read 'subject 001' in block letters, and a camera pointed directly at the tank itself. Tracy reached out to the frosted glass cover, unsnapping it to reveal the inside of the apartment, and stepped back, waving a hand at the glass. Inside was a woman about five inches tall, middle aged, missing a leg, facial scars on her left side, sitting in a comfortable looking chair.

"My mom died on paper." she said "She's legally dead, but as you can see, my dad found her in the wreck after the police declared her dead. Her leg was crushed off before she compressed all the way, and there was enough... biological material in the wreck that they assumed she didn't make it."

Tracy put her hand on the glass, barely aware we were here "My dad's been working to fix her ever since."

The woman, Tracy's mom, waved gently at her, and gave us a sad smile. She didn't say anything, just watched us through the glass, her gaze resting on

Tracy. Tracy's fingers pressed into the glass until her fingertips turned white, lost in her own world. I looked around at the others to see what they were thinking. Marissa and Quince looked somber, which was understandable, they'd more than likely known this lady since they were kids, and had just gone through a roller coaster of thinking she was alive, then dead, then finding out she was compressed and still injured from the accident. Kensey met my eyes, and looked at me seriously, nodding to me like she was confirming something, but I had no idea what.

"I love you, mom..." Tracy whispered, tapping the glass, and she leaned away, turning back to the rest of us, tears in her eyes "If there's *any* way to help her, any chance I get my mom back, back to normal at least, I will to do *everything* I can to make that happen."

"Yeah, no- of course." Marissa said, her sour mood gone "I'll do anything to help as well, I- I had no idea..."

She grimaced "I still don't know how that will help convince my mom though, but we *really* need to find a way to convince her now."

"It was already pretty urgent." I said, glancing up at her

"Yeah, but- you know what I mean." Marissa said "Now it's like, even more personal."

"I'd like to help any way I can too..." Quince said "What do we need to do?"

Tracy took a long shaky breath and swallowed "We need to- we need a break-through. We need something that will prove that we can un-do the virus."

"Is it possible?" Marissa asked "I mean, fuck, I'd have heard about it if was, right?"

"You wouldn't have." Tracy said, shaking her head firmly "We're the only lab working on this stuff, and we don't talk about stuff publicly until it's ready. But we're *almost* ready."

"So if we do the breakthrough, what then?" Quince asked

"Then people stop selling Miss Lund their stocks, my dad keeps majority control, and we get to keep the lab. I get to save my mom, and we get to *cure* everyone who needs it." Tracy said

"Oh fuck, yeah that's like, an actual serious plan, yeah." Marissa said, uncrossing her arms "I'm on board, but seriously, what do you need *me* to do?"

"This is the hard part." Tracy said "I kinda sort of... need all your blood."

"That's some serial killer sounding shit right there..." Kensey muttered

"I *like* my blood though." Quince said, taking a step back "Do you need *mine* too?"

"It sounds bad, but you guys have uncompressed blood without the genetic triggers, we need more of *that* to study where the particles go when they're infected. We can use your blood as a baseline or a mixer to run tests on the compression rates." Tracy said "Your blood won't be *taken*, just swapped out with blood we've already run the tests on, ok?"

"Like, you pull the blood out one arm and pump it in another?" I asked

"We have an exchange transfusion machine..." Tracy said "It's both sides in one arm, but it kinda works like that, yeah."

"Ok, so what, we set up an appointment?" Marissa asked

"If you're ok with it..." Tracy said "I've been trained on how the machine works, I was going to ask if you're ok with me taking your blood right now."

"That seems really dangerous to do without a doctor here." I said "We should wait, right?"

"We don't have *time* to wait, we need to get the blood in stock before the night shift. I want to make the breakthrough tonight, if possible. There's not many more stocks left to buy before Miss Lund *owns* this place." Tracy said, rolling up her sleeve "Look, I already did it to myself, see?"

Sure enough, there were bits of gauze on her arm, with a tiny bit of blood seeping through. I looked at Marissa, she was frowning, but she wasn't saying no...

"Come on, Missy, this is dumb, at least tell her to call in another person to do it for her, she's an *intern*." I protested

"*I'll* do it." Quince said "I'll swap out my blood..."

"I'll do it too then, I guess" Marissa said, glancing at Quince and petting me softly

"Ok, thank you..." Tracy sighed in relief "Come on, the exchange transfusion machine is over here."

She lead us into still another room, this one with another dual airlock that protruded into the room, and we found ourselves in what looked like a garage or a warehouse, with rows and rows of tall metal shelves full of medical supplies. Blue bay doors lined one wall, and the rest of the room was lit in dim, hanging fluorescents. There were large tanks up close to the ceiling with hoses trailing down close to the floor, and a table-bed in the middle of the room with a big square box next to it. Tracy walked up to the machine and pressed a button, and a whirring noise started, filling the room. She turned to us and pointed to Marissa and Quince, her finger going back and forth between the two of them.

"Ok, who has what blood type?" she asked

"Uh, I'm O positive." Marissa said

"I think I'm A positive?" Quince said, shrugging

"Marissa, we'll start with you then." Tracy said with a tight smile "The process takes up to three hours, and the lab workers will be here at eight to start their shift, so we need to get the blood out of you *now* or they won't have time to run the experiments."

"O-ok." Marissa said "Uh, will I be knocked out? Or..?"

"Nope, we'll be here keeping you company, it's ok." Tracy said "Quince, if you could bring some chairs over?"

"I'm nervous," Quince said, dragging some office chairs over "is this legal? Will they be allowed to use the blood if there's no one official here to take it?"

"*I'm* official, damnit, I work here." Tracy said "Come on, Marissa, get on the table, we've got a lot to do."

"This feels really stupid," Kensey said "I don't like this either."

"Well, you and Quince can complain about it later, we're doing this." Marissa said "All my life I've wanted to give a 'fuck you' to my mom, and this honestly might be my best shot at it."

"Won't this hurt you too?" I asked her "This would be *your* company soon enough if you don't fuck up the deal."

"I'm sure she'd rather help people like you than to have a lab, Amber." Tracy said, helping Marissa up onto the bed "Just think, you could gain up to three or four feet back!"

"Yeah, but I'd still be all short." I said, frowning

"It's way better to be short than to be tiny." Kensey said "Fuck, if this works even a little, I might be a real person again..."

"You can still live with me, if you like." Quince said "Even if you get bigger, I don't care. We have guest rooms and stuff."

"Aw, that's sweet of you!" Kensey said "I'll have to think about it."

"So like, is this something we might be able to do tonight?" Marissa said, wincing as Tracy poked a needle into her arm "Like, am I going to actually be able to hold Amber in my arms as we fall asleep or something else gay like that?"

I climbed down onto her chest and gave her a hug, pushing my face into her hoodie to make it feel more 'real'. I wanted to be able to hug her for real, but as long as I was close to her, that's what mattered.

"I don't think- um." Tracy said, poking the other needle in "Well, if we *do* manage to find where the extra material goes, we might be able to run some tests, yeah."

She sounded unsure, and it sounded like she was lying, but I hadn't expected her to be able to 'fix' me today in the first place.

"So- a-h-h-h, ugh, *fuck*, that feels weird." Marissa shuddered as the machine kicked in, blood filling both tubes going to her arm "It's kinda cold..."

"It'll warm up in a second." Tracy said "Just- we gotta wait it out now."

Tracy's hands were shaking as she pressed the buttons on the machine, checking the readout and making sure the needles in Marissa's arm were in place. She must be nervous, this was a last resort for her, for her mom. If she didn't get the breakthrough she was looking for, her mom could be used for any number of horrible experiments, and she might lose her all over again. I could understand her nervousness. I looked around the room for something to take her mind off the blood transfer, and saw a big TV in one corner.

"Hey, Quince," I said, pointing "wanna see if you can cast to that?"

"You want to play music or something?" she asked, pulling her phone out of her purse and setting the bag on the floor

"No, I was just thinking, we never *did* get to watch Freaky Friday."

Quince grinned "Oooh, perfect! Trace, can I..?"

"Uh, y-yeah, g-go ahead." Tracy mumbled, still looking at the machine, tears in her eyes "I- I'm just- yeah, let's watch a movie."

Quince set Kensey on Marissa's chest with me and ran over to see if she could move the tv closer, and I smiled at Kensey.

"Kinda feeling a little hopeful about this, how about you?" I asked

"I'm waiting to see." she said, frowning "It's just- hm. I just want to wait and see."

"We gotta t-try." Marissa said, shivering "If we h-have th-the power to t-try, we n-need to. It's th-the r-right thing t-to do"

"Yeah, that's a good way to look at it." Kensey nodded, and took my hand in hers, squeezing it gently

As Quince dragged the TV stand over to us, my stomach filled with butterflies, and I wondered if we *were* doing the right thing. It *felt* like we were doing something wrong, but we had the passes, Tracy worked here, her dad owned it, and people were coming in later to help us, so it couldn't be anything that'd get us arrested or anything, right..?

~~~

"I'm n-not feeling great." Marissa said "I'm all dizzy and my guts hurt..."

"That's normal." Tracy said, her jaw clenched "You just have a few more minutes to go..."

"You seem tense, was watching the remake right after a bad idea?" Quince asked

"What?" Tracy asked "No, uh, I'm just distracted."

She checked a readout on the machine and swallowed hard, her eyes watering. I hugged Marissa's neck tightly and took a deep breath. It was close to six in the evening already, not enough time to finish replacing Quince's blood as well before people showed up. Hopefully they didn't mind too much, maybe they could mess with Marissa's blood for a while until Quince was drained or something. Kensey stood up and popped her back, making Missy groggily glare at her for getting footprints on her chest

"Hey Quince, come get me, I'm guessing Amber and me will be using you as a sofa next, and I need to stretch before then." she said

"Yeah, get- get her off Marissa, and here, Amber, come with me." Tracy said, reaching out for me

I climbed into her hand, feeling it tremble and I felt nervous again, maybe we *were* doing something illegal after all? She set me on the flat part of a close by shelf and turned back to the tubes, checking how they went into Marissa's arms. She poked them and Missy flinched, pulling away slightly with a glare. Tracy stood up straight and lightly slapped herself in the face, taking a deep breath.

"Quince, I need to get more needles for your turn, could you go to the room with the little machines and get some?" she said "They'll be next to the blood-drawing station."

"Uh, yeah, can I peek at some class Bs on my way there?" Quince asked "I've hardly got to see any, and that was the whole reason I *came* on this tour."

"I- just don't bother them, knock first before you take the frosted screen off." Tracy said, shooing her away with a wave of her hand

"Yes!" Quince said, pumping her fist "Come on Kay, let's find ourselves some new tiny friends."

As Quince headed for the airlock, Marissa shifted up on the bed, looking groggy and a little worse for wear.

"Is it almost done?" she said, her voice heavy "I want to get these tubes out of me..."

"Y-yeah, just," Tracy said, flinching "let me..."

She shut off the machine and carefully removed the needles from Marissa's arm, wrapping a bandage around it and tying it closed. She stared at Marissa for a moment, and put her hand on her chest, breathing heavily.

"Are you ok?" I asked "You look like you're about to puke."

"Yup, yup yup. I am fan-*tastic*." Tracy said, looking around "Marissa, just lie there for a moment longer..."

I heard a muffled thumping and glanced over to see Quince and Kensey, still in the airlock. Quince was waving at us, pointing to her keycard, then to the door and shaking her head. It wasn't letting her through? Was she trapped in the airlock? I waved at Tracy to get her attention.

"Hey, I think Quince is stuck." I said, pointing

"Yeah, I know." she said simply, pulling on one of the hoses connected to the ceiling, something dripping from the end.

"Ok, um, M-Marissa? L-lay still, ok? I want this to fully cover you so there's no accidents." she said, holding the hose up

"Accidents? Trace, what are-" Marissa said, before being cut off by a blast of water to the face.

I shrieked, what was going on?! Marissa sputtered and held her hands up to catch the water, but Tracy kept spraying until she was fully soaked, her body, the bed, the machine, all dripping wet. I walked over to the edge of the shelf and glared at her as Marissa indignantly tugged at her hoodie and tried to wring her hair out.

"You fucking *bitch*, what was that? I was a little sleepy so you decide to *soak* me?" Marissa growled sitting fully upright "What the fuck?"

"No, it- Marissa, I'm so sorry..." Tracy said, still shaking "I need to save my mom, this is the only way..."

"What did you do?" I asked "Wait- did *you* trap Quince? That was on purpose, wasn't it? What is this?"

"She wasn't even supposed to *be* here, Amber!" Tracy yelled, her voice cracking and her tears finally falling "I just- there's only one way to save my mom, I can't stop Miss Lund from getting the lab, it's too late. No matter *how* much blood we have, we'll *never* find out where the extra mass goes, this- the *only* way to make sure my mom stays safe is to make sure Miss Lund cares enough about class Bs to actually *help* us instead of stripping everything, and there's only one way to make *sure* she cares..."

Marissa stared at Tracy, her eyes wide, then she looked at the machine, and she shuddered violently "Oh, gods, Trace, *no*, fucking *tell* me you didn't do what I think you did..."

"I did, Marissa." Tracy said, the tears dripping off her face mixing with the contaminated water pooling on the floor "I replaced your blood with the blood of people who had the compression mutation, I'm sorry, I had to... We never even needed your blood, it was a trick."

"I'm- but- I'm *immune*..." Marissa muttered

"Not anymore." Tracy said, sniffling "I'm so sorry Marissa, I'll take good care of you here, we'll keep you with Amber, even. I just..."

"Can you undo it?" I asked "Quick, give her the un-mutated blood back! It took hours and hours before the infection set in for me, we have time!"

"...No." Tracy said "This is grey-water from *years* of compression experiments. We don't have hours, we have minutes."

"I am going to fucking *kill* you." Marissa snarled, sliding off the table and balling up her fists

Tracy stepped back "Do it, I don't give a fuck." she said tiredly "I knew what I was doing. I'm saving my mom from yours, I don't care about myself anymore. I threw my only friendships away for this, I'll lose whatever I need to."

"Missy, don't!" I yelled "She's our only way out of here!"

Marissa glanced over at me, her expression softening, and she reached out to touch me. She never got close enough though, she doubled over and moaned in pain, collapsing to the floor in a ball. I screamed and ran back and forth on the shelf I was on, looking for a way down, I could knock the racks off and slide down them, but if she was about to compress, and I got caught up in it-

She moaned again, and the ground around her split and cracked, the noise louder than I expected, making me jump.

"What was that?!" I asked "Why is the ground breaking?!"

"The part she's on is compressing with her." Tracy said, still looking tired and dead inside "She's already started..."

Marissa moaned again, and grabbed the shelf I was on for support, her body blurring. It looked like vibrations, some kind of twisting, shimmering glass. I could see her body melting away, getting smaller as she struggled to stand back up. She pulled herself to her feet, the ground under her splintering and cracking, making her sink, but her head was already below the shelf I was on. She'd lost at least two feet already. There was a twisting metallic noise as the part of the shelf she was resting against compressed under her touch and the whole thing shook, knocking me to my butt.

"It- it *hurts*, it's n-not s-supposed to hurt I thought?" Marissa wheezed. I peeked over the shelf to see her grabbing her chest, the side of the shelf and the floor still folding in on themselves as she got smaller still

"Marissa!" I screamed, slapping my hands against the metal "Missy, no! Please, Tracy, help her!"

"I'm not getting anywhere near her." Tracy said "I'd lose a limb. It's- it's going to be ok. I'll take really, really good care of you two, I'll get Quince to hang out with us still, and if she can be *normal* about it, maybe even Henri, I promise, it's going to be fine."

She bent down, crouching on the edge of the dusty circle Marissa was compressing in and ignored the pen I threw at her "Marissa, I *will* fix you, and your mom is going to help me do it. You'll be ok, I swear to you."

"F-fuck you, you f-fucking *bitch*." Marissa mumbled, and vomited under the shelf

It buckled again and I braced myself as I was knocked over again, dropping to my hands "Tracy, please, you know what Miss Lund will do her if she sees her like this..." I said, fighting off tears.

Our life was *ruined*, we couldn't go back to her room, we couldn't play our games, or go to school together like we used to. Marissa's whole future was ruined now, and I was willing to bet Henri would use this as blackmail of some kind to get *me*, leaving Marissa all alone to be a lab rat for her mom. I curled up in a ball, I wanted to jump down and hug Missy, to tell her everything is ok, but getting that close, I'd compress too, and I doubted I'd survive if I was much smaller than I was now.

"Miss Lund will see her as her daughter, one that needs help." Tracy said "She has to. She'll keep the focus on helping class Bs, and she'll give money to make sure they're safe."

"Sh-she'd r-rather m-me b-be *dead*." Marissa grunted, her voice barely reaching me

"That's not what I heard." Tracy said "I just want to say again how sorry I am, I care a lot about you Marissa, but my m-"

There was a wrenching noise, and the shelf I was on collapsed, and I screamed, sliding straight into the support beam on the side. It went down fast, the boxes of pens and lab equipment tumbling off around me to the ground, and I slammed into the metal hard as we made impact. I opened my eyes and moaned, I was at an angle, so the shelf hadn't hit the ground- was Marissa crushed?! I scrambled up and climbed the side of the shelf to look around. I couldn't see Marissa, but Tracy... The shelf had landed straight on top of her. I scuttled along the side of the shelf to get a better look, and had to brace myself as the shelf shifted again. Marissa must still be compressing under this somewhere...

Tracy was face down on the ground, the shelf at an angle over her, one of the support beams on her head. I gasped when I saw blood running from under the beam and pooling on the floor under her, she'd taken a hard hit to the head... She was actively bleeding, that meant she wasn't *dead* dead, right? Or was there enough blood in someone to let them bleed even without a heartbeat? She was in an uncomfortable position, her legs splayed and her body bent in half with her face on the concrete, maybe she *was* dead...

I turned away, and looked up at the airlock. Quince was slamming and kicking the door as hard as she could, waving at me and shouting, but I couldn't hear her. I was too short to use the keycard anyway, she was stuck in there for now. I picked my way through the fallen shelf to the middle, my heart beating quickly. I needed to know if Missy was ok... The shelf shuddered and tipped, and held still. She had to be done compressing by *now* right? I crested the top of the shelf and look down. Way below me in a pile was a familiar hoodie curled up in a ball, the ground cracked and split around it, no movement at all.

My breath caught and I slid down the shelf, hitting the ground hard. I ran over to her, slowing down as I got close. What was that I'd read about the virus kicking back in after initial compression? Something about the compression particles could stay in the area now, and re-trigger the infection? Something like that... I had to get her out of here before she re-compressed. I stepped up to her, and bent down. The hoodie was almost my size, maybe a little too big, but the lump inside it wasn't. I reached out and lightly touched Marissa's shoulder, and she jerked upright with a gasp.

"That stupid fucking fucker!" she said, her face wild with anger "Fucking- fuck her and her fucking mom, fuck *FUCK* fuck!"

I gasped at her and fell back, she was- she was *small*. Not my size, not really, but close to it. It was alien and wrong to see her so tiny, so much like me, like she was even smaller than she really was. I was almost worried I'd break her if I touched her, but she wasn't *that* compressed, she just seemed that way because I was used to her usual size... I stood back up quickly and pulled her to her feet, and looked down at her in shock. She was barely as tall as my shoulders, if that. Her anger melted away into horror and she spun in place, looking around at her surroundings, taking it all in. She flapped her hands and looked around for something to say, but her arms dropped to her sides and she sagged, quiet tears running down her face.

"I'm- fuck, I'm really- I just..." she mumbled "I'm gonna be in a lab my whole life now..."

"Not- No, we don't know that." I said "It's ok, it might be ok..."

"Tracy is going to grab us and put us in fucking box..." Marissa said, her stare vacant "Everything I ever loved or wanted is gone now..."

"W-well, n-not everything?" I told her, waving at myself

She looked at me and blinked, then her eyes flashed with anger and she opened her mouth to snap at me, but lost the energy before she started. She tried to run her hands through her hair but her hoodie hadn't compressed as much as she did and she just ended up slapping herself in the face with wet sleeves. She sobbed and sank to her knees, shaking.

"Why hasn't she just grabbed us already?" she said "I just- I just want to get this nightmare over with..."

"She's- um, I think she's dead." I said, bending down next to her "The shelf fell on her."

Marissa looked at me, wild eyed, then barked a laugh, harsh and mean "Get *fucked*, bozo. Killed by a fucking shelf." she said with an angry glare

"Y-yeah..." I said, putting my hand on her shoulder, feeling how fragile it was compared to just a few minutes ago "We... need to get you to a source of uncontaminated water. If we don't wash you off, you might start compressing again any minute."

"Fuck, wouldn't want *that*, huh?" she snarked "Wouldn't want to be even smaller and more useless than completely small and totally useless, right?"

"We need to have a game plan." I said, ignoring her muttered growls as I led her through the remains of the shelf "Once we get you- and me since I'm touching you- washed off, we need to figure out what we're going to do."

"I guess just wait until the late shift shows up and get boxed." she muttered

"I don't think there's a late shift." I said "I think she lied about that."

"Then I don't know, live in the walls like ra- uh, mice?" she said, waving her hands wildly

"Here's a valve, it says it's 'water for control group." I said, pointing to a nozzle on the wall "Look, I think I can turn the lever…"

She boosted me up and I used a conduit to shimmy up to the spigot, and kicked the lever as hard as I could, a stream of water gushing out. i dropped to the floor and set my bag aside before I stepped into the stream, shuddering as the cold water rushed over me, soaking me and my clothes. I scrubbed for a moment, then stepped aside for Missy to wash, clothes and all. She growled at the temperature and didn't wash as well as I'd have liked, but at least she was 'clean' of any potential compression particles and genetic materials now.

"Tracy isn't going to be a problem." I said "Quince is locked up and can't get out, and even if she *was* out, she can't take care of us because, let's be honest, she's going to be a suspect, they'd *never* let her adopt the girl she might have helped disable."

I looked at where Quince was trying to pick the card reader with a hair clip and sighed "And both of your parents are out too."

"Oh, yeah, I guess they're both… ugh…" Marissa said, her fire dying down slightly

"Yeah, no offense, but I don't trust either to come pick us up, much less care for us."

"Not that my dad legally *can* after this past Sunday." she mumbled "Are you saying we need to call your mom? She… was nice to me, I'd be ok with that."

"I don't think so." I said "If word gets out about this, your mom is going to do whatever she can to get you."

"Maybe. Maybe she'd just pretend I died." Marissa said sullenly

"No, I think she'd want you, to test on, yeah, but she *needs* to control you if she can. If she heard my parents had us, she'd use her lawyers to fuck them up and get you under her control, and they wouldn't be able to fight back, they have no money."

"Fantastic." Marissa frowned "*I'm* out of resources. I'd say Darcy, but she's still out of the country, and I think she'd forget about us in a week and let us starve even if she *did* adopt us. Maybe my hitmen could do something if I can still access my accounts..?"

"I have a better idea." I said "It's a stupid one, it's not very safe, and it's going to hurt our pride to do it, but..."

"Oh, *fuck*." Marissa said "Just- please promise you won't let her touch me."

"I'll do my best..." I said, hugging her to my chest, warmth filling me despite the freezing water we were both covered in

I kissed the top of her head gently and savored the feeling of pressing my girlfriend into my chest, my arms around her, hers around me, and I knew it'd be ok. We had each other, no matter what, we'd be ok. I squeezed her gently, and she returned the squeeze, her arms tightening around my ribs in the same places her fingers used to. I let myself hold the glow for a moment, feeling the love and connection for just a bit longer before I finally broke away and pulled my tablet out of my bag.

I looked at Marissa, quietly crying, her hands pulling at my sleeve, and I gave her a nervous but supportive smile.

"It'll be ok, she's our friend, she'll make sure we're ok, I know she will." I lied, and called Henri

# Chapter Thirty

Henri's car smashed through the wall of the lab, sending debris across the room as she skidded to a stop. I hugged Marissa to my chest huddled in front of the airlock, braced against the door. As Henri's car stopped moving, Quince banged on the clear plastic from within the airlock to get Henri's attention and gestured at us wildly. I stood shakily and helped Marissa to her feet, still pressed against the door to the airlock. The car shook as Henri tried to open the driver's side door, but the crash had dented it in and she couldn't budge it. She slammed her hands on the steering wheel and shook it, finally climbing over into the passenger's side and bursting through that door instead, stumbling out and onto her feet. She straightened up and grabbed her sleepover duffle bag out of the passenger's side floorboard and looked around the room, scanning for us.

Her eyes fell on us as she noticed Quince pointing, and she dropped the bag, rushing over to us as her shoes slapped on the concrete floor. Marissa hissed and curled up closer to my chest, her body shaking. I hugged her to me and put my chin on her head as Henri jogged up to us.

"She's so big..." Marissa hissed, her fingers digging into my top "Fuck, she's- I can't even- I can't do this..."

"It's ok, she won't grab you, it's ok..." I said gently, petting her head

Henri kneeled in front of us and stared down, her eyes wide "Oh my, you really *were* compressed." she said, reaching out to us

"Henri I *just* told her you wouldn't grab us!" I said angrily

"I- Amber I need to pick you two up, we need to make our escape." she said, her eyes locked on Marissa

"Let Quince out, let *her* pick us up for now." Marissa said "I don't want you touching me, I don't trust you..."

"No, don't!" I said quickly

Marissa pulled away from me and glared "Why the fuck not?"

"If Quince is still locked up when the cops show up, she'll have an alibi." I said "She'll be a suspect, yeah, but she'll get out on bail if she's even arrested and be cleared quickly, we need her to stay in there for now or she might lose Kay."

"That's stupid." Marissa mumbled "I just- I don't want Henri to touch me."

"Why do you not want me to pick you up?" Henri asked "Someone will notice the hole I made in the wall soon, and I would *like* to be out of here before then."

"You're going to squish me or something!" Marissa yelled "You'll squish me so you can finally have Amber!"

Henri narrowed her eyes and scooped both of us up in her hands, standing up. Marissa screamed and curled up on top of me, her heart racing.

"You misunderstand something, miststück." Henri said calmly "There is no danger from me anymore, because there is nothing you can do to keep Amber from me. Why squish you? You cannot do anything to keep us apart."

"Henri, stop!" I yelled "She's *terrified*, just stop scaring her!"

"She *should* be terrified." Henri nodded "I could do any *number* of terrible things to her... I could crush her, I could leave her here, I could put her in the car exhaust until she passes out, I could break her arms so she could never hug you again, I could do so so many things."

Marissa pushed her face against me and growled "Just fucking *do* them, then!" she yelled

"..." Henri took a breath "No. I will not. I will be polite to you, and put up with you, for now. I do not fancy myself a bully, and I want Amber to remain happy."

"Then why list all those terrible things you want to do?" I asked, kicking her palm

She closed her hands around me, pressing Marissa into me as she looked at me closely, her blue eyes darting over my face like she was memorizing it

"I want her to appreciate that I am *letting* her live." she said simply "I want her to understand that the *only* reason I'm helping her is to keep you from hating me, and I would discard her in a moment if it meant helping you even slightly more."

"I didn't *ask* you to let me live, fuckwit!" Marissa barked, trying to turn around to see her "If you're going to treat me like shit, then just stomp on me or something!"

"Just let me help Amber and stop whining." Henri said "For now, I am getting you both out of here. I have some of your things in the duffle, Amber. I had Parker pack them up and I swung by for them. He was more than happy to help, but I did not tell him our plan."

"What *is* the plan?" Marissa asked "If we go back to Amber's old place we'll be found."

"We are going to the airport, of course." Henri said "I am making sure Miss Lund cannot get her hands on you ever."

"Oh, fuck..." I groaned "No, no no no, Henri, *please* no."

"It is the only way, Amber." Henri said, wincing

"What's the only way?" Marissa asked "We're going to her house in Europe I guess?"

"It's- nothing." I said, looking back up at Henri and trying not to think of what was coming next "How are we getting to the airport? Your car is all smashed up."

Henri frowned, and looked back at her smoking car "I... had not thought of that."

She looked around the room and blinked, staring at Quince who'd resorted to leaning against the wall sullenly once she'd realized Henri wasn't freeing her "Where did Quince leave her purse?"

I pointed to the area next to what was left of the table, and Henri walked over, giving Tracy's limp form a wide berth and digging through the designer bag, pulling out Quince's phone, her charger, and her pepper spray, setting them on the table before finding what she was looking for. As she walked back past the airlock to the hole in the wall, she held up the car keys and jingled them at Quince. Quince gasped and threw herself against the side of the airlock again and again, trying to break it with her shoulder but with no luck.

I made eye contact with Kensey, who was sitting on the card reader, as we left the area, and she gave me a small wave, her expression worried and hurt. I felt a pang of sadness when I realized I'd most likely never see her again. I smiled sadly at her, or tried to, and then we were out of the building, Henri swinging the duffle bag onto her shoulder with the hand that wasn't carrying us. I saw Quince's sports car on the far side of the lot, the gold paint shining in the late afternoon sun. Henri squared up, and marched towards it with purpose. I only hoped she knew what she was doing...

~~~

I huddled on the seat surrounded by blankets and hugging Marissa tightly. We'd changed out of our wet clothes finally, but my wardrobe was far too big for Marissa, and she was practically swallowed by the poncho she'd picked out. I was trying to lay close to her so she wasn't so cold, but her teeth were still chattering and I could feel her trembling through our thick clothes. She gave a violent shudder and huffed, annoyed.

"Gods, Amber, w-were *you* always this cold?" she muttered

"Yyyup." I said "It's why I was ok being in your pocket all the time, you were so, so warm..."

"Ugh, I wish I could say the same about you." she said "You're b-barely warmer than I am."

"So, about my car?" Henri said, glancing down at us from the driver's seat "Are you sure it will be ok?"

"Fuck, yeah, it's *fine*." Marissa rolled her eyes "The guys I use are used by like, D-Darcy's entire family. It'll be like we were never there, no car, no security footage we don't want, none of your f-fingerprints on stuff, and I'm g-guessing Quince will even testify she *let* us b-borrow her car if questioned, so there'll be no gta charges."

"I- ok, so just there, you said there would be 'no car', I am concerned." she said, frowning

"You can't keep it, it has too much heat." Marissa snapped "Th-they'll get rid of it for you."

"I *liked* that car..." Henri said with a pang of hurt "I had it for five years, I bought it with my own money. I wanted to have it brought over to my home eventually."

"What does that even mean? 'Heat'?" I asked Missy "She crashed it, we're not even being looked for yet."

"W-whatever." Marissa said "I'm doing her a favor."

She cuddled up closer to me and spoke under her breath "I kinda just wanted to f-fuck her over, s-so I told them to crush it."

I held back an eye roll and sighed, hugging her closer to me "Henri, do we have a plan for what we're doing once we get to the airport?"

"Ja, I called my papa on my way to pick up the stuff from Marissa's house and I got him to charter a private jet." she said "We should be off the ground by midnight."

"Ok, that's good." I said "He didn't ask any questions?"

"He did not." she said "My call woke him up, he was very tired. I will have a hard conversation waiting for me once we land."

"I hope h-he's ok with th-this." Marissa said "H-how are we g-getting past the security?"

"Well, we are on a private flight, so I will be using a private gate, with a metal detector instead of a scanner..." Henri said, her voice quiet

"And?" Marissa said "They'll still go through the luggage. Small or not, my bones still show up on an xray."

There was an heavy silence and I pulled Marissa closer to me, shuddering "It'll just be for a while, it's ok..."

"I'm still confused." Marissa grumbled "This had better work."

"It will, it will." Henri said confidently "I just- ah, I will need to stop by the drug store first for some things."

Marissa shot me a look, confusion making way for comprehension, bleeding away into horror. I quickly buried her face in my chest before she could start screaming and held her tight. It'd just be for a while... That's all I could tell myself, it'd just be for a while...

~~~

Marissa lay on the tray in the jet, sobbing, her chest shaking violently as she caught her breath, her hands clawing at nothing. I lay in a similar state, coughing as I got my wind back, hugging myself and trying not to shudder. I reached over and snagged her hand as it swung, bodily pulling her over to me. I hugged her with my free hand, my nose wrinkling at the latex smell that stuck to her, and I sat up, pulling her with me so I could hug her better, our skin warm and comforting as I held her.

"It was only for a few minutes." Henri sighed from behind us "Less than half an hour, we are on the plane now, it was fine, you see?"

"B-bath." Marissa said "Or b-bleach, either one."

"You did not even *touch* anything, you are perfectly clean-" Henri started before I cut her off

"Henri we smell like the inside of a guy's wallet, I need to get clean too before I put my clothes back on." I snapped "Just- fuck, can we just get cleaned up?"

Henri sighed, but picked us up, bringing us to the bathroom, snagging the carafe for tea on her way. She set us on the side of the sink, and stopped it up, running the water to fill it, then poured the hot water from the carafe in, heating up the water. She poked a finger in and frowned, thinking for a minute, then she ran a little more water and tried again, nodding. I was still holding Marissa to me closely, trying to ignore the fact we were both in our underthings and were about to take a bath together. It wasn't the time for things like that, Missy was still shaking and hiccuping, and I doubted it was because of the temperature on the plane.

"Ok, the water is ready." Henri said plainly "Get in and I will put the soap on you."

I poked my toe in, feeling that it was hot, but not too hot. Not as hot as the soup she'd dropped me in, at least. I slipped all the way in, my legs resting on the sloped side, and gave Missy support as she climbed down too. I held out my hands for the soap, and Henri dripped a small bit of hand soap into my and Marissa's palms. I lathered up over my underclothes, not watching Marissa do the same, I'd feel guilty looking at her like that while we felt like this... I finished soaping up, and slid under the water, letting the water and soap wash away the film of 'product' that was on me. This hand soap would *kill* my hair, it'd be rough and unpleasant for days. I tried not to think about that as I stood up again, wringing it out with my fingers.

"Ok, Amber, let me dry you off..." Henri said, plucking me out of the water and wrapping me in paper towels as I struggled and kicked back

"I can do it, I can do it!" I yelled angrily, and she set me on the sink, her expression smug

"Was that so bad?" she asked "You know, when we tried to do this before, we ran into a snag, but now..."

"Oh, fuck off." I growled, pulling Marissa up and handing her the paper towel

"Hm, that is not polite language to use for the person who is saving you from being used as lab rats." Henri said haughtily

"Fuck. You." Marissa said "Look, if you want to fucking be like this, then just leave me on the tarmac. I'm not putting up with your entitled attitude."

"*MY* entitled..?" Henri said, her eyes widening as she picked us both up to go back to her seat "Oh, I- you- Do *not* tempt me, Marissa. Amber would get over you soon, you are not *that* valuable to me."

"If you hurt her, I'll kill myself!" I said, pulling Marissa close again

"Amber- no, stop." Marissa said, pushing me away "I'm- you're not- this is too weird, just stop."

"W-weird?" I asked, letting her slip back "Weird how?"

"You're being too, I don't know, protective of me, I guess." she said quietly "You'd *kill* yourself? Really?"

"Her being protective of you is the only reason you are not still at the lab." Henri said, dropping us on the tray gently "She 'loves' you, and that is enough for me, but it is the only reason you are here."

"I know, but- *I'm* the one in charge here, but- it feels like maybe I'm *not* anymore, and I *hate* that, it makes me feel- I just hate it, ok?" Marissa said, grabbing her poncho and some sweats

"I- uh..." I said, unsure how to deal with this "Marissa, I still see you the same, I just know like, you're smaller now. You're still in charge, I'll follow your lead, I promise!"

"*I* think you two should- oh?" Henri said, turning as the door to the plane opened and she scooped us onto her lap.

I tumbled down onto her skirt, the soft material not doing much to stop me from knocking against her leg. I flailed, trying to sit up, but her hand pressed down on me, holding me in place. I wiggled around and looked for Missy, had she landed ok? I saw her legs sticking up out between Henri's thighs kicking wildly, and I winced. Being held upside down was bad enough, being *pinned* upside down? I hoped she could breathe...

"Hello, Miss Burkhart?" a voice came from above us

"Ja, are you the pilot?" Henri asked

"I am, I see you've requested no flight attendants on this particular flight, is that correct?"

"That is correct, I do not want to be disturbed." she agreed

"I see, well, It's not legally required for this plane, but I'd highly encourage you to-"

"No thank you." Henri said plainly "I wish to be alone."

"Ok, that's not a problem. I'll just get the pre-flight check done, and we'll be on the way, sound good?"

"Yes. Thank you."

I heard sounds of walking, and the closing of a door, and Henri finally pulled me back onto the tray, dumping Marissa behind me. Missy staggered to her feet and stomped to the far side of the tray, dropping down to a sitting position facing away from us, her arms crossed.

"Ah, she is so moody." Henri sighed "I do not understand her being so upset, I am doing all I can to keep her alive and with you, am I not?"

"You're being inconsiderate." I said "She's just had her whole life ripped away and you're just enjoying it."

"I do enjoy it, a bit." Henri agreed "I think seeing her like this helps me to deal with a lot of my past issues with her."

"Henri, she's still a person, she's my girlfriend, and she deserves for you to like, I don't know, understand that she's scared right now, not threaten her and treat her like she's worthless."

"I do not *care* if she is scared." Henri said "And no, I do not think she is worthless, just not as valuable to me as she is you."

"I can hear you, you know." Marissa said over her shoulder

"I am aware. I simply do not care." Henri said back "Now, Amber, let us discuss how we will be living once we get to Germany..."

I didn't want to think about that, I didn't want to think about *anything*. I just wanted to lie down and cry. I couldn't even *start* to process what things look like now, would I ever see my mom and Appa again? Would Marissa actually be allowed to stay with me? Would I be treated like a non-human toy or would Henri actually respect me as a person now? I had no safety, no one to call and get me out if things got too bad. Henri was that person before, the balance of her and Marissa keeping me secure and mostly unbothered about how I'd be treated.

Henri was technically an international smuggler now, or she would be once we left the country. It was a direct flight from New Jersey to Germany, and we'd need to be... smuggled in through customs, but hopefully that was less of an ordeal than getting *on* the plane. I felt dry and unpleasant from the hand soap, I was so, so tired from the long stressful day, and my arms and legs ached from climbing up and down the shelf. I knew Missy was most likely in just as rough of a shape, if not more- she'd mentioned the compression *hurting* for some reason- but she wouldn't admit it, not in front of Henri.

"I don't want to talk right now..." I said "I just want to pass out, did you get my bed?"

"No, no furniture, just your clothes and electronics, that was all I told Parker to get." Henri said "I can hold you in my lap and you can sleep?"

"No." I said firmly "Marissa? I need you, I'm too cold and I don't want to sleep alone. Henri, make a nest in your bag for us."

"I am *not* letting you two sleep together like that, I just got you for myself and I do not approve of-" she started

"I *do* not care, Henri, we've *been* sleeping together, and I'm freezing. I need a bed-warmer, and she's bed-warmer-sized."

"*You're* the bed-warmer, not me." Marissa said sullenly, coming over beside me "But I'm still shivering, I need someplace warm too, yeah."

Henri huffed, but slid her duffle out from under the seat next to her and rooted around in it for a moment "Fine, there, a lovely nest for you two to nap in. When you wake up though, I *do* need to talk about the living situation." she said, mildly annoyed

The duffle bag had been rearranged so a sweater- one of my old ones- was on top, with the arms folded over the chest, making a 'bed' of sorts. I pulled Marissa to me and held her tight as Henri lowered us into the bag. I shimmied under the sleeves and Marissa followed, her body cold and clammy next to mine. Hopefully she'd warm up soon, if she was too cold for too long, she could get brain damage...

"Alright. Sleep well, I guess." Henri said, looking down at us with un-masked disappointment "Amber, I love you..."

I curled up, facing Marissa, and waited for her to close the bag again, plunging us into near-darkness. I felt Marissa's breath on my face, not as strong as it had been when she was a giant, but still 'her'. She'd had a mint earlier in the waiting room, and I caught the faint hint of the familiar icy scent and she curled up close to me. I remembered the first day I'd been hers, her minty, frigid breath washing over me. She'd changed to cinnamon soon after. I'd thought little of it at the time, but it'd been to get closer to me without making my eyes water, knowing her. I pulled her head into my shoulder and hugged her close to me, feeling the 'nest' warm up.

"You keep doing that, I don't like it." Marissa said softly

"Doing what?" I asked, pulling away

"Putting your head over mine, I don't like that." she said "I don't like being reminded that you're taller than me, scoot down."

"I- sorry, ok." I said, feeling a pang of something deep inside

I scooted down until I was deeper inside the sweater than her, and she pulled me to her chest, reversing the positions until she had her chin on my head. It was weird, and I had to curl up slightly to feel like I was actually being 'held' by her, but it was cozy. I pushed my face into her chest and breathed in, her unique human smell so much less noticeable at this size. I was sad, I'd grown to enjoy it, knowing it was her, smelling her on my clothes, feeling safe when I was around her. It was still there, it was just muted greatly, and I wondered if Henri's smell would cover up ours as she carried us around.

"I'm still your girlfriend, Amber." Marissa whispered to me "And we have a very particular relationship, as girlfriends."

"You mean, you still want to play around?" I asked, hopefully

"It's part of dating me. It'll be harder at this size, but I think it'll be more intimate." she hissed "I'm more used to full sized partners, after all."

"We may have to get creative..." I said, clutching her poncho "You're a bit smaller than me now"

"I still know how to make it hurt." she whispered "The good kind of hurt, I have lots of tricks."

"I'm excited to see what you can do." I said, balling up my hands and pressing them into her

"Mm, yeah." she said "It might be even better for me this way; getting to boss you around, getting to bully and torment you, all while you look down at me, not able to fight back or do a thing despite your height advantage..."

"I- yeah, I wouldn't fight back..." I said "I respect the dynamic, I do."

I felt a slight flutter in my chest at that. I *did* respect the dynamic, I knew where I belonged, where I wanted to be. I was relieved in a way, that despite the big change, the vast difference of power and control gone, flipped even, that she still wanted me. She valued me aside from her innate power over me, but still wanted to *create* that power over me even when it didn't exist, because that's how she loved me, how she expressed herself in a relationship, and she still *wanted* it with me.

"I love you, Missy." I told her, closing my eyes

"You'd better." she said back, sullenly "It'd suck to love someone as much as I love you and have them not feel the same."

"I'm gonna get some sleep, fight off the jet lag, ok?"

"Yeah, my whole body hurts, I need to sleep too. Just- stay here, and let me hold you, pet. I don't want you wandering off while I need you close, ok?"

"Of course, Lady M." I said gracefully, and pulled my arms closer around her as I drifted off

~~~

We'd managed to stay in the bag, curled up on each other like ants for the whole flight. Henri had peeked at us multiple times, and whispered my name to see if I would 'wake up', but I lay still and faked sleep until she got bored and closed the top of the bag again. It wasn't that I was avoiding her, I really *was* tired and I was so, so comfortable with Marissa hanging onto me, but at the same time... I didn't want to have the hard conversation she'd been asking me about before our nap. It could mean me finding out she saw me as a pet still, and I couldn't deal with that right now.

The muffled sounds of the plane shifted around us, and there was a thump, jolting us and making my head knock into Marissa's. She swore and groggily sat up, rubbing her eyes and popping her back. She groaned, and rubbed her limbs gently. She must have still been sore from the compression. I didn't remember feeling that myself, was it because the compression particles were just in her blood? Or because she'd compressed so quickly? Either way, it sounded like she was tender and aching. The bag opened up once again and Henri's pale face peered down at us from her seat and she nodded.

"That woke you up I see. I almost woke you up several times, but I was unsure if I should. We have just landed in Frankfurt."

"What time is it?" I asked "It's pretty bright out."

"It is..." she checked her phone "just past two."

"I hate time zones..." Marissa muttered "I slept for fourteen hours and only got eight hours of sleep total, how fucked is that?"

"I never understand how they work, I get mixed up." I admitted "Is Frankfurt where we're getting off? Or are we still going?"

"No, we will get off at Stuttgart." Henri said "But here we will go through customs and passports. It's not as bad since I am a german citizen, but they will still search my bag."

"Ohhh *fuck* no, no no no, you *can't* make me do that again." Marissa said, her words sounding like she was demanding, but her tone bordering on pleading

"I did not plan on doing *that* again." Henri said "I brought some undershorts that are very tight, I will put you and Amber pressed against my tummy, one on either side. Customs does not require a full-body scan, and you two should clear the pat-down."

"Oh thank the gods..." Marissa sighed, slumping against me "I was about to just ask you if I could just try to sneak through security on foot."

"I am sure it was not *that* bad." Henri said "I was careful, you were safe and-"

"It's the *idea* of it Henri." I said "Just never bring it up again, ok?"

"Ok, I will not." she said "I do need to change into my shorts and get you two in place though, it will be tight, and hard to breathe. I have a little 'give' on my stomach so it will not be too bad, but you'll need to be careful and breathe deeply."

I cringed, remembering the jeans pocket. I bit my lip and grabbed Missy's hand, clenching it tightly "This'll be hard, but after this, we're good, right? Just get through customs, get back on the plane, and we're home free?"

"Yes, once we get to Stuttgart, my father will be there with a car to pick us up, and we will be safe." Henri said, plucking us out of the bag and digging through for her shorts

"We can do this, we've got this." I said, half to myself and half to Marissa as we were set on the tray

"I can't believe it's so much work just to avoid being used as a lab rat..." Missy complained "Ugh, if Tracy wasn't already dead, I swear I'd have put a hit out on her for this, who the fuck did she think she was?!"

"It is a lot of work, ja." Henri said, shimmying the shorts up under her skirt "Just keep that in mind. Remember all I did all this for *you* when we get to where we are going."

She reached out, picking up Marissa and pulling her waistband out "Stay very still, try to stay in the groove where my tummy and hip meet."

She slid her hand into her shorts, and pulled it out, sans-Marissa. I swallowed hard, it was my turn now, and my heart was pounding. Marissa had no idea how bad it'd be, but I had the misfortune of having experienced it before. I took a deep, deep breath and closed my eyes as Henri carefully picked me up and brought me close to her stomach.

"Stay safe, Klein Fee..." she murmured, and the world was sealed off.

It was hot, it was tight, I could barely get a breath out, what little air I had was stale and humid, and I fought the urge to writhe as Henri exited the plane. I couldn't hear what was going on around me, just muffled noises and the rush of the crowded airport. At one point I felt fingertips play across me quickly, and I fought not to move or twitch in response, but they moved on, and I felt Henri walk further and sit, her action crushing the air out of me. She slid down in her seat, relieving some of the pressure, but I was fighting to draw in air, to stay awake. I could only imagine what Marissa was feeling at her smaller size, she must be practically dead by now...

After an eternity of waiting, she finally moved again, and I felt her stand, the air rushing into my little pocket, my chest swelling with oxygen. She walked quickly and with long strides, and before long, we were in a quiet place, the noise of the airport gone. She stopped, and her fingers dipped down into my hiding spot, scooping me up and sliding me out, the sweat making me cling to her skin painfully.

I crested the fabric and found myself back on the plane, being set on the tray once more. A moment later, Marissa joined me, pale and choking for air but not getting any. I crawled over to her, the world still foggy, and I climbed on top of her, taking a deep breath and pressing my lips onto hers, forcing the air into her lungs. She flailed and hit my side with the heel of her hand and I rolled off, the both of us panting in the cool, clean air of the airplane.

"F-fuck, Amber..." Marissa whispered, her voice rough and raspy "I c-can't do this, I really can't, I want to die, I can't *do* this."

"You can, I know you can." I said, laying my hand over hers "I did it for weeks and I'm still ok, you can do it, I'll support you, I'll be here for you."

"I d-don't want support, I want t-to just be ok." she croaked "I'll never be ok again, I'm like this until I d-die."

"I will do whatever I can to help the two of you retain your humanity." Henri said solemnly as she looked down at us with a look of sadness "Marissa, I do not like you, but even still, I will ensure you are treated as a person should be."

"Stop *looking* at me like that..." Marissa said, turning away from her "I don't need your 'humanity' or empathy or fucking pity or whatever, I *need* to be my old self again."

"I cannot help but pity you." Henri said "To see *you*, so strong and bold and commanding, brought so low that you cannot even look me in the face, it engenders pity of the highest order."

"Well, fuck your gender pity or whatever." Marissa said "Just ignore me and let me hang out with Amber and I'll be fine."

"That brings us to what I needed to discuss with you two." Henri sighed "Amber, we *do* need to discuss the living situation once we get to my home."

"I figure we'd just do what I did in Marissa's house, I just live on a desk or something in your room, and I have my own apartment or house. It worked for me and Missy..."

"*We'd* have our own apartment or house. Together, in the same one." Marissa corrected me "That's non-negotiable."

"Ok, I can concede that." Henri agreed, much more readily than I expected "But you might not be in my room with me, I do not like the warm quite so much as you two. We have many rooms in our manor, we could set one up with a dedicated thermostat and build a custom home for you there, if you like?"

"You'd be ok with that?" I asked "With us not living with you?"

"You would still ride with me in my pocket as I lived my life, if you allow that." Henri said "I would simply come to get you in the mornings or when I needed you."

"That puts me being pretty lonely all day." Marissa complained "I'd be stuck with nothing to do but look at whatever that app Amber likes is called."

"A *lot* of people do nothing but look at AntMound all day." I said "Uh, but maybe you could ride with me in her pocket?"

"That's too dangerous." Marissa said "She could like, pull me out and pretend to drop me or something, I still don't trust her."

"And I do not wish for her to be that close to me that much." Henri "She is quite mean and that would get old fast."

"Well, fuck." I said "Can we, like, work out a schedule then?"

"As if me and Henri are your divorced parents?" Marissa asked "I've been putting up with that for years already, it's a mess."

"I could do that." Henri said "I get you afternoons and early evening, Marissa gets you mornings and nights."

"I *guess* that works?" Marissa said "It's weird, but I could see that working out, sure."

"So, unless there's a change, we'll be doing that?" I asked "I'll bounce between you two, but Marissa and I will have our own room?"

"I think that works, yes." Henri said "I only have to convince my father..."

"He seems nice though, from what I've heard over the phone." I said "He'd be fine with it, right?"

"Amber, I have to tell him that I am dropping out of college, I am moving back in, I am now an international human trafficker, and I *may* need to tell him I'm gay, if he does not accept the excuse that I just love you as a friend enough to ruin my whole life."

"Oh, shit." Marissa said, looking at her with a frown "You're really fucking up your whole life for this..."

"Yes." Henri said quietly "I am, and I do not regret it, but I do want to make sure I make it worth it."

"*All* our lives got ruined, if you think about it." I said quietly "My parents are lost forever to me, and I won't even be able to *talk* to anyone in Germany, I'll just have you two."

"We will be fine, I know we will." Henri said "We must be, really. We have no other option."

"Fuck." Marissa said, leaning onto my arm and holding tightly "If you put it like that, I guess we'll be ok after all..."

I braced myself, feeling the rumble of the plane as it took off, shaking and swaying in the air as we made our last jump of the trip. Flying away to Henri's father, to her manor, to our new home. I felt butterflies in my stomach, both full of anticipation and fear, and I did the only thing I knew to do, and held Marissa close. If I had her, anything, even a new country and a new language and a new dynamic for my best friend would be ok. I just needed her...

# Epilogue

*Two Weeks Later*

I yawned as I sat up, the doll bed I'd slept in the night before shaking slightly, rousing Missy from where she'd been sleeping next to me. She reached out and grabbed my thigh, making me wince as her fingers dug into the bruises she'd left on me last night. I flexed my leg, feeling them pulse lightly with a mild pain, and I pushed her hand away from my leg. I swept the hair off her face and looked down at her groggy, bleary face and grinned. It felt different, more important somehow, to see her like this, in my bed, at nearly my size.

"Whrblst..." she said eloquently, curling up to a sitting position, her legs under her chin

"Good morning, Missy, sleep well?" I asked

She yawned and shrugged "My arms hurt from last night. It's a lot more work than I expected roughhousing with someone bigger than yourself."

"It shouldn't have been *that* hard, I let you win." I said "Besides, you're the sporty one."

"Don't *tell* me you let me win, that takes the fun out of it." she said, punching my shoulder

I laughed and pushed her over, making her squawk indignantly "Think there's still any of those little flapjacks Mrs B made us left?" I asked

"I think you ate all those last night." she said "Besides, those made me sick."

"You'll get used to it, Kensey said she tried a little bit of Quince's quiche yesterday afternoon and was mostly fine." I said "I bet it's just a matter of your body learning how to process it."

"I still would rather have compressed food." Missy said "They say we're not supposed to eat the regular stuff you know."

"Yeah, yeah, I know." I said "I'm gonna go find breakfast then, see what Henri bought us."

"Uh, actually, no, you're not." Marissa said "I'm bringing you breakfast in bed, just chill out here, I'll heat something up. Flapjacks, if there's any left, one of those little meals if there's not."

"Aw, that's sweet of you, but I gotta pee, soooo I'm getting out of bed." I said

"Then get *back* in bed after." she said, glaring at me "I can't get you new clothes and toys for your birthday like I planned, at least let me get you breakfast in bed."

I felt my face flush and I smiled at her "Aw, ok... I'll get back in bed, I guess. I'm still bummed we didn't get to have that party you wanted for me."

"You would have hated it." she said "I was going to use you as a cake topper and get drunk and make fun of you the whole time."

"Even after we started dating?" I asked "That was still the plan?"

"Uh, *yeah*? It was a good plan. I don't know how the 'getting drunk' part would have worked with my issues, but I'd have made an exception." she said, rolling her eyes "Look, just go pee or whatever and I'll be back with food in no time."

She rolled off the bed and onto the dollhouse floor, pulling her woolen blanket with her as she shuffled out of the room to the stairs. We didn't have a custom home yet, just an old antique that had been in the estate since the late

1800s, but Henri's mom had hired a very famous craftsman to design something specifically for us. It'd be done in a month or two, and it'd have heated floors and running water when he was done. Until then, we'd have to make do with what we had.

It was fancy, but we had to step around the outer walls to get to the other rooms, which was precarious on the second floor, and we'd had to have little stairs build on the outside to get down to the bottom floor. Luckily, the Burkhart family gardener knew his stuff, and we'd had a *mostly* functional home a day or two after arriving. It was missing running water and most rooms didn't have electricity, but we had bottled water and one room with an us-sized electrical outlet for the TV, my game system, and our charger.

I carefully gripped the wall and swung around the edge of the house into the 'bathroom' and did my stuff in the mini chemical toilet Henri had gotten us until we got our regular house, and washed up a bit before heading back to bed. It wasn't bad so far, living here. Henri's father had been *furious* at her dropping out of school to run away with me and Missy, but after some explaining, and some calls to the school, he'd decided that if she could pass her current classes via proctored remote exams, he'd let her go to a local school to finish up the remaining year on her degree.

Mrs Burkhart was a harder sell, she was distraught that Henri would come home after spending so long on her own, and called herself a 'failure of a mother', or, at least that's what the translator on my tablet said. I think it had something to do with Henri's older brother being a jobless traveler; Henri was the golden child, and seeing her drop out had flashed Mrs Burkhart back to when her son had done the same. She'd even threatened to make Henri find another home for us if she didn't promise to find a job and start working full time until the next school year started, which seemed fair to me. Then again, I'd *always* had summer jobs growing up, Henri'd never worked a day before in her life.

It took me and Marissa making friends with Mrs B; dancing with her fingers, showing off our clothes and my little tv, and in general acting much more innocent and sweet than I'd ever seen Missy behave prior, to get her to settle down long enough to explain things properly. She still wanted Henri to get a job, but after getting to know us better, she dropped the threat of making Henri adopt us out completely.

I slid back into bed and wondered if she'd done anything for my birthday, she seemed to see us as a second chance at raising kids- despite us both being full grown adults- and was trying hard to be there for us in ways that make me slightly embarrassed. She'd try to clean our dollhouse, make us treats despite Marissa not being able to eat big food yet, and try and comfort us in broken english when we were homesick. I knew Henri was planning something, and I wouldn't be surprised if Mrs Burkhart was in on it too.

"Do you want fake eggs or fake rice?" Marissa yelled up at me, shaking me out of my thoughts "I'm making fake bacon and fake chopped steak, with cheese on it."

"Eggs, please!" I called down

Twenty one years old... I didn't *feel* twenty one, I felt somewhere between fourteen and forty. I'd had so many experiences and stress over the past five weeks that it was like I'd aged well past my years, but at the same time I felt so fragile it was as if I was a kid again. I made a nest in the bed, leaving room for Missy for when she came back up.

It was going to be a weird birthday, the first time I wouldn't have my special birthday soup for dinner. My mom had worked hard making sure she could make it vegetarian for me when I first stopped eating meat, substituting the beef for mushrooms and buying veggie broth. It wasn't my all time favorite dish, but the seaweed and kimchi were *so* good together, and the fact we only got it on birthdays made it feel so much more special.

I could still call my parents though, a video call, later in the day. It was nine here now, so for them it'd be... three in the morning? The call would have to wait. I know I was more than likely going to have another video call with the Quince and Kensey later, we'd had one every day since I'd gotten here. They'd been calling almost every day to give me updates on the situation back home and tell me how sad they were Marissa and I'd left.

The situation was... not good. Tracy had lived after all, but she hadn't woken up yet. She had broken her spine and suffered major clotting in her brain, so the doctors weren't hopeful that she'd wake up at all, and if she did, she'd have serious brain damage and more than likely be unable to walk. I couldn't feel *too* bad, she'd tried to keep me in a box and have her dad do experiments on me after all, but I did really wish things had gone differently. She was the most sane of the girls, or so it'd seemed before the incident.

Miss Lund was another story entirely. She'd managed to get her hands on the lab in the end, buying out the majority of the stocks and absorbing it into her own company. There was no word on if she'd stayed true to her word and kept the research going to help undo the compression for her daughter's sake, but she hadn't closed the lab, which was a good sign. In a surprising turn of events, she'd actually given up all rights of guardianship over Marissa, not even *trying* to get her back. Her legal claim would have been shaky as it was since Marissa was over eighteen, and Henri had been confident she'd win, but it was a relief to not have to go through the legal battle. It was still a sticky situation with Henri crossing borders with us before we were registered to her, but it looked like we'd officially be Henri's soon, as long as the paperwork went through.

I took a deep breath, smelling the breakfast before I saw Missy's head cresting the stairs, a half-lidded smirk on her beautiful face.

"Mm, I'm getting hungry." I said "I can smell it and it's making me want it."

"Yeah yeah, here it is, don't drop it." Marissa said, handing me one of the plates. The food looked, well, it looked compressed, but it was made with love, and that weighed out any amount of odd textures.

She climbed into bed next to me and curled up, her own plate on her knees and took a bite of her bacon, the flat, fake-marbled stick of protein crunching as she chewed. I ate some of my eggs and savored the syrup she'd put over them, just how I liked, and wondered how I'd gotten so lucky to have someone like her in my life, demanding to be in charge, but still willing to serve me breakfast like this...

"I love you, Marissa." I told her, kissing her cheek

"Ew, you got sticky on me..." she said, wiping her cheek, but she returned the kiss a moment later "I love you too, Stress Toy."

She took a bite of the steak, spearing some of her eggs with the fork at the same time, and chewed thoughtfully.

"Hey, you know how Henri is planning something for later?" she asked

"Yeah?"

"Can I spoil it?"

"No! That would be so mean!" I said, shaking my head "Let it be a surprise!"

"Laaaame..." she sighed, taking a sip of water from the cup on her nightstand

"If she wanted me to know, she'd have told me already." I said "I can wait."

As if we'd called her, the door to our room opened, and Henri walked in, fully dressed and awake, a rarity for this early in the morning. She dashed over to us and sat at the table we were on, a bright grin filling her face.

"Hello birthday girl!" she said "Breakfast in bed, huh? So fancy!"

"Hi Henri!" I said "I'm taking it easy today, Missy made it for me!"

"Well, try not to take it *too* easy..." she said "We need to be at the airport in two hours!"

"We- huh?" I looked at Marissa, confused. She smirked at me and poked her tongue out.

"Happy Birthday!" Henri said proudly "My parents got plane tickets for your parents and Quince! Kensey's coming too as a carry-on, even, they are landing here around eleven! They had a red eye flight, it was a struggle to get it all worked out in time, but they will be here for the party tonight!"

"Wh- uh, *what?*" I asked, my heart racing, barely believing what I'd heard "Henri, you beautiful blue eyed goddess! Thank you!"

"It was *my* idea, really." Marissa said, poking me

"No, *you* just asked if Quince could come, it was *my* idea to invite the Parks too, and *my* father's money that paid for it." Henri said, bopping her on the head

"I'm so happy..." I said, smiling and fighting off the tears "Thank you, both of you, I wasn't expecting to see any of them again for a long, long time..."

Henri smiled and leaned into the dollhouse, kissing my head gently "I want you to be happy, Klein Fee, I will do whatever I need to do to make that happen, I told you."

"You're doing a pretty good job so far..." Marissa begrudgingly admitted "She's a lot more relaxed here, and she's smiling more this week than I've ever seen her."

"That's because I'm starting to feel *safe* again." I said "I have you here every day with me, and Henri and her mom doing what they can to care for us, and Mr Burkhart doing his best to help us too, I just... I just feel loved."

As I smiled at the two girls smiling back at me, I knew there was nothing else to say, I *did* feel loved, I felt like I was *important* to them, like I made their lives better by being in it. I knew they certainly made *my* life better. I'd need to get up and get dressed soon to go see the rest of the people who loved me and cared about me, but for now I sat there, soaking up the warmth of Henri and Marissa's presence, basking in the feeling of being valued.

*Fin~*

# About the Author

Erica H. Campbell is an up-and-coming queer author in her late 20s. She lives in the southeast US with her sister and a turtle named Inertia. In her free time, she enjoys tabletop games, board games, and cooking vegan meals for her friends. You can contact her directly at SylifiPublishing@gmail.com

The original draft of this book, artwork of the characters, and other upcoming novels by Erica Campbell are all available for free on https://sylifi.neocities.org

www.ingramcontent.com/pod-product-compliance
Ingram Content Group UK Ltd.
Pitfield, Milton Keynes, MK11 3LW, UK
UKHW040049120326
468911UK00005B/312